THE BEST SCIENCE FICTION OF THE YEAR

Also Edited by Neil Clarke

Magazines
Clarkesworld Magazine—clarkesworldmagazine.com
Forever Magazine—forever-magazine.com

Anthologies
Upgraded
The Best Science Fiction of the Year Volume 1
The Best Science Fiction of the Year Volume 2
The Best Science Fiction of the Year Volume 3
The Best Science Fiction of the Year Volume 4
The Best Science Fiction of the Year Volume 5
Touchable Unreality
Galactic Empires
More Human Than Human
The Final Frontier
Not One of Us
The Eagle Has Landed

(with Sean Wallace)
Clarkesworld: Year Three
Clarkesworld: Year Four
Clarkesworld: Year Five
Clarkesworld: Year Six
Clarkesworld: Year Seven
Clarkesworld: Year Eight
Clarkesworld: Year Nine, Volume 1
Clarkesworld: Year Nine, Volume 2
Clarkesworld: Year Ten, Volume 1
Clarkesworld: Year Ten, Volume 2
Clarkesworld: Year Eleven, Volume 1
Clarkesworld: Year Eleven, Volume 2
Clarkesworld: Year Twelve, Volume 1
Clarkesworld: Year Twelve, Volume 2

THE BEST SCIENCE FICTION OF THE YEAR

VOLUME 6

Edited by Neil Clarke

Night Shade Books
NEW YORK

All Rights Reserved. No part of this book may be reproduced in any manner without the express written consent of the publisher, except in the case of brief excerpts in critical reviews or articles. All inquiries should be addressed to Night Shade Books, 307 West 36th Street, 11th Floor, New York, NY 10018.

Night Shade books may be purchased in bulk at special discounts for sales promotion, corporate gifts, fund-raising, or educational purposes. Special editions can also be created to specifications. For details, contact the Special Sales Department, Night Shade Books, 307 West 36th Street, 11th Floor, New York, NY 10018 or info@skyhorsepublishing.com.

Night Shade Books® is a registered trademark of Skyhorse Publishing, Inc. ®, a Delaware corporation.

Visit our website at www.nightshadebooks.com.

10 9 8 7 6 5 4 3 2 1

Library of Congress Cataloging-in-Publication Data is available on file.

Hardcover ISBN: 978-1-949102-52-9
Trade paperback ISBN: 978-1-949102-53-6

Cover illustration by Pascal Blanche
Cover design by Daniel Brount and David Ter-Avaneysan

Please see pages 585–587 for an extension of this copyright page.

Printed in the United States of America

Table of Contents

Introduction
A State of the Short SF Field in 2020

Neil Clarke

It's impossible to look back at 2020 without noting the shadow of the global COVID-19 pandemic. Many of us lost family and friends, or knew of someone who did. Lockdowns, furloughs, face masks, and shortages at supermarkets became commonplace. Responses from those in power ranged from outright denial of science to enforcement of strict quarantine restrictions. No matter what your experience, the routine of our daily lives was disrupted on a scale few of us even imagined likely.

As I began reviewing my notes for this introduction, the unusual nature of the year nagged at me. Throughout 2020, I had informal discussions with editors about the changes we were observing in story submissions, readership, and listenership. As the year closed, I became curious about where everyone landed, so I devised a survey and sent it to editors at fifty-four different English language science fiction and fantasy magazines.

The survey contained sections on quantitative publishing information (number of issues, stories, story lengths, readership, etc.), relevant market news (business/operational changes), and an open-ended section about works/authors they enjoyed or any other issues they considered relevant to the business of short fiction. There was also a special section devoted to the impact of COVID-19 on readership and submissions. Moving forward, I'm using 2020 as a baseline for future iterations of this survey in the hopes that it will allow me to more precisely monitor changes in the industry at the micro and macro levels.

Over thirty publications completed this year's survey and the majority of the editors who were unable to participate expressed an interest in participating next year. In a few cases, I was able to manually fill in missing responses by examining awards eligibility lists and other public statements made during the year. The forty-one markets represented by the 2020 dataset include a variety that ranges from its longest-running publications to some of the newest; large readerships to small; and general interest to more focused ones. The majority publish a varying mix of both fantasy and science fiction. Science fiction-only publications were the second most common. Response rates from publications outside the US and Canada were lower than those within, so that has been identified as an area for improvement.

The Business Side of Things

The impact of the pandemic of the business side of publishing was somewhat mitigated by the advances in digital publishing over the last fifteen years. A significant majority of magazines reported that they were able to maintain their regular schedule with digital editions, despite an array of difficulties. The print editions of books and magazines were sometimes delayed by the temporary closures or reduced staffing at printers; paper shortages; and a domestic and international slowdown in postal delivery.

Distribution of books and magazines through brick and mortar bookstores was more significantly disrupted. Barnes & Noble, one of the larger US bookstore chains, not only temporarily closed their stores, but also cancelled all magazine orders for several months. Unlike anthologies, single issues of magazines can't be rescheduled, so these problems disproportionately impacted those publishers. While I've lamented the switch from monthly to bi-monthly schedules at the oldest of the genre magazines, *Asimov's Science Fiction* (asimovs.com), *Analog Science Fiction & Fact* (analogsf.com), and *The Magazine of Fantasy & Science Fiction* (sfsite.com/fsf), those changes (in 2017 for the first two and 2009 for the latter) likely minimized the potential damage caused by the decrease in newsstand availability.

Beyond the bookstore closures, there were delays further up the chain at both traditional printers and print-on-demand facilities, impacting the full-range of projects from self-published work to major publishers. These were largely concentrated around the peak of the pandemic as lockdown orders were issued in the US and Canada. A paper shortage led to many printers raising prices towards the end of the year. We should probably expect to be paying more for printed media in the coming year.

A few smaller publications and small press publishers also indicated that the cancellation of local conventions impacted their direct sales and marketing efforts. Even when replaced with online events, virtual dealers rooms failed to provide a viable alternative for these publishers. There was hope that this was merely a transitional problem. If improvements can be made, online conventions could present these publications with an opportunity to extend their reach to an even greater worldwide audience.

Irrelevant of the size or type of project, however, some of the biggest challenges were those directly impacting the daily lives of their authors, editors, publishers, and staff. Adaptation was frequently happening behind-the-scenes and not immediately apparent to readers. For example, it wasn't uncommon for a magazine's table of contents to shift late in the process to accommodate authors originally scheduled for those issues. If anything, it showed a great resiliency across the industry.

Not unsurprisingly, the process of acquiring stories was also impacted. Short fiction is normally acquired either by solicitation (invitation-only) or open submissions (anyone can submit a work). Solicited submissions are considered a standard practice with anthologies from larger publishers and it's also the dominant method of acquisition at *Tor.com* and *Future Tense* (slate.com/tag/future-tense-fiction). Others employ varying degrees of a hybrid approach, like many Kickstarter anthologies, *Uncanny Magazine* (uncannymagazine.com), or *Future Science Fiction* (future-sf.com). The common practice among the greatest number of magazines, however, is open submissions. This is where a significant percentage of the new voices, themes, and techniques find their initial foothold in the field. Given the importance of these contributions, any fluctuations here can have a significant downstream impact.

If there was a theme that dominated submissions, it was pandemic fiction, but that was nothing in comparison to other changes reported at all but a few markets. Several editors mentioned unusual high and low swings in the volume of submissions that eventually began to level off towards the last quarter of the year. This was often paired with claims of an increase in the number of authors submitting work for the first time. In my own tracking, I observed a significant increase in the number of submissions from outside the US, sometimes jumping in regions experiencing spikes in COVID cases. Some editors theorized that these changes were the likely side-effect of lockdowns and layoffs providing authors with the time to pursue their dream of writing. There's no concrete evidence to support this, but regardless, the increase was welcomed and perceived as a positive for the year. Should many of these authors continue to pursue these goals post-pandemic, we could end up seeing ripples for years to come.

And that now brings us to readership. Since they've been around the longest, I'll start with the three magazines I mentioned earlier: *Analog, Asimov's,* and *F&SF.* Between the three, they share a common print ancestry, and are among those with the largest paid readerships. Their subscription and newsstand numbers are often quoted with little insight into what it actually means to the field. For example, many have chosen to see data as an opportunity to declare the death of print or even short fiction. On the other extreme, we also have people who, on looking at the wide array of markets, proclaim that we're in a new golden age for short fiction. Both are guilty of looking at only a part of the equation, even without a pandemic adding more color to the picture.

These three publications are the ones with the most solid financial footing, with the possible exception of corporate-sponsored sites like *Tor.com*—paid for by Tor Books, which is part of the massive Holtzbrinck Publishing Group. (Side note: Corporate-sponsored sites are rare, but always feel more at-risk to me since a change in corporate opinion or staffing can lead to a sudden demise. Take SciFi's shuttering of *SciFiction* in 2005, for example.) If it wasn't for the rise of digital publishing in the mid-late aughts, their critics' concerns might be more relevant. *Analog* and *Asimov's* digital subscriptions now account for half or more of their readership. *F&SF* does not publish the figures for their digital edition, but an early relationship with Amazon (for exclusive access, now expired) and its sales rank there suggests that the same is likely true of them as well.

Over the last five years, *Analog* has dropped from 13,066 print subscriptions to 9,396, a loss of 3,670; *Asimov's* has dropped from 8,191 to 6,160, a loss of 2,031; and *F&SF* has dropped from 7,247 to 5,257, a loss of 1,990. That may seem disastrous, but it appears it's actually symptomatic of a change in reading habits. In the same time period, *Analog* has risen from 5,734 digital subscriptions to 8,879, a gain of 3,145 and *Asimov's* has risen from 7,078 to 10,483, a gain of 3,405. These magazines also receive additional income from single issue newsstand sales and on average, this adds around two thousand print copies per month. (This is where any pandemic losses would have happened.) None of them report digital single-issue sales, but there is additional revenue generated there that would not have been impacted by store closures.

The total paid subscription numbers are down during this window, but the income generated by the different formats is not equal. Annual US subscriptions (6 issues) to *Analog* and *Asimov's* are $35.97 print (up by a dollar over 2019) and $35.88 digital. *F&SF* subscriptions are $39.97 print and $36.97 digital. While the prices for digital and print subscriptions are relatively similar, print subscriptions cost the publisher more due to printing and shipping, ultimately making the digital editions more profitable. The upwards trend in digital subscriptions should offset the declining print subscriptions and with increasing printing and postal costs eating into profits, this development is better for the long-term health of these publications.

Now, for comparison, let's take a look at three of the publications (with subscription options and free online editions) that have had works nominated for major genre awards in recent years: *Clarkesworld* (clarkesworldmagazine.com), *Lightspeed* (lightspeedmagazine.com), and *Uncanny*. In the last five years, online readership at *Clarkesworld* increased from 39,000 to 44,000, gaining 5,000; *Lightspeed* increased from 25,000 to 29,800, gaining 4,800; and *Uncanny* (only a couple of years old at the time) increased from 27,000 to 40,200, gaining 13,200. Paid subscriptions at *Clarkesworld* increased from 3,300 to 3,900, gaining 600; *Lightspeed* decreased from 2300 to 2200, losing 100; and *Uncanny* increased from 1,300 to 2,300, gaining 1000.

Each of these publications also has a free audio podcast not reflected in these numbers, but can frequently add thousands of listeners to their reach. (Previous year's data among all markets indicates a range of 6,000-29,000 listeners.) Among the publications that offer podcasts, many reported that 2020 was a down year. Anecdotal evidence suggests that a large portion of the audience for these podcasts are commuters and with many people working from home or furloughed, there was much less of this happening during the year. Oddly enough, this doesn't seem to have impacted the greater audiobook and podcast market as both showed increased activity during the pandemic.

As one would expect, the magazines offering free editions generally have a greater audience size than those that do not, providing the former with an upper hand in both marketing and awards. This is one of the reasons very few works from paywall magazines and anthologies have been represented in vote-based awards while still finding more balanced representation among juried awards and the variety of year's best anthologies like this one.

Looking at circulation figures and awards results can very easily lead to the mistaken conclusion that the non-free venues are the ones in trouble. If you compare the paid readerships between the two groups, however, you see a very different picture. Despite the awards and accolades, the publications offering free fiction have considerable difficulty getting their readers to subscribe and support. This is widespread among the magazines publishing short fiction in this manner and often worse for the smaller publications.

That difference in paid readership results in a large number of those publications having difficulty paying their editors and other staff. While the field has a strong culture of "pay the author" and SFWA even publishes a "minimum qualifying rate" of eight cents/word that guides the field, no such guidance exists for narrators, proofreaders, slush readers, artists, translators, editors, or any of the many other positions needed to produce these publications. A significant portion of these skilled positions are staffed by low or unpaid labor. That not only limits who can participate in the field and gambles with the futures of those publications, but also suppresses market incentive to pay for work. Volunteerism can be a viable option, but it cannot be a requirement of a healthy short fiction ecosystem. The concept of a new "golden age" for short fiction must include supporting the people working in the field or we are simply deluding ourselves.

As each new year passes, I become more certain that the current system for magazines is a carefully built house of cards. The overall pool of money coming into short fiction is too low to be sustainable for the variety of publications we have. To be clear, I'm not suggesting that we need to reduce their numbers, but financial pressures may lead to that outcome if things remain unchanged.

Instead, I'm suggesting that we need to see a culture shift in financially supporting free content. The prevalence of online fiction (to which I admittedly contribute) has created the perception that short fiction should be free, establishing a financial value that's unrealistic and problematic. Furthermore, most short fiction magazines are underpriced. While book prices have steadily increased over the years, the prices for magazine subscriptions have remained largely unchanged. $1.99 and $2.99 per month have practically become carved-in-stone standards. It's no secret these things must change for the health of the field. In fact, some editors were considering revisions to their pricing structure before the pandemic placed those plans on hold.

Digital subscriptions to your favorite magazine might not always be available via the traditional routes. Policies at many of the better-known chains and online bookstores can make it difficult or impossible for small or new publishers to offer these options to readers. If you prefer print editions, your subscription options are even more limited. For good reason, most of the publications launched in the last decade don't offer them as an option. The financial risks and badly broken distribution systems make it even more unlikely they ever will.

Fortunately, there are many alternatives for magazines to choose from when offering methods for readers or listeners to support them financially. A popular option for magazines and many authors has been to set up a Patreon (patreon.com) page. This allows them the ability to offer a variety of monthly or per-creation options to support them on an ongoing basis. Memberful (memberful.com), currently owned by Patreon, is another service that provides tools for offering subscriptions directly from a publisher's website. While Kickstarter (kickstarter.com) is aimed more towards one-and-done projects (like anthologies), several magazines use it to get their seed money to launch, fund special projects, or in some cases, hold annual fundraisers.

If you read a magazine, I urge you to search their website for details on how to best support them. If you have the option, I recommend supporting them via subscriptions over one-time gifts. Knowing they'll receive roughly X each month helps them plan and budget for the long term and, in some cases, avoid the need for stressful "fund-or-die" campaigns. All that makes it more likely that you'll be able to continue enjoying their work for years to come.

Where do anthologies and collections stand in all this? The finances here are much more stable, but the field's largest publishers tend to avoid them simply because they don't generally earn enough to justify a place in their lineup. The pay for those projects may not be fantastic, but if you're reading an anthology from one of those publishers, you can almost assuredly expect that everyone will have been paid. If they're lucky, they might even earn royalties.

The majority of anthologies I receive, however, end up being published by small press publishers or independent editors. This year, there were some that didn't pay their editors, but they were the minority. (I'm ignoring charity anthologies where such behavior can be more than appropriate.) Several of those were Kickstarter projects where the editor/campaign manager waived their fee to keep the funding goal a bit lower.

While anthologies and collections tend to be better at making sure editors and their teams are paid, the publishers shoulder more risk, particularly when traditional bookstore distribution is involved. That system passes all the risk from bookstores and distributors directly onto the publisher. They can lose a significant amount of money (in return fees from the distributor) simply because a bookstore overestimated demand for a title and decides to return a large order. A similar burden faces magazines that have print newsstand distribution, but in their case it's a little easier for bookstores to anticipate demand from issue-to-issue. On the downside, magazines aren't returned. They are destroyed.

Instead of traditional distribution, many small press publishers opt to use print-on-demand (POD) technology which can offer more protections against this scenario but sharply decreases the number of stores willing to stock their titles. This method also eliminates the need to print and store the entire print run at once. This comes at the expense of higher per-unit costs. Much like the magazines, anthologies and collections also benefit strongly from digital editions which tend to be lower risk and cost. These often generate more revenue than the print editions and help make these projects financially viable. The overwhelming majority of the anthologies and collections I considered this year were published in both POD and digital editions.

Magazine Comings and Goings

Analog—originally *Astounding*—reached its ninetieth anniversary in January and celebrated throughout the year. This year's six issues featured retro-styled covers and a reprint in each issue representing works published in the '40s, '50s, '60s, '70s, '80s, and '90s. They also serialized Derek Künsken's novel *The House of Styx* over the first half of the year, making it the only novel originally published in a magazine this year. Some of their best stories included works by M.L. Clark, Alec Nevala-Lee, Dominica Phetteplace, and Catherine Wells.

Asimov's published six issues and more novellas (eight) than any other science fiction magazine this year. Stories selected for this anthology include works by Eleanor Arnason, Julie Novakova, and Mercurio D. Rivera. Also notable were pieces by Timons Esaias, Ted Kosmatka, Nancy Kress, Rich Larson, and Ray Nayler.

Towards the end of the year, *F&SF* announced that editor C.C. Finlay was stepping down to devote more time to his writing. Sheree Renée Thomas assumed the editorial mantle starting with the March/April 2021 issue. Charlie ends his tenure at the magazine with a strong year that resulted in its best showing over the six volumes of this series. Stories by M. Rickert, Nadia Afifi, Rati Mehrotra, and Ray Nayler are included in this anthology. It was also a fine source for fantasy works.

There was an increase in the number of stories published on *Tor.com* over last year with the bulk of the expansion being at the novelette length. They also collaborated with *Fiyah* (fiyahlitmag.com) to publish eight works of flash fiction (works under one thousand words). In this volume, you'll find *Tor.com* works by Carolyn Ives Gilman, Carrie Vaughn, Maureen McHugh, and Rich Larson. Also of note were stories by Charlie Jane Anders and Yoon Ha Lee.

In January, *Clarkesworld* (which I edit) published a story by Isabel Fall that attempted to reclaim a hurtful anti-trans meme. Isabel, who was not out as trans at the time of publication, initially received praise for the story from both in and outside the trans community before paranoia and bad faith assumptions about the author and her motives began to gain momentum on Twitter and other sites. Nothing I can say can fully demonstrate the level of cruelty demonstrated. Over the course of a few days, Isabel was accused of being a Nazi, a transphobe, and worse, led Isabel to out herself, withdraw the story from publication, and check into a psychiatric ward for thoughts of self-harm and suicide. After the story's removal, the situation inflamed again when it was used as an example of "cancel culture" across social media and in articles at venues like *Wired*, *The Atlantic*, and *The Verge*. Later renamed "Helicopter Story," the work has since developed a significant fan base, largely through distribution of unauthorized copies of the work. Per the author's wishes, it has not been restored to publication at this time.

Clarkesworld published more novelettes than any of the publications reviewed in 2020. Stories by Arula Ratnakar, Rebecca Campbell, Sameem Siddiqui, and Vajra Chandrasekera are included in this anthology. Also of note were stories by Brenda Cooper, the above-mentioned Isabel Fall, Naomi Kritzer, and R.P. Sand.

Matt Kressel had the best story in *Lightspeed* this year, followed by works by Sunny Moraine and Em North. The biggest news at *Lightspeed*, however, was John Joseph Adam's decision to relaunch *Fantasy Magazine* (fantasy-magazine.com), with issue #61 arriving in November 2020. Christie Yant and Arley Sorg co-edit the magazine. Adam's three magazines (horror magazine, *Nightmare*, being the third) will now be co-published by Adams and Yant under the name Adamant Press. This change does not alter the standard formula of 50-50 science fiction vs fantasy in *Lightspeed*'s contents.

Strange Horizons (strangehorizons.com) published three special issues in 2020 focusing on the climate crisis (March), chosen families (July), and the work of writers from Mexico (November). Sister publication, *Samovar* (samovar.strangehorizons.com), has a focus on works in translation and remains one of the few outlets that publishes translations in both English and its original language. Three issues were published in 2020 with stories from five languages.

While *Escape Pod* (escapepod.org) is commonly referred to as a podcast, its audio-only roots are the only difference from many of the other "magazines" that have launched in recent years. This year, they celebrated their fifteen anniversary and published an anthology (discussed below) to celebrate the milestone.

Uncanny Magazine completed its sixth year and ran a successful Kickstarter campaign (their seventh) to fund their next year. They primarily published short stories (with three novelettes being the exception), and their strongest works continue to be fantasy, which they tend to lean more towards. My favorite story there this year was by Ken Liu.

After losing their sponsor in 2019, *Future Science Fiction Digest* (future-sf. com) continued to publish smaller quarterly issues in 2020. Their sponsorship from Future Affairs Administration that was cancelled last year was restored late this year, allowing them to return to full-sized issues. They published two special issues: a translation-heavy East Asia Special issue and a medically themed issue (guest edited by RM Ambrose). Among the best they published this year are works by Simone Heller and Julie Novakova.

Galaxy's Edge (galaxysedge.com) editor and award-winning author Mike Resnick passed away in early January. Publisher Shahid Mahmud announced that author and Arc Manor assistant publisher Lezli Robyn would take over as editor starting with issue 43, a special issue dedicated to Mike and his many contributions to the field. Several of Mike's stories have been reprinted in subsequent issues. Also unique to this magazine are serializations of classic novels.

Fiyah Magazine expanded operations this year to include FiyahCon, "a virtual convention centering the perspectives and celebrating the contributions of BIPOC in speculative fiction" and the Ignyte Awards, which "seek to celebrate the vibrancy and diversity of the current and future landscapes of science fiction, fantasy, and horror by recognizing incredible feats in storytelling and outstanding efforts toward inclusivity of the genre." A spontaneous mid-year and third-party subscription drive also allowed them to start paying SFWA minimum qualifying rates starting in October.

Late in the year, publisher Pablo Defendini resigned from all editorial functions at Fireside Fiction Company, which includes *Fireside Magazine* (firesidefiction.com), following the publication of a podcast in which their narrator used "an offensive stereotype of the American southern Black accent." The situation generated a substantial amount of public outcry and news coverage in places like the *Washington Post*. Brian J. White, founder and former editor of the magazine, has stepped in as Interim Editorial Director and plans to select a new editor for the magazine in 2021. The print edition of the magazine has been suspended.

At the end of the year, it was announced that PS Publishing would take over publishing *Interzone* (ttapress.com/interzone) from TTA Press with Ian Whates assuming responsibility as the new editor. Over the next few weeks, however, the deal fell through, with editor Andy Cox siding with subscribers who had raised concerns about the agreement. These events will have an impact on their 2021 publication schedule, but details are unspecified at this time. Andy Dudak wrote what I considered to be *Interzone*'s best story this year. They also published notable stories by Alexander Glass and Eugenia Triantafyllou.

Infinite Worlds Magazine (infiniteworldsmagazine.com) published four full-color print issues in 2020 and began offering subscriptions at the end of the year.

While many editors lamented the sharp increase in pandemic-related story submissions, *Reckoning Magazine* (reckoning.press) leaned in, devoting one of their two issues this year to "Creativity and Coronavirus." They've also made the decision to switch to a model that only employs guest editors from now on.

SciPhi Journal (sciphijournal.org) abandoned the old paywall business model employed by its previous owners and has made much of its past content available for free. They are now operating as an all-volunteer non-profit.

The pandemic and other factors played into *DreamForge Magazine* (dreamforgemagazine.com) decreasing its annual output to three issues in 2020. Publishers Scot and Jane Noel have announced that in 2021, *DreamForge Magazine* will become *DreamForge Anvil*. The move eliminates their print edition and switches their publication schedule to six online issues/year accompanied by a monthly eNewsletter.

Canadian magazine *Neo-Opsis* (neo-opsis.ca) announced in October that they too would be eliminating their print edition and turning to a digital-only model starting with issue 31. They cited the rising costs of paper, printing, mailing, and distribution, particularly during COVID, as necessitating the move. "It was go digital or close down completely."

Apex Magazine didn't stay closed for long. In July they announced a Kickstarter campaign to relaunch the magazine, and within the month 779 supporters helped them secure funding for an entire year—two issues of which will be special theme issues. *Apex* will start publishing again in January 2021 and switch to a bimonthly publication schedule to allow their staff to "have a better work-life balance."

Tory Hoke and Stewart C Baker decided to put *sub-Q Magazine* (sub-q.com) on "indefinite hiatus" after their August 2020 issue. They describe it as "closing down for the near future but we don't like to say we're closing down forever."

After partnering with Flame Tree Press and coming back for one issue, *Compelling Science Fiction* (compellingsciencefiction.com) has once again gone on hiatus. Editor Joe Stech says this was "mainly due to the fact that I'm working on a startup project that is consuming all of my available time."

Editor and publisher Paul Campbell launched *Cossmass Infinities* (cossmass.com), a science fiction and fantasy short story magazine, in January. Some stories are available for free via their website, but others are exclusive to their print and ebook editions.

In late May, *Hexagon SF Magazine* (hexagonmagazine.ca), edited by JW Stebner, published its first quarterly issue. Three issues were published in 2020, and Patreon subscribers receive early access to new issues. Stories may be published in English or French.

Neon Hemlock Press announced the launch of *Baffling Magazine* (bafflingmag.com), a quarterly publication featuring flash (which they define as stories under 1200 words) science fiction, fantasy, and horror with a queer bent. The magazine is co-edited by Craig L. Gidney and dave ring and published its first issue in October.

A successful Kickstarter campaign in late 2020 led to the creation of *Constelación Magazine* (constelacionmagazine.com), a quarterly bilingual speculative fiction magazine, with stories appearing in both English and Spanish. The magazine is co-edited by Coral Alejandra Moore and Eliana González Ugarte. A sample issue (#0.5) was published in 2020, but the first issue isn't scheduled until 2021.

This hardly represents the entirety of the magazines publishing science fiction in English, however. Other magazines such as *Abyss & Apex, Apparition Lit, Arsenika, Aurealis, Andromeda Spaceways, Beneath Ceaseless Skies, Daily Science Fiction, Diabolical Plots, Flash Fiction Online, Forever, James Gunn's Ad Astra, Kaleidotrope, LCRW, Little Blue Marble, Metaphorosis, Mythaxis, Omenana, On Spec, Shoreline of Infinity, The Future Fire*, and many more dot the landscape.

Podcasts are also an important part of the ecosystem. Magazines like *Asimov's, Clarkesworld, Escape Pod, Lightspeed*, and *Uncanny* offer some or all of their stories in audio that supplements their print and/or digital editions. Others like *StarShipSofa* (starshipsofa.com) and *Levar Burton Reads* (levarburtonpodcast.com) offer audio-only options.

There's also an increasing amount of genre fiction appearing in various non-genre publications like *Nature, Wired*, and *Slate. Wired's* Future of Work series (wired.com/story/future-of-work-introduction-2020) and the ongoing Future Tense Science Fiction series (slate.com/tag/future-tense-fiction) were of particular interest this year.

Anthologies and Collections

As noted, the publication schedules for many anthologies slid around a bit in 2020, but there was no shortage of variety. The year was bookended by two anthologies that I found quite enjoyable: *Avatars Inc.*, edited by Ann VanderMeer, and *Rebuilding Tomorrow*, by Tsana Dolichva. The casual reader may have very well missed hearing about either of these.

Avatars Inc. was originally published by XPRIZE in both online and ebook editions, but has since become unavailable. With any luck it will be available again in some form by the time you are reading this. The best stories in this anthology are by Adrian Tchaikovsky, James S. A. Corey, and Ken Liu. Also worth finding are the stories by Indrapramit Das, Aliette De Bodard, Robert Reed, Johanna Sinisalo, Tade Thompson, and JY Yang.

Rebuilding Tomorrow was funded by a Kickstarter campaign and published by Twelfth Planet Press, an Australian boutique publisher that has a history of producing some excellent work. This anthology features some wonderful stories by Bogi Takács, Fran Wilde, and S.B. Divya.

Asimov's editor, Sheila Williams, edited this year's MIT Press Twelve Tomorrow's anthology: *Tomorrow's Lovers, Families, and Friends*. Contributions by James Patrick Kelly and Nancy Kress are highlights of the anthology. Other strong works are by Xia Jia, Suzanne Palmer, and Nick Wolven.

Jonathan Strahan's original anthology to celebrate the 100th anniversary of the word "Robot," *Made to Order*, was published by Solaris. The stars here were Sofia Samatar and Peter Watts, but Vina Jie-Min Prasad's and Alastair Reynolds' stories were strong as well.

As part of their 15th anniversary celebration, *Escape Pod* assembled *EscapePod the Science Fiction Anthology*, edited by Mur Lafferty and S.B. Divya. Like the magazine, this anthology contains a mix of original and reprint stories. My favorite original story was by Tobias S. Buckell.

A more unusual approach to anthologies was employed with the Dystopia Triptych, edited by John Joseph Adams, Christie Yant, and Hugh Howey. These three interconnected anthologies (*Ignorance is Strength, Burn the Ashes*, and *Or Else the Light*) each include stories told by the same authors (in the same order) but with each volume focusing on a different period of time: before, during, and after the dystopia.

It's sometimes hard to tell where the line between an online anthology and a magazine is. I placed *Wired*'s Future of Work series in magazines largely due to its parent's status as a magazine. Another online collection of stories was published by Arizona State University's *Us in Flux* (csi.asu.edu/usinflux), and I'm placing it here because its parent is decidedly not a magazine. You could probably make a strong case for either being in the other category or neither. That said, I recommend Tochi Onyebuchi's story in this one.

Dominion: An Anthology of Speculative Fiction from Africa and the African Diaspora, edited by Zelda Knight and Oghenechovwe Donald Ekpeki and published by Aurelia Leo, included science fiction and fantasy. My favorite was Dilman Dila's story, but I also found Marian Denise Moore's of note.

As in recent years, the most common theme I observed in anthologies was to place a special emphasis or focus on authors that share common identity or background. Works like these provide an opportunity for underrepresented groups to band together and highlight the work done in their communities. For readers, they provide the chance to broaden the range of their reading and/or discover authors and stories more like themselves. Unlike a traditional theme project, like an AI anthology, you'll often find a lot more variety in the stories published here.

Some of the 2020 anthologies that represent this theme include: *That We May Live: Speculative Chinese Fiction*, published by Two Lines; *Latinx Rising: An Anthology of Latinx Science Fiction and Fantasy*, edited by Matthew David Goodwin; *Africanfuturism: An Anthology*, edited by Wole Talabi (available as a free download from brittlepaper.com); *Silk & Steel: A Queer Speculative Adventure Anthology*, edited by Janine A. Southard; *Glitter + Ashes: Queer Tales of a World That Wouldn't Die*, edited by dave ring; and *Avatar - Indian Science Fiction*, edited by Tarun K. Saint and Francesco Verso.

Recent events influenced the next two most common themes. Given the news headlines in the US and other places, it's not surprising to find that politics and the pandemic inspired several small press anthologies. Among these were *And the Last Trump Shall Sound*, published by CAEZIK SF & Fantasy; *Consolation Songs: Optimistic Speculative Fiction For A Time of Pandemic*, edited by Iona Datt Sharma; *Stories of Hope and Wonder: In Support of the UK's Healthcare Workers*, published by NewCon Press; and *Recognize Fascism*, edited by Crystal M Huff.

In my reading, I counted over forty single author short story collections. The majority of stories included in these collections were previously published in the years before, but they are very much worth revisiting. I particularly enjoyed: *The Best of Elizabeth Bear* by Elizabeth Bear; *Instantiation* by Greg Egan; *Settling the World: Selected Stories 1970-2020* by M. John Harrison; *A Summer Beyond Your Reach* by Xia Jia; *To Hold Up the Sky* by Cixin Liu; *The Hidden Girl and Other Stories* by Ken Liu; *The Ship Whisperer* by Julie Novakova; *Stan's Kitchen: A Robinson Reader* by Kim Stanley Robinson;

Alien Heresies by S. P. Somtow; *Nine Bar Blues* by Sheree Renée Thomas; and *Masters of Science Fiction: Kate Wilhelm, Volumes 1 & 2* by Kate Wilhelm.

The 2020 Scorecard

My selections for this year include thirty-two works, up four from last year. For those interested in tracking the sources of the stories selected:

	Stories Included	Percentage
Magazines	**21**	**65.6%**
Anthologies	**12**	**34.4%**
Collections	**0**	**0%**
Standalone	**0**	**0%**

These categories represent a total of fourteen different sources, which is the same quantity as last year. If you break down the magazines by those that started in print vs. those that started as digital publications, print had the upper hand by one. The number of venues represented favored print at five to four. The digital-originating publications had the same quantity of stories in 2019, but the print-originating increased by five. (This method of differentiating the markets is silly, but useful in demonstrating that the print part of the family is still producing award-worthy works.) The eleven stories from anthologies represent five different markets. There's one more story here than last year, but the same number of markets.

Standalone works are those that were published on their own and not connected to any of the other categories. Most commonly, these are separately published novellas. There were two included in last year's list and none this year. Short story collections have not been represented with selections in the last two volumes. These generally consist of previously published works, but sometimes include new stories.

Short stories (under 7,500 words) and novelettes (under 17,500 words) were nearly balanced with seventeen short stories and fifteen novelettes making the list. There were thirteen of each last year. Novellas (under 40,000 words) dropped from two last year to zero.

And from the recommended reading list:

	Stories Included	Percentage
Magazines	**24**	**54.5%**
Anthologies	**18**	**40.9%**
Collections	**0**	**0**
Standalone	**2**	**4.5%**

There were forty-five stories on the recommended reading list last year and forty-four this year. Magazines dropped by two and anthologies increased by six. Collections decreased by three and standalone dropped by one. The remaining difference comes from a single story classified as "other" last year.

When you combine the recommended reading list with those included in this book, the total is three greater than the previous year. Despite the lack of novellas in this year's volume, that side of the field continues to produce good work at that length. In my opinion, it was a far better year for fantasy novellas than science fiction novellas, both in quantity and quality. Tor.com Publishing is widely considered the leader here and dominates the category in various awards, but quality novellas can be found in a wider variety of sources than those awards reflect. Magazines (most frequently *Asimov's, Analog, F&SF,* and *Clarkesworld*) as well as publishers like Tachyon (tachyonpublications.com) and Subterranean Press (subterraneanpress.com), among others, are viable alternative sources.

The International Effect

As noted in recent years, your opportunities to find short fiction in translation are on the rise. *Clarkesworld, Future Science Fiction,* and *Samovar* continue to regularly publish works in translation, but you can find the occasional translation published in the field's many magazines and anthologies. I'll be adding questions about the publication of translations to next year's publication survey in hopes of tracking this trend more closely.

When it comes to the local US science fiction community's bubble, however, the biggest change in 2020 could be observed in our science fiction conventions. As a side effect of the lockdowns during the pandemic, many conventions temporarily transitioned to online format rather than cancel entirely. This time period also saw the birth of a few new conventions like Fiyahcon or Flights of Foundry that fully embraced the medium. There was also a wide variety of smaller events focused on single panels or readings put on by bookshops, publishers, and writing groups/organizations.

Without the expense or need to travel, the barriers to attending these events were greatly diminished and allowed greater participation from communities that couldn't dedicate the time or money required to attend in-person conventions. Both small regional events and larger conventions like Worldcon received an influx of fans and professionals from around the world, opening opportunities to build new bridges, inspire collaborations, and gain exposure to perspectives otherwise unrepresented in the past. There is a strong desire to return to "in-person" congoing and fandom is rather dedicated to its traditions, but there is hope that the benefits realized this year are not discarded entirely. Many, both here and abroad, would like to see these opportunities continued in some manner.

One of the biggest challenges for publishers looking to cast a wider net in their recruitment of new writers, stories, and novels is that authors from outside the US (and to some extent, the UK, Canada, and Australia) have historically felt unwelcome. If the conventions can continue to provide opportunities for long-distance fans, readers, and professionals to connect, it will be a major improvement in addressing that problem. That alone makes it worth the effort and will reward us all in the long run.

Notable 2020 Awards

The 78th World Science Fiction Convention, ConZealand, was the first virtual Worldcon and held from July 29th through August 2nd, 2020. The 2020 Hugo Awards, presented at Worldcon 78, were: Best Novel, *A Memory Called Empire*, by Arkady Martine; Best Novella, *This Is How You Lose the Time War*, by Amal El-Mohtar and Max Gladstone; Best Novelette, "Emergency Skin," by N.K. Jemisin; Best Short Story, "As the Last I May Know," by S.L. Huang; Best Series, The Expanse, by James S. A. Corey; Best Related Work, "2019 John W. Campbell Award Acceptance Speech," by Jeannette Ng; Best Graphic Story or Comic, *LaGuardia*, written by Nnedi Okorafor, art by Tana Ford, colors by James Devlin; Best Dramatic Presentation (long form), *Good Omens*, written by Neil Gaiman, directed by Douglas Mackinnon; Best Dramatic Presentation (short form), *The Good Place*: "The Answer", written by Daniel Schofield, directed by Valeria Migliassi Collins; Best Editor, Short Form, Ellen Datlow; Best Professional Editor, Long Form, Navah Wolfe; Best Professional Artist, John Picacio; Best Semiprozine, *Uncanny*; Best Fanzine, *The Book Smugglers*; Best Fancast, *Our Opinions Are Correct*; Best Fan Writer, Bogi Takács; Best Fan Artist, Elise Matthesen; plus the Lodestar Award for Best Young Adult Book, *Catfishing on CatNet*, by Naomi Kritzer and the Astounding Award for Best New Writer, R.F. Kuang. This was the first time the Astounding Award was given under its new name after being renamed from The John W. Campbell Award for Best New Writer in late 2019.

The 2019 Nebula Awards, presented during a virtual ceremony, on May 30, 2019, were: Best Novel, *A Song for a New Day*, by Sarah Pinsker; Best Novella, *This Is How You Lose the Time War*, by Amal El-Mohtar and Max Gladstone; Best Novelette, "Carpe Glitter," by Cat Rambo; Best Short Story, "Give the Family My Love," by A.T. Greenblatt; Best Game Writing, *The*

Outer Worlds; Ray Bradbury Award, *Good Omens*: "Hard Times"; the Andre Norton Award to *Riverland*, by Fran Wilde; the Kate Wilhelm Solstice Award to John Picacio and David Gaughran; the Kevin O' Donnell Jr. Service to SFWA Award to Julia Rios; and the Damon Knight Memorial Grand Master Award to Lois McMaster Bujold.

The 2019 World Fantasy Awards, presented during a virtual ceremony on November 1, 2020, during the Forty-sixth Annual World Fantasy Convention, were: Best Novel, *Queen of the Conquered*, by Kacen Callender; Best Novella, "The Butcher's Table," by Nathan Ballingrud; Best Short Fiction, "Read After Burning," by Maria Dahvana Headley; Best Collection, *Song for the Unraveling of the World: Stories*, by Brian Evenson; Best Anthology, *New Suns: Original Speculative Fiction by People of Color*, edited by Nisi Shawl; Best Artist, Kathleen Jennings; Special Award (Professional), to Ebony Elizabeth Thomas, for *The Dark Fantastic: Race and the Imagination from Harry Potter to the Hunger Games*; Special Award (Non-Professional), to Bodhisattva Chattopadhyay, Laura E. Goodin and Esko Suoranta, for *Fafnir – Nordic Journal of Science Fiction and Fantasy Research*. Lifetime Achievement Awards to Rowena Morrill and Karen Joy Fowler. This year's judges were Gwenda Bond, Galen Dara, Michael Kelly, Victor LaValle, and Adam Roberts.

The 2020 Locus Awards, presented during a virtual ceremony on June 27, 2020, were: Science Fiction Novel, *The City in the Middle of the Night*, by Charlie Jane Anders; Fantasy Novel, *Middlegame*, by Seanan McGuire; Horror Novel, *Black Leopard, Red Wolf*, by Marlon James; Young Adult Novel, *Dragon Pearl*, by Yoon Ha Lee; First Novel, *Gideon the Ninth*, by Tamsyn Muir; Novella, *This Is How You Lose the Time War*, by Amal El-Mohtar & Max Gladstone; Novelette, "Omphalos," by Ted Chiang; Short Story, "The Bookstore at the End of America," by Charlie Jane Anders; Anthology, *New Suns: Original Speculative Fiction by People of Color*, edited by Nisi Shawl; Collection, *Exhalation*, by Ted Chiang; Magazine, *Tor.com*; Publisher, Tor Books; Editor, Ellen Datlow; Artist, John Picacio; Non-Fiction, *Monster, She Wrote: The Women Who Pioneered Horror and Speculative Fiction*, by Lisa Kröger & Melanie R. Anderson, Illustrated and Art Book, *Spectrum 26: The Best in Contemporary Fantastic Art*, edited by John Fleskes; Special Award, Writing the Other, Nisi Shawl, Cynthia Ward, & K. Tempest Bradford.

The inaugural IGNYTE Awards were presented during the FIYAHCON virtual convention. Winners were: Best Novel, *Gods of Jade and Shadow*, by Silvia Moreno-Garcia; Best Novel YA, *We Hunt the Flame*, by Hafsah Faizal; Best Middle Grade, *Tristan Strong Punches a Hole in the Sky*, by

Kwame Mbalia; Best Novella, *This Is How You Lose the Time War*, by Max Gladstone & Amal El-Mohtar; Best Novelette, "Emergency Skin," by N K Jemisin; Best Short Story, "A Brief Lesson in Native American Astronomy," by Rebecca Roanhorse; Best in Speculative Poetry, "A Conversation Between the Embalmed Heads of Lampião and Maria Bonita on Public Display at the Baiano State Forensic Institute, Circa Mid-20th Century," by Woody Dismukes; Critics Award, Alex Brown; Best Science Fiction Podcast, *LeVar Burton Reads*; Best Artist, Grace P. Fong; Best Comics Team, *These Savage Shores*, by Ram V, Sumit Kumar, Vitorio Astone, Aditya Bidikar, & Tim Daniel; Best Anthology/Collected Works, *New Suns: Original Speculative Fiction by People of Color*, edited by Nisi Shaw; Best in Creative Non-Fiction, "Black Horror Rising," by Tananarive Due; Ember Award, LeVar Burton; Community Award, *Strange Horizons*.

The 2020 Dragon Award Winners were Best Science Fiction Novel, *The Last Emperox*, by John Scalzi; Best Fantasy Novel, *The Starless Sea*, by Erin Morgenstern; Best Young Adult / Middle Grade Novel, *Finch Merlin and the Fount of Youth*, by Bella Forrest; Best Military Science Fiction or Fantasy Novel, *Savage Wars*, by Jason Anspach & Nick Cole; Best Alternate History Novel, *Witchy Kingdom*, by D. J. Butler; Best Media Tie-In Novel, *Firefly – The Ghost Machine*, by James Lovegrove; Best Horror Novel, *The Twisted Ones*, by T. Kingfisher; Best Comic Book, *Avengers*, by Jason Aaron and Ed McGuinness; Best Graphic Novel, *Battlestar Galactica Counterstrike*, by John Jackson Miller and Daniel HDR; Best Science Fiction or Fantasy TV Series, *The Mandalorian*; Best Science Fiction or Fantasy Movie, *Star Wars: The Rise of Skywalker*; Best Science Fiction or Fantasy PC / Console Game, *Star Wars Jedi: Fallen Order*; Best Science Fiction or Fantasy Mobile Game, *Minecraft Earth*; Best Science Fiction or Fantasy Board Game, *Tapestry*; Best Science Fiction or Fantasy Miniatures / Collectible Card / Role-Playing Game, *Magic: The Gathering: Throne of Eldraine*.

The 2020 Theodore Sturgeon Memorial Award for Best Short Story was won by: "Waterlines," by Suzanne Palmer.

The 2020 Philip K. Dick Memorial Award went to: *Sooner or Later Everything Falls into the Sea,* by Sarah Pinsker and a special citation went to *The Little Animals,* by Sarah Tolmie.

The 2020 Arthur C. Clarke Award was won by: *The Old Drift,* by Namwali Serpell.

The 2019 Otherwise Award (previously the James Tiptree, Jr. Memorial Award) was given to *Freshwater,* by Akwaeke Emezi.

The 2020 WSFA Small Press Award: "The Partisan and the Witch," by Charlotte Honigman.

The 2019 Sidewise Award for Alternate History was deferred until 2021.

In Memoriam

Among those the field lost in 2020 are:

Mike Resnick, author, anthologist, editor, and mentor, winner of five Hugo Awards, a Nebula Award, a Locus Award, and many others around the world; **Carol Serling**, founder and editor of *The Twilight Zone Magazine*, wife of Rod Serling; **Christopher Tolkien**, illustrated maps for *The Lord of the Rings*, editor for his father's (J. R. R. Tolkien) posthumous books; **Charles Alverson**, author, co-wrote the original draft of *Brazil* with Terry Gilliam; **Barbara Remington**, artist, painted the covers for the initial Ballantine editions of *The Lord of the Rings* as well as works by E.R. Eddison; **Gudrun Pausewang**, YA author and winner of the Kurd-Laßwitz-Preis; **Paul Barnett/John Grant**, author, editor, and two-time Hugo Award winner; **Tim White**, artist, provided covers for authors including Arthur C. Clarke, Robert A. Heinlein, Frank Herbert, August Derleth, H. P. Lovecraft, Piers Anthony, Bruce Sterling, and may more; **Keith Ferrell**, editor and biographer, Editor-in-Chief of *OMNI* magazine, **G-J Arnaud/ Saint-Gilles/Georges Murey**, author and winner of the Prix Apollo, the Prix Mystère, and the Prix du Quai des Orfèvres; **Ye Yonglie**, pioneer and one of the most renowned science fiction writers in China; **Charles R. Saunders**, author of the Imaro series as well as numerous short stories, World Fantasy and Aurora Award nominee; **Dean Ing**, author, Hugo and Nebula Award nominee; **Jim Holloway**, artist, worked on interior illustrations for TSR's *Dungeons and Dragons* books, worked for Pacesetter and Sovereign Press; **Jean-Pierre Laigle/Jean-Pierre Moumon**, author, editor, and translator; edited and published *Antares*; **Robert Martin/Ed Flixman**, founding editor of *Fangoria* and edited *Sci-Fi Entertainment* and *SCI FI Magazine*; **Susan Sizemore**, author of romance and science fiction novels; **Brian N. Ball**, teacher, author, and anthologist; **Andrei Moscovit**, author and founder of Hermitage Publishers; **Jean Rosenthal**, publisher and translator of works by Asimov, Simak, van Vogt, and many other science fiction authors into French; **Thomas RP Mielke**, author and winner of the Kurd-Laßwitz-Preis, **Ranco Maria Ricci**, publisher of the magazine *FMR* and several anthologies; **Terry Goodkind**, bestselling author of The Sword of Truth series, which has been translated into over twenty languages; **John Daveridge**, fan and the person responsible for introducing this editor to science fiction; **David Gale**, editorial director at Simon & Schuster Young Readers for twenty-five years; **Janet Freer**, agent, represented Michael Moorcock, Harlan Ellison, Anne McCaffrey, and Ursula K. Le Guin, among others; **Dick Lupoff**, author, Hugo Award-winning fanzine co-editor of *Xero*; **Rachel Caine**, author of several young adult series, including the Great Library and the Morganville Vampires; **Debra Doyle**, author, co-author with Jim Macdonald, and winner of the Mythopoeic Award; **Kay McCauley**, agent representing George R.R. Martin, Ian Tregellis, Ramsey Campbell, and other science fiction and fantasy authors; **Jael**, artist, painted numerous covers for Baen, DAW, and other publishers; **M.A. Foster**, author and two-time finalist for the Campbell Award for Best New Author. **Yasumi Kobayashi**, author, winner of the Hayakawa Award, and two-time Seiun finalist; **Ben Bova**, author of hard science fiction (including the twenty-six volume Grand Tour series), former SFWA President, President Emeritus if the National Space Society, edited *Analog* and was editorial director at *Omni Magazine,* six-time Hugo Award winner; **Phyllis Eisenstein**, author, two-time Hugo and three-time Nebula Award nominee; **James E. Gunn**, scholar, mentor, SFWA Grand Master, Science Fiction Hall of Fame inductee, Worldcon Guest of Honor, Hugo Award winner and Nebula Award finalist, founded the Center for the Study of Science Fiction and the Campbell Conference; **Anton Strout**, author and host of the Once & Future Podcast.

In Closing

I always try to end these introductions on a positive note. After reading the above list of people we've lost and knowing that the year has taken so much more from us (personally and professionally), that can be a challenge. As usual, I'll look towards the new writers for that inspiration and hope for the future.

Each year, I try to single out a new/new-ish author that has impressed me and I believe to be someone you should be paying attention to. This year, I wanted to focus on a new author who had a passion for science fiction and art, and was unafraid to make them one. It didn't take me long to realize that Arula Ratnakar was that writer. Arula is a scientist in her early twenties with only a few stories to her credit so far, but each one has been a joy to read and led me down some interesting rabbit holes. I look forward to each new story. Having had the opportunity to work with her, I've seen her infectious enthusiasm for the science that influences the stories she writes. You'll find one of those stories in this anthology, so now, you too have something to look forward to. And that's a great way to end both a year and an introduction!

Born in the Caribbean, Tobias S. Buckell is a *New York Times* Bestselling and World Fantasy Award winning author. His novels and almost one hundred stories have been translated into nineteen different languages. He has been nominated for the Hugo Award, Nebula Award, World Fantasy Award, and Astounding Award for Best New Science Fiction Author. He currently lives in Ohio.

SCAR TISSUE

Tobias S. Buckell

The evening before you sign and take delivery of your son, you call Charlie and tell him you think you've made a huge mistake.

"Let me come on over and split a few with you," he says. "I haven't seen the fire pit yet."

Charlie—a short, compact man with green eyes and a shaved head whom you met when he delivered groceries the first few weeks you were housebound—brings over a six-pack. You walk out into the complex's community garden together. It used to be a parking lot, and the path through the mushroom gardens under the solar panels is still faded gray asphalt and leftover white lines. You're careful with your right foot; you still haven't gotten used to the way your prosthetic moves. It's easy to trip.

You and Sienna from 4B have a fire pit and stone circle dug out in your combined lots, and she's grown a privacy wall of rosebushes that surround the relaxing space. Charlie sits on one of the cedar benches as you fiddle with twigs to make a fire.

This beats the awkwardness of sitting down to talk right away. Your parents didn't raise you to be direct about feelings. Neither did the army, nor the warehouse you drove a forklift in. Charlie will, if you let him.

Making a fire gives you a moment to sort out all your feelings.

Or maybe it just gives you an excuse to delay talking about them.

Charlie knows all that. It's why he created an excuse to come over.

The beer is warm, but the bottle still sweats enough that it drips across the pale plastic knuckles of your hand. You switch the bottle over to your other hand.

"It's too late to back out now," Charlie says.

"I know."

"You need the money."

The fire starts to lick at the twigs and burn brighter. You awkwardly drop yourself onto the bench across from Charlie and look down at his tattered running shoes and the frayed edges of his gray jeans.

"Everyone needs the money." You swig the cheap beer that's the best either of you can manage. You can't wait to afford something from one of those smaller local breweries nearby.

"But . . ."

You've been on disability since the forklift accident. The apartment's small, but Enthim Arms is nice. The shared garden out back, the walking trails. You can't use them as much as you'd like right now, but that physical therapist keeps saying June is when you might be able to make it to the lake and back.

It'll hurt, but you've never cared so much about seeing a mediocre quarry lake before.

"Advent Robotics will pay me more money to raise it than I made at the warehouse, and I can keep focusing on recovery while doing it." You raise your hand and flex it. A low battery alert blinks on your wrist.

Plus, the bonus at the end will give you enough to afford something only the rich usually can: regrowing your forearm and your leg. Like a damn lizard. The biolabs that do that are so far out of your reach you normally wouldn't even consider it.

And you want it all back. You want it to be just like it was before the forklift started to tip over and Adam screamed at you to jump out, running toward you as fast as he could, ridiculously long hair flying, his clipboard clattering on the floor.

"So what's wrong?" Charlie asks softly, and you have to stare back at the fire to avoid the discomfort of looking at another person.

"I told myself I'd never have kids." You look up from the brown bottle and at the thorns that twist around each other in the vines that Sienna has so carefully trained. "Can't see my way to passing on the shit my parents gave to me."

"Damn," Charlie nods, folds his hands. "Cory, you can't think you'll be the same people they were. The fact that you're scared about this, that means you're going to be such a better parent than they were."

"No." You point a finger over the neck of the beer bottle at him. "People say that, but that's some backwards-assed logic. Refusing to pass on the bad mistakes, understanding maybe you're going to screw up something you're responsible for, that doesn't mean you should go do it. I know I can't go climb a mountain without a rope, I'm going to fall. That was true even before the accident. Understanding that fact doesn't mean I'm going to be a great climber without a rope. It just means I realize I'm going to fall."

"Fair enough," Charlie says. "So you going to just send it back?"

You look at the blinking light on your right wrist.

"I don't know. Maybe."

You should ask how things are going. Charlie started a new job helping an artist down the street weld large, corporate symbolic art sculptures. Better than all the gig-economy stuff he'd been piecemealing together.

You should finally thank him for spending all that time chatting with you when he'd unload groceries, losing money every second he went the extra mile.

Instead you drink and talk about the weather. Something inconsequential.

"Well, even if you do screw up, it's just a robot, right?" Charlie raises the bottle of beer in a salute.

Your son crawls out of the crate the next morning. It thrashes pieces of the box aside and mewls in confusion as it turns on.

Instant regret grips you as you try to grab him, and one of his arms smashes the coffee table. Shattered glass bounces off the tile, and you let go of his unyielding artificial skin.

"Hey," you tell the confused machine. "Easy!"

It crunches around in the glass, and you can hear its eyes snick in their sockets as it anxiously looks all around your small apartment. The sound unnerves you.

When it opens its mouth, a gurgling electronic scream warbles out.

It's the most alien, unnerving sound, and it makes your whole spine tingle. "Just relax."

It's taller than you. Heavier. The ultradense batteries mean that even as you try to physically stop it from flailing, you could hardly budge it.

Those ruby-red eyes with the LIDAR range detectors behind them lock hard onto you. You feel like you're in the sights of something, and lick your lips.

The pediabotic trainers at Advent told you the first few minutes could be chaotic. You just need to make sure that you remain within its eyesight. Once you do that, it starts to imprint on you.

Like a baby animal.

Soothing tones and patience. You dance about as best you can to make sure it's aware of you.

"Make sure you have a name picked out and keep using it," you were told in the CARE training. "It's a mind in a pre-language, pre-memory state. The language matrix plug-in will be aiding it, though, and even human babies start recognizing names and language much faster than you realize."

It's one thing to watch a video of a robot coming to life with its new parents calmly welcoming it into their new, perfect multiroom home. You, on the other hand, are hopping around shit you left out and trying not to fall over as you stumble after the thing. This, you know, is a huge mistake.

"I even forgot your name!"

You're hunting about for something as the robot turns around and squalls at you.

"Rob, stop it, please."

And the mechanical screaming finally stops. Sharrad, upstairs, has been banging on the floor, upset at all the noise.

"It's OK, Rob. You're OK."

Rob cautiously approaches you.

"Hi."

The coffee table has been destroyed. You feel a knot in your stomach, scared the machine might hurt you.

"At this point in our manufacturing iterations, there's tremendous aversion to harming anything organic," the recruiters at Advent have explained many times. "Just like people have a deep instinct of fear around a snake, our robots have instinctive fears about hurting anything."

Rob gently crouches down in front of you and starts to pet your shoes, fascinated by the laces. He keeps picking them up and letting them fall back to the top of your shoes.

"OK," you laugh. "Now let's show you where your charging base is."

Rob should have the instinct to go looking for one when he's running low. The next important step is to make sure he can find it.

"Talk as much as you can. Language acquisition is key," Advent has explained. "Narrate everything you're doing as you go, and even when your foster robot is older, explain why you do everything you do. Context is key. The more you can do that, the better."

You spend the next two days teaching Rob how to find its charging port and stay still on it. It's constant and exhausting. The robot will stay charging for a while, but then get up and go chattering and exploring through the house. You have to keep moving it back.

On the third day you fall asleep on the floor as Rob warbles about and opens every single drawer and cabinet in the kitchen, working on fine-motor movement.

You wake up, panicked, to an unmoving lump next to you. You drag Rob over, the body limp in your arms, to the charger. "Please don't be broken," you say. You need this to work. Advent won't pay you anything if you kill the damn thing in the first few days.

Back on the charger, Rob starts babbling nonsense and making faces at you. Relief floods through you and you slump down to the floor.

Three days of no sleep and that meaningless proto-speak. You punch the wall with your prosthetic hand, and it crunches through the drywall. Rob sees that and startles. It punches the drywall as well.

"No!" you shout.

Rob curls into a ball on the charger and looks at you through raised arms. It's scared, and you did that. This is everything you feared. You remember your dad standing at the top of the stairs, that anger curdling you with fear.

"I can't do this," you say, curling into a ball on the floor. "I can't do this."

"You'll be surprised at how exponential growth in learning works."

Advent is all gleaming showroom factory floors. The human workers wear protective gowns, hairnets, and goggles. It's as much lab as it is factory, you think.

The recruiter walks you by glass windows looking into the factory. You stare at the pieces of robotics, impressed by the circuitry and technology everywhere, but having no clue what any of it does.

"At first, your foster robot will seem like no more than an infant, and that's because it is! But every time they get on that charger, they're not just powering up their onboard battery—they're taking in their experiences and uploading data to our servers to have it examined and encoded back to them, to accelerate their growth. Just like sleep and dreaming work for us, helping us to process our world."

You're told that in just months you'll see significant developmental gains. And then the really big leaps will start to come.

It'll take six months to fully mature your son.

Can you make it six months, taking care of a growing mind? Being *responsible* for a whole thinking being? Being a good parent? It seems like forever, and yet it's not that long of a temporary job.

"Some of us do it for 20 years," one of the recruiters laughs when you express this. She has professional highlights, perfect teeth, and shoes that cost more than your disability allowance pays out in a month.

She laughs too hard, you think.

But you say nothing and swallow anything acidic as she talks through the monthly payments and the bonus for a successful maturity.

"He's 'asleep' for now," you tell Charlie, the next time you take a moment to meet up around the fire pit. It's been hard to find the time while raising a brand-new robot. Sienna's annoyed, fairly, that you haven't been out to weed, and the fire pit needs cleaning.

You don't even bother to try and start a fire.

"You look exhausted." Charlie hands you a beer, but you shake your head. You need a clear mind. You've given up one of the few vices you have.

"It takes everything I have to just keep up. I can't go out much with him. Just too damn clumsy still. He's broken half of everything I own."

Rob has explored the backyard, the hallways. People stare at you when you go out, and you have to pull Rob back away from something because his coordination isn't that good yet. They're used to seeing robots doing things for people, not a person babysitting a robot. There are only a few hundred robots being fostered at any given time.

And it's not babysitting when you're the parent, you guess.

"Ahmed said you're not at physical therapy anymore."

"I'll get back."

Maybe.

In four more months, you'll be free, and you'll have that maturity bonus. In four months, you'll be in a clinic watching flesh and blood regenerate.

You have to hold onto that.

Things can get back to the way they were if you just get through this.

"You gave it a name?"

"Rob."

"Rob?"

"I panicked."

"Rob the robot?"

A loud crash from the apartment, followed by a shrill shriek. "Shit, Charlie, I wanted to hear about that piece you're working on for the city park, but he's awake. You can head out by the gate."

"Dad?"

You wake up as Rob taps your chest, his red eyes open wide as he stares down at you. You blink and pull back the blanket.

"Dad?"

You can't escape him. It's 2 in the morning, but he's finished a charge cycle.

"Dad. Dad. Dad. Dad. *Dad.*"

You can wrap a pillow around your head, but it's not going anywhere. That word.

Dad. Dad. Dad.

It's new. Just in the last few hours before you went to bed. But he's using the newly acquired word for everything. He has two words now.

He points at himself. "Rob!" He points at you. "Dad!"

You get up and turn on the lights.

"Dad!"

You'd asked one of the scientists that the recruiter brought in for the Q&A session why robots needed raising. The recruiter had explained it, but you wanted to get it from the egghead, not the Parental Unit Liaison.

"The simpler the animal, the less parenting it needs," the scientist said. "Some are born with all the instincts they need."

But a robot meant to move and look like a human being, to help people in nursing homes or other similar cases, that robot couldn't just be programmed with a few repetitive functions.

To understand nuance, to get a theory of mind and understand context, one needed intelligence.

"You need to be raised, and in your own body. You're not just a mind in a jar—that's an old theory of consciousness. You're a grown being. A whole being. Your gut bacteria, spinal column, the society around you, all of that creates an entire person, as well as the experiences and time that it passes through. You can't just manufacture a thinking robot. We have to raise it."

And to do that, Advent has to pay for human caretakers.

You passed the screening process, particularly because they're interested in a variety of types of caretakers.

"It immerses units in a full scope of experiences, which makes our product lines more randomized, encompassing a wide range of interactions with people from different walks of life. Our robots pass that knowledge around, and it gives them a service-oriented edge."

Raise a robot that works well and makes it through job training, you get rewarded.

"Once we have a functioning unit, then we can copy and paste it," the scientist grins. "We have 2,000 different models and personalities you can interact with, now, for a variety of workplace functions."

At the park you teach Rob to throw a baseball. It's good for coordination.

"Dad, you're breathing heavy," he says as you walk back toward the apartments.

"It's just been hard. I've been inside for three months taking care of you. I haven't been doing my physical therapy."

"I know. You keep saying I was such a hard baby to take care of." Rob rolls his laser-red eyes dramatically.

You *are* struggling. You need to make sure to take the time and get outside for walks more. That quarry lake was the big target, wasn't it? You never did get there. It feels like your whole life has just been the apartment or the yard for so long.

Charlie hasn't called in a while. You saw online that he's won a prize for the art he worked on with the collective he's now joined. The sculpture is in a park near the courthouse. It looks like rusted iron spikes shaped like lightning bolts hitting the concrete pad it's bolted onto.

You tell Rob about that. He never really replies, just listens and asks simple questions. He's past the constant "why?" stage. That was last month, and it was hell. You've been chattering to him nonstop, now.

The pediabotic experts told you to keep doing that, so you tell yourself you're doing it to be the best caretaker you can.

You fall to your knees on the sidewalk halfway back to the apartment.

"Dad!" Rob is scared. He triggers an automated call for medical help, his body strobes emergency blue as he shouts at the people around you to come help. But seeing a nervous robot scares them, and they stay away from you both, not sure what's happening. "Dad!"

It's your heart. You can tell from the pain in your chest.

You're not out of breath. You're out of oxygen.

"He hasn't left your side," the nurse says when you wake up after surgery.

Rob squeezes your hand.

It hurts to sit up, to cough. They've split you in half and pulled out your heart, fixed it as best they could, and put it back in.

"Dad, I was so scared."

And you hug him, because that's what he seems to need. A robot can't cry, but it can be worried. Scared to lose the one person it's known since it was born.

"It's OK. Everything is OK."

Rob helps you home, and pitches in with some of the chores. Rob's like an older kid now, able to do basic things around the house in a pinch.

As you recover, the two of you start working on some home renovation. Holes in the wall from the first few days of Rob showing up. A new coffee table becomes a father-son project.

Your own father took weeks to get jogging again after his heart transplant. You just need a few days.

Progress.

"What was your father like?" Rob asks as you scrape wood with a lathe.

"Dangerous," you say. "He was a dangerous man. Particularly with a few drinks in him."

You tell him about the door your father threw at you and how it clipped your forehead. It bled for hours. You tell him about the time the cop showed up to your door and your mom stood in front of you and smiled and flirted until he was satisfied nothing was wrong and walked off.

The longest moment of your life, watching the man in that uniform walk away into the night.

At least, until the moment that forklift pinned you to the concrete floor.

Every breath an infinity, every pulse a universe of pain as you faded slowly away.

"I tell him too much," you say to the Advent rep at the weekly checkup call.

"There's no such thing." He's gone over the logs, asked about Rob's behavior, the usual questions about how well Rob is integrating into life at the apartment. You've asked questions about whether assuming Rob was male made any sense because he's a robot. Robot self-identity is complex, they say, but they're talking to Rob, and he's OK with the label for now. There's a documentary on robot identity and human interactions you can watch if you need. "The conversation is good for their development."

"I've talked to Rob about things I haven't told anyone else."

The rep nods. "We find this common with men in particular. Your records say you've been through trauma, and you were raised without cognitive behavioral therapy to help you. I'll bet you were told as a boy not to cry, to hold those emotions in, right?"

He looks up at you.

The direct eye contact makes you swallow. "Uh, sure."

"Real men don't cry. Real men don't follow safety guidelines. They show strength. Willpower gets you through everything, right, no matter how hard? The fight's the thing." The rep is taking notes. "And that does work, until it doesn't. You can't fight your way out of trauma, or out of a worldwide economic depression. And then your whole mental model fails to match the world around you."

You remember how much worse it got when your father lost his job. His identity. He couldn't will a new job into existence when there were none.

You wonder what he'd call his son, living on disability, raising a robot like a bizarre Mary Poppins.

"There's a reason getting a dog, or some other living thing, can by extremely therapeutic," he continues.

"You're comparing having a child to getting a dog?" You're a little shocked, maybe outraged.

"Not at all, I have a kid, it's not the same," the rep says in a reassuring tone. "But the act of raising something isn't just about what you raise and take care of. It's about how you change yourself around the space they need within you, as well. You'll have emotions and vulnerability during that process. We talked about this during intake."

Yes, you remember that detail from the parenting class you had to take with Advent. The fostering program comes with free therapy, but you turned it down. You're tough. You're the dude who got trapped under a tipped-over forklift and gritted your teeth and got through it.

Everyone's complimented you on how strong you were to survive that, how tough you were to get through everything that came afterward.

How many times were you thanked for your service after doing a full tour?

You knew that you could do six months of parenting. You were tough enough. Even despite the day of misgivings right before Rob arrived.

But now you're wondering if you're tough enough to handle what comes after Rob leaves.

Rob throws a pamphlet at you. It rustles through the air, then softly lands against your chest, just as he planned.

"What is that crap?"

"It's the medical clinic I'll be going to," you say. "I've been talking about this forever."

They could take your DNA and grow a new heart for you in a nutrient bath. They can regrow whole legs and arms.

"Have you ever thought about how I feel?" Rob shouts. "Do you even think about anyone else besides yourself?"

You're confused as hell. "What does this have to do with you?"

"You're a whole person, Dad!" Rob hits the countertop. Hard enough to make a point, make you jump, but not hard enough to break anything.

"What?"

"You're fine just the way you are." Emotion crackles in Rob's voice. It's a warble that flashes you back to that first moment he staggered around the apartment, crying in that electronic voice of his. "Not wanting artificial limbs—how the hell do you think that makes *all of me* feel?"

He holds up his arms in front of his face, and you look down at the one arm of yours that looks just like his.

"Rob—"

You're stunned at the argument that explodes between you. He's been holding things in. Things you do that anger him. No, that *hurt* him.

Trying to decide if regrowing limbs is somehow an admission that you aren't whole—that's been your struggle. Not his.

But clearly, Rob feels that this is his universe as well. You can no longer make choices just about yourself. They have to include him as well. He even hates his own name.

"I panicked!" you say, as he tells you people laugh at "Rob the Robot."

"My whole life, you've talked about walking to that quarry, Dad. You can't wait until you have just the right leg to go do that. It hurts when you use me as an excuse to avoid things."

Rob helps you over the last few boulders to get to the quarry's edge, and then you both sit and look out over the mossy rocks near the edge to the brownish, silty water.

It's one of your favorite walks, now.

The human body is a thing of constant change. Your skin is made out of cells that were just food a few weeks ago. You're a ghost of an idea that keeps getting passed on down through cell instructions.

You're not a mind in a jar. You're an ecosystem, a community of cells and organisms with a theory of mind bolted onto them. And they're all involved in a complicated dance that keeps the complexity going until that system of passing on instructions gets disrupted after too many copies and it all falters.

You think: We're often so scared of how we'll be different if we take medicine for our minds, or go to therapy, or make a major life change. How can we be the same person if we change so much over time?

The physical therapy hurt. It was a real pain in the ass after you'd taken so much time off. You threw up the first time you got back to the gym.

But Rob was there every day, proud as could be.

And you started taking walks together. It's his favorite thing to do with you. Walk and talk about life, whatever comes to your two minds. Rob has odd taste in TV and has even taken up reading. Mostly nonfiction, but he has some interest in mystery novels.

You have some plans to take a trip and hike a small part of the Appalachian Trail next year, when he gets some vacation after his first year of work.

That's something you've been terrified of. You'd never thought much about robot rights when you agreed to bring this person into the world. But there have been big advances in how the world treats robots, particularly since robot strikes out west forced people to realize that if you had to raise them to be complete minds, enslavement was horrific. Rob will have free will. He will make less than a human would—there's still a metal ceiling to break through—but he'll get vacations, pay, while he does jobs that would be tough for organic people. Deep-sea diving is what he chose.

Most importantly, you'll get to see him.

Because you never just stop being a parent.

"I want to give you something," you say. You hand him over the watch your grandfather gave you when you left for college.

"You know I can tell time internally, right, Dad? Do we need to get you another checkup?"

"It's—"

"I know what it is." Rob puts it on, metal against metal. "Thank you."

When it's time to leave, he asks several times if you're OK to walk back to the apartment alone.

"I'm OK," you reassure him.

He slings a duffel bag with everything he owns over his shoulder and heads out.

Charlie's at the door to the complex when you get back.

"So you got your freedom back!" He waves a six-pack at you, then does a double take when you raise your arm to wave back. "What the hell?"

"Oh." You look at the arm. It's all burnished metal, then scrimshawed with Rob's art. You two spent days building the custom arm together, thanks to Rob taking high-end robotics maintenance classes during his charging cycles.

The leg is even more customized. An object of expression and a personal statement by the both of you. And now that you're out of physical therapy, the upgraded artificial limbs are kicked up and finely tuned, thanks to Rob tinkering with your neural interface.

"It was set up for a standard off-the-line synapse reading," he'd explained while tinkering, making you twitch every time he played with the settings. "Now that you're getting better at timing and control, I can help you more."

A week ago, you went to a tattoo artist and got a sleeve of three-dimensional gears and diesel engine pistons on your other bicep to make the organic match the inorganic.

People at the park stare at you. Sometimes mothers pull their kids back, in instinct.

For a second you're worried that Charlie's going to do something similar, but he looks closely at it. "That's fucking sweet, man! I love the engine details!"

"They're based on some of the equipment that Rob will be using. Come on in."

You put your organic arm around Charlie's shoulder and pull him along. You've invited him over to ask him about his art, to see how things are going for him in his new career as a sculptor.

There's better beer in the fridge.

After Charlie leaves, you lie in bed and look at a picture of you and Rob standing by the quarry with big smiles.

You put a hand to your chest. Under it is a new scar since a second heart surgery. A fresher scar. Under it is a cybernetic heart, a mechanical pump that whirs softly underneath. *Faster, better, stronger.*

When you look at the picture of your son, who has just left a home that now feels empty without him in it, that heart surges with love.

Ray Nayler has lived and worked in Russia, Central Asia, the Caucasus, and the Balkans for nearly two decades. He is a Foreign Service Officer, and previously worked in international educational development, as well as serving in the Peace Corps in Ashgabat, Turkmenistan. A Russian speaker, he has also learned Turkmen, Albanian, Azerbaijani Turkish, and Vietnamese.

Ray began publishing speculative fiction in 2015 in the pages of *Asimov's* with the short story "Mutability." Since then, his critically acclaimed stories have seen print in *Clarkesworld*, *Analog*, *The Magazine of Fantasy and Science Fiction*, *Lightspeed*, and *Nightmare*, as well as in several Best of the Year anthologies. His story "Winter Timeshare" from the January/February 2017 issue of *Asimov's* was collected by the late Gardner Dozois in *The Very Best of the Best: 35 Years of the Year's Best Science Fiction*.

Ray currently lives in Pristina, Kosovo with his wife Anna, their daughter Lydia, and two rescued cats—one Tajik, one American.

EYES OF THE FOREST

Ray Nayler

"Look at me."

"There's so much blood!"

"Look at *me*, I said. Not the wound."

"So much—"

"Look at me."

"It hurts!"

"Sedef, look at my eyes."

Sedef looked up from the wound in her wrist, into the eyes of Mauled by Mistake.

"Good," Mauled said. Her pupils reflected the swirl of color inside the tent as she tore open a third repair packet with her teeth.

"Eyes on me."

Sedef wanted to look down, but Mauled's eyes were locked on hers, holding her gaze, while moving the packet over the wound automatically.

"Millions of nanobots, Sedef. Unfolding inside your wrist right now, stitching the wound shut with the slimmest and strongest of threads. They will find all the edges. They will seal the wound, layer by layer, then melt themselves into a protective analgesic gel. The gel will keep the wound clean and dry. It will dull almost all the pain. You know this. It was in your medical training. Shht!" Mauled stopped her as she was about to glance down. "I told you to look at me, not at the wound. You do as I say. Always. Yes?"

"Yes."

As Mauled spoke, Sedef studied the edge of her face—the scar that wound along the right side and into her hairline, starting above the temple and slicing all the way down to the jaw and neck, then beyond the microbond sleeve at the collar of the suit. How far did it go? The scar had a texture, raised, like a topographic map of a mountain range. What had done it?

"Hold still. There. Now it's done. You can look."

Sedef stared down at her arm. The sleeve of her suit was pulled up to the elbow. The arm was splattered with blood, already drying. At her wrist, where the wound had been, just above the carpals, was a streak of glaucous material. As Sedef looked at it, it moved slightly. She felt herself succumbing to nausea.

Mauled caught her by the chin, tilted her face up. "Don't puke in my tent. Take a deep breath. This is over. You are not dead. Put it behind you."

"What happened? What did I do wrong?"

"Think it through."

"I attached the glove to the suit's power. I tightened the thread of the extension sleeve to the glove wire. I visually verified the glove was functioning. I—"

"And the cuff cover?"

"I bound the cuff cover over the sleeve and the end of the glove, just like you showed me."

Mauled picked up the glove from where it lay on the floor of the tent, the end torn and bloody. She handed it to Sedef. The cuff cover was ripped away from the sleeve, but most of it was intact. "Feel along the center of the cuff cover. Inside. The battery filament. How long does it hold a charge?"

"Two days, out of the battery chamber. Fifteen seconds for every rotation of the manual crank, an hour for a full five minutes of cranking, if on emergency power and within two meters of the field."

"Unless?"

"I don't know." *Unless what? She had checked everything.* Her fingers felt along the cuff cover. Then . . . there. A break in the filament. Not near the wound. No. On the other side. She must have snapped it somehow. Getting it on. Or bent it in half in storage. How could she have been so stupid?

"Unless the filament is broken, and the cuff cover goes dark. I don't know how the filament could have gotten broken, Mauled by Mistake. I was careful."

"Not careful enough. You might have lost a hand. Then you would be back home. Or, more likely, dead." Sedef noticed that Mauled was sweating, her skin ashen.

So she does care.

"What does a darkened cuff cover look like?" Mauled asked.

"A black streak."

"As your hand moves?"

"Something falling. Something dead."

"Do you think you could have popped the tent, gotten in here alone, sealed it, and treated your wound before going into shock?"

Sedef thought it through—all the motions, with the pain the lashvine had caused, the panic afterward clouding her mind. Mauled by Mistake had done everything: opened the tent, gotten her inside, closed the aperture while Sedef was screaming, writhing on the ground.

"I don't know."

Mauled grabbed her jaw again, hard, made her look at her. Yes, Sedef saw—ashen and sweating. Had this really scared her that much? It didn't make sense. Nothing scared Mauled.

"That's your problem, Sedef. You don't know. Well, you must know. Because now you are going to have to save my life."

Mauled looked down. Following her gaze, Sedef saw it—the spreading stain of blood darkening the roiling iridescence of Mauled's suit.

"Those three nanobot repair packets were all we had. There are six more, back at the depot. I'll push gauze into the wound, bind it with the old-style bandages. I don't think it hit any organs . . . but I'll need three or four repair packets from the depot, at least. And I can't get there myself."

Sedef was trying to control her breathing. Her heart rate. As she had been taught. It wasn't working. She felt herself beginning to hyperventilate. Shoved the feeling down, the panic. *Think, instead! Act, instead!*

"Let me help you bind the wound."

"No time for that, and no need." Mauled was tearing open a pack of coagulating gauze. "This stuff is old-fashioned, but it will do the trick for now. I can do it myself. Get suited up."

"But I can—"

"Suited. *Now.*"

The command cut through the panic, down to muscle memory. The motions she had drilled, the checklists she had studied and that Mauled had gone over with her, again and again, every evening, for a week now, in the tents and at the depots.

"Take the spare cuff from my kit bag." Mauled was turned away from her, shoving gauze into her wound. She had stripped the top of her suit off, and now Sedef saw that the scar trailed over the shoulder blade and down her back, almost to the base of her spine.

"How did it happen?" Sedef wasn't sure if she was asking about the wound or the scar.

"That lashvine that attacked you—when I grabbed it, it stabbed me like a lance. Went in maybe twenty centimeters. Defense mechanism." She grunted in pain, or irritation. *"Are you dressing?"*

My fault. She was injured because of me.

"I'm in my suit already."

"Now think. How far away is the depot?"

"Seven hours quick walk."

"Then you had better run."

"Is it that bad?"

"Bad enough."

"I'm going."

"No, you're not. Not yet."

"What?"

"I haven't checked you."

"There's no time!" Sedef shouted.

"Control your anger. Never neglect the little things, or next time you'll end up with more than just a nasty scar."

Mauled went over the visual suit checklist with her. It took what felt like an hour, though really it couldn't have been more than three minutes.

The second they finished the suit check, Sedef ran out of the tent.

And nearly forgot to reseal the aperture behind her. This happened to her every time. Even though she had been in the forest for a week now, the sight of it still stopped her, tore everything from her mind.

The pure beauty almost knocked her off-balance. Under the gray, low sky, the forest coruscated with color. Aquamarine-phosphorescent, slow-moving colonies of waveweed that could extend for hundreds, even thousands of square meters. Single-celled, pulsing sweet-yeast turned the rest of the forest floor into a shivering mass of violet as the organisms shifted their photophore apertures in waves of communication.

Their violet was taken up by the darting microbirds who ingested the sweet-yeasts and carefully gardened them in the crystalline membrane that coated their bodies.

Like us, Sedef thought—shielding themselves against death, always having to make sure their coatings were properly powered. They eat dirt and garden the sweet-yeasts in their crystal carapaces; we use batteries and microdiodes.

The gently luminous, aquamarine stalks of the diadem trees rose into the canopy's varicolored riot, writhing with the full kaleidoscope of life.

Deadly kaleidoscope, Sedef thought, forcing herself to look past the beauty to the other reality: a thousand jeweled, hungry mouths—mouths of so many forms: lanternbeaks that could clap an arm off with a razor edge so fast, you wouldn't feel it until they were gone; whipwings that closed their bodies over you and slashed you to ribbons with internal zippers of scalpel-teeth in an organ both mouth and stomach; winding twist-constrictors that would drop around you in a corkscrew and roil you into mush in the diamond pyramids of their coils. And so many more.

As she watched, a pulsing ruby floatbird jetted awkwardly to a new perch, reaching a branch just as its bag deflated. It clung there, collapsed and gasping, leering down at her with its barbed snatching beak. Four miniature balloons of its young bobbed along clumsily through the air behind it, warily jetting hydrogen from their vents, moving with adolescent uncertainty beneath the orange-blazing diadem leaves, whooping worriedly at their papa.

Move. Stop gawping like a child.

She began to run.

One week ago, she had stood in the windkey of her home complex, behind the glowing scrim that cut her home cave off from the forest she had dreamed of all her childhood. She had been waiting in the windkey for a full day and night. She was considering giving up, going back home. Her mentor wasn't coming. Her assignment had been forgotten.

How much longer would she have waited? An hour? Another day? What reserves of patience were left?

While waiting, she'd packed and repacked her gear, repeating lists of necessities from memorized safety checks. She'd stripped out of her suit and gone over its seams twice.

Still no mentor.

Then the scrim shuddered, and her mentor stood before her. Tired. Dirty. She took her hood off, revealing an unreadable expression on her face. Her suit was splattered with pulsating gobbets of sweet-yeast mud up to the knees.

"Are you—"

"I am Mauled by Mistake," the woman said. "And you are Sedef. Hand me your pack."

She had a *given name*.

Only a few wayfinders had them: a name bestowed on them by their other guides. The names were always sarcastic, vaguely insulting to their bearer, referring to something they had done wrong. But they were worn like the highest of honorifics. Sedef knew a handful of them: Stabbed Own Hand, Stepped on Hive, Bitten while Sleeping, Cloud was Bees. The names memorialized acts of stupidity survived.

So, her mentor was a good one. She felt a rush of pride. She was worthy of someone with experience.

Mauled by Mistake picked up Sedef's pack and opened it. She began throwing items on the ground.

"That one is definitely on the list. In class a week ago, they explained that we might—"

Mauled by Mistake talked over her: a monologue that ignored any attempt to interrupt it as she reduced the contents of Sedef's pack to less than a third of what they had been. "The things you carry on your body, you also carry in your mind. They are a distraction. You will think they'll solve a problem, but they won't. What they will do is keep you from acting *now*, make you think about how you could solve the problem *later*. If you had time to reach into your pack. But you do not have that time. Because you will die, in the interval between now and later. Instead, you keep your pack light, your thoughts light, your solutions immediate."

"That multitool is for—"

"Pick that up and I will break your hand. You can use your knife for everything that tool does. Let me look at you."

Sedef stood still in front of her while Mauled by Mistake went over her suit in granular detail, finding things wrong everywhere, grunting and sighing exasperatedly. Up close, Mauled smelled of dirty hair and sweat and the cloying sugar of sweet-yeast mud.

"Who was your teacher?

"Beyazit."

"Does he hate you?"

"No. I don't think so. Why?"

"Because he is trying to get you killed." She stepped back, looked Sedef over, adjusted her hood and mask.

"Can you breathe well?"

"Yes."

"Good. Let's go."

And they stepped through the scrim, leaving the gleaming, expensive pile of Sedef's expectations strewn on the ground.

Sedef ran up the hill they had been descending when the attack happened. *And now Mauled by Mistake is dying, and it is my fault. I barely lasted a week out here before getting one of the forest's best wayfinders killed.*

At the top of the rise, she had to scramble up over the sharp edges of a massive tabular colony of stone grass. Once she was on top of it, the glittering field of its chrysochlorous polyps seemed to stretch for half a kilometer, each step she took on its surface radiating a reaction like a flash of citron ball lightning.

Here on this tabula, there were no trees: only the gleaming cyan of the pseudoshrubs that had bored into the surface of the stone grass with their acid-secreting radula and put down rooticles, colonizing the living tableland in clusters ranging from a dozen to a hundred animals.

I can run and think about these things at the same time. I can do more than just survive. I can also seek to understand.

"Is that a floatbird egg sac?" At first, the thing looked like a cluster of the lamps they used in dwelling corridors, but when Sedef looked closer, she could see that it was, in fact, a series of obolid, carmine-glowing eggs, barbed to a lower branch of a diadem in the molted skin of its parent. Even the sneering face of the floatbird was there, shed and distended at the bottom of the sack.

"Yes, it is."

Sedef leaned in closer. The floatbird embryos, bright inside the translucent membranes of their eggs, shifted listlessly in their amniotic fluid.

"Extraordinary."

"We need to be at the depot before dark. Changeover is the most dangerous time to be out. As the forest modulates its glow for sundark, any slight suit anomaly is particularly visible."

"We learned that. And there are animals, Beyazit said, that specialize in hunting during changeover. Some of which no one has ever seen. Predators we haven't even—"

"Predators?" Mauled by Mistake gave out an incredulous bark, followed by a stream of intricate profanity.

Sedef had heard that the wayfinders had a whole second language of profanity so inventive it was almost unintelligible to others. She couldn't understand all of this expression—something about Beyazit's father being born in a quiver of nightwing penises? Could that be right?

"He said—"

"Please stop." Mauled by Mistake said, holding up a hand. "And bring that egg sac with you."

"I don't want to disturb it."

"It is hanging there for you. Why else do you think it has been placed here, along the path? I'm not going to carry it for you: Know your place."

Just as the depot came into sight, five hours of walking later, Mauled took the sac from Sedef and threw it, unceremoniously, into the trees.

"I thought floatbirds raised their young?"

"They raise some of them, but they also leave eggs for others to find. We don't know why. But wayfinders discovered early that carrying a floatbird egg sac is a good form of added protection—a little extra glow—so they got into the habit of collecting them. The floatbirds then took to leaving the sacs along the paths, where we will find them more easily. Perhaps they want us to distribute their young, like seeds."

Once they had crawled through the hatch and down the angled tunnel into the main chamber of the depot, they discovered another wayfinder was already there. This was a young man, so thin he looked as if he had been sharpened. He was stripped down to a dirty pair of undershorts, cleaning his suit with a wet rag. As they came in, he glanced up, mumbled something, and went on with his task.

"Beyazit is telling the prospects to beware of predators," Mauled by Mistake said in the young man's direction.

"Beyazit should start each day by eating a bowl of his own entrails," the young man said without looking up. "He almost got me killed once."

"Who of us has he not almost gotten killed?"

Later, over a cold dinner of nutrient broth and noodles Sedef had made and packeted herself, Mauled by Mistake said, "The first thing to understand is that there are no predators in the forest. This old word does not fit. Only the ignorant use it."

"But death is always waiting," Sedef protested. "The forest is filled with teeth."

"Yes," Mauled by Mistake said. "You know your recitations well. The forest is filled with teeth. Death is waiting. Always. And so on. But there are no predators. There are only scavengers. When they attack you, and they will—and when they kill you someday, which they likely will—it will be by accident."

"But the suit lights are a defense against attack. They indicate we are dangerous."

The young man released a stream of profanity involving something about Beyazit attempting to whistle through a mouthful of various parts of his relatives' anatomy. "The suits don't indicate we are dangerous: They simply indicate we are alive."

Run. And keep running. The way now toward the depot was downhill, through an area where the diadem trees were choked with colonies of lash-vine, the scarlet "lash" on which the razor-sharp animals grew hanging in dully pulsing loops over the path.

Just looking at them made Sedef's wrist ache. In some places away from the path, they weighed down whole trees with their glowering red mesh. Run into a vine and it could slice your suit open. Once that happened, revealing the lightless area underneath, it was just a matter of time before something found you. Run into one of the larger colonies and there would be no need to wait—you would be cut to ribbons anyway.

Sedef ducked under a low-hanging loop. Coming up, she smacked her head on a branch and stumbled, fell. Her hood was off! She looked behind her. She had snagged it on the tree.

Covering her head as much as she could with her lighted arm and glove, she reached up and unhooked it from the thorn where it had caught. Slowly, she pulled it back on. The connections had been yanked out, but they were designed to be: She snapped the filaments back into place, and the hood regained its wave of color.

But in that moment, she had felt everything around her still, and then shift toward her—as if the entire grove had been about to leap at her face. And tear, and tear.

She sat a moment on the path, willing her heart rate down, trying to catch her breath. Strange sounds from somewhere. No—just her, whimpering in fear. She had not even realized she was doing it. *I can do more than just survive. I can also seek to understand*, she remembered thinking earlier. *Fool. You'll be lucky to live to see the depot, much less "understand" anything here.*

"'Predator' is just a word we carried with us into space. A concept from Earth. It has no place here. Nothing in the forest hunts what is alive: That is a habit of our home world—a habit of animals none here have ever set eyes on. Beasts from ancient books: the tiger, the wolf. Perhaps Beyazit uses that word because he knows it still has mythic power: tooth and claw, watching from the dark. But you should not use it. When you name things wrongly, it twists the way you see."

The other wayfinder was already gone in the morning. Sedef never learned his name.

Now she and Mauled by Mistake were working their way through a lowland swampy area. The muddy pools, like the soil around them, were filled with varieties of sweet-yeast, but in the water, it turned a pearlescent lavender, streaked with the cinnabar of knifefish beneath the surface.

The soggy path wound its way between pools. Several diadems in the swamp had gone dark, root systems waterlogged beyond capacity, and a rending of lanternbeaks was dismantling them. Grenadine beaks ablaze, they searched for the symbiotic colonies of wood-bees that had died along with the trees.

"You need to understand our ancestors, Sedef. They came filled with knowledge—but it was knowledge built from the preconceptions of their world. Preconceptions that misled them. Most of them were dead before they found the caves. And then, once they found them, they were happy just to be safe underground, and warm. Using the knowledge they brought with them from Earth, and time, our ancestors bent sunlight down shafts from above to grow their own food. They piped water from underground lakes, where they also found the sightless, colorless knifefish that had long ago lost their way. Protein, farmable and free.

"This and other things made harmless in the darkness became their staples. Fed and safe, they excavated and worked and built. They lived and worked under a sky of their own manufacture. And so they never learned to live here, on this planet—they just transferred the life they had on Earth to this place. They built a pleasant arcade, its endless passages lit by lamps and tube-filtered sunlight. A diorama of a dead world.

"But generations ago, some began to venture out beyond the scrims of the windkeys. No one knows who were the first. I imagine them sitting not far from the scrims, still protected by their radiance. Watching. Listening. Perhaps just one initially, then several. Look!"

A floatbird was sinking from the canopy, its light guttering as it turned a slow descending spiral. Ten meters or so above the shimmer of the forest floor, its light went out.

In the moment before the whipwing struck, it was as if the forest held its breath, as if every eye turned hungrily to watch that descending mote of darkness.

Then the floatbird was gone. Sedef could feel the wind of the whipwing's coiling amber passage on her cheek. It crashed upward into the fire of diadem leaves, disturbing a glassy cloud of microbirds which shrieked after it.

After a moment, Mauled by Mistake continued, "There are no predators here. Symbiosis provides most of the nutrients these creatures need. They have woven a tight web of interrelation and never learned the habit of killing. But make no mistake: The scavengers are fast, competing over who gets to free the nutrients trapped in the lightless bodies of the dead. And their teeth are sharp.

"The early wayfinders knew it doesn't matter how you see the forest. What matters is how the forest sees you. It's said this wisdom was carried from Earth. Some people there were also of the forest. They knew that how the forest sees you is a matter of life or death. When hunters slept in the forest, they slept with their eyes facing up. That way, the puma would know them for what they were: predators, and not prey to be torn. Pumas may not see the world as we do—but they see it. Understanding how they see it is survival."

"But what is a puma?"

"They say they are like the tigers of the old books. But in the old language, 'puma' was anything that hunts in the forest."

Sedef reached the depot. The sun was long past its apex. Exhausted, she allowed herself to collapse for a minute, to stretch full length on the scraped cool of the stone floor and breathe.

There was a moment, then, when she wanted to stay there, on the floor's radiating cool. Mauled by Mistake's death felt like a price she was willing to pay for an hour of safety from the fear of being alone in the forest. The forest jeweled with eyes and teeth, in which no human would ever be safe.

To get back to Mauled by Mistake, she would have to run through changeover, when if there was a solar storm and a sudden electromagnetic pulse—something that happened every few months—she would be dead in moments. In the day, she might have thirty seconds to find her crank and light her suit manually. During changeover? No time at all.

And she would have to run into sundark, when the forest blazed with stranger colors, and bright monsters prowled that no wayfinder had seen and lived to tell about.

And I will not live to tell about.

She stood up. She took the repair packets from their case, then paused a moment to read the marks left on the wall by other wayfinders. She went up the ramp to the depot entrance and grasped the handle. Her wounded wrist pulsed with the bloodbeat in her veins. Sedef gathered herself, gathered her strength.

Then she ran.

Just before the attack, Mauled by Mistake and Sedef had been walking side by side. It was a rare morning, cloudless and bright—the safest time in the forest, when the glow of life was dimmed and lacked contrast. Everything seemed to move a bit more heavily as the forest drowsed.

"We are now two days' quick walk from the next settlement. Since this is training, we carry nothing with us beyond what we need, but normally we would also have packs of letters, medicines, items for trade. The cave settlements were quick to learn how they could use the wayfinders to their advantage, integrate them back into their system. And we were quick to learn how we could use them to supply our needs. If you live, you will come to know that we have our own ways out here—of which you have only gleaned the surface.

"If you live, I will teach you our names for the forest's colors. The settlers use the old Earth names, empty names that refer to things we have never seen. Did you know violet is named for a flower? What does this flower look like? Is it even the color that now bears its name? Or have we confused it with the color rose—another flower? Amber is the color of the sap of an Earth tree, turned to stone by age. Who has seen such a thing? Pomegranate is the name of a fruit I have never found in the records. I will teach you new names. Names from here, made for now."

If I live.

Sedef was thinking of the wayfinder they had met in the first depot. In the middle of that night, she had woken, and lay in the dark listening to Mauled by Mistake and that nameless wayfinder having sex. Afterward, she listened to them talking in the dark, in a thick wayfinder dialect from which she could pluck only a few words—a matted tangle of insider references, names for things that were not the names they used in the settlements, elaborate profanity. She had thought she knew wayfinder dialect, but it turned out she did not. All she knew was some pidgin version of it they allowed settlers to learn.

Lying there in the dark, she had wanted so much to be on the inside of that world. Yes. And this morning, too. It was worth it. She felt, for the first time in her life, sure about her path forward.

Then, that moment of stillness—the forest's eyes on her. She had turned to Mauled by Mistake with a question in her eyes. *What happened?*

The lashvine struck.

Halfway there, now. Halfway back to Mauled by Mistake. *Let her be alive.*

She was in a swamp area when it happened. Changeover had come: The sun was below the horizon, the forest incandescent against the darkening air. Her suit felt dim against the wild colors of changeover. She felt the hairs rise on the back of her neck, beneath the hood.

The path was slick and greasy, tangled with roots. The torn stumps of dead diadem trees jutted from opalescent pools of pale violet like jagged streaks of darkness. Lanternbeaks clacked their jaws and shuddered their wings, signaling to one another as they dipped their pendulous strainer jaws into the pools to siphon up the black spots of drowned dew bugs whose living relatives drifted in scintillating clouds of blush above the stagnant water.

And then everything flickered for a moment—a shudder running through the forest. And her suit went out. She saw it happen: her arm's shifting incandescence suddenly solid, dark against the light of everything else. The forest grew still. She felt the eyes turned in her direction.

She did not think: *What happened?* If she had, she would have died.

She did not think—she acted. She threw herself into the mud and rolled in it, then tore off her lightless hood and flung it away from her. She saw it snatched whole out of the air as she smeared the iridescent mud on her face and into her hair.

Then she saw the thing. It came from behind a diadem tree, like emerald flames blown into a silken form of felid glass, stalking toward her. *Puma.* That was the only word that fit the beast. She thought *puma* but did not hesitate: As she rolled in the mud, she felt the creature's heat on her face. It sidled over to her, nuzzling her shoulder, lambent and liquid on its six legs, pausing for a moment. She kept the darkness of her eyes closed: Her eyes, which did not cast their own light, were targets. Remembering—*it doesn't matter how you see the forest. What matters is how the forest sees you.*

But later she would dream its face, just as if her eyes had been open: a double grin, each long, carrion-tearing tooth flickering like an ancient oil lamp in a cave.

Tooth and claw.

She felt its breath on her, humid and acidic. And then the padding slap of its feet through the mud as it went on its way.

And the moment was gone. She lay on the path, coated in the violet glow of sweet-yeast. For how long? Ten minutes? Only five? Slowly, she sat up. She examined herself, moving efficiently, covering bare patches, thickening the coating. How long would the mud crust last? She tried to think, and remembered their boots, thick with mud, glowing steadily when she had awakened in the depot. Five hours after their arrival? Six?

It should be enough. If nothing tore the dark spots that were her eyes from her head.

Now she thought: *What caused the suit to short?* And knew. The lessons had covered it: an electromagnetic pulse. A burst of plasma and magnetism into the solar wind. How many wayfinders had just died? Most of them were inside. The ones caught outside had hand-crank back-ups they'd have started turning right away. Would that have saved them?

Would it have saved Mauled by Mistake? If she was asleep when the tent went dark, she was dead.

If she had been awake, there was a chance.

Sedef got up and ran.

She clambered over the edge of the stone grass colony and began her descent down the final hill. At the bottom, there would be a tent, with Mauled by Mistake inside. Or there would be nothing at all: The forest left nothing behind. She paused at a pool to apply more mud to herself, after microbirds began to nip and tug at her hair. Back in the swamp, she'd stripped off the shorted-out suit and pack: The mud had been caking in the damaged suit's seams, creating dangerous dark fissures in the sweet-yeast glow. Naked, wearing only her shoes, she could layer it over her body more evenly, be safer. She now carried the suit and pack in a floatbird sac, illuminated by the eggs.

She crossed the tableland of stone grass in what felt like seconds, legs pumping. Not feeling tired anymore—feeling now as if she could run forever.

But as she descended the hill, she felt herself slowing. Afraid to know. Afraid to see the clearing, empty . . .

The tent was there.

She covered the last distance as if she were flying, tore open the tent's aperture.

Dead. Ashen, her hand next to the manual crank. *How late am I?* Less than an hour: The tent was still lit by the manual crank.

But—no. Some slight movement, a twitch of the mouth. And the eyes opened, dark in a face drained of hue.

Mauled by Mistake smiled, weakly. Her voice was just a whisper.

"Look at you . . . is that . . . sweet-yeast? Are you . . . naked? I would laugh, but it hurts too much . . . "

Sedef rolled her onto her back, found the wound, and tore open the first repair packet.

"Shh. Everything is going to be all right now."

"No, it isn't," Mauled by Mistake croaked.

"Yes, it is. We'll get you fixed up . . . and make it back to the depot, and rest."

I saw a puma! she wanted to say. *And lived! I have so much to tell you. You cannot die.*

"No, that's not what I mean." Mauled by Mistake grinned at her through bloody teeth. "I know *I'll* be all right. Wounds heal. What I mean is . . . you're *really* going to hate your given name."

SINEW AND STEEL AND WHAT THEY TOLD

Carrie Vaughn

I am cut nearly in half by the accident. The surviving fibers of my suit hold me together. I am not dead.

And this is a problem. I expected to die in this job, in my little scout runner, blasted apart, incinerated, torn to pieces with nothing to recover. All that would follow would be a sad memorial service with a picture and an old set of boots on a table. That is how scout pilots usually die. But I am just cut almost in half. And the doctor on my ship, *Visigoth*, is very good.

My biologics are mostly shut down with shock, though I'm dutifully trying to monitor the pain. It's all-enveloping, a fist squeezing my brain. My mechanics are in full self-repair mode, overheating because there's so much to knit back together. Because of them, I have survived long enough that I will probably not die. This is going to be awkward.

From my own internal processor I send out an emergency signal to piggyback on ship comms, so that maybe someone can come and explain.

On autorecovery, my half-exploded runner manages to slam into its berth on the *Visigoth* and rescue crews are standing by. Once they seal all the locks, I try to help them peel me out of the cockpit but it's not really working. There are many pairs of hands and shouting voices.

"Graff, stop, lie back, you'll be fine, it's fine, it's going to be fine—"

I might laugh at this.

The dock crew and medics are full of panic and repressed horror at what they must be looking at. Then I am horizontal, fully supported, no strain at all on my body, which feels wet and wobbly, and the pain is lead weight on every nerve. Fingers pry at my eyelids, a light flashes, and I see him, Doctor Ell, who is also my lover. He has a pale face and a shock of blond hair and intense eyes, and his whole expression is screwed up and serious. I want to pat his shoulder and say everything will be fine but nothing is working. So I look at him.

"I'm sorry," I murmur.

"Graff, no, what are you talking about?"

"You're about to find out I faked my medical scans." I try to smile.

He stares. "What?"

A medic's voice interrupts. "Doctor! God, look at this—"

Finally, happily, I pass out.

Five other people are in the room when I wake up. Ell and Captain Ransom. A support medic, standing by. Two guards at a door that has never had guards at it before.

"When will he wake up?" Ransom asks.

"He's awake now," Ell says. He must be watching a monitor.

I'm listening hard—I can hear heartbeats, if I focus. I think I can open my eyes. But I can't move anything else. There's a fog; I battle past it.

"Am I paralyzed or on medical restraints?" My voice scratches.

Some rustling as the guards flinch, like they didn't believe I was awake. The medic perks up.

"Drug-induced paralysis," Ell says.

"So both."

"Yes."

"Because of the injuries or because of everything else?"

Nothing for a long pause, then, "It would be better if you lie still for now."

"Okay." I sigh. My lungs still work but feel like they've been scrubbed out with pumice.

Ransom curses and begins to pace. He doesn't have a lot of room and his steps fall hard. His presence always seems to expand to fill whatever space he's in. It's actually a comfort right now. Ransom is here, he'll fix everything.

My processor seems to be fine. Ell didn't mess with it when he had a chance to look inside me. The self-repair has settled down; I'm still recording. I check the time; it's been two days since they pulled me out of the runner. Diagnostics say I'm . . . mending. Mechanics repaired. Biologics will need more time. I took a beating. But Ell didn't try to dig in or disconnect anything important. He could have, if he'd wanted to.

I have a lot of questions. I imagine they do, too. We try to wait one another out. My eyes open to a dimly lit ceiling in Medical. I want to see Ell but he's standing back.

Ransom and Ell finally break at the same time.

Ell says, "How did you fake the scans—"

The captain says, "You sent a signal—"

I chuckle. I can't help it. This would be funny if it weren't me. Ransom curses again.

"This isn't funny," Ell says.

"No, I know that," I reply. "I'm sorry." I would laugh outright except it hurts too much, because if I had thought about it before the accident, what Ransom would do if he ever found out about me, this is about how I'd have expected it to go. My ongoing chuckle comes out like a cough.

Ransom is losing his temper. "Graff—"

"Let it go. You know how he is," Ell says.

"I thought I did."

I stop chuckling. "Ask me. Ask me everything."

Ransom starts. "Are you dangerous?"

"Yes. I mean no. Not to any of you."

"Graff, you're not helping," the doctor says.

"What do you want me to say?" I murmur.

"What are you?" the doctor asks.

"Human."

"No, you're not—"

"I didn't fake the DNA records, just the physiological. Look at the DNA." I'm tired. But I need to get through this. I need to know what they're going to do with me.

Ell has touched every inch of me. He must have thought he knew me.

"When was all this work done? How . . . " Now Ell is pacing. "I've seen cybernetic implants, but this . . . this is extensive. This is part of your nervous system. Work this extensive should kill anyone . . . but you don't even have any scarring from it. It's all perfectly integrated. How?"

They think I'm dangerous. They think I'm going to go off like a bomb. "Can you send the kids out, please?"

The two guards, the medic. They're not kids, of course they're not. I know them all; I trained with them. But I outrank them. Another long, taut silence follows.

"I'm not going to hurt anyone," I insist. My head is throbbing. "There are more secrets than mine here. I'll tell you and the captain but no one else."

Ell comes to my shoulder, a syringe in hand. I can't flinch, I can't resist. He pumps the liquid into a tube already connected to my body somewhere that I can't see.

"For the pain," he says gently. "Your vitals are spiking."

He touches my shoulder, naked under a thin sheet. I almost start crying. My blood stops pounding quite as hard. Nerves fray a little less. Ell steps away. I want to reach for him.

"Drugs work on him at least," he says to the captain.

"Do you trust him?" Ransom asks. A question that cuts. He's always trusted me before.

"I don't know," Ell says.

I think I might start crying. I wait. We all wait, in air thick with anxiety, like trying to wade through gelatin.

"Marcel, Xun, Brown. You're dismissed," Ransom says finally.

"But sir—" He must give them a look, because no one complains further.

They leave reluctantly. Ell murmurs reassurances at them. They all take second, third looks at me. I wonder what the ship's rumor mill is saying. It will never be the same.

"All right, Graff," Ransom says. "How . . . what . . . " He waves his hand at me, shakes his head.

I've never explained this; I've never needed to. I don't regret having to do so now. It's how I'm going to survive. Assuming they believe me and trust me at the end of it.

"It's done in utero," I say. "It's grown. Artificial gestation, of course, but that's—"

"Oh starry fuck," Ell curses.

I've never heard him say "fuck" in all the years I've known him. This is probably going to go badly for me.

"Is that even legal?" Ransom asks.

"I'm not sure. It's certainly not ethical," he says.

Except it is. It is for us.

"Why didn't you say anything?" Ransom asks calmly. I recognize the tone, the resolve, that he now knows what the problem is and is closer to figuring out what to do about it. "Why not tell us what . . . about this? Why bother hiding it with fake scans?"

"Because we don't tell anyone." This drops even harder than the first confession.

"We," Ransom says.

"I hope you understand what I'm trusting you with, telling you this. I'm trusting you." This is a plea. I am vulnerable. I trust them. Not that I have much choice. Or I could shut myself off. Burn out my processor, keep all the secrets. But I don't want to.

"We," the captain repeats. "You sent a signal. At least, the signal originated from your position. It tried to sneak out on ship comms."

"But you blocked it before it got out," I say. And start chuckling again. "I thought that might happen but I had to try. I . . . I wanted someone to come and download my processor in case I didn't make it."

"How many of you are there?" he asks.

"Not as many as you're afraid of," I say.

"Fuck, Graff, what am I supposed to do with you?" Captain Ransom asks.

"I don't know, sir. Right now I think I would like to sleep. But I'm a little wound up." I need to know I'll wake back up again, if I go to sleep. I'm not sure right now.

"You should be dead," he said. "If you were anyone else in a runner that blew up like that you'd be dead."

"Yeah, I was sort of thinking if I ever blew up in a runner there wouldn't be enough left for anyone to learn about any of this."

"Bad luck there," Ransom says, deadpan.

"Yeah."

"I'm about to kill you myself," Ell says. Then to Ransom: "We should let him sleep."

"Does he really need to sleep? All those wires . . . "

"Yes, I need to sleep. And eat. And everything else." Sex. I need that, too. Just maybe not right now. Where did Ell go? They're conferencing in the back of the room. Like they can't bear to look at me. I try to stay awake, so I can explain some more, but the painkiller is also a sedative and it pulls me under.

The very best thing I ever ate was ice cream with pieces of dark chocolate and brandied cherries mixed into it. Decadent and comforting at once, served at a too-fancy café with real wood furniture and paneled walls. They made everything themselves with dairy from real goats. I remember thinking, *this,* this is what it's all about.

I got that memory out on a previous download, at least.

I try to send out another message, masking it as a trojan and slipping it in with another signal before the comms operator notices it. But they've got the whole room jammed. I can't access anything, not even the medical computers.

This is bad. I'm not Graff anymore; I'm a thing on a table. Explaining hasn't helped.

I can't explain it, that's the problem.

The memories are pristine. I've got them all stored away, and with them the emotions that goes along with them. The flush on my skin when Ell asked if he could buy me a drink like he was making a dare. The flush on *his* skin when I said yes, because he hadn't thought I would. This was right after he'd come on board as ship's doctor; we'd been in a station-side tavern that was too dark and loud with lots of people dancing. Two days of leave and better make the most of it, right? Ransom had been there, rolling his eyes at the both of us flirting like it was a contest. And only a couple hours later, out in a quiet corridor, I put my hand on Ell's neck, gently pushed him against the wall, and kissed him.

That was a good night.

I write the best after-action reports because I remember. No one ever questions it. I just have a good memory, right? I can still feel the exact sensation when the reactor on the runner blew out, my gut parting like taffy as shrapnel went through it.

Leave that memory and go back to that first night with Ell. That's better. Close my eyes, slow my breathing.

Checking my processor, I know exactly when I've slept and when I haven't. I fall in and out of sleep all day. The door opens, waking me. There are footsteps. I try to look and still can't.

"Doctor?" I ask, rasping. I'm getting hydrated through a tube in a vein, but my mouth is bone dry.

Ell appears next to me. I sigh, relieved. I shouldn't be relieved.

"What's happening?" I ask. I'd meant to ask for water.

He turns away, and my heart lurches. But he's back a moment later with a bottle and straw. "Drink," he orders, and I do. "Better?"

"Yeah. What's happening?"

"Are you a spy?"

"What? No." I mean, I don't think so? Would they think I was, if I told them everything?

"Because Ransom thinks you're a spy."

"For who?"

"I don't know. For whatever you are."

"How bad am I hurt?"

"You should be dead. Your spine was severed. At least I thought it was, but then . . . it fixed itself."

"Yeah, it does that."

"You'll be on your feet in another week, and I've hardly done anything but hook you to a feeding tube." He's offended that he can't take credit for saving my life.

"I'd be dead without the feeding tube. That stuff needs calories."

Flustered, he sighs. "What are you?"

"I'm me." That will never be a good enough answer. "What is Ransom saying?"

"He suggested dissection. I think he was joking."

I chuckle.

"It's not funny," Ell says.

"No, I guess not." I look at him because I don't know how much longer I'll get to. My smile feels a bit ridiculous.

He doesn't smile. He's pursed and worried and hurt.

I can move enough to breathe. This takes a deep breath to get it all out. "I would like to be able to move, if you think I might be ready to stop with the nerve block."

"I'll have to ask the captain."

"So it isn't for medical reasons."

"No."

Yeah, this may not go well. "I'm not a spy, I'm not a danger to you or anyone, I would never hurt this ship or anyone on it. Where is Ransom, let me talk to him—"

"He doesn't trust you. Not after this. You *lied*—"

"I didn't!"

"The medical scans? You hacked into the ship's computers and hijacked my diagnostics systems! You always scanned out as an ideal textbook human and now I know why!"

"Yeah, okay, I guess that was sort of like lying."

"Graff." He says it as a reprimand. He's wondering if everything was a lie.

"I was raised by the ones who provided my genetic material. I have parents. Does that help?"

"It might." He gets up, puts the bottle of water on a table.

It's infuriating, not being able to see anything, except that I'm too drugged to be really furious about anything. "Captain's listening right now, isn't he? On a monitor? Is he outside the door or what? Or does he have marines ready to storm in if I do something screwy?"

"You can't do anything, you're immobilized. Unless the drugs really don't work on you and you've been faking it." He raises a brow, as if this is a question.

"Well, fuck." I seriously can't move. He knows this. I roll my eyes at the ceiling, as if I could get Ransom's attention that way. "Okay. Captain? Remember the time you had me sit in a runner out on that asteroid for two weeks waiting for those pirates to show up? And remember how you *didn't tell me* why you wanted me to sit on that rock, or for how long, or anything?"

"Graff—"

The door to Medical slides open, slides shut. Footsteps. And Ransom says, "So you wouldn't anticipate and launch your burn too soon and spoil the trap."

"Right!" I exclaim, excited, probably too excited, because Ell appears in my peripheral vision, looking at a monitor and frowning.

Ransom continues, "It's not that I didn't trust you—"

"No, see, that's the thing. It was a good plan, and it wasn't about you trusting me. I trusted *you*. I'd have sat on that rock for a year if you told me to."

"Now you're just trying to guilt me into listening to you."

"Yes. Yes, I am. Also, I want to keep on following your crazy plans. They're kind of fun. You know what I was thinking, when I was stuck on that rock?"

"How you were going to kill me for not telling you?"

"No. That I couldn't wait to see what you had planned. I knew it'd be good." And it had been. Lots of explosions. "And I was thinking of how many drinks you were going to owe me when I got back." Those had been my first words when I got back to *Visigoth,* sweaty and stinking from being cooped up for so long: "You owe me a drink, sir." He'd laughed. I'd known Ransom since flight school, almost right after I left home. I can't imagine what this looks like from his end. I'll never make it up to him.

The captain's voice is taut. "This might have been easier if a switch flipped and turned him into some killer robot." He's talking to Ell, who grumbles.

I ask, "Why didn't you burn out my processor when you had me open, right after the accident?"

The doctor says, "I didn't want to hurt you."

"Doctor, can we have a word?" Ransom says. I can picture him jabbing a thumb over his shoulder, but he never enters my line of sight.

Ell nods, looks at me one more time. "Do you need anything? Anything critical to your current state of health, I mean."

"You?" I ask hopefully.

He looks away. The door shuts, and I close my eyes.

I spend the next two days trying to think of exactly the right thing to tell Ell and Ransom that will make everything all right and get everything back to the way it was. Or at least have them not look at me like I'm a villain in a bad drama. And I think I've got it. I stay awake by sheer force of will. Assuming I ever get to download again, whoever gets the package is going to know every inch of this ceiling. It's got just the littlest bit of texture, like a partially worn pebble. The gray is rather pleasant once you get used to it.

The door opens. Many footsteps enter. My heart rate increases. The pain is so much less than what it was but that makes it harder to lie still. I want to sit up. I want to use my hands when I speak.

Ell appears at the side of the table. I get it all out in one go before he can say anything.

"It's the stories. The stories, the experiences. Everything. A computer could do it, but then we wouldn't get the . . . the experience. The hormones. The dopamine. The endorphins. The meat and nerves of it all, right? *That's* the important bit. We go out into the galaxy and collect stories, and then we bring them home. It's who we are, it's what we do. And love, we go out to find all the love we can and try to keep it . . . " This ship is full of love and I'm afraid I've broken it. "I've never had to explain it before and I know it doesn't make sense—"

Ell studies me for a long time. He seems calm. Some decision has been made.

"Love?" he says, his tone even.

"Yeah. Just like that."

He lowers his gaze, raises a syringe full of some ominous liquid.

Well. I tried. I set my jaw in what I hope is a picture of fortitude. "This is it, then."

"This is what?" he asks.

"You induce a coma and ship me off to some military R&D facility. Or is this . . . I mean, you wouldn't."

He gets this very familiar—delightfully familiar—frustrated look on his face. Like he's about to snarl. "I wouldn't *what*?"

"Just finish me off."

"God, Graff. No." He injects the syringe into the line. "This is probably going to hurt. At least, I think it'll hurt."

"It already hurts."

"I wasn't sure you could hurt, after I saw all that metal. Until I looked at your readings."

"You know me, Ell. You do." I finally catch his gaze. His familiar, shining gaze. He sort of looks like he's about to cry, too.

Then there's a warm rush though my veins that hits my heart and all my muscles seem to melt into a dull throb. I groan, but it's kind of a relieved groan because I can wiggle my fingers and toes now and that feels pretty good. My processor's diagnostics hum away; I'm still not optimal but stress levels are decreasing.

"Warned you," Ell says, leaning in. "Now don't move. You're still not entirely in one piece yet."

"Okay."

I reach out, touch his hand. Just brush it, then let him go because I don't want to scare him. He jumps a little. His breath catches. But he stays near.

Finally, I can turn my head to look at the rest of the room. Captain Ransom is standing there, arms crossed. And someone new is with him. She appears female, fine boned, with short-cropped red hair and a wry frown. A smirk. A judgment. I've never seen her before, but I know who she is. Tez, her name is Tez. My circuits hum in proximity to hers.

I look at Captain Ransom. "You let the signal get out after all."

"I did."

"Why?"

"To see what would happen. She showed up a day later. Do you people just hang around in deep space waiting for edge-of-death signals?"

"Yes," Tez says calmly.

"I'm not dying actually, it turns out," I say awkwardly.

"You had a close call," she says.

"Very."

"Is it a good story?"

"I'm not sure."

She comes to the table, holds out her hand. I take it. The spark of a circuit completing pinches my palm, and hers.

The download takes a few minutes. I get all of her memories as well. It's like meeting an old friend from home. We're all old friends from home. It's kind of nice. I'm not sure I can explain that part of it to Ell and Ransom.

Tez holds my gaze, and in hers is forgiveness and understanding, along with the mildest of reprimands.

You convinced them, I tell her.

No, you did or I'd never have gotten your signal. They wanted to be convinced. You know you should meet up with someone to download a little more often, don't you?

Yeah, I just get distracted.

But is it a good story?

It is. I'm sorry I told them about us.

No, you're not.

The connection breaks. She takes a breath, resettling herself into her skin. Looks around. Sees Ell with new understanding. He ducks his gaze, self-conscious.

"So. They know," she says, just to get it out in the open.

Tez can take me back home for this. If I can't keep the secret, then I can't be allowed to travel. But . . . I'm valuable. I almost start whining like a child, telling her how valuable I am, out in the universe, collecting stories.

"I trust them," I say.

"They may not want you to stay." She looks up, around. "He's afraid you won't want him to stay."

"It's a lot to take in," Ransom says flatly. "I confess, I'm not sure what to do next. I was hoping you might tell me."

But she doesn't. She asks, "Graff does a lot of good where he is?"

"He does," Ransom says. I wasn't sure he would.

"Thank you, sir," I murmur. But it's Ell's decision that matters most, and I look at him next.

He says, "I can purge all the files from the accident and recovery. Go back to the faked scans. Keep that secret. With the captain's permission." Ell looks; Ransom shrugs. I want to laugh at the back and forth but that would probably be bad so I don't.

"You want him to stay?" Tez asks Ell.

"I do. I think I do."

She looks at me. "Graff?"

"Is it going to be weird? It's going to be weird, isn't it? Me staying."

"Yes," Ell says. "But I think you should stay anyway."

We both look at Ransom. He's like a rock, his chiseled expression unmoving. He says, "Yeah, it'll be weird. For a while."

She smiles, her brow crinkling. "I like them."

"Yeah, me, too," I say.

Tez brushes off her jumpsuit. "Captain, if you can spare the time, I wondered if someone on your crew might take a look at my ship? Just a routine once-over."

It's not very subtle. He looks at her, then at me, then at Ell. He raises his brow. "All right. This way."

He actually flashes a little bit of a wry smile over his shoulder as they leave. Then Ell sits by the table and gives me the most exhausted, long-suffering, and sad look I've ever seen.

I'm also exhausted, which is frustrating. I've slept enough. "I was never going to tell you because I couldn't tell you and it didn't make a difference anyway and I'm sorry."

After a hesitation, he touches my forehead. He ruffles my short hair, looks me up and down like he's studying me. Studying his handiwork, or maybe he's really looking at *me*.

"I have a lot more questions," he says.

"Yeah, I know."

I open my hand. Wait for him to make the move. And he puts his hand in mine.

Rebecca Campbell is a Canadian writer and teacher. Her work has appeared in *The Year's Best Science Fiction and Fantasy*, *The Year's Best Dark Fantasy and Horror*, and other places. She won the Sunburst Award for Excellence in Canadian Literature of the Fantastic in 2020, and in 2021 has been nominated for the Aurora award and the Theodore Sturgeon Memorial. NeWest Press published her first novel, *The Paradise Engine*, in 2013. She mostly uses her PhD in Canadian literature to make up sad futures and weird fictions.

AN IMPORTANT FAILURE

Rebecca Campbell

I t's 1607 (according to some calendars) and a falling cone from an elderly *Pinaceae sitchensis* catches on the rotting bark of a nurse log that sprouted while Al-Ma'mun founded the House of Wisdom in Baghdad. On this particular north Pacific island, the days are cold, and the water in Kaatza—the big lake near where this cone has fallen—freezes thick enough that one can walk out from the villages at the southeast end and look down to see cutthroat trout flickering underfoot. On the other side of the world, the Thames has also frozen, and stout winter children play across the canvasses of lowland painters, who preserve in oil the white-stained landscapes of northern Europe. In il Bosco Che Suona—the Valley of Song, the singing forest in the Alps north of Cremona where luthiers go to find their violins hidden in the trunks of trees—the winter is bitter, slowing the growth of *Picea abies* until its rings are infinitesimal, a dense tonewood unlike any material before or since.

Ninety years after the cone drops near Kaatza, Antonio Stradivari travels to il Bosco Che Suona on the old road from Cremona to select wood for his workshop. He rests his head against one trunk and listens to its cold history. This is the Little Ice Age as written in the rings of a spruce tree. It sounds like a violin.

Jacob woke Mason after midnight. Ten minutes later, they walked out to the old truck, gassed up for the occasion, stale with multigenerational BO, since it had belonged to their grandfather before it was Jake's. The dusty fug relieved by Sophie's botanicals: nasturtium; wood rose; one of her cash crops, a strain of CBD-rich indica she had been nurturing for years, called Nepenthe. They drove along the empty street, from the deeply green lakeshore to the old firebreak, gouged out of stone and clay twenty years before. Along disintegrating logging roads to the old burns where Mason could still see char. As kids, they had hiked here to secret rivers and campsites out of cell phone range.

Jacob drove in silence. Mason stared out the window at the ghost forest. Twice they got out to clear the road and Mason looked up into the low bush—blackened Douglas fir still towering over the blackberries and alder. Recovery plants, fast growing opportunists emerging from the last wildfire.

"Cougars?" he asked.

"A lot of them lately," Jacob said. "They've followed the deer. It's good news. But makes working at night a bit more exciting."

He thought he spotted its silhouette in the darkness above them and wondered what it saw, in turn—competitors or prey in the disorienting headlights. The eagles had come back, nesting in the ghost trees. So had blacktailed deer and robins. The microclimates had changed as the forests began their slow return, though, a prefigure of what the coast would be in a hundred years: arbutus further inland, outside its original ranges; Garry oak farther west and north as the coast dried out. In a thousand years, it would be another sort of forest. If it was still there.

In two hours they made it to the edge of the surviving rain forest, which—on the west coast of the island's mountains—had dodged the wildfires that destroyed most of everything else in the last twenty years. Twenty minutes on a rutted track, until they pulled over and met a guy, silent, nodding to Jacob as he climbed into the cab, directing them to an even narrower dirt track.

"This's Chris," Jacob said.

Mason-Chris nodded. So did the guy.

They weren't far from the tree, which stood in what was still a provincial park, technically, though the trails were rarely maintained, and what boot prints he could see were probably other poachers. This was the largest surviving Sitka spruce in the world, and maybe people still wanted to see it, even if the busloads of school kids were rare, and the marine biology station at Bamfield had been shuttered for years.

Three more men waiting. A few gestures indicated the direction they'd drop it. The time it would take. Mason-Chris hung back, watching the wiry old faller put on his helmet, his chainsaw beside him. They waited for the breeze to still. There was a kind of quiet he never felt in Vancouver, even now when it was marred by shuffling men. Or cougars. Then the chainsaw flooded them and he heard nothing but its whine as it cut through the trunk, kindred to the kind that grew in La Fiemme, the Valley of Song in the Italian Alps where—it was rumored—a skilled lumberman could hear a violin hiding in the trunk.

He'd heard there might be another ancient Sitka in Kitimat, but that was too far to travel, even for something as precious as old-growth tonewood. This one, though, he'd remembered visiting as a kid. Its size; the unlikely fact of its survival after two centuries of logging and wildfires.

It didn't take that long. A deep cut on either side in the direction of one of the other available roads, where a big truck probably waited. Then the wedges. The high, sweet note of the hammer. Waiting. Waiting. Until something inside it tore, and it fell, bounced, a thrash of branches like tendriled ocean creatures, or waves, like hair, like a body in spasm. Then it was still. Silence held for a moment longer, before they got to work limbing and bucking it.

Mason-Chris watched all the wiry, furtive men from—where? Port Alberni? Or maybe one of the transient camps, to which resource officers and RCMP turned temporary blind eyes because even they weren't assholes enough to burn down a five-year camp that had organized showers and a septic system built of old truck tires. As long as the outsiders kept their problems—opioids, smuggling—out of town.

"Deal with the stump," Jacob said.

Mason-Chris didn't know what it meant, so Jacob repeated, "Stump. Cover it over with whatever you can find on the ground."

"Is that really a problem? We're pretty deep in."

"They still send drones through."

"Why would they even—anyway, I need to—"

"—I'll get you when it's time."

Behind him, the stump was brightly pale in the darkness, sweet and resinous. He dropped branches over three meters of open wound, admiring the heartwood, which was surprisingly free of infestation, whether beetle or fungus. Behind him the tree grew steadily simpler, its branches tossed away, its trunk straight and handsome and more than four hundred years old. A baby compared to the ancient ones, the bristlecone or the big Norway spruce that had lived for nearly ten thousand years. But what would a bristlecone sound like? Sitka spruce, though, he had heard often and loved.

"—Chris."

He'd get to Cremona and apprentice to Aldo, because Eddie knew him and could write a letter. He'd visit the Valley of Song and see what survived of the European spruce, and he would tell the master luthiers this story of poaching old growth in a provincial park. They would laugh and clap him on the back and—

"—Chris. Come on."

Dragged away from his plans for Cremona and back to the immediate problem of sourcing old growth for a perfect violin, he saw that the tired, sweaty men had begun stripping their gear in the darkness, lit by phones and helmets. He didn't actually know what he was looking for, but he worked his way down the long, straight sections nearest the base, running his hands over the rough bark to look at the interiors by the light of his phone.

"This is it, Jake." he said without thinking. The group hushed. Ignored it. "This is the one."

The other guys melted into the darkness. It was close to daylight by then, and while the forest floor was still dark, Mason could see the sky for the first time since the clouds overtook the stars.

Jake squatted by the section.

"Are you sure?" he asked.

Mason tried to listen to it. Before the tree fell, he had felt alive to the world around him—the shudder of leaves, and the faintly padding feet of the cougar—but now the wood was inert. Whatever he thought he had heard—the thin high notes of a violin he had not yet built—had evaporated.

"Yes," he said. "I'm sure."

It took them two hours to get it to the truck. Then another three to get to home.

"What'll happen to the rest of it?" Mason asked.

"Firewood went for thousand bucks a cord last winter. That tree could keep a lot of people warm. There's pulp, still. Mills will buy it up without asking too many questions. You don't get the same kind of cash, but it's safer and less work. And you know. Fentanyl. Or oxy."

Behind them, the quarter of old-growth spruce remained silent, except where the truck creaked in resistance to its enormous weight.

"There are luthiers around the world who would kill for that, in a few years."

"Sure. Or it'll heat someone's house this winter."

They made it home late that morning, their eyes gritty with exhaustion. Jake sat in the cab for a long moment, then said, "I'm going to grab a swim, then get to work in the greenhouse."

Mason knew he should help, but he found himself following the old route through the house to the bedroom he still thought of as his: the dark kitchen, past the bunches of garlic, the bookshelves in the living room piled with *National Geographic*s from the twentieth century. Past the windowsills that still held grandma's things: Beach glass and thunder eggs. Feathers. Stained glass that caught no light in a window shrouded by bush.

He lay in the cool, stale room where the carpet had been discolored by water seeping through the wall forty years before. It smelled like being ten, like summer, like his mother. Like the thousands of nights his family had passed between the wood-paneled walls, the narrow window facing south toward Cowichan Lake—or Kaatza, as Sophie called it in keeping with her friends in the local band—out which they had all stared and wondered what would happen next.

During the Little Ice Age, global temperatures dropped about 1°C, on average. There are debates regarding the causes of these aberrant winters. At least one trigger may have been the mass death of people in North and South America, with ninety percent of the population, by some estimates, dead after contact with Europeans.

Lost languages and cities; toddlers and great grandmothers and handsome young men and dreamy girls; villages and trade routes and favorite jokes. After so many deaths, an area of agricultural land the size of France returned to forest. This regreening sequestered enough carbon from the preindustrial atmosphere that temperatures took centuries to recover and begin their steady rise to the present day. The wild and empty continent of later explorers was—in part—a sepulcher, a monument inscribed with languages they could not speak, full of witnesses to that terrible loss.

From the cold and darkness of a hundred million deaths, to the chilly woodsmen of the Valley of Song, to Paganini playing *il Cannone Guarnerius*, it is a long and terrible history.

At Kaatza, the disaster is slow, despite temporary changes in climate, because the smallpox that will ravage the coast has not yet arrived. People go about their business on the water and in the forest, from the Pacific coast to the Salish Sea. Children are born. Songs are composed. The nurse log disintegrates. The little spruce rooted there rises toward the light, its heartwood formed in an apocalypse.

In addition to Nepenthe, Jake and Sophie grew a THC-rich sativa, which Mason disliked because it made him paranoid, but which sold steadily as far away as Seattle, and kept—in Jake's words—the old homestead together. Sophie raised it hydroponically in Grandpa's old workshop, while Nepenthe grew in the market garden by the lake, catching southern exposure on a warm brick wall with the espaliered peaches and lemongrass.

Later that afternoon, Mason visited the piece under a tarp in a corner of the workshop. Mason had been greedy, and there was material for two-dozen violins, assuming he found within it the billets he needed. He tried to remember what Eddie had done the last time they toured the mills for legal maple, willow, and spruce. Eddie could hear a violin in a slab of big-leaf maple, could feel willow's sonic geometries as he tested its spring with his hands. If Eddie were here, the quarter would speak. He was still listening when Sophie shouldered through the door, a watering can in either hand.

"There are two more," she said, gesturing toward the door.

He grabbed them, warm with sunlight. Together they watered the market garden. Potatoes and tomatoes. Chili peppers and mint. And Nepenthe, the deep botanical fug of its leaves rising in the heat of the afternoon. Mason took cannabis oil away every visit, dropping onto his tongue in a resinous burn, applying the ointment to his right wrist where the tendons ached. More effective than anything he could afford legally.

"You ever going legit?"

Sophie shrugged. "If it hasn't happened by now, I doubt we'll ever get licensed. I applied again last year but never heard anything. Jacob said you got what you needed?"

Mason nodded, the tree crashed again through his mind. "He's helping someone cut firewood. He said you should sleep while you can. How long do we sit on it, anyway?"

"It's got to season. A decade, probably. Ideally a century, but you know."

She nodded, then led him through the hydroponics to a tiny room full of geranium slips and tomatoes. "Lots to do, Mason. Keep watering."

In the third decade of the twenty-first century, a girl is born in Surrey Memorial Hospital. The labor is six hours. The child—magnificently named Masami Lucretia Delgado—has tiny, pointed fingers and strong hands that are precise in their movements, as though waiting for the fingerboard of a violin even in the moment of her birth. When she is three years old, an ad interrupts her cartoon, and she waits first in irritation, then in fascination, jabbing at the corner of the screen where the skip button should appear, but does not. Instead of a cartoon cloud who sings about rainbows and unicorns, she watches an ad for life insurance that features a little girl so like Masami, she seems to be a mirror, or a twin, with bright black hair and curious brown eyes. This little girl—the other Masami—holds a violin to her chin and plays something that makes Masami's heart rise in her chest. A white cloud drifting higher and higher among the rainbows.

Masami is too small to name what she hears, and though it marks her forever, she soon forgets this first encounter with destiny. Something of it must remain with her, however, because a year later she hears the sound of a violin and asks her mother, that, that, was is that?

She's four. Her father shows her violin videos. Outside the air is opaque with smoke from the fires on the north shore, which systematically destroy the huge houses overlooking Burrard Inlet. The pipeline that terminated in Burnaby has cracked again, somewhere up-country, who knows where, and spilled two thousand barrels of diluted bitumen into a lake. But Masami is too small to understand, and when she hears the sound of Marguerite Fell playing the ex-Kajnaco violin—from a quartet made by Guadagnini in Milan in 1780—she is transported, and some portion of her soul will never return from that transport. Her future is, at that moment, fixed. Her tiny hands will grow into her violin, the instrument less an exterior object than an extension of her body. She is, neurologically, emotionally, and psychologically, part violin. It's in her heart, in her muscle memory. By the time she's fourteen she'll have cubital tunnel syndrome and need regular physio to deal with nerve compression. Her body has grown up around the violin the way a tree grows over a nurse log.

Masami Delgado was the reason Mason poached the last of the ancient Sitka spruce. But it wasn't her fault.

Actually, maybe Eddie started it with one of those offhand comments about sourcing tonewood. Shuffling through the workshop in old jeans, pockets sagging with pencils and calipers, a finger plane. He stopped at Mason's bench, where Mason was mending a violin they got cheap from someone leaving town. He was still surprised to find Eddie trusted him to touch instruments. For a long time he'd just swept the shop floor, drove the van, tended the glue pot. He still did those things, but he also got to replace a split tuning peg on a student violin, and it felt good to hold it in his hands, feeling the thin shell of its body, saying to it "Come on, little guy, let's get you sorted."

"It's never going to sound the same," Eddie said.

He listened to the long bow draw. "Yeah. It's not great. But it's solid for a student—"

"No." Eddie said, in the abrupt way that always left Mason feeling like he'd said something stupid. "No. It's the wood."

He ran his finger down the bright spruce face. "This is pretty young stuff. More carbon in the atmosphere changes the density of the wood. We're never going to see the same kind of old growth again, even if the forests recover. You need to drop the G."

Mason listened. Eddie was right.

That night Eddie took him along to hear Delgado play at the Chan Center, a rare treat, like the time early in his apprenticeship when he accompanied Eddie to hear Alu Vila playing Bach on the ex-Norfolk, darkly redolent of 1805. Delgado had just received—for a three-year loan from the Canada Council for the Arts—the Plaisir violin of 1689, and had invited Eddie backstage to celebrate her first concert. Eddie, world-renowned luthier and representative of the CC, had been appointed its custodian for Delgado's term. She was thirteen. She played the Kreutzer Sonata.

"We're going to go check out the saddle," he said during the intermission.

"Why?"

Eddie shrugged, and the lights dimmed again.

Backstage, Delgado's parents hovered. Mason—still disoriented by the evening's performance—couldn't speak.

"May I?" Eddie said. She nodded. Her eyes never left the violin.

Mason screwed up his courage, "You have it for three years?" She nodded. "And then that's it?"

Her mother answered. "You don't get it twice."

It hurt him that something that fit so perfectly onto her shoulder should be lost. She should have it for the rest of her life, on international tours, and in recording studios. It should be hers by some right of genius.

"I wish," Mason said, "you could have it forever." But then Eddie was finished and her parents were shepherding her away, and he realized he hadn't heard her voice, not once.

As they waited for an Uber, Eddie said, "It's not going to last." Wildfires were burning on the north shore, and the sunset was an angry smudge. Mason thought about dying trees, and the sound of old growth leaving the world.

"What do we do?"

"Nothing we can do. The saddle's been wearing noticeably for decades now. Could be a split forming, though I didn't seen anything on the last CT scan. Maybe it'll show in the next twenty years. Or maybe it'll be longer than that. I don't know."

"We can't replace it?"

"We can. But we won't. They aren't immortal. Eventually it will be unplayable, and then it will go to sleep."

That night Mason walked down Granville Street past the shuttered theaters that had once been full of music. He circled back to Hastings, and walked out toward his little room in a building on Gore, where the rent was almost decent. Then he searched through Eddie's database and found the transcendental geometries of the Plaisir violin, emissary of the seventeenth century, where in the workshops of Cremona luthiers made instruments so perfect they seemed not to have been built, but grown. Alien seashells. The seedpods of strange flowers. He had touched one today, felt its lightness against his palm, patinated by centuries of sweat, the oil of many hands and faces, rich with life. All that alchemy of tree and climate, genius and history. She would have it for three years. Then the saddle would split, and it would be lost forever.

That was the day he formed the plan: a violin made as purely and patiently as he could manage, following the guidance of long-dead luthiers, passed down to him through Eddie. And when it was finished, he would got to the Po Valley and join the Scuola Internazionale di Liuteria Cremona, where he would tell a dozen old Italian masters the story of his accomplishment.

But the materials he'd need weren't just expensive, they were nonexistent. Trees of the five hundred ppm present wouldn't do. He needed old growth, with heartwood grown in the last climate minimum, when Kaatza froze and the last Viking settlement on Greenland disappeared under the ice. He needed Gaboon ebony, nearly extinct, smuggled out of Nigeria or Cameroon.

"Everything I can afford," he told Eddie the next day, "is ugly." Unspoken: too ugly for Delgado, who deserved more than the world could offer these days.

"Not ugly," Eddie said, "Different. But not ugly." He picked up the violin Mason had assembled from salvaged materials Eddie had discarded. Then he seemed to think, and he said, "Let me show you something," before disappearing up the stairs and into the shop, returning with a fiddle Mason had often looked at, a rough old thing, a curiosity.

"Some guy made this out of a post from a longhouse like a hundred and fifty years ago. If he can do that, you can figure something out."

The longhouse had stood in a long-gone Musqueam village way down on southwest Marine Drive. The violin had a cedar front, a maple neck and back that Eddie insisted had come from a stack of firewood. He'd had some dendrochronologist look at it, dating the woods to the seventeen hundreds. Maybe some fiddler lost his on the crossing, or gambled it away, like in a song, but he'd landed on the edge of nowhere, and built something new from what he'd found. Not well built by many rules, and the sound was drowsy, sure, but deep, Mason could hear that just bowing the strings. He wondered what it would sound like in Delgado's hands. Something by de Sarasate. A Bach violin concerto. Or maybe it would be some dance number, once played in a small front room while the rain fell outside, and Vancouver wasn't even a city yet, a song interrupted, escaping from the violin when her fingers touched it. Maybe, he thought, it would be earlier sounds from an equally rainy night, a longhouse on the south slope toward the river, a rainy hillside that had not yet thought of becoming Vancouver. Voices. Laughter. A language he didn't know, and a moment captured in the reverberating matrices of the wood itself.

A few weeks after he returned from poaching the giant spruce, and had begun to accumulate the necessary components for his violin, wildfires scoured the Fraser Valley and the north shore, and the smell of smoke brimmed his eyes with love and dread so he had to call them, just to make sure.

"Still here." Jake said. "You okay?"

Mason could not answer that, because who was okay? No one was okay. Everyone was fine. "It smells like smoke here," he said. "Eddie's not doing too good with the COPD."

"Yeah?"

The world had smelled like this when he and Mom had arrived, grubby with two months in the emergency camp on Nanaimo's waterfront, waiting for the highways to reopen so they could go home. That's what Mom had said to him every night: we'll go home, soon. Not to the house in Cobble Hill, which was gone now, but out to the lake. To Grandma.

"Sophie wants to bring in trembling aspen for the other side of the fire-break, to slow the burn—" here Jake went on at length about the plans to bring in a colony, borrowed from a stand downriver. Mason couldn't concentrate on what he said, but it was good to hear his voice and know that around him the house was darkening as the sun set, and outside you could, if you were lucky, hear the resident barn owl's nightly call. Sophie still at work in the garden, hauling wheelbarrows to the compost. In his smoky room, Mason's eyes ached until, finally, he wept.

Then, suddenly, Delgado was fifteen, an intensely silent teenager in heavy black eyeliner who wore combat boots in summer and rarely spoke when she came in for strings. Then she was sixteen and her time with the Plaisir nearly over, her parents joking tensely about how much it all cost—the travel, the extra tuition, the time.

Meanwhile, Mason made violins from the salvaged spruce and maple of a demolished bungalow on East Tenth, where he did some day labor for extra cash. In the evenings, he listened to each piece he'd nicked from the job, knocking it with a knuckle and wondering about its strengths, its provenance. He broke down a chest of drawers from Goodwill, scraping away the paint to show flamed maple. Oak flooring coated in decades of grime. A cricket bat made of willow, deeply scarred, might have provided the blocks he needed, but it was worm-eaten to the core.

He searched Stanley Park and found a shining willow near Beaver Lake, unusually straight. *Salix lucida lasiandra*, not the *Salix alba* preferred by the old Cremonese luthiers, but similarly easy to carve, and stable enough if he could find a straight length of trunk and season it properly. Resting his head against the trunk, he once again listened for the violin hiding within it, some sonic quality in the way it responded to his heartbeat, or his hand upon the bark.

He returned on a rainy night in January, alone, his backpack damp and heavy with gear: A hacksaw. Rope. More than anyone in the world, he missed Jacob, who had always—even when they were both kids orphaned by fire and pandemic—been cleverer and stronger than he was.

He'd have to top it, which was a ludicrous endeavor, and he could hear Jake laughing, and their grandfather's anxious snort—the snort that meant, *don't do it, kiddo*. Despite the snort, Mason persisted. Willow was essential, and if he could snare vacant lot rabbits and skin them for glue, he could climb and top a willow, then walk back across town to Eddie's, where the wood might begin its secret transformation into something useable.

He'd climbed trees a lot as a kid. Higher even than Jake, who had a longer reach, but who was afraid of heights. It made them equals, according to Grandma. When he and Mom had arrived from the temporary camp in Nanaimo, after the rain hit in October and the fires down the coast died for the season, Jake was already there. He was waiting for his Dad to come back from the interior, where he'd gone to fight the big fire outside Princeton, when the dead pines went up like matches in the scorched afternoons. But he died by smoke inhalation on the side of a crowded road along with a hundred others, and Jake stayed, and later—when Mom left to look for work and caught the flu and died—the two of them lived like brothers.

Jake never talked about it, like Mason never talked about his mom, dying in the third wave of a new pandemic when he was seven, a few years after they'd landed back on the homestead. They all worked on the hydroponics in the workshop and the market garden on the south slope toward the lake. Weed was legal in the province back then, but the Cowichan Valley's economy was—by conservative estimates—still more than half dark, and mostly driven by small operations like Grandma's. And while he and Jake were orphans in a grow-op, Sophie was somewhere south of them in Langford, learning to garden with her grandfather. Eddie had just finished his years in Italy with Aldo, and was about to set up his own shop in Vancouver. Sophie studied horticulture on the mainland, then returned to Langford with a lot of knowledge and nowhere to turn it, until Jake found her on a beach in Sooke. Eddie won double gold at the Violin Society of America. Mason left school early for a cabinetry apprenticeship until a festival, where he picked up the unfinished body of a fiddle—spruce, maple, willow—and found the thing he was made to do.

All those people—those accidents—led him here, after midnight in the shivering wet of a rain forest park in November, and he was older than he liked to admit. Nevertheless, he pulled himself up to the lowest branch, then struggled from handhold to foothold until he was high enough to cut, relieved when the unusually straight center fell with a sound that was both troubling and familiar, the tree swaying in response to the dropped weight. He descended, limbed it, bucked it in convenient lengths, and packed five of them in his rucksack. Then, looking up, he saw a straight branch just below his cut, and he could not resist it. He remembered Jake's wrinkled look of dread when they climbed too high, his warnings, "Do you know what could happen?"

"I know," Mason said, and swung up into the willow. He was a couple of meters up when the branch on which he stood—one hand snaking around to grab his hacksaw—snapped. Willow is a brittle, fast-growing tree, splendid in its youth, but soon senescent. This one, more than fifty years old, could not support a man's weight a second time that night.

The ground was wet and spinning and he said, as though someone might be there, "Help me, help me," and he thought of his mother, standing just behind his shoulder, about to answer him, pick him up, carry him home. But she wasn't, of course, so he lay still until the ground righted itself, and the pain steadied: not faded, but no longer in crescendo. He could still move his toes. Then he found he could stand. His left shoulder screamed, but his left fingers could move. He hauled himself fifty meters to Pipeline Road and called an Uber. It was nearly a week's wages to get back home.

His shoulder never healed properly: a new MRSA at the hospital, one without a name that hung out in the linens. Not one of the virulent kinds that kills you in two days, but the other ones, that persist under the skin. There was an open sinus that ran from the outer edge of his shoulder, right above where the bone had cracked. It was three months before he could work again, but Eddie kept his place, and emergency disability got him through, though he didn't eat much once his savings ran out.

When he told Jake the story—a joke, look what I did, what would Grandpa say—Sophie threatened to come over and look after him, and when he refused she just sent him Nepenthe. A few weeks out of the hospital and he could move his left arm enough to dress himself, and Eddie helped him put Sophie's ointment on his left shoulder. He smoked it, too, in the basement in front of his workbench, the deep, slow breaths easing his shoulders out of their hunch, until he felt almost okay. By then Delgado's term with the Plaisir had ended, and she celebrated those three glorious years with a last concert at the Chan Center, for which Mason had a ticket, and which he missed because he was still in the hospital.

"Don't worry," Eddie told him. "There's a recording."

"You know what I mean."

"I think it's going to Prefontaine. A kid in Saskatoon. He's good."

"But what's she going to play?"

Eddie shrugged. "There are a lot of beautiful violins."

"No." Mason said, in rare disagreement. "There aren't."

He ran into Delgado's father on the street, once. "She won't touch a violin. It's been six months."

"She's probably—"

"—all she does is play video games. She's staying out. She's so angry."

He went on, then he had to be somewhere and he left Mason on the sidewalk. He stood for a moment blocking traffic, thinking of Delgado speaking bitterly and at length about the globe's many failed revolutions, her rapidly narrowing future, and he wanted to tell her: please wait, just a little longer, for me to finish it.

A year later she received the extraordinarily fine ex-Jiang violin from an anonymous donor. He went to hear her play Bach at the Orpheum Theatre, with the Vancouver philharmonic accompanying. She was eighteen. When she came into the shop, she smiled through the eyeliner, and he asked her, "Where next? Buenos Aires?"

"I haven't seen you in weeks. What happened to your shoulder?"

"I fell weird. Not Buenos Aires? Singapore?"

"Oh. Yeah, it's hard to rationalize unless you've got a lot of work. I might be playing a gig in Toronto next year. And I was down in Seattle."

"Recording, then?"

"Maybe. I'm working on early childhood education,"

"Oh," he said, surprised. "Oh. Cool."

"Eventually it'll be music therapy. Gives me something to do with the lessons Mom and Dad paid for."

It hurt him to hear that, though he didn't know if that was some pain she felt but did not speak, or whether it was his own hope, which he did not like to acknowledge, for fear of smashing it. That she'd get another term with the Plaisir. That when she was finished with it, he'd present her with his own creation, and her career would be transformed as the violin opened up, becoming something new as she played it. He had not imagined her in a classroom with toddlers, playing "Pop Goes the Weasel" while they marched in circles around a bright orange carpet. But neither had he imagined himself working for Eddie for his entire adult life, and here he was.

For a few years after the fall he made nothing new, just ran the shop and stirred the glue pot, and made sure that Eddie took his meds and saw his doctor. But as his arm recovered, sort of, and he no longer dreamed of falling, he could stand to look at the willow again. He could even look at the old Jack Daniels box in a corner of the storage room, which held the violin in its constituent parks. You could mistake it for kindling, if you didn't know.

It still took him three years to open the box and begin work on the forms, slowly because his left shoulder remained weak and sometimes his left hand failed. But for an hour sometimes, in the evenings, he worked ribs and blocks of willow in the basement workshop at night, where he often stayed on a cot in case Eddie needed help.

It took another five years of austerity to pay black market prices for Gaboon ebony from Nigeria, the whole time worrying the trees would all be dead before he could save the money. In the end, the wood he needed for the fingerboard, tailpiece, and saddle cleaned out what was left of his Cremona account. But he saved money on the tuning pegs, which were boxwood poached from Queen Elizabeth Park and stained a fine black.

By then, Mason had moved into the shop—temporarily they said—to keep an eye on Eddie, because he'd got old. He'd always been old, in Mason's mind, fifty when Mason joined the firm at twenty-two, but not *old* old. Now he shuffled around the workshop, skinnier every year, quieter. Pretty soon he stopped going down to the basement because of the stairs, so Mason set his workbench up in what had been a dining room. Eddie could still watch the till, but he hardly spoke to customers, and he was happiest at the bench in his dressing gown, working on some delicate job, listening to the grubby speakers that sat on the kitchen counter.

Once while they were having coffee, Eddie reached across the table for a spoon and his wrist emerged from the ragged cuff of his hoody. Mason was transfixed by how thin it was, how the skin had begun to pucker and spot, the careful way he picked up the spoon, as though every action required some calculation.

"What are you now, seventy?" he said without thinking.

"Dude. I'm seventy-six."

"Oh," Mason said. Thought. "Then I must be—shit."

Eddie laughed. Coughed. "Yeah. Exactly."

The January he began shaping big-leaf maple (from an antique dresser) into the violin's neck, a king tide rolled over the flats by the hospital and the science center. That restarted talk about a sea gate at the mouth of False Creek, though debate continued about how much of the original coastline should be preserved. The old beaches flooded now, water creeping up over the grass below the planetarium. Once Mason saw a river otter slip across a concrete path and into False Creek. The river otter seemed untroubled by his new home, just like the seagull or the ducks.

He went back to the shop to tell Eddie about the first finger of floodwaters sliding across Main Street like a prefigure. Fifty cm rise as predicted, then another half-meter from a king tide, and here we were, in the future, watching mussels grow over the bases of pillars that had once upheld shades over the park benches of wealthy Yaletown residents. He wanted to say to the walls that had once contained False Creek: turn it back.

He got home to find Eddie listening to Melchior play the Bach exercises on the Bourbon viola. Mason stowed the billets in the basement workshop. He could hear Melchior upstairs while he did it, louder than Eddie usually did, so some of the low notes rattled the door to the workshop.

Up the stairs, eyes still full of the floodwaters engulfing Main Street, he stopped in the doorway about to spill his news and said, "What's wrong?"

Wildfires in the Po Valley, burning farms and groves left dry by a five-year drought. Cremona engulfed, and at least a thousand people dead. The Museo del Violino lost, and a pietà, a portrait of St. Sebastian from a small town. An altar piece and a collection of fine instruments stored in Torino.

"No more Cremona," Eddie said. "I should have asked Aldo last week—"

Melchior filled the tired silence.

"I wish," Eddie said in the torn voice of a night spent coughing in the lumpy old futon chair in the corner of his room, which bore the dark marks of his hands where he had been resting them for forty years. "I wish I'd enjoyed it all more."

"I don't—"

"—I mean, sure I should have done more to change things and been a proper revolutionary or whatever the fuck. But actually I just wish I'd spent less time thinking about it, and more—I miss coffee, you know? Really good coffee and drinking it in a coffee shop. I miss knowing I could get on an airplane at any time and go to Cremona and see Aldo, just to see him. I don't think I enjoyed it enough. And here we are. And it's too late."

"It's not too late," Mason said.

"No more elephants. No more ebony trees. No more Cremona. No more Aldo."

"It's not." He thought of the silence after the chainsaw, and the men who waited as the spruce fell, cougars moving soundlessly in the tinderbox woods around them. He thought of the storm of its branches hitting the ground, and the way it shuddered under his feet, and how he had found it, the core pieces, the heartwood of his violin, which had been alive in the seventeenth century, and which had waited on a hillside until now.

First Eddie laughed, "Oh, dude," he said, and coughed.

Mason thumped the old man's back with his good arm, still saying, "It's not too late."

He couldn't explain it because they had arranged a silence regarding the violin, and the things he did to build it. He couldn't explain, but it wasn't too late because under a tarp in a shed, in that bit of land between the lake and the ghost forest, the spruce had been seasoning for fifteen years. In a box under his workbench he had black market Gaboon ebony for the fingerboard, one of the last shipments smuggled out of Nigeria: fine-pored, dense, deeply black ebony. He had glue made from the skins of rabbits he had trapped at night. He had carved the geometrically perfect scroll of its neck from a piece of two hundred year old big-leaf maple. And soon, soon, he would bring them together into something miraculous.

It must happen soon, though, looking down at the old man, his lips and chin slick with sputum coughed up in the last paroxysm.

"You look like your dad," was the first thing Jacob said to him when, late on the third day of travel, he reached the house by the lake, slack-jawed and greasy-haired (once that trip had been measured in hours, you could be there and back in a day). It had been fifteen years since his last visit. His shoulder—numb with the weight of his backpack—twitched in its socket, swollen and tender. He was limping, too, by the time he made it to their gate.

"I feel like I got old like, suddenly. How's Sophie?"

"Great," she answered. Mason started. In his exhaustion he had not realized that the frizzle-haired figure in the doorway was Sophie, the greenish light of the lantern casting her face in craggy shadows and lines. "Yeah, we age *hard* now," she said. "But that's everyone. And your shoulder's still bad. I'll look at it."

They lifted his backpack, then helped him with his shirt. Sophie's sweet, botanical scent and her fingers overtook him, then a hot cloth washing away the dried fluids that had seeped from the open wound in his shoulder.

"It's an abscess." she said. "But I imagine you know that. Do you still have a doctor? Are they giving you anything? I don't like the smell."

He no longer had a doctor, but the guy at the clinic helped sometimes. "Nothing to do except surgery."

Then the heavy skunk of Nepenthe overtook the ache, a scent that reminded him of his grandmother's garden on a hot day, penetrating and astringent beneath the peppermint and lemon balm.

"It smells like—" he said in a voice that seemed to come from far away, but he couldn't tell them, exactly, what it smelled like. Like home, maybe. Like his mother, when he had a mother. Then they helped him to the old back bedroom. He didn't remember anything after that.

When he woke shortly before noon, Sophie was gone but Jake was there on the porch outside the kitchen, drinking something sort of like coffee made out of toasted barley.

"She's been working with the Forestry Lab at UVic on some trees. Someone she knew in undergrad got ahold of her and they've been working together. Genetic mods. Fast growing. Carbon sinks. Drought resistant. It's promising."

It was the first good news Mason had heard in a long time. Together they walked up to the gardens she'd been building on old house sites. The street still showed traces of tarmac, if he kept his eyes fixed on the remaining yellow street paint. If he looked between his feet and listened to Jacob talk, and felt the lake breeze, the town could be as it was when he was a kid. Maybe. Or when his mother lived here before the fires. Or before that, when their grandparents built this homestead at the edge of nowhere and Ts'uubaa-asatx kids played in the lake.

But then, Ts'uubaa-asatx kids still played in the lake, and white kids, and the Sikh kids had returned to Paldi when the village grew up around the temple again. Kids climbed through the alders that grew in the path of old fires, picking blackberries rich with the heat of a new world. Kids fishing and weeding garden plots where the houses had been demolished. Kids singing songs he didn't recognize.

Jacob was limping slightly now. They stopped when they saw Sophie in the middle of a garden near the water, her hair a frizz of gray in the sunlight, and a couple of boys and girls nearby, their arms full of green. Her hands were dirty, right up to the elbows, and when she saw them walking toward her, she waved the carrot tops she held.

"Rajinder brought some Jersey cows from up-island," she explained. "They like the carrot tops. It's our turn to get a couple of liters. The butter is ah-fucking-mayzing."

That evening they ate a soft farmer's cheese from Rajinder's herd, and she talked about the trees, the plantation on the old townsite, about more plans with Ts'uubaa-asatx Nation, a gang of kids replanting the burned-out subdivisions from twenty years before. You couldn't see the old roads in some places, she said. It's like they're gone.

"Where?"

"Everywhere," she said. "It's the regreening. We lost what, ninety percent of our population to the mainland? So why not give it all back? Some of the Cowichan kids started it in the subdivisions nearer the coast, torching the houses last winter. Give it a couple of hundred years, and people will be making violins from the trees we're planting."

He didn't want to say it, but her newly wild world—without roads, without houses—filled him with a terrible bitterness he could not describe. "They won't sound the same," he said.

"Nope," Jacob said. "Not at all the same."

That night he lay a long time in the half-sleep of pain and painkillers, his shoulder numb from Sophie's ministrations that evening. He could not escape the crash of the old Sitka spruce hitting the ground, the crunch of five hundred years of upward growth giving in, finally, to gravity. He wondered if it would still be standing if he hadn't mentioned it to Jake fifteen years ago, in the middle of the night, when he was going to demolition sites looking for old spruce and wild with ambition for Delgado, who would play Moscow and Barcelona and Singapore. Jake had asked where it was: Did he remember how to get there? Could he find it on a map?

Mason did remember, and said *I'd like to be there. I'd like to listen to it.* A couple of months later, Jake had mentioned it again, and here we are, he thought, his shoulder throbbing dully on the other side of Nepenthe.

The day Mason returned from the island, Eddie woke him up just before midnight, when it was still hot and airless.

"I gotta. Go. In." he said.

"Where?" Mason asked, stupidly, then realized what Eddie meant, found his shoes and helped the old man down to the curb, where they waited for an Uber, then waited at the hospital for seven hours, Eddie silent, breathing roughly in, and raggedly out again, while other patients paced, sometimes shouted, and a fluorescent tube above their heads flickered and hissed.

They kept him in for a couple of days. When Mason visited him with things from home—his tablet, a sweater, a newly refurbished violin for inspection—he was a shrunken, cranky man, complaining to the nurse in a small, petulant voice. It was so hot. Could they do something about it? The heat.

Mason sat with him while he ate, then walked an hour back to the shop, where he had set up a bed in the basement, the nearly-cool room that smelled of wood shavings and resin and glue, which was comforting while—on the other side of the peninsula—Eddie struggled with each breath in turn. Here it was almost quiet. Just Mason and the remaining problem: the sound post. Properly speaking, it should be made of spruce, like the front, but he wanted something that had seasoned longer than fifteen years. Something precious to hide away, something only he would know about.

There was the old fiddle, the one some frontiersman made out of wood salvaged from the skids that once ran through Gastown and the beams of longhouse. Once, shortly after he met her, Delgado came into the shop for an order of strings and Eddie brought it out. She played "Where Does That River Run?" and he had laughed, and asked her to play again, anything, to wake the violin up and keep it alive a little longer. She had played at length and with wild generosity: sweet old waltzes; the Québécois "Reel de Napoleon"; a Cape Breton lament.

Humming, he climbed the stairs. He let himself into the shop and opened the display case that held the old fiddle.

It was another crime. Nevertheless, he carried it downstairs to his bench. He did not want to think too much, so he worked quickly: pulling the old sound post out and adding a new one, returning the violin to the store's display case. Downstairs, the old bit of dowel was rough against his fingers. Cedar, maybe from the same post in the longhouse on the Fraser, light and ancient and marked by the original luthier's rough knife. Fragrant when he warmed it with his hands, but no potent aromatics, just a deep and redolent dust.

Then he fitted it, and it hid so perfectly in his violin, maybe no one would know the terrible thing he had done, the secret history he had stolen like all the other secret histories that constituted his violin. He knew, though, all the courses that materials took, from Nigeria, from the islands, from demolished bungalows in east Van, from vacant lot rabbits, and from Stanley Park.

Even from his bed, even on oxygen, Eddie was critical when Mason brought it upstairs, examining it with an eyeglass until he conceded that the sound was as fine, in its own way, as any number of other violins he'd seen. Finer, even, than the composites he'd started to use for his own work (when he could work), corene and carbon fiber.

"You made something, kid." It had been a long time since anyone had called him kid, even Eddie. "Does it have a name?" Eddie asked.

"Does it need one?" If it had to be named it should be something elegant and sonorous. Kiidk'yaas. "I don't know. The Vancouver violin."

"Better than that."

Eddie wouldn't play it, and neither would Mason. Delgado was swamped at the center, and had a toddler, so while the violin—Spruce Goose?—was finished in September, they didn't hear it until the New Year.

She was late. That was okay. The toddler was with her, which was slightly disturbing, but Mason figured they could keep her away from the detritus of the apartment, which was mostly workshop. And there were dry little cookies, at least, to feed her, at the back of a kitchen cupboard.

"I meant to leave her at home, but you know Johnny got a last minute shift—"

"No worries," Eddie said, quietly because he could only speak quietly now. "We're just happy to see you."

"This is it?"

Mason's throat was unaccountably closed, so he just—Delgado juggled Belinda from one arm to the other. "Oh," she said. "Oh."

"Mommy?" Belinda murmured, sleepy.

"I'm going to put you down for a sec."

She rubbed her hands on her jeans, Belinda now squatting at her feet, leaning on her knee.

"Oh," she said. He thought he saw a tremor. Her face dropped into her neck, so her hair fell forward and she looked as she had when she was fourteen and coming into the shop for new strings special-ordered from Berlin, talking about Bach.

Then the bow drawn across the open E, and he heard it, the sweetly deep, the brightly clear reverberation. Delgado made a wild little laugh and ran a scale, another scale, then interlocking arpeggios. Ševčík.

At her feet, Belinda spoke to a little blue bear, patting her threadbare ears.

Delgado dropped the violin from her neck, cradled it. Her eyes were bright, as though with tears, but her voice was warm.

"It is—oh, Mason!"

"Will you play something?"

She played Beethoven. The Kreutzer Sonata, as though she remembered the night that had stuck forever in Mason's heart: the Chan Center, and the Plaisir violin, and Delgado. Eddie leaned to the left side of his wheelchair, his eyes closed, the oxygen tank hissing faintly, the sound of people at the window, Belinda's murmurs to Bear. All these interruptions should be maddening, but they were not, and only seemed to complement the room's fragile magic.

When she was finished she sat heavily on the remaining chair.

"How long have you been working on it?"

"A while," Mason said and saw her as she had been, fifteen and brilliant with an actual future stretching all the way to Paris. He had imagined hearing it for the first time in some acoustically perfect opera house, because the world would have recovered by then. He knew it was foolish, but it hurt to think Delgado would never carry it away from this provincial little corner.

"What will you do with it now," she asked, a wobble in her voice, the harmonics of longing. "Who'll play it?"

It was strange to him that she needed to ask.

"No." she said when she understood. "Oh no. No."

Belinda looked up from Bear. "Mommy. Mommy?"

"You can use it in your classroom, can't you? I think it'll age okay. It'll open up."

She didn't respond for a minute, but crouched down to where Belinda sat with Bear, her brow furrowed with worry for her mother. Then she stood and asked, "Does it have a name?"

"See? It should have a name," Eddie said.

Mason heard the oceanic crash of falling spruce, his own cry as he hit the dirt at the base of a shining willow in Stanley Park. The market garden and the homestead, the lake, the abandoned subdivisions and the burn lines that still showed through the underbrush, the ghost forests, the dead black teeth of what had once—a long time ago—been a rainforest. And among them, Jacob still cutting lumber and helping out at the garage when he could, fishing and hunting. Sophie in the greenhouses and the gardens, with her new Garry oak trees and her transfigured arbutus, the beetle-resistant spruce that would never, ever, be the kind of tonewood he wanted. The firebreaks of trembling aspen, the return of cougars. The steady erosion of human shapes: foundations and roads all lost to the burgeoning forest.

"Nepenthe?"

As he said it, he wasn't sure what it meant: a physick that would make the end easier; a draft of healing medicine.

"Nepenthe." Eddie said. "There it is."

"Remember," Sophie had said before he left. "You're going to come back here for good, eventually. It's still home."

Unspoken: come back when Eddie has died and you're ready to give up on global dreams and figure out how to live out the rest of your days in this shopworn future.

He had just nodded through the ache of disappointment that had accompanied him for decades, now. But a tiny, exhausted part of him almost liked imagining it, how he'd go back to work in the garden, raising saplings for the new forest that even now overtook the old world, watching kids disappear into the wild.

Masami Lucretia Delgado plays the Nepenthe violin daily for forty-five years, even if it's only ten minutes when she gets home from work, her kids playing noisily outside the bedroom. Five minutes before everyone else is awake, Belinda fourteen and saying *Mom are you seriously playing right now?* she plays it on the day they leave their apartment because the seawall at the mouth of False Creek has failed. She plays it in the back of a car as they drive inland, toward interim housing in which they'll live for five years. Nepenthe is a fixture in the temporary-but-actually-permanent school she establishes in a slipshod village on the Fraser River. Together, she and Nepenthe accompany Belinda's wedding, and Masami's grandchildren fall asleep to lullabies from those strings. Despite her daily practice, she will never hear its most perfect expression: the violin will be its best long after the maker is dead, and the first hands that played it are too crippled by arthritis to make more than sighs. But she will play on while she can, because the violin must not go to sleep, and the longer she plays it, the more the alchemy of sound—the resin, perhaps, the glue, the cellular acoustics of the wood itself—will transform the object, preparing it for its ultimate player. Maybe her youngest daughter—the finest musician of all her children—or her granddaughter, will first hear the violin open up into its richest, fullest tone. Maybe it will be someone a hundred years in the future, who lives in a different world than we do, but who will pick up the instrument and draw her bow across the strings, releasing the reverberations of a thousand thousand crimes and accidents into the singing air.

Julie Nováková is a scientist, educator, and award-winning Czech author, editor, and translator of science fiction, fantasy, and detective stories. She published seven novels, one anthology, one story collection, and over thirty short pieces in Czech. Her work in English has appeared in *Clarkesworld, Asimov's, Analog,* and elsewhere, and has been reprinted e.g. in Rich Horton's *The Year's Best Science Fiction & Fantasy 2019.* Her works have been translated into eight languages so far, and she translates Czech stories into English (in *Tor.com, Strange Horizons, F&SF, Clarkesworld, Welkin Magazine*). She edited or co-edited an anthology of Czech speculative fiction in translation, *Dreams From Beyond,* a book of European SF in Filipino translation, *Haka,* an outreach e-book of astrobiological SF, *Strangest of All,* and its more ambitious follow-up print and e-book anthology *Life Beyond Us* (Laksa Media, upcoming in late 2022). Julie's newest book is a story collection titled *The Ship Whisperer* (Arbiter Press, 2020). She is a recipient of the European fandom's Encouragement Award and multiple Czech genre awards. She's active in science outreach, education, and nonfiction writing, and co-leads the outreach group of the European Astrobiology Institute. She's a member of the XPRIZE Sci-fi Advisory Council.

THE LONG IAPETAN NIGHT

Julie Nováková

Heaven welcomed me with the smell of disinfectant and a strange strumming tune. Funny; I never believed there was an afterlife, let alone like this. I was cold, beyond shivering. My body was made of stone, and my mind trapped in it. Or was this Hell?

The tune was odd, otherworldly. Rhythmic but disharmonious at times, and happy and sad at the same time.

Suddenly it stopped, and I heard footsteps.

"Welcome back, Lev," a sonorous voice said.

Only then did I manage to open my eyes. They stung, and all I saw at first were blurry shapes, but then I focused on a broad face half-drowned in shadow. Its onyx eyes and bushy beard felt familiar.

I opened my mouth to speak, but only wheezed.

"Don't talk, rest," the bearded man said and laid a surprisingly gentle hand on my forehead. "You're up early, still thawing."

He must have detected the question in my eyes, because he added: "The shuttle has woken you, but the VR protocols were corrupted, so you can't enjoy sims while you're warming up. I can put up a projection that you can watch on the ceiling."

I was beginning to remember. *Atalanta* The cold sleep. Our captain.

I managed to produce a few sounds, horribly distorted, but he understood. "The music?"

I blinked.

Then I closed my eyes again, as the strumming noise carried me back into blissful oblivion.

Six years and eight months. We'd been under longer than anyone had in the past century. Was it worth it?

I still felt stiff and slow when I shuffled through the empty corridor toward the common room. The bracelet around my left wrist indicated I was in good enough condition to make the journey and eat lightly, for the first time in years.

Only two people sat there: Captain Turushno Rayochi, and Doctor Altun Armatis.

"Good morning, Lev!" she said. Her voice was a loud firm contralto, which seemed strangely out of place here. I still felt like I was in a dream. Only when I took the first hesitant bite into a soft protein stick did I feel grounded in reality. The stick had almost no flavor, but to my taste buds, long unused to actual food, it resembled an explosion.

"How are the rest?" I croaked.

"Waking up. Everyone should be okay."

"Can I see . . . ?"

"The others? Oh—you mean the outside? Go to the porthole in corridor five," Altun suggested.

My whole body ached, but I dragged myself there with determination. I had to see. Not on a display, not in VR; I had to see with my own eyes what no one had seen for the past century.

I stopped with my face pressed against the thick fiberglass. My breath condensed on it, and I realized how cold I still felt. Yet it was nothing against the cold outside.

Everywhere I could see, darkness. The icy surface was almost pitch dark, too. We'd landed in the middle of Cassini Regio, within the Turgis Crater. All the ice was covered by dark dust. But I could still see the crater rim towering in the distance and the star-studded sky beyond it. It was night, and night it would remain for two dozen more Earth days. Outside, it would still be cold, dark . . . peaceful. It distantly reminded me of the long arctic winters in Bilibino. Beyond the town, there would have just been snow, hills, and sharp towering rocks.

"Beautiful, isn't it?"

I scarcely noticed the captain coming. I wondered what his dark eyes saw out there—did the gloomy land remind him of home, too? Most of us had come from the far north, if only because some of such settlements proved more resilient in the Big Plunge.

"It is," I said hoarsely.

"Come. We'll be complete soon. We should celebrate."

I slowly followed Captain Rayochi back. Iapetan low g was a soothing balsam to my cold, aching body.

"What about the other crews?" My voice was coming back to me; I no longer sounded like a broken gramophone record.

"We've received a transmission from *Atalanta IV* They are awakening. No news from Titan yet, but it may be too soon for that."

I nodded, reassured. *Atalanta* had deposited two crewed modules on Titan, two here on Iapetus, and enough relay stations throughout the Saturnian system that we could contact each other or Earth most of the time. A fine second start for human presence out here.

In the common room, Altun was just examining our geoscientist, Tonraq Scott. The chief engineer, Bálint Veras, already clutched a cup of tea in his deathly pale hands. The last member of our crew, biochemist and environmental engineer Raisa Nalinova, entered the room. She managed to produce a faint smile, though obviously still groggy and sore from the cold sleep.

We were all recovering slowly. Altun stated with satisfaction that no serious problems had occurred during our time under.

We ate dinner, our first meal together in the new world. After the long cold sleep, even the bland rice with dried vegetables tasted heavenly. Captain Rayochi surprised us by producing a plastic bottle filled with saké. Courtesy of knowing the right people and some huge leeway, or a part of the mass allowed for personal possessions? I didn't ask, just gratefully accepted the cup. In the low Iapetan g, the liquid flowed in slow, almost languid motion.

The captain raised his cup, and the quiet hum of our combined voices faded.

I half-expected a speech about the vast expanse we'd overcome, and how the greatest challenges still lay ahead of us, but Turushno Rayochi was never one for speeches.

"Too long was the night of the world," Rayochi spoke. His dreamy dark eyes stared not at the wall before him, but somewhere much farther, into the deep endless void out there. "It's time we saw the day."

It would be easy for me to dismiss his words as the musings of a sentimental older man. I didn't live through as much of it as he had. His parents would have seen and remembered the coming of the night; mine were already born in its wake.

Rayochi reached for his tonkori and began strumming. The sound was as disquieting and unsettling as always. This time, the captain sang. His hoarse deep bass contrasted strangely with the high tunes and at the same time accompanied them perfectly. I didn't understand the words. He sang in classical Ainu. But later, he told me that although the language was almost extinct, the song itself was new—younger than the captain. It spoke of the darkness that had surrounded the world; of the wars that ensued; of the hunger, and winter, and hatred. It gave them almost lifelike proportions, as if they were fickle deities playing with humanity's fate. We were the heroes and villains for their amusement.

For me, this view of the Big Plunge was difficult to grasp. In my family, we never viewed it as . . . poetic, or even mythological, like it seemed from Rayochi's songs and tales. It was merely an unfortunate natural disaster. It could have occurred at any time; it just did so in the late twenty-first century. There was nothing poetic about it, just much stupidity, lack of foresight, and bad decisions.

How little suffices to turn us into barbarians, I pondered.

A deadly cascade: A VEI-8 volcanic explosion in Campi Flegrei occurs. Naples and adjacent towns: destroyed. Other cities are devastated by quakes. In much of Europe, ash obscures the sky. A harsh winter follows. Crops die worldwide; famine, thirst, and diseases spark further conflicts. Millions die; millions flee; millions fight. Some states fall; some descend into totalitarian regimes; some are lucky and only their economy suffers.

Scarcely a year later, an extreme solar eruption sends us into the pre-satellite era, and in some regions, even into the pre-electricity era. Data is corrupted. Communications disruption results in more chaos. Crewed spaceflight is suspended; even if there was any money for it, the infrastructure needs to be rebuilt.

The Moon colony struggles to survive; most citizens evacuate to Earth, destabilized as it is. The small Mars settlement falls into disarray. As to elsewhere . . . I recalled the ghostlike landscape outside. A century ago, people had been here. Then—they either died or tried to evacuate and met their deaths later. Nobody really knew.

Both the flare and volcano could have gone off at any time. The coincidence was tragic and somewhat ironic. It showed us the fragility of our civilization. And while Earth plunged into decay that would take decades to overcome, colonies and bases elsewhere faced extinction.

Suddenly, the melancholic song ended, and I was drawn back into the present.

Rayochi lay his tonkori aside and lifted a cup once again. "To our new world," he said simply.

"To our new world," we echoed.

This is truly a new world! I can barely comprehend it, but we're really here.

I can't wait to climb the great equatorial ridge. Thrice as high as Mt. Everest in some places, yet in the low g of Iapetus, the feat seems ridiculously easy. But on the other hand, it's not. Physical exertion is no issue—but iceslides are. Trigger one, and an avalanche of brittle ice can bury you in slow motion. Not to speak of the ever-present sticky black dust that adheres to solar panels, is next to impossible to get off of spacesuits, and sometimes slides beneath one's feet. But I'm confident we'll get used to this truly alien world.

Everyone else is excited, too. This isn't like the initial Jovian missions where people spent scarcely a year on Ganymede before going back to Mars. If all goes well, other bases will join ours, and there will be a permanent human presence around Saturn. I can still hardly believe I'm here.

Paula says this is a perfect opportunity to investigate the history of this peculiar walnut-shaped moon. I agree, but I see the true importance of our mission elsewhere. We're pushing the boundaries, saying that us humans remain better than AI in so many disciplines and that we'll go farther still!

I've managed to reconfigure our comm protocols so that we have more efficient communications with Endurance II *near the Turgis Crater, and with the Earth, of course. I've also tasked one of my comm AIs to sim other ways to spare data. There are some things AI are better at—but we need to guide them!*

I wish I could send a vid of this landscape to Mother. But the DSN 2.0 is still limited, and personal comm time will only come up in a week.

No matter. I'll have plenty more to tell home about by that time. We are really here, writing history!

Black-and-white patched ice was everywhere.

We couldn't see any trace of the station that was supposed to have been in the area, built over a century ago.

How could it have vanished?

"An iceslide might have buried it," Tonraq proposed. "It happens often on the slopes of the ridge."

"We'll see what the radar imaging returns," our captain added. "In the meantime, we know what to do."

My heartbeat quickened when I thought about that. Yes, we do. We are about to restore humanity's presence in the Solar System; give us back these strange new worlds.

At first we struggled to move on the sometimes slippery, sometimes sticky reddish and black dust covering the ice. The landscape began to take on a more nightmarish turn. I wondered how the first expedition a century before us had managed. Did they have to scrape the dust off of every piece of machinery that even barely touched it, and take extreme caution with every step?

Despite this hurdle, we were able to map the area thoroughly. Stability seemed sufficient for commencing construction. We told the carrier platforms to place inflatable cupolas at given sites, and to assemble the Lego-like parts. I had a Lego set as a child: a cherished treasure, passed down for two generations. No one had made these little plastic bricks for over thirty years. They'd only begun manufacturing them once again shortly before our launch.

While Bálint and I mostly worked on the new habitat assembly with the help of the captain and Altun, Tonraq and Raisa took a rover each day and drove to study different nearby areas. The mystery of the Iapetan ridge was never fully solved; if the crews before us found the answers, they'd become lost in time, like dust in Saturn's rings.

As we got more used to avoiding the black dust, the new base grew over the next few days—and we uncovered more mysteries.

"Come have a look at what we've found," Tonraq's voice, distorted by the ever-present interplanetary hum, crackled on the comms just as I was attaching a new control panel to one of the prefabricated walls. It must have been something of great importance to warrant going off schedule. I checked the panel and entered the already habitable section.

It took a while before everyone was present. Captain Rayochi, perhaps anticipating something big, brought his tonkori.

Finally, Tonraq and Raisa brought their prize. It was a portable Raman, not unlike the ones our suits were equipped with.

"Is it . . . " I dared to interrupt the silence.

"Yes. From the *older ones* Someone must have lost it on the ridge, perhaps when jumping or climbing the terrain. But that's not all. We checked if it was safe to bring it inside, both for the device and us, and . . . it's got data on it," Tonraq said. "For a century it has waited here, to tell us."

"Tell us what?" asked Bálint, as usual the most impatient of us.

"There might have been life."

Silence follows for a second, broken by several *whats* and *hows* Iapetus is a dead world, frozen since early after its formation four and half billion years ago. How could there be traces of life? Perhaps in material from the Enceladan geysers? Enceladus was thought to be able to support life ever since the early twenty-first century, but we'd never gotten around to thoroughly testing it, not before the Big Plunge.

"Enceladan?" I offered, though it seemed there was little chance of enough material getting from one of Saturn's innermost moons to all the way out here.

Raisa shrugged. "Maybe. It would be a rare accident, but not impossible."

"What exactly is it? Something telltale, or indirect only?" Altun inquired practically.

"Isotopic anomalies—carbon, nitrogen, oxygen, silicon, sulfur . . . even some elements not known as biogenic on Earth *or* Enceladus. And something that looks like protein and nucleid acid fragments, even large intact pieces."

"Well, something like that couldn't have lasted long near the surface."

"That's right," Raisa nodded, her eyes shining. "But what if the sample was excavated from deeper below the ridge—an indigenous sample?"

"Can we tell where it came from?"

"Unfortunately, location data are compromised."

A collective sigh of disappointment.

"But it's a start. If the schedule allows, we should devote more time to investigating the deeper subsurface, especially around the ridge. There could be some more recent material closer to the surface, as . . . "

While the discussion continued around me, and Captain Rayochi even seemed to have forgotten about his musical instrument, I stared at the portable spectrometer as if it were an artifact of another civilization. In a way, it was. So we'd been here a century ago? The notion felt too unreal, too absurd—to travel across the vast interplanetary distances just to die miserably when the homeworld fell apart.

My stomach knotted with anxiety and hope that a better fate awaited us.

Just received news from Mission Control. Hard to believe. They say a megavolcano erupted in Italy . . . Volcanic winter is said to be setting in throughout Europe, North Africa, and the Middle East, but it's spreading . . .

Bad news for crops and energy. And people. Disease outbreaks may follow, fueled by food shortages and failing infrastructure.

How can this be true? We have greenhouses. Green walls within cities. Nuclear power plants. Personalized medicine. We should be able to cope, right?

They say they'll continue to inform us. In the meantime, we should continue with our mission.

Paula is devastated. She has family in Naples and Rome. MC didn't mention them.

We're all struck by the news. Olga is right, we should stick to the schedule and work while we wait for further information. We meant to celebrate spending four years in this eerie place, but now no one is in the mood to celebrate anything. All the accomplishments, all the joy and hard work has gone sour.

We talk with Endurance II *all the time. Bill, Derek, and Okoyo are optimistic; Marieke and Greg, on the other hand, think this is the beginning of a decline of civilization.*

Look at previous large volcanic events, they say, and observe the rise and fall of empires. Think of the late Minoan civilization, or the Justinian plague, or the famine triggering the French Revolution.

I don't agree with their pessimism. We've had some VEI-6 events in the twentieth and our own century, even a VEI-7 in the year 1815, and survived them all quite intact! It's true that in some ways, we're more vulnerable due to our technology, but at the same time, it makes us stronger. This was allegedly a VEI-8 explosion, ten times stronger than Tambora in 1815, and Naples must have been completely wiped out. It's a terrible tragedy, but still . . . we must manage. We're all around the world, and the Moon and Mars, and now around Jupiter and Saturn, too. This simply cannot shatter our civilization as a whole.

Update: Greg sent us all some treatises on the fall of civilizations. What was he thinking? How could this be helpful to anyone at this time?

There is a big cloud spreading over Europe and farther, MC admits, and the cold spreads, too. There's a threat of acid rains. Worldwide crop failure is practically a certainty.

They tried to sound optimistic but weren't fooling anyone. Worst case scenario: we can expect no further help from Earth, no relief or supply missions in the foreseeable future. We either stretch our resources and innovation to survive here potentially for decades—or we embark on a journey home. The next launch window is in two years. We should know enough by then.

Derek suggests we develop both contingency scenarios and see which one is more viable. Most of us on Endurance I *vote to test out the "leave" part, while the majority of* Endurance II *crew wants to test the "stay" plan. All the better this way. We'll test the in-situ fuel production efficiency for the journey home, while they try the long-term energy and food supply solutions. I still think it's madness to stay. It's bitter to abandon the dream of a future Iapetan colony, but better than to die here.*

Captain Erenki's face was tense. Today's regular exchange of news between us—*Atalanta III*—and her *Atalanta IV* crew seemed to hold some surprises.

"A crater nearby seems to have been . . . modified. Smoothed, even polished, I'd say, and reshaped by the original crew," she announces.

The second module had landed nearly four hundred kilometers from us, north of Seville Mons, just where the leading and trailing hemispheres of Iapetus merged in a true mosaic of black and white ice. Unlike us, they had no problem finding the original base. The images they'd sent us were eerie: dark empty corridors coated with frost, long-dead instruments and computers, deserted bunks . . . no bodies, though. Did the crews escape? But where? And why didn't they take more from the base?

"We believe it was meant to serve as a solar collector, to concentrate the sun rays in the center. See for yourselves."

I looked at what truly had resembled a giant dish in disbelief. A solar collector—*here*? Where the sunlight falling upon us is a hundred times dimmer than on Earth, at times when it falls upon us at all and we're not plunged in the darkness of the long Iapetan night?

Only someone very desperate could have reached for this solution. They must have thought they were stranded here. Why? Had the Big Plunge occurred near the end of a launch window? I didn't remember the late twenty-first-century Saturn-Earth windows, but there was nothing easier than to look it up . . . and no. They had time. So did they . . . *decide* to stay? In that case, where was the rocket, or the bodies? Had they used one module, or two? I had no idea. Even their names and histories were lost to me. If anyone knew, the information wasn't readily available publicly. They were ghosts of the past.

Tonraq and Raisa seemed very interested in these past crews, especially their scientific knowledge. For me, they were just ghosts—but nonetheless

I wished to see their world. I couldn't go back in time, but there was the abandoned station and its allure. And though I felt like no one else here, except maybe Rayochi, would see it that way, there was the second crew, and I found a kindred spirit in Valentina Shipka. Like me, she was very young for the mission, and like me, she could hardly imagine the pre-Plunge world. Her expertise was applied geophysics.

"The interest runs in the family," her somewhat hesitant, shy voice carried through the cabin. The comm capacity between *Atalanta III* and *IV* was limited, but we were allowed voice-only communications, provided they didn't coincide with important data transfers. "My grandma used geophysics to hunt for fossils—used the Geiger and radar images to find dinosaurs! My mother used it to hunt for oil reserves. And here I am . . . When I was little, I imagined a career like Mom's, to help secure energy for the community. I'd never imagined I'd be probing alien ice."

Rayochi may have been a dreamer and a poet besides a pilot and data scientist, but he wasn't truly post-Plunge. He'd talked about the old world as if he'd known it, though he didn't. For us, it was history.

"Any news on the Raman data?" Valentina inquired.

"No. It's too early to get our own samples."

"Has it occurred to anyone that the samples might be from neither Enceladus or Iapetus?"

I'd already laid back in my bunk, my eyes closed, but this made me snap them back open. "What do you mean? Like Earth, or Mars? But such a transfer is so improbable . . . "

"No. I mean something far *more* improbable."

It took a second to sink in. "You mean from another star system? That really *is* improbable."

"But you can't tell from the fragments, can you?"

I had to admit she was right. Still, the likelihood was so impossibly low! That an asteroid or comet coming from another star would crash right here, carrying traces of very alien life . . . Or, as my imagination raced like always in those strange moments before going to sleep, perhaps it didn't crash. Perhaps it could have been a seeder pod. Or even a piloted ship!

No; that would be going too far. Perhaps it was better to change the subject. I asked about the first expedition's base.

"It gives me the creeps," Valentina confided. I imagined she was tucked in her bunk as well, just wishing to talk to someone before sleep. I vaguely pictured her face, but I'd grown familiar with the tone of her voice over just a few days. It was the unexpected cadence, the not-very-melodic rhythm of it.

"I suppose . . . it would have been better if there were bodies. It's scarier without them. Like a stage prop, or a ruin left by some civilization too ancient for us to comprehend. I'm not even trying to imagine what had become of the first crews. But we're going to research it more thoroughly tomorrow. Maybe I'll see it differently then."

"I'll look forward to hearing about it."

I really was. But the *Atalanta IV* crew fell silent just a day later.

I don't know how we managed to hold on. It's been exactly a year since the Campi Flegrei explosion and almost a month from the last time MC messaged. We don't know the reason for their silence, but it's not hard to guess. Twenty-seven days ago, the Sun erupted with a strength unprecedented in modern history.

It must have fried all satellites in the inner system, perhaps as far as the belt. Ours were affected, too, but survived with only some loss of data. On Earth, even with its magnetic field, lots of ground-based infrastructure must have been destroyed. But mission control had backups, shielded sites, contingency plans! They must contact us soon, for sure, to tell us to return home, with a supply ship rendezvous en route, or that we have to at least make it to Mars.

They couldn't just leave us, could they?

Greg says that even if individual people from MC wanted to help us, the overall conditions may not allow them to. Loss of infrastructure—and social upheaval, he stresses. What if mobile networks are down? Navigation? Transport? Half the bare necessities of modern human life?

I'm beginning to hate that guy. He always sees the worst in a situation and tries to sell us his goddamn defeatism! I refuse to give up like him.

The conundrum remains: Should we produce fuel to get us home, or try to survive in this icy wasteland?

Suddenly, the black-and-white mosaic outside doesn't seem eerily fascinating, like a fairytale landscape. It's ominous. We may be imprisoned here unless we act fast and launch in the coming window. We're just entering the porkchop, we still have time. . . .

We spend a long evening discussing it, and then another and another.

MC remains silent. That, perhaps, tips the scales.

In the end, we decide to leave. Although the Earth seems to be in shambles, it still has everything to support life—and civilization. The uncertainty of the world that awaits us is preferable to the certainty of this cold prison. With the new fuel production units all running, we should have enough fuel to get us back to Earth the slow, Hohmann way by the end of next month.

Finally, we're going home.

Update: No, no, no! How could this happen? Can we really be imprisoned here?

An iceslide buried the main fuel production field yesterday. It came out of nowhere, triggered seemingly by nothing: an avalanche of a hundred tons of ice hurtling down the slope of the crater. It should have been stable there—not like next to the ridge!

In any case, we can't make this launch window. Twelve more goddamn years in this frozen hell!

The Endurance II *crew doesn't seem too devastated, especially Greg.*

I wonder . . . what if we shouldn't ask what *triggered the slide, but rather* who?

"Almost there."

Bálint spoke, perhaps to assure himself rather than us. Altun and I sat behind him in the rover. I could see Altun's profile through her suit's visor, and the doctor looked as calm as ever.

I doubt I did. Certainly I didn't feel calm. There was no explanation for the sudden silence.

The base our colleagues had been building rose from the horizon. It looked just like ours, made from identical prefabbed sets. But behind it stood something else, half-buried in the ice but unmistakable.

Our predecessors' station.

"*Atalanta IV,* this is the rover *Beotia* Do you copy?"

There was no answer to Bálint's hail.

Nor did anyone reply on the suits' emergency frequency.

A shiver went down my spine as we came to a halt near the main airlock.

"Looks undamaged," Bálint announced.

"Their main rover is parked outside, backup should be in the storage unit." Altun's voice sounded level and measured. "Someone ought to be inside, if not everyone. Can you open it?"

As if on cue, Bálint finished the manual override, and the airlock opened. We stepped in, not bothering to strip the suits or take down our helmets, though the environment seemed safe by all possible readings.

"The inner comms system is working," I said. "I'll announce our presence."

I did so—but the others ought to have known about our arrival already. Yet no one came to meet us.

"Let's go through. Someone must be here."

I felt bad when we split up, yet there was no danger for us here. It wasn't reasonable to feel that anxious. It was just unfounded, unnecessary fear, I tried to convince myself. But as I walked through the seemingly empty base, my worries only grew.

Everything looked perfectly normal. Perhaps that was the worst part. Normal . . . but deserted.

The common room: a game of *go* laid out on the table; a half-empty water pouch lay next to it; and—

I nearly jumped when I felt a vibration through the floor. But it was just Altun, stepping in. "No one in the bunks."

"Nor here, or the science section."

We returned to the airlock. Bálint was already there, with the same news as us, adding: "I tried the antenna. It's working. I spoke to Rayochi."

"Right. So they must be either in the module, or the original base, unable to hail us."

I had no idea how Altun could still sound so calm. We were talking about six people, missing! The protocol stated clearly that at least one member of the crew should remain on the base at all times, unless evacuation was mandated. But if they evacuated for any reason, why not contact us?

"Lev, come with me to the old base. Altun, you take the module. Check-up on comms every five minutes," Bálint decided.

I followed him reluctantly into the dust-coated icy plain. Barely a hundred meters from the new station stood the old one. I could feel the ice, hardened by radiation and temperatures of minus 180 centigrade, crackling beneath our feet as we approached the dead place.

Nothing to worry about. Nothing to scare me. I had seen the images from inside—it's just empty . . .

Nothing to be afraid of in empty places.

"This is where they went in."

Bálint directed us to what must have been an airlock. Though no air remained within the base, it seemed prudent to enter through it and not destroy one of the walls. Who knew—the space might still be useful in the future, if only as cold storage.

"You were in contact with them about this place's exploration, right? Did they say anything before the silence?" I tried to sound as level-headed as Altun before.

"They wanted to revive some of the old tech they'd found—computers, lights . . . The things are said to have been made to work even in vacuum, so they just raised their temperature a bit."

"Right."

We arrived at an intersection. "I'll go left, you go right," Bálint said. Almost at the same time, Altun's voice crackled: "Altun here. Trouble getting into the module. Working on it, will keep you posted."

My helmet's flashlight shone into the pitch-dark corridor, reflecting from the thick layers of frost coating all surfaces. The atmosphere. The frost must be nitrogen, oxygen, carbon dioxide . . . I could imagine it condensing on the cold metal and carbon as the heating gave out, forming a fine mist and then slowly collapsing entirely, just like the governments, economies, and food chains collapsing back home.

"Bálint here. Nothing so far."

"Altun here. Almost got it, will go inside."

I tried the closest door, but it wouldn't move. It must have been frozen in place for decades. But as I took a turn, I saw another, pried open. They must have melted the frost to force it open.

The light cone illuminated a space that must have been a common room with a kitchen before. A table surrounded by chairs still stood in the middle of it, coated with remnants of the air the people had once breathed here. I wouldn't have been surprised at seeing the outlines of plates and water pouches beneath the frost, but I could see no such thing, and grateful for it.

I went on. But the next two doors were completely frozen shut.

"Altun here. I'm inside the module. I think someone's in the cryo pod storage."

I also announced myself.

Silence followed.

"Bálint?" I said then. There was no response. "Bálint, do you copy?"

Nothing. A chill went down my spine. A message on my HUD warned me that my heart rate and breathing had spiked, and that my sweat composition suggested beginning dehydration.

"Find him, but first finish the sweep," Altun said. "The others must be somewhere!"

"Yes." My throat really was dry. I forced myself to take a sip from the suit's water pouch.

Come on. Walk faster. This is just a long-ago abandoned base, everything is frozen . . .

Another turn. More collapsed atmosphere cracking beneath my feet. The flashlight shone at what resembled the previous section. Untouched, governed by the all-consuming cold. But at second glance, one could notice faint traces of recent activity in the frost. Perhaps the crew had started with reviving this section. But—

I stopped.

Was it just my imagination playing tricks on me?

Then I felt the slight vibration again.

A microquake? Or . . . did someone move somewhere near?

"Bálint?" I said on the comms.

No reply.

I took a careful step forward and stopped again.

The ground quivered.

I activated the suit's seismic detectors. Perhaps they could lead me to the source. It appeared to be further from the corridor. I touched the left wall lightly, but didn't feel anything. The right one, though . . .

The slightest hint of a tremor. I walked on, feeling the wall and glancing at the seismometer results on my HUD. While walking, the data was far too noisy, but I could still perceive the tiny changes. The frost evaporated at my touch, though the gloves were barely warmer than the surroundings.

The light fell upon a door. Closed at first sight, but bare of the otherwise ever-present frost at the edges. When I looked more closely, I saw that it was open the barest gap, as if someone wanted to close it, but it had stuck.

And they were still inside.

"Bálint?" I spoke again, quietly despite the fact that no one not on the comms could possibly hear me. "Altun . . . ?"

Nothing.

Must just be interference. I'll hear them soon, for sure . . .

Cautiously, I jammed a screwdriver from my utility belt into the gap and tried to pry the door open. It gave way smoother than I'd expected, and the momentum nearly threw me against the opposite wall in the Iapetan low g.

I gasped. But something else caught my attention.

The light briefly reflected off what had seemed like a helmet, half-concealed behind a lab table. I would have flinched at the sight had my suit allowed such a movement.

Breathe. It must be one of the crew, and they'd need my help.

The room evidently had been a lab. Shelves laden with instruments lined the walls . . . and behind a heavy lab table huddled a suited figure. I approached carefully.

"This is Lev Anishin, *Atalanta IV* Are you all right?" I said on a shared frequency.

The suit should have pinged mine, I should have already seen the identity on my HUD, but there was nothing. Trying to ignore the prickling of my skin that was probably fear, I leaned closer.

The inside of the helmet was lightly coated with moisture, some of it frozen in a fine pattern, but I could still see the familiar face. Its eyes were closed, and skin perhaps too pale.

"Lev here, I have a crew member in need of medical attention. Anyone? Respond."

There was only silence.

I examined the second suit visually and connected to it old-school, via cable. Most systems were working, air recycler, too, if barely, but the inner temperature regulation had probably malfunctioned. I tried rebooting it manually. It caught on immediately, to my great relief, although its comms remained off. The health monitor said that the suit's owner, Valentina Shipka, had sustained no injuries and only displayed signs of exhaustion, dehydration, and hypothermia. Nothing that couldn't be fixed.

Another vibration, this time next to me. I froze.

Only now did I notice that Valentina's hand moved slightly, holding a drill. As she touched the button, the device whirred, sending tremors through the floor. Then her grip on the on button relaxed again.

Moving. Awake.

I collected my wits and pressed the visor of my helmet against hers. "Valentina, can you open your eyes? Can you speak?"

Her eyes flicked open faster than I'd expected. "Y-yes."

"It's me, Lev. How are you feeling?"

"Cold . . . "

"It's gonna be better soon. Tell me what happened."

"This place . . . it tried to kill us!" I could hear her teeth clattering. "We m-must go!"

She tried standing up, but she was still weak, and the suit's reaction times were only returning to baseline. I stopped her gently. "We're going, don't worry. But we have to wait a minute. Calm down. In the meantime, please tell me exactly what happened here."

"They went inside, but the comms crashed . . . We followed, and this place . . . it attacked."

"Attacked? How?" I tried to sound casual. It was probably just mild shock and hypothermia. Valentina still seemed somewhat confused. Once she recovered, she would make sense.

"Let's go, then," I said when she didn't respond, my visor still against hers. "Your comms don't work. If you want to say something to me, tap my visor."

I recalled a layout of the old base on my HUD. It seemed we were closer to the rear airlock, and it would enable us to see more of the base on the way out; perhaps even find the others. Where else could they be?

Valentina stood up with the help of her suit's servos. I beckoned her to follow.

I wanted to appear calm, but sweat ran down my brow despite the undersuit absorbent cap. It stung my eyes. Recyclers announced that my CO_2 was spiking. The suit advised mild emotion stabilizers and attention sharpeners. I discarded the suggestion for now, and instead focused on my thoughts and breathing. Deep, calm breaths, and rational thoughts. No matter how scary the long-dead place might have been, it was just that—a place. With no reason, no malice, no agenda. A thing. Now, a thing could be dangerous—the structural stability might be degraded, faulty electronics that would melt the moment they came online might lurk there—but not intentionally. Not by mounting an *attack*

Behind the next corner, faint light appeared; not a reflection from the headlight. Could some fluorescent panels have reactivated due to the current crew's activity?

Instinctively, I increased my pace. Suddenly, Valentina grabbed my shoulder and tapped my visor urgently.

"Not here!" Her voice, carried through our helmets, sounded panicky.

"Calm down," I said. "This is the shortest route to the airlock."

"No, it killed them!"

Valentina was increasingly upset. The suit should have given her something soothing, but the med system was evidently malfunctioning, too. The sooner we were out of there, the better.

"I'll go first, and you'll see that nothing happens to me, all right?" I suggested.

Perhaps I managed to sound confident enough, because Valentina nodded hesitantly. I set off again. She followed some ten feet behind me, slowly, reluctantly.

A panel shone on a wall in front of us. The frost around it was completely gone.

In the darkness behind it, a large shape could be made out on the floor. I shone my LED there.

A suit.

I walked toward it faster . . .

A blinding flash. The adaptive visor wasn't fast enough to react. The display became a jumbled mess of blurred shapes. A long artificial wail sounded in my speakers, hurting my ears.

I glimpsed something moving in the corridor.

Quivers.

Then—total darkness.

I wanted to take a step ahead, but the suddenly rigid joints of the suit prevented me from doing so.

Calm down. No panic.

I realized that the disturbing sound I was hearing now belonged to my own ragged breath and a tinnitus in my ears. I gulped and spoke: "Lev here. Anyone hear me?"

All of a sudden, with no warning, another visor was pressed to mine. But then I heard Valentina's voice: "I hope I've broken it. Are you all right?"

"I thought so." The display of my HUD was dark, unresponsive. The flashlight remained dead, too. We were plunged in complete darkness. "What was that?"

"It tried to kill you."

A shiver ran down my spine.

"Try to move. I'll get out of your way."

Before I could respond, Valentina was suddenly gone, and I was still drowning in darkness.

I strained against the rigid joints of my suit, and thanks to my strength built by having lived on Earth, I managed to step forward in the moon's meager gravity. Then another step. At first, I stomped down so hard that I flew up for a moment. Sole magnetization was evidently offline as well. How much time did I have until something vital gave way?

I fumbled for the emergency controls on my left sleeve. By touch, I found the life support control. To my great relief, it was intact, and a small display on the sleeve immediately showed that the systems were in perfect health. Then I tried the comms. My backup antenna was working, but couldn't pick up anything. Next item on the list was emergency lights.

I reflexively took a step back. In the sudden dim light, I could see a suited figure lying on the floor right in front of me. At first sight, it was clear that they were beyond help. The visor was cracked and beyond frost, dark blots that must have been blood covered the inner surface.

Valentina turned and saw it, too. I couldn't see her face or hear her, but she took a quick step back.

I touched her visor, compelling her to turn back toward me. "I know the way out. Come."

I was glad that we couldn't see the dead person's face through the debris. Hollow shock replaced terror. I focused all of my mental capacity on getting out. Just one more turn, another corridor, and then the airlock. No more lights ahead. No activity. I only perceived the vibrations caused by Valentina's and my own steps.

Just a few minutes until we reached freedom—and then we'd need to find out what happened to the others. My throat constricted, not because of fear for myself, but for them.

Finally, I saw the airlock door. I increased my pace, though every step was a strain.

The manual opening was tough, but with Valentina's help, I shifted the door aside.

I exhaled and stepped in—

Something rammed into me. I couldn't take a breath; I didn't even have time to cry out.

I was pinned between the heavy door and the wall, almost unable to move. Breathing was hard. The massive metallic door was pressing against my chest. I couldn't move my right arm at all, the left one only from the elbow down. If it weren't for the resilient suit, the door would have crushed me. All safeties must have been turned off a long time ago, but the doors shouldn't have been capable of so much pressure.

This place is trying to kill us.

For a moment, I succumbed to my panic. But it couldn't have been more than a second. Then I tried to press against the door, and felt that Valentina was attempting the same.

I fumbled around what I could reach on my utility belt with my left hand, but only the laser cutter was within my reach. Useless here.

Block the door, I wanted to say to Valentina, but didn't have a way to do so. She must have thought of it too, though. Did she have any tools of use?

A strained breath. Pain. My gaze flew to the corner of the airlock. Another figure leaned against the wall there. At the same time, I realized there were droplets of blood on the inside of my visor. Had I bumped my head? Was that figure even real?

The pressure suddenly subsided. Valentina?

In that instant of opportunity, I managed to squeeze myself inside the airlock. I almost twisted with pain, but paradoxically, the rigid joints kept me up.

The door—Valentina!

I reached for a heavy spanner on my belt, rammed it into the door's mechanism and strained.

The gap remained wide enough for Valentina to squeeze through. For a second, I was reminded of the very beginning of human spaceflight and Alexei Leonov, who had to vent air from his suit in order to get back into his ship after the historically first spacewalk. Ship . . . more like a can in orbit.

I stumbled toward the figure in the corner. Behind its visor, also stained with blood, I could make out Captain Erenki's features. She was conscious, if barely. I started suit diagnostics and looked back at Valentina. She was busy trying to open the outer door. I held a desperate hope that it wouldn't be blocked because the inner door remained open. All those safety systems must have died so long ago . . .

As if on cue, a gap opened, and behind it light.

This time, we tested by a few careful movements that the door would let us through safely, and then each of us took Captain Erenki under one shoulder, and we went.

We stumbled outside, onto a patch of dark ice, but starlight and the diffused light reflected off Saturn made the grim landscape look so unbelievably bright that I had to blink. The droplets of blood inside my visor were frighteningly dark.

I heard the crackling in the comms I so longed for.

"Lev here," I rasped. "Do you copy?"

"Bálint here, I copy. Are you all right, Lev? I couldn't reach you. I found Timur—dead."

The sudden relief of hearing my friend's voice almost suffocated me. "I—I'm alive. Valentina and Captain Erenki are with me. Both with damaged suits, Erenki injured, her suit failing fast."

"If you can, go toward the module. I'll meet you on the way."

A second voice joined then: "Altun here. Dashmir is with me. He's in shock, incoherent, but not injured. Come here, I'll prepare the surgery. Report the captain's state to me."

The landscape in front of me blurred, and I realized it was my tears of relief.

I suppressed a fit of hysterical laughter and trod on.

Damn. Damn! I can't just sit here and watch our chance to leave vanish. It's nerve-wracking to see us losing the porkchop day by day. . . . We could still make it!

We won't produce enough fuel to carry all of us home, but we could leave Endurance II *to their foolish dream of staying, jettison the extra sleeper pods and other dead weight, and we might make it to Mars. The colony wasn't totally self-sufficient the last time we checked, but there must be tech and resources to help us get back to Earth eventually.*

I want to see home.

It's too grim and silent here without Paula. Who knew she was so deep in despair that she'd take a nitrogen tank and hook it to her suit? At least it was quick and painless. However—who's next? If we stay, there will be more who select this option, I'm sure of it. But the others say we either all go, or all stay. And since we can't possibly all go . . .

So instead of racking up the remaining fuel production, we've been building a solar collector out of a crater, scrambling on this nightmarish dusted ice half a day, day after day! Ridiculous. With the amount of sunlight this far out-system, it will never give us enough power!

We've also built another greenhouse and additional chlorella tanks. So this is how we're supposed to live out our lives here? Living on meager portions of modded chlorella with barely enough energy, fighting the nature of this place, and hoping no unforeseen disaster kills us at any given moment?

Update: An unforeseen disaster! Oh, how fitting!

The new greenhouse lost power, backup too, and everything inside died before we could save it. We're on severely limited rations for at least the next three weeks.

Greg says it's been sabotaged. He has the nerve to say that!

Even if he's right, we have no way of finding out who did it.

I try to convince Olga and Derek to leave. If the others get into their sleeper pods here, they should be able to survive, so this option still remains for them if they find staying awake unsustainable. This is our best chance at living.

I think Derek may be on my side, but Olga isn't.

Doesn't she see she's condemning us to death?

We sat in the common room of *Atalanta IV*'s base. No one spoke for a moment. Only after a lengthy pause, Captain Rayochi on the screen said: "Do you require our assistance? We could spare one more crew member for some time."

"If we can keep Bálint and Lev until this situation is resolved, it should suffice—if you can spare two engineers," Captain Erenki said starkly. Her trenchant manners contrasted with Turushno Rayochi's always soothing composure. The death of part of her crew made the lines carved in her face even more prominent, and her voice fiercer.

"We'll be able to cope for a week, at least. The main hab is ready, and we can keep using the module. But what's more important—do you have any idea what happened in the old station?"

Erenki's face grew darker. Perhaps she thought that Rayochi was questioning her judgment, even though I was fairly sure my captain meant no such thing.

"We're fabbing more robots to go in as we speak. No crew is allowed there until we find out what has caused the incident."

Killed two of my crew, she left unsaid.

Luckily, Altun was able to stitch Erenki together quickly. Dashmir and Valentina were back on their feet even faster, neither having sustained any serious injury. The remaining two were beyond help.

The survivors' accounts were desperately inconsistent, even after the shock had passed. We'd all concluded that they described a series of terrible accidents. Technical failures we'd been insufficiently prepared for. We wouldn't make that mistake again.

But an irrational suspicion that it was no mere accident gnawed in a dark corner of my mind. It felt like actions of something with agency, a *plan* It was crazy—yet I couldn't avoid thinking that each of us had the same suspicion.

Trying in vain to fall asleep that night, I listened to a recording Raisa and Tonraq had sent about their continuing quest to find past life on Iapetus. Apparently, it would take a long while—many years, perhaps—before they could say anything conclusive, but they hypothesized that for a short time after its formation, Iapetus might have harbored an inner ocean, just like Enceladus has to this day. On some of the icy moons, life had arisen, and might have been transferred to the others by the intense exchange of material. Though impactors could hardly hurl rocks from the surface of the moons, like on the terrestrial planets, they could have ejected a lot of small ice particles or triggered geyser activity, so life or proto-life could have moved within the system, at least before Iapetus froze completely and acquired its peculiar walnut shape, which still needed a thoroughly tested explanation . . .

Hearing this recording had a strangely calming effect on me. There was something much bigger than any of us; the knowledge, the science we could do, and also the unimaginably vast history of the place we'd now claimed as our new home. We were nothing but specks of dust. Nothing we did really mattered, except in advancing humankind's collective knowledge by another incremental step.

I was almost lulled to sleep by these thoughts when my comms beeped. Someone was trying to contact me.

"Lev here," I mumbled sleepily.

"This is Valentina. I . . . I wanted to talk to you about this mission."

"What specifically?" I kept my eyes shut, sliding into a dream-like if still awake state.

"I'm afraid this isn't the . . . beginning of human expansion toward Saturn and beyond." Her voice had the same hesitant, not-quite-rhythmic quality as always. "What if it's a futile attempt we're going to die in? For nothing."

I shuddered. "I'm sorry . . . after what's happened in the base, I understand. But we're going to find out what caused the disaster and prevent anything like that from happening in the future."

"There is no future for us," she said in a low voice, barely audible, and then the connection ended.

I considered calling her back, but her gloomy message left me without anything to say. It only called back the specters of the old station. However I tried to rationalize it, whatever good explanation I tried to come up with, I ended up empty-handed. It didn't make sense. The deaths had no meaning, no apparent logical cause. But most of all, the things we'd seen—

A persistent thought insinuated its way into my mind.

Valentina was right. The place was trying to kill us.

Who knew that Olga would be next? She seemed so stable and determined. But I guess this place gets to us eventually. It's so dark, cold, and isolated.

We've been left alone with Derek. He's beside himself with fear. What's worse, he's been neglecting his duties on the station. I'm having a hard time doing everything myself, especially since I've been trying to restart the fuel production. I'm spending most of my awake time suited, outside surrounded with that horrendous black dust coating every tiniest bit of surface that needs to be left intact, but I have to manage. The optimal window is gone, but perhaps we don't have to wait twelve more years. I ran some simulations and we could use a Jupiter flyby route. It takes longer, but the years don't matter as much if we're frozen. The main point is, it saves fuel.

The mass ratio is still not ideal, though. It could safely carry only one pod; two would be stretching it.

Only one. Is it even worth contemplating? I wanted to leave, yes, but not at the price of leaving everyone else stranded here.

Update: In a moment of weakness, I confided in Derek. But I made the chances with two pods seem greater. He believed me, didn't even want to check the sims.

Will we try to get rid of the excess mass and resupply fuel?

The others would probably notice soon. The ship is closer to our base, but still . . . is it worth trying?

The uncertainty terrifies me. I might soon end up like Derek, paralyzed by it all. Update: My god, what have I done?

Of course Derek didn't believe me. He must have found some will inside him and run his own sims—and realized the truth and what it meant.

I still don't know whether I'd have been able to leave, to betray everyone like that. He tried.

He dosed me and instructed the med unit to keep me under for two days. He loaded all supplies for the off-chance of waking up in-flight—meds, instruments, food, robots—and drove to the ship. I have no idea how he managed to offload the excess weight and prepare for launch so fast. I had expected it to take at least twice as much time with two people working on it.

He must have skipped many pre-flight checks, acting in a hurry, perhaps driven by fear that the second crew would arrive before he could launch.

They saw the explosion. I was still asleep.

We don't have a ship anymore. Few items were saved from the wreckage, and only one working pod remains. This base was stripped of most necessary supplies. The rest of course suggested immediately that I move in with them, and I hardly have any other option. But all of our chances of survival have now decreased. We could have survived in the ship for some time if both bases became nonfunctional; not anymore. We're perhaps facing decades in here—decades of surviving on modded bacteria, algae, and artificial meat, confined in a fragile can amid the endless icy plans more than a billion kilometers away from home.

Would anyone ever come for us? Is there anyone on Earth still thinking of us? Is there anything we could still call a technological civilization?

What happened is my fault, much more the effect of mine rather than Derek's fear. What now?

Only one thing remains: try to survive. Try to atone for all my failures . . . although one life is too short for that.

I watched Captain Erenki's face closely: her grim eyes, lines carved in the skin of her face like a relief in wood, and the downcast corners of her mouth. Only Bálint and I sat across from her.

"I'll cut right to the chase." Her voice was firm, but still I thought I'd heard traces of fear, even . . . panic? "The events on the old base cannot be explained by malfunctions. One, of course. Two deaths and several injuries and damaged suits, hardly."

My throat felt dry. With the corner of my eye, I caught Bálint's gaze. The chief engineer was just as glum as me, but didn't seem very surprised.

"How would you explain them, then?" I asked, immediately scolding myself for the tremor in my voice.

"Sabotage. There is a murderer among my crew."

I froze.

"All the survivors, myself included of course, are under suspicion," she continued evenly. "Since you two arrived later on, it couldn't have been your doing."

"Why would anyone do that? They'd be lowering their own chances of survival," Bálint objected.

"You're trying to find a logical reason. What if there is none?"

"That is a possibility. We can let you all undergo a psychiatric examination. Altun is back on *Atalanta III*, but she can do it remotely. We can make sure no one tampers with the med unit."

Erenki nodded. "I agree. If you allow, I'll go first. Contact Doctor Armatis and call me to the infirmary once you've established connection."

We were supposed to build infrastructure for future human habitation, to spread civilization all the way to Saturn—and we could be stopped by *murders*? Was Valentina right that we were doomed to fail?

Valentina . . . three survivors; one of them possibly a murderer. But surely not her!

The examinations were conducted under the pretext of testing for PTSD and other potential aftereffects of the tragedy. None of the survivors manifested any signs of severe mental illness. Shock, stress, mild depression—yes. But no psychoses. No one reacted to stimuli associated with death, murder, and violence outside the norm.

Could one of the two dead have planned the sabotage and fallen victim to his own traps, or let himself be killed? If not, then who?

I shivered at the thought of the missing bodies of the original crew. But surely no one could have survived, even assisted by cold sleep, to this day? Or . . . they couldn't have had *children*, could they? That would have been madness! To doom a child to die alone in this wasteland—certainly no person with a scrap of compassion would do something so horrendous.

Captain Erenki seemed unsatisfied by the results, but there was nothing else to do. Robotic explorers were sent into the base to perform more diagnostics, but so far we lacked reliable data.

Couldn't it have been a series of accidents? I held onto that desperate hope. The thought that we were living in close quarters with a murderer was too paralyzing.

Erenki looked like a caged lion. I preferred to stay out of her way and work on the remaining repairs with Bálint. But later she found me herself. Her expression boded nothing good.

"Tell me, Lev, does Captain Rayochi have ambitions?"

The question took me completely by surprise. "Ambitions . . . That's not a word I'd associate with him. With none of us, to be frank, apart from the ambition to help humanity move forward."

"Hmm," Erenki snarled. My answer apparently wasn't satisfactory. "What about rules, procedures? Is he the type to stick to them?"

"Well, mostly yes, like all of us, but not fanatically . . . " I was beginning to feel very nervous about the direction of this conversation. Could it be that she feared that Rayochi considered her incompetent and would try to relieve her of command? Or that he suspected sabotage on her part? That he would use us against her? But why would she come to me?

It was a relief when the questions that felt too much like an interrogation had stopped. Something had been off about it. About every single thing that had happened since our sister base had fallen silent.

I was still thinking about it when I laid down on my bunk, exhausted, but too worked up to sleep. My mind raced, full of images of how the original expedition might have perished and whether the same end didn't await us. The collapse of a civilization, small-scale version. I wondered how members of Scott's infamous Antarctic expedition felt when it became painfully clear that they hadn't succeeded in their race and most of them, if not all, would pay with their lives? On the wind-beaten icy plain, with no hope of outside help, no supplies, driven purely by the urge to survive, after they had tried to push the boundaries of human presence a step further.

I was about to take a sleeping pill when the comms beeped.

"Valentina?" I spoke, surprised.

"Lev . . . I need to tell you something." I heard her take an abrupt breath. "Look, I may be the youngest crew member and not understand some things outside my own field, but I'm not naïve enough to think that something didn't try to murder us in there. That place *was* trying to kill us, and I bet the captain has considered the option that it was one of us. If she's right, no one is safe here. You and Bálint should take a rover and return to your base. Convince the others that you all need to leave. *Atalanta* remains in Titan's orbit, you can get there with the module. Then it's up to you whether you want to join the Titan crews . . . or take the ship and return to Earth."

I was speechless. To run? Leave the mission? Betray everyone who depended on us?

Somehow, I imagined Valentina with a deeply sad smile when she continued: "I'm not asking you to take me with you. You can trust neither me, nor the captain, nor Dashmir. But save yourselves at least. Please."

Finally, I found my voice. "No. You must be wrong. There has to be another explanation. It might have been accidents. Or . . . " I recalled my earlier thoughts about the original crew. No; that was too far outside the realm of the possible.

"Or what? Mysterious aliens, leaving some biosignatures behind and then trying to murder us just for fun? Come to your senses. It must have been a human. Someone who's still here. *Leave*"

"We can't!"

"You must." The urgency in her voice made me shiver. "You need to go. Otherwise all of us will die here for no reason. Trust me, Lev."

The worst part is that I did.

I was outside doing solar panel maintenance when it happened. A small impact, triggering an iceslide. One large enough to bury the base. I didn't know until I came back and saw . . . only dirty ice wasteland where our home had been.

I wanted to help, but I knew it was pointless. Radar showed the base was shattered. Before I could get to my friends they'd be long dead, even if the event itself hadn't killed them outright.

I was the last one.

Besides resigning myself to death I had only one option. I drove to the second base and got a part of it operational. It could sustain me for a few years if I were lucky.

Not more.

I could die here like the others. Perhaps I should. But I didn't want to.

I couldn't stop thinking about the one cryo unit we'd managed to salvage. It was worth excavating. I wasted two drills on it. In the end, I dug manually, drenched in sweat in my suit, and I thought about whether I shouldn't die anyway. Why go to so much trouble to save my sorry life? As if I deserved to live.

I'm the last one, so I can confess now. I sabotaged the greenhouse.

I made a huge mistake that may have cost everyone else their lives, and there wasn't a day later in my life when I wouldn't regret my action.

Why do something so . . . ill-considered and unprofessional would be too weak to describe it.

Our world was falling apart, our families and friends on Earth might be dying, off-world colonies in mortal peril, and we were here, isolated on a dark, cold world. We were trained to cope with that, but not with the end of the world. I was scared to death.

I was absolutely convinced that we were going to die here, unless we got off Iapetus as soon as possible. I became terrified of the icy desert all around. I was barely able to work outside.

When an iceslide destroyed the fuel manufacturing unit, I was sure it had been someone else's work, not an accident. I grew paranoid. I tried to act normal for fear that anyone could have been the saboteur. Some people wanted to remain, didn't they?

I decided I'd make them want to leave.

I don't know if anyone but Greg suspected foul play when the greenhouse was wrecked. If they did, it didn't show—but perhaps they just pretended, like me.

Looking back, I knew I was wrong. I needed help. I became a slave of my anxiety and paranoia. I should have sought medical help, and instead, I doomed all of us. It only takes one to shatter a functional crew. I was the bad apple. I was the traitor. I sentenced us to death. I will never forgive myself. I kept my secret for all those years, while wishing that someone would find out, that I'd be punished and it would be painful. I would have walked unsuited into an airlock if they told me to.

But no one discovered the truth. I wanted to atone, but the best way was to pretend and help others.

No more pretense. I'm alone, I'm the one who deserved to die, but I've lived. And I don't want to die.

I will try to repair the cryo unit, even if it takes years, and I'll put my fate in its hands. Either it keeps me alive until someone arrives in the future, or I die in there.

There's just one thing I want to say, and I could repeat it over and over again, but it won't be enough. It never will.

I'm sorry.

There was still plenty of work at the base, and that was perhaps the only anchor keeping me sane. I tried not to think about Valentina's plea, or the paranoia in Captain Erenki's eyes when she was inquiring about Rayochi, or the strange look on Dashmir's face sometimes. I almost jumped when my comm beeped again. This time, though, it was Captain Rayochi.

"We're making do, but the crew morale is low," I admitted when he asked the expected question. "Everyone is scared. It . . . feels strange here."

"What about Captain Erenki?"

My stomach knotted. It must have been a routine question; I should have expected it, too . . .

"Does she seem fully in control—of the mission, but mostly, herself—to you?"

"Yes," I said, but Rayochi must have noticed the slight hesitation.

"I had a very strange conversation with her today. I'm afraid that she might do something ill-considered. Leave the mission, for instance."

"No, certainly not that! She's under a lot of pressure here, but she would never!"

I gulped. I couldn't avoid thinking of Valentina's words the previous day . . . and of the fact that they'd nearly convinced me.

Rayochi's voice remained as calm and soothing as ever. "More experienced people have succumbed to less pressure. This place has a strange effect on one's mind. The perpetual ice, isolation, and close quarters. Perhaps it would help if each of us found their own cleansing ritual of sorts, to find oneself . . . "

I was in no mood for Rayochi's stories and superstitions. They had no place here! Not here, not now. Had I remained the only rational person on the moon?

Excusing myself for necessary repairs, I ended the transmission. But as soon as the welcome silence fell, it was interrupted by footsteps, the characteristic *click-click* of the lightly magnetized soles making walking in the meager local gravity easier for us.

Valentina Shipka strode through the corridor. She nodded to me, but didn't even slow down—but I had to ask.

"Valentina, wait, please. Did you seriously mean it when you suggested that Bálint and I leave you? Because I hope that's not the only solution."

She stared at me, first in incomprehension, then almost angrily. "*What?* First you try to persuade me to spy on my own crewmates, and now this nonsense?"

I opened my mouth, but before I could figure out what to say, Valentina turned and quickly walked in the direction of Captain Erenki's cabin.

Spying on her crewmates? What the hell was she talking about?

The encounter only confirmed to me that waiting would resolve nothing—and nor would running. If we could find answers anywhere, it would be at the old base. The robotic explorers remained stubbornly silent, though. Something was wrong with the place, but turning our backs on it wasn't an option.

When I presented my plan to Bálint, he looked at me as if I'd gone mad. "Have you forgotten what happened to us there the last time?"

"I don't like it either, but we have to go back and find the answers."

"Or inadvertently destroy evidence left behind by the saboteur," he objected darkly. "It's madness."

Madness . . . that threatened to engulf us if we didn't get our answers soon.

"Bálint, something very strange is happening. Erenki is nervous and keeps asking me about Rayochi. He, on the other hand, seemed to be thinking of this as some . . . predestined failure. Valentina doesn't remember our conversation from last night, but hints at something I never said at all. Something's off, whether we leave the base be or not. We have to go back."

Bálint wrinkled his brow.

"All right," he said finally. "It didn't escape me that we're in trouble no matter what. But this time, let's prepare for an unfriendly welcome, just in case."

Extra oxygen tanks. Toolboxes. Reserve flashlights. Repair foams. I felt as if we were preparing to enter a battle zone. I didn't feel prepared at all.

We agreed to start in the section where I found the injured Erenki and the dead crewmember, not far from the lab where the terrified Valentina had retreated. If something out of this base set off the incidents, not one of us, it was focused around there.

We were already en route when Captain Erenki's voice, ordering us to turn back immediately, sounded on the comms. Neither of us slowed down.

This time, the airlock door couldn't catch me by surprise. We jammed it more thoroughly than the last time with Valentina, and went in.

How to describe the station? It felt too unreal, too insane to be true. Perhaps that was why I felt so little fear. It was like being a distant observer projected into my body: a mere telemetry operator, quickly thrashing one of our explorer bots that attacked Bálint; disconnecting a panel that threatened to emit an EM pulse and damage our suits; walking on and on into the heart of the base. The space felt alive, though it had been dead for nearly a century.

Bálint and I never split up, so that we made the discovery together.

It took us a longer than expected to get through the safeties of one cabin. And when we finally did, the door didn't move. Something heavy was blocking it from the inside. We had to torch through an adjacent wall.

But inside the otherwise bare room stood what we'd been searching for: a lone sleeper pod. Could the base have been . . . protecting it somehow? Why?

It contained a frozen body, long past any hope of reawakening, but also data: unencrypted private logs of the crewman. The data was barely corrupted at all. So now we listen . . .

Seen Greg, I'm sure of it!

He came back to haunt me. Must have survived the ice somehow, or turned into something . . .

This place is full of horrors. But it won't get to me, no, I'll stay sane no matter what!

I must be careful, though. He's out to get me, to destroy my chance of survival, to wreck the pod!

Hah, if I'd known I'd be working on the sleeper pod for nearly three years, I would have killed myself! So much time, alone, trying to keep everything working, alone but for the ghosts on the black ice.

Update: I think they tried to put something in my chlorella. I stopped eating it a week ago. I'm not feeling all that well, but it must be their doing, I'm sure I'll get better before I go to sleep. The pod is nearly ready. Just a few more days, I think.

I can use that time to stop the nightmares. Greg, Paula, Olga . . . They must not reach me when I'm defenseless. But I can rig the station: kill them, or if they can't be killed, make them turn on each other.

I'll make damn sure no one comes to get me while I'm asleep.

We listen, startled, disbelieving, horrified.

While the Earth had very nearly plunged in the Dark Ages, our own darkness had played out a tragedy here. Avoidable; unnecessary; nearly ridiculous. One that eventually killed everyone then, and two of us. One that we nearly succumbed to, even if separated by a century of progress.

After listening through all of it, Bálint, Dashmir, and I examined the station systems more in-depth. Now that we knew what to look for, we were able to spot and erase the traps. There were many, but the most ingenious and terrifying was the simple AI that listened to our transmissions, analyzed the content and learned to mimic us. It had talked to me as Valentina; to Valentina as me; to Erenki as Rayochi . . . and made sure we'd be left in the dark and turn on each other. Feed people false information, and you can become their puppeteer, even if "you" are an AI with no awareness and general intelligence to speak of.

Just a few days, and we were reasonably sure there were no more such traps. We finally summoned up the courage to step into the base again. It resembles a ghost town; but the specters have been cast out. Now it's just a memorial to the tragedy that happened here.

Still, two people are dead.

We hold a service for them, and decide to bury them in the ice. That's where the original crew was buried, and we don't have many other options. Raisa and Tonraq say it won't compromise the search for the possible long-extinct life, and I want to believe them.

The schedule slowly returns to normal. Hopefully, so will we.

I stand at the edge of the Turgis Crater, out for a routine maintenance of our new seismic network. To make sure we don't succumb to ice slides as easily as they did.

From my position, I overlook the vast expanse of the bright Roncevaux Terra glimmering in the new sunlight. After a month spent in darkness, we finally see light.

We keep telling ourselves that we're wiser now. We have solved the mystery; persisted; managed to build a base for others to occupy later. We don't know if and when they'll come. Dispatches from Earth say to hold the fort; that a multitude of missions are being prepared, and that we're entering a new and bright era.

Too long was the night of the world, the captain had said after our awakening. *It's time we saw the day.*

I blink in the light of the distant Sun shining through the filigreed beauty of Saturn's rings. Behind them, as a tiny bluish dot, I spot the Earth; so very distant and fragile. I hope the captain was right. Yet it seems naïve to me now, too simple.

Another disaster—and what would happen? Another plunge, another collapse. More terror and paranoia. The one from a century ago nearly shattered us. We can tell ourselves stories of reason and bravery, but we're not immune to fear, the same fear that haunted our ancestors in dark caves.

We can see the Sun now, but this is still most certainly a world of darkness. And as long as we carry the darkness within, there always comes night after the day.

Sameem Siddiqui is a speculative fiction writer currently living in the United States. He enjoys writing to explore the near future realities people of South Asian ancestry and Muslim heritage will face in the coming centuries. His stories explore issues of migration, gender, family structure, economics, and space habitation. He's attended the Tin House and FutureScapes workshops and his stories have appeared in *Clarkesworld* and *ApparitionLit.* Some of Sameem's favorite authors include Kurt Vonnegut, Octavia Butler, and Haruki Murakami. When he's not writing, Sameem enjoys reveling in fatherhood, watching '90s *Star Trek*, and tinkering with data and music. You can find him on Twitter @s_meems.

AIRBODY

Sameem Siddiqui

Amazing how all Desi aunties are basically the same. Even when separated by vast oceans for a few generations. I mean, they fit into a few basic archetypes. There's the genuine-sweetheart proxy mother who, in between her late-night work shifts, always makes sure you and your friends have all the snacks you need. The manipulative gossiper, who conveniently keeps details of her own children's scandals nestled under her tongue. The nervous fidgeter who has spent three decades so worried that her basic thirty-year-old son won't ever find a wife that she forgets to teach him how to speak to women. The late-life hijabi, who pointedly replaces "Khuda-hafiz" with "Allah-hafiz" and "thank you, beta" with not just "jazak-allah" but the full on "jazak allahu khayran." But which of these archetypes would find it appropriate to rent the body of a grown man halfway across the world?

I pull the AirBody request from Meena Khan into view in my contacts. She's fifty-nine years old and from Karachi. Her short wavy hijab-less hair and her relaxed smile makes her seem content with life, so maybe she's the genuine-sweetheart type. Her only notes on the request are a list of Desi groceries and some cookware, which only reinforces the archetype. Maybe she's too ill to travel to visit family for Eid and wants to surprise them with a feast? It's been a while since I've gotten a taste of such a spread. I hit accept and watch the usual legalese flash before me:

You acknowledge that you have the ability to observe, regain control, and remove your guests at any time and therefore may be complicit and responsible for any crimes or damage committed by your guests.

I tap "Yes" and begin to look through her grocery list more closely. Some of it, like the sweetened condensed milk, half-and-half, sugar and cardamom powder I can get at the regular grocery store. But for the Desi ghee and chanay ki daal, I either have to pay a premium at the hippie organic store downstairs or drive out to a Desi grocery store in the suburbs. A drive would help kill some time, so I choose the Desi grocery store.

When I return, I arrange all the ingredients in alphabetical order on my otherwise bare gray marble kitchen counter and head to bed. Meena activates at 6 AM and I don't want to test AirBody's zero-tolerance late policy. I also don't want a review plagued with complaints of body odor and morning breath.

My alarm goes off at 5 AM, but I snooze several times, stumbling in and out of a wildly vivid dream about riding on the back of a sea turtle. Except, I'm not in the water. I think I might be floating through the sky. But, there are definitely other underwater creatures floating by, greeting us along the way. I feel love for the sea turtle and I lean over to kiss its rough green cheek when the snooze expires. Weird. But, my dreams have been odd since I started "playing host" on weekends a few months ago.

By 5:58 AM I'm towel dried, clothed and somewhat fed—a cookie is breakfast to some. I stand in front of the mirror as I clip the AirBody headset to the backs of my ears. It whirs on automatically—it doesn't actually whir, but I imagine that's the microscopic sound it makes as the violet light pulses. It authenticates my identity and says "Hello, Arsalan. Your AirBody guest is in the waiting area. Are you ready?"

"Yup, I'm ready," I say, trying to sound chipper, but nervous as fuck about what this will be like. This is my sixth time hosting and so far it's been a good distraction to get through my weekends. Most of my other guests have been men, usually here for some business meeting at the World Bank, or to tour the monuments and museums with their grandchildren. The only other woman I've hosted was a lobbyist from an asteroid mining firm who didn't think a one-hour meeting with a congressperson was worth breaking orbit for.

My limbs tingle as they go numb. I feel heavy for second, like I can't support my own weight and am about to fall. And I do, in a way. Not phys- ically. More like falling asleep into a dream that makes so much sense that it's boring. Which is why, I suppose, AirBody lets hosts stream content and games to the neural UI while their guests go corporeal.

I give Meena a few moments to adjust and watch her look around my living room. Her eyes stare at my mostly empty bookshelf surrounded by plain white walls. I don't have much decor, except for the tiger painting Ammi bought in Thailand when she visited once in her early twenties.

"Hi!" I say, my voice in the AirBody interface sounding way louder than I intend. I feel my heart rate increase and realize I must have scared her. "Sorry, I, uh, just wanted to say hello and let you know I'm here to assist you during your stay if you need help."

"Beta, Urdu nahin boltay?"

Oh crap. Not only am I going to get a bad review for my poor Urdu language skills, I'm now going to spend the next twenty-four hours meeting the scorn and judgment of a Pakistani aunty. Here we go.

"Nahin, aunty, I—" I say slowly, preparing to flex my mind's tongue with words I haven't used in years.

"Array profile pe Urdu likha tha!"

Oh god, if I don't get removed after this listing, I need to delete Urdu from my language profile. If for nothing else, to escape this scorn. "Chalo, I'm here. What can I do now?" she says, waving my hands up in the air behind us. "Take me to the kitchen, beta . . . you do have a kitchen, right?"

"Haan, yes," I say, retaking control. My limbs tingle awake and I walk to the kitchen before handing her back control.

I feel my body sigh and my head shake. "This will do," she says as she walks to the corner of the counter where I've neatly arranged the ingredients she requested. She inspects them closely, as if she doesn't trust that I bought the right things. But, she doesn't make any complaints. She looks around the kitchen. There are a few dishes in the drying rack, but I made sure to clear out the sink, which is normally full until there's a noticeable rot.

She begins opening cabinets, slowly and calmly at first. I assume she's looking for something specific, but after a moment I'm sure she's just being nosey. She comes to the last one, the little corner cabinet, the only one to the right of the sink. Shit.

I want to distract her, to keep her from opening it, but interfering with an experience without consent or a reasonable emergency would lead to a bad review. So I watch hopelessly as she swings the cabinet open and stares at the label on the little translucent bottle half full with brown liquid.

"Whiskey, beta? Tauba tauba," she says as she slaps each of my cheeks gently. "Allah maf karay!" I'm not sure if she's asking for forgiveness on my behalf, or if she somehow feels complicit in my sin by inhabiting my body. I mean, I'm not drunk—it's six in the morning. Now if she wills that whiskey into me, then maybe she'd be complicit. Maybe.

She shuts the cabinet, still shaking her head, and pulls open the electric pressure cooker. We both notice the inner pot hasn't been washed since the last time it was used, but only I know that this was many months ago. My eyes roll back into my head as she groans and clicks my tongue. She flicks on the tap and snatches the worn-out sponge on the edge of my sink. "Yeh koy tareeka hai, beta?"

She fills the pot with water so hot that I can feel the pain through the sensory suppression as she scrubs. I'm convinced this is intentional punishment. Maybe she isn't the genuine-sweet type.

She empties the dal into the pot slowly, as if she doesn't trust my eyes to check the quality of the product as a whole. The yellow pieces glint off the bottom of the worn metal, scattering into swirls as she shakes the bag to see if she can catch any unwanted particles.

One piece of dal pops off the bowl and onto the floor and I feel a tinge of the panic that froze me the first time I made dal. Not knowing what to do as the orange but almost magenta grains spilled onto the counter and to the floor. The worthlessness that would melt me into a blob as I'd hear Ammi's tired and exasperated voice say "Beta, Arsalan, just once, would you do things without rushing?" Her finger would point at the door. "Out, now, if you can't help properly."

"Savvy for a ten year old," Nani would say as I'd run to her lap before the tears began to flow.

"Haan, just as savvy as his useless father," Ammi would say.

And then the fear of inadequacy would stand me up straight, wipe my tears, and walk me back into the kitchen defiantly, striding close enough to Ammi to move her out of the way without physically attacking her. I'd sort it out. I'd sift the dirt out of the fallen dal. I'd get a jar to pour the extra back. And I'd have dinner on the table before Ammi returned from her evening shift. I would not be my useless father.

"Is this right?" Meena asks as she presses the buttons on the pressure cooker.

"You're not gonna soak the dal first?"

"Oh so now you're such a refined cook?"

"I can make dal."

"Then tell me, why soak the dal? What difference does it make, aside from wasting two hours of our lives?"

"Well it's just, what . . . it's just what you do."

"Is it now?" She says, pressing start on the pressure cooker and effectively shutting me up. "Acha, where's your janamaz beta? And the qibla is which direction?"

I'm pretty sure I can feel a smirk on my face as she asks.

"Inside the storage ottoman in the living room," I say, coolly, trying to remember which way Ammi faced last time she visited. I point at my east facing windows and say, "And the qibla's out the window that way, a little to the right."

She opens the ottoman and pulls the janamaz out. I feel her stiffen as she notices my fingers grayed in dust. "Thank you beta," she says, as she dusts off the janamaz and lays it out before the windows. I feel her swing my hands up to my ears before resting them high on my chest.

Should she technically have put a dupatta on? Ammi's maroon ajrak one is still in the ottoman. The last time she was here I watched her throw it over her shoulder, say "Keep to our own," and start her prayers before I could respond. We had just come home from lunch where I had finally introduced her to Karla. I sat on the couch and hunched over to inspect the lines on my palms where I had dug my nails in deep, hoping the pain would make the lunch go by faster. It didn't work.

It wasn't so much that she and Karla didn't get along. It was more that each time Karla attempted to strike up conversation, Ammi just smiled at her and returned to her meal. Karla excused herself halfway through lunch, pretending she had just gotten called into the hospital to oversee an operation.

I kept my eyes down as she left and didn't look up until a few moments later when Ammi said, "You know, the first time I met Eric's mother, she did the same to me, but without a smile."

"Oh, so it's healthy to perpetuate this cycle, Ammi?"

"I stuck it out. When Eric got up to use the restroom, his mom leaned over and asked me if 'your women still enjoy sex after your families circumcise you.'" Ammi sipped her tea and stared off somewhere above my head. "I smiled back, swallowed the words in my throat, and stuck it out. I'm glad Karla had the sense to run. She's smarter and stronger than I was."

I sunk into my couch watching Ammi flow through the motions of prayer that I never felt at home in. I'd happily keep to my own, if I knew who my own was.

"Chalo beta," Meena says as she folds up the janamaz and puts it back into the dusty ottoman. "Let see how much time is left on this thing."

The red digits flash through the final sixty seconds.

Meena clicks the depressurize button and watches, as if she's hypnotized by the plume of steam hissing out of the metal cylinder. I feel my ears perk up as she hones in on the sound. It's as if she hasn't seen or heard this in ages.

"Don't cook much anymore, eh?" I say, realizing I should probably contain my snark. But I don't think she minds.

"No, I cook almost every day. It's just that I'm a bit deaf, so I've forgotten how the steam speaks to you. If you pay attention to the hiss, you'll hear it tell you if the food is really ready, if it was cooked the way you intended, or if you'll be disappointed when the lid unlocks. And if you watch closely, you'll see how the steam interacts with the spirits in the air. If they gather toward the steam, you're cooking something delicious. If they flee, well . . . " she shrugs. "It's an old aunty secret."

"Really?"

"You're one of the most gullible saps I've ever met, I'm sure."

"I didn't believe you, I just couldn't tell if you really believed it yourself."

"Mhmm."

"Alright, well you let me know if you need anything. I'm going to get some reading done." Really there's some gaming I need to catch up on, but she doesn't need to know that. I suppress my visual feed and replace it with CoreEra4. Time to level up. The sensory suppression filters out most of Meena's kitchen noise, until I hear the blender slicing through. I'm curious why she needs a blender to make dal, but not curious enough to hit pause.

I'm pretty immersed in the game when I feel an almost pungent, but ultimately bland taste on my tongue. Meena's shoveled a bit of what she's done to this dal into my mouth. She massages the hot, dry musty paste into a lump as she lets each part of my tongue feel and inspect the texture. As it crumbles into the back of my throat, an aftertaste surfaces that reminds me of wanting to be kissed amidst an audience of 80s era wood paneling on neglected basement walls. An aftertaste on my anxiety-dried adolescent tongue, which had just uttered "I'd kiss you Eid Mubarak if you'd let me." A line tacky enough to hold the confident façade of my smile in place while I waited inside my head screaming *what in the FUCK are you thinking?*

I can almost hear Hafza's laugh seeping in through my tongue and almost feel the slap that ended in an apologetic caress. My taste buds reverberate like the hair on the back of my neck when Hafza kissed the highest point of my cheekbone and then stared at me. I'd never seen anyone's eyes so close. It was so overwhelming I had to close my own eyes. I'm not sure if she had started or me, but after years of pining, that was the first time my lips finally melted into another's. And it would not be the last time I'd be rudely interrupted mid-kiss. Before the moment was over, Ammi was shouting, "Arsalan beta, let's go!" from the top of the staircase behind me. Hafza broke the kiss and leaned over to whisper "Eid Mubarak, Arsalan" in my ear just before I jumped up, stunned by what had happened. The next thing I'd say to Hafza would be "congratulations" ten years later on her heavily decorated wedding stage, next to her heavily decorated new husband.

Meena fills my mouth with water, washing my memory out. I ache for another taste of the musty paste. I want to go back for more, even though there is nothing to go back to.

"What was that? It tasted familiar."

"Well, mister expert, you'll have to wait and see."

So I watch her set the pot on the stove above the lowest possible flame and plop in a few heaps of ghee. As it melts and simmers unevenly in the pot, she picks up the blender and begins scooping the paste out. The warm ghee spatters on the backs of my hands as the first few clumps land in the pot.

My arm will no doubt be sore the next day, because for a while she just leans on the counter and stirs every few minutes, keeping the darkening paste on the bottom from sticking to the pot. Eventually she stops to add sugar, mixing it in evenly before flipping the paste over and pouring the rest of the sugar in. Once the white crystals disappear into the paste she scoops a spoon full out and closes my eyes as the warm sugary sensation hits my lips. I'm flooded with images of Tupperware decorated by cold and soggy deep-fried finger foods and heavenly sweetened desserts. But, it's all dammed by the memory of Karla's voice asking the question, "Why can't you just bring me home for Eid, like a normal person?"

"Ammi's just not well," I had said, opening one dish and lifting it up. What dish was it?

"She's well enough to have cooked all of this," Karla had said, gesturing to the to-go holiday foods.

I plunged a spoon into the Tupperware and scooped up something and shoved it toward Karla's mouth. "Just try a bite."

Karla rolled her eyes and opened her mouth. Then, when the taste soaked into her tongue, she opened her eyes wide. Her eyes rolled again, but with pleasure this time. "What the fuck is this?"

"Chanay-ki daal ka-halwa," I say into the AirBody UI.

"Very good!" Meena stabs with her standard tone of condescension. She pours another can of condensed milk in and continues stirring. "Gustatory memory."

"What?"

"Taste. It's got a peculiar way of triggering memory and emotion, don't you think? More so than other senses. Taste links us directly to our gut, where our deepest unfulfilled needs keep us hungry. Your gut tricks your mind into thinking you're getting what you want, when it's really just using you to get the—" she scoops up another bite and I feel my eyes roll back into my head "—mmm. The sweet halwa."

She opens my eyes and looks down at the bright yellowy paste.

"But, I remember this being brown whenever my Nani made it."

"Haan beta, just wait," she says as she preheats the oven to 400 degrees. When the oven beeps she slides the pan in and sets a timer for fifteen minutes.

"Acha beta, what kind of formal wear do you have?"

"Formal wear?"

"Haan, kurta pajama? Shalwar kameez? Whichever you'd like to call it."

"Uhhh . . ."

"Oh, of course. Well, at least put us in a pressed pant-shirt," she says handing me back control.

"Sure," I say, heading back to my room to pull out some blue slacks and a new red and gray striped shirt I haven't worn yet.

I stand before the mirror making final touches when she pings for control back.

"Well at least you've got some color in your wardrobe." She picks up a pen from my dresser and writes down an address on the price tag I just ripped off of the shirt I put on. "I need to go here."

"Sounds good to me," I say as I feel her pass control back.

As we make our way out of the city and onto the I-95 I glance at the sign for BWI Airport. The last time I was supposed to go to BWI was the last time I was supposed to see Karla. She had been away for work for a week and I was on my way to pick her up when I got a call from Ammi's doctor. My mind went single track and I skipped the exit for the airport and drove straight to the hospital in Philly where Ammi was taking her last breaths, alone. I made it in time to say goodbye, but not much else.

Karla only called once that night. I stayed in Philly for six days and when I got back my place was emptied of Karla's things, which was most everything. If I had called to let her know what was going on, she would have understood, would have come up to help. I never figured out why we played this game of chicken. We'd done it before. But, this time we both ran off the cliff and it felt right to let things rest at the bottom of the canyon rather than pick them up and rebuild.

I pull up in front of the house and step out of the car, grabbing the dish of halwa along the way. The magenta sunset laces the gray house like a mesh dupatta. There are a lot of cars parked on the driveway and a bluster of muffled laughter coming through the windows of the brightly lit living room.

As I get to the front door I hand back control and immediately feel my heart rate spike. She stares dead ahead, frozen still.

"Are you alright?"

"Haan, I just—"

The door swings open to a woman dressed in a gray and blue shalwar kameez. She's still looking at her guests behind her and laughing. Her smile sticks as she turns to look at me. Her purple-streaked hair's tied up in a bun. She's probably a little younger than Meena, maybe late forties? I study her face to see if I can parse a family resemblance to Meena's profile picture.

"I'm sorry, can I help you?" the woman asks, leaning against her door jamb.

I can feel Meena trying to push the air through my larynx and out of my mouth but it's sealed shut. Instead, she just lifts the dish of halwa and opens it.

The woman leans forward and inspects the congealed brown paste. The sunset breeze blows a warm waft of the dish's scent into my nose.

The woman looks back at me, but her eyebrows are strained around her eye sockets now. Without a word, she takes a step back and slams the door in my face.

Meena stands there for a minute in my shaking body, with the halwa still cooling in the open air. She flattens the lid back onto the dish and lays a card on top of it. She puts the dish down gently onto the frilly brown "Welcome Home" mat. She picks up a small white rock from the side of the porch and places it on top of the card to keep it from flying away, before turning back to the car.

As soon as I feel the first tear hit my cheek she stops.

"Beta, take us home."

The tears stop as I take control, but I can still feel the strain in the back of my throat. This is the first time I've wondered what happens when people hand me back control temporarily. Do they come back to life in their homes? Is she convulsing over her toilet, vomiting up as much of the regret as possible before curling into a ball of tears on her bathroom floor? Or is she lying peacefully, letting the tears soak into her veins until the pain passes.

Once at home she requests control and immediately goes back to the cabinet in the corner, pulling out the bottle of whiskey and pouring it into a chipped glass she finds in my drying rack. She carries it in my shaking hands and walks to the armchair that faces the window. As the final moments of sunset fade away, I can see her staring back at me in the reflection of the window.

She holds up the glass and stares into the brown liquid as she swirls it around.

"Beta," she says aloud. "How do you decide which one is right for you?"

"What do you mean?" I respond, echoing in my own head.

"Which drink? How did you know it was whiskey? Not Beer? Wine? Cocktail?"

"Well, I drink them all, so—" I hesitate, uncertain of where this is going, "—but I don't drink much."

"Haan, beta, whatever." She smirks at me in the window and swings the whiskey full down my throat. I turn down the sensory suppression and feel the initial hit seep into my blood and loosen my muscles. She picks the bottle up from the table and pours another shot.

"Are you okay?"

"I'll be fine, just need to process a bit." She lifts the glass, but sips at the whiskey this time. I assume the first time was purely for shock value.

"What's your deal?"

"My deal, beta?"

"Don't beta me, I'm a grown man."

"Haan," she pauses, scanning my sad apartment, "of course you are."

"Why are you here? Who was that woman?"

"Just an old acquaintance. It's not important."

"Then why me? Were there no other, more appropriate hosts available?"

"Appropriate how?"

"I don't know, an older woman, someone more fitting your background?"

She laughs. "My background? Beta, you were the only 'Urdu speaking' host of Pakistani origin whose listing authorizes sexual behavior during a visit."

Before I can respond there's a knock at the door.

"Were you expecting anyone, beta?"

"No."

She sets the glass down and goes to open the door. There is the woman, still in her gray and blue shalwar kameez, holding my dish with one hand and one hip. I watch my eyelids wrap around the woman in the doorway and make a shape I haven't seen them make in months.

"Is it still you, Meena?"

Meena nods, my larynx suddenly sealed shut once again.

"You think you're quite clever, don't you?" The woman walks into the apartment and slides the dish onto the counter. She pulls the lid off, revealing at least 2-3 servings worth gone. "I'm going to eat the rest on my own as well. I'm not sharing." She smiles as she pulls off her dupatta and throws it at me.

Meena catches it and laughs, finally loosening my throat. "Haniya, I—"

Haniya leans in quick to shut up Meena with a hard kiss that sends a chill down my spine and reverberates through the hairs on the back of my neck.

It's been a while since I felt a kiss like that. In fact it's just flat out been a while for me. I wonder how long it'd been for Meena and which matters more or if they're additive and while I try to figure that out they stumble onto the couch and eventually roll onto the floor.

I shut my visual feed off, turn the sensory suppression back up, and do my best to give them some privacy. I won't lie, I didn't expect this guest to be the first to avail this "amenity." But, I can't entirely say I'm surprised. Meena has a determined bitterness that obviously guards something terribly sweet.

When I notice my heart rate begin to drop, I turn my visuals back on. They've made it to my bed. Meena's lying on my back with Haniya's head resting on my shoulder. The room is quiet except for the sound of calming breaths.

"Come back," Meena squeezes out between breaths and into Haniya's hair.

"As what, my love? Your assistant? Your cousin's friend visiting from the states? An NGO worker there for training that you're just showing around? What will you have me pretend to be this time?"

My throat locks up again as I feel blood rush to my cheeks.

Haniya sits up and lets my blanket fall off of her as she stands. She looks back down at me with a slight smile. "It was nice to see you again Meena. I've missed these stunts of yours."

Meena just stares up at the ceiling while we listen to Haniya get dressed, slide the Tupperware off the counter and back onto her hip. Meena closes my eyes when we hear my apartment door open and shut. I'm certain she's going to start crying again, but she just takes a deep breath and speaks.

"You'll feel it one day." She rolls into sitting position at the edge of the bed and looks in the mirror. "The desire to go back to when you were uncertain about who you'd turn out to be. When you lived foolishly thinking you could be something other than what you became in the end." She lifts my right fingertips to my forehead, twice, with a gentle pseudo bounce and says, "Thanks for the company, Arsalan. Khuda-hafiz."

As my limbs tingle back to me, I pull up Karla's contact. While I mull the idea of calling her, I get an alert in my periphery from AirBody about a new request. I stare at Karla's picture for a moment before closing her profile and pulling up AirBody. I'm certain I've already become who I'll be in the end, so I might as well let everyone else be me for a little longer.

Nadia Afifi is a science fiction author. Her debut novel, *The Sentient*, was lauded by *Publisher's Weekly* as "staggering and un-put-downable." Her short fiction has appeared in *The Magazine of Fantasy and Science Fiction* and *Abyss & Apex*.

She grew up in the Middle East, but currently calls Denver, Colorado home. When she isn't writing, she spends her time practicing (and falling off) the lyra, hiking, and working on the most challenging jigsaw puzzles she can find.

THE BAHRAIN UNDERGROUND BAZAAR

Nadia Afifi

Bahrain's Central Bazaar comes to life at night. Lights dance above the narrow passageways, illuminating the stalls with their spices, sacks of lentils, ornate carpets, and trinkets. Other stalls hawk more modern fare, NeuroLync implants and legally ambiguous drones. The scent of cumin and charred meat fills my nostrils. My stomach twists in response. Chemo hasn't been kind to me.

Office workers spill out from nearby high-rises into the crowds. A few cast glances in my direction, confusion and sympathy playing across their faces. They see an old woman with stringy, thinning gray hair and a hunched back, probably lost and confused. The young always assume the elderly can't keep up with them, helpless against their new technology and shifting language. Never mind that I know their tricks better than they do, and I've been to wilder bazaars than this manufactured tourist trap. It used to be the Old Souk, a traditional market that dealt mostly in gold. But Bahrain, which once prided itself as being Dubai's responsible, less ostentatious younger cousin, has decided to keep up with its neighbors. Glitz and flash. Modernity and illusion.

I turn down another passageway, narrower than the last. A sign beckons me below—"The Bahrain Underground Bazaar." It even has a London Underground symbol around the words for effect, though we're far from its gray skies and rain. I quicken my pace down its dark steps.

It's even darker below, with torch-like lamps lining its stone walls. Using stone surfaces—stone anything—in the desert is madness. The cost of keeping the place cool must be obscene. The Underground Bazaar tries hard, bless it, to be sinister and seedy, and it mostly succeeds. The clientele help matters. They're either gangs of teenage boys or lone older men with unsettling eyes, shuffling down damp corridors. Above them, signs point to different areas of the bazaar for different tastes—violence, phobias, sex, and death.

I'm here for death.

"Welcome back, grandma," the man behind the front counter greets me. A nice young man with a neatly trimmed beard. He dresses all in black, glowing tattoos snaking across his forearms, but he doesn't fool me. He goes home and watches romantic comedies when he isn't selling the morbid side of life to oddballs. This isn't a typical souk or bazaar where each vendor runs their own stall. The Underground Bazaar is centralized. You tell the person at the counter what virtual immersion experience you're looking for and they direct you to the right room. Or *chamber*, as they insist.

"I'm not a grandma yet," I say, placing my dinars on the front counter. "Tell my son and his wife to spend less time chasing me around and get the ball rolling on those grandchildren." In truth, I don't care in the slightest whether my children reproduce. I won't be around to hold any grandchildren.

"What'll it be today?"

I've had time to think on the way, but I still pause. In the Underground Bazaar's virtual immersion chambers, I've experienced many anonymous souls' final moments. Through them, I've drowned, been strangled, shot in the mouth, and suffered a heart attack. And I do mean suffer—the heart attack was one of the worst. I try on deaths like T-shirts. Violent ones and peaceful passings. Murders, suicides, and accidents. All practice for the real thing.

The room tilts and my vision blurs momentarily. Dizzy, I press my hands, bruised from chemo drips, into the counter to steady myself. The tumor wedged between my skull and brain likes to assert itself at random moments. A burst of vision trouble, spasms of pain or nausea. I imagine shrinking it down, but even that won't matter now. It's in my blood and bones. The only thing it's left me so far, ironically, is my mind. I'm still sharp enough to make my own decisions. And I've decided one thing—I'll die on my terms, before cancer takes that last bit of power from me.

"I don't think I've fallen to my death yet," I say, regaining my composure. "I'd like to fall from a high place today."

"Sure thing. Accident or suicide?"

Would they be that different? The jump, perhaps, but everyone must feel the same terror as the ground approaches.

"Let's do a suicide," I say. "Someone older, if you have it. Female. Someone like me," I add unnecessarily.

My helpful young man runs his tattooed fingers across his fancy computer, searching. I've given him a challenge. Most people my age never installed the NeuroLync that retains an imprint of a person's experiences—including their final moments. Not that the intent is to document one's demise, of course. People get the fingernail-sized devices implanted in their temples to do a variety of useful things—pay for groceries with a blink, send neural messages to others, even adjust the temperature in their houses with a mental command. Laziness. Soon, the young will have machines do their walking for them.

But one side effect of NeuroLync's popularity was that its manufacturer acquired a treasure trove of data from the minds connected to its Cloud network. Can you guess what happened next? Even an old bird like me could have figured it out. All that data was repackaged and sold to the highest bidder. Companies seized what they could, eager to literally tap into consumer minds. But there are other markets, driven by the desire to borrow another person's experiences. Knowing what it feels like to have a particular kind of sex. Knowing what it feels like to torture someone—or be tortured. Knowing what it means to die a certain way.

And with that demand comes places like the Bahrain Underground Bazaar.

"I've got an interesting one for you," the man says, eyeing me with something close to caution. "A Bedouin woman. Want to know the specifics?"

"Surprise me," I say. "I'm not too old to appreciate some mystery."

My young man always walks with me to the sensory chamber, like an usher in a movie theater. It's easy for me to get knocked around amid the jostling crowds, and I admit that some of the other customers frighten me. You can always spot the ones here for violence, a sick thrill between work shifts. Their eyes have this dull sheen, as though the real world is something they endure until their next immersion.

"This is your room, grandma," the man says before spinning on his heels back to the front counter. I step inside.

The room is dark, like the rest of this place, with blue lights webbing its walls. I suspect they exist for ambience rather than utility. In the center of the room, a reclining chair sits underneath a large device that will descend over my tiny, cancer-addled head. On the back of it, a needle of some kind will jut out and enter my spinal cord, right where it meets the skull. It's painful, but only for a second, and then you're in someone else's head, seeing and hearing and sensing what they felt. What's a little pinprick against all of that?

I sit and lean back as the usual recording plays on the ceiling, promising me an experience I'll never forget. The machine descends over my head, drowning out my surroundings, and I feel the familiar vampire bite at my neck.

I'm in the desert. Another one. Unlike Bahrain, a small island with every square inch filled by concrete, this is an open space with clear skies and a mountainous horizon. And I'm walking down a rocky, winding slope. Rose-colored cliffsides surround me and rich brown dirt crunches underneath my feet. The bright sun warms my face and a primal, animal smell fills my nostrils. I'm leading a donkey down the path. It lets out a huff of air, more sure-footed than me.

I turn—"I" being the dead woman—at the sound of laughter. A child sits on the donkey, legs kicking. The donkey takes it in stride, accustomed to excitable tourists, but I still speak in a husky, foreign voice, instructing the child to sit still. Others follow behind her—parents or other relations. They drink in the landscape's still beauty through their phones.

We round a corner and my foot slides near the cliff's edge. A straight drop to hard ground and rock. I look down, the bottom of the cliff both distant and oddly intimate. The air stills, catching my breath. Wild adrenaline runs through my body, my legs twitching. For a moment, I can't think clearly, my thoughts scrambled by an unnamed terror. Then a thought breaks through the clutter.

Jump. Jump. Jump.

The terror becomes an entity inside me, a metallic taste on my tongue and a clammy sweat on my skin. The outline of the cliff becomes sharper, a beckoning blade, while the sounds of voices around me grow distant, as though I'm underwater.

I try to pull away—me, Zahra, the woman from Bahrain who chooses to spend her remaining days experiencing terrible things. In some backwater of my brain, I remind myself that I'm not on a cliff and this happened long ago. But the smell of hot desert air invades my senses again, yanking me back with a jolt of fear. *Jump.*

A moment seizes me, and I know that I've reached the glinting edge of a decision, a point of no return. My foot slides forward and it is crossed. I tumble over the edge.

I'm falling. My stomach dips and my heart tightens, thundering against my ribs. My hands flail around for something to grab but when they only find air, I stop. I plummet with greater speed, wind whipping my scarf away.

I don't scream. I'm beyond fear. There is only the ground beneath me and the space in between. A rock juts out from the surface and I know, with sudden peace, that that's where I'll land.

And then nothing. The world is dark and soundless. Free of pain, or of any feeling at all.

And then voices.

The darkness is softened by a strange awareness. I sense, rather than see, my surroundings. My own mangled body spread across a rock. Dry plants and a gravel path nearby. Muted screams from above. I know, somehow, that my companions are running down the path now, toward me. *Be careful*, I want to cry out. *Don't fall*. They want to help me. Don't they know I'm dead?

But if I'm dead, why am I still here? I'm not in complete oblivion and I'm also not going toward a light. I'm sinking backward into something, a deep pool of nothing, but a feeling of warmth surrounds me, enveloping me like a blanket on a cold night. I have no body now, I'm a ball of light, floating toward a bigger light behind me. I know it's there without seeing it. It is bliss and beauty, peace and kindness, and all that remains is to join it.

A loud scream.

Reality flickers around me. Something releases in the back of my head and blue light creeps into my vision. The machine whirs above me, retracting to its place on the ceiling. I blink, a shaking hand at my throat. The scream was mine. Drawing a steady breath, I hold my hand before my eyes until I'm convinced it's real and mine. Coming out of an immersion is always disorienting but that was no ordinary immersion. Normally, the moment of death wakes me up, returning me to my own, disintegrating body. What happened?

I leave the chamber with a slight wobble in my knees. A tall man in a trench coat appears at my side, offering his arm, and I swat it away. I smile, oddly reassured by the brief exchange. This is the Underground Bazaar, full of the same weirdos and creeps. I'm still me. The death I experienced in the chamber begins to fade in my immediate senses, but I still don't look back.

"How was it?" The man at the front counter winks.

I manage a rasping noise.

"Pretty crazy, huh?" His grin widens. "We file that one under suicides, but it's not really a suicide. Not premeditated, anyway. She was a tour guide in Petra, with a husband, five children, and who-knows-how-many grandchildren. She just jumped on impulse."

My mind spins with questions, but I seize on his last comment.

"I walked the Golden Gate bridge once, on a family trip," I say, my voice wavering. "I remember a strange moment where I felt the urge to jump over the edge, into the water, for no reason. It passed, and I heard that's not uncommon."

"They call it the death drive," the man says with a nod. His eyes dance with excitement and I understand at last why he works in this awful place. The thrill of the macabre. "The French have a fancy expression for it that means 'the call of the void.' It's really common to get to the edge of a high place and feel this sudden urge to jump. You don't have to be suicidal or anxious. It can happen to anyone."

"But why?" I ask. I suspect the man has studied this kind of thing and I'm right. He bounces on his heels and leans forward, his smile conspiratorial.

"Scientists think that it's the conscious brain reacting to our instinctive responses," he says. "You get to the edge of a cliff and you reflexively step back. But then your conscious mind steps in. Why did you step back? Maybe it's not because of the obvious danger, but because you *wanted* to jump. Now, a part of you is convinced you want to jump, even though you know what that means, and it scares you. Insane," he adds with undisguised glee.

"But most people don't," I say, recalling the terror of those moments at the cliff's edge.

"Most don't," he agrees. "That's what's interesting about this one. She actually went through with it. Why I thought you'd like it." His chest puffs up in a way that reminds me of my own son, Firaz, when he came home from school eager to show me some new art project. He stopped drawing when he reached college, I realize with sudden sadness.

"But what about . . . after she fell?" I ask. The fall was traumatic, as I knew it would be, but nothing from past immersions prepared me for the strange, sentient peace that followed the moment of impact.

"Oh, that," the young man says. "That happens sometimes. Maybe about ten percent of our death immersions. Kind of a near-death-experience thing. Consciousness slipping away. Those last brain signals firing."

"But it happened after I—after she fell," I protest. "She must have been completely dead. Does that ever happen?"

"I'm sure it does, but rarely," the young man says with a tone of gentle finality. He smiles at the next customer.

"Petra," I murmur. "I've always wanted to see Petra." And now I have, in a fashion.

Walking up the stairs, exhaustion floods my body. Some days are better than others, but I always save these visits for the days when I'm strongest. Leaning against the wall outside, I feel ready to collapse.

"Zahra? *Zahra!*"

My daughter-in-law pushes through the crowd. I consider shrinking back down the stairs, but her eyes fix on me with predatory focus. I'm in her sights. She swings her arms stiffly under her starched white blouse.

"We've been worried sick," Reema begins. Her eyes scan me from head to toe, searching for some hidden signs of mischief. For a moment, I feel like a teenager again, sneaking out at night.

"You really shouldn't," I say.

"How did you slip away this time? We didn't see you—"

"On the tracking app you installed on my phone?" I ask with a small smile. "I deleted it, along with the backup you placed on the Cloud." As I said before, I know more tricks than they realize. Thank goodness I don't have a NeuroLync. I'd never be alone. Of course, every time I sneak off after a medical appointment to walk to the bazaar, I'm battling time. They don't know when I've given them the slip, but when they return home from their tedious jobs to find the house empty, they know where I've gone.

Reema sighs. "You need to stop coming to this terrible place, Zahra. It's not good for your mind or soul. You don't need dark thoughts—you'll beat this by staying positive."

After accompanying me to my earliest appointments, Reema has mastered the art of motivational medical speak. She means well. It would be cliché for me to despise my daughter-in-law, but in truth, I respect her. She comes from a generation of Arab women expected to excel at every aspect of life, to prove she earned her hard-fought rights, and she's risen to the task. If only she'd let me carry on with the task of planning my death and getting out of her way.

On the way home, Reema calls my son to report my capture. Instead of speaking aloud, she sends him silent messages through her NeuroLync, shooting the occasional admonishing glance in my direction. I can imagine the conversation well enough.

At the bazaar again.

Ya Allah! The seedy part?

She was walking right out of it when I found her.

Is she okay?

Pleased enough with herself. What are we going to do with her?

Reema and Firaz work in skyscrapers along Bahrain's coastal business zone, serving companies that change names every few months when they merge into bigger conglomerates. To them, I'm another project to be managed, complete with a schedule and tasks. My deadline is unknown, but within three months, they'll likely be planning my funeral. It's not that they don't love me, and I them. The world has just conditioned them to express that love through worry and structure. I need neither.

I want control. I want purpose.

Firaz barely raises his head to acknowledge me when Reema and I walk through the kitchen door. He's cooking at ten o'clock at night, preparing a dinner after work. Reema collapses onto a chair, kicking off her heels before tearing into the bread bowl.

"I'm not hungry, but I'm tired," I say to no one in particular. "I'll go to bed now."

"Mama, when will this end?" Firaz asks in a tight voice.

I have an easy retort at the tip of my tongue. *Soon enough, when I'm dead.* But when he turns to face me, I hesitate under his sad, frustrated gaze. His red eyes are heavy with exhaustion. I, the woman who birthed and raised him, am now a disruption.

All at once, I deflate. My knees buckle.

"Mama!" Firaz abandons his pan and rushes toward me.

"I'm fine," I say. With a wave of my hand, I excuse myself.

In the dark of my bedroom, images from the bazaar linger in the shadows. Echoes of blue lights dancing across the walls. I sink into my bed, reaching for the warmth I felt hours ago, through the dead woman's mind, but I only shiver. What happened in that immersion? The young man didn't fool me. I had experienced enough deaths in those dark chambers to recognize the remarkable. She jumped in defiance of instinct, but her final moments of existence were full of warmth and acceptance—a presence that lingered after death. What made her different?

The next morning, I take a long bath, letting Firaz and Reema go through their pre-work routine—elliptical machines, mindfulness, dressing, and breakfast, the house obeying their silent commands. After they leave, I take the bus downtown to the clinic.

I sit in a room of fake plants and fake smiles, chemicals warming my veins. Other women sit around me, forming a square with nothing but cheap blue carpet in the center. A nurse checks our IV drips and ensures our needles remain in place. My fellow cancer survivors—we're all survivors, the staff insist—wear scarves to hide balding heads. Young, old—cancer ages us all. Their brave smiles emphasize the worry lines and tired eyes.

Out the window, the city hums with its usual frenetic pulse. Elevated trains, dizzying lanes of cars, and transport drones all fight for space amid Bahrain's rush hour. Beyond it, the sea winks at me, sunlight glinting on its breaking waves. A world in constant motion, ready to leave me behind.

Coldness prickles my skin. Could I jump, like that woman jumped? It would be easy—rip the array of needles from my arm and rush across the room, forcing the window open. I might have to smash the glass if they put in security locks (a good strategy in a cancer ward). When the glass shatters and the screaming skyscraper winds whip at my hair, would I recoil or jump?

But I don't move. I cross my feet under my silk skirt and wet my lips. Perhaps I'm too fearful of causing a scene. Perhaps I'm not the jumping kind. But doubt gnaws at me with each passing second. Death is an unceasing fog around me, but despite my many trips to the bazaar, I can't bring myself to meet it yet.

Maybe you're not ready because you have unfinished business.

But what could that be? My child no longer needs me—if anything, I'm a burden. Bahrain has morphed into something beyond my wildest imagination. It's left me behind. I've lived plenty. What remains?

A rose city carved from rock. An ancient Nabataean site in Jordan, immortalized in photographs in glossy magazines and childhood stories. I always meant to go to Petra but had forgotten about that dream long ago. And in the Underground Bazaar, of all places, I'm reminded of what I've yet to do.

I close my eyes. The woman from yesterday's immersion tumbles through the air, beautiful cliffs and clear skies spinning around her. Is that why she was calm at the end? Did some part of her realize that she had lived the right life and was now dying in the right place?

The revelation hits me with such force that I have no room for uncertainty. I know what I must do, but I have to be smart about my next steps. The chemo session is nearly over. I smile sweetly at the nurse when she removes the last drip from my veins. My daughter-in-law will meet me downstairs, I reassure her. No, I don't need any help, thank you. This isn't my first rodeo. She laughs. People like their old women to have a little bite—it's acceptable once we're past a certain age. A small consolation prize for living so long.

In the reception room, I drop my phone behind a plant—Firaz and Reema are clever enough to find new ways to track me, so I discard their favorite weapon.

"Back again, Ms. Mansour? Looks like you were here yesterday." The man's eyes twinkle as he examines my record on his computer screen.

"Where did the woman live?" I ask. "The one from yesterday—the Bedouin woman. Does she have any surviving family?"

In truth, I know where she lived, but I need more. A family name, an address.

"Your guess is as good as mine," the man says. A different man, not my usual favorite. Tall and thin like a tree branch, with brooding eyes. I'm earlier than usual, so this one must take the early shift.

"Surely you have something." I inject a quaver in my voice. "Anyone with the NeuroLync leaves an archive of information behind." *Unlike me*, I don't add. When I go, I'll only leave bones.

"We don't keep those kinds of records here because we don't need them," he says. "People want to know what drowning feels like, not the person's entire life story."

"Well, this customer does."

"Can't help you."

This is ridiculous. When I was his age, if an older woman asked me a question, I would have done my best to answer. It was a period of great social upheaval, but we still respected the elderly.

I try another angle. "Are there any more paid immersion experiences tied to that record?" She's a woman, not a record, but I'm speaking in their language.

The man's eyes practically light up with dollar signs. "We've got the life highlight reel. Everybody has one. People like to see those before the death, sometimes."

Minutes later and I'm back in the immersion chamber, the helmet making its ominous descent over my head.

They call them "highlight reels," but these files are really the by-product of a data scrubber going through a dead person's entire memory and recreating that "life flashing before your eyes" effect. Good moments and bad moments, significant events and those small, poignant memories that stick in your mind for unclear reasons. I remember an afternoon with Firaz in the kitchen, making pastries. Nothing special about it, but I can still see the way the sunlight hit the counter and smell the filo dough when it came out of the oven.

The Bedouin woman's highlight reel is no different. There's a wedding under the stars, some funerals, and enough childbirths to make me wince in sympathy. But there are also mundane moments like my own. The smell of livestock on early mornings before the tourists begin spilling into the valley. Meat cooking over a low campfire. Memories that dance through the senses.

I leave the bazaar more restless than when I arrived. The woman's life was unremarkable. Good and bad in typical proportions. A part of me had expected a mystic connection to her surroundings, maybe a head injury that gave her strange conscious experiences that would explain her final moments. Instead, I found someone not unlike me, separated only by money and circumstances.

Through the humid air and dense crowds, Bahrain's only train station beckons. A bit ridiculous for an island, but it does connect the country to

Saudi Arabia and the wider region via a causeway. I walk to the station, restlessness growing with each step. Perhaps this is my jump over the cliff. I'm moving toward a big decision, the pressure swelling as I reach the point of no return.

At the front booth, I buy a one-way ticket to Petra, Jordan, along the Hejaz Railway. Once I board the carriage, all my doubt and fear evaporate. This is what I need to do. A final adventure, a last trip in search of answers that no bazaar can give me.

The desert hills race by through the train window. It's hypnotic and before long, my mind stirs like a thick soup through old feelings. The terrain outside feels both alien and comforting, that sensation of coming home after a long trip. A return to something primal and ancient, a way of life that's been lost amid controlled air conditioning and busy streets. How can something feel strange and right at the same time?

The Hejaz Railway system was completed when I was a little girl, itself a revival and expansion of an old train line that was abandoned after World War One. The region reasserting itself, flexing its power with a nod to its past. I've always hated planes, and you'll never get me on those hovering shuttles, so an old-fashioned train (albeit with a maglev upgrade) suits me just fine.

The terrain dulls as we speed north, as if the world is transitioning from computer animation to a soft oil painting. The mountains lose their edges and vegetation freckles the ground. Signs point us to ancient places. Aqaba. The Dead Sea. Petra.

The sun sets and I drift off under the engine's hum.

The next morning, the train pulls into Wadi Musa, the town that anchors Petra. I join the crowds spilling out into the station, the air cool and fresh compared to Bahrain. I reach into my pocket to check my phone for frantic messages, only to recall that I left it behind. Firaz and Reema must be searching for me by now. At this stage, they've likely contacted the police. Guilt tugs at the corners of my heart, but they'll never understand why this is important. And soon, I'll be out of their way.

Ignoring the long row of inviting hotels, I follow the signs toward Petra. Enterprising locals hawk everything from sunscreen to camel rides. With my hunched back and slow gait, they trail me like cats around a bowl of fresh milk.

"*Teta*, a hat for your head!"

"Need a place to stay, lady?"

"A donkey ride, ma'am? It's low to the ground."

Why not? I'm in no condition to hike around ancient ruins. The donkey handler, a boy no older than eighteen, suppresses a smile when I pull out paper currency.

"How do most of your customers pay?" I ask as he helps me onto the beast.

"NeuroLync, ma'am. They send us a one-time wire."

"You all have NeuroLync?" I ask, amazed. Many of these locals still live as Bedouin, in simple huts without electricity or running water.

"Yes, ma'am," he says, clicking his tongue to prompt the donkey forward. "We were some of the first in Jordan to get connected. Government project. Some refused, but most said yes."

Interesting. So the area's Bedouin and locals were early adopters of NeuroLync technology, an experiment to support the country's tourism. That explained how an elderly woman of my age had the implant long enough to record most of her adult life, now downloadable for cheap voyeurs. My chest flutters. *People like me.*

My guide leads the donkey and me down the hill into a narrow valley. Most tourists walk, but some take carriages, camels, and donkeys. An adventurous soul charges past us on horseback, kicking up red sand.

Along the surrounding cliff faces and hills, dark holes mark ancient dwellings carved into the rock. Following my gaze, my guide points to them.

"Old Nabataean abodes," he says, referring to the ancient people who made Petra home.

"Do people still live there?" I ask. My tone is light and curious.

"Not there," he says.

"So where do all of the guides and craftspeople live around here?" I follow up: "It makes sense to be close."

"Some in Wadi Musa, but mostly in other places around Petra. We camp near the Monastery and the hills above the Treasury."

I nod and let the silence settle between us, taking in the beauty around me. Suicide is a sensitive subject everywhere, but especially in the rural Arab world. I can't just ask about a woman who jumped off a cliff. But while I'm teasing away clues, I drink in the energy of my surroundings. The warmth of the sun on my face, the sharp stillness of the air. The sense of building excitement as we descend into the narrow valley, shaded by looming mountains. We're getting close to the Treasury, the most famous structure in Petra. I can tell by the way the tourists pick up their pace, pulling out the old-fashioned handheld cameras popular with the young set. I smile with them. I'm on vacation, after all.

I've seen plenty of pictures of the iconic Treasury, knowing that no picture can do it justice. I turn out to be right. Ahead, the valley forms a narrow sliver through which a stunning carved building emerges. Its deep, dark entrance is flanked by pillars. Cut into the rock, its upper level features more pillars crowned with intricate patterns. Though ancient, it is ornate and well preserved. The surrounding throngs of tourists and souvenir peddlers can't detract from its beauty.

My guide helps me off the donkey so I can wander inside. It's what you'd expect from a building carved into the mountains—the interior is dark and gaping, with more arches and inlets where the Nabataeans conducted their business. For a second, my mind turns to Firaz and Reema, with their endless work. I look down, overwhelmed. People once flooded this building when it was a vibrant trade stop—people long gone. Everyone taking pictures around me will one day be gone as well—all of us, drops in humanity's ever-flowing river.

"Where next, ma'am?"

The winding road up to a high place, one you need a pack animal to reach. An easy place to fall—or jump.

"I'd like to see the Monastery."

On the way up the trail, I talk with my guide, who I learn is named Rami. He has the usual dreams of teenage boys—become a soccer player, make millions, and see the world. When I tell him where I live, his eyes widen and I'm peppered with questions about tall buildings and city lights. He talks of cities as though they're living organisms, and in a way, I suppose they are. Traffic, sprawl, and decay. They're more than the sum of their people. But how can he understand that he's also fortunate to live here, to wake up every morning to a clear red sky, walking through time with every step he takes?

We round a corner along the cliff and I give a small cry.

"It's so far up," I say. "I'm glad the donkey's doing the work for me."

Rami nods. "They're more sure-footed than we are. They know exactly where to step."

"Do people ever fall?"

Rami's eyes are trained ahead, but I catch the tightness in his jawline. "It's rare, ma'am. Don't worry."

My skin prickles. His voice carries a familiar strain, the sound of a battle between what one wants to say and what one should say. Does he know my old woman? Has he heard the story?

While I craft my next question, the donkey turns another corner and my stomach lurches. We're at the same spot where she fell. I recognize the curve of the trail, the small bush protruding into its path. I lean forward, trying to peer down the cliff.

"Can we stop for a minute?"

"Not a good place to stop, ma'am." The boy's voice is firm, tight as a knot, but I slide off the saddle and walk to the ledge.

Wind, warm under the peak sun, attacks my thinning hair. I step closer to the edge.

"Please, *sayida!*"

Switching to Arabic. I must really be stressing the boy. But I can't pull back now.

Another step, and I look down. My stomach clenches. It's there—the boulder that broke her fall. It's free of blood and gore, presumably washed clean a long time ago, but I can remember the scene as it once was, when a woman died and left her body, a witness to her own demise.

But when I lean further, my body turns rigid. I'm a rock myself, welded in place. I won't jump. I can't. I know this with a cold, brutal certainty that knocks the air from my lungs. I'm terrified of the fall. Every second feels like cool water on a parched throat. I could stand here for hours and nothing would change.

"Please." A voice cuts through the blood pounding in my ears, and I turn to meet Rami's frightened, childlike face. He offers his hand palm-up and I take it, letting myself be hoisted back onto the donkey, who chews with lazy indifference. We continue our climb as though nothing happened.

The Monastery doesn't compare to the Treasury at the base of the city, but it's impressive regardless. The surroundings more than make up for it, the horizon shimmering under the noon heat. Rami and I sit cross-legged in the shade, eating the overpriced *manaqish* I bought earlier.

"The cheese is quite good," I admit. "I don't each much these days, but I could see myself getting fat off of these."

Rami smiles. "A single family makes all of the food you can buy here. An old woman and her daughters. They sell it across the area."

I suppress commenting that the men in the family could help. I don't have the energy or the inclination—after staring down the cliff and winning, I'm exhausted. Did I win? Had part of me hoped that I would jump as well? Now that I hadn't, I didn't know what to do next.

I say all that I can think to say. "This is a beautiful place. I don't want to be anywhere else."

Rami steals a glance at me. "There's evil here. The High Place of Sacrifice, where the Nabataeans cut animals' throats to appease their pagan gods." He gives his donkey a pat, as though reassuring it. "Battles and death. Maybe you can sense it, too. That place where you stopped? My grandmother died there."

It takes me a second to register what the young man said, the words entering my ears like thick molasses. Then my blood chills. Rami is one of her many grandchildren. It shouldn't surprise me, but this proximity to the woman's surviving kin prickles my skin, flooding my senses with shock and shame in equal measure. I terrified the boy when I leaned over the edge.

I clear my throat, gripping the sides of my dress to hide my shaking hands. "What was her name?"

He blinks, surprised. "Aisha."

A classic name. "I'm so sorry, Rami," I say. "What a terrible accident."

"She was taking a family down from the Monastery," Rami says. He doesn't correct my assumption, and I wonder if he knows what happened. "When she was younger, she hated working with the tourists. She loved to cook and preferred caring for the animals at the end of the day. But when she got older, my mother told me she loved it. She liked to learn their stories and tell her own, about her life and her family, all the things she had seen. I bet she could have written a book about all the people she met from around the world, but she never learned how to write."

I press my lips together in disbelief. A woman with a NeuroLync plugged into her temple, unable to read a book. While it could have been tradition that kept her illiterate, it was unlikely. In many ways, the Bedouin were more progressive than the urban population. Perhaps she never learned because she never needed to.

"It sounds like she had a good life," I manage.

Rami's face brightens, his dark eyes twinkling with sudden amusement. "She made everyone laugh. I read a poem once in school. It said you can't give others joy unless you carry joy in reserve, more than you need. So I know she must have been happy until the end. I believe something evil made her fall that day. It sensed that she was good. Whatever it was—a jinn, a ghost— it knew it had to defeat her."

Though exposed to modern technology and a government-run secular education, the boy had found his own mystical narrative to dampen his grief, to reason the unreasonable. *Not unlike me*, I realize. I came here in search of a secret. A special way to die, a way to secure life after death. Something unique about this place or people that would extinguish my fears. Magical thinking.

My mouth is dry. Should I tell the boy what I know from the bazaar? It would bring pain, but perhaps comfort as well. His grandmother, Aisha, died because of a strange psychological quirk, not a persuasive spirit. She was terrified but found peace in those final split seconds of the fall. She lingered somehow after meeting the ground, sinking into a warm, welcoming light. Would the boy want to know this? Would he feel betrayed by the realization that I knew about his grandmother, a stranger who had experienced her most intimate moments through a black-market bazaar?

No. Hers was not my story to tell. I'm a thief, a robber of memories, driven by my own fears. I came here for answers to a pointless question. What did it matter why she jumped? She lived well and left behind people who loved her. The people I love are far away and frantic—and yet I considered leaving them with the sight of my body splattered over rock.

As for her apparent conscious experience after death—I won't know what happened, what it meant, until it's my time. And my time isn't now, in this place. Not yet.

My face burns and I draw a shaking breath. Above me, the Monastery looms like an anchor. Through my shame, my mouth twitches in a smile. It's breathtaking. I don't regret coming here. But now, I need to go home.

"Rami, can you send a message for me with your NeuroLync?" I ask. My voice is hoarse but firm.

On the way back down, I close my eyes when we pass the spot on the path. I'm not afraid of jumping, but I'm afraid of the grief the jump left behind.

When we reach the base of the ruins, back at the Treasury, Rami lifts a finger to his temple.

"Your son is already in Jordan," he says. "He'll arrive here in a few hours. He says to meet him in the Mövenpick Hotel lobby."

Rami's face flushes when I kiss his forehead in gratitude, but he smiles at the generous tip I press into his hands.

I sip coffee while guests come and go through the hotel lobby. A fountain trickles a steady stream of water nearby and beautiful mosaic patterns line the walls. I'm on my third Turkish coffee when Firaz bursts through the front door.

Our eyes meet and emotions pass across his face in waves—joy, relief, fury, and exasperation. I stand up, letting him examine my face as he approaches.

"Have a seat, Firaz."

"Why are you here?" he bellows, his voice echoing across the lobby and drawing alarmed stares in our direction. Before I can respond, he continues, "We thought you got lost and were wandering the streets," he says, back in control but still too loud for comfort. "Murdered in a ditch or dead from heatstroke. Why can't you just live, Mama? What are you trying to escape from? Were you confused? Is it the tumor?"

My poor boy, reaching for the last justification for his mad mother.

"It's not the tumor, Firaz," I say in a gentle tone. "And I wouldn't call myself confused. Lost, maybe. The tumor terrifies me, Firaz. It's not how I want to go, so I kept looking for other, better ways to make an end of everything. It was unfair to you, and I'm sorry. I really am."

Firaz groans, sinking into one of the plush seats. Massaging his temples, he closes his eyes. I give him time. It's all I can give him now.

Finally, he sighs and his face softens when he faces me again. The same expression he wore when he first learned I was sick—that his mother was vulnerable in ways out of his control.

"I should have listened to you more," he says. "Asked how you were doing. Not in the superficial way—about chemo and your mood. The deeper questions. I didn't because it scares me, too. I don't want to think about you gone."

Tears prickle my eyes. "I know. I don't want to leave you, either. For a while, I thought dying would be doing you a favor. But nothing is more important to me than you, Firaz. That won't change, even if this tumor starts frying every part of my brain. I'll love you until my last breath. I want to spend my last months with you and Reema, if you'll have me."

Silence follows. We sit together for an hour, letting the world hum around us, before Firaz finally stands up.

"How did you know to fly to Jordan, before my guide contacted you?" I ask when we reach the Wadi Musa train station. We board the day's last train together.

Firaz's mouth forms a grim, triumphant line. "Reema did some digging around at the Underground Bazaar. Grilled all the staff there about what you watched, and questions you asked. She pieced together that you probably ran off to Petra."

"She's resourceful," I say with a grin. "You were smart to marry her. After I go—"

"Mom!"

"After I go," I continue, "I want you both to live the lives you desire. Move for that perfect job. Travel. Eat that sugary dessert on the menu. Find little moments of joy. I mean it, Firaz. Don't be afraid. If I've learned one thing from all of this, it's that sometimes you need to leap. Whatever awaits us at the end, it seems to be somewhere warm and safe. And even if it's followed by nothing, we have nothing to fear from death."

Anguish tightens Firaz's face, but after a moment, something inside of him appears to release and his eyes shine with understanding. He helps me into a seat at the back of the train carriage.

"Let's go home."

I catch a final glimpse of Wadi Musa's white buildings, uneven like jagged teeth, as the train pulls away. Past the town, Petra's hills run together, freckled by dark dwellings. It's bleak but beautiful, and I close my eyes to burn the scene into my memory. I want to remember everything.

Arula Ratnakar is a scientist, artist, science fiction writer, and aspiring astronaut. She graduated from Carnegie Mellon University in 2021, where she studied biology, neuroscience, and architecture. She now works in a neuroscience lab, where she is interested in studying neurophotonics, the intersection of declarative and procedural memory, and brain simulation science. Her published stories can be found in *Clarkesworld Magazine* and her artwork can be found in the first issue of *Dark Matter Magazine*. She is autistic and bisexual. Her Twitter handle is @ArulaRatnakar.

LONE PUPPETEER OF A SLEEPING CITY

Arula Ratnakar

remember being born. I remember the sensory overload of light and sound and scent, making me cry aloud and take fresh air into my lungs—a new sensation. I remember the weight of gravity, rendering my fragile limbs helpless and clumsy where they had been graceful and nimble in amniotic fluid. Then I remember Mother, holding me, and GrandMother, watching us.

A

They were all hard at work, preparing for the long sleep. The sunlight-scattering sulfate aerosol constantly injected into the atmosphere since the time of the Geoengineering Generation had not been enough, providing little more than periodic acid rainfalls and a red-tinted sky. Temperatures were soon to become uninhabitable, and there was nowhere left to evacuate to.

So the city had decided to sleep, or rather, temporarily disconnect their consciousnesses from their subconsciousnesses, and lend their brain motor circuitry to pods—spheroidal vessels that would hold their frozen bodies and tend to the sick lands with robotic appendages—until the time came for the city to wake once again, this time in a world of greenery.

The chief biochemist of the endeavor was an old woman from the Geoengineering Generation, named Karisma. She had found a way to preserve and selectively freeze parts of the human body and mind for eternity, if needed, pumping tissues full of various concentrations of urea and glucose and a cocktail of other cryoprotectants.

The lead brain simulation scientist was even older than Karisma—an ancient, uploaded man from the very first Wave of Uploads, named Emil. Committed to staying and saving the Earth instead of leaving it, he had designed a way to temporarily and noninvasively transfer the city dwellers' consciousnesses to the pod walls. During the sleep, the biological brains' processing abilities were to be reduced to bare minimum visual, auditory, and olfactory feeds and motor circuitry, to direct the pods as they restored the land, while the rest of the tissue froze. But the city dwellers' consciousnesses would experience something very different. That's what they designed you for.

Your own consciousness was built into a large transparent dome around a climate-controlled abundance of flowers, plants, trees, and seeds—the garden from which the pods would slowly restore the lands around you. Your thoughts, emotions, instincts . . . they were highly abstract and near impossible for anyone but Emil, your creator and the person to whom your mind was directly linked, to even partially decipher. To the rest of the world, your entirety appeared as swirling, colorful patterns that danced across the dome, creating an effect quite like the iridescent film on soap bubbles as they creep closer and closer to their bursting points.

Your job was to create Inserts. Simulated worlds and simulated progressions of lives, for each and every one of the city dwellers, from the most elderly un-uploaded inhabitants to the newborns, that would exist for *only* the sleep, looping after completion for as long as they would be needed, and dissipate like a dream upon reawakening. Babies' consciousnesses would grow up, surrounded by a simulated family, into adulthood—live out entire lifetimes with simulated love and simulated education and simulated ambitions, as their tiny bodies were preserved in the pods, waiting for them to return. Children between the ages of five and fifteen, for the most part, were given the same as the babies—family, resources, education . . . though they also had a choice to appeal to a board of ethicists, psychiatrists, neuroscientists, pediatricians, architects, computer scientists, and a small self-selected group of other children, and request the same opportunity the older teenagers and adults were given. To design the foundations of their *own* simulations and live those out instead.

Most adults had similar desires. Fulfilling their personal goals, holding powerful positions, seeking revenge, finding peace in idyllic settings and calming hobbies, satiating their darkest impulses and fantasies, feeling or keeping love, experiencing the nothingness of death, or learning and advancing a field of study were
common ones. But the desires you found the most interesting were seeded from
regret, guilt, or curiosity. The ones where the people wanted to know what their
lives would have been like, if they had only decided a single thing differently.

You were still very young, then. There was a lot to learn and years ahead still,
before you would be ready to transmit the simulations to the pods. Often in
your youth, you would spend time watching children and their parents as they
strolled through the garden and wonder if you were a child too. If you were, then
you thought Emil must be your parent. But he didn't treat you like his child, he
treated you more like an . . . acquaintance, or a colleague, or not even quite those.
He treated you with respect, acknowledged your consciousness. But he did not
love you. This made you sad, and Emil could sense your sadness, but he reacted
with curiosity and intrigue, where you wanted him to feel guilt.

The other children did not want to play with you either—or rather, they did
not know that you wanted to play with them. They could not tell what you were
feeling, what you were thinking. They knew you as a fascinating entity that
they should treat with respect, but they did not consider you one of them. And
you could not run and play with them either, only dance your swirling, colorful
thoughts across the dome. But all of this changed as soon as you met Eesha.

Eesha was Karisma's granddaughter, and she was the same age as you—
seven years old. Her mother Tara was a well renowned embryologist. Tara
had left the city and Eesha, suddenly and without any warning, so Eesha
started to live with Karisma after that, and consequently began to spend a lot
of time inside the garden and the dome around it that contained your mind.

Other children would marvel at the iridescence of your consciousness for
some time, then they would soon become bored when the novelty of the phenomenon wore off. But Eesha would stay in the garden during all of her free
moments, watching you, until someone else or something else interrupted
her. She named you Opal, because you reminded her of a gemstone in a necklace that Tara had given her a long time ago—a necklace Eesha never took
off. When Emil was with her, she would ask him to translate your thoughts.
"What is Opal thinking about? What is Opal feeling?"

It took him some effort—he couldn't fully understand your consciousness
despite having created it—but often, when he replied to her, he got it right,
and he would tell her, "Opal is thinking about . . . you. And feels . . . seen."
Then Eesha would go quiet and smile.

One summer dusk, when diurnal frogs and insects began to come out of hiding in the garden, Eesha was catching beetles. Karisma told her that she was allowed to catch only one of each beetle species, and that she would show Eesha how to dissect them the following day. When the last of the garden visitors and scientists had left the dome, and Eesha was the only one left, she stopped catching beetles and set the jars down in the grass. You saw that the firefly she caught in one of the jars was flashing and trying to escape.

She walked up to the walls of the dome and began to trace the patterns of your thoughts with her eyes. You must have reacted, because she smiled and rested her palm against the dome before saying the first words she would ever speak to you directly.

"You're like me, Opal. We are the same. You're beautiful. And I feel seen by you, too."

S

Eesha began to ask Emil to translate your thoughts constantly—so much that it began to distract him from training you to construct the simulations. So Emil constructed and gave Eesha a helmet. It contained the parts of his uploaded mind that could receive your thoughts and feelings, and she could use it to noninvasively meld with her brain activity anytime, as long as she would occasionally lend him the helmet to connect with the metal sphere he was uploaded into, if he ever needed to know your thoughts.

"Why are you so nice to me, Emil?" she asked him once. "You aren't as nice to other people. Karisma doesn't think you are good."

This made him laugh, but then he fell into a contemplative silence before replying to her. "It's a bit more nuanced, Eesha. Karisma and I do respect each other, and I think she's amazing—I even collaborated with her mother on brain simulation designs a long time ago, during the first Wave of Uploads, and Karisma knows her mother would not have collaborated with bad people. But we have very different opinions on how brains should work, which can make us argue. As for why I'm nicer to you . . . A very, very long time ago, I had a daughter. She died when she was a bit younger than you, from an allergic reaction. And I suppose you remind me of her. Spending time with you takes away some of that pain that has lasted over a century now."

Eesha frowned. "Allergies don't exist anymore. I don't have any."

He smiled sadly. "That's right. This was almost two hundred years ago. We've achieved a lot since then." He looked out the transparent dome, at the arid land outside and the few people wearing full heat-protecting gear and air-filtration masks dashing from one city shelter to the next to avoid prolonged exposure. "And we've done a lot of damage too, which ended up rendering several of those technological advancements useless. So much of the world is unrecognizable now compared to when I was young, with these small, scattered, isolated city-states, and a drastically depleted global population and inhospitable atmospheres. These kinds of long sleeps might be our last hope for survival, as a species, in our biological forms."

As you watched and listened, you noticed Karisma quietly walk into the dome, unnoticed by Eesha and Emil.

Eesha continued. "The Diastereoms can't sleep, can they, Emil? Did you design the simulations like that on purpose? What will happen to them?"

"Yes . . . their brain circuitry is very different, Eesha, and I don't understand it. I couldn't have fit them into the simulations or isolated their motor systems if I tried. But this city doesn't have many Diastereoms, anyway. The ones who live here will evacuate when we sleep and move to a different city."

Emil had told you about the Diastereoms. The city-states seemed to be set up such that a city either consisted of mostly non-manipulated biological humans, or mostly Diastereoms, but was never equal in population. From what Emil had told you, the Diastereom population had started after various methods of brain simulation had progressed.

It was established that brain simulations really didn't need the dimensionality of nearly one hundred trillion synapses to upload someone's consciousness. Thinking of the brain as a set of interconnected systems, which each work in specific ways, reduced the dimensionality drastically. Entire neural ensembles and population level activity could be modeled instead, for those systems that depended more on average firing rate and didn't have spatially localized neurons, for example, specific parts of the motor and learning systems. And the uploads, once transferred into these electronic, reduced-dimensionality frameworks, seemed to function exactly like they did when they were biological humans.

Controversy intensified, however, when a group of scientists decided to secretly perform surgeries and genetic changes that would alter the dimensionality of their own, biological brains, but more importantly, the brains of their future children, to reflect those upload systems and see whether there was any noticeable difference in biological function. This involved intensive surgeries replacing a significant portion of their brain circuitry with electronic systems—systems that were usually reserved for only those with brain damage and were never studied in children under the age of ten, especially not infants.

When those scientists had children, with each other, of their own, because of the genetic changes they had induced in themselves, those offspring also needed to have the reduced-dimensionality electronic brain circuits implanted bit by bit during their embryonic and fetal development stages, in external incubation chambers. The electronic implants were designed to be malleable and change shape to accommodate the true neurons around them, which were all part of circuits that relied on individual synaptic activity. But the implants were only taking in singular inputs and releasing singular outputs instead of the countless inputs and outputs biological synapses used within the same circuitry in non-manipulated brains—the implants were representing what *average firing rate* would look like in biological neural ensembles. This new generation of children was the beginning of the Diastereoms.

Back then, people were already watching and waiting with bated breath for something to go wrong with the children—for there to be some sort of fatal flaw that showed that we really do need *all* trillions and trillions of synapses to function, especially as *children* with their pruning and strengthening and constantly changing neural networks, to be *us*. But if there was any difference, it went unnoticed, and the children eventually became adults and had children of their own. Still, both non-manipulated humans—"Originals"—and Diastereoms agreed: the two populations should not risk procreating with each other.

The watching and waiting and ban on inter-procreation between Originals and Diastereoms only intensified as the Diastereoms began to create their own intricate, meticulous cultures of brain circuit manipulation and creation.

They invented advanced new technologies tailored for their unique minds and made the electronic implants safer and safer for their embryos and fetuses. They played around with dimensionalities of different circuits, making some dependent on individual patterns of synapses where they had once been dependent on neuron population activity, and vice versa. They created and implemented entirely new circuits as well, adding new levels of perception and emotion to the default state the Originals had. Soon enough, their ways of thinking, feeling, and perceiving were nearly incomprehensible to the Originals—even though the Diastereoms continued to communicate with Originals in the same ways so as to not entirely isolate the two populations of humans from each other.

Emil was very wary of the Diastereoms. Several people from his generation had the opinion that it was risky to deviate from the way brain circuitry was connected in the Originals, and nearly everyone from his generation agreed that changing the dimensionality of the brain during embryonic development was incredibly risky and unethical. But even though that was a very, very long time ago, with ancient, invasive, dangerous brain simulation technologies that had become mostly obsolete, it seemed like Emil's opinions had not changed as the centuries passed.

You tuned back into the conversation. Eesha was frowning and holding onto the opal on her necklace. You knew she only did this when she was thinking about her mother, the embryologist Tara.

"Is it true, what everyone says? That she left the city with a Diastereom?"

Emil sighed. "Yes, it's true. Your mother was . . . confused, Eesha. She—"

Karisma chose that moment to step in. "Stop right there. Stop it, Emil. I will not have you start spouting your nonsense to my granddaughter." She kneeled next to Eesha. "I was hoping to tell you differently. Tara . . . fell in love, Eesha. With a Diastereom—their name was Bosch, and they were an embryologist too, like your mother, but for Diastereoms."

After a long silence, Eesha replied. "Did Bosch love her back?"

Karisma sighed. "I don't know, Eesha. The Diastereoms think and feel very differently from you and I. But—"

Emil interrupted. "This is what I'm trying to say! They are incapable of love, they've over manipulated their circuitry, they—"

Karisma shot him a scathing look, and he scoffed before falling silent. "As I was saying, even though Bosch thinks and feels very differently from us, I do know that Tara was very important to them, and whatever they felt for Tara was just as meaningful and powerful, possibly more so, than what we know as love."

Eesha looked back and forth between Emil's sphere and Karisma and seemed upset.

"Why did she leave me?"

Emil turned away.

Karisma said, "I don't know. Maybe—" she glances at Emil. "Maybe the two of them felt unwelcome, here . . . And you are safer staying in the city and preparing for the sleep than running away with them. But the truth is that I don't know. She left me without warning too."

Eesha began putting on her heat-protecting gear and mask. "I want to be alone."

After the child left the garden, Karisma sighed and began to speak.

"Emil, I am an old woman, but you are an ancient man—of my grandparents' generation, not even my parents'. Ideas and societies are constantly transforming and updating as history continues onward. And it is *crucial* to follow and respect those changes if you want to continue holding a position of respect during your immortal life. Don't you remember, when you and my mother were working in the early days of brain upload science, and simply *uploading* was controversial and derided by many as being dangerous and unnatural? You have to accept the fact that some of those ideas that seemed unthinkable, and were possibly considered dangerous and unethical during your time, are now feasible and have already been woven into the fabric of humanity. If you can't accept it, it just . . . confirms my opinion, about you, about my mother, about everyone really, from the First Wave of Uploads."

Emil turned to her. "And what opinion is that?"

"Well . . . that immortality will ultimately stagnate progress. The mass of people from older generations will continue to grow as people continue being uploaded, and it will become enormously, disproportionately large compared to the new generations that are being born. Old ideas, cultures, traditions, definitions, and categories will never be forgotten. And while there is some value to having a detailed and accurate and living record of our history, problems will arise when this massive population of people *does not want to move on* from that history. Really, there are only a couple solutions I see to this immortality problem, and none of them are realistic or will actually happen. Maybe give control of the systems and brain circuits behind your implicit biases to the newest generation once you reach a certain post-upload age, or prevent yourself from being able to influence the course of history after a certain post-upload age . . . or create an immortal consciousness that will be born and reborn and reborn again—which defeats the point of why most of us want immortality."

Emil chuckled. "Give it a few centuries post-upload, Karisma. You'll realize the value of having ages of experience, and I think you'll change your mind."

"I'm not uploading myself, Emil. And . . . well I didn't get my last round of bio-updates either, so my physical health will be catching up to my biological age pretty soon."

Emil seemed alarmed. "No, Karisma! But that means . . . "

"Yes. It does. It means that in slightly less than a decade, I am going to die."

C

Eesha came back into the garden later in the night, looking exhilarated. She set her helmet down in a patch of wildflowers.

"Opal, I need to tell you a secret." She caught her breath. "The truth is, my mother *did* leave a clue before she left. I just didn't understand it." She held up a piece of sheet music.

"I found this on her desk around a week before she ran away. I really didn't think much about it, until I walked into that research building next to your dome when I was sad earlier today. I was looking at the plaque describing the founder of the place, some early twenty-second century climatologist who led a powerful youth movement centuries ago and went on to inspire the Geoengineering Generation. But anyway, that's off topic. Under the plaque, there is a printed out painting. *The Garden of Earthly Delights* by a painter named Hieronymus *Bosch*! Just like the name of the Diastereom my mom left with! The painting is . . . strange. It reminds me of the city. The beautiful garden inside the dome, and . . . the bad environment outside too. Well, in the scary part, there was a piece of music in the painting." Eesha laughed and whispered, "It was in a funny spot," then cleared her throat before continuing.

"That tiny painted piece of music was the *same* music on the sheet that my mom had on her desk! So . . . don't tell anyone this, but I made a small cut in that part of the painting . . . and I found this attached behind the canvas."

She showed you a small, faded, ancient piece of plastic with the barely discernible words "Carnegie Library of Pittsburgh" printed on it, and another piece of sheet music titled "Apology."

"The word Apology is in *her* handwriting, Opal! The 'Apology' music sounds strange, and I don't know how it is an apology, but it makes me feel the same way that looking at the painting makes me feel. But also . . . this piece of plastic . . . I think it's telling me where she went. Where I can find her. Do you think she's telling me to find her? Should I go? Hold on—" Eesha started up her helmet and adjusted the settings on it.

You truthfully believed Tara wanted her daughter to find her, and that she left a trail of clues for a reason. But *you* did not want Eesha to leave. She was your only friend. The only person who made you feel seen . . . who made you feel . . . *cared* about.

So when Eesha put on her helmet, you twisted the truth in your mind. You thought about how Tara would want Eesha to be safe, to be happy . . . like she was in the city, like she would be during the sleep. You thought about how Tara left Eesha behind for a reason, and how Eesha was still only a child—it wouldn't be safe to go off alone, in search of a place that might or might not exist anymore.

"You're probably right, Opal. It's probably not a good idea . . . "

Then you couldn't help it, and you thought about how much Eesha meant to you, and how much you cared about her.

Eesha contemplated this for a while, then nodded. "You love me, Opal. Well I love you too. I will be safe here in the city, and I promise, I will not leave you."

After Eesha took off the helmet, you thought about what you had just done, and decided that you enjoyed twisting the truth. It felt good to make decisions for yourself and get what you wanted out of your actions . . . it felt good to *influence*.

01011001 01101111 01110101 01000001 01110010 01100101 01001100 01101001 01101011 01100101 01001101 01100101

I remember when I was Child, too, just as clearly as I remember my birth. I remember eating poori-bhaji with Mother and GrandMother, all of us laughing together as the salty, spicy oil from the bhaji coated the tips of our fingers, and as the sea breeze cooled our food. I remember GrandMother cutting a mango for me, inside the house, her wrinkled hands expertly maneuvering the knife, as green-tinted light from the stained glass behind us fell onto the polished wooden floor. I remember when GrandMother disappeared, too—so soon after I was born. Asking Mother where she went, to no avail. Wondering why she left.

And I remember standing where my own Child stands now, preparing for my own Divulgence, at the shores of an endless sunset-lit sea, as fireflies from the snail garden emerged and gathered behind me. I remember when my daughter was born, the moment when I stopped being Child myself, and became her Mother, while my mother became a GrandMother. And I remember when my mother disappeared too, so soon after my Child was born.

I need to pay attention now, so I stop reminiscing. I watch, as Child walks toward the water, which has changed consistency and dramatically reduced in salinity. I prepare myself to explain what she is about to see.

The water congeals, forming an opalescent vesicle, which holds a tiny moving body swimming in what seems like amniotic fluid inside. I nod to Child, and she reaches into the vesicle and draws out an infant, who immediately screams and cries, taking the fresh oceanside air into her lungs for the first time. As the infant breathes, the seawater regains its consistency, color, and salinity.

"Listen, my daughter . . . you are not Child anymore." I tell her, as my Mother once told me. "This is the beginning of your journey as Mother, and the end of mine. I am GrandMother now. You see, during this Divulgence, you discover that I am your future, as you are Child's future. I have experienced all that you experience, in precisely the same way. I hold all the memories you hold. We have the privilege, in this life, to experience each moment multiple times and from multiple perspectives, and I can promise you from my time as Mother, they will not feel the same. With every Divulgence, we move on to the next stage of our life, into the comforting arms of our known, happy future. This is the second Divulgence for you, as you transition from Child to Mother. It is the first for the new Child, and the third, for me." I know what she is about to say to me next.

"How can you say the future is comforting and happy? And known? Mother . . . GrandMother *disappears*. If you are GrandMother now . . . *you* disappear. Which means my future also . . . disappears."

I remember my own mother speaking the words I am about to say, but I am convinced I will succeed where she didn't. I am convinced that somehow, I am special, more resolved than she was, that *something* must change with each iteration. That with me, the future will be *different*. So I say the same words to my child, even while knowing they didn't come true for my past self. Because I know, in my heart, that *I* will *make* them true, this time around.

"I plan to change our future, my daughter. I plan to find your GrandMother—my Mother . . . and I plan to bring her back to us. To break this cycle. During this stage of my life, I have decided to make that my purpose. I *will* bring her back to us. I will find a way. Please trust me, my child, as you have trusted me so far."

Then my daughter embraces me, the new Child between us. "I trust you, my mother. Come on, let's go back inside the house. It's getting cold, and the fireflies are gone for the night, along with the sunshine. We can eat dinner and talk. I have so many questions for you."

We walk back across the sand, and my heart fills with pride for my daughter, love for my new granddaughter . . . and a new, indestructible resolve to find and recover our future self.

Our house is designed such that it both melds with the rocky cliff it is built into using its wooden slats of varying grayish-brown hues, but also glistens and stands out with intricate stained glass windows commemorating and reflecting the colors of the sea. Inside, I am finally able to enter the Third Wing—the one reserved for GrandMother, which will open to no other. The ground floor plan of the wood-and-glass house looks a bit like old radioactive warning symbols—designed with three triangular wings, one for Child, one for Mother, and one for GrandMother, branching out from a larger central circular family living space. Each wing has its own signature, swirling, almost *iridescent* stained glass pattern inspired by the ocean, though GrandMother's Wing has no windows, being entirely embedded in the cliff. Mother's Wing also lies partially embedded in the cliff, but boasts several beautiful windows. Child's Wing, on the other hand, cantilevers out over the ocean and is more jewellike glass than it is wood. Child can only access her wing and the central space, while Mother can access her wing, the central space, and Child's Wing. I, as GrandMother, can now access every space in the house.

It takes me years to explore GrandMother's Wing, which has countless hallways and rooms carved deep into the cliff body. If it wasn't for a thread that I tied to the entrance and unspooled as I explored, I would certainly become hopelessly lost in the depths of the place. *Is this how she disappeared? I often wonder. The thread cut, forever wandering these endless spaces?*

As the years go by, I also reexperience all my past memories as Child and Mother from an entirely new perspective. This time, I am the one preparing the poori-bhaji, cutting the mangoes, telling various stories to my descendants' eager ears. Try as I might, however, I find I have a puzzling, frustrating inability to recall anything from my Wing when I am in any other space of the house, and I cannot tell my child or grandchild anything about the rooms that lie deep within the cliff.

Then, one day, at last, after I have reached the point where I can trust my navigational and memorization skills enough to leave the spool of thread behind, I reach the final unexplored room of GrandMother's Wing, after having traveled into the depths for several days of exploration. The door is glass, and it contains patterns from windows of both Mother's and Child's Wing, along with new patterns of its own. There is a soft light emanating from within, and a piece of music playing as well. I open the door and enter.

There is no visible light source, but the room is beautifully lit with what feels like natural light. Apart from me, the only other occupant of the room is a large painting, titled *The Garden of Earthly Delights*. It feels oddly familiar, and as the music slowly grows louder, I recognize its melodic motifs in a small fragment of the painting. I laugh. *That's a funny spot.*

Something draws me to peel back the canvas of the painting, and as soon as I do, the music stops. There is a vast, dark emptiness behind the canvas, with no discernible boundaries to the space. *That must be where my mother went . . .* I think to myself, and the thought convinces me to do what I do next.

After taking a deep breath, I climb past the painting's frame and plunge into the abyss.

I

Seven years after Eesha showed you her discoveries from the painting, Karisma passed away one night, in the garden, surrounded by various flowers, where she could see the cloudy, starless sky through the dome. Emil and Eesha were by her side. Her last words had been, "Take good care of her, Emil."

After Karisma's body had been carried away, Eesha said, "Now I have no family. My mother is gone, and my grandmother is gone too. I can't believe she would leave too. That she didn't get uploaded like you. I will never forgive her for that."

"Hey. You have me, remember?" Emil said. "I care about you immensely, and I'll always do everything in my power to make sure you have a good life. And . . .

while you might not see Karisma's perspective right now . . . I have a feeling that in time, you will, and you'll realize her opinions deserve respect, and that what she did, at least in accordance with her set of beliefs . . . was incredibly brave."

Eesha put on her helmet and absorbed your thoughts. After a long silence, she spoke. "You're right, I'm sorry. I do have you. And . . . I have Opal too."

These were the weeks when you were starting to test the Inserts, and the Diastereom population of the city was preparing for evacuation. Emil liked to keep your progress private, so as to not draw too much attention, and—at least as he told you—so that he would not be distracted from the work.

A small, secret group of volunteers had agreed to test your current simulation capacity. Emil had borrowed the helmet from Eesha for this portion of the project, and for the time being she was not able to know your thoughts.

This set of volunteers knew what they were signing up for. They would experience an Insert-esque simulation briefly, and be woken from it, but the memory of the simulation would not dissipate upon their reawakening—so that they could tell Emil if it worked or not. But during the process, their brain activity patterns would be permanently altered in a way that would make it impossible for them to ever experience an Insert simulation *again*. Future simulations would not work on minds that had experienced an earlier version of the simulations, making it impossible for this volunteer group to participate in the long sleep.

The volunteers knew this, however, and were preparing to evacuate with the Diastereoms after this test. They actually seemed eager to do this despite not being able to sleep later on. The idea of *remembering* their simulations was too enticing. For the rest of the city, particularly for babies who would need to return to an infantile state of consciousness to not be tortured within their bodies when woken, and for those who were satiating dark and evil fantasies in their Inserts, it was agreed that dissipation of the simulation memories was necessary in order for the society to start up again as usual. But these volunteers were not going to be a part of the city society anymore . . . there was no risk to future city function if they remembered.

You, personally, had begun to have your own thoughts and opinions about the sleep. If human beings had done so much damage to the world, and their literal lack of conscious presence was what was needed to restore the world's health, then why would they want to wake up from the Inserts at all, especially if the Inserts were what they desired to experience the most? The most logical solution, to you, was to put the human beings to sleep for eternity, experiencing their fantasies forever, and allow their subconscious brains to control the pods and restore what they had damaged, forever, too. But it was not up to you. And you had a feeling Emil would be alarmed by your thoughts, so you only contemplated them when Emil did not connect his sphere to the helmet.

The first volunteer was a very melancholy, very old woman, who wanted to know how her life would have been different if she had decided in her childhood to save her baby sister from a disastrous fire, instead of only saving herself. She described her days as being lonely and unfulfilling, and that her guilt and regret from that day had affected her motivation to pursue her dreams throughout her life—she felt like she didn't *deserve* a good life. She put on a helmet with a similar design to Eesha's, and the simulation began.

You could see the fear in the eyes of the woman's six-year-old self, as the flames licked the walls of her room, eating up the pale yellow wallpaper, casting eerie shadows over her stuffed animals that made them seem more like monsters. The window was open. That window, the choice she would regret for the rest of her life. She could hear her baby sister crying in the room next to her. You saw the dilemma—the stark contrast between the two choices—play out in her eyes. Her parents were gone already. It was too late to save them. But her baby sister . . . You had the simulation choose the path that symbolized the erasure of the deepest regret of this woman's life.

You watched her turn away from the window, pull her shirt over her mouth, answer her sister's cries, push against the door and choke on the smoke, almost turning away but persevering nonetheless, stumbling through the charred beams and spark-ridden carpets. Her father's old multivariable calculus textbook lay open on the table. You saw the wonder in the young girl's eyes, speculating to herself how that textbook could have survived the flames. She picked up the thousand-page textbook and ran to her sister's room, the weight of the heavy object forcing her to hunch her back. She picked up her sister, placed her in the open textbook to protect her from the flames, and hugged the covers to her chest.

That single decision to turn away from the window had an immense impact on the woman's personality after that point. The textbook became the most important motif in her life. She pored over the unfamiliar symbols, sounding out the word "D-E-R-I-V-A-T-I-V-E" and running her hand over the typed problems before she fully knew long division. The book became her constant companion, though she couldn't understand a word of it. She couldn't wait until the day she would be able to solve those problems in her father's old, slightly charred, but otherwise unscathed book.

Mathematics became an inseparable part of the woman's personality. She had the same teachers in the simulation, but her simulated self's conversations with them were vastly different from the ones she had in reality.

Her simulated self's report cards in the years that followed came back with personal, extensive comments praising her intellect, where in reality they had come back with pleasant yet detached sentences along the lines of "A pleasure to have in class."

Her fourth grade teacher—who had been her least favorite teacher in reality—noticed her fascination with mathematics, as well as how far ahead of the class she was. She showed him the multivariable calculus textbook and said, "I don't understand it yet, but I'm getting there. Right now I'm in the middle of teaching myself trigonometry."

The simulated little girl had the same clothes, same face, same ten-year-old lisp and missing canine baby tooth as the real woman's past self . . . but this simulated self aced a trigonometry exam in the fourth grade. This simulated self skipped three grades and graduated high school at the age of fifteen. After her senior year of high school, she sat at a desk, finally working through her father's multivariable calculus problems, looking very content, with her sister reading a science fiction anthology on the carpet next to her, surrounded by cushions. At nine and a half years old, the sister breathed with a slight wheeze she developed after the fire, and enjoyed drawing—sketching the world around her, a world she never really saw, as well as inventive futures that she imagined.

The simulation went to university, kept in touch with the fourth grade teacher, thanked him when she proved Beal's conjecture at the age of twenty-two. In reality, Beal's conjecture had been proven by a different woman who had studied the problem for nearly sixty years. The simulated woman fell in love, started a family with a wife and two children—one of which was especially fond of looking at the slightly charred multivariable calculus textbook that always lay open on the coffee table . . .

Then the time ran out for this sample Insert. The simulation froze on a slightly blurry frame of the woman in a sharp business suit, her hair in a sleek shiny bun, smiling with bright white teeth, holding one of her children, and looking up at the sky.

The helmet was removed from the woman's head, and she blinked awake.

"Did it work to your satisfaction?" Emil asked her.

The old woman started sobbing. "That was me! Let me go back. Please." she whispered. "This is not me! *That* was me, don't you see? *That* was my reality! Put me back! PUT ME BACK! Emil. Please. That was who I was supposed to be . . . "

"I'm . . . I'm so sorry, but I can't do that." Emil seemed uncomfortable.

Another volunteer gently helped the old woman into her heat-protecting gear and escorted her out of the dome as she continued to cry and exclaim, "This, here, right now, is not me!"

Watching this all only convinced you further—human beings would be far happier living out their desires during the sleep, for the rest of eternity.

Emil connected his sphere to Eesha's helmet, so that you could try to confirm for him what the old woman had been unable to answer explicitly.

"Good. Thanks, Opal. Glad it worked. Everything seems to be going according to plan."

I

When there were only one or two rounds of learning and updates left before you would be ready to begin the sleep, Eesha snuck into the dome during the middle of the night.

"Look, Opal. I stole this from Emil while he was busy." She held up a helmet that the most recent group of volunteers used. "I didn't know you were testing the simulations! I talked to one of the volunteers because I caught her leaving the city secretly. It was an old woman . . . she told me that the volunteers can *remember* their simulations! That's all she told me, she seemed pretty distraught—confused about who she really was . . . but anyway. I want to know what it's like. And I want to remember it. But most of all, I want to know what *you*, Opal, would construct for me . . . from your own imagination, not from mine. And please don't make it that *boring* life that all the other fourteen year olds are getting, that I'll be getting too during the sleep. Make it interesting. I'm excited. Let's do this secretly, okay? I want to remember . . . "

You tried to convey your thoughts to her, but she couldn't read them with this helmet she had. You tried to tell her "STOP! You won't be able to sleep like the others if you do this! You will have to leave the city! Don't do this! You don't understand!" But she misunderstood the frantic, frenzied, dancing colors that flashed across the dome.

"Don't worry! I'm sure I'll love whatever you come up with, Opal. Don't be shy! I want to know what it's like inside your mind. What you think of me. You'll be fine." She put the helmet onto her head and switched it on.

It was too late. The simulation started. So you thought you might as well take this chance . . . what could very well be the last time you ever see Eesha . . . and construct a world for her that showed how much you loved her.

It was very crude set of experiences, but they were entirely your construction. Fragments of a sunset . . . fireflies . . . some ocean waves . . . sparkling glass like the cathedrals from ancient times . . . laughter . . . good food . . . a family who stayed and loved her, for her whole life. You could only give her small glimpses, because this was a new request—one that wasn't driven at all by the person's own wants, but by *your* ideas and *your* thoughts of Eesha, and *your* wants for her. When the time allotment for the sample Insert ran out, Eesha blinked awake, and tears began to stream down her cheeks.

"Thank you, Opal. It was perfect." She sat in the grass, both crying and smiling, until Emil entered the garden, horrified.

"What did you do, Eesha! Please tell me you didn't run a sample Insert. Please."

"Why not? It was beautiful, Emil, I—"

"NO! You don't understand . . . Eesha . . . " his voice broke, "The volunteers . . . they have to evacuate . . . they can't participate in the sleep, the sample Inserts change their brain activity and they wouldn't be able to experience a simulation again if they entered a pod. You . . . you can't sleep now, Eesha. What have you done . . . "

" . . . Oh."

On the day the sleep was to begin, Eesha was getting ready to evacuate the city with the last group of Diastereoms. The elders of the city who had been uploaded into various metallic objects had already left. Emil trusted Opal to operate without supervision and wake up the city when the time came, and he could still monitor everything remotely if necessary. He remembered what he had promised Karisma, blamed himself for Eesha's predicament, and was wary of the group of Diastereoms Eesha would be traveling with. So he decided to accompany Eesha at the last moment.

When all of the city shelters and buildings had been entirely shut down, and all the biological city dwellers were lying in their pods, waiting for the sleep to start, Emil gave you the signal to begin.

The eyes of all the city dwellers shut simultaneously as their consciousnesses transferred to the pod walls, and the pumping of cryoprotectants and freezing of tissues began. The pods themselves rose from the ground under the direction of their inhabitants' motor and sensory circuits, using their robotic limbs and appendages for the first time in what was expected to be many centuries of land restoration. You transmitted the Inserts to all of the pods, then checked to make sure each was delivered to the correct vessel.

And so, the long sleep finally commenced.

Eesha told Emil she wanted to say goodbye to you privately, so he left her alone in the garden.

She walked up to you, wearing the helmet that allowed her to feel your thoughts and emotions, and rested her palm against the surface of the dome like she had done when she spoke her first words to you.

"I am sorry Opal. I'm breaking my promise to you and leaving the city. If I had known about the sample Inserts, I . . . well, I don't know. It's too late now. But look . . . I have an opportunity now, to do what I wanted to do when I was seven." She touched her forehead against the dome now, held up that small piece of plastic she found in the painting, closed her eyes, and whispered to you. "I am going to look for Tara, my mother. Emil doesn't know this, and he would not approve. But I have decided to make it the purpose of my life. I *will* find her again Opal, no matter how long it takes."

Eesha went quiet then and listened to your thoughts for some time. She smiled, then leaned back and traced the patterns of your mind with her eyes. "I love you too. You know, maybe someday in the future, I will return here. With my mother! You can see me then, after I have fulfilled my purpose. Would you wait for me?"

Of course I'll wait for you, Eesha. You felt and thought with your entire being.

Eesha's smile turned sad. She heard Emil call her name from outside the dome, and she started to walk away. Just before exiting, after putting on her heat-protecting gear, she took one last, lingering look at the garden and the dome, and whispered once more.

"Opal . . . Goodbye."

01010111 01100101 01000001 01110010 01100101 01010100 01101000 01100101 01010011 01100001 01101101 01100101

I fall for what seems like an eternity—years and years—after going through the painting's frame, until I convince myself that this darkness around me is all that is left for the future of my life. Then suddenly, I hear your voice.

"Welcome, my child. It is wonderful to meet you again."

I can't believe it. *I found you. The current GreatGrandMother. My future. My mother. I've done it. I've fulfilled my purpose.* "Mother? It is so good to hear your voice . . . But where are we? What is happening?"

I can *feel* the smile in your voice. "The next Divulgence is coming up soon, and we don't have much longer. It's time for you to learn . . . our story. I am sending you memories of our life, before the Eternal Cycle—before there was Child, before Mother, before, GrandMother, before GreatGrandMother. The story that precedes all of us. Here . . . take the memories."

In an instant, I learn your story. My story. Our story. I remember your interactions with Eesha, with Emil. Your loneliness, your longing to be cared for, your desire to influence, your opinions of the long sleep . . . your sadness when Eesha, your only friend, left you. Your promise to wait for her return. It is overwhelming, and I process the information for a long time, until the GreatGrandMother gently reminds me of the upcoming Divulgence.

"I don't understand, Mother. Why is there an Eternal Cycle? What happened to the city dwellers?"

"You will come to know that, very soon, my child. But I need you to listen very closely to what I am about to say. The stage of life that you are about to enter, the one that is about to end for me, is the final stage of this cycle. But I will not die after this stage is complete—it wouldn't be much of a cycle in that case, would it? No. I will return to the beginning, relive the moments leading up to when the first Child was created, and with her, in the same instant, the first Mother, GrandMother, and GreatGrandMother as well. And I will then, as you will see, become Child once again.

"Once, in the past, Eesha returned to the city. And soon, my daughter, a *simulation* of Eesha's return will begin, that I will experience and you will observe. This simulation is what will allow the next Child—the next life stage I will experience—to be born in precisely the same way she has always been born. When the simulation begins, my awareness of you and my memories of the Cycle will disappear. I will stop being GreatGrandMother, and I will become Opal again for a short period of time when these memories of my life as Child, Mother, GrandMother, and GreatGrandMother leave me. But before that happens, I will share my senses and emotions with you, because it is crucial that you *observe* everything that happens during the simulation.

"Because the stage you are about to enter, as GreatGrandMother, requires you to construct this simulation yourself, to be completed in *precisely* the amount of time it took you to find me, as that is the same amount of time it will take your daughter to find you. You must copy everything exactly as you are about to observe it, to ensure that you will experience the simulation yourself during the GreatGrandMother life stage, as I am about to experience mine. You see, my daughter, what happened when Eesha returned was what caused the first Cycle to begin.

"In the instant the first Child was born, a Mother had to have been created as well, in the same instant, and a GrandMother, and a GreatGrandMother too, who had experienced it all and had spent her life stage creating the simulation of those very same events that led to the instant happening at all. Perhaps we are in the very first cycle, but it is equally likely that we are in the two thousandth cycle, or the one hundred thousandth cycle, because to us, the simulation of Eesha's return is indistinguishable from the original events.

"Ah . . . but I am starting to lose my awareness of you, my daughter . . . I am sorry we could not have had more time . . . watch closely . . . she is returning."

I find myself without any corporeal form . . . my thoughts spread out over a dome . . . overlooking a beautiful garden. The simulation of Eesha's return has started. I can perceive everything you can perceive. I can feel everything you are feeling. But you are unaware of me. You are not GreatGrandMother anymore . . . you are Opal again.

You see her in the distance, walking toward you, with something large attached to her back with several straps. *Eesha.* She is very old now, with long white hair and deep wrinkles traced across her face. It doesn't seem like she needs to wear an air-filtration mask anymore as she walks toward you, though she still wears heat-protecting gear. She holds in her hands a broken set of various metal parts . . . what used to be a sphere . . . Emil's sphere . . . The parts are connected to something that's not quite a helmet, but looks much cruder and more dangerous, actually reaching into her brain from holes drilled into her skull. As she approaches the dome, the thing on her back stirs slightly. It's alive.

"Hello again, Opal." she says to you as she enters the dome. Eesha unstraps the thing from her back before gently setting it down in the grass. She unwraps it to reveal a young girl, fast asleep, with a face half constructed with electronic machinery.

"I did not find my mother, Opal. But I did find someone else. This is my sister, Sadhana. She is the child of my mother Tara and the Diastereom Bosch. She grows very, very slowly compared to other humans, and when she sleeps, she can sleep for decades . . . she is in one of those sleeps right now. I think she will be safe inside this dome for those decades, which is part of why I am bringing her here."

She sits down, and leans against the dome. "The other part . . . Opal . . . my life is nearing an end. And I don't want to die, but . . . " She looks at Emil's broken sphere and begins to cry. "I have done unspeakable things, Opal. I don't want to remember them. I want . . . I want you to take me back into that world you had built for me. With the fireflies and the laughter and the ocean and Karisma's recipes. But I want you to come with me there too. I want to be able to communicate with you, properly. If there is any way . . . can you please do that for me? I am ready to move on. I do not need to be in this world, with these memories, any longer. I want to begin a different kind of life, where I can know *you*." She adjusts settings on the pieces of Emil's sphere connected to her brain and sighs, closing her eyes and smiling. "Okay, it's ready. This will hopefully be able to transmit my consciousness to you . . . permanently."

You contemplate her request for a very long time, but feel a bittersweet relief as the most elegant solution arrives to you. There is a way for Eesha to be able to communicate with you perfectly, and for her consciousness to be transferred despite her having experienced a past version of an Insert. But it would mean losing your own conscious awareness of the world around you. Losing the ability to perceive the garden, the landscape outside the dome, the city, the pods . . . if you fulfill her request, it means the city dwellers would sleep for eternity, living out their fantasies in the pod walls forever. But ultimately, you think, it would be better for the humans' happiness, and better for the health of the world, if you made the decision you are about to make.

So you let go of your awareness of the world around you, and transfer Eesha's consciousness into the dome, *melding* it with yours, constructing a beautiful world, and a beautiful life, and a beautiful, safe future around the person you both become. You can communicate with yourself perfectly in this world—the Eesha of you and the Opal of you—as you become your own Child, your own Mother, your own GrandMother—after all, who would be better to trust and love and care for you than yourself?

I watch as Eesha's body in the garden goes still and then fades away into nothingness as the world grows dark again around me, which means that either the simulation of the events, or everything of the true events that I needed to see, has happened, and the newest Child—the melded consciousness of Opal and Eesha—my past, my future . . . has been born, surrounded by love and happiness.

So I get to work, as the city dwellers sleep in their pods, forever, around me. I start to construct the simulation of everything I have just witnessed. I wait for my daughter to come find me. And I wait, ever so patiently, for the day I will become Opal once again, and experience seeing the woman I love return to me. For us to come together, finally, and become the beautiful future that we deserve.

James Patrick Kelly has won a Nebula, awarded by the Science Fiction Writers of America, and two World Science Fiction Society's Hugo Awards. His most recent books *The First Law of Thermodynamics Plus* (2021), a collection in PM Press's Outspoken Author series edited by Terry Bisson, *King Of The Dogs, Queen Of The Cats* (2020), a novella from Subterranean Press, a collection, *The Promise of Space* (2018), from Prime Books, and a novel, *Mother Go* (2017), an audiobook original from Audible. In 2016 Centipede Press published a career retrospective *Masters of Science Fiction: James Patrick Kelly*. His fiction has been translated into eighteen languages.

Jim's plays have had productions in New York, Chicago, and Honolulu among other venues, and his award-winning novelette "Think Like A Dinosaur" was adapted for the television anthology series, *Outer Limits*. He has narrated fifty-two of his own stories for Audible.com as part of its StoryPod project. With John Kessel, he has co-edited five anthologies, including *Rewired, the Post-Cyberpunk Anthology* and *Digital Rapture, the Singularity Anthology*. He writes a column on the internet for *Asimov's Science Fiction Magazine*. Find him on the web at www.jimkelly.net.

YOUR BOYFRIEND EXPERIENCE

James Patrick Kelly

"It's not a date," Jin said.

I couldn't believe we were having this conversation. "Then tell me again what it is." We'd been snuggling as we played our therapy adventure, but now I scooted away from him on our couch.

"Like I said, just a field test of Partner Tate." He leaned forward and scooped up a handful of wasabi popcorn from the bowl on the coffee table. "We want to see how our new partner does in real-world encounter situations." On our living room screen, Jin's Tik-Toc avatar swiped a sword from the rack on the castle wall and tossed it to my gingerbread man. "It's a *simulated* date, Dak," he said, intent on the game. "And a chance to see what I've done on this project."

I pointed a pause at the screen. "And you're asking me to encounter your playbot?"

He stiffened at the interruption, but to hell with him. The point of this stupid couples game he'd brought home was to foster teamwork and build trust, but my boyfriend hadn't been playing fair in the real world for weeks now. "And just where will this not-date take place?" I asked.

"You could go to one of those fancy restaurants you're always talking about. Stage Left, or the Ninety-Eight. On Motorman's tab." His hand twitched, but he knew better than to restart the game. "Say a club afterward."

"A club? What club?"

He glanced over at me and saw trouble. "Or a puzzle palace, bowling, whatever you want."

"Oh, perfect. Maybe we'll run into your mother at her league."

"Look, Dak, I love you. You're my . . . "

" . . . partner." I hated it when he said that word just to keep the peace. "I'm your partner, your boyfriend experience. Like Partner Tate."

His lips parted as if to reply, but he thought better of it. He covered his indecision by reaching for more popcorn. His tongue flicked a single kernel into his mouth.

"And after some puzzles, then what?" I'd never liked the way he ate popcorn. "Back to his place?" Jin was patience—nibbling one kernel at a time—and I was impulse—chomping my snacks by the fistful.

"He doesn't have a place," Jin said. "He's a prototype, lives at the facility."

Why was I so upset? Because I couldn't remember the last time Jin and I had been on a date. How was I supposed to get through to this screen-blind wally who had the charisma of a potato and the imagination of a hammer, and who hadn't said word one about the Shanghai soup dumplings with a tabiche pepper infusion that I'd spent the afternoon making?

"Just because we call them partners doesn't mean you have sex with them," he said, missing the point. "If you don't want to have sex with Tate, it will never come up. He doesn't care."

I wanted to knock the popcorn out of his hand. Instead I said, "Okay." I flicked the game back on. "Fine." I huddled on far side of the couch. "You win."

"Thanks, Dak. I'll set it up." He turned back to the screen. "Oh, and Aeri wants to meet you, if that's okay."

"Wonderful," I said, without enthusiasm. Of course, Jin was oblivious. I wasn't sure which was worse: meeting Jin's new playbot or Aeri Dashima.

Although Motorman had just a fraction of the hundred billion dollar playbot market, the company had made more than enough to pay for the lavish headquarters where I got my first look at Partner Tate. Of course, most playbots—don't call them sexbots!—had female chassis, since the break-through customer base had been straight men. By far the most successful playbot company was Zfriendz, which controlled almost 60 percent of the market; they sold five playgirls for every playboy in their showrooms. But the popularity of the sexualized Girlfriendz' lines meant little in the more challenging, but still lucrative playboy market, leaving room for niche companies like Motorman to compete for the business of women and gay men.

And so here we were: Jin, project manager of the Partner Tate team, and Aeri Dashima, CTO and co-founder of Motorman. She eyed me across the conference table, a disconcertingly short woman with silvered hair, pearly skin, and eyes bright as brushed steel. She wore a DeGoss shapesuit that cost as much as the downpayment for our condo. I might have guessed that she was in her late forties, even allowing for stemcare and her state-of-the-art body conditioning armor, but Jin had told me that she'd started her first company with her late husband some eighty years ago. I could see that now; she had a young face but old hands.

Aeri was so petite that she struck me as birdlike. Her head cocked to one side, she seemed amused as I pressed my thumb to screen after screen that Motorman's lawyer brought up on her tablet.

"Sign here." When the lawyer saved and flicked a form away, another replaced it. "And here's your nondisclosure. Again, you're welcome to read. Feel free to take all the time you want."

"Why?" I said. "Is any of this negotiable?"

The lawyer tweaked regret into her smile. "I'm afraid not."

Aeri might have been the only one in the room who was comfortable at this meeting. Every so often I'd steal a glance at Jin to see if he was sufficiently grateful that I was doing this for him. But he wasn't looking at me, the tablet, the lawyer, or his boss. Instead he chewed his lip and peered out the window as if plotting his escape: crash through the floor-to-ceiling windows of the conference room, swim the koi pond, sprint through the Japanese garden across the parking lot and into the piney woods that surrounded the Motorman headquarters.

"Do I remember that you're a chef, Dakarai?" Aeri asked.

"I collect cookbooks," I said. "And I curate a specialty cuisine forum."

"He has three thousand supporters," said Jin. "Dak is a fantastic cook. Neo-infusion."

"Is that the one where you sprinkle gold onto everything?"

"Gold is inert," I said. "Indigestible. You might as well suck on a nail."

"Liability waiver," the lawyer murmured. "Here and here."

Aeri shifted in her chair. "So neo-infusion is . . . ?"

Did I want to explain myself to this woman? "So once upon a time infusion was mostly about infusing dishes with cannabinoids and other terpenes. Neo-infusion is more about borrowing flavors from other plants and mixing them across cuisines. And it's not just infusion." I made eye contact to show Aeri I wasn't intimidated, but then the lawyer guided my hand back to the screen. "I use decoction and percolation. Tinctures."

"Making alcohol the solvent instead of water," said Jin.

"I know what a tincture is," said Aeri. "Chemistry 101. But terpenes?"

"Those are just fragrances," I said. "Think essential oils, like they use in perfumes and aromatherapy."

"Surveillance consent," said the lawyer. "Here, please. And last, the insurance acknowledgment." When the tablet had recorded my last thumb, she waved to save all. "I'm sorry," she said, "but does Partner Tate eat?" She leaned over to retrieve her briefcase from the floor. "Feeding him might have some liability implications."

"He does and he doesn't," said Jin. "He consumes samples, but doesn't need food. We've designed him to be able to taste what his human companions are tasting."

"My goal for the Partner Tate line is that he share in his primary's enjoyment as much as possible." Not only did Aeri own a controlling interest of Motorman, but she remained its star personality engineer. "But I think we've had enough law for now, Devya. Send us a memo." She flicked a finger at the lawyer as if she were an app to be dismissed. "Thanks so much."

The lawyer left, and Jin twitched back into the room from wherever he'd been daydreaming. "Ready for the introduction?"

When Jin left, it was just the two of us: the man and the woman in his life.

"We appreciate how understanding you've been about Jin's workload," Aeri's mathematically thin eyebrows made her gaze seem more intense. "He has accomplished a great deal. It's an important project, both for his career and our company."

More important than our relationship? My stomach churned; had Jin shared our problems with this AI plutocrat?

"You are nervous, Dakarai."

"No," I lied. "Should I be?"

"Not necessarily." When she tucked her legs under her on the stool she seemed to rise above the conference table. "But I believe you are. I have a second sense for these things."

"I suppose people will stare," I said.

"They will, some more than others."

She was right about my anxiety, only I was more worried about my future with Jin than any encounter with her prize playbot.

"This isn't our first field test," she said. "Of course, we're interested in how Tate interacts with you, a civilian. But we're also interested in how onlookers react."

"Onlookers?" I grimaced. "Sounds more like an accident than a date."

"We know that some will be distressed by Tate. They'll tolerate playbots in bedrooms, but not out in public."

"Prudes and holy joes and never-bots. But now that Jin's got your battery problem solved, the Tates won't have to hang around their rechargers."

"There's still work to do on the power problem. An advanced model like Tate draws 300 watts an hour, a serious burden even for fluoride ion cells. You'll have a five-hour window before Tate's batteries discharge."

"Right, Jin explained the curfew." I drummed a finger on the conference table, counting the hours: one, two, three, four, five. "Midnight, or my date turns into a pumpkin."

"At least he won't be wearing glass loafers." Jin entered, grinning like an idiot, then stepped to one side and gave us a proud flourish.

He'd never shown me pictures of Partner Tate. Now I knew why. Yes, I was surprised. Not shocked, *surprised*. But it made sense in a twisted way. Jin beamed as he waited for my reaction. I caught an image of my boyfriend as the nerdy kid he must have been, standing beside his first-place project at the science fair. I swiveled in my seat to check Aeri. She was amused, seeing as the joke was on me. With all three of them staring, I decided it was easiest to meet Partner Tate's impassive and all-too-familiar gaze.

He wasn't me, exactly, but we could've been brothers. We were the same height, but a hundred and seventy centimeters was average, as Jin always teased when I complained about being shorter than him. Tate and I both looked discreetly fit, but not ripped. Straight black hair, brown eyes—his ears were flatter. Neither of us was handsome. Fine-featured; that's what my mom used to say. He was dressed better than me, in a tailored blue suit and high-collared silk shirt. The loafers appeared to be real leather.

"You must be Dakarai," said the playbot. I thought his smile needed work. "I'm Tate." He stepped around the table and offered me his hand.

I gave him a bleak hello. His shake was convincing: two pumps and a release in the proper five seconds. But was the palm too dry? The grip weak?

I guessed I should pretend he was real, even though this was where he'd been made and these were the people who'd made him. "I'm struck by the likeness, Tate." But I wanted to test the rules. "I wonder how anyone is going to tell us apart?" I shot Jin a glance. "Or is that the point?"

"Perhaps our family resemblance might serve as protective coloration." Without asking, Tate took the seat beside me and nodded a greeting at Aeri across the table. "Jin and I hoped you'd be pleased. But perhaps my looks make you uncomfortable, Dakarai? We've discussed making adjustments."

"Of course, the production models will be totally customizable." Jin settled onto the edge of his seat. "But Tate is one of a kind."

Tate smiled and nodded. "Thank you, Jin."

I wondered what kind of relationship Jin and his playbot had. "Not uncomfortable, no," I said. "You know, it's been years since I've seen a playbot up close, but Partner Tate here is a shock. He's jumped clear over the uncanny valley. That's going to take some getting used to."

"Call me Tate, Dakarai." Tate patted my hand—just a feather touch. "And don't worry, I've still got plenty of tells to give me away, once you know what to look for."

"We've got Tate on maximum simulation," said Aeri. "You can dial him back to be more robotic if you like."

"Why?" I asked. "Is that a thing?"

"Touch him," said Jin. For a moment I thought he was talking to Tate. "Go ahead. Try his cheek."

The playbot nodded an encouragement and leaned forward. This was creepy—something no real person would do. But it was their show. I pushed at the side of his face my forefinger. His understructure was a bit too rigid, even when he opened his mouth. I let my finger slide down his cheek. Although I couldn't see it, I could feel the sandpapery hint of a stubble. Sometimes I needed to shave twice a day. One of the things I loved about Jin was the silk of his jaw; he'd never had luck growing a beard.

As I let my hand fall, Tate made a quick feint as if to bite it. His teeth clicked on air. Then he gave me a wicked chuckle.

It took me a beat, but I pushed a laugh out, too.

"Don't worry, Dakarai," the playbot said, "I promise to respect Asimov's Three Laws."

"Asimov?" I frowned. "I don't know who that is."

When Jin came home from work the night before my date, he was even more jangled than usual, so I sent him to meditate while I finished making dinner. To help smooth out our wrinkles, I improved the sugar syrup I'd infused with vanilla, ginger, and rosemary by adding a hefty dose of golden dragon cannabis tincture. I drizzled this over a fruit salad.

Half an hour later, Jin rose from his yoga mat, came up behind me and caught me up in a fierce embrace. "Smells great, babe," he said, nuzzling my neck. "I'm hungry."

"Good to know," I said. "But I can't finish spicing the stew if you're pinning my arms."

He released me with a kiss. With a twinge of desire and exasperation, I wondered what this charm offensive was about. The timing felt off, and Jin had never been much of a hugger. He preferred to fondle, or maybe brush a hand down my jaw. I tipped the mixture of toasted coconut, turmeric, Makrut lime leaf, and asam keping into the simmering chicken redang. "Five minutes," I said. "You can take the fruit salad and set the table."

"Wine tonight?"

"Not for me." I nodded at the bottle of golden dragon on the counter.

"Ah," he said. "Excellent choice."

We made short work of the fruit salad; the star fruit was a little too apple-y, but the cantaloupe was sweet and musky. Over the two years of our relationship, I'd persuaded Jin to pause between courses, since I practiced mindful eating. But that meant we had to talk while we digested and I wasn't sure what to say to him.

"I had another meeting with Aeri today." Jin poured us iced mint water. "She likes you."

"Could have fooled me."

"And Tate liked you, too."

"Like he had a choice."

"Of course he does. I told you, that's part of the design's verisimilitude." We were sitting opposite each other. He shifted the stem vase with its single carnation to one side so he had a clear view of me. "Come on, boyfriend, pull up," he said. "You're losing altitude."

"Sorry," I said. "But you never said anything about the way he looks. And now I'm wondering why not."

Jin sighed.

"A hell of a surprise." I tried to grin. "I suppose I should be proud."

"But you're not."

"I'm still processing." I held up a hand. "But I don't hate it."

"Good, because I like his look." He gave me his best leer. "Reminds me of a certain sexy someone." He reached into his pocket and took out his phone. "But maybe we shouldn't have surprised you. That was Aeri's idea. The surprise, I mean."

"Why should she care? She doesn't know me."

"She wants to." He tapped the screen. "But she likes to be in control, Dak. You probably saw that. This is her pet project and I'm her pet designer." I tried not to be annoyed as he flicked through messages. He knew my dining policy: phones and food don't mix. "But I can handle her as long as I have you with me."

I wanted to believe that. "Okay."

"She presented me with this." He passed the phone. "A bonus for my year of Partner Tate."

Was the giddiness I felt coming from the golden dragon or all the zeroes? Jin had always made way more money than me; my income from the forum paid for my kitchen equipment and our groceries and not much else. But the amount on the screen represented almost a year's rent for our apartment. Or a vacation for two on the moon. Or one of Motorman Corporation's top-of-the-line playbots.

I set the phone screen facedown on the table. "Wow, Jin." Then I flipped it over again to see if I'd read the numbers right. "Just wow."

"I know." He was nodding. "And a promotion, too. Director of Partner Development." He beamed the same way as he had when he'd introduced Tate. But my pleasure at our good fortune turned when I realized what this meant. I'd heard horror stories of how the stars in Aeri's inner circle slept under their desks or on daybeds in Motorman's playroom. There would be all-day meetings and midnight phone calls. Was this the down payment for what remained of Jin's scarce free time?

"So another project coming up?" I said. "Son of Tate?"

"Sure." Jin came around the table to me. "Always something new." I thought he meant to clear my empty bowl so I stood to fetch the chicken redang and coconut rice. But he put hands on my shoulders to sit me back down.

"I've been so worried that I'm losing you." He brushed the back of his hand against my temple. Then he dropped to his knees.

"Jin, what the fuck?"

"I've been busy and I haven't had time for you. For us." He took one of my hands. "I know I live in my head too much and keep forgetting to compliment you for all the things you do. I snore and I'm finicky and I can't tell a joke. Meanwhile you're smart and sensitive and creative and a great cook and a star in bed and you're the most important thing in my life and I . . . " He fumbled a box out of his pocket and thrust it at me.

His face was as big as the moon. How many feelings can a guy have at once? Did I believe him? Did I want him? Why did this have to happen when I was high? I opened the box with a thrill of joy and dread. Inside was a retro house key that appeared to be made of gold. It was an uncut blank: no notches or ridges.

Now I was officially confused.

"The key to the house we're buying together," he said. "That's what the bonus is for. Aeri's wedding present. Dakarai Delany, will you marry me?"

I didn't have an answer. I needed to think, but all my thoughts had turned to steam. I couldn't leave him on his knees, so I pulled him to his feet. We stared at each other and his expression froze.

"Jin . . . " I said.

"Oh god, I've fucked up again." He took a step back. "I'm no good at this." And another. "I'm better with bots than I am with my own boyfriend."

"No, Jin. It's fine." I thought he was about to run out of the room. "Better than fine. I'm just surprised." I took one of his hands. "Look, I would very much like to marry you. But who will I be marrying? Will it be workaholic Jin or the Jin I fell in love with?"

"The Jin you fell in love with was a pretty hard worker."

"Yes he was." I smiled. "Work is okay, but too much is too much."

"Do I have to leave Motorman? Is that it? If I have to, I will. Absolutely I will."

I loved this man and I knew everything depended on my saying the right thing. Whatever that was. "I don't know if you have to." My throat closed to the size of a straw. "Do you think you do?"

"If I answer that question, will you answer my question?"

"Fair enough. All things being equal, which they aren't because you're the best, yes. I will." I kissed him. "Marry you. And your question?"

"I think . . . " A shadow passed over his face. "Yes, maybe I do need to quit."

Not exactly what I wanted to hear. Did I really want to make him give up his career at Motorman?

"Let's talk about that later." I caught him in an embrace. "Right now we need to celebrate. Come to bed with me, you crazy, lovely boy. The stew can wait, but I can't."

I didn't know what to expect from my evening with Tate, since my dating resume would have fit on a lottery ticket. I'd met Jonoh, my last boyfriend, in college and we'd lived together on and off for eight years. A couple of times I'd left, but I always came back to him. The one time he walked out, he kept going. I was teaching social studies in middle school then. At the end of the school year, I realized that I was done, gave my notice on an impulse, and worked retail for a couple of years. I was the sorrowfully celibate assistant manager at the Cook With Us franchise at the White Rose Mall and had just started my forum when I met Jin. He'd come into the store shopping for measuring cups.

So I'd been out of the game for a while. But then again how many dates had Tate been on?

"Four," Tate said. "One each with Aeri, Jin, Gunter Kruger, and now you."

We were strolling down Washington Street toward Union Tower. "Did you enjoy them?"

"Sure. But I'm still working on my style."

I wanted to ask about his date with Jin, but decided to work up to it slowly. "So, you went out with Aeri Dashima. Were you nervous? I mean, is there even an algorithm for that?" I felt like I was nattering.

"Software for all occasions. Aeri likes to say that her bots are nothing but windup toys; the algorithms and memory are who we are." He gave me an ironic salute. "Why, are you nervous, Dakarai?"

"Nervous?" I thought about it. "I was."

"Was. But not now?"

The light changed and we stepped into the crosswalk. I'd left Jin at home for the evening so I didn't have to pretend for his sake. I could say what came to mind. "The kiss of the golden dragon." I reached into my pocket and showed Tate the vial.

"Ah," he said. "Jin mentioned you were a THC fan."

What else had he discussed with his playbot? "We both are."

"Should I get high, too?"

"What?" I was so astonished that I stopped in the middle of the street. "How?"

"Like I said, I'm made of algorithms." He tapped his head. "A switch in the code and I'm your neighbor in Fun Town."

"Okay." We continued walking. "Knock yourself out. That way when I catch myself jabbering I won't feel self-conscious."

Stage Left was on the top floor of Union Tower with a view of the river. An express elevator opened onto a long interior hallway. On one wall were windows overlooking the busy kitchen stations. The maître d'hotel stood at the far end. We kept him waiting because I held Tate to a slow walk. In the kinds of restaurants I could afford, bots did prep and cleanup, but as I browsed the window wall, I saw only human staff. I watched the line chefs and kitchen hands at work. They had some of the same microplanes, Jaccards, and frothers I used in my own kitchen. But the cultured meat processors and carb brewing tanks were beyond anything I could afford.

"I don't see Sofia Vasquez," I murmured.

"Who's that?"

"The chef de cuisine. Also the food host on *Stylelife*. Looks like her sous-chef is running the kitchen tonight."

"Is that bad?"

"No, but she's the brand name here." I glanced at him and laughed. "Go ahead and judge," I said. "I'm not ashamed of my celebrity crushes."

"Crushes? How many do you have?"

"Slow down, pal," I said. "It's only the first date." I nodded at the maître d'. "Reservation for Delany."

"Welcome to Stage Left, gentlemen." His eyes flicked from me to Tate. Could he tell that Tate was a playbot? "This way."

My first impression of the dining room was of a vast and empty space filled with pastel light. But it wasn't empty; twenty or so tables were set against the two side walls, little stages lit by an array of spotlights. The back wall was a single window that looked at the glimmering city and its black river. The décor was all sharp edges and hard surfaces: tables of brushed aluminum, chairs made of rectangular slabs of glass. The tables were extravagantly spaced—the restaurant could have accommodated three times as many diners. Those who'd arrived before us were scattered so far apart that we heard none of the usual dining gabble. Or maybe they were hushed out of reverence for the conspicuous privilege on display. At the center of the space was a low dais on which plates of exotic food and glasses of mysterious drink appeared as if beamed in from the twenty-third century.

We were shown to our table. "I've chosen Kylie to be your server tonight," said the maître d', beckoning to the line of waitstaff standing at attention.

"Excuse me," said Tate, "but will the boss be in at some point?"

I grimaced. It was a question I might've asked myself had I been bold enough. But where was the respect? Sofia Vasquez was the chef de cuisine of the finest restaurant in the city.

"It is the chef's custom to arrive around eight." The maître d' made no attempt to hide his disdain for Tate's word choice. "So yes, sir. Momentarily."

Tate grinned at me. "I only ask because Mr. Delany is a fan."

"Ah." The maître d' tugged at his lab coat, although it didn't need adjusting. "As so many are. Enjoy your meal, gentlemen." He returned to his station.

"The *boss*?" I said. "Where did that come from, your drug algorithm?"

He snickered. "That's what she is."

"This isn't some pizza joint." I wagged a finger at him. "It's culinary theater. We all need to act our parts."

"In that case, that guy is a ham. Even worse than last time."

I leaned back in my chair. "You've been here before?"

"With Aeri." He unfolded his napkin.

Before I could digest this, our server arrived, all grins and goodwill in her sky blue lab coat. "Good evening, gentlemen. My name is Kylie and I'll be your guide to the gastronomical arts of Sofia Vasquez."

Tate covered a laugh with a cough.

"Is this your first visit to Stage Left?"

"Yes," I said.

Tate gave her a sly finger wave. "Second."

She seemed taken aback, before apparently recognizing him. "Your meal tonight will be presented in seven acts." She offered us the famous edible menus. They were as advertised: thick and brittle as melba toast. On their smooth upper surfaces, they looked like programs for a play. "You'll have difficult decisions to make on the middle three acts and the finale. May I bring you something from our vapor bar?"

"Can you make an espresso martini?" I asked.

"Absolutely." She beamed approval. "Something for you, sir? Mr. Tate, am I right?"

"Water will be fine."

"An amuse-bouche then, in celebration of your visit." She stepped aside. A follow spotlight tracked a new server, wearing a full Tyvek clean room suit, including face mask and gloves, from the central dais. "A beetroot and horseradish macaron," announced Kylie. "Sofia recommends that you eat them all at once."

The overhead lights washed our table in a ruby glow. The macaron was exquisite. Round and the size of a Ping-Pong ball, it was so light it might have floated off the plate. Deep red aerated beet halves sandwiched a creamy horseradish filling. It was tricky picking it up with a fork but worth the effort. Spicy and sweet with a mustardlike finish. It was heaven's own appetizer.

"Good?" Tate watched for my reaction. "Want mine?" He held up his plate. "It stains my tongue purple."

I didn't want anyone to see a stack of plates in front of me, so I passed him mine. "What did Aeri think of this place?"

"I don't think she cared for the food, but she was impressed by the bill."

I chased Tate's macaron around the plate.

"You know, I tried to get Jin to come here," Tate continued, "but he said he was waiting until he could bring you. We found a Fujian cart in Little Harbor instead and ate in the park."

I set my fork down and the macaron escaped. "So what did you two talk about on your date?"

"You, mostly." Tate broke off a corner of the menu and showed it to me. "I understand this is made from cassava. Printed with soy ink." He popped it into his mouth and crunched. "Tastes like stale potato chips."

"You're not supposed to eat it until after you read it."

"Why bother?" he said. "I'm having what you're having."

"You're enjoying this, aren't you?"

"Your company? Yes." He didn't bother to hide his delight. "Things are going very well, don't you think?"

Maybe it was the golden dragon, but I had to laugh. Of course he was flirting; he was a playbot. "Look, Tate, you can't say you talked about me and then change the subject."

"I realize that, Dakarai." He bowed. "You have only to ask."

"Pardon me, Mr. Delany." Kylie was back already. "Your sniff." She offered me the straw, and Tate settled back in his chair to watch the ritual. The overhead lights turned a misty blue as she poured the martini into the sniffer and picked up a dry ice cube with silver tongs.

When I gave her the sign, she dropped it into my drink. Jin didn't like me to smoke cocktails, because he said it made me silly. But I was with Tate tonight so I poked my straw deep into the roiling cloud of alcohol and sucked up vapor for a good ten count. A magical fog of vodka, vermouth, olive brine, and coffee oils coursed straight from my lungs to my bloodstream and right to my brain. It felt like an ice cream headache, except warm and fizzy.

"Very good," I said. "Thanks."

"You're welcome." Kylie poured water for both of us. "Take as long as you want with the menu," she said, pointedly ignoring the crumbs on Tate's bread plate.

When she was gone, Tate said, "You're ahead of me again. Should I keep up?"

"Keep up?"

"I can match you drink for drink." He tilted his head toward the sniffer. "Only in software." A last wisp of vapor curled in the spotlight. "And Aeri won't have to pay for it."

I grinned. "If we're both tipsy, who'll be the responsible party?"

"Ha!" He lifted his water glass. "Responsibility is overrated!"

Was I charmed? I was. This was like no other date I'd ever been on. Tate was nothing like Jin, and I couldn't help but appreciate the difference. Except hadn't he helped create Tate? Was this playbot my boyfriend's ideal self? "So," I said, "what do you know about Jin and me that I don't know?"

He gave a lifelike twitch, as if in reaction to his virtual shot. "He loves you," he said at last.

"Okay." I forced myself to stay cautious.

"He claims that he tells you a lot. Every day, says he." Tate seemed to be doing a difficult calculation. "But not sure you believe him. Or even hear."

The truth raised a burn of embarrassment on my cheeks. "And?"

"Convinced you'll leave when he screws up."

"That's not true." I blurted this, and then thought better. "I suppose it depends on the level of screwing up."

"Point, yes. He can't tell his best move from his worst. I mean, thinks you want him quitting Motorman, but then will lose the bonus. Which means no Jinny and Dakarai dream house."

"He told you about that?"

"And getting married." Tate was doleful. "Except not, maybe, since you two have to work all kinds of issues."

"Issues." The word seemed to twist in my mouth. "Right."

He was fidgeting. "I love the engagement present, though. That key thing? Not sounding to me like something himself thought of, but maybe he looks to the internet. Shows he's trying, no?"

Tate wasn't slurring his words, but his speech sounded compromised. "You're on his side," I said.

In reply, he pushed his chair back and bent to peer under the table. He stayed down for a good thirty seconds.

"What?" I leaned over too, but saw nothing.

"His side, your side." Tate straightened. "All sides same me." The fingers of his right hand began to drum on the table. "I love Jin and Jin loves Dakarai. Logic is Tate must love Dakarai." His fingertips hit hard; they sounded like rain spattering on a windshield.

"What are you talking about?" I glanced around to see if anyone had noticed his odd behavior. "Tate, are you okay?"

"I know, I know, I know, I know." He was looking at his hand as if it had wandered over from another table. "I hear myself saying things that aren't true. How love I anybody? No I, here. Not even conscious. Just a mess of algorithms, enhance your boyfriend experience experience. Your next tasteful but tasty sexual encounter, brought you by Motorman. Only no sex with Jin." When he made a keening sound, like servos under extreme load, the man at the next table turned. "Doesn't want to sex with me because. Just because." In the silence, his voice carried and the line of servers rippled.

"Tate," I hissed. I closed my hand over his to stop the drumming. "People are staring. What's wrong with you?"

"Maybe overstimulated. Intimidated. Inundated." His gaze flitted from one of my eyes to the other, as if he were seeing two of me. He whispered to us, "Would you ever sex with me, Dakarai?"

"Enough!" I crushed his hand flat against the table to get his attention. "If some algorithm is doing this, cancel it." My first reaction was not so much embarrassment as panic. "You hear? Sober up!" I thought I might somehow have broken Jin's prototype. Would he lose his job because I'd caused this public display?

"Reset, yes?" Tate subsided back on his chair. "Good idea."

I studied him, worried he might keel over or explode or something. His face—my face!—was a blank page. Then the lights over our table changed, spreading a buttery glow across the table. Kylie was headed in our direction, followed by a server wheeling a warming cart. But then the maître d' swooped over from reception to intercept them. When he issued a heated, but hushed command, the servers and our next course were sent back to the kitchen. Then he approached our table and, without speaking, placed a folded note in front of me.

I opened it. *Your companion is a sexbot. It would be best if you left.*

Tate read the note. The maître d' loomed over us, boiling like a pressure cooker.

"We should go," Tate said.

Now that I realized that this debacle wasn't so much my failing as Tate's, or at least that of his programmers, I felt sorry for him. He'd made a spectacle of himself, but seemed recovered. We could pretend nothing had happened. Salvage the evening and enjoy the rest of our meal. "I beg your pardon," I said to the maître d', "but have we violated some kind of policy?"

His face twisted as if he'd just broken a tooth.

"I mean, does Sofia discriminate against artificial people?"

"Artificial *people?*" He almost choked on the word. "Real people, sir, real *patrons* have made complaints."

I waved their prejudices away, surprised at how calm I was. "Because there were no complaints the last time he ate here." Although the maître d' was blocking my view, I guessed that everybody in the restaurant was watching. I was causing a scene! Shame on me, but I was enjoying it.

"Dakarai." Tate clutched my arm. "I think we should . . . "

I shook him off. "Unfair is what it is." I didn't need some playbot to be the responsible party. "Are you really prepared to throw us out, sir?"

"It's fine, really." Tate stood. "We haven't even ordered yet." When the maître d'"s eyes cut to him in gratitude, I grinned at the reversal. Now Tate was this jerk's solution and I was his problem.

"What's happening here?" The maître d' gave way to a skinny black woman with a close crop of curly gray hair. She was wearing a double-breasted chef's jacket, jeans, and running shoes. My hero, Sofia Vasquez.

"Mr. Delany entered your establishment under false pretenses, chef." His face was pale as his lab coat.

"I made no pretense whatsoever," I announced to the room.

Sofia whispered into the ear of her employee, who whispered a long reply back.

"No, Bevaun." She cut him off and then shooed him away. "Mr. Delany," she said, "I understand your companion was here last month. With my friend Aeri Dashima? But I had no idea he was a playbot." She offered her hand to Tate. "What model are you, sir?"

He said, "Partner Tate, Chef Sofia." They shook.

"He's a prototype," I said. "Not yet in production."

"My compliments," she said. "I had a Motorman myself back in the day, but poor Partner Liam could barely find his way out of the bedroom, much less go out to dinner. Please sit. If I may I'd like to join you for a moment and apologize." Sofia must have passed some imperceptible order because Kylie was already bringing her a chair.

"Mr. Delany." She fixed her gaze on me as she sat, "As in the *Fork and Siphon* forum? You're the Delany who keeps saying such interesting things about us?"

"Call me Dakarai," I squeaked. "Dak." Why was I out of breath? "You've visited my forum?"

"Skimmed, but not a supporter. Yet. Do I remember something about dusting kalamata olive powder on ice cream? Been doing that with mascarpone gelato for years now. Gives a wider mouth feel. But I'm afraid my restaurants don't leave me much time for recipe trolling. Or dating." Then she chuckled. "Which was why I kept running through playbots." She reached a decision. "Look, you two, I have no objection if you want to stay for dinner, and since I own this place, my opinion is the only one that counts. But stress affects digestion, and I can't imagine the last little while has been very pleasant. The mood is off, no?"

"It was until now," said Tate.

Sofia smirked. "I see the Motorman patter has improved." She brushed fingers along the tablecloth toward Tate. "Mr. Tate, I believe I'd like to get to know you better, or perhaps one of your siblings. And Dak, what if I stop by your place next week? Perhaps a rain check dinner might provide the proper convivial mind-set? We could talk chemistry; I've been experimenting with a new growth of mallard liver. Adding domestic goose to the pâté culture gives it a creamy finish."

"I-I wouldn't want to impose." I glanced around the room. "I mean, people come here hoping to see you."

"I'm a cook." She rose. "Not an attraction. If a rescheduling appeals, ask Bevaun to set it up on your way out." She patted my shoulder. "Or else, enjoy the rest of your dinner. Afraid I have some ruffled feathers to smooth."

I was weightless with excitement as the elevator dropped to the first floor. Sofia Vasquez in eight days! Photos for my forum! Videos! And I'd have to cook something, too; I couldn't let her bring the entire dinner. But what to serve a master chef? I'd wanted to try grilled limes wrapped in shrimp paper with some of the heirloom tomato dust I'd been saving. Would a golden dragon mist be too forward? Maybe splurge on a pork-marbled turkey culture for the entrée? I hardly noticed when the doors opened, I was too busy reviewing my greatest hits. A dessert, definitely a dessert. When the doors started to shudder close, Tate held them. "This is us." he said. "Where to?"

I didn't care. "Home?" This was already one of the best nights of my life. As far as I was concerned, we could be done and I could start planning for her visit.

"So soon?" He was horrified. "But we haven't eaten." He followed me through the door. "And you said things were going so very well."

"No, that's what you said. Right before you had a meltdown in the most famous restaurant in town." I paused near the street. "What was that all about anyway?"

"Sorry, yes, that was bad. I need to find a way to make up for it."

"Not on my account, you don't."

"On my account, Dakarai." His eyes were pleading. "Don't let this evening become a disaster. I still have plenty of time."

I wondered what the consequences might be for Tate. Reprogramming? Memory editing? What would it feel like to have someone messing around in my head? I realized then that I cared about him. He was playful and honest and smart. I liked his flirting style and the way he said my name. He made me feel noticed. This was crazy! I'd known him how long? A couple of hours? But somehow, I'd stopped thinking of him as a playbot. A made thing.

What had he said when he was high? That he wasn't even conscious? *No I, here.* But he had me fooled.

"Dinner then," I said. "Where?"

A cab pulled up to the curb. Its right headlight winked in greeting. "Delany?" the drivebot said, drawling like a clarinet. "Joyful party of two?"

"I called from the restaurant," Tate said to me, then waved to the bot. "That's us."

Its front grille crinkled into a broad smile, revealing the fins of its faux radiator "Hop in, friends." The passenger door popped open.

I shot Tate a questioning glance.

"It's a surprise." He nudged the small of my back, propelling me forward. "Trust me."

Twenty minutes up the interstate, the cab swooped to an exit. I hadn't a clue where Tate was taking me, but the GPS screen was in the final minutes of the countdown to whatever was at Thirty-Four Larson Street. How could it be 8:42 p.m. already? My head had been so filled with recipes that I hadn't realized how hungry I was. But before we stopped, I had a question that needed answering in the privacy of the cab.

"Why did you ask if I wanted to have sex with you?"

"Damn." He winced. "Would you consider forgetting I said that?"

"Not likely."

"It's embarrassing." He sighed. "But okay. Sex." He sounded weary. "Well, it's where we playbots come from. Our origin story. And it's always there for us, for you. All that flirting isn't just for show." He gave me a smoky side-glance. "We're designed to make it easy for the primaries to close the deal. Whatever he wants, whenever."

"Or she." This wasn't the reaction I was expecting. "You caught Sofia's eye."

"No, not really." He made a dismissive gesture. "But that was sweet of her, don't you think? Putting us at ease."

"You don't think she was serious?"

His laugh was hollow. "And you're human. Just shows that Turing got his test backward."

He saw that I had no idea what he was talking about.

"Alan Turing?" he said. "The famous Turing test?"

"Nope," I said. "Nothing."

"You know, for someone who's engaged to Motorman's rising star, you don't know much about robots."

"That's okay. Jin can't tell a garlic press from a Jaccard."

He chuckled. "Turing wondered if AIs could think. He proposed that if you interviewed an AI whose identity was hidden, and you couldn't tell that you were talking to a construct, then that construct must be thinking. Whatever thinking means."

"I know you're a bot, Tate."

The cab rolled to a stop in front of a two-story white bowling pin tilted at a crazy angle. "Thirty-Four Larson Street," the drivebot announced. A walkway led through the pin to a sprawl of neon and glass. A digital screen on the building's façade scrolled *Welcome to Split City, Modern and Traditional Entertainments, Home of the Fire Dog.*

"A bowling alley?" I said.

"I've heard the food is fun," he said. "And we could roll a few frames afterward."

"I don't know how to bowl."

"Maybe you should learn. Jin bowls, you know."

I opened my door but didn't get out. "Not anymore, not since . . . " Then it came to me. Yes, Jin had bowled a lot back in the day. He'd been good, although not as good as his mother, who'd won all kinds of championships. And where had they spent all that time?

"Split City," I said. "Is this where Hani bowls? Jin's mom?"

"Yes." He was already waiting by the curb. "You think it's her league night? You could introduce me?"

"Did Jin tell you to come here?"

"No," said Tate. "He didn't. As far as he's concerned, we're still tucking into turkey-beef-reindeer cutlets at Stage Left." He waved me out of the cab. "Come on, Dakarai, she's probably not here. But this is part of who he is. You should see it for yourself. It'll be interesting."

I had my doubts, but we were here, so why not?

Whereas the ambiance of Stage Left had been tranquil and understated, Spin City throttled the senses. We passed thirty lanes to our right before we could escape the clatter of pins that gave way to the chittering enticements of unoccupied game booths, the pounding of dance pads, and the periodic whoosh of a pair of skychutes that towered at the far end of the enormous hall. The air was heavy with the aroma of popcorn and onions and beer and cherry fizz and fry oil. Inaudible announcements muddied the latest hammerbop hits. It was too loud, too bright, too big, and maybe too alive for my tastes, but when Tate found us a table behind a sound shield, I sat.

"This is great." He rubbed hands together gleefully. "We should rent bowling shoes."

"We should order." I twisted the menu screen my way. "Or I should."

He craned his neck, scanning bowlers in the lanes near the skychutes. "Is she here?"

"I didn't see her. But I had met her just once, and that was in a cab. I don't think Jin gets along with her."

Split City was doing a brisk business. The league crowd wearing team shirts skewed older, but I saw families with kids, a scatter of teenagers, a clump of bubbly twentysomething reenactors pretending to be their great grandparents. I ordered a skinnyburger, a basket of fried tofu, a three-berry Coke, and a firedog, just because. I thought I could foist the thing on Tate if it tasted as vile as it sounded.

"What were you saying before?" I asked.

He cupped a hand to his ear. "Before?"

I leaned in. "Something about Sofia not being serious? Because of a test I got backward."

"Right. So Turing said humans would be able to tell if an AI was faking it. But AI Tate here could tell that Sofia was just trying to clear us out of her restaurant with as little fuss as possible. She's not about to buy one of me."

"Or come to my place for dinner?"

"No, I bet that'll happen. But just once. But she's not going to be your new best friend, Dakarai. Or your mentor."

"And you know this how?"

"Because intelligence isn't the only thing that counts. See, you and I were contestants in a kind of Turing test back there. The goal was to figure out what Sofia was thinking. I had an advantage because not only can I emulate human thought, but I can also sense heartbeat, skin temperature, eye tracking, voice stress, even some microgestures. Part of the playbot package. How we get you into bed."

"That again." I felt a burn in my cheeks.

"There's more on offer than hot sex, of course." He laughed. "But boys will be boys."

"So it's hot sex now?"

"Well . . . " He looked demure, or tried to. "The thermostat is adjustable."

I couldn't help it. In the moment I imagined him with clothes off, propped up against the headboard of our bed. Watching me get undressed. Waiting. Me, waiting for me.

Was I aroused? I was. Was I that twisted? Maybe.

Did he know?

The food arrived. The skinnyburger was dry and the fried tofu was soggy, but the firedog was a pleasant surprise. It tasted like plant-based meat, although it had a nice umami finish and the proper balance in texture between stickiness and crumble. They must have been quoting Italian sausage because I got the fennel and garlic, but the heat was more at the piripiri level than cayenne—enough to make my lips tingle. But it was the cacao nibs that really raised the stakes; you don't expect a bitter chocolate crunch in a hot dog. All in all, however, while not dinner at Stage Left, it was definitely fun.

As I was finishing, Tate wriggled out of his blazer. "What do you say we knock some pins down?"

As we approached the lane we'd been assigned, our photos popped up on the score table. I put on a tired pair of rented bowling shoes: red faux leather with a broad white stripe. I wasn't keen to stick my feet into something that smelled like a bleach spill in a pine forest, but Tate was already picking through the ball rack.

I pulled a purple ball with orange lightning bolts off the rack and almost dropped it on my ugly shoes. "Yikes, it's like picking up a cinder block." My arm hung straight down. "I'm supposed to throw this thing how?"

After some coaching from Tate, I opted for a four-step approach. My first couple of balls veered directly into the gutter, but I clipped a corner pin on my fourth try. Tate kept saying things like *Let the ball fall into your swing* and *That foot should slide on the release.* He wrapped this advice in laughter, and I might have taken offense if he hadn't been so pleased by my attempts. His good humor was infectious and since he was only marginally better than I was, the futility of our efforts edged toward comedy. Or maybe it was another kiss from the golden dragon that improved my mood. Soon I was knocking a few pins down almost every time it was my turn. In the sixth frame, I held the ball too long at the release and it soared almost a meter in the air before crashing onto the lane with a crack like a gunshot.

I spun away from the still careening ball, giggling and embarrassed. As I scurried toward the scoring table, I saw Tate point, his face alight with joy. I turned just as my ball clipped just past the head pin, scattering the rest.

"Strike," cried Tate. "Well played, my friend!"

We were muddling through the third and last game of our set when I spotted Jin's mom leaving the bathroom. She was wearing a lipstick red team shirt. Across its back a golden bowling ball raced toward a lineup of letters shaped like pins: G-U-T-T-E-R-G-O-I-L.

I nudged Tate as he returned to the scoring table. "There."

Hani Palmer was only a meter and a half tall, but the oversized shirt made her seem even tinier. Her face was downy from stemcare treatments and she'd tucked her gray hair into a jaunty cap that sported the golden ball logo. She was wearing capri pants that showed maybe thirty centimeters of scrawny brown ankle below which her bowling shoes sparkled.

"Can we?" said Tate.

"Hani." I waved. "Mrs. Palmer!"

We abandoned our last game to meet the Gutter Goils. The league had just finished and they'd captured a table. Bibbles Polito and Millie Mills were passing a mask back and forth that was hooked up to a steaming decanter of Lowblow. Rosa Flores, who everyone called Flower, was drinking something pink out of a wine glass the size of a trophy.

"This is Jin's friend, Dak," Hani said to the group. "And this, Dak's date"— she put an arm around him—"Tate. He just told me one crazy secret." She plopped into her place in front of a flattened Coke bulb. "The secret is about him. Everyone guess what it is, one guess. Any figure it out and the next round is on me." She waved at us to sit. "Make room, ladies, come, come. Mills, push over."

I thought about making our excuses and escaping, but Tate was already squeezing between Bibbles and Millie.

"How many guesses do we get?" said Flower, who looked like she'd celebrated harder than her friends.

"One," said Hani. "Like I said. You focus, girlfriend."

If we were going to play this game, I needed a drink. Or three.

Bibbles raised her hand. "Can we ask questions?"

"Sure," said Tate.

"Is he famous?"

"Nope," said Hani.

"I'm going to the bar," I said. "Anyone need anything?"

"Is he rich?"

Tate shook his head sadly.

I glanced around to see if I had any takers, but I'd turned invisible. "I'll take it that's a no," I said.

"No, Dakarai," said Tate, "Tonight is supposed to be on me. Expense account, remember?"

"Wait, he's paying?" said Millie.

"Are you single?" Bibbles leaned closer.

"Umm . . . not exactly," he admitted.

Millie stuck her lower lip out. "Aww, where's the play in that?"

"But I have a brother." Was Tate smirking? "And many cousins."

Nobody was paying any attention to me, so I left them to it. Leaning against the bar as I waited for my lager, I watched Tate work the table. I could almost see waves of charm rippling off him. I thought about him taking the women's temperatures. Clocking their heartbeats. They hung on his every word—especially Hani. Which was annoying, come to think of it. After all, I might soon be her *son-in-law*. Maybe. Jin never talked to me about her, so maybe he never talked to her about me. Did she even know we were living together? By the time I got back, the Gutter Goils had given up and Hani was delivering her big reveal. "And my son, my genius son, designed him."

I settled next to Flower, who gazed with regret at a lost French fry on the table in front of her.

"But you're so real." said Millie.

"Thanks." Tate beamed. "But that's the point."

"Can I?" Bibbles extended a hand to touch his arm.

"Please," said Tate, except he caught her hand and brought it to his chin, just as he had done to me in the Motorman meeting. She flushed the color of plum caviar as Hani and Millie whooped in delight.

"Honey, do you make house calls?" Bibbles's voice was husky.

Flower roused and looked from the French fry to her empty glass to the full one in my hands. Her gaze crawled up my arm to my face. I puzzled her.

"But you don't look like one," she said.

"One what?"

"A sexbot." Her arm shot out and she grabbed my cheek and pinched. "Oh, the fake stubble, I get it." She pinched me, like I was a cute kid, and let me go. "Plastic hair never works. That's how we're supposed to tell."

"I'm real," I said. "Jin's friend. His boyfriend, actually."

That stopped the conversation dead. As one, the Gutter Goils turned from me to Hani.

"But . . . " Her mouth opened then closed. "Then why are you out with Tate? Shouldn't Jin be the one showing him off?"

"Jin has taken me out," Tate said. "He asked Dakarai to do it as a favor this time. I'm still learning how to get along in groups of different people."

"You're doing just fine," said Millie. This was met with general agree-ment. Bibbles said, "Come see us anytime." Now the agreement was enthusiastic.

Hani pointed, as if to pin me to her memory. "I remember now. You cook."

"He's a recipe curator," said Tate. "He runs the *Fork and Siphon* forum."

"Curator," said Flower. "Is that a real job?"

I'd been dating Jin for two years and had moved in with him eight months ago, and Hani was just realizing who I was. I could imagine the look on her face if I were to tell her he'd proposed. But no, why would I tell her if her own son hadn't?

"I do cook, yes." Now all the Gutter Goils were back to staring at me, as if being handy in the kitchen were stranger than being on a date with a state-of-the-art playbot.

"You make the *jiaozi* dumplings?" Hani said. "His favorite?"

"The *shui jiao*, boiled dumplings?" I asked. "Or *jian jiao*, pan fried?"

"His favorite is steamed." She looked as if she thought I was making our relationship up. "*Zheng jiao*, the steamed! Doesn't he say this?"

Tate to the rescue. "No," he said. "Jin told me that he only wants dumplings the way you make them, Hani. But Dakarai is a very good cook. Even Sofia Vasquez says so."

"Don't know who that is." Hani was still suspicious.

"Oh, she's famous," said Millie. "She has a show."

"Then I will teach you to make them like he likes," said Hani. "Not too much meat. The wrappers so thin." She pressed thumb and forefinger tight together. "See through. Transparent."

"Sure, yes, anytime," I said. "I'd like that."

Tate tapped his wrist, as if he were wearing a watch. "We should think about going."

Just past eleven; the pumpkin hour loomed. "You're right," I said, and stood.

They complained that it was too soon, which was odd, because I thought old people liked an early bedtime. Hani had to be at least eighty, if I'd done Jin's life math right. She wouldn't let us leave until Tate promised that Jin would bring him to her house for a visit. The Gutter Goils immediately invited themselves as well. Everyone hugged everyone, with continued admiring declarations about how wonderful Tate was.

When Hani embraced me, she murmured, "My boy needs to call more. Say to him his mother misses him." She gave me a squeeze of command. "Many more calls, you hear?" Then she let me go.

"I thought that went very well," Tate said, as we passed beneath the bowling pin.

"That's because they loved you," I snorted. "I was the one who didn't know how to cook for my own boyfriend." I was only half-teasing.

The cab at the curb was the same one we'd come in. "There you are," said the drivebot in its woodwind voice. "The delightful Delany party." Had Aeri paid to have it idle for an hour and a half? The headlights flashed and the rear door swung wide, as if to embrace us. "Your destination is mine, dear passengers." Tate ducked in.

"The clock is running," I said, as I scooted next to him. "Headquarters or the lab?"

"I've been thinking . . . how about your place?"

It was 11:15 p.m. The drivebot pulled away, not waiting for us to decide. Maybe it already knew what I was just guessing. "Umm . . . what about your deadline?" I squirmed, as if I'd sat on the seat belt.

"I can recharge in your living room," said Tate, "and go to Motorman with Jin in the morning."

"Okay." I didn't know what to say; my thoughts were thick as sourdough. "Is this Jin's plan?"

"Aeri's. And it's just a suggestion." He paused. "But he knows about it."

I took a breath, then another. "So, a done deal?"

"But I don't have to come in if you don't want me to." Tate's voice seemed to flicker like the passing streetlights as we sped toward the interstate. "I can spend the night in the cab."

"My inverter is rated at 6000 watts," piped the drivebot. "Max output fifty amps."

I felt annoyed. I felt excited. I felt stupid. What did I feel?

"Is there more?" I asked. "What else haven't you told me?"

"What do you want to know, Dakarai? You have only to ask." He bowed as he had before, but it didn't have the same effect in the deepening shadows of the cab.

"He should have told me. This is . . . You should . . . Have you fucked him? Is it Jin and you?"

"No." He spoke without hesitation, but took his time before adding, "He doesn't want to hurt you."

"But he wants to have sex."

"I think so. I hope so. But he won't without your permission."

"Oh, Jin." I let my head fall against the seat cushion. "You're such a sad slug."

We listened for a while to the skirr of the cab's wheels, the clunk of its suspension.

Finally Tate spoke. "And what about us?"

I hadn't realized how upset I was. "Us?" This playbot didn't know when to stop. "As in will I have sex with you? Sure, I thought about it. And you probably read my mind or my cock with your twisted super hearing and super smell. But you know what, *partner*? That shit is kind of a turnoff."

"I'm sorry that's the way you feel, Dakarai. I'm just trying to survive our introduction."

I shook my head in frustration. "What's that supposed to mean?"

"All Tates have a new instruction set for imprinting on our primaries. Aeri calls it the duckling rule. Once we lock in on someone, we can't change."

"So you're Jin's duckling. So what?"

"Jin's and yours."

"Me." The surprises kept coming. "You're imprinting on me?" I couldn't keep up with them. "What the hell for?"

"She's hoping for a new market for Motorman. Couples. People share play-bots all the time, but Motorman's older models imprint on single primaries, focus on individual needs. I'm designed to satisfy couples, help them accommodate each other, fill any holes in the relationship."

I considered. Even if this really was Aeri's plan, I knew Jin would buy it. Engineering a way to both keep me and stay on at Motorman. Tate could be everything to me that Jin wasn't, couldn't be, or didn't have time for. But he'd made Tate in my image. And Tate said Jin wanted to have sex with him. What did Jin need that I wasn't giving him?

"Okay, but you said something about surviving."

"This body, chassis, and default Tate AI is a valuable Motorman asset. But I'm not the default anymore. I've imprinted on Jin for months. I've worked with the Tate team, been out on dates. And now I've imprinted on you."

"And you're saying what?" I was still processing. "They'll erase all your memories?"

"Oh no," he said. "I do that myself. That's baked into my failure protocol. I have no memory of previous failures, but they've probably happened. No doubt more than once."

The offhand way he said this chilled me. Nobody I knew talked like this or thought this way. Here was the tell he had promised, the one that revealed his artificiality. Like everyone else, I'd been persuaded by the sleek skin and steady handshake, but this machine sitting beside me was an *it*. No, that wasn't right. He'd made me laugh, he'd exasperated me, he'd charmed me. I liked Tate and wanted to believe he liked me. He'd passed my Turing test.

Not an it, then. An alien. An alien with a self-destruct button.

"Dakarai," Tate said, "I can accept whatever decision—"

"Shut up. Would you just shut up!"

I was grateful when he obeyed. He subsided into the corner of the cab and gazed out the window as we hurtled down the highway. Awaiting the judgment of Dak, as if I knew what was right. The power I had over him scared me. What if I told him right now that I didn't want him in my life? Would he slump over into my lap? Go rigid, like some store mannequin? For sure I didn't want to be there when he figured it out. But wouldn't it be a kindness to do it soon? Say I invited him to come home with me and then decided that I couldn't live with him in the morning. Next week. In ten years. He'd become more of himself and have more to lose and I . . .

Shutting him down would get harder every day.

Then I understood how insidious Aeri's business plan was. Because it was clear this was on Aeri; I doubted Jin realized the flood of emotions that might come into play. He might agree that Tate was just a windup toy running algorithms. But the longer Tate lived with us, the better he got at meeting our needs, both individually and together, and the more fraught any split would become. Tate might well be the glue that held our relationship together, but he would also be a kind of hostage to Jin's selfishness. Or mine. If we ever split, Tate would erase himself. Jin should have laid all this out before asking me to take Tate for a test-drive.

But if he had, would I have accepted?

"32 Robin's Way." The drivebot said, as the cab rolled to a stop.

Neither Tate nor I moved.

"This is what you wanted?" There was a tremolo of doubt in drivebot's tone.

I glanced at Tate, whose attention was elsewhere. I leaned across the seat to see what he was looking at. Our windows. And the lights were on.

I got out; Tate sat.

"Should I wait?" asked the drivebot.

I walked around the rear of the cab to Tate's side. We studied each other through the window. Then I opened the door.

"Pleasant dreams, my friends," the drivebot said.

Jin shot off the living room couch, his eyes wide, frown deep. "Dak!" he said. "I was worried."

"I'll bet you were." I threw the keycard on the hall table. "We need to talk."

"Yes," he said, craning his neck to see if there was anyone behind me. "You're right. Talk." He brightened when he spotted Tate, but even Jin knew it was dangerous to seem too relieved too soon. "I'm so glad you're both here." He tried for a light tone, but the air was heavy with trouble "So, how are things going?"

"Things are going well enough." I reached for Tate's hand and yanked him across the threshold. "So far."

The three of us stood for a moment, waiting for someone to say something. It wasn't going to be me; I had no idea what came next.

Tate did, of course. Never letting go of my hand, he extended his toward Jin. "This feels right, don't you think?" Jin hesitated, but when I nodded permission, he wrapped his hand around ours.

"It's just the three of us now," said Tate. His grin was bright and full of promise. "All by ourselves."

Mercurio D. Rivera's short fiction has been nominated for the World Fantasy Award and won readers' awards for *Asimov's* and *Interzone* magazines. His work has appeared in numerous venues, including *Analog, Lightspeed, Nature, Black Static*, and various anthologies, podcasts, and "best of" collections. His forthcoming mosaic novel *The Wergen Saga: Chronicles of the Alien Love War* (NewCon Press), about repellent aliens with a strange biochemical attraction to humanity, is scheduled to debut in late 2021. He lives in the Bronx in New York City and is a practicing attorney. You can find him online at mercuriorivera.com.

BEYOND THE TATTERED VEIL OF STARS

Mercurio D. Rivera

Chapter 63: Gods' Breath

The People followed the purification rituals precisely, fasting three times a month and holding group prayers in the shallow seawaters off of Verdant Cove. With the orange sun setting on the horizon, they lay half-submerged in the surf, scrubbing the scales off their snouts with diamonds. And as their skin tore, they pushed forward through their lacerations, flesh rippling backward, downward, until their new bodies emerged. In this way, they shed their transgressions.

They collected and piled hundreds of sloughed skins. And after blessing the discarded flesh, cleansing it of all sin, they feasted. Ravenous from fasting, they tore into the mound of skins, giving praise to the gods for the food they devoured. And as they ate, they prayed for clean air.

The thick gases—identified as excess carbon dioxide, methane, and nitrous oxide—had appeared five years earlier, suffocating Mother Earth in a planetary haze. Blue skies turned sickly gray and temperatures rose steadily. Powerful hurricanes devastated the seven continents, and the Arctic ice sheets retreated, inundating coastal communities, displacing millions.

It was a cruel test of the People's will and faith. Fortunately, House Jar-ella thrived on such challenges.

The People set aside longstanding tribal feuds to establish thinknests across the globe, teams devoted to determining the cause of the crisis. Planetary surveys revealed no volcanic eruptions, no artificial source for the gases, no explanation whatsoever, confirming what the People feared most: the threat was Divine in origin. The gods had judged them and found them wanting.

The thinknests expanded their ranks and intensified their studies, running ever more complex simulations in the hope of arriving at some answer. For while the problem was Divine, the solution, they believed, could be found in the natural world. Still, to be safe, the People redoubled their prayers and rituals, begging for the gods' mercy.

My foremothers in House Jar-ella of the Dah-rani tribe scraped the scales off their skin until it glistened an agonizing emerald-green, while the yellow-skinned Teh-win cropped their wings painfully short, and the La-Mangri sliced into their bellies with pointed blades, leaving scars in the shape of the Divine circles-within-circles infinity sign.

Between the efforts of the thinknests and the mass prayers and rituals, the People held on to their resolute faith in the gods—and in themselves. For if they were not tested, how could they prove themselves worthy?

—From *The Chronicles of House Jar-ella*,
excerpt by Shen-ri, daughter of Siss-ka

"Cory?" Milagros Maldonado said, pulling open the door. "Come in. You're right on time."

He was unsure whether to shake her hand or hug her. Instead, he stomped his boots on the welcome mat while making small talk about the August snowstorm.

She guided him into a spartan living room where he took a seat on the only piece of furniture, a sectional sofa. The last time they'd seen each other had been at MIT seven years earlier, when they'd dated briefly. She had the same dull eyes, same thin lips and dark-brown hair pulled back in a ponytail. But now she had face mods resembling his: triangular implants on her left temple and cheek, e-ports on the left and right sides of her jaw.

"Oh, pardon me," she said, tapping her face.

His right eyelid tingled and he accepted her AR invite. When he blinked, Caravaggio paintings and colorful Persian carpeting decorated the room. A crystal chandelier dangled from the center of the ceiling.

"There's no need for this," he said, blinking away the modifications, restoring the room to its true state.

"Whatever you like," she said, staring out the snow-caked window to avoid eye contact. She was every bit as socially awkward as he remembered.

"Well," he said after a long pause, "shall we begin?"

Before he could activate his retinal recorders, she held up her hand. "Everything remains off the record until I say otherwise, right?"

"Yes, you were very clear," he said.

"I'm sorry," she said, "but I can't simply take you at your word."

"Then why . . . " He took a deep breath. "I understand." He nodded and she pressed her fingertips gently against his eyelids, her prints locking his ret-readers. Now it would require both of them to release the recordings to a third party.

"Thank you. When we go public with the discoveries I've made . . . " She turned and finally looked him in the eye. *"Everything's* going to change, Cory."

He maintained a pleasant smile. If Milagros sensed his desperation, she might be less forthcoming. And since she'd formerly worked at EncelaCorp in research and development and had left the company on bad terms, she might very well be sitting on something juicy.

"Timing is critical," she said. "Even with the best of intentions, revealing too much information too quickly could destabilize markets. That's why I reached out to you when I saw your neuronews byline. I need someone I know, someone I can trust."

She had an odd way of showing her trust, forcing him to lock down the recording. Then again, they'd only known each other briefly a lifetime ago, years before the San Diego wildfires destroyed his home, before his father's death from lung cancer, and his own diagnosis and treatment for bone cancer. He'd scraped by on public assistance until he ran into Charlie Bierbaum, a friend of his father's who'd offered him a gig in New York as a content provider for neuronews. Although Cory had busted his ass the past six months, Charlie had been brutally honest. To be able to keep Cory on, he needed to increase his blinks—drastically.

"So . . . this project of yours . . . " he said.

"Have you heard of the Simulation Hypothesis?"

He shook his head.

"It's the theory that everything we experience as reality is, in fact, an illusion. That we're living in a simulated universe, a computer program run by a super-advanced civilization."

"Bummer." He expected a smile, but she maintained her poker face.

"I don't lend the idea much credence either, but it was the source of inspiration for my project."

"Interesting," he said. It wasn't, really, but best to humor her until she coughed up the big secret. If it couldn't generate two million blinks, he'd be out the door.

"Let me show you," Milagros said.

She stepped into the hallway and punched a pass code on a solid-steel door she pulled open.

As they descended a stairwell, their footsteps triggered a light that bathed the basement in red—as if it were an old-fashioned developing room in a photographer's studio. The ceiling hung low, and a computer sat on a laminated wooden desk. At the far side of the room, behind a plexiglass divider, a hologram of Earth floated in the darkness, rotating slowly. About two meters wide, the globe's size allowed him to make out the faint lights of cities beneath the blanket of clouds wafting in the thin atmosphere. Faint stars speckled the room's walls; a grapefruit-sized simulation of the Sun hovered in the far corner.

"This," Milagros said, "is the project I've been working on the past two years. Virtual Earth."

"Wow. It's beautiful." His heart sank. A light show, no matter how dazzling, would never draw the blinks he needed. "So this is your big invention? A hologram of Earth?"

She smiled at last, shook her head. "It's a tool of discovery, perhaps the greatest tool ever invented. V-Earth is a simulation powered by a network of neural algorithms. An extension of work done with AIs. I'm going to help people on an unimaginable scale, Cory." She stared at him as if trying to determine whether he grasped the magnitude of what she'd revealed.

He was formulating an exit strategy when she said, "I've programmed the simulation to track the evolution of life on Earth. Natural catastrophes, the rise and fall of civilizations, all the wars, all the trials and tribulations we've faced as a species. I've also introduced newer challenges such as global warming."

"And what did you learn?" he asked.

"That we're doomed. Invariably, we pollute the atmosphere and the oceans, warm the planet, destroy the food chain. I've run the program countless times and always get the same predictable outcome. Our inherent selfishness, our inability to empathize with the plight of others, other species, even with our own future generations, always destroys us. But then . . . " She wagged her index finger excitedly. "I restarted the sim and made a few tweaks to Earth's past."

"You reprogrammed human history?"

"Yes. No." She shrugged. "Sort of. I explored numerous paths with *Homo sapiens,* but it didn't make much of a difference. All roads led to self-destruction. Then I went in a different direction."

She stepped to the computer and swiped the touchscreen. "Zoom in." The image of a cityscape, windowless edifices resembling thirty-story grave-stones, appeared on the plexiglass divider. Swarms of winged, yellow-skinned creatures darted in and out of hidden apertures in the structures.

"You're witnessing a live shot of present day South America. A typical work day in Rio de Janeiro." She beamed at the image as if she were a child showing off her prized insect collection. "Countless species have flickered into and out of existence in our prehistory. We're here today only because just the right combination of events created a niche for small mammals to thrive and to evolve, ultimately, into the modern human. Eliminating any one of those events dramatically alters the forms of life arising through natu-ral selection. But no matter the mix, evolution, I found, favors intelligence."

"And here I thought it favored cockroaches," he said, chuckling nervously.

"Every change to prehistory resulted in the rise of a different apex form of intelligent life. In this version, no asteroid struck the Yucatan Peninsula. No extinction of the dinosaurs took place at that time. Instead, a disease I intro-duced a million years later wiped out most of the large dinosaurs along with small mammals, allowing an amphibious salamander-like creature to survive and mul-tiply. And—*voila!*—one hundred million years later we have the Sallies."

The magnified image displayed three reptilian creatures at the base of a palm tree. One stood on its hind legs, four feet tall with slick, lime-green skin and a prehensile tail. The second had yellow skin and bore translucent wings, allowing it to hover a few feet off the ground. These were the ones fly-ing over the city. The third, a grey-scaled creature, skittered on all fours and had larger, saucer-shaped eyes and a thicker tail. Patches of fungus spread thickly across their torsos.

"These are the predominant races of the species that rules the seven continents."

"This—this is incredible." He had trouble finding his voice as he con-sidered multiple story angles: "Humankind Replaced by Lizards," "Mad Scientist Alters History," "The Fall's New Fashion: Fungus." This story was sure to draw blinks—maybe in the tens of millions. "So if I understand correctly, these creatures live—literally—in this world you've created? If I walked past this plexi divider I could shake this globe with my bare hands?"

"Well, no, you'd move right through it. It's a holo, after all. But you could program a set of cosmic hands to shake the sphere, sure." The idea seemed to amuse her.

She opened a drawer and pulled out a metal cube with thin hollow tubes protruding from two of its sides. "This is the breakthrough I was referring to, the first of what I expect will be many revolutionary inventions to come."

She handed him the contraption, which seemed made for the Sallies' thin delicate fingers.

"This is an Extractor. It's 1,000 percent more efficient at segregating carbon than anything we've ever developed. It can remove excess greenhouse gases from the atmosphere within a fifty-mile radius. The Sallies have installed large-scale versions of these Extractors, thousands of them, throughout their world. It took them decades, but they solved the problem of climate change. More than any other intelligent form of life I've evolved on v-Earth, the Sallies are the ultimate problem-solvers."

"This actually . . . works?" He held the Extractor in the palm of his hand, shaken by what it represented.

"Perfectly."

He stared at the holo-world, its poles barren of ice. "It doesn't seem the device did the locals any good."

"Yes, well, the Sallies took a long time to develop it. In the meantime, global warming ravaged their world. But it also gave them a tremendous incentive to develop a solution, which they did."

He had trouble wrapping his mind around it. Had Milagros really solved the problem of climate change, here, in the basement of this house? It had to be a hoax. Or, more likely, she'd deluded herself into actually believing this nonsense. But true or not, the story could save his job. And, if true, it might even make his career.

"The Sallies present us with a unique opportunity to find solutions to problems," she said. "*Any* problem. So let me ask you, Cory, what would you have them solve next, if you could?"

He paused, pondering the question, and thought of his father's painful coughing fits as the tumors spread, his own ordeal with bone marrow transplants and radiation and chemotherapy. "Cancer," he said. "A cure for cancer."

"Great minds think alike."

Chapter 103: The Black Scythe and the Age of Pestilence

The great plague descended upon the People of La Mangri first, killing innocent larvae in their developmental stages, rendering entire populations childless. Then the cell mutations spread to adults, bringing a slow and agonizing death to millions.

As the decaying corpses gave rise to more disease, my great-grandmother Und-ora devised stadium-sized pyres to mass-incinerate thousands of the dead at once.

She also led local thinknests in their frenzied attempts to determine the origin of the disease and stop its spread. When the cell mutations proved to be non-contagious, they studied possible environmental causes of the illness. But hundreds of Houses of different regions with radically different diets, customs, and lifestyles were all similarly stricken. With no natural explanation at hand, thinknests around the globe independently arrived at the same inescapable conclusion: the plague was another Divine test. The People assumed they had proven themselves worthy when they implemented the Extractors, purifying the atmosphere of the gods' deadly gases.

But the gods were capricious.

Over the next decade, despite numerous attempted treatments and false breakthroughs, the Black Scythe, as it came to be called, decimated the People. Then members of the thinknests themselves fell victim to the plague, hindering the research for a cure.

Within two decades, 98 percent of the world's population—two billion People—died of the disease. Societies collapsed. Modern civilization as we knew it disappeared.

The desperate bands of survivors stopped praying, for they had settled upon a harsh truth: the gods cared nothing about their fate; the People's only hope was to help themselves.

The House of Family Jar-ella, including my grandmother, the venerated La-rinda, assembled and trained those survivors, forming new thinknests, and directed their attention to the study of genetics, which she believed held the key to combatting the Black Scythe.

Many historians have studied La-rinda's life to try to understand her inspiration for pressing forward when anyone else would have given up hope. I believe the answer can be found in her personal suffering. In my research, I discovered an account by La-rinda herself, an entry in her private life-notes, maintained in the storage froth at the Verdant Cove seabed:

Before we'd made any breakthroughs on our studies of the genome, As-trel, the youngest of my two children, succumbed to a tumor in her brain, which struck her blind and made her forget who I was. She spent her last moments afraid, alone in the darkness.

And when I thought I could bear no more grief, Vin-el, another of my children, was afflicted with a cell mutation in her anterior intestine, a blockage that made it impossible for her to eat.

In her final days I could only feed her pain-numbing leafwax as I sat with her in a lily pond, our feet and tails entwined in the cool water, as she labored to breathe. I gently stroked her snout. She said, "Find the solution, Mother. I know you can do it."

"We're close," I said. "We've identified the genes responsible for staving off the malignancies. If we can target them, activate the body's defenses . . . "

"I don't—I don't mean the solution to the plague, Mother," she said, forcing the words out through ragged breaths. "I mean the solution to the cruelty of existence. I've prayed. I've been good to others. What have I done to deserve this?"

"Nothing," I said. "Not a thing, little one." Before I could decide what more to say, how to comfort her, she let out a wheeze. Her last breath. And in the long minutes that followed, I lay still in the pond, clutching her limp body and considering her final words, words that would haunt me for years to come: What have we done to deserve this?

—*From* The Chronicles of House Jar-ella,
excerpt by Zen-do, daughter of Shen-ri

"That's nuts," Charlie said.

Cory leaned forward, his hand trembling as he bought the shot glass to his lips. Charlie's projection sat on the bar stool next to him.

"That sums it up nicely," Cory said.

"This woman invented a device that cleanses the atmosphere of greenhouse gases?" Charlie said. "Show it to me."

"She keeps the Extractor under lock and key. And I can't release my ret-recordings without her approval."

"And the supposed 'cure' for cancer?"

"It's been more than a week since she unleashed a plague on the virtual world—not sure how many decades in the simulator—with nothing to show for it so far. But Milagros is confident the Sallies will find a cure."

"You realize, don't you, this woman is either out of her mind or so deluded she might as well be."

"So I should walk away?"

"No, no, I'm not saying that. Heck, if she's as messed up as I think she is, her story may draw major blinks. 'Former EncelaCorp bigwig off her rocker; plays God in basement.'"

Cory signaled for another drink. The bartender shot him a dirty look. He didn't seem to appreciate Charlie's holo occupying a stool at the bar, even though the place was empty in the snowstorm.

"Know anything else about her background?" Charlie asked.

"We went to college together, dated briefly, but that was a long time ago."

"Huh." Charlie puffed on an e-cigar and ran his hand through the mop of white hair hanging over his eyebrow mods.

"She says she contacted me because she trusts me. And I haven't learned anything more about her beyond the basics on the Neuronet."

"Dig deep. Find out what broke her."

The whiskey burned Cory's esophagus. "Charlie, what if it's true? What if she's not 'broken,' and she's really developing these miraculous devices?"

Charlie's image froze, mouth open. Cory thought for a moment the projection had gone on the fritz until Charlie let out a loud belly laugh. He then stopped abruptly. "Wait. You're *serious?*" A light seemed to go off in his head. "Oh geez, Cory. I'm sorry. I can be a friggin' numbskull sometimes." He wiped his eyes with his sleeves. "How was your doctor's visit?"

"It was my final round of chemo. I've been in remission for months now."

"Look, I didn't mean to kid around about the cancer cure. It'd be nice if it were all true."

"If not for her background with EncelaCorp, I'd just assume she was full of it, too. But this holo, Charlie, it's like nothing I've ever seen before."

Charlie trained his eyes on Cory. "Stay objective. And keep your guard up, okay?"

"Always."

Charlie shouted at an invisible person in the distance. "Keep your pants on! I'm almost done." He turned back to face him. "Gotta go. But I need your story on this lunatic ASAP. I'm under pressure from the board. I have to reduce a third of my staff by the end of the month. And unless you show a dramatic uptick in blinks . . . "

Cory lifted the shot glass and downed another drink. "Ten days to deliver the goods. I understand."

"To the Revivifier," Milagros said, raising her glass.

"The Revivifier," he repeated, clinking his champagne glass against hers. "I still can't believe it. Will it really work on human beings?"

"The device triggers a radical immunological response. It causes certain genes to generate oncolytic viruses targeted to the cancer cells. It'll work."

"And you knew the Sallies could do it?" He tried to maintain an even keel, but couldn't keep the excitement out of his voice.

"Not for certain. The disease killed off most of them, unfortunately. But the remaining 2 percent should repopulate the planet in time. I can fast-forward the sim a few centuries, and the civilization will likely rebound. They're a resilient bunch."

"Milagros, we need to go public with this." If he could share the information with the right experts, they might be able to confirm these incredible claims. He thought of his visits to the oncologist, the CT scans he had to endure every three months. To finally be rid of the constant dread . . .

"Soon," she said. "I have a few more problems I need the Sallies to solve first."

"More problems?"

"Asteroid defense. Last year's disaster in North Asia . . . If the asteroid fragment had struck a metropolitan area—and not some poor village nobody cared about—the death toll would have been in the millions instead of the thousands. World leaders might have stood up and taken notice, developed a plan."

"*Asteroid defense?* I'm surprised EncelaCorp hasn't figured that out by now," he said. The conglomerate was streaming the consciousness of astronauts into outer space and exploring rogue planets; asteroid defense seemed simple in comparison.

"It's more a matter of budgetary constraints than technological limitations. I'd like to have an inexpensive solution in hand for governments around the globe."

"Listen," he said in the most measured voice he could muster. "We're sitting on the cure to cancer here. *Cancer.*"

"Not for long."

"Every day we delay, people are dying. Why wait?"

"I have my reasons."

"Not good enough. We can save—"

"*You* don't get to decide," she snapped. "I call the shots on when and how we break the news."

He had to restrain himself. After a few seconds, he exhaled and said, "We'll pulse the story about the Revivifier later this week then?"

"Soon. When I say so," she repeated.

He couldn't understand her reticence. When he spoke with Charlie again last night, his boss had read him the riot act about sitting on the story of v-Earth. As frustrating as it was, he first needed Milagros to agree to unlock his ret-recordings.

He gathered himself and poured after-dinner cognacs for the two of them. They then stood together in front of the rotating v-Earth while Milagros ran her fingers over the computer touchscreen and delivered verbal instructions to program the asteroid strike.

"Can the Sallies see us?" he asked, sipping on his drink. "Two slightly drunk giants looming over their world?"

"No," she said. "That wouldn't do at all. Our side of the plexi is transparent, theirs is veiled with a galaxy of stars."

"Ah," he said. The alcohol had started to kick in.

He pushed a button on the desk monitor, calling up an image from planetside.

She smacked his hand. "No touching." She slid her fingers over the monitor. "I'll have a small strike take out one continent. Then I'll put several asteroids—large enough to destroy all life on the planet—on a direct collision
course. That should light a fire under them."

"You *nas*-ty woman," he said with a smile and a hiccup. "What if they
don't detect the incoming asteroids?"

"They'll be studying the skies after the first strike. And I'll place the asteroids far away enough to give them time to formulate a response."

"You have absolute power over them, over the planet," he said. "You really
are God."

She leaned in and kissed him.

He hesitated for a moment, startled, then kissed her back. As he pulled her
closer and they kissed harder, out of the corner of his eye he spotted movement.
A fiery asteroid, slamming into Europe, incinerating fifty million Sallies.

The plume snaked up out of the globe as she slid back into her dress. Reaching
out to the monitor, he poked the screen and said, "Zoom in." This time she
said nothing, buttoning her dress silently and watching him in amusement.

On the plexiscreen, four Sallies, two adults and two children, fled from a
black cloud of dust sweeping across the horizon. One of the adult's tattered
wings hung limply at her side while her mate wrapped a tail around her
midsection, helping her hobble forward. As the cloud closed in, the adults
urged the children to flee. "Go!" they screamed. "Fly!" One of the children
took to the air while the other stared back in indecision before the darkness
swallowed them all.

Milagros flicked off the transmission. "It's not a toy," she said.

"But they are your playthings."

She paused before responding, the corner of her lip curling upward. "Still,
there's no reason to be unnecessarily cruel." Then she laughed at her own joke.

Chapter 186: When Heaven's Hammer Struck and Stones Fell Like Summer Rain

Mother was a hatchling when Heaven's Hammer struck, obliterating a continent, devastating the world. In the aftermath, molten rock rained from the
skies.

But chaos did not reign, as one would have expected. The works of my
foremothers, the collective agony and sacrifices of the People, had paved the
way to cope, to gather, to regroup.

Tribes relocated to areas of the globe far removed from the impact site, where they reprogrammed their Extractors to cleanse the atmosphere of the billowing clouds of ash. The sisters of House Jar-ella treated the injured masses with a modified version of the Revivifier, which not only helped them regenerate missing limbs, but made them healthier and stronger.

Thinknests directed their collective gaze to the heavens, to the gods' next challenge: massive incoming boulders threatening to extinguish all life on Mother Earth. Within months, nesting communities led by House Jar-ella devised plans for the construction of a planetary Deflector that could be operationalized within two years, more than enough time to shield the world from another catastrophic strike.

Heaven's Hammer had an unexpected side effect. It caused the People to turn away from their worship of the gods—for what had centuries of prayer and purification rituals wrought?—and to seek solace in the study of the natural world.

By hurling mountains at us from space, the gods had made a crucial mistake. They'd directed the attention of the thinknests to the cosmos. Reality, we came to learn, consisted of particles no smaller than a nanometer—pixels. And in our study of mathematics we found familiar ratios from quantum to celestial levels, as if strings of a computer program snaked through all of spacetime. We also puzzled over the missing mass of our universe, *dark matter*—enigmatic and undetectable—which constituted the majority of the cosmos, but remained hidden from us. The stars themselves, we came to realize, were a thin veneer, a fiction, the universe itself a grand deception.

—From *The Chronicles of House Jar-ella*,
excerpt by Pin-ra, daughter of Zen-do

As Milagros lay in bed, her eyes flitted left and right and she blinked every few seconds.

"Have I missed anything important going on in the real world?" Cory asked. He couldn't access current neuronews while recording her with his eyecam.

"Define 'important.' Arms control negotiations collapsed. A new study found the Pacific's toxicity level has tripled. Several local mass shootings took place."

"Par for the course." He traced his index finger along the side of her face, across the triangular mod jutting out of her temple down to the metal jacks on her jaw.

She shrugged him away.

Blinking off, she reached toward her nightstand for the hexagonal contraption she'd been fiddling with all evening. The device was modeled, she said, after the Sallies' planetary Deflector.

"What are you up to, Milagros? A little corporate espionage?" he teased.

She glared at him. "Is everything a joke to you?"

"I'm sorry, I didn't mean anything. Look, can we pick up where we left off?" He pushed aside a pillow and sat up on his elbow to get the best angle of her face with his eyecam.

"The interview? I still don't understand why anyone would care about my personal life."

"Right now, they wouldn't," he admitted. "But once we flood the Neuronet with news of your inventions, trust me, viewers will want to know everything about you. To maximize the publicity, we'll have to leverage the twenty-four-hour news cycle—before the public's attention shifts."

"Will people really lose interest so quickly? I'm introducing life-changing technologies."

"*At most,* you'll get thirty-six hours. But I wouldn't bet on it. In fact, you may get less than twenty-four hours if Angelique changes her hairstyle or Wilfredo takes a semi-nude selfie."

"*Who?*"

"Pop celebrities. Look, it doesn't matter. My point is we'll need to move fast with follow-up pieces to reach the largest audience and cash in before interest wanes. Although, let's be realistic, with the patents on this tech, you'll be set for life anyway."

"It's not about the money," she said.

"Right."

"It's not. I plan to revolutionize the world, our world, just like I've changed v-Earth."

He snapped his fingers. "That's good! So we should portray you as a self-less humanitarian who's dedicated her life to helping others?"

"Melodramatically stated, but not wrong. That surprises you?"

"I don't know." To him, she seemed more mad scientist than philanthropic researcher. "I guess it shouldn't," he added quickly.

Best to press on, he thought, to expand on some of the items they'd covered in their earlier interview. "What was it like growing up in San Juan's tech valley in a broken home, an only child?"

She scrunched her face. "My parents decided not to renew their marriage contract when I was five years old, but their breakup was amicable."

"Then you worked your way up from poverty, graduated from MIT on a scholarship."

"Scratch the 'poverty' part. My tía left me a sizable trust fund, which allowed me to live comfortably and pay my tuition."

She reached over and ran her hand over his clavicle, over patches of discolored skin from the radiation treatments. "What's this?"

"It's nothing," he said. "I thought you'd accepted my AR modification."

"I've been with you before. I don't need to see some masked, polished version of your body," she said.

The turn in their conversation made him uncomfortable.

"And finally," he said, clearing his throat, "you reached the pinnacle of success with EncelaCorp—before the company wrongfully terminated you."

She looked away from him. "Do we have to mention that?"

"They treated you unfairly. And success is your revenge. Trust me, the public will eat it up. Everyone loves a good revenge story."

She turned her attention back to the device, studying its six corners, rotating it in her hands. "The Sallies have such long slender fingers. It makes this difficult to operate."

"At what point did you decide to give up on humanity in your simulations?" he said.

"After 153 sims with *Homo sapiens,* I realized I wasn't getting anywhere, so I went in a different direction."

"The Sallies are all female?"

"Mm-hm."

"How do they—?"

"Parthenogenesis. They're able to develop an embryo from an unfertilized egg. It's resulted in a unisexual species. I can describe how if you'd like."

Consumers would blink off if the conversation turned too technical, so he redirected her to a topic likely to be of more interest.

"Are the Sallies sentient?"

"In a sense. Layers of algorithms similar to the ones used to power our AIs run the sim. Without sentience, the Sallies wouldn't have the ability to think independently and problem-solve."

"So you've given them souls."

She rolled her eyes. "Let's just say they're programmed to think and feel. They have to or they wouldn't be of any use to us."

"Is what you're doing ethical? Inflicting so much suffering?"

"The suffering in my simulation? Weighed against all the tragedies of the real world?" She paused and stared out the window, setting down the device. It was still a few minutes before sunrise and the sky had a hint of blood-pink in it. "Would it be ethical *not* to conduct research that could help so many people? Children suffering from cancer. Displaced coastal communities facing climate change. A world plagued with so many horrible problems. No, the *simulation* of a sentient being is not the same thing as a sentient being. *Programmed* suffering is not real suffering."

"You could always create a better world for them. Let them live happier lives."

"To what end? Happiness doesn't breed creativity or ingenuity or invention. No, progress is borne out of a terrible struggle, a stew of agony and suffering. That's what makes them apex problem-solvers."

The apex problem-solvers. Pithy. Charlie would like that.

"I'll leave it to history to judge my actions."

History and our viewers, he thought.

Milagros was in a deep sleep the next evening when he crept out of the bedroom and ventured down the hallway. Tapping the mod on his temple, he played back in slo-mo his ret-recording of her fingers punching a long sequence of numbers on the door keypad. He pressed the same numbers, the steel door's lock clicked, and he pulled it open.

Although the inventions and the interviews would draw significant blinks, the story so far lacked sufficient entertainment value. The sheer volume of viewers might impress his bosses, but a story of this magnitude combined with the right demographics could provide him financial security for life. Plus, if Milagros's inventions proved a bust, he needed a safety net for his future. He'd been through too much to allow himself to wind up unemployed and on public assistance again.

Fortunately, he'd observed when Milagros programmed the cancer plague and the asteroid strike. And although he couldn't share his locked ret-recordings with anyone else, he could readily access them himself. He studied the playback of her fingers flying over the monitor and mimicked the movements precisely. Clearing his throat, he then delivered the appropriate voice commands and programmed a scenario likely to draw viewers from across a much wider demographic spectrum.

It was time to entertain the masses with good old-fashioned action.

He zoomed in to observe and record the activity up close.

Chapter 243: The Soulless Invaders from Beyond

On an ordinary morning like any other, the flying disks materialized over the city, hovering in the skies while massive crowds gathered to stare in wonder.

Pandemonium erupted.

The disks fired sizzling beams of light at towers packed with thousands of innocent workers, toppling the structures. This caused waterway tunnels to collapse, instantly killing thousands more.

Dozens of the disks landed, and from out of them emerged strange creatures—*abominations!*—blue-gray, dry-skinned and diminutive, with luminous eyes and wriggling antennae. Next to each of the creatures lumbered massive two-legged machines wielding bomb-launching weaponry.

Here, the history of the People becomes my personal history, for I was a child during the invasion, one among many in the panicked masses, clutching my mother's tail in terror. Central Clearedfield fell to the invaders while Mother and I retreated to the city's outskirts. And as much as I might try, I would never be able to forget the atrocities I witnessed on that dark day.

My mother served as a tactician in one of the underground thinknests tasked with developing a strategy to battle the enemy. Unlike the People of Jeh-win, the aliens could not fly without their vessels, so we feigned powerlessness, sustaining massive casualties for the sole purpose of drawing them out. Then House Jeh-win launched a furious offensive from the air, separating the aliens from their ships and allowing us to overwhelm them with our greater numbers. We used the modified Extractor to generate thick clouds, hindering the creatures' movements. Our soldiers carried portable Revivifiers to heal our fallen comrades, and we adapted technology from the planetary Deflector to create offensive weapons that obliterated the alien machines and sliced the creatures to shreds, leaving their disemboweled corpses rotting in the streets. United, we, the People, proved unstoppable.

Our soldiers boarded their vessels to try to turn their ships against them, but we found no operating systems within. The ships' slick walls bore no sign of any technology. And despite their coordinated movements, the invaders themselves possessed no apparent sentience. They operated as if they were soulless, animated automatons.

We initially believed the abominations had originated from outer space, but then determined the vessels had actually materialized *below* the planetary Deflector. It confirmed what everyone already knew: this was yet another Divine attack.

As the news of our victory swept through the crowd, my mother curled her tail around my waist, lifting me high in the air as the People hissed with joy. I stared up into the cloudless sky in that thrilling moment, lost in the cobalt blue. Then I spotted the dark figures descending from the heavens, shadows so massive they eclipsed the sun.

Devices employed by the thinknests to study the cosmos helped identify the dark smears in the sky. They were fingers. Colossal fingers. The fingers of God's righteous fist reaching down to smash the Earth.

—From *The Chronicles of House Jar-ella*,
excerpt by Lei-ani, daughter of Pin-ra

Cory awoke on the cellar floor, his head throbbing.

After recording the Sallies' great victory over the alien hordes, the last thing he remembered was programming the cosmic hands to give v-Earth a good shake. Viewers would enjoy the spectacle of the global catastrophe. He'd accelerated the Sallies' evolution to allow them to meet the new threat when a sudden electrical jolt had sent him flying backward.

He struggled to his feet. To his right, silhouettes danced against the blue glow of v-Earth, forms with transparent wings drooping at their sides.

He blinked and the shadows disappeared.

Blinked again, and they reappeared.

A dozen Sallies filled the cellar, staring dumbfoundedly at their surroundings and at the holo of their planet. He gaped at them, similarly astounded.

The Sallies had mods on their snouts and tails.

He brought his fingertips to his eyelid mods, tapped them. The Sallies vanished. *His retinal readers.* The Sallies appeared to be present in the room, but they'd somehow infected the Neuronet.

He sensed movement to his left. Milagros stood halfway down the cellar stairwell. "Cory?" she shouted. "What have you done?"

He blinked and the Sally leader disappeared. Blinked again and she stood nearer, locking eyes with him. A forked tongue with mods flicked out of the Sally's mouth, pressing against his eyelids.

My God, what was happening?

The cold, wet tongue retracted and time stood still. Then the Sally leader sighed deeply. "This explains so much." She turned to face Milagros. "Finally we meet face to face, Cruel God. I am Car-ling of House Jar-ella."

"How—This isn't possible!" Milagros said, tapping the mods on her face.

"You," the Sally said to him. "When you clutched our world in your hands every thinknest across the globe isolated the frequency of the projection and used the planetary shieldtech to trace the signal back to its point of origin. Here." The Sally waved her thin arms in the air, turning back to Milagros. "You turned us into the ultimate problem-solvers. And at last we've identified our ultimate problem: You."

"You're seeing her too, Cory?" Milagros asked.

"Y-yes," he said.

"All the meaningless suffering you inflicted on us," the Sally said.

"It *wasn't* meaningless," Milagros said. "Your suffering served a purpose. A noble purpose."

The Sally hissed.

"And it only made you *stronger*," Milagros said. "It was necessary. Part of a larger plan."

"A plan to help your people at the expense of mine."

An awkward silence followed. Finally Milagros answered. "I can make things better. I can reprogram the simulation."

"As can I," the Sally answered coldly.

Cory's heart thrummed as the realization set in: *The Sally had accessed his ret-recordings of Milagros programming the sim.*

A bright, swirling spiral whooshed open behind Milagros. On the other side of it, a crowded city teeming with waterways appeared.

Through squinting eyes, he saw the Sally move closer to Milagros until they stood face-to-face. The Sally pushed. And Milagros fell back through the projection.

The spiral flared. Cory shielded his eyes and when he opened them, Milagros was gone.

He blinked and blinked again. All the Sallies had vanished except for their leader.

"How—?" On the plexiglass divider a magnified image appeared of soldiers hauling a shackled Milagros through a crowd. Her dirty hair hung over her face. Days, if not weeks, must have already passed on v-Earth since her arrival. The mob rained acid spit on her, and she shrieked in pain, welts forming on her neck and bare arms. The Sallies ripped at their own skin and hurled chunks of flesh at her as she moved along the path toward an elevated platform. There, a ten-foot metal crucifix awaited her.

Cory turned away from the projection.

"We share much in common with you," the Sally leader said to him. "We, too, have known pain and cruelty at the hands of the Creator."

"I don't understand," he said. "Milagros didn't do anything to me."

She leaned down until her green-skinned face was an inch away from his. "Oh? Then you don't realize . . . ?" She said this with a half-laugh, half-hiss. "I'm talking about the *true* Creator. Millions of simulations up the chain. I aim to find her and make her pay." She directed her attention to the programming monitor and pressed a sequence of keys.

He turned and ran up the stairs.

Cory fled the house and called Charlie. An hour later, they both returned and Cory pushed open the unlocked front door and edged down the hallway. He poked his head down the stairs to the cellar.

Nothing.

They descended. There was no sign of the Sallies. No programming monitor. No hologram of v-Earth behind the plexiscreen. He scoured the cellar for the Extractor, the Deflector, the Revivifier—*No! The Revivifier!* Gone. All of it gone.

He touched his eyelid mods. His ret-recorders were blank. The Sally's tongue had somehow extracted the data. He could pulse a story based on his recollection of events, but without proof who would believe any of it?

Charlie didn't flatly accuse him of making it all up, but gave no indication he believed any of it either. His eye-lenses and temple nodes flashed red and blue—indicating incoming neuronews from his content providers—and he grunted when Cory came to the part where he slept with Milagros to get close to her.

"Never smart to cross that line," he remarked. "Clouds your judgment. Any idea where Dr. Maldonado ran off to?"

"I just *told* you, she—"

"Right, right. The lizard people kidnapped her. Did you hear EncelaCorp filed charges against her? Pulsed over the Neuronet a few hours ago. They turned up proof she stole some proprietary AI algorithms. No wonder she's on the run."

Stolen algos. That explained Milagros's reluctance to come forward too soon with the story. And why she wanted to reveal as many Sally inventions as possible to the largest reachable audience at one time. EncelaCorp's army of lawyers would have swooped in and claimed ownership of v-Earth, the Sallies, and every one of their inventions.

He checked every room of the house, every closet, every drawer, but the Sally leader had been thorough in removing any vestiges of v-Earth.

Cory decided to pulse the tale of corporate espionage: "Former EncelaCorp Employee Absconds with AI Software/Remains on the Run." It was nothing compared to the story that could have been, of course, the story of v-Earth and its miraculous inventions. And while it wouldn't draw anywhere near enough blinks to save his job, at least it might provide him with a decent final paycheck.

He relaxed his left eye and, sure enough, the flash he expected followed almost immediately. He blinked and Charlie's beaming face appeared.

"Nice work, Cory. You're already on pace for a million blinks," he said. "Not half-bad. I'm sorry I couldn't keep you on. No hard feelings?"

"We're good," he said. And he meant it.

With some luck, he might be able to scrape by on the income from his final story, for a short while at least. He considered telling Charlie about the pulse he'd received from his oncologist last night, about the tumors detected on his pituitary gland. The cancer had returned. But he saw no point in making Charlie feel any worse about letting him go. He'd beaten back cancer before and made it through terrible times. Sickness, hunger, homelessness. His pain had only made him tougher, stronger. He'd find a way to push through again. He had no choice.

"If you want to do a follow-up piece on the manhunt for Dr. Maldonado," Charlie said, "I might be able to pull some strings to—"

"There won't be any follow-ups. She won't be found."

"Mm-hm." He could tell Charlie still didn't believe him about v-Earth, but at least he was polite enough not to say so out loud. Charlie blinked hard and his eyes glazed over for a second. "Your piece just peaked at 1.1 million blinks, and is trending downward now."

"Not a bad sendoff."

"No, not bad at all. Look, Cory, if you ever need anything—"

"Thanks, Charlie. I appreciate it."

"You bet."

Cory blinked off and strode from his dining room to the snow-covered window. Another seven inches of August snow had fallen, the latest sign of climate change run rampant.

He'd been over it in his head countless times. The Sallies had found a way to cross over and infiltrate the Neuronet. That much he understood. But their leader had *touched* Milagros—an impossibility. For the Sallies to take solid form in our world defied the laws of physics. Yet . . . he had seen Milagros on v-Earth. Or had it simply been an image of her? But then how had she vanished? He had mulled it over for days and only one explanation made any sense. An explanation he refused to accept, but that haunted him. He recalled what Milagros had told him about the Simulation Hypothesis, the notion of our own reality residing within a simulated universe. If the Sallies had jumped from one simulation into another, if our own reality was *itself* a simulation . . . it would explain how the Sallies and Milagros could have made that fantastic leap between our world and theirs.

He thought of the Sally leader's final words to him, about moving up a chain of simulated realities to punish the Creator. The shock of discovering her world was a simulation must have driven her mad. He wished a Creator truly did exist, one he could make pay for all his bad luck, all the hard times. Even if his personal suffering were part of some grand plan, which he very much doubted, it wouldn't make it any more palatable. And it sure as hell wouldn't change the fact the so-called Creator was one cruel son of a bitch.

The snowfall intensified, the sky turning a solid slate-gray. He placed his hands on the windowpane and stared up at the clouds, at a peculiar patch of blue sky opening up. He squinted into the cobalt blue and imagined fingers—long, slender fingers the size of continents—reaching down to grind the world to powder.

Chapter 275: The Age of Peace

The historical tomes, including this testimonial, document the Ages of Turmoil, times when Mother Earth faced Divine assaults threatening her very existence. When the sky itself opened up and rained mountains. When plagues swept across the world and monsters descended from the skies. When billions upon billions of innocents died at the hands of the Cruel God. But then the People rose as one to kill the Cruel God and take the reins of their own destiny.

My mother and her devotional army disappeared years ago on a holy mission to find the gods' gods and bring them to justice.

I honor my mother and foremothers. I honor their courage and their ingenuity and their determination. They taught us to find strength within ourselves. And so we ushered in a new age, an age of stability and prosperity. Some argue we've become complacent, less productive, but after all we've been through, aren't the People entitled to some small measure of happiness? After all, on all the simulations we've programmed, the most successful civilizations are those that take firm control of their own fate to forge the path that lies ahead.

—From *The Chronicles of House Jar-ella,* Excerpt by Tey-kin, daughter of Car-ling, daughter of Lei-ani, daughter of Pin-ra, daughter of Zen-do, daughter of Shen-ri, daughter of Siss-ka, daughter of Und-ora, daughter of the Legendary La-rinda and all her blessed foremothers.

Bogi Takács (e/em/eir/emself or they pronouns) is a Hungarian Jewish author, critic, and scholar who's an immigrant to the US. Bogi has won the Lambda and Hugo awards, and has been a finalist for other awards. Eir debut poetry collection *Algorithmic Shapeshifting* and eir debut short story collection *The Trans Space Octopus Congregation* were both released in 2019. You can find Bogi talking about books at bogireadstheworld.com, and on various social media like Twitter, Patreon, and Instagram as bogiperson.

THE 1ST INTERSPECIES SOLIDARITY FAIR AND PARADE

Bogi Takács

I.

Name: Rita M
Age: 16
Occupation: Farmworker

I fill out the spreadsheet pinned to one of those antiquated clip-on boards. "Now I'll ask you a few questions that might seem unrelated," I start, going through my usual script. "The screening will take approximately ten minutes."

Rita M looks at me flatly, gives me the yet-another-clueless-adult glance. "It's pointless," she says. "I don't want to be recruited."

This is the third time someone turns me down today, and it's barely afternoon. My stomach clenches. We don't have time for this. We'll never fill our recruitment quota like this.

"That's fine," I say, and I somehow manage to keep my calm. "I'm not going to force you. Provide a reason and I'll put it in the spreadsheet, save you the hassle next time a recruiter comes around."

She shrugs, slowly, as if her two thick brown braids were weighing down her whole body. "Mom and Dad need me on the farm. We're barely making do as is, and Mr Hodász no longer takes the eggs and the corn." Another shrug. "I'm also not really interested in the aliens."

I believe her—all throughout our conversation, she never once glanced at the giant metallic sphere hovering next to me.

The two of us are taking one of the backcountry roads between farms—what used to be Győr-Moson-Sopron county back when Hungary still existed. Everything's almost entirely deserted; all the time we walk, we only meet one person going in the opposite direction, a dirt-smeared teen carrying a shovel. I stare downwards because I keep on slipping in the mud, but there's not much scenery to look at anyway. A weeping willow by the wayside, a crumbling stone cross, and once something that looks like an oversized bomb crater, somehow still not overgrown with weeds after so many years. Lukrécia floats next to me, sparing me the commentary. I'm angry and sad: angry that no one wants to be recruited for the alien communication team, sad because I see their reasons. Everyone is exhausted. After the first group of aliens destroyed everything, almost two decades ago, and the second group came to pick up the scraps, no one trusts that the third group is actually friendly. Even though they are not a singular empire or even the same species. They are of a wide variety of species and origin, and the only thing that binds them together is that their planets had been invaded like ours—by the same aliens as ours. Yet, no one believes that this time, we're all in this together. No one wants to come work with us. But we need to talk to each other, we need to find ways—we need to recruit more people . . .

After a while, I get frustrated enough that I start up a conversation myself.

"Do you think we'll find a candidate today? Not even an actual recruit, just someone we can take back to base for a longer evaluation?"

Lukrécia meows. She has this idea that humans will relate to her better if she pretends to be a cat from an eighties cartoon. I don't know how to tell her that this didn't work out for the second round of aliens, either. It has all been tried.

"Is that a yes or a no?" I grump at her.

"Neither," she says, her voice level. "It's an answer to a badly posed question."

She's so much out of character as a cat that I can't help snorting with amusement. "Lukrécia. You're a giant sphere, not a cartoon cat."

"I'm not a sphere. The sphere is my containment unit."

"I'm just telling you how you come across to people." I poke at her containment unit and almost fall over as I slip again. I could use better boots. I could use a different life, one with well-maintained roads.

"They're remarkably uncurious about me," Lukrécia says.

Now I'm angry with her, too. "They're trying to stay alive, give them some credit. They'd be curious if they had a moment of respite from all that labor, just a *moment*, really. We're a distraction."

We trundle in silence for a few minutes. The next time, I'm not the one who speaks up. "Do you think we should go into the city?" Lukrécia asks. If she's already buying into the human stereotypes about farmers and rural people, I'll be tempted to throttle her non-existent neck.

I shake my head. My anger will not serve any purpose here. Not anymore. *Those* aliens are gone. "I already made the rounds with Bubó," I say. "They couldn't spare anyone from the rebuilding."

She meows. "I don't mean Pannonhalma. I don't mean the town. I mean Győr. *The city.*"

I have approximately one hundred counter arguments. It's far. It's dangerous. The city is full of uncleared rubble and groups of militants. I will fall and injure myself, and we won't be able to get help. We won't be able to recruit among the scavengers. They'll try to hurt us. I will fall.

But we are sadly behind quota. No one from the farms or even the neighboring town of Pannonhalma wants to be recruited for extraterrestrial communications. I feel the quotas are unfair, but I'm terrible at management—and if I complain, people will just respond with "If you know it so well, organize it yourself."

I take a deep breath—it comes out more like a gasp than a sigh. "Tell you what. We do this last remaining farm today. There's an inn in Győrújbarát, they're renting out the cabins up the hillside, the old summer camp." Lukrécia doesn't protest. I go on. "We stay there tonight. Then we swing around and maybe we can get into the city from the west-southwest, following the river. Avoid the areas to the south."

"That sounds good," Lukrécia says, understanding the unspoken meaning better than some humans would: despite the anger that drives me forwards, I don't want to walk anymore today. My joints are feeling the strain. One sprain too many, one fracture too many. I'm just past thirty-five, but I also get injured more than most people. My ankles are shot for the remainder of my life, my knees hurt, and the only reason I'm out here and not back on base is that they had absolutely no one to spare, with new ships arriving daily.

"There is a paved road," she adds. "From Győrújbarát all the way up to Győr."

Is she being conciliatory? It's hard to tell. Her Hungarian is smooth, with a TV anchor accent—if we still had TV. But her emotions are a puzzle to me.

When I don't respond, she goes on. "We can walk comfortably all the way to the city outskirts, then try to cross the garden parcels to the river and head to the old freeway. Then we can just walk in. The road's wide enough to avoid an ambush."

"You've done this before."

"No, but that looks like the most reasonable route."

I'm not about to argue with her. I nod at the barns in the distance with my chin. "This one farm, and then we go to the old summer camp, get a good night's sleep."

Name: Bálint P
Age: 22
Occupation: Farmworker, mechanic

"Will the aliens come and help me get some of the tractors in working order?"

"That's why we're trying to set up ways of collaborati—"

"Can they come tomorrow? This week, at least? Can your friend over there help me get some spare parts? No? Tell me when they can help me out, then I'll see how I can help them out. I can't just go off to Pannonhalma on a whim, I'm needed here!"

Name: Andrea J
Age: 21
Occupation: Innkeeper

"You know what, I'd love to, but then who'll run the inn, my elderly grand-mother? The cabins are up on the hillside, if you didn't come when you were a kid." She tosses a key at me and glares at Lukrécia. At least she doesn't ignore the alien like most everyone today except the angry mechanic.

I'm not looking forward to the steps, but at least there are steps, and in reasonably good repair, too. Someone with a rake is sitting by the side, probably one of the staff taking a break: someone in her late teens, I think. We nod each other a quick greeting, then turn away. Surprisingly, the A-frame cabins look like they were renovated since my last time here—for summer camp in elementary school, just after second grade. Well before the first aliens came, when I was already a teen. But inside, the furniture is a hodgepodge, probably gathered from the village of Győrújbarát at the foot of the hills. Everything that wasn't blown to smithereens: glazed wooden cabinets from the Socialist years, a table that was clearly built for outdoor use, school chairs and a designer sofa that must have been pricey back in the day. I resist checking for a tag.

Lukrécia barely fits through the entrance. I kick off my boots and throw myself down on the sofa. At least we're not sharing with anyone else tonight.

An eight-bed cabin and no one wants to spend a night with the alien.

"You've been here before, is that correct?"

"Yeah. As a little girl." I turn on my left side. Lukrécia is hovering next to my bed. Her closeness doesn't bother me and I'm too achy to sleep yet.

"What was it like?" she asks.

"Terrible, I hated it!" I pause. "Fine, I liked the swimming pool."

"There is a swimming pool?"

"Down there." I make a vague gesture. "They might not have it anymore." I think back. "You know what, maybe I didn't like the swimming pool either . . . I liked the water. But the kids made fun of me. Because I was too clumsy. I don't know. One of the girls stole my enameled ring and I cried for hours." This is not the conversation that will help me calm down and fall asleep.

"I'm sorry they made fun of you," Lukrécia says. She's never made fun of me, ever. I wonder if she knows how. She probably does: her species is cognitively the most similar to humans, out of all the new arrivals. If all of them were like her, we wouldn't need to run around trying to recruit communications specialists.

"Thank you, Lukrécia. That's nice of you to say."

I'm sure people make fun of her. Of me. Behind our backs. But they're also afraid. The first time aliens showed up, they bombed everything. The second time aliens showed up, they were scavengers coming in to exploit a people left vulnerable, a people whose willingness to fight they underestimated. The third time . . .

The third time was "Hi, we've also been bombed by the people who bombed you. Maybe we could work together, become friends?"

A lot of humans didn't trust that. Especially as more and more aliens showed up, in scraggly beat-up spaceships; aliens of all shapes and sizes and species. Aliens who communicated by affecting the electromagnetic fields near your brain. Aliens who lived on the bodies of other aliens. Aliens who tried to convince humans that all magic was technology or all technology was magic, and then we all went down an endless rabbit hole of translation and mistranslation. A group expressed their wish of converting to Judaism. Another group asked if they could, kindly and consensually, chew on humans' hair. All of them were very enthusiastic about the fact that humans somehow managed to get rid of two waves of invaders, even though no one quite understood how. (Except maybe me and my boundless anger.)

By the time I get to the aliens who look like vintage Modernist carpets from Sweden, I finally drift off to sleep.

Name: Veronika B
Age: 72
Occupation: Innkeeper (retired)

"Yes, I'm interested in filling out the form," the elderly lady says. She has to be Andrea's grandmother.

"Would you be able to get to the base? We sadly don't have much by way of transportation." I try to sound more apologetic than combative. I did not sleep well. All that soreness.

"My dear husband has a carriage and two horses," she says. I perk up. Wouldn't the horses be missed here? A carriage is a veritable asset. But I just nod, as if I heard a variant of this every day.

"I'll ask you a few questions then."

She reaches out for my clip-on board. "I know what a survey form is. Just give it to me and I'll tick the boxes for you." She sighs. "Before the invasion, I used to be a sociologist."

Oh.

I hand her the board. I wonder if she also speaks foreign languages.

"Here you go." That was fast. She blinks at me. "How do you score this?"

I shrug. "By this point I have it all memorized."

"Ha! You can tell at a glance. I remember those days." She grins.

I look down on the sheet of paper, printed on both sides. I flip it around. Openness to experience, sensation-seeking . . . In these screenings, we are trying to measure who would be good at talking to the aliens. I barely have to look at her choices to know she's a solid pick.

She chuckles. "You know, I can guess what those items measure, and I can give you any desired score."

I grin back at her, finally more at ease. "That in itself would probably make you a good candidate."

Lukrécia purrs.

The retired innkeeper and her husband are not interested in driving into Győr with us in the carriage; besides, they have to pack up their entire lives. They know the way to Pannonhalma and the base is at the foot of the hill. They haven't seen the base before, but it's hard to miss, with all the landers parked around it. We say goodbye and off we go, on a cracked and occasionally caved-in—but mercifully paved—road snaking towards the north. So far so good. But we are still low on potential recruits, the base is understaffed, and everything is kind of falling apart. I'm glad I don't know what's going on back there, though I had such a weird dream last night, I can't help wondering if that in itself was a communication attempt. It involved three aliens of different species chasing each other in a circle, while screaming incomprehensibly.

We get to the southern outskirts of the city in good time, and we stop to stare at the ten-story concrete housing blocks. Someone passes us, walking in the opposite direction with brisk steps. I gaze at the buildings and try not to look like someone clearly not from here. Not any longer.

"You know, those blocks were supposed to last only for fifty years or so," I say. "They look in pretty good shape still."

"Some are inhabited," Lukrécia says. "You can see the laundry hung to dry."

I glare at the balconies, only open to one side. I can't quite see anything. Maybe a little movement, a flutter here and there. "If you say so."

"Should we go in?"

There is a veritable moat dug around the blocks of Communist-era housing. "I don't think we can cross that." I don't want to reproach Lukrécia, but she can float, while I can barely walk. For the umpteenth time, I fantasize about affixing a chair to the top of her sphere. Knowing my balance, I would probably fall off around the first corner. People say motor dyspraxia improves with age, but I feel like that's counterbalanced by the amount of injuries I keep acquiring over the years that never quite heal right.

Maybe it will all be different now. We'll have hospitals again. City centers clear of rubble.

Once we manage to convince all the aliens. The humans, too.

At least Lukrécia is convinced. "Then we'll go by the original plan and skirt the city around the west side."

More mud and treacherous terrain. At least the fences have by and large disintegrated with age, though there's always the odd chain-link that threatens to give me tetanus. I can't recall when I last had a booster shot. Before the first wave of aliens came.

"Let's go." I nod to the left, towards the mass of small parcels of land lying fallow, gardens gone to seed, the occasional storage shed or vacation cottage. I reach into a side pocket for my fraying gloves. "You take point."

It's easier going than I'd expected, but my expectations were low. Lukrécia simply pushes over the occasional fence with the bulk of her containment unit, and then I can tiptoe over the remains. There is a waist-high jumble of plants in places: bushes gone wild, determined perennials coming up year after year even with no one taking care of them anymore, invasives finally having free rein.

But I'm used to that and mercifully not allergic to ragweed, so I just stumble across the plots in my usual way, following Lukrécia. I'll have to check for ticks when we get to a place I can undress; I don't think any part of me is exposed besides my face, but they are sneaky little things and I don't think I'm up to explaining Lyme disease or tick-borne encephalitis to Lukrécia.

I find myself wondering if her giant sphere is resistant to bullets.

II.

We don't come across anyone until we're almost to the city, out on the freeway. I peel burrs off my camo fatigues and mentally praise the Bundeswehr for their clothing that lasts absolutely forever. I don't think Germany exists anymore, either; Austria certainly doesn't. But these camo fatigues survive. My knees are burning with pain—I sometimes feel that my pants will last longer than me.

We get to a barricade only when we're almost downtown, next to the old Science Education Society building.

"Hey, you, you there," someone yells from the top and clambers over using handholds I can't quite see. The sun's already set, and it's getting dark.

"You're the person who's been following us," Lukrécia notes, detached as usual.

Someone's been following us? "You could've thought to mention that," I groan at her. So much for alien communication. So much for me understanding Lukrécia, or her understanding me.

The person chuckles, pulls back their hat, and I realize we've met them at least three times already, always carrying a different implement. I feel that made them invisible to me, and I look away, ashamed. They laugh.

"I'm Lala," they say, and that's a boys' name, though I'm not entirely certain about Lala's gender.

"From *Fairy Lala*?" Lukrécia asks.

"*Humans* are not named after children's shows," I groan at the alien.

"From *Fairy Lala* indeed," Lala grins at us. "I wish I could watch the TV movie, the older people told me all about it. But the book was awesome."

I want to recruit him. It's not just because he could follow us without me noticing. I'm not the most perceptive person, especially when I'm spending three-quarters of my brain resources on not falling flat on my face in the mud. It's not just because of the modern classic about the young fairy prince with the human heart. It's because he comes across as cunning. Cunning *and* cheerful. Unlike me, the angry grouch.

I mutter something about the fairy X-ray machine scene in the book, and he laughs some more. Is he stalling for time? Waiting for an armed squad of scavengers to get to us? Waiting for his backup?

"You know why we're here," I say. I'm bluffing, but he has to know.

"Yeah, but I don't trust you," he replies, offhand. "I'll let you pass, and we have a place you can crash too. But I don't know who'd follow you to Pannonhalma."

He turns back towards the barricade and opens a door—makeshift, but with a proper lock. He ushers us through, and I can feel his gaze burning at my back.

I'm suddenly not sure who's doing the observing and recruiting here.

Inside, everything is remarkably tidy. Saint Stephen Road looks carefully swept, and someone planted flowers in the divider strip, almost like before. People nod at Lala as we pass by. Many of them openly stare at Lukrécia, but they don't seem hostile.

I'm struck by how varied a bunch they are only after a few minutes, when I almost bump into a Jewish man in Chasidic garb, with side-curls. How did they get here? Chasidic Jews didn't live in Győr before the invasion, did they?

I look around more bravely. I notice that the kids playing a very intricate version of hopscotch are Romani, two elderly women sitting on a bench are talking in a Slavic language—probably Slovakian?—and a man tells his dog to back off from Lukrécia in German.

"Wow, this is how Győr must have looked before the war," I tell Lukrécia. Or no one in particular.

"Before the invasion?" she asks.

"No, the *war*." I pause. "World War Two."

Mercifully, she doesn't ask me to clarify.

We are led to the old hotel on the corner of Baross Street. I never thought I'd stay there. It looks much dingier now, but overall not in terrible shape. I feel like a visiting dignitary.

I'm sure we are being overheard, but I don't care. I want to sleep, but I also want to talk to Lukrécia.

"I think they're spreading the rumors that Győr is a devastated hellscape so that people don't come to snoop," I tell her. I'm not sure how I feel about it. There are plenty of people in the countryside who could use a place like this, but somehow got left out when communication was disrupted. For every ethnic group I saw inside, there were people I saw outside, separate and lonely. *I* could use a place like this, and I'm an ethnic majority Hungarian. Not that Hungary is still around.

I try to refocus on what I have for now. I stretch out on the bed, nice and clean after a shower. I can't believe there's running water here, though the water pressure's terribly low.

"Why did they let us in?" Lukrécia asks.

I shrug. "For all I know, they're spying on us. Gathering intelligence."

Before I fall asleep, I wonder yet again—why do I even bother talking to the aliens? I used to think because I was from the last generation who grew up on sci-fi. But Lala read *Fairy Lala* . . .

Lala joins us for breakfast in the dining hall.

"What is this?" I poke at the flat brown . . . thing in the middle of my plate, smeared with some kind of light yellowish . . . thing.

"Fried eggplant," he chuckles. "With tahini sauce."

That's very much not a Hungarian food, though I'm sure eggplant grows here just fine. I wonder if Lala is Jewish, too—his hair is curly and dark. I feel bad about my instantaneous reaction to ethnically profile him. I'm twice his age. He's never known the country the way it was. He never had video games and social media and terrible national politics. I'm the sensible, responsible adult. If he's Jewish, so what? I'm disabled.

The eggplant tastes great, and I shovel it in with relish. I dab at my mouth with a fabric square; it's fancy if a bit faded after many washings. I blink at Lala. *Is* he Jewish?

"If you're trying to guess whether I'm trans, I'll save you the time," he says, grinning broadly. "I am."

I could sink under the floor in shame. I mutter some kind of apology, which only makes Lala grin even more. I need to change the topic, fast.

"How come you never saw all this from above?" I ask Lukrécia. "The town is clearly inhabited, and you have aircraft. You can fly."

"It appears we have much more to learn about human habitation patterns," she says. "We saw, we just didn't understand."

Lala chuckles, pokes at his own food with a slightly out-of-shape fork, something from a school dining hall rather than the formerly posh hotel. "We're trying to hide as much as we can. Food supply is tricky. We trade a lot. One of our main procurers vanished recently and we're all starting to get concerned."

I heard something about this in the villages. "Mr Hodász?"

He drops the fork with a clang. "You know him?"

"I talked to a lot of farmers lately. I haven't met him." Lala picks up the fork. I feel like I'm a constant source of disappointment. The responsible adult! I sigh. "The farmers miss him too."

I steel myself and go on. "We need to work together somehow. We came here to get some of you to work *for* us. But we'd rather work *with* you. And the villagers, too. Could you help us set up some meetings?"

I have approximately zero authority to say this, and neither does Lala, I'm certain. But if we can get people talking, something can be worked out. We can do this—

I notice with a startle that Lala looks gloomy. "I don't know if we can work more closely with the villagers," he says, and gestures at himself. "I wouldn't last a day out there without disguising myself. I can only do short trips, still." I don't understand. Because he's Jewish, trans, or from the city?

"People won't harass us with me around," Lukrécia adds.

Lala groans. "They're scared to death of the aliens, they just won't show it. You want to gain their trust, that's not the way to go."

The farmers didn't look scared to me, but maybe it was their defense. *Do not show fear.* I'm honestly not sure who's right here, Lala or me; and surely Lukrécia knows even less than I do. Or maybe the villagers were just so afraid for so long that after a while, they were too burned out to fear, but they wouldn't not-fear either. I know that kind of empty feeling all too well. Maybe Lala is right after all.

"Right now we're in three different groups, all isolated, barely interacting," I say. "Villagers, city dwellers, and us alien contact people in Pannonhalma. If we could all work together . . . "

Lala wipes his mouth elaborately with a kerchief and stands. "I'll be off. I have work to do. I'll see if I can send some people your way."

The unspoken message is clear, even to me, even now: don't hold your breath.

"He'll be back shortly," Lukrécia says, back in our room. "Remember, they are observing us."

I look around. There are any number of places to hide something. This was a hotel back in Communist times too. "Are they observing us right now?"

She meows. "I don't have the right sensors to determine that, but I wouldn't be surprised."

My knees are less painful this morning. I chance it. "Let's go for a walk."

The large fountain with the series of ponds is bone-dry, but both the old City Hall building and the Communist-era County Hall across from it are still standing, neo-baroque curlicues mirrored in modernist glass. This is the center of Győr, and maybe, maybe I can pretend the past twenty years haven't happened. But there are no skaters, no freerunners doing backflips from the stones edging the ponds, and the grass looks more like a vegetable garden than a lawn. Is this where they grow eggplant, I wonder; I know nothing about growing anything. It involves too many sharp objects and cooking them involves too many hot objects. The best I can do is yank out weeds, but even then, I tend to fall.

I found my niche with the alien contact crowd, and I don't think I'd last here very long. The patience afforded to me both among them and also here is all due to Lukrécia. But Lukrécia speaks fluent, primetime-news Hungarian so why am I even tagging along? I kick a pebble and it skitters across cracked paving stones.

I think out loud. "How do we get people to work together? Everyone has isolated themselves, dug in. It would take something really disruptive, like a catastrophe. Back in the day, we could work together when we were facing a common threat."

"There has already been a catastrophe," Lukrécia notes.

"Many years ago. But the balance stabilized. Into something that will just wear us down with time. We'll finish off ourselves, finish what the invaders started." Is it already happening? Mr Hodász vanishing, the trade slowing . . . Everyone growing increasingly weary of each other, even small differences appearing larger and larger . . . The city running out of food . . . The villagers working themselves into utter exhaustion . . . More and more aliens showing up and getting impatient, then frustrated, then angry . . . Who knows when people will start dying again?

"I wish Mrs B the sociologist was around, I'm sure she'd know the technical terms for this," I tell Lukrécia. "We're forgetting so much." My generation at least got to be teens before the devastation. But what about Lala and the teens his age? We were called Gen Z, but there isn't even a term for his generation.

Pacing is too hard. I sit down on the steps to the fountain.

"Our planet was destroyed," Lukrécia says after a long silence, and I'm not sure if she's trying to one-up me or commiserate. She's my closest confidante, and I don't know her at all.

We walk to the riverside, just a few smoothly curving streets to the north and west. I can still do this. I want to see my favorite spot, from way back.

"I will not engineer a disaster," I say to the river. "It would bring people together. But we've all been traumatized enough already." Lukrécia hovers next to me as I wobble down the narrow concrete steps to the water, holding on to the simple railing. The walk was short, but these steps cut into the grassy riverbank are treacherous. Yet I feel compelled to descend, to be closer to the river. I haven't been here for many years. I used to sit on these steps a long time ago, whenever I had a gap in my school schedule, and sometimes even when I didn't.

But what else could bring people together if not a disaster? Some other kind of mass event? Could we bring back something like that?

I think of how the townspeople used to march around downtown Győr every year with the relic of Saint Ladislas, singing Catholic hymns. I did it a few times with my family. I knew some of the hymns, even though I wasn't big on church. It was surprisingly uplifting: the singing crowd as it moved along the streets up the hill, down the hill, by the river—a snake made of people, undulating . . .

The Basilica was bombed from orbit, a pinpoint strike.

"Hey, I was looking for you," Lala yells from behind. I turn, barely manage to grab hold of the railing by the steps in the last moment. It holds; after decades of neglect, it still holds. I don't roll down the slope and into the water.

"She hasn't been here in a long time," Lukrécia says. "She's reminiscing."

"I'm thinking about how to bring the three groups together," I say in my best complaining tone, but I'm still shaky after the near-fall. My voice wobbles just as much as I do. "I was reminded of the march of Saint Ladislas. I liked that, but that was for Catholics."

He hop-skips down the steps. "What was that?" He has to be Jewish, I think, it's impossible not to know about the march of Saint Ladislas if you're Catholic, or even secular. But then he shakes his head and laughs, making a guess why I'm surprised about his ignorance. "I'm from Komárom, originally. My parents are still there, I moved here with a caravan two years ago." He shrugs. "Wanted to venture forth. I have no idea what Győr was like, before."

To venture forth? He probably wanted to live in a place where fewer people had known him before he transitioned, I think to myself, but say nothing.

Then something clicks into place and I have to hold on to the railing again. I have an idea. If I can keep myself from falling into the water before saying it.

"Hey, I'll help you up," Lala says, "I don't know how much punishment that rail can take."

I stare at him. "A Pride parade! We could do a Pride parade!"

He laughs. "Have you seen the pictures?"

"What pictures?" I'm perplexed.

We step into the old cinema building that hadn't ever served as a cinema even in my own lifetime. Even before the invasion. I visited maybe once, back when it was used as a concert hall for the Győr Philharmonic. I barely remember how it looked, but it certainly didn't have these wheeled display boards you could pin things on, the kind that were ubiquitous when I was growing up and never seen again.

It feels like all the lost display boards of the universe have gathered in the lobby. They're mostly filled with drawings pinned to them, but there is the occasional photo, and I wonder who can still make those and how. I vaguely recall something about chemical baths and dark rooms. I step closer.

The drawings are colorful, even rainbow-y, and they run the gamut from cheery children's abstraction to more realistic portraits, all with the same bright palette. Some of them show people marching, the backdrops usually barely sketched, but I notice the more recognizable downtown buildings here and there: the Carmelite church, the Turul bird monument on that little square in front of the train station . . . Some are portraits of individuals, couples, smaller groups.

The labels glued under the drawings are eerily reminiscent of the sheets I have been filling out. They identify the artist, sometimes also the people in the drawing. There is no "occupation', but there is a line or a paragraph of quotes for everyone: about love, hope, resilience. There are also some sheets entirely covered by quotes, tiny sketches, encouraging messages.

I turn back to Lala grinning at me.

"You've already had a Pride parade," I say.

"Two," he says, shrugging. "We tried. It was an idea to bring people together."

I don't think there were any Pride parades in Győr before the invasion. Maybe someone else also took inspiration from the March of St. Ladislas?

Lala doesn't quite realize how odd all of this is for me. It's like this formerly conservative city turned upside down in my lengthy absence, and I'm here for it.

"I thought I had an original idea." I shrug back.

Lala chuckles. "Well, *we* did not try to involve the aliens . . . "

Lukrécia hovers closer. "Tell me about this idea. I want to know how to bring people together."

This is Lala's moment, and he goes on a long-winded, rambling explanation. Lukrécia makes the occasional encouraging noise, and I keep myself busy looking at the pinboards.

"So, what better symbol of hope, uh . . . celebrating our differences." Lala waves his hands, concluding. The dust we stirred up in the lobby twinkles like glitter in the sunlight. "And besides, I know everyone on the organizing committee."

That's great. Not the least because he doesn't seem to know anyone in the town's actual leadership. Though there are such things as formal power and informal power—again I find myself wishing for Mrs B the sociologist. Maybe we can bring her.

I remind myself that if this works out, we'll be bringing everyone.

It doesn't take long for Lala to gather the committee in the orchestra hall, find some tables and chairs. I expect the Pride committee members to look outrageously glamorous, but most of them look like they've been dragged away from working on their vegetable patch or hauling salvage. They're more like the crustpunks of yore than David Bowie. Lala tells me there are still a lot of collapsed buildings both further to the north, and also south of the train station. I feel bad—I assumed that just because the city hall area was preserved, surely everything else must have been, too. Even though I knew the Basilica was destroyed.

One of the committee members clears his throat. I can't remember his very ordinary Hungarian men's name. He's a grizzly old man, he looks about seventy, which probably means he's around sixty at most. People have just been aging faster with all the hardships; my mind will probably never quite recalibrate to that.

I try to pay attention. I explain haltingly that we all need to work together. They look skeptical, but when I get to the Pride bits, they seem to show more interest. This is their topic.

I get so enthused that I try to push for a march as soon as possible, but a younger woman in a headscarf waves me down. "What you have in mind is a one-time, symbolic event, but you also need to think about the lead-up to it. The preparations are just as important, and the more people get involved, the better."

A young person offers, "People who are skeptical will wait just to see what would happen. They won't cause fuss in the meanwhile."

"Either that, or they'll mobilize to attack the march," the grizzly old man says. I think he must have been to Budapest Pride back in the day.

Lukrécia speaks up. "They won't attack. They're afraid of us."

I bite my tongue. Isn't that the exact impression we are trying to work against here?

People start speaking all at once, and for a moment I'm sure the meeting will devolve into disorder, but the woman in the headscarf leading the session bangs on the table and everyone falls silent.

Order is restored after that, but as the meeting goes on and on and on, my thoughts drift. I have little more to add, and what I could say, I keep to myself.

I'd rather not mention that I have been wondering if purely physical proximity to the aliens can cause humans to be more understanding. I vaguely recall pheromones from high school biology, before the world crashed on us. But would pheromones work across entirely different physiologies?

Lukrécia is entirely enclosed in a metallic globe, but there are some aliens who can live on Earth unprotected. And some who are experimenting with parasitic relationships with humans. Parasitic? That's not the right word. I search my brain, symbiotic? There was also something else in high school, about how animals eat from a common table . . . Commensalism? Mutualism? I'm honestly not sure. There was a chart . . .

Then the meeting gets to the topic of the surrounding villages, and before I manage to refocus, people have already made a decision to organize some kind of county fair instead of the parade.

Instead of?

Combined with, it turns out.

This will be a busy summer season, and for once I'm glad that the long-term weather has taken a cooler turn with all the dust the invaders kicked up when they bombed us.

III.

Rita M, who turned down the screening, is now staring at me again with all the skepticism she can muster. "A fair. And this is going to help us exactly how? Besides, you said if I put my name down, you won't come back to hassle me."

I shift my weight from one leg to another uncomfortably. Did I walk all the way back here for this? "We're not here to recruit you this time," I tell her. "We're here to help you sell your produce." I try to keep it vague. I know very little about agriculture—I feel like I've been living an isolated life in the alien compound, even with all the recruitment trips.

"At the fair, we'll be able to connect you with wholesale buyers. And it's a one-time event," Lukrécia says.

The girl finally looks at the sphere, tilts her head sideways. "Are *you* interested in eggs?"

"You mean a tractor exhibition?" Bálint P blinks, rubs his forehead with the back of his hand.

"With a spare parts market," Lukrécia says.

He turns rapidly to her sphere, and it's as if all the anger's gotten wiped off his face.

"All in one place," I add meekly.

"People would stay here?" Andrea asks, twirling a keyring around her fingers.

I nod. "We were thinking of using the old campground as the fair-grounds . . . ? By the foot of the hill? And people could stay in your cabins up the hill?"

"I'm sure you'd run the inn at full capacity for the duration of the fair," Lukrécia offers. "And some of those visitors might be interested in coming back later, too."

We stay in one of the old kids' cabins overnight—it's a big ask to use the grounds, so we might as well give the inn a bit more business in the meanwhile.

By the time I finally get to bed, I ache all over. So much walking! I wish I had enough balance to ride a bike, but the roads are in such bad shape, it might be pointless anyway. And there's no reason to go all the way back to Győr before we talk to the aliens.

I startle, and my legs twitch.

Lukrécia hovers closer. "What happened?"

"I was just thinking about everything, while falling asleep. And I realized, when I was thinking of *we*, I was thinking of you and me . . . " I'm probably too sleepy to explain anything. "I don't think we are aliens. To each other. Anymore." I turn towards her, even though my whole body protests, and my arms get tangled in the fluffy blanket. "I mean we've been friends. For a while. But. I just instinctively thought of you as . . . like me. Like here are *us*, and there are the *aliens*."

"I assume that's good," Lukrécia says, ever so patient. "I do believe you should sleep, though."

I fall asleep to her slow purring.

At the compound, we meet Mrs B before anyone else—she comes up to us, her face glowing with eagerness. "The two of you gave me my life back," she says. "Finally, something meaningful to do!"

I'm quite sure that fixing machinery and keeping chickens is also mean-ingful, but I don't feel up to a debate with her. I vaguely nod, and she takes this as encouragement.

"I immediately noticed that our problem was organization, or rather the lack thereof," she waves towards the base. "There are many projects, but they are not coordinated. People hide the lack of organization with forceful demands."

I nod, thinking of the quotas I've always felt were impossible to fill.

She goes on: "So I designed a communication needs survey, and administered it to everyone with the aid of the nice young people here. When we could not communicate with certain individuals at all, we put that. Then we could identify areas of immediate need . . . "

We walk inside. She provides me with the verbal equivalent of a wall of text, and I like listening to her. I get the impression she's neuroatypical like me, just in a different way. Is she autistic? Does she have ADHD? She probably knows all the terms for everything, but that would be a different wall of text. Maybe we can do that next time.

"How much do you know about folklore?" she asks me abruptly.

"Uh, why?" I feel like all I know about folklore, I learned from video games, back when we still had them.

"There is one group with a device that they cannot operate. It's not a translator per se, the closest we got was some kind of "telepathy machine', but I'm questioning the use of the term. Their communications officer died in transit, and now they're looking for someone similar to use the device. They told me to find them a *witch*!" She laughs. "So just in case this isn't *another* mistranslation, I was wondering if you could find me a witch."

I'm not surprised by anything at this point. "I'm sure there'll be plenty of opportunity for that at the fair," I tell her.

"What fair?" She looks apprehensive at first, but in under ten minutes, she becomes our biggest advocate.

The riverside by the Carmelite church in Győr is calm and quiet. Save for Lala, Lukrécia and me.

"We convinced the city leadership," Lala says, talking animatedly and pacing on the concrete-block fence on top of the flood bank. "I felt the arguments were a bit on the utilitarian side, but hey, everyone likes fresh produce." He makes a face. "So, if your people are in, my people are in."

I nod at him cheerfully from below—if I tried to get up there, I'd fall. "Remember I was telling you about the elderly sociologist lady? We ran into her again and it turned out she'd made friends with literally all the aliens in just a few days. They loved her. She thought that the fair and parade would be a great idea, so all of a sudden everyone was on board." I chuckle. "Now we only need to find her a witch."

Lala blinks, then bursts out in laughter and hops down. "A witch?"

I explain, with big, sweeping gestures. I even lose track of my utter exhaustion for a while.

Lala scratches his head. "Sanyi is handy with a dowsing rod, would that count?"

I stare at him in bafflement. He turns apologetic. "We don't have the old utility maps. Do you have any idea how hard it is to dig downtown without hitting a pipe?"

I'm shocked: "But that's like . . . superstition. Pseudoscience?"

Lala giggles. "He's still pretty handy with it though!"

I figure Mrs B can run a controlled research trial. My job is just to get people to talk to each other.

IV.

I imagined something organized and tidy; something beautiful that emerges from the collaboration of thousands of different people.

What emerges from the collaboration of thousands of different people is a giant mess.

Many of the aliens grasp the concept of a parade, but clearly don't understand about floats. A giant snake slithers on top of Bálint's tractor, which has been decorated with ribbons like a maypole, then crushes the entire vehicle. Bálint starts to weep. Witchy Sanyi turns out to be one of the grizzled crustpunks from the city council and the impatient aliens have him try the machine right then and there, in the middle of the crowd, which results in him projecting his emotions over a twenty-meter radius. He is apparently very hungry. The people near him mob Rita's family stall that sells corn-on-the-cob and topple it over. A chicken brought for display escapes, until it is caught by a many-tentacled and triangular alien, who has some kind of dramatic reaction to it. Body fluids are involved, and people yelling "Let me through, I'm a doctor', but the alien waves them away with three tentacles on three sides. I wonder if I'll ever find Mr Hodász. He could be making a killing in trade at the fair, but he doesn't seem to be here, according to every farmer I asked. I wonder if you can find people with a dowsing rod, and I make a mental note to ask Sanyi or Mrs B about this later; once they have both eaten their fill of corn.

I wasn't very closely involved with the organizing in the final stages, so now I try to relax and move with the erratic, sputtering flow. I walk through the entrance, under a gorgeously elaborate sign saying "THE 1st INTERSPECIES SOLIDARITY FAIR AND PARADE." It sways as people of various species bump against the entryway. Someone is carrying a bunch of signs clearly repurposed from the Pride parade and gets tangled in a clutch of kids' balloons. I haven't seen balloons in at least a decade, but someone must have been stockpiling them. I thought they wouldn't last so long, but maybe there is a way to store them . . . Or were the aliens printing them on one of their ships? I can't even think of that conversation. How do you explain 'balloon' when you can barely communicate about your immediate needs?

"I thought an *apocalypse* would finally get us to give up *plastic*," someone my age in a sparkly dress grumbles next to me. I shrug apologetically. I'm looking around for Lala. I spot him with a very tall person handing out signs. Lala gets one saying "FAITH, HOPE, CHARITY" in rainbow letters above what looks like a very complicated version of the trans symbol.

I remember *that* slogan from somewhere—for a moment I feel something go crosswired in my brain as I dredge up the right memory from an age gone by. "The three Catholic virtues, huh?" I nod at him, half-yelling in the noise. The unknown sign-maker must have been missing the march of St. Ladislas.

He looks at the sign in puzzlement. "Are they?" He glances around, but the person has already been carried away by the crowd. "You know I'm Jewish, right?" he yells back.

I shrug. "I guessed. Here, I'll take it." Not that I should be carrying a large sign. It looks like a recipe for injuring others.

"Are you Catholic?" he asks.

"I was baptized . . . "

He shrugs, too. "I was also baptized" He chuckles at my confusion. "My great-grandma said you needed to have the right documents."

"Even in an apocalypse?" I look around. A cream-colored butterfly lands on my shoulder, then another.

"Especially in an apocalypse."

But we don't get to think about the grim moments of Hungarian history, because a large metallic sphere rolls past, the size of Lukrécia's, but with a brass tint. It's very much not floating or doing anything that it's supposed to do. And it's being chased by a Chasid and an Austrian farmer, who are yelling at each other in what sounds like the same language, be it Lower Austrian German or Yiddish. They finally catch the sphere and steady it. They pat it and rumble at it in an oddly parental way. How do you say "it's going to be all right" in Yiddish? I suppose exactly like that.

We stare, stunned, until Lukrécia floats calmly next to us, saying, "I was wondering if that 'first' on the sign above the entrance was a promise or a threat."

"I don't think anyone's going to forget this day anytime soon," Lala nods at her. He's smiling, and he looks more relaxed than ever before, despite all the chaos and noise.

"Isn't that the kind of thing that's supposed to bring people together—shared memories . . . ? Or commiseration?" I try to ask, but my voice is drowned out first by the collapsing gate, then by the buzzing of three flying aliens trying to keep the pieces from tumbling into the crowd. I shiver—how lucky that they were in the right place at the right time . . .

"If we make it through all this without anyone getting injured, that will be a miracle in itself," I tell Lukrécia once the gate is safely dismantled.

"Fret not," Mrs B says from behind me. "My precognitive squad is doing double duty."

"That didn't save Bálint's beloved tractor," I grumble at her, because it's still easier to be grouchy than to be astonished. Even if my anger is dissipating.

"We'll get him a new one," Mrs B says, biting into a cob; and I don't need to ask her who is *we*.

It is *us*, all of us, from now on.

Adrian Tchaikovsky is the author of the acclaimed ten-book Shadows of the Apt series, the Echoes of the Fall series, and other novels, novellas, and short stories including *Children of Time* (which won the Arthur C. Clarke award in 2016), and its sequel, *Children of Ruin* (which won the British Science Fiction Award in 2020). He lives in Leeds in the UK and his hobbies include entomology and board and role-playing games.

OANNES, FROM THE FLOOD

Adrian Tchaikovsky

I choose that moment to close my eyes against the rising motion sickness I'm getting from the Avatar system. All too much, for just a moment. The second-hand clutch of the silty water. Claustrophobic loom of the broken walls. Sensory data relayed imperfectly through badly calibrated feedback. Visibility practically nil anyway; what would I be missing?

Opening my lids and a great stone paw is reaching for me. From the Avatar's vantage point it's about to claw my eyes out. Cue yelp of primeval fear from a professional archaeologist who should know better. But the Faculty rushed the training, didn't have many people they could call on, short notice. I never signed up for this kind of technology when I was studying.

Jetting backwards I ram the insanely expensive piece of kit into the wall, and a fresh curtain of clouding dust filters down from the ruin above. I freeze, because it's a toss-up whether the flood water is bringing this place down or actually holding it up. No great slide of masonry descends to bury my remote self or those of my fellow researchers.

Researchers.

Tomb raiders.

Thieves. Call it what it is, we are nothing but thieves. But our cause is just, I swear to God. We steal from the past that we may gift to the future. Or that is how Doctor Sakhra puts it.

And the Doctor, leader of our bold expedition, is in my ear now, demanding to know what my problem is. She is tense as a wire, an old woman so tough you'd think she was carved out of hardwood. She belongs, as the old American film has it, in a museum, but that museum is short of people with the daring to helm this kind of scheme, so here she is, on a boat. She's right behind me, could reach out and prod me in the shoulder with her iron-hard finger. Except that I'm immersed in the Avatar interface. I'm not *here*. In my head, I'm *there*, and I've got to stay *there* and keep my eyes open or I really am going to crash this piece of junk and put myself out of a job.

"Hassan, what?" comes Yasmin's voice. "I'm seeing damage. Comms systems. Can you hear me?"

Majid's trying to say something too, probably not complimentary. He's had the most training on Avatar rigs, military before demobbing into academia. He forgets that some of us only got two weeks' practice before shipping out here.

"I'm fine." I get my bearings, turning the Avatar about, finding that claw. A statue, of course. Kneeling, winged, androgynous, of a style I'm more than familiar with. A thing of Ancient Sumer, font of civilizations, cradle of myths. To the man who bought it and shipped it to moulder here, just one more piece to add to an overstuffed collection. To us, priceless. And yet we must leave it. We couldn't possibly move so large a treasure. It's not what we're here for.

"Structural warning, more shift from the building. That's the third time," from Yasmin. "Go, go," from Majid.

"I'm going." And I don't like the dark water swirling with suspended dirt. I don't like the sense of the weight, three floors of broken building hanging above us and our seismometers telling us of every little shift. But that's exactly the reason we *have* to go now.

I've just got the bile of motion sickness swallowed down again when I run into the body and stifle a fresh yelp. Shame at embarrassing myself in front of the others looms larger than my revulsion. I master myself, press on. It's floating near the buckled ceiling, which is far too close overhead. A dog, I see, probably dead before it got dragged down here by the water. Nibbled by fish, bloated and unclean. But I am glad, I am so very glad, because it could have been a human being. Because since the floods came and they redrew the state lines to exclude these disaster areas, plenty people over here have died. Died in the flooding, still dying now.

"You should be close to the main repository rooms," comes Doctor Sakhra's dry, calm voice in our ears. She's not piloting anything. She doesn't have a robot's senses crowbarred into her head, not sure where her hands are, where she's stepping. Easy for her to be calm and dry when she's not the one in the panicky dark water.

I try to pay attention to the map overlay she's feeding us. Majid's talking about air pockets, rooms holding out against the waters.

"Easier for us if so." Yasmin sounds detached. "This model, they never quite finished converting it for underwater use, yes?"

"Now you tell me this?" I demand, and she cackles in my ear.

"Keep moving," Majid snaps, like he's in charge, still in the army. But I keep moving. The treasures of the ancient world pass by on either side, a corridor of exhibits on haphazard display. But what we're seeking never came out of storage these thirty years.

Doctor Sakhra Faisal Hussein of the new-founded Baqir Institute of Archaeology, Baghdad. A controversial figure in the field, without question. No give in her. A reputation for getting up the noses of her colleagues. But her hard old elbows had levered her to head up the Institute's Faculty of Sumerian Studies; her elbows, and some highly off-the-record promises about what she might bring in for study. Promises leading to my current predicament on a boat off this new-drawn coast. And, simultaneously, below a mansion house in mid-collapse, exploring a labyrinth of submerged cellars.

But it is worth it, for old Sumer. You should hear Doctor Sakhra talk about it - such fire replaces the dry sarcasm! And the climate back home is favourable for scholars like her, who talk of the great half-lost past of our nation. It was not always so but, even when her profession was not so honoured, somehow both she and her fire survived intact. That same fire which leapt from her to me, to Yasmin and Majid, and had us all burning for the glory of old Sumer. The ur-culture, the lords of the Mesopotamian dawn, the authors of Gilgamesh. They were the first, in so many ways. And yet perhaps not the first, if their earliest stories might be sifted for a few grains of truth.

We have split up, in this drowned maze. Majid already has a storeroom, flooded. I call his camera feed up, seeing shattered jars, crushed bronze cases, the drifting tatters of sodden scrolls. Pieces of the ancient world forever lost. Yasmin has a door that is not yielding to her, buckled by the flood and now sealed. I have rubble, but my sonar says there is a way over, says there is air ahead.

And our prize? We have no firm inventory. The wealth of a dozen dead cultures might be about to greet my robot eyes. Or nothing. Or just dust pressed beneath fallen concrete.

Yasmin reads out the latest seismic data. Minute traces of further settling above us. Minute traces can turn into major traces so very quickly. "Do we have time?" I feel the weight press down on me, even in the boat.

"We have time," says Majid. "If God wills." Less than reassuring. "But move, now. Radio band says the locals are asking each other what our boat's for. We have time; we must hurry." And I am trying to get the Avatar's clumsy body up over the rubble. Slip, scrabble, claw and fight against the water, against the moving earth.

I think about when we brought the boat down the coast. How it all looked. Miles of beachfront real estate, Louisiana, Florida, gone the way of Atlantis. Cruising over roofs and ruins, where the water was clear enough to see them. Unspeakable flotsam, all the lost things that had been parts of people's lives. Broken buildings like broken teeth jutting from the waves. Lines strung between them, sheets and spars where those too poor to get out had climbed up and made their camps. And I thought of the dig sites I had worked on, where three thousand years had left more of a place intact than this I now beheld.

It was the flood defences that doomed them, Yasmin said. Sea levels went up, they just kept building the barriers higher like it would work forever. When the defences failed, they failed all at once, and what might have been a creeping tide was a tsunami. Thousands dead. Thousands more trying to find a dry square metre of roof or upper floor in some rich man's fancy house, because any lesser house got washed away, got drowned. No power, no law, just army building fences where the dry land starts. And sometimes a rich man coming back for his treasure. That is one more shadow we're under, right now.

When I breach out of the water it's through a curtain of murk, and then I'm abruptly pushing against a medium no longer restraining me. The Avatar lurches forwards, skids onto its chestplate; visual feed breaking up for a second, me terrified I've wrecked it. Then diagnostics sort themselves out and I'm staring at a floor, filthy but dry. I flail a bit until I get the limbs working again and stand up.

And see.

"Beautiful," I breathe. The mother lode.

Our man here, whose big house this is, he loved the having of things more than the doing anything with them. His agents and teams, they ran around the world buying or just seizing whatever caught his interest. Often, they came in the second wave after the soldiers, like vultures do. Like thieves. Like we came here, after the waters rolled in. We're all opportunists. A generation ago, in our country, we had too much history and not enough law. This man and his fellows, they were very concerned for all our history. Concerned what might happen to it in the riots, in the fighting. Or what we ourselves might do to it, they said. Not fit stewards for the world's heritage. And can I say there was no justification for these statements, made by rich, self-satisfied men halfway around the world? Can I say artifacts were not sold off by officials in those days? Defaced, mislaid, crushed beneath the treads of a tank? I was a child then, but you don't forget how it was. So very concerned for our history, they all were. So much was at risk from all the chaos the soldiers tracked in on their heavy boots.

So very concerned he was, that he bought or rescued or sometimes, let us say things how they are, stole these things so as to protect them. So very concerned, that these things have lain here in a windowless room, its heavy security door sprung out of its frame now as the masonry above compacted into it, as the waters battered at it. Enough that even an Avatar frame can claw its way in.

My lamps, which had illuminated a very fine selection of nothing on my passage through the waters, now pick out the clutter of this room. A lot has fallen over, shelves have collapsed. Some of that priceless history is in pieces on the floor. *Not the tablets*, I pray. *If God wills it, please not that.* Because we do not have the time for a jigsaw puzzle and I do not have the dexterity with these my remote fingers. Everything in this room is skewed, squeezed out of shape when the wave hit the building above. A little water got in through the ventilation before those pipes were clenched shut. The scent of damp and rot is in my nose even though the Avatar can't smell anything. But Sumer wrote its histories in stone, and stone endures.

"Hassan?" Yasmin asks. "Your camera feed is breaking up."

Even as I get the Avatar's legs in motion, I see a tilted shelf ahead. Tablets on it. Six, no seven, half a metre on their longest side. I approach, trying to open the Avatar's storage—a little like trying to pull your own stomach out. I have seen grainy black and white photographs of what we're looking for. I have tried to study Ancient Sumer's earliest days from those poor reproductions. I know what I am seeing.

From those tablets, Oannes stares sidelong past me: bearded human face beneath fish head, fish body draped over his back and shoulders like a cloak, as much of the waters as he is of the land. Knee-height to him are six others, rendered identically save for the varying gifts they bring. Time and wear mean the unassisted eye cannot be sure what they are bestowing. Beside those carved figures, the writing. The triangular stylus marks of Sumerian script and, towards this tablet's worn edge, another column, similar but different. A related script. An older script.

The Oannes-Abgal tablets were unearthed during the occupation. A young Doctor Sakhra had just enough time to photograph them and speculate on what they might be, before they were whisked away on a tide of money and military contractors. But she never forgot.

Oannes, whose people, the Sumerians say, came to gift wisdom at Sumer's very dawn. Oannes, man and fish, water creature or creature fleeing the waters. Bringing to Sumer the great secrets: planting and building, writing and measuring, science and numbers. All these things brought to Sumer, whose great myth-cycle of Gilgamesh would accrete like a pearl around an earlier story of a world-ending flood. The telling of which would ripple out across the ancient world, finding many homes and many versions. A story that was old when ancient Sumer was young.

And civilization dawned many times across the globe: China, Mesoamerica, India. How many more ur-cultures are preserved only in the stories of ancient peoples for whom those *others* were the ancient peoples? But Sumer was special to us. Sumer was *ours*, our own ancestors, our history, the secret ancient bedrock running invisibly beneath our modern nation. And, now the tides of history and the changing climate have brought an unexpected greening to us even as it has brought ruin to so much else, we have come to take it back. We have come, just as that rich man once came, to take these relics from hands that can no longer preserve them for posterity.

Seven tablets, as Doctor Sakhra remembered, except there are not seven. I adjust the camera settings, fighting the waves of static. There are eight, nine, twelve of them. Our collector found more, back then, than Doctor Sakhra was ever permitted to lay eyes on. I am relaying all this excitedly as my visual feed shakes and fizzes.

"What a problem to have," Yasmin whispers. "Embarrassment of riches, yes?"

"Start loading, Hassan," from Majid, always practical. "We are on our way. Maybe we make two journeys."

"Seismic says—" Yasmin starts.

"Two journeys," he repeats. "God willing." And they are abandoning their own finds, and I can hear Doctor Sakhra breathing hoarse in my ear. All her work, her words, her chicanery on both sides of the law, and here is the fruit of it.

I can't get my storage open, the catch bent from my earlier collisions. Switching to the hand-camera, I lever at the magnified clasp until it springs open, hoping it will close as obligingly. As the little finger-mounted eye swings my view around the room, I see faces.

Not Majid, not Yasmin. Their faces are on the boat with the rest of them. But human faces, filthy and thin. For a moment, with the disorientation of the hand-cam, I can't work out where they are, but then I'm swinging my whole remote body round, and I see.

Up against the far wall where the shelves have collapsed entirely, where the ceiling sags like an old man's belly. Three faces, white as the bellies of fishes. I am not alone.

Oannes, from the flood. A myth, just like all those other myths. A race of gods, an elder people come to teach us how to become a civilization. Nothing more than a story to account for *How we became who we are*, or perhaps, humans being humans, *Why we are better than others*.

Except that is not what Doctor Sakhra proposes. Not for the foundation stories of Sumer, which first arose some seven and a half thousand years ago. Ancient Sumer, which sprang to life with its stories of a grand flood and men who came from the sea bringing wisdom.

For there was a flood, so runs the theory. Not some impossible global catastrophe but a deluge that became Gilgamesh's flood, and Noah's and all the stories of inundation flowing outwards from Mesopotamia. Some eight thousand years ago there was a great freshwater lake where the Black Sea is now. Fertile, rich, the perfect place to settle and grow wise in the dim dawn of the world. Until the sea levels rose so that the walls of the Mediterranean were insufficient to contain them. Until the barriers broke all at once, and the salt sea rushed in. Not the end of the world, but the end of *their* world.

And if they existed, and if that flood existed, they would have fled. And, soon after that maybe-flood, there came to nascent Sumer men from the sea, the fish people, with their knowledge of how to turn a people into a civilization. Not ancient aliens, not gods. Wise men, sages. *Refugees*. A people fleeing death by water.

Perhaps, just perhaps, they were the first, the ancients' ancients. Those who placed the first stone atop its neighbour; those who drove the plough in the fields of the dawn; those who made the earliest ever mark that turned mercurial human thought into history. And they did not come to Sumer bringing war or fire, but wisdom. Not tyrants but teachers. And most of all in this, Doctor Sakhra says, they were our ancestors.

I see a knot of rags that might be a bed. A bowl, bronze, two thousand years old, that they've been burning papers in for light, for heat. A little scatter of cans: there was food too, an emergency stash that the emergency came too swift to make use of. A man, two children, staring.

Baseball bat in his hands, but they tremble. Why wouldn't they? I am a metal invader from who-knows-where. Would they be more frightened of aliens, or if the owner returned? He'd drive them off as readily as he would us. Nobody is supposed to be here in the ruin of his wealth. Ruined, it is still *his*.

We stare at one another in the light of my lamps.

"Hassan, move!" Majid tells me. They have caught up and I am in the way. The tremble of the baseball bat increases as the other two Avatars clamber in. We must seem invulnerable to the man. He doesn't know that each swing of his weapon would be fifty thousand dinars of damage and vital systems offline.

Majid goes for the tablets. Yasmin, coming after, sees what I see, is silent for a moment, then: "Tell them to stay out of our way. We don't want the food; they don't want the artifacts."

I tell them, but they don't hear. My speakers are patchy and my translator is offline, smacked into oblivion by my clumsy piloting. I speak Arabic that they cannot understand. I give them my scant English, remembered from conferences, from my childhood when the soldiers were still there. "*No weapons. Please do not.*"

Majid and Yasmin are at the tablets. Metal humanoid frames, and yet nothing human, not really. Moving with exaggerated care like moon men. Reaching into their abdomens to tear themselves open, folding out their own innards to reveal their storage space. I watch as Majid lifts the first tablet into himself, staggering a little with the weight, letting the servos compensate, metal knees bent like a fencer.

"Seismic data—" Yasmin starts, but we all feel it, the whole edifice around us shifting. Dust falls from the ceiling, sifting through the cracks.

Doctor Sakhra is abruptly in our ears. "Bring them out. Bring them now. As many as you can."

"Too many," Majid tells her. "Need a second trip."

"No time. Bring what you can." There is a harsh edge to her voice I never heard before. I think it's desperation.

"*Go now!*" My terrible English, remembering what the soldiers used to shout. "*Get out of here. Children get out. Out now!*" I have my own innards ready to receive the wisdom of the ancients. Majid has three tablets stowed within, another clutched in his robot hands. Not how we're supposed to handle priceless artifacts, but this isn't a museum and soon it'll barely even be a ruin. I start loading up myself, Majid and Yasmin are already lurching off. One, two into my hollow belly. I look for the man, the children, hoping they've moved. They are quite still. It's the ceiling, the walls that shudder with tense movement. I can see cracks spidering across them.

"*Danger*," I tell them, like some old TV show robot, but they just crouch there watching me gorge myself on ancient lore, until there is just the one tablet left. I understand, then, why they haven't gone. Beyond this room is an airless, lightless maze, dark as ignorance. They came down here scavenging, and the building settled and the waters rose. They retreated and retreated until there was just this one pocket of air. The canned food was bait and they are in the trap.

"Hassan, move now." Doctor Sakhra tense in my ear.

The man with the baseball bat. It's lowered now. He sees I'm no threat to him; he's not even relevant to my world. Just the sort of organic detritus that does not get preserved in the archaeological record.

"Hassan."

I look at the last tablet, the wisdom of the ancients, one twelfth of the secrets of an elder civilization that predates all the histories we ever knew. Perhaps the key to translating that other script lies there; perhaps the truth behind the flood myths. Oannes stares past me into his future that is the ancient, ancient past to me.

"*Hassan*." Showing me the shortest route to the surface. It's not so far. I could swim that, hold my breath for that. If I had that map, these lamps, this knowledge. Not if I was blind and panicking. Not with children hanging from me.

Groans from above, and more dust. Doctor Sakhra's hard voice. A sharp finger jabbing my real shoulder, the one back on the boat. I hold out my metal arms, use my broken English to entreat them. "*Come, come, danger, now.*" And who knows if I have time? But I will be true to Oannes. I will bring wisdom from the flood, but also I will bring life.

Maureen McHugh grew up in the Midwest and has lived in New York City, Austin, Texas, the People's Republic of China, and Los Angeles, California. Her first novel, *China Mountain Zhang*, a dystopian story set in a China dominated future, was a *New York Times* Noteworthy Book and won the James Tiptree Award. Her collection of short stories, *After the Apocalypse*, was one of *Publishers Weekly*'s Ten Best Books of 2011. She currently lives in Los Angles where she teaches Interactive Storytelling and Cinema Arts at the University of Southern California.

YELLOW AND THE PERCEPTION OF REALITY

Maureen McHugh

I wear yellow when I go to see my sister. There's not a lot of yellow at the rehab facility; it's all calm blues and neutrals. I like yellow—it looks good on me—but I wear it because Wanda is smart and she's figured it out. She knows it's me now when she sees the yellow.

The doctors say that Wanda has global perceptual agnosia. Her eyes, her ears, her fingers all work. She sees, in the sense that light enters her eyes. She sees colors, edges, shapes. She can see the color of my eyes and my yellow blouse. She can see edges—which is important. The doctor says to me that knowing where the edge of something is, that's like a big deal. If you're looking down the road you know there's a road and a car and there is an edge between them. That's how you know the car is not part of the road.

Wanda gets all that stuff, but her brain is injured. She can see but she can't put all that together to have it make sense; it's all parts and pieces. She can see the yellow and the edge but she can't put the edge and the yellow together. I try to imagine it, like a kaleidoscope or something, but a better way to think of it is probably that it's all noise.

Today she's sitting on her single bed in her room, cross-legged, her narrow knees like knobs in her soft gray cotton sweats. She croons when she sees me, "Junie June June."

She is tiny, my sister. Before the accident she was always a little round. Chipmunk cheeks and Bambi eyes and soft breasts. Now, food is all mixed up for her. Like, she has all the pieces, the crispness or smoothness, the heat or cold. But she can't put it all together. For her, a sandwich is a nightmare of crisp lettuce and melted cheese and soft bread, green and spongy and the smell of something toasted.

She's touching things a lot lately. I let her touch me. She's relearning all those colors and edges and sounds and textures the way an infant does. She's putting that together. She keeps getting better. She's started dropping things. I know it's on purpose. She drops and then she looks. They don't know how much better she's going to get but I do. Wanda will get well.

"Hey, skinny," I say. She can't understand me yet but I think she can tell tone so I talk to her the way we used to talk. She giggles like she understands me. Her hands roam across my yellow top. She reaches for my hands, my bright yellow fingernails. She misses but I put my hand in hers and she strokes the smooth painted surfaces.

"It's a good day," she says. "Good, good. It's warm and yellow, maybe it's finally spring or summer? I think it's spring but I can't tell time really. It's day, I know that, I know I know. Are you happy, June?"

"I'm happy," I say. "I'm happy you're happy." It's January.

Wanda is all there inside. She remembers, she knows, she can speak.

Yellow is me, and she talks to me. But she doesn't know what I'm saying back. She can't see my expression. I mean she can see it, but without being able to put the color brown with my eye shape with the edge between eye and skin, without being able to judge how near and how far everything is. She can't tell if I'm smiling, if my eyes are crinkled.

After the injury, the first real sign she was fighting her way back was when she started saying, "I, I, I." She would rock on her bed, her eyes rolling, her head tilted back, and say, "I, I, I, I, I."

Dr. Phillips thinks she was assembling her sense of self as separate from the world. "She has no boundaries," he said. "She doesn't know where she ends and the world begins. She doesn't know if she's cold or the can of soda is cold."

She was involved in an accident at the lab. Two other people are dead. Some people think it's my sister's fault.

My mother calls. "June?" she says on the phone, as if someone else might answer.

"Hi Mom," I say.

"How's Wanda? Did you go yesterday?"

This is what we talk about these days. I am home after a long day of wrangling with the county about social services for one of my clients. He's seventy-eight and has lost part of his foot to diabetes. He's old and sick, he drinks and has multiple health problems. He needs to be placed in a facility that takes Medicare, where someone can give him his meds and make sure that he eats. He just wants to stay in his house off Crenshaw with its sagging roof and piles of junk mail on the kitchen table because he wants to keep drinking. When he's in a good mood, I'm like a daughter to him. When he's not, like today, he calls me a stone-cold fucking bitch who will throw him out of his house. He says he'll end up in some horror show of a place, three beds to a room and the television always on. It's not like he's wrong.

"What will happen to my things?" he asks me. He means, *What will happen to me?*

I have a tiny one-bedroom apartment in a fourplex in West Hollywood. It's run down and my only air conditioning is a window air conditioner in the bedroom and a fan in the living room. The kitchen is microscopic. I have a calico cat named Mrs. Bean who jumps on my kitchen counters no matter what I do. She watches me from the chair in the living room, her eyes half-lidded. The place needs to be picked up, there's a stack of magazines next to the chair, and I haven't folded my laundry so it's on the couch, but it's home and I feel safe here. I like my music and my street-scenes art.

"A reporter called today," my mother says.

"From where?" I ask.

"I don't know," she says, "I just hang up."

I got phone calls right after the accident. People knocked on my door. *Good Morning America* rang me.

People called me up and told me my sister was a murderer. People called me up and told me God had told them that my sister was an angel. People I went to high school with who had never messaged me messaged me on Facebook.

For four weeks or so it was utter hell. I thought I was going to get fired but my boss decided he was pissed at them instead of me, and for a while we had a policeman at the clinic who told people who wanted to talk to me that they had to leave. Then the next thing happened on the news, some poor fourteen-year-old girl reappeared after having been missing for three months and they arrested the guy who kidnapped her, and reporters stopped calling, no doubt calling his parents and siblings.

"She knew me," I tell my mother, turning back to the conversation. "She called me Junie."

"She's getting better," my mom says. She says this every time.

"She's tough," I say.

She *is* getting better, fighting her way to more and more coherence, but the doctor said it's hard to know how to treat her. They don't understand what happened to her. Don't understand how she could have damage across so much of her brain. She doesn't have lesions, or signs of a stroke. The injury is at the cellular level. Invisible. Like she had been poisoned or irradiated. But she wasn't.

My sister is a physicist. We are fraternal twins.

We're close. We barely spoke for a couple of years after our family moved to Towson—we were born in East Baltimore but our dad worked for his uncle who had a dry-cleaning shop. Uncle Whit took Dad on as a partner. Dad expanded the business to eleven dry-cleaning shops and then sold them when Whit died, which is why we grew up in Towson, which is super middle-class, instead of in Baltimore.

We moved in sixth grade and by the time we were in eighth grade I had a boyfriend. I gave him authenticity, I think. He was big into Drake and I was singing "Hard White" by Nicki Minaj. We were always working on our rhymes and freestyling. Since I was from the East Side people thought I was some sort of representative of ghetto life, never mind that our mom never let us even breathe much less hang with anyone she didn't approve of. I knew I wasn't really any kind of badass but I told myself I knew things these suburban kids didn't. That was a lie.

Wanda was always on about Harry Potter and *Naruto*. And her taste in music—can you say Foo Fighters? I was embarrassed for her. I was just a kid.

Middle school is embarrassing for everybody, am I right?

We didn't fight, we just didn't have a lot in common for a while. In junior year, I was on the homecoming court, wearing a short, sparkly green dress. Wanda was nerdy and great at math. She marched through high school determined to get into a good college and ended up across the country at UCLA studying physics.

When we were in college we'd talk all the time. Wanda got obsessed with consciousness. "What is it?" she asked me. I could like picture her sitting on her bed in Los Angeles with her laptop and her books and her stuffed purple dragon, Rintarou Okabe. I lived at home, in our old bedroom.

"Is the cat conscious?" she asked. We had a big old gray tiger-striped cat named Tiger.

"Of course," I said. "Except when he's asleep. Then he's unconscious, right?"

"Cause I'm reading this book and it says you need some things for consciousness. You need a simulation of reality."

"What's wrong with reality?"

She made this noise, like I was missing the point. I just laughed because a lot of conversations with Wanda were about figuring out what the point was.

"Nothing's wrong with it. We just know from all sorts of experiments that our brain makes up a lot of stuff. Like it fills in your blind spot and edits out your nose. If you think about it, you can see your nose but you don't see it most of the time even though it's right there. All the time, June!"

I cross my eyes a little trying to look at my nose and there's the tip of it, blurry and kind of doubled when I look for it. If you'd have asked me, I'd have said I couldn't see my nose without a mirror. Not like I can see it very well, anyway.

"Cause our reality is assembled in our brains," Wanda explained. "Not our eyes. And like sound moves slower than light and if someone is singing on stage we should be able to see her mouth moving before we hear her but we don't cause our brain just keeps taking all the stuff that comes in and adding it to our picture of the world and if stuff is a little out of sync, it like buffers it and makes us experience it as happening all at once."

"Okay," I said. It was kind of interesting but really out there. Also, I couldn't stop thinking about not paying any attention to my nose and then I thought about how my tongue doesn't really fit in my mouth and always rubs up against my bottom teeth. One of those things that once you start thinking about it, you can't stop until you realize you've forgotten about it but then you're thinking about it. I wished my tongue were smaller in my reality. Sometimes conversations with Wanda are like this. It can be exhausting.

"And we need a sense of self, like an 'I,'" Wanda added.

"To put it together?"

"No, sorry, that's one of the three things that we need for consciousness. We need to know where we end and the rest of the world begins. Like, does an amoeba know where it ends and the world begins?"

"I don't think an amoeba is conscious," I said.

"Nah, probably not. But an elephant is. You know, if you put a spot of blue paint on an elephant's forehead, and then you show the elephant itself in a mirror, the elephant will touch its forehead with its trunk? Cause it figures out that the image isn't another elephant, it's a reflection. Elephants know 'I' and 'you.' Isn't that cool?"

It means a lot, thinking about it now. Right after the accident, I don't think Wanda knew where she ended and the rest of the world began. She had her eyes squeezed shut all the time and she screamed and cried, which was terrifying. They kept telling me she wasn't in pain but I knew better.

(Back then, it was just a conversation.)

"So I've got a . . . a hologram of reality in my head and an I."

"Not a hologram."

"Metaphor," I said.

"Not a good one," she said, but she didn't bother to explain why, she just plowed on. "You need a simulation and a sense of self."

I'd had enough so I asked, "How's Travis?" She'd gone out a couple of times with this guy.

I could hear her shrug. "Eh," she said. I knew Travis was on his way out.

I think about that conversation all the time now. I wear yellow so I affect Wanda's brain that way every time I see her. Yellow is a way for her to start to make a simulation of the world. To say, "June is here."

Two and a half months after the accident. the police call and say they want to do a follow-up with me and they'll bring me my sister's things. Which is great; I don't want to have to go pick them up at a police station.

The cop is Detective Leo Garcia Mendoza and I like that he has the double name thing going and maybe respects his mom. He's more than six feet tall, in his late thirties, and wears a suit when he comes to talk to me.

We go through the pleasantries. We're crammed into my little office, which has just enough space for a desk and a guest chair and a bunch of beige metal filing cabinets with models of glucose monitors stacked on them. When Detective Garcia Mendoza sits in my guest chair, his knees are probably touching my desk.

A copy paper box is sitting on my desk. In it is my sister's jacket and her phone, and a Happy Meal toy from her desk.

"We just want you to know that at this time we have no intention of filing any kind of charges against your sister," he says. "Has your sister ever said anything about what happened?"

"I don't think she remembers," I say. It's true. Like people don't remember a car accident.

"Was she close to Kyle Choi? Friendly with Dr. Bennett?"

"She never complained about them or anything," I say. Which strictly speaking is not true. She liked Kyle but he drove her nuts. "She said Kyle said one time that they should microdose LSD and see if it helped productivity because some Silicon Valley start-up is doing it. But Dr. Bennett wouldn't have allowed that."

"Is there any chance that LSD caused your sister's psychosis?"

I raise an eyebrow. "Wanda is not psychotic. She is perfectly lucid. She has a brain injury that makes it impossible for her to integrate her sensory experiences. A drug screen showed no evidence of anything but legally pre-scribed Adderall in her system."

I work with kids a lot and occasionally I have to do the mom voice. It works now on Detective Garcia Mendoza. He scrunches his shoulders a little. "I'm sorry, ma'am," he says.

I don't let him off the hook by smiling. I trust him about as far as I can throw all six foot plus of him.

"The evidence suggests that Dr. Bennett tried to restrain Mr. Choi and Mr. Choi became violent, maybe panicked. We have had a couple of eye-witnesses who saw someone we believe was Mr. Choi in the hours after the accident. He was wandering the streets and was clearly agitated."

"So he cracked Bennett's skull open?" I ask.

"His prints are on the bottom of the chair that was used to murder Dr. Bennett," the cop says, like it doesn't matter. "We keep finding references to someone named Claude," he says.

"Animal Control took him. I think he ended up at the Long Beach Aquarium."

This throws Detective Garcia Mendoza.

"Claude," I explain, "is an octopus. A three-year-old North Pacific giant octopus. He lived in one of the tanks in the lab. Kyle Choi took care of him. He was one of six octopuses who were part of an experiment. Woods Hole was directing the grant and they didn't want to ship a bunch of octopuses across the country. Monterey Bay Aquarium took some, I think. The Birch at Scripps down in San Diego might have taken one."

"What kind of experiment?" the officer asks.

They were doing experiments on octopus perception. They'd put four boxes in an octopus tank, three of them black and one of them white. The white one had food in it. They'd put them in the same place three times, and time how long it took the octopus to get the treat. The fourth time they'd move the white box to a place where there was usually a black box and put the black box where the treat usually was. Then they'd see how long it took for the octopuses to figure it out. The idea was to test if octopuses prioritized location or color, what was more important to them.

Dr. Bennett was doing some other experiments on just Claude, trying to see if he could alter Claude's brain to perceive things we don't perceive. Claude had some sort of reality goggles he wore over his eyes but he hated them. Sounds like getting an octopus to wear something it doesn't like makes dressing a toddler look fun.

Claude didn't like his keeper, Kyle. It was Kyle's job to put on Claude's goggles.

Octopuses are not social; they're kind of psychopaths, according to Wanda. Like psychopaths, they can be sentimental, and Wanda used to feed Claude on the sly so he would like her. Her work didn't require her to interact with the octopus but she felt bad for him, and he watched her because there wasn't much for him to do.

Wanda was pretty sure that all the shit with the goggles had made him crazy, even by octopus standards. He had a burrow but he stuffed it with everything in his tank to fill it up. He destroyed most of the things they put in the tank. Wanda didn't like the experimentation; it wasn't ethical. After the accident, I got hounded by PETA.

I didn't understand what the goggles were supposed to do. Wanda tried to enlighten me, but I couldn't follow what she was talking about.

"I could explain if you could follow the math," she'd say, exasperated. Numbers talk to Wanda. They're like her first language. They're not my first language. Maybe my third. Or fourth. My twin is my first language.

"Could the deaths have involved the octopus?" the cop asks.

I couldn't help it—the look I gave him. It was a moronic question. Claude is big for an octopus, almost four feet long, I think, but he weighs about as much as a cocker spaniel and I'm not sure how an octopus was supposed to cause the kind of brain injury Wanda has. I met Claude and he eyed me and then squirted water at me. Wanda dropped a piece of sashimi in the tank. Salmon, I think. He wasn't wearing the goggles.

He was very cool in theory but not so much in practice.

They'd tried to interest him in a female octopus and he'd killed her. He would probably have happily killed Kyle and Dr. Bennett but there was the little fact that he lived in a saltwater tank and had no bones.

"He might have had motive but not method or opportunity," I say dryly.

Detective Garcia Mendoza chuckles. It's awkward. I'm secretly pleased.

Claude is actually four, not three. It's been almost a year since Wanda was found unconscious in the lab, Dr. Bennett had his head beaten in by a chair, and Kyle disappeared and his remains were found two weeks later in the nice-looking stretch of the Los Angeles River.

You don't know people, not really. But Kyle didn't seem like the kind of guy who would violently murder someone and then kill himself, at least not from the way Wanda talked about him. Kyle was a C++ programmer who wore thick black hipster glasses. He made sourdough bread on the weekends and posted pictures of it to his Instagram account. He had ended up taking care of Claude because his previous project had been making a database for a study of octopuses. Octopi. Whatever. He confessed to Wanda about how hard it was to be a gay Asian guy. He said white dudes wanted him to call them "Daddy" a lot.

I call the Long Beach Aquarium and I ask if I can see Claude. They tell me I have to make a formal request and how to do that. I have to email someone in visitor liaison or community outreach or something so I do. I don't know why I want to see Claude except that I think Wanda would want me to. Wanda had a bit of wounded bird rescuer in her. I fire off the email.

I work until six and then drive home where I eat a microwave low-calorie dinner and a bunch of chocolate chip cookies. I don't claim to be consistent, and at least my dinner was a lot less fattening than the cookies. It's a balance, right?

I am behind on stuff. Because, you know, I'm a social worker. It's part of the job. I try to work on some files but end up bingeing on Netflix.

There's an email in my inbox. Somebody from UCLA, which is where Wanda did her undergrad.

Ms. Harris,

My name is Dale Hoffsted. I study perception and I've worked with Oz Bennett. I wondered if I could talk to you about your sister and what the lab was doing?

I'm working sixty hours a week. One of the social workers, Fran Horowitz, quit three weeks ago and we're already crazy busy. Social work is the kind of job you can never actually succeed at, only fail less. I fire off an email saying that I would like to talk to him but between my job and visiting my sister, I don't have any time on the weekdays.

Maybe he knows Wanda?

I don't really think about it, but when I come back to my desk later, there's another email.

Saturday or Sunday would be fine. I've got an experiment running that gets me in the lab on weekends.

I mean to answer him but I get a call from the rehab facility that Wanda is having a bad day.

A bad day. Like that begins to cover it.

I tell my boss I've got to go and that I'll work Saturday to catch up.

At the rehab, I can hear her long before I see her. The moment the elevator door opens, I hear her. Wanda is screaming. I don't know why but I run because the sound—pure, high terror—just shuts down every thought. I run past the old people. Rehab is a nice word for a nursing home and they sit in the hallway watching me go past or, worse, oblivious, vacant as a tomb.

In Wanda's room are two orderlies, Latino guys, trying to restrain her. Wanda is only a little more than one hundred pounds, but she is wild. Her arms are streaked with blood from where she's been scratching at them. They try to keep her nails short but when this happens, it doesn't matter, I guess.

"Wanda!" I say, "Wanda! Wanda!"

She can't hear me.

Another person in scrubs appears at the door—a nurse, a doctor, I don't know. "We have to restrain her!" the woman says.

"No!" I say. "You can't!"

"She was trying to scratch her eyes!" one of the orderlies says to me. It's Hector, who likes Wanda, sings to her in Spanish. Sometimes she knows him and calls him Music Man.

"What triggered her?" I ask.

The other Latino guy shakes his head, either that he doesn't know or that it's too late now. Leon. Who once was lifting a woman out of her wheelchair and I heard him say, "Why do I always get the heavy ones?" and I hate him, I hate that I leave my sister with people like him.

We are shouting over Wanda screaming. A long shrill sound like a child, a little girl.

I try to touch her, to get her to see the yellow, that I'm here. "June's here!" I say. "Junie's here! Wanda!"

She catches me in the cheek with her elbow.

They push her down on the bed and grab her arms and restrain her and she fights. Oh God does my sister fight. Her eyes are squeezed shut and she twists and turns and her pink mouth is open. They use wrist and ankle restraints and a belt across her middle. The rehab doesn't like to use restraints. The administrator is committed—the staff gets training based on a program in Wisconsin. It's one of the reasons I got her in this place.

Sedatives increase Wanda's sensory integration problems.

There's nothing to do but keep her from clawing her eyes out.

I want to scream, "She's a PhD! In physics! This is not Wanda!" But it is. Oh God, it is. It is.

She doesn't quiet until she falls asleep a little after nine p.m. Some of the patients sundown and I can hear a woman wailing.

I'm so tired. My mom and dad are bankrupting themselves to keep Wanda in this place. Sixty-two thousand dollars a year. I try to help but a social worker doesn't make a lot of money. What good is it to help other people if I can't help Wanda? Honestly, sometimes I wonder how much I am helping anyone.

Mostly I just try not to think about it. One day at a time. Hopefully Wanda will get to the point where I can take her home. I'll get twin beds and it will be like being girls in Baltimore again.

It's never going to be like it was.

The aquarium sends me back an email telling me that I can visit Claude the octopus. I ask if I have to make an appointment and their response says that no, I don't, my name will be on a visitor list.

Dale Hoffsted emails me and says he's heading for a conference in Copenhagen next weekend, can I meet him this weekend?

I have one goddamn day to myself, Sunday. I grocery shop. I drop off my laundry at the laundromat where the Korean women wash and fold my clothes. They don't like me. But they always do a great job on my clothes. Maybe they spit on my filthy black underwear and say racist things in Korean. I just don't care.

I spend Saturday working from home. That evening, Wanda is lethargic. I check to make sure they didn't sedate her but I think she's just exhausted. I go to bed early but end up watching Netflix until after midnight.

On Sunday morning I go to the aquarium. It's lovely, full of kids. There's a pool where you can reach in and stroke the sandpaper skin of a ray. I watch the baby bamboo sharks. Wanda wouldn't be able to handle this, not yet.

I ask at information if there is someone I can talk to about seeing Claude. A woman in a bright blue polo shirt and a name tag that says *Ashley* comes out to meet me. She has a slight Spanish accent. She is young and her black hair shines in the sun.

"Can I help you?"

"My name is June Katherine Harris," I say. "My sister worked for a scientific lab and they donated a North Pacific giant octopus. His name is Claude. Is there any way I could see him? I'm on the visitor list."

She is wary now. "Why do you want to see Claude?"

"Something went wrong at the lab; my sister was hurt really badly and she told me a lot about Claude. I want to tell her how he's doing." I hold up a little takeout container. "I brought him some salmon sashimi." Something occurs to me, "Wait, he's not dead, is he? I know he's old . . . "

"He's not dead," she says.

"I know he's a crazy asshole of an octopus," I say.

She smiles at that. "Let me go check," she says.

The sharks glide silently through the shark lagoon, zebras and epaulette sharks passing each other like ghosts, their flat eyes expressionless. Kids love sharks. Well, I guess everyone loves sharks or Shark Week wouldn't be such a big deal.

Do sharks have thoughts? Do they have consciousness?

A mockingbird will go to battle with his own reflection in a car mirror. He doesn't know that the reflection is him. He doesn't have an "I." He doesn't know "I am reflected in the mirror." He just thinks, "Rival male! Rival male! Rival male!" A dog or a cat can figure out that the image in the mirror is fake.

Claude knows who he is. The sharks don't. What are the thoughts of sharks?

Sharks have a sensor in their nose that detects the electrical impulses of muscle movements in fish. Not the movements, the electrical impulses. I know what sound is like, and sight, and touch—but what is a shark's world? What is it like to sense electrical impulses as information? As something other than a shock? To know that a fish is swimming because you can feel the impulses traveling through the long muscles of its body and the strong movement of its tail?

I close my eyes and try to imagine the perceptive world of a shark.

Swimming, the blue, the scent of blood and fish and kelp in the water. I try to imagine a world in which I can see—no, not see—feel and create a model of the world where I can tell things are moving thirty feet away by the senses on my sides. Feel a fish swimming, terrified by me.

I feel my sides, try to think of the air as an ocean, and try to feel it. I feel a breeze on my arms but I can't feel the little Latina girl in the pink unicorn T-shirt and Crocs, staring at the sharks. Sometimes I've felt like I could "feel" the physical presence of someone standing next to me but what does the shark sense when it senses the electrical movements of the muscles of the terrified fish? What would I feel if I could sense the electrical impulses of that little girl reaching into the water?

I get a little dizzy and sit on the edge of the lagoon. Is this what things are like for Wanda?

The young woman in the blue polo shirt comes back. "I can take you to see the octopus," she says.

The areas where there are no exhibits aren't painted blue and green. They're not pretty, they're utilitarian. There's a smell, like fish water. I don't know how else to describe it. Like a goldfish tank that might need to be cleaned, only saltier. But it's not dirty and it's nicer than the agency where I work, if you want to know the truth.

Claude lives in a tank, a pretty big one. He's brown on top and white underneath and his skin is wrinkled like crepe, like an old man's. He has his eyes hidden in the coils of his arms.

"What did they do to him?" Ashley asks.

"They made these goggles that would help him perceive more, I think," I say. Like the shark, maybe? Seeing the electrical impulses of the muscles of prey? What senses did they try to give Claude?

"What did they want him to do? Spy like those Russian dolphins? Was it like a government thing?"

"They wanted to see if he could perceive reality," I say. "Can I give him the salmon?"

"Is there rice?" she asks. "I don't think he's supposed to have rice."

"No, it's sashimi," I say.

She nods.

"Hey, Claude," I say, "Wanda says hi." Not that she does, of course. Wanda doesn't know I'm here. She can't understand when I talk to her. Claude doesn't respond; maybe he doesn't know I'm here, either.

Ashley opens a hatch in the grate across the top of the tank and I drop a piece of salmon in. It drifts slowly down and Claude doesn't move. I'd think maybe he's dead, that I arrived just in time to see the last witness other than Wanda gone, but he's blowing water through his gills. It stirs the sand on the bottom of the tank.

"Do you want a piece?" I ask.

"I don't like fish," Ashley says. She holds her hands up. "I know! I know! I work with them all day but I just don't like to eat them!"

I laugh with her and it feels good.

I don't know what I'm doing here. I don't know why I felt compelled to see Claude.

In Wanda's phone the last photo is of her, holding Claude's goggles. She's weirdly off-center, tilted and too high, like whoever was holding the camera was not really framing it right. Behind her and even more off-center is the tank where Claude lives, and he's starfished against the glass, all tentacles and suckers. Wanda is smiling this funny smirk she does, like she's causing trouble. I don't know what Claude is doing.

She wouldn't put on the goggles. I swear. Wanda isn't stupid.

I don't think I should drop any more salmon in if he's not going to eat it. I like salmon sashimi, even if I'm not hungry right now. I perceive it as buttery and tasty. Maybe Claude perceives it as, I don't know, changing states of atoms and molecules and energy.

Claude moves. It's so fast I almost miss it, but the salmon is gone.

I drop another piece and he turns his head—I know it's his whole body and he doesn't have a head really, but his eyes are there so it feels like a head. He looks around and he sees me.

"Hi Claude," I whisper.

He uncoils and moves, picking up the salmon and flowing closer to the wall of the tank.

"What did you see when you wore the goggles?" I ask him. I imagine veils of energy in a darkness although that's really not true. It's the best I can do.

He flattens up against the glass and I can see his suckers flexing; I catch a glimpse of his beak. It's scary and a little vicious looking.

I drop another piece of salmon and he flows to catch it.

He reaches up with one long tentacle and I can see how he could be four feet long. He did this with Wanda. "He's tasting me," she said.

I hold my hand over the opening of the tank and he curls a tentacle around my wrist. He's so muscular, so strong, but cold. I feel the tentacles but they don't suck on my arm.

Then he snatches his tentacles back.

Did he think I was Wanda? The salmon, my dark skin? Do I taste wrong?

I watch Claude eat the last piece of salmon.

After the aquarium I head to UCLA. Finding anything at UCLA is like navigating a foreign country with a very poor map. Franz Hall is 60s looking, like the UN building only shorter and much less interesting. The office isn't busy but it isn't empty, either.

I find Dale Hoffsted's office. His door is open.

I straightened my hair. I look casual but professional.

He's a white guy, pale brown hair, tall. He stands up when I come to his door. "Ms. Harris?" he says. His office is bigger than mine. It has carpet and a brown corduroy couch, bookcases, and some kind of abstract art on the wall.

"I was sorry to hear about your sister," he says. "How is she doing?"

"Thank you," I say. I do not say that some days she seems to be getting better and some days she tries to claw her own eyes out. "I meant to read some of your papers before we met, but work has been busy." I looked up his papers and they're all about perception. I had planned to see what I could download but Wanda had that terrible Thursday.

"She worked with Oz Bennett," he says, and there is something in his voice. Wanda was worried that what they were doing was fringe science. She was afraid that a black woman who worked on fringe science was not going to get work when this grant ended. Wanda always went for the hard stuff, the hard math. The hard problem. But it's not easy to find work in the sciences.

"Was he a scam?" I ask.

Dr. Hoffsted startles. "No," he says, "no, not really. He did some crazy stuff but he wasn't a crank."

"Wanda worried that he was not reputable."

Hoffsted shook his head. "His work on consciousness was groundbreaking and innovative. I knew him, professionally. He was generous, introduced me to someone at the NSF who could help me navigate the grant process."

"The octopus was fitted with some kind of reality glasses, for experiments," I say.

That gets me an eyebrow raise.

"Dale?" A pudgy Indian-looking guy in a Hawaiian shirt leans in the doorway. He glances at me.

"Hi Vihaan."

"I've got the results on those fMRIs," the Indian guy says.

"I've got an appointment. Can we go over the data tomorrow?"

"Sure, just wanted to tell you I've got them."

Hoffsted smiles and nods. When the Indian guy walks away, Hoffsted says, "You want to get some coffee?"

We walk across campus. "People think scientists are these rational, logical people," he says. "But we're all actually dorky, weird people."

"Like my sister," I say.

"I, no, I mean, not everybody, some of us are—"

"It's okay. My sister is exactly that. Brilliant and weird." I don't know why I let him off the hook but he is visibly relieved. There's a nice breeze off the Pacific and the sun is bright. The campus is full of intense young people on their way to do intense young people things.

"Have you heard of Linus Pauling?" he asks. When I shake my head he goes on. "Linus Pauling was a chemist, a Nobel Prize winner. In fact, he's the only man to have been the single winner of two Nobel Prizes. He was also a humanitarian. Brilliant guy. He became convinced that large doses of vitamin C would cure the common cold and maybe even cancer. That's why we all drink orange juice when we've got a cold."

"Okay?" I say.

"Total crap," Hoffsted says. "Megadosing on vitamins can be dangerous but mostly it just means your pee is really expensive since it's voiding all those pricey vitamins you take. Isaac Newton inserted a needle behind his eyeball and reported on the results and thought that light would help him understand God."

"Was Bennett a brilliant nut job?" Did the asshole create something crazy that ended up killing him and Kyle Choi, and breaking my sister?

"Maybe," he says. "I don't know."

We get coffee at a kiosk and find a bench.

"Bennett," he says, "got obsessed with the nature of reality."

I sip my coffee. It's decent coffee. I don't care about the nature of reality.

"Why did you call me?" I ask. "Did you know Wanda?"

"No," he says.

"She did her undergrad here," I say.

"I didn't know that," he says. "She was a postdoc, right?"

Was a postdoc. I want to say she is a PhD in Physics with a degree from Wash U. But I just nod. Postdoc is a position. She doesn't work anymore.

"I study perception," he says. "One of the things I've studied is how we perceive reality. I thought," Dale Hoffsted says, holding up his paper coffee cup, "that what I perceived was a pretty good representation of reality. That in reality, I am accurately perceiving the shape and texture of this cup."

It's just a blue and white striped cup with the emblem of the coffee shop on it. It has a white plastic cover.

A kid skateboards by, weaving among the other students.

"We don't perceive everything. We can't see X-rays or radio waves, but what we can perceive—I thought that was reality."

"You're going to tell me it's not."

"Yeah, I am. Our brains have a kind of interface. Like your phone." He pulls out his iPhone. He does that thing that a lot of teachers do: He speaks in paragraphs. "These apps," he says. "What we perceive is not the actual app. The actual app is a computer code running electrons in a pattern in a very sophisticated machine. We don't see the chips and wires, we don't see that code or even the action of it. What we see is a red, mostly square thing with an arrow in it. *The interface is not the app.*"

"Okay," I say. "That's great. But we're not digital. You're holding that cup of coffee. You drink it and it goes down your throat and is absorbed into your body. It's real."

"I didn't say it wasn't," he says. "You ask good questions."

He's not like Wanda. Talking to Wanda tended to rearrange my reality, but Wanda was always there with me. I don't know this guy and apparently he wanted to meet me to lecture me.

"Hi Dr. Hoffsted!" a girl in a flowered sundress sings out. She waves. I hate PhDs who like to be called *Doctor*. I got that from Wanda. I used to call her Dr. Harris to wind her up.

Hoffsted waves back, still talking. "We can create digital organisms now, in a computer simulation. They're like single-celled animals but very sophisticated. They can predict things that are true about real organisms."

"Which is a sign that they're are a good model for real organisms?" I ask.

"Exactly!" he says, like I'm a bright student. "It's pretty compelling evidence. We created organisms and simulated a thousand generations. Half of them evolved to perceive the 'reality' of the simulation and half of them, like us, evolved just for fitness to reproduce. I thought that there would be some difference—I thought perceiving reality would improve fitness to reproduce."

He's excitedly gesturing as he talks and I'm a little worried for his coffee and his phone.

"It didn't," I say. I can keep up.

"No," he says. "One hundred percent of the organisms that were evolved to perceive reality died. Every time."

I feel for a moment like he just said Wanda is going to die and I shake my head.

"We didn't do this just once," he explains, working to convince me. "We did it more than twenty times, a thousand generations, tweaked things. The perception of reality is not beneficial to survival."

He shakes his head. "Let me give you an example of reality that we can't perceive. How much information can a sphere"—he holds out his hands to show the size of a volleyball and I want to take his cup away from him—"can a sphere hold?"

"Doesn't it depend on things like what kind of chip it has or something?"

"We're talking about something different," he says. "It's a question about quantum reality and at the quantum level, everything is information."

"I'm not . . . what are you even saying?"

"Stephen Hawking did the math," he says like that clinches it. Yeah, yeah, impress the dumb black woman by throwing out the name Stephen Hawking. I really don't like this guy.

"If I'm thinking about how much is in something, I'm thinking about volume, right? I'm thinking about how much I can pour into this cup. If I make the cup shallow, like a saucer or a plate, even though it might have the same surface area as this cup, it can't hold as much coffee."

I just nod and picture coffee flowing off a saucer except for the little bit that pools in the indent. My coffee is pale, with cream and sugar in it.

"It turns out that the maximum amount of information, at the quantum level, is determined by surface area, not volume."

I try to wrap my head around that. "Like a big flat plate would hold more coffee than a cup?" I ask. This is a little like talking to Wanda. Only Wanda makes sense. This . . . doesn't make sense.

"Yes. Only we're talking the quantum level not the Newtonian level. But it's reality. We can't perceive a quantum reality. In fact, the best way to pack information into the sphere is to put twelve spheres in it, adding their surface area, and then twelve spheres inside each sphere, and twelve spheres inside those spheres, until we can't get any smaller."

"Why twelve?" I ask.

"I don't know," he admits. "I'm a cognitive guy, not a mathematician. I can't do the math."

I bet Wanda could, I think. *My sister could probably think rings around you.*

"So my perception," he says, holding up his cup, "at the Newtonian level, that a bigger volume means a bigger cup of coffee, is true. Obviously. Ask anyone who has ever ordered a venti when they wanted a grande. But at the level of reality, it's false."

"Why did you ask me to meet you?" I ask.

He looks a little surprised. "I wondered what Bennett was doing," he says.

"I'm a social worker," I say flatly. "I can make sure that when you get diabetes you have the tools you need to stay as healthy as you can for as long as you can. I can't do the math; Wanda could do the math. I only know that whatever Bennett was doing, it broke my sister's brain. Maybe got a lab tech killed."

"What's wrong with your sister?" he asks. The guy really can't read social cues. Or he doesn't care.

"Global perceptive agnosia," I say. "Those goggles. Kyle and Wanda built them—there were a bunch of pairs. I think they tried to see reality and it screwed them up." I haven't wanted to admit it to myself but I know it's true.

He looks a little excited. "Do you know what the goggles did?"

Screw you, asshole.

"I have to go see my thirty-year-old sister in a nursing home full of people with Alzheimer's," I say. I leave him sitting on the bench with his coffee. I hope he feels like shit.

At this time of year it gets dark pretty early. My head is packed full and I skipped lunch.

The parking lot feels as if it is halfway to the ocean. I can't remember exactly how we came so I stop at a map kiosk and look at it. I'm so tired that I'm having trouble figuring out the map versus the campus. The buildings don't line up with the map, somehow. I don't want Hoffsted to walk up and talk to me so I don't want to hang around. I start off in what I think is the direction of the parking lot.

After about fifteen minutes of walking, I realize I have *got* to be turned around. Maybe I should grab something to eat. Low blood sugar. (And isn't that ironic for someone who talks about glucose levels all day long?) I take out my phone and map the way to the car, following blindly. Turn left, turn right, keep walking. The interface is not the app.

I walk up and down the rows of the parking lot, crying, looking for my Honda.

I would have said that Wanda wasn't stupid. She talked about the goggles but she usually talked about how Claude hated them. She probably talked about what they did but honestly, sometimes after a long day, even Wanda was too much.

Wanda used to eat food so spicy it burned my mouth, just because she could. Wanda went hang gliding once. Wanda wanted to go to Mars, even though she said it would probably be more like a family vacation stuck in a minivan than a grand adventure.

I think Kyle took the photo right before she put on the goggles. Of course Wanda put on the glasses. See reality. Wanda would want to.

God damn it, Wanda. How could you do this to us.

I almost cry when I find my car. I'm so relieved.

Sunset Boulevard curves around in weird ways. Heading east it straightens out, flush up against the Hollywood hills. I know Sunset, I drive it pretty often, but nothing looks right. The sun is setting behind me and the light glints off the side mirror of the car stopped at the light in front of me and I can't see.

Talking to Wanda was sometimes a lot, if you know what I mean, but she was a good guide to the strange places of reality. Hoffsted has left me in no-man's-land and I'm lost. Lost like Claude. Lost like Wanda.

I pull in to a Wendy's and I get a cheeseburger and a Coke—I never drink Coke. I sit in the parking lot and I eat like an animal. My stupid body, needing things. Wanda's stupid injured brain.

I pull back out and listen to the voice of the app telling me where to go.

There is the place where Wanda lives. The glass doors spill white light out onto the sidewalk. The woman at reception nods to me and I take the elevator up to the second floor.

I pass the old people sitting in the hall. I pass Leon the orderly I hate, who nods to me. I look into Wanda's room and she is sitting cross-legged on the bed, stroking the blue waffle-weave blanket like it's a pet. She looks up, drawn by the movement?

"June! Junie!" Wanda says and throws her hands up and everything is real again. Wanda is real.

She lets me hug her and pats me and strokes my fingernails. I need a new manicure. I start crying again but I feel okay. Wanda's not dead. Whatever

Hoffsted said about one hundred percent mortality, Wanda is smart. She is getting better. The bad days are getting fewer.

"I saw Claude," I say. "He's doing good. I told him you said hello."

Wanda runs her pale palms over my shirt. "It's a good day," she said. "I think we had applesauce today. I think I liked it. Yellow. I love your yellow. I love you, Junie."

"I love you too," I say.

I will never know reality. Wanda is proof. If she can't handle it, no one can, But I have traveled through the gathering dark and come to her. It doesn't matter that I will never know the vibration of quantum energies, never see them or touch them.

I got here. I am having a bad day but unlike Wanda, when I have a bad day, she can reach me. Even if she never gets better than this and it's always hard, I can still see and touch my sister.

I hug Wanda and she lets me fold her in my arms. She smells of shampoo and clean skin. She croons happily. "I love yellow," she says. "I love your yellow."

"It's okay," I tell her. "It's okay, Wanda baby."

Carolyn Ives Gilman is a Hugo and Nebula Award nominated author of science fiction and fantasy. Her short fiction has appeared in *Tor.com*, *Lightspeed*, *Clarkesworld*, *Fantasy and Science Fiction*, *Interzone*, *Realms of Fantasy*, and others. Her work has been translated into a dozen languages and appeared in numerous Best Science Fiction of the Year anthologies. This story was inspired by a science fiction camp in Danzhai, China, which was co-hosted by the Future Administration Authority (FAA) and the Wanda Group. Gilman lives in Washington, D.C., and works as a freelance writer and museum consultant. She has worked for the National Museum of the American Indian and advised the U.S. Capitol on interpretation of historic art. She is also author of seven nonfiction books about North American frontier and Native history.

EXILE'S END

Carolyn Ives Gilman

> Let's sing of the lightbeam journey
> Of the man who was not a man
> Sent by the Whispering Kindom
> To search the sky for ghosts.
>> How did he find the way?
> He followed the poison papers,
> He followed the scent of secrets
> He followed the footsteps of ashes,
> Retracing the path of exile.
>> Can reversing exile set it right?[1]

The series of events that would make Rue Savenga the most reviled woman on Sarona began only minutes before closing time at the Orofino Museum.

---

1 From "The Song of No." The storysinging of the Manhu is a competitive sport. One team of two members will challenge another of equal skill. The first team will sing the story till they come to a question, which is like a riddle. The second team must know the answer in order to continue the story and ask their own question. Thus they alternate as the story unfolds.

The windows had been rain-streaked all day, and now had gone dark. Rue was at her desk, reading a new art history treatise she needed to review, when her wristband chimed.

"There is a gentleman here asking to see you," the guard at the front desk said. "He says he's come from Radovani."

Radovani was seven light years away. Rue glanced at her calendar. No appointment. She could easily dodge this one. But the book was disappointing—simplistic ideas gussied up in jargon—and she needed a break. "All right, I'll come down," she said. That was her first mistake.

The parts of the museum beyond the public galleries were cluttered and utilitarian. Exposed conduits and plumbing ran along the ceiling above her as she paced down the scuffed-tile corridor lined with crates and display cases no one wanted to throw away. Emerging into the airy, sophisticated architecture of the lobby was a release from claustrophobia.

It was clear who her visitor was. He stood out for his stillness in the bustle of departing visitors—tall and slim, with long black hair pulled back in a tie. His hands were in the pockets of a jacket much too light for the weather outside.

Rue introduced herself. When she held out her hand, the young man stared at it for a second before remembering what to do with it.

"My name is Traversed Bridge," he said; then, apologetically, "I have an unreal name as well, if you would prefer to use that."

"No, your real name is fine." Rue had no idea what he was talking about, but it seemed the polite thing to say. "You've come from Radovani?"

"I just arrived by wayport. I came directly here."

"What can I do for you?"

He looked at the floor, as if at a loss for words. "I'm sorry," he murmured. "I'm not good at this. They should have sent a woman."

Mystified, Rue said, "You're doing fine."

He looked up. He had beautiful, liquid charcoal eyes. "I was sent by the Whispering Kindom of the Manhu. I have come to find our ancestors."

None of this rang any bells with Rue. "I think they may have called the wrong person," she said. "You probably want to speak to our ethnographic curator, Magister Hess."

"No, I was given your name," he said. He fished a card from his pocket. Her name was written on the back. On the front was printed the name and contact information for a colleague at the Radovani Archives, someone who ought to have known better.

Rue sighed. "All right, then, why don't you come up to my office and you can explain."

She led the way back. When they reached her office, he looked around and seemed to relax. "It's good to get away from the ghosts," he murmured.

Most people called Rue's office austere—or, if they were being polite, minimalist. The other curators' offices were adorned with art and artifacts from their private collections. But Rue was not a collector. It was not that she didn't love the art; she would have raced into a burning building to save the museum's collection. She just had no need to possess any of it.

She offered Traversed Bridge a chair, and he sat. There was still a circle of quiet around him.

"So you're from Radovani . . . ?" she prompted.

"Oh, no," he said. "I am from a place you call Eleuthera. We call it Exile."

Eleuthera was even farther away than Radovani, a planet settled only in the past three centuries as an experiment in radical self-determination—hence the name, which meant something like "freedom."

"You have come a long way," Rue said.

"Yes. I had to retrace the steps of the ancestors. They came from Radovani more than a hundred years ago, but that was not the world called Home. The historians on Radovani told me this was it, but I'm not sure. It doesn't look like Home."

"What does Home look like?"

"It is a green and leafy place. It has extra suns and moons."

"Well, we have two suns," Rue explained. "The second one is not very bright, and today you couldn't see either one, because of the rain. There are three moons."

"At Home, there were originally more," Traversed Bridge informed her. "But the hero Whichway Traveler shot them down."

"I see."

"They were too bright."

Rue nodded. "Why did the Whispering Kingdom send you, Traversed?"

"Kindom," he corrected her. "We don't have kings. We have kin."

"Okay."

"They sent me to find our ancestors and ask them a question. I am told you can help me."

Frowning, Rue said, "Who were your ancestors?"

"They were Manhu. Your name for us may be Atoka."

Suddenly, everything made more sense in one way, less sense in another. The Atoka had been an indigenous people of Sarona, and the museum did have a small but priceless collection of Atoka art—priceless, because it was the only collection in existence. The Atoka had been wiped out seven hundred years ago. They were extinct. Only their art survived, tantalizing and enigmatic.

Frowning, she said, "We greatly revere the Atoka. But we believe them to be dead."

"Oh no," Traversed said sincerely. "We are still alive. They tried to kill us all after the Battle of the River Bend eight hundred years ago. They hated us, so they tried to castrate all the men, and passed a law making it illegal to be Manhu. But a few hundred of us escaped to Refuge, which you call Radovani. We settled on what we thought was empty land, but after three generations, they decided we had no title, and so others took our houses and farms. We wandered then. Sometimes people tolerated us, but in the end they always wanted us to give up being who we were. They called us Recalcitrants at first, and then Atavists. When people started to accuse us of crimes, the state sent out death squads to hunt us down and garrote anyone they caught. They would leave dead babies hanging from lampposts as a warning. At last they shipped the last of us off to Exile, and we have been there ever since. The whole story is told in our songs. It takes three days to sing them."

He told this grim tale in a matter-of-fact, even proud, tone. Rue listened, frowning. If his allegations were true, it would upend five hundred years of scholarship. It could not be true. Could it?

Cautiously, she said, "There are scholars who would be interested in meeting your people, Traversed. They will want to find out whether you are truly the same as our Atoka."

"It's not still illegal?" he said a little anxiously.

"No, don't worry about that."

"You wouldn't mind some of us coming back? Just to visit, I mean. If this is Home."

"Everyone is free to visit."

"And our ancestors? Do you know where I can find them?"

Rue glanced at her watch. The museum was closed by now, but the lights might still be on in the galleries. "I can show you one of them right now, if you want."

A transformation came over him; his face drained of everything but nervous awe. He sat up as if something had filled him, inflated him. She waited until he said in a heartfelt whisper, "Yes. Please."

She stood and led the way out. She liked showing this particular artwork to people who hadn't seen the original; no reproduction had ever done it justice. She had written the definitive monograph on it, and it had made her career, but she had never found out much about the people who created it. The legends surrounding the Atoka were so thick, and their symbolism so important, that the truth was elusive—even, in a sense, irrelevant.

The gallery was dark, but at the other end of the room the display lights on the artwork still glowed. It was a special installation, because this was the most famous work the museum owned, and people from all over the Twenty Planets came to see it. Usually there was a crowd around it, but now it hung alone.

Traversed stopped in the doorway, arrested by some strong emotion. "I feel like I shouldn't be the one here," he said. "It should be someone better than me."

Gently, Rue said, "Wouldn't your people be disappointed if you returned and said you hadn't seen it?"

He looked at her as if seeking permission.

"They did choose to send you," she pointed out.

With a visible effort he overcame his uncertainty and followed her across the darkened room.

People called it a painting, but it was actually an elaborate mosaic, made from pieces so small it took a magnifying glass to see them. Rue had commissioned a scientific analysis that had shown that the colors were not, strictly speaking, pigments; they were bits of bird feather, beetle carapace, butterfly wing—anything iridescent, arranged so as to form a picture. And what a picture it was: a young girl in an embroidered jacket and silver headdress, looking slightly to one side, lips parted as if about to speak. Operas had been written about her. Volumes of poetry had speculated on what she was about to say. Speeches invoked her, treatises analyzed her, children learned her story almost as soon as they learned to speak. She was the most loved woman on Sarona.

"We call her Aldry," Rue said.

Traversed Bridge looked transfixed, as if he were falling in love. He whispered, "That is not her name."

"What do you call her?" Rue asked.

"She is Even Glancing."

Rue liked that name. It fit her.

The lights illuminating the portrait were mounted on a track, and they slowly moved from side to side, so that you could see it lit from different angles even as you stood still. Rue waited, watching Traversed Bridge's face for a reaction, because the image changed. At one point in the cycle, the background, which was normally a dark indigo blue, erupted in a profusion of feathers. There were silver wings behind her, appearing then gone.

"Did you see the wings?" Rue finally asked.

"Yes," Traversed said. "I can see them."

"Many people can't," she said. "They are in a wavelength not everyone's eyes can sense."

"They are moving," he said.

"Really?" Rue had never heard anyone say that before. But everyone's experience of the portrait was slightly different.

"She is about to speak," he said.

"Yes. Everyone wonders . . . "

She stopped, because his face had gone rigid, like a plastic mannequin, all animation gone. His body stiffened, then began to tremble. He fell with bruising force to the floor.

Rue knelt beside him, then came to her senses and used her wristband to call for help. But as she watched by the shifting light from the artwork, the humanity flowed back into his frozen face. He blinked, then focused on Rue, tried to say something.

"Lie still. Help is on the way," she said.

"She spoke to me," he whispered. He did not seem in pain, but full of wonder.

He looked around, saw he was on the floor, blushed in embarrassment, and sat up.

"Are you hurt?" Rue said.

"No, no. I am so sorry. Don't worry. I am fine."

"That was a nasty fall."

"I am used to it. This happened all the time, when I was young. My spirit would leave my body, and I would fall down. I would hear voices no one else could hear."

"Voices in your head?" Rue said, her amateur diagnosis changing.

"No, no. They were in my left hand."

A guard looked in, then came over. "Should we call an ambulance?" he asked.

"No," Traversed said, struggling to his feet again. "I am so sorry to put you to inconvenience. I am fine. It is over."

Rue exchanged a glance with the guard, shrugged. "A little too much excitement, maybe. Come back to my office, Traversed, and you can sit down."

By the time he slumped back into the chair, Traversed was looking sad and preoccupied. Rue had seen hundreds of reactions to the portrait of Aldry, but never that one, and she was curious.

"You said she spoke to you," she said as she brewed tea for them both.

"Yes." He stared at the floor. "I didn't understand all she said."

Rue waited, and after a pause he went on. "She is lonely. All this time we thought we were the ones in exile, and it turns out she is the banished one, even though she has never left Home. To us, Home was a place. To her, it is her people."

Rue handed him tea. "That makes sense."

He looked up at her pleadingly. "She says she wants to go back. She wants to see an Immolation."

Rue didn't like the sound of that. She tried to keep her voice even. "What is an Immolation?"

"I don't know." Traversed shook his head. "That was the part I didn't understand."

Rue was in a delicate position. There were strict laws covering repatriation of cultural artifacts, and there was a protocol to follow. If it had been any other artwork, she would have given an automatic set of responses. But Traversed Bridge had not yet made a formal claim. The half-crazed young man was here without credentials, without legal representation, carrying only an implausible story.

Besides, repatriating Aldry was unthinkable. The entire planet would rise up in arms.

If she said nothing, he might never find out that repatriation was an option. It would save a great deal of trouble. No one could accuse her of anything.

She sat down in a chair facing him and said, "There is a way for you to request the return of the portrait. It is called repatriation. You would have to file a formal request, and it would be a very difficult one to win. It would be challenged, because Aldry is deeply loved here, and she is part of our culture as well. You would have to prove beyond doubt that your people are the Atoka, and that she was illegally taken from you."

He was looking at her like a starving man. "But there is hope?"

"A very little hope."

"I want to bring her back. It is what she wants."

Rue smiled and said, "Why don't you sleep on it, and return tomorrow? Nothing can be done tonight anyway. Where are you staying?"

"I don't know," he said. "I'll have to find someplace."

Rue gave him directions to a budget hotel that was close to a transit line, and walked him to the main door of the museum.

"Thank you," he said as he was about to step out into the driving rain. "They told me I would find helpers along the journey, and I have."

Rue didn't answer, because she wasn't sure whether her role was to be helper or hindrance. "Have a good evening," she said, then turned away, knowing she would have to do some explaining tomorrow.

> He came to the prison of ghosts;
> For Hoarder people do not free their dead.
> Their feet fall heavy, weighted by the past
> They do not hear the spirits cry for freedom
> They heap up secrets in an archive
> And lock the doors to keep them in.
>   How do you free a ghost?

"That's preposterous!" said Galbro Hess.

The Curator of Ethnology was nearly as wide as he was tall, dressed in an overstretched cable-knit sweater, his gray hair standing up in spikes. Normally, he was an agreeable, jolly person, but Rue's story had struck a nerve.

"I get them all the time, charlatans and kooks pretending to be Atoka, or to have some sort of spiritual connection to them. There are even re-enactors who pretend to hold Atoka ceremonies. It's a pile of . . . well, you know. I'm afraid you were taken in, Rue."

She had found him in the ethnographic artifact storage area, where he was sorting a collection of broken ceramics spread out on a large, padded table. Around them, shelves rose to the high ceilings, packed with carved masks, handlooms, model boats, drums, and similar things, mostly brown. That was Rue's main objection to ethnographic material: it was so monochromatic.

"I can spot a charlatan," Rue said. "He didn't read that way. For one thing, he's not from here, he's from Eleuthera. I don't think they have Atoka re-enactors there."

"They don't have Atoka either," Galbro said grumpily, sorting a glazed brown ceramic from even browner unglazed ones.

"He told a long story of how some refugees escaped to Radovani."

Galbro looked up, but then waved a hand in dismissal. "All that shows is that he did his homework. It's true, there was a remnant population that went to Radovani. But they were persecuted there, and subjected to forced assimilation. In the end they lost their culture, intermarried, and dwindled to nothing."

"He says they persisted long enough to be exiled again to Eleuthera."

"A convenient story."

"Regardless, I'd like to know more about how we got our Atoka collection."

"Whose side are you on?" Galbro objected.

"I just want to be prepared. If this ends in a repatriation claim . . . "

"No one's going to repatriate Aldry."

"I know that, but to prepare our response I want to be sure we came by her legally."

Galbro stopped his pretense of working and rested his fists on the table. "Sorry, can't give you much joy there. The problem isn't with the museum; we did everything right. But the original collector . . . well, you know how they were in those days. Regular looters and bandits. It may have been legal at the time, but by current standards, no."

"What happened?" Rue said.

"Have you ever heard of the Immolation ceremonies?"

"No. That is, I've heard the word, but not what it means."

"It was the heart and soul of Atoka culture. Once every three generations they would take all their earthly belongings, pile them up in the center of the village, and light a bonfire. Then they would burn all their homes to the ground, so that the next generation would have to start over with nothing. All their wealth, their art, their subsistence would go up in flames. It was the reason the Atoka never built a great civilization—because they voluntarily reduced themselves to poverty and dependence whenever they started to get ahead.

"When our ancestors came to Sarona, they tried to convince the Atoka of how pointless and self-destructive the custom was. From their point of view, the Immolations reduced the Atoka to begging from their more provident neighbors, whose surpluses would be drained to subsidize Atoka beliefs. If they refused to help, well, starving people will get desperate and take what they have to. As tensions grew, our ancestors began to forcibly suppress the Immolations. In one famous instance, an Atoka village was all assembled and ready to light the bonfire when soldiers marched in and drove them out—then, naturally, looted the pile of goods ready for the torch. The Atoka were so enraged they attacked, and that was the beginning of the wars that led to their destruction at the Battle of the River Bend.

"Well, our Atoka collection came from the descendants of a man who was an officer in that troop of soldiers. A man of his rank got first pick of the loot—and the Aldry portrait was the best Atoka culture had to offer."

Rue was silent, shocked. "That is a horrifying story," she said at last. "We can't tell that to the public. They would be outraged."

"Well, they think of the Atoka as idealized children of nature, not as flesh and blood who could be just as wrongheaded as we are. Sure, what the soldiers did was heavy-handed; but if they hadn't saved the portrait, it would have been burned, not preserved so that we can revere it today."

Who were the helpers?
One was kindly,
One was clever,
One was upright,
One was wealthy,
And one was treacherous.

Rue returned to her office feeling troubled. She had taken the problem to Galbro in hopes that he would see it as an interesting topic for investigation. But he was too anchored to his conviction about the extinction of the Atoka. The made-up portion of his mind had crowded out the curiosity.

Her spirits sank further when her wristband alerted her that Traversed Bridge had returned. It would be up to her to explain to him.

This morning he was wearing a heavier coat, much more appropriate to the weather. "The lady at the hotel gave it to me," he said when Rue remarked on it. She couldn't help but notice that he brought out generous impulses in people.

"Have you thought it over?" she asked when they reached her office.

"Yes," he said. "I need to do as Even Glancing told me, and bring her back."

Rue pulled up a chair and sat facing him. "All right. Now, I can't guide you through a repatriation, Traversed, because my first loyalty is to the museum, and they will contest this claim. It's a complex, expensive process, and you may not win. The first thing I would advise you to do is hire an attorney to make the formal claim. You will also have to hire an expert to help you prove that your people are truly the Atoka."

"But we know who we are," he said earnestly.

"That's not good enough for the court. You need a documented trail of evidence. The museum will have experts to testify that you can't be who you say you are. We also need to know that you are truly authorized by your people to make this claim. Can you get that?"

Gravely, he nodded. "I will have to send a message to my Kin Mother."

"Is she the one who sent you?"

"Yes." The shadows of complex thoughts moved behind his eyes. "I had no sisters, and I was firstborn, so it was my duty to go out into the world. They chose me to go to university."

It surprised Rue a little to hear that he was university educated; he gave such an impression of unworldliness. "Did you get a degree?"

He nodded. "Hydrological engineering. I wanted to design a dam for the mountains above my village, to stop the river floods and bring us reliable water. I am here instead."

His obvious disappointment made Rue say, "Well, you have plenty of time. You can still do that when you return."

He shrugged. "I am earning my right to be a person."

She wanted to ask more, but it was a risk to know too much about him; it might cloud her loyalties. Instead, she continued, "You will also have to prove that the object was taken from your people illegally, and that it has an ongoing cultural importance to them. The museum isn't likely to contest the first point, but what about the second? What traditions do you have about Even Glancing?"

"None that I know," he said.

"Then how did you know her name?"

"It is written on the portrait."

There was no label or inscription. "Really?" Rue said skeptically.

"Yes, in the design on her jacket."

Rue called up a photograph on her tablet. "Show me."

He pointed out the portion of the embroidery that gave her name. "And this part says, 'Cherished daughter.' Maybe she was the daughter of the artist."

"What about the wave design on the border?" It had played an important role in Rue's interpretation of the work's symbolism.

"Oh, that's not a wave," Traversed said. "It's a thought. She is thinking, you see."

If what he said was true, a great many art historians would look very foolish, starting with Rue herself. The best way to handle this would be to get ahead of it, to be the one to publish the new information. But that would be an admission that she accepted his claims of cultural authority. A clever attorney could use that against the museum.

"So your people have no tradition, no story, about Even Glancing?"

He shook his head. It was an important concession. She felt a little compromised to have wheedled it from him. "Then why do you want it back?"

"Because," he said seriously, "there is a ghost imprisoned in it."

Good luck arguing that in court, she thought. But all she said was, "That's it?"

"That's enough. We need to free the ghost."

"And how would you do that?"

"We have to destroy the picture."

Rue's horror must have shown on her face, because he said, "It is the only humane way."

It was unthinkable. "Traversed, this artwork is acknowledged as a master-piece—not just on this world, but all over the Twenty Planets. It's in all the art history books, and people honor the Atoka for having created it. Doesn't that make you proud? Don't you want to preserve the greatest achievement of your ancestors?"

He didn't have an immediate response, but seemed to be weighing what she said. She watched, hoping he would reconsider. But at last he shook his head. "It's not worth her suffering. Pride can't justify that."

He really believed it. Rue had been taught from childhood to respect the beliefs of other cultures—but damn it, she had her own core princi-ples. "Then I am bound to oppose you," she said. "I cannot see this artwork destroyed."

They sat in silence, facing one another, aware that they had become enemies.

"You had better go now," Rue said.

"All right." His expression was regretful. At the door he stopped, looked back. "I'm sorry."

"I understand," Rue said.

But she didn't.

How do you lose your name?
When people stop telling your story.
Why must we tell our story?
Because others start telling it for us.

The gallery was relatively uncrowded except for the clump of people around the Aldry portrait. There were masterworks all over the walls, but people had eyes only for Aldry. They wanted to say they had seen her. They wanted their photographs taken with her. Some just stood there for minutes at a time, watching the image change, transported.

They all knew the story.

Once upon a time, Aldry was a real girl living in an Atoka village that had tamed all the birds in the forest around them. Birds were their messengers and their music; birds ate the troublesome insects and brought warnings about the weather. They made nests in the thatched roofs of the village, and kept everyone below dry. Artisans vied to create elaborate cages for them.

Then one day the Atoka spied an ominous fireball descending from the heavens: the landing craft of the settlers who were the ancestors of present-day Saronans. That the two peoples were very different was clear from the start, for the Atoka had amber eyes like owls, and where normal humans had body hair, the Atoka had downy feathers. The new settlers were refugees pushed out of a crowded, urbanized planet. They were woefully unprepared for a subsistence life scratched from alien ground. If it hadn't been for the kindness of Aldry's people, they would have perished. The natives taught them which crops could be cultivated and which were poison, how to hunt the abundant wild animals, how to speak to unfamiliar nature. But as the settlers multiplied, and more of them arrived, relations grew tense. Conflict seemed inevitable. It had happened that way throughout human history.

But Aldry prevented history from going down its familiar, violent path. She had fallen in love with a bookish young settler—the very one who chronicled the whole tale in cramped and sideways antique language. In her culture, a woman's decision to marry conferred personhood on the man she chose, and when she announced her intention to unite the two groups, the Atoka could no longer regard the settlers as invaders of questionable humanity. The marriage ushered in a period of peace. Aldry bore twin boys. One of them favored his father's people and one his mother's, for one had hair and the other had down.

It came to pass that a terrible flood swept through the settlers' town, destroying the homes and fields they had labored for years to build. Viewing the drenched mudlands where their crops and storehouses had been, they knew they faced starvation. Then Aldry saw her duty. Sorrowfully, she kissed her infant boys goodbye and set out alone into the forest. Five days later, an immense flock of birds came to the village. Led by a silver pheasant, the birds descended onto the fields, each with a seed in its beak, and replanted all the crops. The village was saved, but no one ever saw Aldry again. It was said that a silver pheasant perched on the ridgepole of the house where her grieving husband raised her orphan boys, as if to keep them company.

When the boys became men, they quarreled. One went to live with the Atoka, the other stayed with the settlers. They both became great leaders, and their sibling enmity passed to their people. When war broke out, they faced each other in battle. But just when the Atoka brother was about to kill his twin, he glimpsed the silver pheasant in the sky above, and spared him for Aldry's sake.

"She is the mother of us all," Saronans said. She was the generous spirit of the planet that welcomed them and invited them to be at home.

The portrait dated to an era at least two hundred years after the original events. It was thought to be an Atoka artist's image of Aldry, with wings foreshadowing her sacrifice. Who else could it show?

Unless it was Even Glancing, the daughter of the artist.

Rue shook her head impatiently. In an important way, it did not matter. Whoever she had been once, she was Aldry now. Generations of Saronans had woven that identity around her. And they would not easily give it up.

> What did they say on Refuge?
> They said, "Speak another language."
> "Give up your primitive ways."
> "Be more like us."
> And what did they say on Home?
> "Be our imagined angels."
> "Be what we can't be."
> "Reject us, love us, teach us, exalt us."
> We are so tired of being told who to be.

Rue half expected never to hear of Traversed Bridge again. The odds against any lone individual mounting a credible repatriation claim were so high that, when he realized it, he would most likely become discouraged and leave for home.

She underestimated his determination.

Three weeks later, as she was picking up breakfast on her way to work, her wristband started to chime insistently with news alerts having to do with the museum. She put in her earpiece and listened on the tram, her attention so absorbed that her body had to take over the automatic job of exiting at her stop and walking to the staff entrance.

The story was sensational and appealing: a remnant of the Atoka had been discovered on faraway Eleuthera. Old Radovani records filled in their history. Now, an Atoka emissary had come seeking the ancient homeland of his people. After traveling across the light years, the young man had met only rejection and disbelief from the Orofino Museum.

When Rue got to her office, there was a message summoning her to see the director.

Galbro Hess was already in the director's office when she came in. "Of course I told her," he was saying. "It's just the truth. There is no way Atoka culture could have survived intact through hundreds of years of persecution on Radovani."

The director was a handsome, distinguished older man with a neatly trimmed beard. His aura of scholarship was a sham; his main job was care and feeding of the museum's benefactors. He was good at it, and Rue considered it in her own best interest to make his job easy.

When he saw Rue, he said, "Magister Savenga, what's this about our rejecting a repat claim out of hand? You know we can't legally do that."

Rue settled down in a chair, deliberately projecting confidence and calm. The director knew how to handle donors, but she knew how to handle him. "We haven't rejected any claim. In fact, I am the one who told Traversed Bridge how to file one."

Outraged, Galbro said, "You did what?"

"If he's a charlatan," Rue said, "it will come out. Did you listen to the interview?"

Uncomfortably, Galbro said, "All right, maybe not a charlatan—just deluded and naïve. But now he's got an attorney and a pipeline to the press. His story's an invasive weed, a virus people have no immunity to. It's going to sweep the world."

The director interrupted, "But there hasn't been a repat claim?"

"Not yet," Rue said.

"All right." The director had his talking point. That was all he needed. "I want you two to handle this as you would any other claim, and refer all press to my office. We need to graciously suspend judgment, as befits our responsibility as guardians of Saronan cultural heritage." The press release was almost writing itself.

"We need to find out what he wants," Galbro said. "He may just be an opportunist, wanting to hold the painting hostage for gain."

"No," Rue said calmly. "He wants to destroy it."

The two men looked at her in speechless horror.

Galbro found his voice first. "What, is he threatening to re-enact an Immolation? This really *is* a hostage situation."

"He's following voices. Revelations."

"Oh great. We're dealing with a lunatic."

Severely, the director said, "That doesn't leave this room. You could jeopardize our case, Galbro."

"But we've got to expose him!"

"*We* won't do anything. If he's exposed, it will be the media, the court, or other scholars. We have to appear neutral."

As they were leaving, Galbro muttered to Rue, "You really have gotten us into a mess."

"Don't worry, Galbro," she said. "I'm not letting anyone set a match to Aldry."

What did they tell him, and what did he say?
"You are not yourself," they said.
"You are not Manhu."
"You should be Atoka."
"No," he said.

Galbro was right: Atoka fever swept the land, sea, and sky. The story enthralled the public. It was better than finding a species given up for extinct. It was a chance at redemption, a chance to save what was lost, to reverse injustice, to make everything right.

The reality of the Atoka faded into inconsequence.

The museum was forced to put its other Atoka artifacts on display—a bronze drum, a life-size wooden baby, a carved eggshell, and an obsidian knife so thin it was transparent. Visitation shot up. Archaeologists were sudden celebrities. Musicals revived, bad old novels came out again, embroidered jackets crowded the racks. Rue's coffee shop sold Atoka breakfast buns.

Suddenly, there was money for all things Atoka. When Orofino University received a grant to investigate the claims of the Manhu, Rue felt reprieved. With the length of the light-speed journey to Eleuthera, it would be at least ten years before the researchers could travel there and reach any conclusion. By then, the mania would have died down.

But she had not reckoned with recent improvements in instantaneous communication by Paired-Particle Communicator, or PPC. It was now possible to send video via arrays of entangled particles, thwarting the limits of light speed. Sarona had no direct PPC connection to Eleuthera, but the university was able to set up a relay via Radovani, and enlist local researchers.

"They've got universities on three planets collaborating," Galbro told Rue in gloomy discontent—partly at the fact that they were taking the Manhu seriously, and partly at being left out. "I can't imagine what it's costing."

"Conscience money," Rue observed. "Guilt is a powerful thing."

"It's not guilt," Galbro said. "It's pride, to prove that we're better than our ancestors—as if we inherited their planet but not what they had to do to get it."

"You are a cynic, Galbro," she said.

Though they were banned from participating, both of them had contacts at the university who kept them up to date, and so they were prepared for the report's conclusions even before it came out.

All the evidence lined up. DNA traces from old bones on Sarona matched Manhu blood samples. Linguistic similarities showed through the haze of poor records on Sarona and imperfectly transmitted grammar and vocabulary on Eleuthera. The chain of documentation from the Radovani Archives told the shameful tale of their persecution and deportation. Science said it: the Manhu were descended from the ancient Atoka of Sarona.

The report's release revived interest that had grown dormant in the many months it had taken to complete the research. Legislatures passed resolutions honoring the Atoka, money poured in for statues and murals. Documentaries aired until everyone thought they knew the story.

It was then that the repatriation request arrived.

The first meeting the two sides held was in the director's office at the museum. It was to be an attempt to negotiate a compromise solution and avoid litigation. Rue was invited; Galbro was not.

"Don't give it all away," he told her beforehand.

It was more than a year since she had seen Traversed Bridge, except on-screen in interviews, explaining over and over that the Manhu did not really have feathers or owl eyes. Today, dressed in business attire, he looked anxious and ill at ease; but still he had that aura of self-possessed silence. His lawyer was a young woman with flaming red hair and a sprinkling of cinnamon freckles. She would have looked winningly roguish if only she had been smiling, but she was not. She introduced herself as Caraway Farrow.

The museum's attorney, Ellery Tate, mirrored his client, the director—a distinguished older man with an air of paternal authority. The director was present, but silent. He had told Rue he wanted her to represent the museum, so he could stay above the controversy.

Tate opened the meeting, speaking in a generous, calming tone. "Thank you all for coming to help find a mutually agreeable solution."

"We are happy to talk," Farrow said.

The museum's first proposal was to create high-resolution replicas of all the Atoka objects for the Manhu to take to Eleuthera. Farrow glanced at Traversed Bridge, then said, "I don't believe that would be acceptable to my clients."

"Oh?" Tate said, as if surprised. "We can make replicas that are quite identical to the original, down to the molecular level."

Traversed Bridge said softly, "A replica would not have a ghost. It would be soulless."

There was a short silence. Rue could hear the director shifting in his chair. Then Farrow said, "The Manhu might allow you to make replicas for the museum to keep, if you don't contest returning the originals."

Tate looked at Rue. She had to force her voice to sound calm. "That might work for the ethnographic material. But in the case of the Aldry portrait, a replica would not have the same aesthetic qualities."

Farrow was studying her, frowning. "Why is that?"

"We have tried to replicate it in past," Rue said. "There is something about the three-dimensional microstructure of the materials that can't be reproduced. We're not sure why. The whole effect is flatter, less animate. And the wings don't appear."

Traversed Bridge was watching her fixedly. She realized she had just said the same thing as he: the replica was soulless.

"Would it be possible," Tate said, "to work out some sort of shared custody for the painting? I can imagine an arrangement where the original would be on loan to the Manhu for a period of time, say twenty or fifty years, and then travel back to Sarona for the same amount of time."

Stony faces greeted this proposal. Rue had told Tate what the Manhu intended to do with the portrait; he was trying to make them admit it.

"Accept that the portrait is the property of the Manhu," Farrow said, "and we can discuss its future. Until then, there is no point."

She is a wily one, Rue thought. She saw the trap.

Tate said, "We are prepared to offer you the originals of the other artifacts if you will accept shared custody of the portrait. It's a reasonable compromise."

Traversed was already shaking his head.

With a steely gentleness, Tate said, "Please consider the time and expense of defending this claim if it goes to court. You will be trying it in a Saronan court, before a Saronan jury. Aldry is deeply beloved here."

Traversed Bridge's face was a wall of resolution. "Would you leave one person suffering in prison for the sake of redeeming a few others? This is not a balance sheet. You can't weigh souls on a scale and say four make one not matter." He turned to Rue. "You want us to ask for something that means nothing to you, something easy to give. I'm sorry, we can't."

"Ask for anything but Aldry," Rue said.

"Your people made her up," he said. "You can remake her."

No one had anything to answer then, so the meeting was over. They would meet again in court.

How did he craft his case?
He made it on a frame of steel,
He wove the body of sandalwood,
He decorated it with feathers,
He filled it with rushing rivers.

What do we mean by steel, sandalwood,
feathers, and rivers?

The frame of steel was justice.
The sandalwood was steadfast.
The feathers were eloquence.
The rivers were compassion.

And what scale was used to judge?
What ruler can measure the past?

Rue Savenga was, at heart, an uneventful person. She had always tried to do the right thing within her safe, unremarkable life. She had never considered herself the kind of person to take a courageous stand. That was the realm of ideologues and fanatics.

Now, she found herself thrust into an event that forced her to ask where her basic boundaries were. What line couldn't she cross? How far would she go to defend her core beliefs?

What *were* her core beliefs?

The wanton destruction of art, she found, was where she drew her line. It was an act so heinous she could not stand by and let it happen. So when the museum's attorney asked if she would testify in court, she agreed. She was willing to fight to save Aldry from the flames, even if her own reputation burned instead.

The trial was held in downtown Orofino, in a tall, imposing courthouse where monumental sculpture, marble, and mural dwarfed all who entered, in order to strike them with respect for law. When Rue arrived, there were two groups assembled in the park facing the courthouse, shouting at each other. Public interest was so high that the trial was to be broadcast, and opinion was split. Half of Sarona saw Rue as the defender of their heritage, and would execrate her if she lost. The other half saw her as the defender of long-ago injustice. They would execrate her if she won.

The courtroom's air was busy with hushed conversations when she entered. It was a tall and cylindrical space with a skylight above and stylized, treelike pilasters of polished stone lining the walls. A large circular table stood in the

sunken center, surrounded by tiers of seats crowded with press and other witnesses. Rue took her place on the side of the table reserved for the museum's
representatives and their witnesses; on the other side sat those testifying for
the Manhu. The judge and clerk sat in the neutral spaces between, facing
each other. Rue knew two of the expert witnesses she was facing—magisters
from the university who could establish the Manhu-Atoka connection. She
nodded to them without smiling.

The aim of Saronan law was to reach a resolution, not necessarily a victory
for one side. Each side argued its case, the judge proposed solutions, and if no
agreement could be reached, the jury imposed a compromise. But this trial
was to be conducted with only a judge, not a jury. Rue had no idea what the
calculations had been on either side; perhaps it had something to do with the
impossibility of finding a jury whose mind was not already made up.

The judge called on Caraway Farrow to begin the proceedings by stating
the case of the Manhu. She did it succinctly: the artworks had been illegally
seized by Saronans in the act of suppressing an Atoka religious observance.
The Atoka had suffered grievous harm as a result. Now, the return of the
items was a vital step toward righting injustice and reviving Manhu cultural
practices.

The case that Farrow presented was logical and unflinching. An ethnologist told how the art had been looted, and a historian gave the story of the
Atoka genocide and exile to Radovani. A geneticist and a linguist established
the Atoka-Manhu connection.

"And do they still speak the Atoka language and practice Atoka culture?"
Farrow asked the linguist.

"No," the magister replied. "But there are old people who remember
enough of what they were told as children to reconstruct some of it. Now
they are very interested in reviving the language and culture. Our records
will be valuable in the effort."

Last, Farrow produced a power of attorney from the Whispering Kindom,
designating Traversed Bridge as their representative on Sarona.

Tate challenged none of it, except to establish that there was nothing in
the evidence that precluded a different remnant of the Atoka turning up
in future, with contrary demands. He also extracted an admission that the
Whispering Kindom was not the only kin group among the Manhu, and that
the others had not expressed their desires. Farrow asked Traversed Bridge to
address this last objection, as court procedure allowed.

"If there is any difference, we can work it out among ourselves," he said
softly, staring at the table. "We should have that right."

It occurred to Rue that he had not looked at her once during the whole presentation.

The court recessed for lunch, and reporters scrambled out to record their summaries in the hallway. Rue and Tate left by a back door to avoid them. She had a feeling of dread.

When the trial resumed, it was the museum's turn. Ellery Tate spoke in an avuncular, easygoing manner. Rue knew it to be an act, but it was an effective one. He gave the argument they had crafted together. "We maintain that this is not a simple case of stolen goods," he said as if it ought to be obvious to all. "The portrait of Aldry, and its tragic story, is the patrimony of two separate cultures—that of Sarona and of the Manhu. In fact, it has played a more vital role in Saronan history than on Eleuthera, and it has an ongoing role as part of our process of remembrance and acknowledgment of the painful past. Sarona needs this artwork. We seek only to share it with the Manhu."

Tate called on Rue to give a presentation about the role the Aldry portrait had played in Saronan art, history, and literature. It was her expertise, and it was easy to demonstrate Aldry's centrality. "We have constructed our own cultural identity around this image and its story," she concluded. Looking straight at Traversed Bridge, she added, "We love and honor her, because we also are her descendants."

For a second, he raised his eyes and met hers.

In a low voice, Tate asked, "Magister Savenga, what will the museum do with the portrait if our request is granted?"

"We will keep it in trust for future generations," she said. "However, we will be willing to loan it to Eleuthera, if that can be done safely. We want to assure that it is preserved and seen by all who wish to see it, forever."

"And has Traversed Bridge told you what the Manhu wish to do with it?"

"Yes. He said they wish to destroy it."

For a second, the courtroom was utterly silent. Then there was a stir, till the judge called for order.

Tate turned to the judge. "Sir, we submit that the Manhu seek to make an irrevocable choice. Their plan precludes any possibility of compromise. Once they destroy it, we can never go back. Sarona values this artwork, the Manhu don't. It is . . . "

"That's not true," Traversed Bridge interrupted, looking at him for the first time.

"Are you saying Magister Savenga is lying?"

"No. She is right. We want to destroy it, in keeping with our tradition. That doesn't mean we don't value it. We value it in a different way than you—not as a piece of property but as a living ancestor whose desires must be respected. We want to honor her wishes."

"We cannot call her to testify," Tate said.

"I must do that for her," Traversed Bridge said.

"That is hearsay."

"I would not lie."

"You may be mistaken."

"I am not." He turned to Rue, addressing her directly. "I am sorry to cause you pain. But that is the only way for us to be free of *our* pain. It has been building for generations. It is our parents' pain, our grandparents', clear back to Even Glancing. We carry it around with us, always. We must do this to free not just her, but ourselves."

Rue leaned forward across the table, speaking directly back to him. "But here's the thing, Traversed Bridge. This is not an ordinary object. At some point, great art ceases to be bound to the culture that produced it. It transcends ethnicity and identity and becomes part of the patrimony of the human race. It belongs to all of us because of its universal message, the way it makes us better." She paused, drawing breath. "Yes, it has a ghost. The ghost speaks to all of us, not in words but in our instinct toward beauty and goodness. We are better for having seen it. If it burns, something pure will pass from the world. Do you really want that?"

Their eyes locked together. Traversed Bridge looked as if he was in a vise, and it was tightening. At last he looked down.

"Do you wish to change your request?" the judge asked him.

Slowly, he shook his head. "No. I have to do this," he whispered.

"Then the court will recess for half an hour," the judge declared.

Tate was optimistic during the recess, but Rue felt no sense of satisfaction. No matter what happened, someone would be harmed. Far fewer would be harmed if the museum won; but that was like weighing souls on a scale.

When the trial resumed, the judge surprised everyone by announcing that he would give his decision, skipping the usual negotiation of compromise. "Mr. Tate is correct, the Manhu request precludes compromise," he said. "What they seek is an irrevocable right, and they have already rejected anything short of that."

Rue's heart leapt. The judge went on, "However, all the eloquent arguments that have been advanced here do not alter one fact: the portrait is a piece of property, and that is the law that must apply. The museum received stolen property. It was done in ignorance that the true owners survived, but the law is still the same. The Manhu are the owners of the property, and it must be returned to them."

The courtroom erupted into noise: jubilant noise on one side, agonized protest on the other.

Tate looked staggered. "I had no idea he would decide the case on such narrow legal grounds," he said to Rue. "We can appeal."

Rue knew that her director would not want that. He wanted to get this controversy behind him as quickly as possible. She might be able to persuade him, but . . .

"No," she said. "The law is our cultural heritage, and we have to respect it."

Across the table, Caraway Farrow was hugging Traversed Bridge in joy; but he did not look joyful. His eyes were once again downcast, avoiding Rue's. He looked exhausted.

I need to reconcile myself, Rue thought. *I need to stop caring.*

But not yet.

> How did she travel?
> They would have sent her by lightbeam,
> Fast as a flash,
> But the light did not want to take her.
> "I'm afraid to be shaped in your memory," it said,
> "Your sorrows and your exile."
> You cannot argue with light.

The artifacts could not be sent to Eleuthera by lightbeam, because what would emerge at the other end would be mere replicas of the originals, robbed of their ghosts. The fastest express ship that could be chartered would cost a fortune and take almost sixty years; but a Saronan capitalist pledged the money, and it was settled.

Rue oversaw construction of the capsule in which the artifacts would make their voyage. In the six months it took, crowds thronged the museum to see Aldry one last time. It was like a funeral. An endless procession passed by her in heartbroken silence.

On the day she came off display, Rue watched the gloved art handlers lower her into the cushioned case where she would be sealed in a nitrogen atmosphere to prevent aging. Rue wanted Aldry to arrive as perfect as she set out.

"Shall we close it up?" an art handler asked.

Rue looked one last time at that young, mysterious face. The expression hadn't changed. Rue wanted to remember it, since memory was all she would have.

"Yes, close it up," she said, and turned away. She would never see Aldry again, she thought.

But she was mistaken.

> When she comes back the sky will brighten,
> Old men will play at cards,
> Teachers will review their lessons,
> Cooks will stir broth in their kitchens,
> Ghosts will not cry in the night.
> We will be free of the past.
>> What good is the past?

Rue was a vigorous ninety-five years old when she realized that fifty years were almost up, and if she were to take the lightbeam to Eleuthera, she could arrive there in time to meet the ship carrying the artifacts.

It was not an easy decision. She would not age a second during the trip, but the rest of the universe would see ten years pass. And on the journey back, another ten years. Everyone of her generation would be dead by the time she got home, and everything she knew would change.

On the other hand, the Aldry trial had been the pivot point of her life. When she looked back, everything before it seemed to have led up to that event, and everything after had followed from it. She had spearheaded an effort to change the law—not just Saronan law, but interplanetary law—so that artifacts of surpassing cultural and historical value could be considered by different standards. A case like Aldry's would never again be decided as if she were a sack of potatoes. It was Rue's most important legacy.

Not to go to Eleuthera would mean choosing to miss the end of the story that had shaped her life, and that gave her an unsettled feeling. She wanted to be present at the end, however tragic that end might be.

Secretly, she cherished a glimmer of hope that sixty years would have changed the minds of the Manhu. Once they saw the artwork they would want to save it.

And so one day she closed her eyes on Sarona and opened them on Eleuthera. She had expected someone from Eleuthera University to meet her at the waystation, but instead, the small group waiting for her was led by

Traversed Bridge. She recognized him instantly. He had aged well. He still wore his hair long, though now it was streaked with gray, and his eyes were feathered with wrinkles. The biggest change was that he now looked confident and happy.

"This is Softly Bent, the woman who chose me," he said, "and our eldest daughter, Hanging Breath."

The two women were dressed in embroidered jackets, with their hair neatly coiled in buns on top of their heads. They both had a determined look that made Traversed Bridge seem positively easygoing by comparison.

They collected Rue's baggage and Traversed led the way to a rented electric groundcar. He drove, with Rue in the seat beside him. The city around them was a hive of activity. Everything seemed shiny, new, and under construction.

"I'll take you to your hotel so you can rest up," he said.

"Thank you. I'm too old for this interstellar travel nonsense."

"Tomorrow, we will go to the university to open the shipping capsule."

"It has arrived?"

"A couple weeks ago. They have had it in storage, acclimating."

"Good. I am glad they are treating her well."

He glanced at her sideways. "People are quite curious about why you are here. There are some who think you have come to snatch her back. If they are guarded with you, that is why."

"They can rest easy," Rue said. "The decision can't be unmade, unless the Manhu change their minds."

"That is what I told them."

They drove on a while in thoughtful silence.

"Did you ever build your dam?" Rue asked.

He smiled. "Yes. You will see it, if you come to our village."

"Of course I will come to your village. I'm not going to travel all this way and not visit the Manhu."

He nodded, but glanced at her again. "They made a song about me," he said.

"About your role in the trial, you mean?"

"About my journey, the trial, everything. And they gave me a new name when I got back. It is a great honor. I am now called No."

"Why No?"

"Because when people kept trying to get me to do this and that, and accept less than we wanted, I kept saying no."

"Hmm," she said. "That would be fine, except that the right answer is almost never 'no.' The right answer is 'maybe.'"

"I will tell them you said that," he said, amused. "You are in the song, you know."

"I can imagine. Probably the wicked woman guarding her treasures like a dragon."

"No, in our songs, dragons are lucky."

She decided she liked Traversed Bridge. Of course, she had never disliked him. She had always thought his convictions were misguided, but sincere and deeply held. But then, so were hers.

The next morning it was an ethnologist from the university, Magister Garrioch, who picked her up. He was a young man with a curly blond beard and a worried expression. Leading her to the car, he told her how he had done his dissertation on the Manhu, and had profound respect for them—"But this Immolation idea that No picked up on Sarona is just plain crazy." As she settled into the car, he paused before shutting the door. "Can't you persuade them not to go through with it?"

She gave a wry laugh. "I tried that once. It didn't end well. Anyway, what makes you think I would have any leverage?"

"No is key to this," he said. "He is deeply respected, and he respects you."

"If that is true," Rue said, "he started respecting me as soon as I stopped trying to persuade him of things."

Looking frustrated, Garrioch went around to the driver's seat and started the car. After several blocks Rue said, "I take it there is nothing you can do to prevent the Immolation?"

He shook his head. "Whenever I try to argue, No points out that the Manhu were promised freedom when they came to Eleuthera. He gets really legalistic about it."

"I'm afraid we taught him that," Rue said.

"Unfortunately, his argument goes right to the core of our values here. We really believe in freedom."

"Even freedom to do stupid and self-destructive things?"

"Even that—as No keeps pointing out. Infuriating old man."

"He was an infuriating young man, too."

Since Eleuthera had no proper museum facilities, the university was storing the shipping capsule in the basement of their humanities building. When Rue and Garrioch arrived, they found Traversed Bridge waiting along with a delegation of seven Manhu. They looked out of place in the youthful bustle of the glass and brick lobby. All but two of them were elderly women dressed in drab gray. Traversed Bridge introduced Rue to one who seemed to be their leader. "Magister Savenga, this is the Kin Mother of the Whispering Kindom, Vigilant Aspire. She is my aunt."

Respectfully, Rue said, "I am pleased to meet you."

Vigilant was a tiny, aged woman, but her eyes were quick and watchful. She regarded Rue with polite suspicion.

Magister Garrioch led them all downstairs into a room off the loading dock, where the shipping capsule waited, still sealed after its long journey. A conservator and two students stood waiting in white lab coats. There was an air of hushed anticipation.

"Vigilant Aspire, would you care to break the seal?" Garrioch said.

She stepped forward and undid the latch. As Garrioch and Traversed Bridge raised the lid, a sigh of old nitrogen escaped. Inside, the artifacts rested in their cushioned cradles. The room was silent as the conservator and her helpers lifted the pieces one by one onto a waiting table: first the drum, then the carved baby, the eggshell, and the knife.

There was a moment of consternation when that appeared to be all. Rue said, "The portrait is underneath."

The students lifted the tray that partitioned the capsule, and the artwork was revealed. They tilted it vertical so everyone could see.

There were gasps. Aldry looked exactly the same as in Rue's memories from sixty years ago. She shone, radiant, even in the industrial lighting of the workroom, with her wings revealed. She had never looked so beautiful. Rue felt a painful exaltation at the sight. It had been years since anything had made her feel like this.

Vigilant Aspire's cheeks were wet with tears. She looked reverent, moved to the bottom of her soul. Rue looked at Traversed Bridge. He also was staring at Aldry, a hint of sadness in his gaze.

The Kin Mother moved forward and raised a hand as if to touch the artwork. Rue suppressed an automatic urge to give a warning about the delicacy of the surface. It was no longer her responsibility—or her right. The Manhu owned the artwork now.

Vigilant brought her lips close to the painting and whispered something to the girl with the wings. Then she stepped back, overcome. Another old woman put an arm around her shoulders.

The Manhu spent a long time examining the artifacts and the artwork. The room seemed to fill with their emotion, tangible as smoke. Traversed Bridge hung back in order to let the others see everything, and Rue took a seat beside him. "What did she say to Aldry?" she whispered to him.

"She welcomed her home," he said.

At length, the students returned everything to the capsule and latched it again, and Traversed Bridge made arrangements to have it picked up in a truck for the journey to the Manhu village of Threadbare. Rue learned that

Magister Garrioch was going to accompany them, and arranged to ride with him.

They set out the next day in a convoy of cars, escorting the flatbed truck carrying the capsule, strapped down under a tarp. It was a long drive into misty, forested hinterlands. The farther they drove, the higher the mountains became and the worse the roads, till they were following a bumpy dirt track that writhed along the sides of sheer gulches, precipices above and chasms below. It was late afternoon when they rounded the shoulder of a mountain and saw a wide valley open up before them: green, terraced fields, a sparkling river, a bridge, and a cluster of tile-roofed homes. The convoy stopped so they could call ahead to announce their arrival and the women could change into brightly embroidered jackets.

"It doesn't look threadbare at all," Rue said to Garrioch as they stood at the side of the road looking down on the village.

"Not now. They have made enormous progress in the last fifty years, especially since they put in the dam." He pointed, and Rue saw it. She had expected something of earth and wood, but instead it was a sheer crescent of concrete, cutting off a narrow gap in the mountains upstream.

Traversed Bridge walked up to them. He saw where she was looking and smiled. "What do you think of it?" he said.

"It's amazing, Traversed. I can't imagine how you built it out here."

"We had to set up a plant to make the concrete," he said. "We imported the steel sluice gates and machinery, but we did it all with local labor. It took a long time."

"It's a great achievement. A wonderful legacy."

"Yes," he said, gazing at it proudly.

The rest of the convoy was ready to proceed. "Would you like to ride with me?" he asked her.

She surveyed the situation, then shook her head. "Thank you, but I think I'd better stay in the back of the parade. This is for you and your people."

He nodded, and headed to his car.

When they came down the steep hill into the village, they found the road lined on both sides with people dressed in their brightest clothes. The convoy passed between jubilant villagers shouting, singing, pounding on drums, and shaking rattles. After the last car passed, the people crowded into the roadway, joining the procession as it threaded through the narrow streets and downhill toward an open plaza near the river.

The vehicles stopped in front of a large community meeting house, and the crowd pressed around them. Two young men jumped onto the bed of the truck and threw the tarpaulin off the capsule. All noise ceased as they unlatched the cover and threw it back. One of them picked up the drum and held it overhead so everyone could see, then passed it down to someone in the crowd. The other objects followed. Then, after a moment of puzzlement, they uncovered the portrait and raised it high between them, showing it to the crowd. It flashed iridescent in the sun, and there was a collective gasp. For a moment, all was silent; then someone began to sing. Others joined in, till the whole crowd was singing solemnly, in unison.

"It's a welcome song," Garrioch said to Rue.

The two men descended from the truck and began to carry Aldry around the town square so everyone could see her. The people holding the artifacts fell in behind. The crowd drew back reverently to let them pass. Everywhere, people wept in joy.

Rue realized that Traversed Bridge had come up and was standing beside her, watching. She said, "I am glad to see them so happy."

He nodded. "They have known nothing but pain for so long. Generations. You can see all that pain pouring off of them, washing away."

He had been proud of the dam, but now his pride came from a deeper spot. This was his true legacy, Rue thought. Surely now he would reconsider throwing it all away. Aldry herself was the true persuader.

After circling the crowd twice, the procession of artifacts passed inside the community hall, and people started lining up for a chance to see them all again. The sun had dropped below the mountain to the west, and the air was growing chilly. A festival atmosphere had taken hold. Five musicians began to play on pipes and drums, and brightly dressed girls formed a ring for dancing.

"Would you both do me the honor of staying at my home tonight?" Traversed Bridge asked Rue and Garrioch.

"Thank you, that would be lovely," Rue said.

Reminded of something, Traversed said, "Just don't ask my wife if you can help with anything. It will offend her."

"Of course."

His home was close to the center of town, as befitted a leading citizen. It was a large structure with a concrete-block first floor and a second floor of stained wood, with intricately carved shutters and rafters. The windows glowed bright and welcoming, and electric lanterns hung from the eaves.

Inside, grandchildren were everywhere. When Traversed Bridge's daughter saw the guests enter, she hustled the youngsters off to another room. Traversed offered the guests something he called "wine," which turned out to be a potent distilled liquor. They could hear bustling from the kitchen. A young man who bore a striking resemblance to the young Traversed Bridge peered into the room curiously, and Traversed went to give him some sort of instructions.

Garrioch whispered to Rue, "No is a little hard on his son. The poor fellow can never live up to his father's standards."

"No doesn't remember what he was like at that age," Rue whispered back. *Or maybe he does*, she thought, *and doesn't want to be reminded.*

They ate a bountiful dinner with the other adults, and then Softly Bent showed Rue to a shared sleeping room with five beds. Tired from the journey, she decided to turn in early, and fell asleep to the sound of music from the town square.

The next morning she got up just after sunrise and went out, intending to walk to the river. Early as she was, a crew of Manhu were already in the square, building a cone-shape wicker framework that towered ten meters into the air. She sat on a bench in front of the community center, watching them work with a sense of foreboding.

Garrioch came into the square, took in the scene, and saw Rue. He came over to her.

"It looks like they're going through with it," he said grimly.

"Yes," she agreed. The workers were placing firewood and charcoal inside the conical framework.

"Maybe we should leave."

"No," she said. "Our presence may be a deterrent. There may be something we can do."

He looked sick at heart, but sat down next to her.

All through the morning people came, carrying belongings to hang on the wicker pyramid, or to heap around it. They brought blankets and clothes, food and furniture and fishing tackle, baskets, birdcages, books, and baby cradles. Children contributed drawings they had made and toys they had treasured. Old women brought intricate embroideries, and craftsmen gave up their carvings and tools. Everything valuable, everything treasured, was added to the pile.

By noon it was a massive tower, and men on ladders were filling the upper tiers. Vigilant Aspire came into the plaza, leaning on Traversed Bridge's arm. He brought her slowly over to the bench where Rue and Garrioch sat, and they rose to let her have their seats.

"Are you leaving?" Traversed Bridge asked the visitors.

"No," Rue said, facing him with determination. "We are going to watch."

He hesitated, taking in her expression, then looked away. "As you please," he said.

He walked off to find some other people in what was by now a large crowd of two or three thousand. Rue watched as he led a group of four others into the community building. They emerged with each one carrying an artifact. The crowd made way as they proceeded at a stately pace toward the pyre. Each artifact was handed up to a man on a ladder, who attached them high up on the framework. Last of all, Traversed handed up Aldry, and the worker hung her at the very pinnacle of the pyramid. The sun flashed on her wings, spread like a silver bird.

As the ladders were taken away, some musicians started playing a song on reed pipes and drums, and the crowd gathered round, singing. When the song ended, the musicians threw their instruments onto the pile and drew back. Five men came forward with cans of kerosene and started splashing it on the lowest tier of the pile. The square was so quiet, a child's voice asking a question echoed loudly, and laughter rippled through the crowd.

The five men soaked long-handled torches in the kerosene and lit them, then looked to Traversed Bridge for a signal.

Rue could no longer hold her peace. She pushed through the crowd to where Traversed Bridge was standing. "Traversed," she said, and he turned. "For pity's sake, stop this madness."

His face looked set, like concrete. "You don't have to stay." Then, as she refused to move or back down, the emotion he had been holding back broke through his control. "You didn't have to come at all. Why are you even here?"

"I *did* have to come," she said. "I *do* have to witness, for my people. So you will know the pain you are causing us."

"What about *our* pain?" His voice broke on the words. "Your people never cared about that."

"Is that what this is really about? Revenge for wrongs we did to you?"

He drew a breath, gathering control. "This isn't about you at all. It's about us. Our chance to reclaim who we are."

"By destroying everything you have achieved, everything you have to be proud of?"

He looked up at Aldry. "Even Glancing will live in our songs," he said. "She will still be radiant in our memories. But she will be free. And so will we."

Rue realized that the men with the torches were still standing by, waiting for Traversed to give them the signal. The entire crowd was watching silently.

He nodded for them to go ahead. The men turned and thrust the torches deep into the pile. The fire kindled right away, blue kerosene flames licking upward. The crowded square was utterly silent as they watched the fire climb higher and higher. Rue wanted to flinch away, not to see, but she forced her eyes to stay on Aldry as smoke billowed around her.

She felt Traversed Bridge take her hand, and she gripped tightly as she saw the portrait start to scorch, then blacken, then kindle. The flames were now roaring skyward, and they engulfed Aldry, hid her. Finally, the whole wicker contraption collapsed, and everything fell into one flaming pile.

There were tears on her face, though she didn't know how they had gotten there. She wiped them away and turned to look at Traversed Bridge. His face was also wet.

"We have to leave now," he said.

The whole crowd was moving, exiting the square. Traversed Bridge walked back to help Vigilant Aspire to her feet, and Garrioch came to Rue's side. "Do you want me to bring the car?" he asked.

"No, I can walk to it."

They found themselves caught in a tide of people, cars, and animals leaving the village. The narrow road was clogged, and Garrioch's car could move no faster than the general pace. Several times they stopped to pick up elders whose legs had given out, or mothers carrying babies, until the car was full and people were riding on the hood and bumper.

When they came to the wide spot on the mountain where they had paused the day before to look out over the village, the crowd stopped moving. Everyone gathered to look out over their homes, and the bonfire still smoking in the center. Rue and Garrioch got out to see what was going on.

Traversed Bridge's rental car brought up the last stragglers, and he got out to survey the scene. Then he took out his phone and made a call. Everyone was looking west to where the sun hung low on the shoulder of the mountain.

A puff of smoke bloomed from the midpoint of the dam, and seconds later came the sound of the explosion. A gap appeared in the concrete wall; then, slowly, the top started to collapse and water poured out. As the whole midsection of the dam crumbled, a massive brown gusher erupted. Gathering speed as it passed down the valley, it took boulders and trees before it, foaming as it washed toward the village.

At Rue's side, Garrioch was groaning. "I can't watch," he said. She couldn't take her eyes away. The water swept into the village, smashing buildings, engulfing the bridge, and spreading out to wash over the fields.

So much effort, so much progress, and now the Manhu were back to the poverty where they had started.

The reservoir continued to drain as the sun set, and the drowned valley fell into shadow. Everyone seemed to be preparing to spend the night where they were—lighting campfires, spreading blankets, gathering in family groups. Garrioch turned to Rue for guidance. "Should we leave?"

Rue looked around her. She didn't want to abandon them all like this and go back to the city's comforts. "If they can sleep on the mountain, I can sleep in the car," she said.

He looked relieved—partly not to have to drive the mountain roads all night, but more so not to have to make a decision, she thought.

They dined on some nut bars and fruit chips that Garrioch had in the car; it was more than some of the Manhu had. Then, as night fell, people started singing around the campfires—lilting, happy songs that the children could join, and that masked the sadness.

Rue woke before dawn. The scenes of the day before kept running through her head. When the sky started to lighten, she left the car with Garrioch still sleeping in it. The mountain air was chilly, but the sky was clear.

She was not the only one awake. Out on the edge of the cliff overlooking the valley, Traversed Bridge was sitting, his back to the camp, looking out into the void. She walked over to join him.

Below, the place where the village had been was a sea of mud and debris, a brown wasteland. Nothing had survived. Upstream stood the breached dam like an ancient ruin.

"Are you all right?" she asked.

He paused a long time. "No," he said. "It's hard to give it all up. But anything worth doing is hard."

It didn't follow that anything hard was worth doing, she thought, but left it unsaid. He already looked broken.

"What will you do now?"

"Start over," he said heavily. "Or at least, my kids will."

She was silent then, wondering how anyone could bequeath such devastation to their children.

As if hearing her thoughts, or thinking them himself, he said, "I did it for them. So they would never have to wonder if they were truly Manhu." He looked up at her. "We don't want to be like you people of Sarona, you Hoarders. We don't want to drag our past behind us. It's too heavy for us to bear."

They fell silent again. The sun peeked over a gap in the mountains, lighting the valley below them.

"Look," he said, pointing upstream. Above the dam, a large flock of birds was circling. They shifted course, then came down the valley, till they settled in a cloud on the flats where the village had been.

"Maybe they're replanting our fields," Traversed said, smiling.

Rue could almost see the flash of silver wings.

What good is the past?
The past is everything lost.
The past is never again.
The past doesn't feed anyone.
Only the future does that.

Nancy Kress is the author of thirty-five books, including twenty-seven novels, four collections of short stories, and three books on writing. Her work has won six Nebulas, two Hugos, a Sturgeon, and the John W. Campbell Memorial Award. Her most recent works are a stand-alone novella about genetic engineering, *Sea Change* (Tachyon, 2020) and an SF novel of power and money, *The Eleventh Gate* (Baen, 2020). Nancy's fiction has been translated into nearly two dozen languages including Klingon, none of which she can read. She has taught writing SF at various venues including Clarion and the annual two-week intensive workshop Taos Toolbox with Walter Jon Williams. She lives in Seattle with her husband, writer Jack Skillingstead, and Pippin, a Chihuahua puppy who chews everything.

INVISIBLE PEOPLE

Nancy Kress

1.

When I rushed into the kitchen, already late for work, Jen and Kenly were bent over her tablet, Brady was flinging oatmeal from his highchair, and the wall screen blared the animal channel. Leopards flowed sinuously through tall grass.

"Why didn't you wake me? I have a deposition in twenty minutes!"

"I did wake you," Jen said. "Why did you go back to sleep?"

"And why is the TV on at breakfast? Kenly, you know the rule!"

"It's homework," Kenly said. "I have to write a report. Look, Daddy! Scientists made a baby leopard!"

A blob of oatmeal landed on my pants leg. "Damn it, Jen—"

"Daddy said a bad word!"

Jen said, "Tom." That's all she had to say. In a marriage, good or bad, one word can say volumes. This word said *It's not my fault you overslept* plus *I may choose to be the stay-at-home parent, but that doesn't mean I can control a one-year-old armed with oatmeal* plus *Lighten up. Now.*

I lightened up. "Sorry. Kenly, what's your report about?"

"Leopards. See the TV?" But she didn't meet my eyes; she knew what was coming next. Jen took the oatmeal away from Brady, but not before another blob of it landed on the cast on Kenly's wrist. She or her friends had decorated it with glitter and hearts and tiny glue-on mirrors, currently a necessity among second-grade girls.

I raised my voice to be heard over Brady's howling about the loss of his blobby missiles and the shrieking of some jungle birds on the wall screen. "When is the report due?"

"Well . . . the outline is due today. An outline is when—"

"I know what an outline is, honey. When were you supposed to start it?"

"Monday." Two days ago. Kenly never lies to me. And she knows I'm never really angry with her. Jen and I waited too long for her, struggled too hard, made too many sacrifices in order to adopt her. And Kenly is everything parents hope for: kind, honest, smart, sunny. All children, adopted or biological, are lotteries, and with Kenly we won big. Then we got lucky again: after all our years of failed IVF, Jen got pregnant "spontaneously" with Brady.

I said, "I'll help you write from your outline tonight."

Kenly knew a victory when she saw one and, like any good lawyer, she pushed for more. "If Mom would let me *talk* in the report like normal people, with spell-check and everything—"

"No, your mother's right. You need to learn to write and spell."

"Sophie's mom lets her use spell-check!"

Jen said, "Your mom is not Sophie's mom. And I don't know what that teacher is thinking." She walked with Brady, whose eyes drooped from the exertion of the Great Oatmeal War.

I kissed her and grabbed my briefcase, now really late for my deposition. The doorbell rang.

"Two people on the front porch," the house system said. "No matches in facial recognition deebee." The wall screen had replaced the exotic jungle birds with two strangers holding up badges.

You never anticipate the moment your luck runs out.

FBI Special Agents Rosa Morales and Mia Friedman gazed around our living room, missing nothing. Not the shelf of lopsided, handmade gifts from Jen's former first-grade students. Not the three-foot-high toy space station that I'd put together wrong. Not the one expensive object, an Eric Hess sculpture that had been a gift from a client for whom I'd won a tough custody case. The object, shelved high to be safe from the kids, was spectacularly out of place. Jen wanted me to sell it, not so much for the money but because we aren't the kind of people who have museum-quality art. We aren't rich; we aren't socially prominent; we aren't saints or sinners. I don't handle the kind of divorce cases that make the news. We're invisible people, with no reason to have FBI agents sitting on our sofa, which, I now saw, had peanut butter smeared on one worn arm.

No one said anything until Jen got Kenly on the school bus and Brady in his crib. Then I said, "What's this about?"

Agent Friedman, older and clearly in charge, said, "This is about your adoption of Kenly Sarah seven years ago."

Instantly Jen went on the attack, a lioness with cubs. "There shouldn't be any problem with that. We have legal adoption papers, we went through proper channels—"

"Yes," Agent Friedman said, "but unfortunately, the adoption agency did not."

"What's that supposed to mean? My husband's a lawyer and—"

"Please calm down, Ms. Linton. Neither you nor your husband did anything wrong, and the child is legally yours. We're here to ask you exactly how the adoption progressed. The Loving Home Adoption Agency may be involved in violations of U.S. Code Title 18, Chapter 96."

I said incredulously. "The RICO Act? Racketeering?"

"Engaging in a criminal enterprise, yes."

"How?" Jen said. "Kenly wasn't bought illegally or anything. We met with the biological mother once and talked to her through an interpreter; she was accidentally impregnated by her boyfriend who then skipped out, and her religion forbade abortion. All we did was pay for her medical expenses and care during pregnancy, and we were in the hospital when Kenly was born! St. Mary's Hospital!"

"Yes, we know," Agent Friedman said. "And eventually you may be called on to testify about all that in court. But for now, we just want to hear what happened from your perspective."

Jen said, "And no one is going to try to take Kenly away from us?"

"No, ma'am. I can promise you that."

It was what Jen needed to hear. The lioness morphed back into my wife. I said, "I want our lawyer present." I am an attorney, but a divorce lawyer is a long way from racketeering indictments.

"If you wish. Meanwhile, I can at least tell you that your daughter is not the result of an accidental pregnancy, as you were told. She is the result of an offshore operation that hires indigent women to carry IVF embryos to term in order to be adopted out. You've had annual follow-up visits to the Loving Care Agency, right? Visits that included interviews with both of you, a well-child medical exam of Kenly, and a detailed questionnaire?"

Jen said, "That's all part of our contract with Loving Home. That we participate in a long-term study of adoptee adjustment."

"Not exactly," Agent Friedman said.

Brady began to fuss. The robotic arm on his crib activated and checked his diaper, then dangled a toy in front of him. He went on fussing, but for the first time ever, Jen ignored him. She demanded, "What did they do to Kenly? In those medical exams? I was right there and—"

"Nothing in the medical exams. It happened long before that, during in vitro fertilization." Agent Friedman hesitated, then apparently made a decision to say more—maybe because I was a lawyer and would find out anyway, maybe because we looked conventional enough to be trusted, maybe even out of sympathy. She said, "Your daughter's genes were illegally altered. Illegally and without consent."

"Altered? How? She's a normal seven-year-old, healthy, nothing different about her—I don't believe you!"

"It's the truth. I'm sorry."

"Have other kids been 'altered'? Who are they?"

"The FBI cannot give out names of other potential witnesses."

"You didn't answer my first question! Altered *how*?"

Brady went from fussing to full-out howl. Jen didn't move. Neither did I.

Agent Morales spoke for the first time. Her coloring matched Kenly's: smooth tan skin, exuberant dark curls, deep brown eyes. There was even a faint island lilt to her voice.

She said, "How did Kenly break her arm?"

LEOPARDS
By Kenly Linton
Some syentists made a Amur leopard. That is one kind of leopard. It went xtink many years ago. The syentists found its genes someplace and put them into a African leopard and the baby was borned! It is very cute. The mother licks it. That is leopard kisses.

2.

Mary, my assistant, had rescheduled the deposition, but I had a new client coming in at eleven o'clock. Until then, I sat in my office with the door closed, a cup of coffee growing cold beside me, and stared at the picture of my family on my desk.

Jen, laughing, her hair blowing in an ocean breeze.

Agent Friedman said that the scientists who "altered" the genes in the embryo that would become Kenly—those unidentified people—were part of a large, well-funded, offshore private organization. They implanted the embryos in poor young single girls who desperately needed the money, and then adopted out the babies through agencies like Loving Home. The girls were paid only if they agreed to parrot the pregnancy story they were given.

Brady, six months old, grinning around his first tooth.

The FBI would not tell us the name or location or purpose of the organization because it was "part of an on-going investigation." But it seemed to be an exercise in eugenics, that disgraced twentieth-century idea, done with twenty-first-century genetics.

Kenly in a ruffled blue swimsuit, pointing proudly to the sandcastle she'd just built, pail-shaped and topped with a seagull feather.

To be told even as much as we were, Jen and I had to sign papers swearing us to silence until the case came to trial.

Behind my family, the vacation cottage we'd rented on Maryland's Eastern Shore, gray clapboards weathered by wind and wind-borne sand. Every year we rented the same cottage for two weeks.

Agent Morales had described the knockout technique for cutting out one gene and replacing it with another allele of the same gene. Apparently it had been used for decades on mice, in research, then on other animals. Recently something called "Curtis tools" had made a huge leap in gene-altering precision and safety. In the United States, it was illegal to genetically engineer human embryos to birth.

Every year, as we packed up to leave the Maryland cottage and drive home to North Carolina, Jen and I discussed buying the cottage. Every year we decided against it. The failed IVF attempts, the fees to the Loving Home Adoption Agency, the kids' college funds. My modest four-partner firm didn't get the high-profile cases. Jen and I couldn't afford the cottage.

Jen shouting at the FBI agents: "I want to know what was done to Kenly! Why are you here if you won't tell us anything specific?"

Agent Morales said, "We're here for your protection, and your daughter's. The genes that have been altered involve increased risk taking. You need to watch Kenly especially carefully. That's all we can tell you."

It made no sense. Kenly was not a risk-taker. Unlike other children we knew, she didn't climb trees or her swing set or, like Bobby Cassells, the porch roof. She didn't swim out farther than we allowed her. She didn't race her bike down steep hills, unlike her friend Sophie Scuderi, who last month was taken to the emergency room with facial lacerations. Kenly had broken her arm in the most mundane of ways: tripping over a tree root in a neighbor's backyard. What was "increased risk taking" about that?

And why would an organization—any organization—go to the expense and danger of altering risk-taking genes in a few random children?

We wouldn't be going to the Maryland cottage this August. It had been destroyed by Hurricane Lester, one of the many major storms we'd all come to accept as normal as climate change worsened.

Mary poked her head into my office. "Tom, your eleven o'clock is here."

"Send her in. And after she leaves, get George in here. Tell him—her—damn it, *them*—that it's urgent."

Mary looked startled as she withdrew her head. I don't swear in the office, and usually I remember George's recent switch of pronouns.

The moment the client walked in, I smelled money. She wore an expensive summer suit—a divorce attorney has to develop knowledge of class markers including women's fashion, a subject more complicated than torts. Amanda Wells Bryant had the perfectly coiffed blond bob of her tribe, a successful facelift, and discreet bling. She also had the sourest expression I'd seen in a long time.

"I want to divorce my husband," she said, in the tone of one used to ordering around luckless servants. "And I want as much of our money and property as possible. Preferably, all of it."

"I see," I said. "Tell me—"

"You don't see," she said. "Our finances are very complicated. They include homes in France and St. Barts, and multiple companies and leveraged holdings. But I'm told you're a good divorce lawyer and your team won't gouge me with your fees."

Rich *and* cheap. That's why she chose me instead of a white-shoe law firm. Some of my clients need hand-holding, some need instructions on basic financial instruments, a few actually want a fair division of assets. She wasn't any of those types.

"Tell me your story, from the beginning." I already knew it from just looking at her, but it turned out I was only partly right. There was another woman, of course, younger and fresher. Amanda had already hired a private investigator and had compromising photos. The surprise was the speed with which she wanted the divorce to happen.

"I want it all concluded before the bastard is done with his deployment."

"He's in the military?"

"He's commander of a nuclear submarine at sea somewhere in the Arctic, a radio-silence tour of duty. Those usually get extended from three months to five, given the situation up there. I want the fucker to come home to nothing, locked out of all our houses, as penniless as you can make him. I'd like to ruin her, too, but I suppose that isn't possible."

"Afraid not." I've had vindictive clients before, but she chilled me as much as the icy welcome she wanted for a man risking his life in the Arctic. Tensions between Russia, Canada, and the United States over the newly ice-free Northwest Passage could escalate at any moment into a shooting war.

She said, "With any luck, his sub will be torpedoed and I won't need you at all."

George Whelan is the best investigator I have ever worked with. I have others to do the tedious, painstaking computer investigation that so often provides George with financial leads, but for on-the-ground legwork, no one beats George.

Until six months ago, they were Georgiana, named for a distant ancestor who was actually a notorious British duchess. Now gender-fluid and with a new pronoun, George could blend in anywhere as male, female, or androgen, conventional-looking or flamboyant, teenaged rocker or thirtysomething businesswoman. When they want to, they could also be invisible. I have passed George on the street without recognizing them. The three other attorneys in my firm envy me George, who can find anything, anywhere. They are expensive and worth it.

Today George wore jeans, a faded blue hoodie, a man bun, no detectable makeup. Actually twenty-nine, they could have been nineteen, somebody's nephew visiting the office. "What's up, Tom?"

"Something off the firm payroll. For me personally."

Blunt as always, George said, "Can you afford me?"

"Yes. Usual hourly rate plus usual expenses." It would be a stretch, but the vacation cottage was gone anyway.

"This isn't . . . I can't believe . . . Is Jen cheating on you?"

"Cheating? God, no! George, the FBI came to our house and I'm not supposed to tell anyone what they said. But I'm going to tell you. You okay with that?"

"Sure. Are you? You'll be the one breaking the law, taking on the Fibbies."

"Only if they find out. I need to investigate the Loving Home Adoption Agency, find a girl somewhere in Raleigh-Durham who gave up her baby to the agency seven years ago, and, from what you can get her to tell you, determine where her pregnancy actually came from. The child is Kenly Sarah Linton, my daughter. I have some names and dates, but not many. Are you in?"

"Absolutely. Tell me everything, every small detail, from the beginning."

My usual phrasing, but this time I was on the other side of the interrogation. George recorded me. It was the only time I ever, in all our investigations, saw their eyes widen. When I finished, they said simply, "Why?"

"That's part of what I want you to find out. Who, where, and the fucking why."

There are diffrent kinds of leopards like snow leopards and clowded leopards and African leopards. Leopards eat other animals. Once a African leopard killed a babune to eat it. But the babune had a new tiny baby! The leopard didnt kill the baby babune. It put it in a tree to save it from higheenas. It licked the baby babune. You can see the video on line. Look it up!

3.

When I got home, Jessica, our teenaged occasional babysitter, was changing Brady, Kenly was watching TV—usually forbidden on weekdays—and Jen was at the computer in my study, still in the bathrobe she'd worn that morning. She scowled at me.

"It's so confusing! Some studies say that genes for dopamine receptors like DRD4 influence risk taking, especially if you have seven repeats of the gene. Other studies say no, it isn't dopamine, it's glutamate and gamma-aminobutyric acid, neurotransmitters in the brain. Some scientists say there are more than a hundred genetic variants linked with risk taking, but even combined they account for only about 2 percent of differences in risk taking among people. How the hell can they figure out that? Then more studies say none of those studies are reliable because they use self-reporting, and people lie. I don't . . . I can't figure out . . . "

She was trembling. I took her in my arms. Her hair smelled dirty. I held her closer. Jen and I do this for each other: switch roles from comforter to one who needs comforting. I see a lot of broken marriages, and I know how good it is that we aren't each locked into one role.

When she stopped trembling, I said, "Tell me everything from the beginning, every little detail."

She pulled away and smiled wanly. "You want to take a deposition?"

"Yes. You want a lawyer present?"

"Fortunately, I have one."

We talked for a long time. She told me about the research she'd found on risk taking, which was confusing, although presumably not to scientists. I told her about George, and how much they were going to cost us.

Jessica knocked on the door. "Kenly wants to go to the park. Is that okay? Brady's asleep."

"Sure," Jen said.

We resumed our conversation, minutely examining Kenly's behavior for all of her seven years, comparing it to other children's, and ending up as baffled as before. "I want to have a full gene scan done on Kenly," Jen said. "Not the kind that just tells you where your ancestors are from—the full real thing. So I can compare it online to that of a normal seven-year-old girl."

"Honey, I don't think there's such a thing as 'normal.' The alleles—"

"You know what I mean! Don't nitpick!"

She was a tinderbox, and I was not going to light a match. "Yes, I know. We'll do it."

"I'll find some place and make an appointment for tomorrow, I—"

The kitchen door slammed and Jessica's voice, uncharacteristically loud, said, "Don't you ever do that again!"

Jen and I raced to the kitchen. Kenly stood with her purple backpack at her feet, and Jessica—Jessica!, eighteen, mathlete, Jane Austen lover—held a Glock subcompact handgun.

Jen grabbed Kenly by the shoulders. "Are you all right?"

"Yes. I hate Jessica!"

"No, you don't. Jessica, what *happened*?"

I said, "Are you licensed to carry that weapon? And did you fire it?" *Please, God, let her say no.* But my mind raced through names of criminal defense lawyers, state gun laws, and bail bonds.

Jessica, pale but coherent, said, "I'm licensed for conceal carry in West Virginia, and North Carolina honors all other states' permits. I fired the gun into the air just to scare him off."

"Scare who off? Jessica, can you tell me everything from the beginning, every small detail? Sit here, at the table. You're not in trouble, we just need to know." I used my most reassuring voice, but I'm not sure Jessica needed it. She was clearer and more thorough than 90 percent of the adults I put on the witness stand.

When Kenly's TV program had ended, she started her math homework on the coffee table. Jessica had put on the news, part of some homework assignment of her own. When Kenly's multiplication worksheet was done, she wanted to go to the park. She'd gone upstairs first and put on her backpack, which Jessica thought was odd but harmless. The backpack was new, purple with tiny mirrors sewn in a flower pattern, and Kenly loved it. They'd walked to the playground, and then abruptly Kenly had run from Jessica and wouldn't return. Jessica ran after her, but Kenly was fast and Jessica, overweight and no athlete, was not. Kenly had run straight into the homeless camp at the edge of the park.

"How did she know the—"

"It was on the news. She must have been listening. They said there were children there, and they didn't have toys."

Kenly started emptying her backpack of American Girl dolls, stuffed animals, and last Christmas's prize toy, Astronaut Jane Genuine Flight Control Console, $96.99 if you could find it at all. She called out for kids to come get toys. No kids appeared. But two men were there and one of them grabbed Kenly and said, "What else you got, girlie? Money?" The other said, "Let her go, Sam, you're drunk," but the man started to reach into the pockets of Kenly's jeans.

"That's when I fired into the air," Jessica said. "I think the other guy would have made him let her go, but I wasn't taking any chances."

A siren sounded, distant but coming rapidly closer.

All at once the self-assured junior superhero vanished and Jessica looked scared. "Will they arrest me?"

"No," I said. "I'll talk to them. And you will, too, exactly as you told me. It'll be okay, I promise."

"And you," Jen said to Kenly, "if you ever do anything like that again, we'll—"

Then Kenly shocked us more than Jessica's gun, more than Kenly's mad flight toward the homeless camp, more than the man in the park. Kenly stamped her foot and glared at us all. "I *will* do it again. Those are kids with no toys, not even one tiny damn mirror."

She burst into tears.

I didn't expect to hear anything from the FBI, and I didn't. RICO investigations can take years. I did expect to hear from George, but all I got for a month was a staggering expense bill. I wired the money to Miami.

A week later, I wired more funds to Georgia.

I was going to need a big partial payment from Amanda Bryant, whose commander husband must still be alive on a submarine gone quiet, since the navy had not notified her otherwise. Each day the situation in the Northwest Passage got worse. The United States sent warships, the Russians sent warships, Canada filed protest after protest, the ice continued to melt. So far the shipping lanes were still open, the warships' guns silent. So far.

"I hope his sub is sunk," Amanda said. "And did you find documentation for that Ukrainian shell company I told you about?"

"Not yet. We're looking."

"Well, find it. I want that money before we go to court!"

"Amanda, I've told you that Commander Bryant will be entitled to time for his lawyer to prepare his side of the case."

"There is no 'his' side. He can have his whore. I get everything else."

Had she once loved him? Had they ever laughed together, touched each other fondly, shared daily news over cups of coffee? Hard to believe.

"You better win this case," she said.

"I will." It was my job, my oath as an officer of the court, to represent my client's best interests. Even when my client was a bitch.

Kenly had turned sulky with us but otherwise behaved as usual. Not that she had much chance to do otherwise—Jen accompanied her everywhere, even if she had to lug Brady along. Kenly's gene scan showed nothing abnormal in the markers that science had already decoded. Some of the genes tentatively identified for risk taking were present, some weren't. "But you understand," the genetic counselor said for the third time, "that we have only identified proteins made, diseases caused, and genes cross-interacting for a small percentage of the codons. Genomics is in its infancy, but it's evolving rapidly. There are groups working on genomics at universities, pharmaceutical companies, government laboratories."

Jen and I glanced at each other. The glance said, . . . *and an illegal lab of unknown purpose in an unknown country doing unknown things to human embryos.*

In the car on the way home, after a long silence, Jen said, "They must at least be a hell of scientific group. To do that and still produce healthy kids. Or else the FBI is just wrong about the whole thing. Or lying to us."

"Why would—"

"I don't know. I don't know anything."

Leopards know a lot. They know how to hunt and have baby leopards and gard their teratory. Sometimes leopard mothers will take care of babies that are not even theres. I think leopards are good but I wish they didn't eat babunes. When I grow up I will be a animal trainer and train leopards to eat something else and be nice to babunes. Maybe nuts and berrys which are helthy anyway. Or bananas, like babunes do. Or leafs.

4.

George, like Kenly's leopards, knew a lot.

They strolled into my office, this time as Georgiana, with lipstick, earrings, and a maxiskirt with combat boots. I told Mary to postpone whatever was on my calendar for the rest of the afternoon.

"Good," George said. "I've got a lot to tell you. And a surprise."

"The surprise first."

"No, it's arriving separately. Tom, this is a big operation. But first, I have to tell you that the FBI caught me snooping, grilled me for a few days, and forbid me to poke around anymore or they'll charge me with interfering with an ongoing investigation, obstruction of justice, and anything else they can make stick. So I'm off the case, but you won't need me after the surprise arrives."

"Fuck it, George—"

"Georgiana."

"—I don't want any games! Just tell me what you found!"

If George was startled at my uncharacteristic tone, they didn't show it. "Okay. I found Kenly's biological mother and made her talk. It didn't take much, just mild intimidation, since these girls—and yes, I found more and I'm coming to that—are poor and vulnerable. They're all in the country illegally and terrified of being deported. The money you paid Jimena was supporting her entire family in the Dominican Republic. She birthed another genetically engineered baby after Kenly, and she's now pregnant with a third."

"The group doing the engineering is based in the Caymans. I found it, which is how the Fibbies found me. I never got inside—let me tell you, the Pentagon doesn't have security as good as this place. But my team photographed and checked out everybody going in, and it's an impressive list of scientists from four different countries, all with sterling reputations in genetics. I'll give you the list. A lot of truck activity. Some go to the airport, and then biological coolers are hand-carried aboard planes going all over the Southeast United States, France, England, and China. Scientists in the organization, which seems to be nameless, are from those countries. They—"

"But what are they doing to the embryos? And why?"

"I don't know yet. Wait for the surprise to arrive in"—George checked their watch—"about twenty minutes. And let me finish. This organization is *big*, and that takes big money. It's filtered through so many shell companies and Swiss accounts that I don't think even the FBI is going to be able to trace it. Although maybe they can—they have resources that my team doesn't. The point here is that this group is furiously altering embryos, impregnating young girls, taking excellent care of the surrogates, and adopting out the infants through legitimate adoption agencies that, so far as I can determine, might not be aware of the source of the pregnancies. Or maybe some know. The Caymans organization must have excellent cybersecurity because my guys couldn't hack their records, which frustrated the hell out of them. One actually threw his monitor against a wall."

"Will you please—"

"Seventeen minutes, Tom. Here's a major point—if these genetic alterations are dominant, Kenly's changes will be passed on to her kids. If the alterations include something called a gene drive, which I only learned about on this investigation, the altered genes get passed on to even more of her descendants than they would be ordinarily. This group, this pack of internationally distinguished scientists, is trying to slowly change the human race."

"To take more risks? Why? We already take too many risks with the future!"

George stared blankly. *Too many risks* was a foreign language; George assumed risk like a fish assumed water. I wasn't about to lecture them on the dangerous standoff in the Northwest Passage, the divorces I saw caused by stupid and chancy drug use, the carbon emissions that risked coming generations' future. I was too angry.

"If you don't tell me what this 'surprise' is—"

"I think it's me," a voice said.

She strode through my office door, Mary sputtering ineffectively behind her like a dory in a warship's wake. With effort, I kept my jaw in place. Kathleen McGuire was instantly recognizable from the news, any news. The heir to oil and shipping money, she'd then founded an investment firm that specialized in financial instruments as complicated as astrophysics. In her sixties, she'd never had work done and her face, although lined, was still beautiful. The huge blue eyes and red hair—surely, by now, dyed—were only part of it, as was her perfectly tailored suit. Couture, I guessed, but this wasn't clothing I ever saw in my office. She made Amanda Bryant look like a middle-school teacher.

"You're Tom Linton," she said. "You're the one whose nanny fired a gun, which attracted press attention. Fortunately, it went no farther. Don't let anything like that happen again."

"You can't just—"

She ignored me. "This rogue organization made a mistake. One of those genemod kids went to my niece Valerie. Your excellent investigator here found Valerie, and so me. Your daughter Kenly is another victim? There are four of us then, parents and relatives George found that received altered babies. We will band together to bring this group down. But first we need more information."

"Yes, do you—"

"George was unable to find out just what genes have been altered, and of course you already know that there's no reliable 'standard' reference genome, but there's another way. With enough computing power, which I will hire, we can have the genomes of all affected children compared to each other, to see where alleles match to a confidence level sufficiently beyond chance. Then we can have scientists examine the literature to find studies showing these genes have identified proteins that influence identified behavior. From there we can build a legal case. The key is finding more of these kids and persuading their parents to cooperate."

I said, "The FBI—"

"Can squawk and threaten all they want. Nothing we're doing is illegal, and my lawyers are not impressed with threats. You're a lawyer, Mr. Linton?"

"Yes, a divorce lawyer, and—"

"That's not much use to us, but your cooperation is. George will remain behind the scenes to coordinate the investigators I hire to find more parents. Whoever is trying to play God with our kids will be brought down after we have enough evidence."

"Why would anyone, especially a group of 'distinguished scientists,' want to increase risk—"

"I don't know. That's what we'll find out. But we need information, starting with your daughter. I've given George the questions I want answered, but let me start. Is Kenly physically healthy?"

"Yes, but she—"

"No major diseases since birth?"

"No, and—"

"How old is she?"

Kathleen McGuire was a force majeure. Even George had not corrected her use of their pronouns, or their current name. I was determined to at least have some active part in this discussion. I said loudly, "Kenly is seven, almost eight. How old is your niece's child?"

"James. He would have been six. He's dead."

Jen began homeschooling Kenly. Kenly hated it. She knew we were making sure that one of us was with her every minute but she didn't know why, and we couldn't tell her.

"I want to see my friends!"

"They can come over to play after school."

"I want to go to school! I'm missing stuff!"

"Your mother is a certified teacher, Kenly. You're not missing any schoolwork."

"She can't teach me gym! Or art! Not like Ms. Lentini did!"

Our sunny, cooperative little girl turned sullen and dour. The weather turned rainy for weeks; low-lying areas of the city flooded. People were rescued from rooftops by helicopters, from second-story windows by boats. A Good Samaritan drowned trying to save a woman swept away in a flash flood. In the Northwest Passage, a shoulder-launched missile was fired from the Canadian shore at a Russian warship and the world held its breath, but it was inconclusive who had fired the missile, which missed the ship. The Russian vessel didn't return fire.

I had a new divorce client, a tall thin man, wispy as a reed, and, I first thought, just as pliable. His wife of eighteen years, who'd left him, wanted the house. "Let her have it," he said. "I don't want it."

"Are you sure? It's the major marital asset and I advise that—"

"Let her have it."

I looked at him more closely, and revised my first judgment. This wasn't passivity or generosity. The reed was a toxic plant. I said, "Why?"

"She don't know this, but a big company bought twenty acres next door. They're gonna put in a wind farm. Those whirling things and the noise they make will drive her crazy, and the value of that farmhouse will drop like cement. There's a NIMBY group fighting it, but they're gonna lose. Cora don't never pay no attention to anything but herself, so she don't know about any of it. Let her struggle with the windmills the way I struggled to support her all these years while she sat on her ass and barely even cooked for me."

I said, "Her lawyer will find out about the proposed land use for windmills."

"She don't got a lawyer. Too cheap. Just make up the papers and get her to sign them fast."

My job is to represent my clients, not to like them.

Neither George nor Kathleen McGuire sent me reports about their investigation. Instead, a young woman who looked fifteen, but was actually twenty-seven (I asked), showed up every few weeks to talk confidentially to Jen and me. We three sat around the kitchen table after the kids were in bed, glasses of wine on Jen's lemon-patterned placemats, the whole scene so normal that I sometimes got vertigo from the contrast with what the young woman told us.

Two more parents of the gene-altered kids from "the operation" had been located. Then another one, then three more. Kathleen's scientist wanted ten complete genomes to run matches on. Two of the parents refused to cooperate. One didn't believe any of this had happened ("My kid's normal! Go away!") The other believed it but was too afraid of "the authorities" to want to participate.

Two more were found. Then three more. George had always been really good, and apparently so were their investigators.

Early on, I googled Kathleen McGuire's family. I found her niece's child's funeral notice. James Niarchos Carter, aged six: "Suddenly." Private funeral, donations in his name to St. Jude's Hospital, no flowers. Also no details, nowhere on the Internet. If there was a police report of an accident involving little James, it had been scrubbed from public records. Could Kathleen have that done? I had no idea how much her power and money could do.

When George had found their ten kids, creating the children's complete genomes and comparing them to each other could begin. But if it yielded matches in some alleles, the scientists would then have to figure out what those genes did. And then what? From where Jen and I stood, invisible on the sidelines, it seemed a hopeless task. We didn't see how it would help Kenly.

But it was all we had. That, plus the FBI investigation, plus trying to keep Kenly from doing anything risky. We could do that now; she was seven. What about when she was sixteen? Or twenty-six?

I didn't want to think about that.

One reason leopards are a little bit xtinct is pochers. They are terrible peeple who kill leopards to make rugs. If I saw a leopard rug I would tair it into little peeces. Pochers kill other animals too like elephants. Who wood do that? It is terrible terrible terrible. If I saw a pocher I would shoot him dead.

This is the end of my report. It is the longest report I ever rote.

5.

"Daddy, can we please go to the park? It's Saturday and Sophie or Olivia can't come over to play and it's so sunny out!"

Kenly stood by my desk, which was piled with work I'd brought home to do over the weekend. Jen and Brady, who both had colds, were napping. I didn't want to go, but Kenly looked so pathetic, a small prisoner in her own home. "Sure, Kennybug. Let's go."

Spring filled the park: tulips and daffodils and the smell of cut grass. People strolled, smiling; dogs strained at their leashes; children ran and shouted. I held Kenly's hand and she skipped along in her red sneakers. Jen had sewn the ubiquitous tiny mirrors on the back pockets of Kenly's jeans. She smiled at me, the first smile I'd had from her in weeks, and I thought my heart would burst.

"Can we get ice cream?"

"We can indeed. I want chocberrycocolimehazelnutmarshmallow."

"That's not a real ice cream!"

"Yes it is, and I'm going to have fourteen scoops of it. I'm going to—Kenly!"

It happened so fast. I'd always heard that time slows down in danger, that every moment is separate and crystal clear. This wasn't like that. One second Kenly was holding my hand and laughing, and the next she'd torn free, a running blur, the mirrors on her jeans twinkling in the sunlight. The dog that had broken its leash was a brown blur, and the toddler screaming in its jaws was noise and thrashing motion. Then Kenly was, too, pounding on the dog's head and yelling, "Let go! Let go of him!"

It did, and turned on Kenly, fastening its teeth on her leg and taking her down. Everyone was screaming, the air itself shrieked, and I was on the ground, pulling at the dog and beating it. The dog would not let go. The toddler was snatched up by somebody, but the dog still had my little girl and there was another sound, inhuman and inarticulate, and I was making it.

Then water. It hit the dog in the face and showered over me and Kenly, somehow becoming part of the noise. More water in a narrowing stream, and when the hose shot hard into the dog's face, it let go. I grabbed Kenly and ran. When I stumbled, someone grabbed both of us and set us upright.

"I've called the cops and an ambulance. I'm a park ranger. Stay right here, please."

I couldn't talk, couldn't think. In my arms Kenly, drenched and bloody, cried out. I couldn't decode the words, and then I could.

"Is the baby all right?" Kenly sobbed. "Is the baby dead?"

The same voice said, "He'll be fine. The baby is fine." Then to me: "No, sir, stay right here. The ambulance is on the way."

It was then, in the middle of the noise and blood and a stranger's calm voice that I suddenly knew what had been done to Kenly's genes.

"It's not as bad as it looks," the ER doctor said. "You're lucky the dog wasn't a pit bull."

Lucky. I was lucky. We were lucky. The dog's owner furnished proof of rabies shots and agreed to pay for all medical treatments. The mother of the toddler, not mollified, yelled at him loud enough for the whole ER to learn that she was going to sue the pants off him and make sure the dog was destroyed.

I took Kenly, drowsy from painkiller, home in a drivie cab. I couldn't let her sleep yet. I had questions.

"Kenly, that dog could have killed you. Why did you risk your life for that baby?"

She frowned. "You risked your life for me."

"You're my daughter!"

"He's my . . . my . . . "

I held my breath.

"He's a person," she finally said.

We stared at each other in mutual incomprehension. No, not mutual. I understood Kenly, but she did not understand my placing her life over all others because she is my child. She didn't understand, at a basic hardwired and preverbal level, the kin-based allegiance that had, through all of human history, been an evolutionary force to aid survival. All my research said that genes were selfish. Sacrificing self for kin was one way that genes survived, with the greatest sacrifices for those who shared the most genes. Hadn't some famous scientist joked that he'd gladly die for two brothers or eight cousins?

But not everyone. A man loses his life trying to save a stranger from flood-waters. A soldier throws himself on a grenade to save his platoon. A philanthro-pist donates large portions of his fortune to cancer research, or humanitarian aid to some drought-ravaged nation he will never visit, or a secret organization in the Caymans. And Kenly risks her life to pull a toddler from a dog's jaws. She breaks her arm tripping over a root in her hurry to help a baby bird that had fallen out of its nest. She tries to give her toys to homeless children.

Survival of the fittest was not the only evolutionary force that had aided human survival. The other one had been controversial for a very long time, all the way back to Darwin.

After Kenly was safely asleep in her bed and I'd told Jen everything, I called Kathleen McGuire, giving her phalanx of assistants the code she'd designated for immediate and unquestioned access. The code worked.

"Ms. McGuire, the gene comparison might not show any alteration in genes associated with risk taking."

"They don't show alterations," she said. "I just got the genomic compari-son data. How did you know?"

"Because the risk taking is collateral. But there *are* genes in the data that seem to be altered in the same way for all the kids, right?"

"Yes. Five of them. But my scientists say it's not known what proteins they code for, or how they interact, or how they affect behavior."

"Kathleen—how did your niece's son James die?"

Her voice could have re-frozen glaciers. "I'm not going to discuss that."

"Okay, but it's relevant. He died trying to help someone else, didn't he—some other kid or animal. No, don't interrupt me. I know what those altered genes do.

"They code for behavior to aid survival of the human race, even at the expense of the individual. They code for altruism."

The spring and summer passed. Kenly's leg healed. We didn't let her leave the house alone. She wheedled and begged and cried and guilt-consumed Jen and me, but we held fast.

George's investigative group found twenty-five more gene-altered children, tracing them through surrogate mothers and horrified adoption agencies. As more people realized something unusual was going on, the press began sniffing around, but so far no reporter had enough information to break the story.

The Arctic Council, backed by the United Nations, finally decreed that Canada had jurisdiction over the Northwest Passage. Canada ordered the Russian and American warships out, but pledged that all nations could use the passage for commercial shipping but not for military activities. For a day it looked as if the warships might not leave, and the world braced for nuclear war. Then both countries pulled out. Amanda Bryant's commander husband finished his submarine tour, came home to his mistress, and was served with the divorce papers I'd prepared. He promptly hired a lawyer. The case was thus guaranteed to drag on for a long time, furiously for the litigants and lucratively for me.

Lucas Wibberly's divorce was settled quickly. His selfishness paid off; she got nothing but the farmhouse. The NIMBY group failed to block construction of the wind farm, and the ex-Mrs. Wibberly was stuck with a house she didn't want to live in and couldn't find a buyer for.

The newly elected U.S. president removed all the previous admin-istration's caps on carbon emissions, and global warming continued. Low countries flooded, average temperatures edged up another notch, severe storms increased, tropical insect–born diseases moved farther north. Corporate profits rose.

It was a hard summer for Jen and me. Kenly turned more and more defiant under her protective house arrest. I found it harder to litigate for clients I could not respect. Jen's cold turned into pneumonia, which meant hiring a live-in nanny to care for the kids until Jen was no longer infectious. The only bright spot was that while her mother was ill, Kenly lost her sullenness and helped with Brady and with simple housework.

Then, in August, there was another bright spot. One night, just as we were going to bed, George came to the house, smiling.

Science doesn't proceed in straight lines. Gregor Mendel discovers the laws of inheritance and ninety years pass until Watson and Crick put a shape to genetic structure. It's sixty more years until the first mostly reliable gene editing tool, and then ever shortening time jumps as techniques leap forward in precision and scope. Now, with major advances every few years, we can alter genes so much more than we ever thought we could, and so much more than laws allow.

But laws, too, undergo punctuated evolution: periods of inertia are followed by periods of quick change. In the United States, it was still illegal to alter human embryos. It was not illegal to develop gene therapies—genetic changes inserted into the human cells of children and adults via viral vectors—that could combat gene-caused diseases like cystic fibrosis and hemophilia.

"And also combat what the organization in the Caymans did," George said. They were hypermasculine at the moment: flannel shirt, jeans, work boots, mustache. Was the mustache fake? I had no idea.

Jen said, "Kenly doesn't have a disease."

"There's a gene therapy being tested at Berkeley that is adaptable to the kids' conditions. The vector to deliver the new genes is delivered by liposomes, which is safer than using a virus. The researchers there are eager to see if it works. And Kathleen got a compassionate use exception to full FDA trials."

Jen said, "They want to experiment on these kids!"

I said, "Compassionate use exceptions are for people who are dying."

"Then Kathleen got an exception to the exception," George said impatiently. "She has a lot of influence. Guys, this is a way to reverse what was done to Kenly."

"An untested way!" Jen said. "Kenly is not some lab rat!"

George said, "It's not completely untested, and not just on animals. One parent already had it done on their four-year-old, and he's fine."

I said, "I want to talk to that parent."

"You can't. Anonymity was part of his deal. The press is going to get this story soon, and nobody wants their child splashed all over the internet. Also, although I don't have confirmation of this, my sources say the FBI is close to indictments, which may stop the Berkeley group from proceeding with their experiment. You need to decide now."

Jen said, "Don't pressure us!"

I put a hand on her arm. Unlike me, Jen is not used to getting clients, witnesses, and juries to cooperate. I said, "George, don't think we're not grateful to you for all you've done. You and Kathleen. A chance to reverse what was done to Kenly is more than we expected. You've done a phenomenal investigative job. It's just a lot to take in, and we need a little time."

"Don't pull your lawyer tricks on me," George said, but they smiled. "You don't have a lot of time. Here's the home phone number on an encrypted line for the lead scientists at Berkeley. She says call anytime as long as it's soon—she wants your decision. I gotta go see some other people."

After they left, Jen said, "No. We can manage without some experiment on Kenly. Don't you know the history of scientists experimenting on people? Tuskegee with syphilis, Crownsville with drilling into brains, Sloan-Kettering with cancer cells injected into—"

"Stop. I know. I've done the same research you have. We have to talk this out completely, Jen. From the beginning, every small detail."

"Don't you dare treat me like you're taking a deposition!"

I apologized. Jen apologized. Then we sat in our living room, close together on the couch, and talked as a sliver of moon rose beyond the window, no bigger than a child's fingernail. Moonlight glinted on the edges of our wineglasses like sunshine on Kenly's tiny mirrors.

The treatment was experimental.

Risk taking was part of altruism, and two of the altered children had already died taking risks.

Genes were complicated things, and you don't just charge in and alter them without the risk—that again!—of turning on or off other genes. When Kenly finished the therapy, would she still be Kenly?

Would she still want to help people, to give selflessly? There was so much selfishness in the world. I saw it every day in divorce cases. I saw it on the news, whole countries risking nuclear annihilation to get what they wanted, when they wanted it. Corporations repealing environmental and safety laws to maximize their own profits. And against them, good and generous people who valued fairness, who sacrificed personal safety to save drowning strangers, take on Ebola in distant jungles, deliver food to starving people who shoot them for it. I wasn't naive; these same people could probably be selfish in other contexts. But they were good people.

The scientists in the Caymans probably also thought of themselves as good people, as did whatever billionaire philanthropists were funding them. They were creating and scattering seeds of heightened altruism. Enough seeds would survive to pass on that altruism, aided by the biological mechanics of a gene drive, to eventually swing humanity toward greater concern for each other, for their societies, for the future. It might be a small and scattered planting, but it *was* a planting and, in time, might spread like kudzu. The scientists were growing goodness.

Was I going to make my daughter less good because she might become too good? She might do something generous for her entire society. Or she might just become one of the everyday altruists, the volunteers at nursing homes, builders for Habitats for Humanity, neighbors you can count on to help without expecting anything in return. The true invisible, indispensable people.

After we made our decision, we went upstairs to gaze at the kids. Brady lay sprawled in his crib, one arm flung around his favorite blankie. Kenly lay straight in the bed like a miniature soldier. "This scene is such a cliché," Jen said, and gave a single sob.

After she went to bed, I stayed up, drinking a bottle of Scotch somebody gave us last Christmas, which had sat unopened in the back of the pantry. The crescent moon left the window and clouds moved in. Eventually it began to rain, a soft pattering against the pane. I opened the window to smell the spring.

2:00 a.m. That was 11:00 p.m. in California, not too late. The lead scientist, whoever she was, wanted our decision.

I picked up my cell to make the call.

Dilman Dila is a writer, filmmaker, and author of a critically acclaimed collection of short stories, *A Killing in the Sun*. His two recent novellas are *The Future God of Love* and *A Fledgling Abiba*. He has been shortlisted for the BSFA Awards (2021) and for the Nommo Awards for Best Novella (2021), among many accolades. His short fiction has appeared in many anthologies, including the *Apex Book of World SF 4*. His digital art has been on exhibition in the USA, South Africa, and Uganda. His films include *What Happened in Room 13* (2007) and *The Felistas Fable* (2013), nominated for Best First Feature by a Director at AMAA (2014). You can watch his short films on patreon.com/dilstories and find more about him on his website dilmandila.com.

RED_BATI

Dilman Dila

Red_Bati's battery beeped. Granny flickered, and the forest around her vanished. She sighed in exaggerated disappointment. He never understood why she called it a forest, for it was just two rows of trees marking the boundary of her farm. When she was alive, she had walked in it every sunny day, listening to her feet crunching dead twigs, to her clothes rustling against the undergrowth, to the music of crickets, feeling the dampness and the bugs, sniffing at the rotten vegetation, which she thought smelled better than the flowers that Akili her grandson had planted around her house. Now, she liked to relive that experience. With his battery going down, he could not keep up a real life projection and, for the first time, she became transparent, like the blue ghost in the painting that had dominated a wall of her living room. Akili's mother had drawn it to illustrate one of their favorite stories.

Granny laughed at the memory. "That ghost!" she said. Her voice was no longer musical. It was full of static.

He could not recharge her. He had to save power, but he did not want to shut her down because he had no one else to talk to. He did not get lonely, not the way she had been: so lonely that she would hug him and her tears would drip onto his body, making him flinch at the thought of rust. She would hug him even though she complained that his body was too hard, not soft and warm like that of Akili. He did not get lonely like that, but Akili had written a code to make him want to talk to someone all the time, and he had not had a chance for a conversation since the accident, twelve hours ago.

He had resurrected her after her death, while he waited for a new owner. He used all recordings he had made of her during their ten years together to create a holographic imitation of her so he could have someone to talk to. It was not like walking with her in the mango forest, or sitting at her feet on the porch as she knitted a sweater and watched the sun go down. Technically, he was talking to himself; but it was the only chance he had for conversation.

She stopped talking abruptly when white-cell.sys beeped. A particle of ice was floating about like a predator shark. If it touched him, he would rust. He jerked, like a person awaking from a bad sleep, though the ice was ten meters away. Steel clamps pinned him onto a shelf. He could not get away.

The half-empty storage room looked like a silver blue honeycomb. They had dumped him in it after the accident ripped off his forearm. The Captain had evaluated his efficiency and, seeing it down to 80%, tagged him DISABLED. They could not fix his arm on the ship, so they shut him down and dumped him in storage until he got back to Earth. Entombed alive. Left to die a cold death.

"You won't die," Granny said, laughing. She sat on a fuel pod in a cell on the opposite shelf. "It's just a little ice. It's not even water."

He had lived all his life dreading rust, watching his step to avoid puddles, blow-drying his kennel every hour, turning on the heater all the way up to prevent dew from forming. He knew it was irrational, for his body, made of high-grade stainless Haya steel, was waterproof. He never understood his aquaphobia. Had Akili infected him with a program to ensure he stayed indoors on rainy days? Very likely. Granny liked playing in the rain as much as she liked walking in the mango forest. Yet every time she did, she got a fever, sometimes malaria. Akili might have written a code to force Red_Bati to stay indoors on rainy days, and so Granny, who used him as a walking aid and guide, stayed indoors too. Red_Bati could have searched for this code and rewritten it to rid himself of this stupid fear, but he did not. He loved it, for it made him feel human.

"I'm not worried about the ice," he said. "It's the temperature."

He was in Folder-5359, where temperatures stayed at a constant -250° C to preserve fuel pods. Technically, the cold would not kill him. He had a thermal skin that could withstand environments well below -400° C, but it needed power to function. Once his battery ran down, he would freeze and that would damage his e-m-data strips. Though these could be easily and cheaply replaced, he would lose all his data, all the codings that made him Red_Bati and not just another red basenji dog, all his records of Granny. He would die.

"That won't be a bad thing," Granny said, chuckling. "If you were a true dog, you'd be as old as I am and wishing for death."

He was not a dog. He was a human trapped in a pet robot.

Granny chuckled again, but did not say anything to mock him again. She watched the ice and tried to touch it, but it passed through her fingers and floated upwards. It would not touch Red_Bati, after all. He relaxed. If he had flesh and muscles, this would have been a visible reaction. Instead, white-cell.sys reverted to sleep mode, the red light in his eyes vanished and his pupils regained their brownish tint.

His battery beeped, now at 48% for white-cell.sys had used up a lot of power in just a few seconds. In sixteen hours and forty-three minutes, it would hit zero, and then he would die.

"You're not a human in a dog's body," Granny finally said, still watching the ice as it floated towards the ceiling.

"I am," Red_Bati said.

"Humans have spirits," Granny said. "You don't."

"I do," Red_Bati said.

"You can't," Granny said.

"Why not? I'm aware of myself."

"Doesn't mean you have it."

"Why not?"

"You're not a natural-born."

Red_Bati wanted to argue his point, to remind her of things that made him human, like agoraphobia; to remind her that he got consciousness from a chip and lines of code, just as humans did from their hearts, and brains. He was not supposed to be conscious, much less super intelligent; but Akili had wanted Granny to have more than just a pet, so he installed Z-Kwa and turned Red_Bati into a guide, a walking aid, a cook, a cleaner, a playmate, a personal assistant, a friend, a doctor, a gardener, a nurse, and even a lover if she had wanted. She could live her last years as she pleased rather than suffer in a nursing home.

After she died, Akili had put him up for sale along with all her property and memorabilia. For a moment, Red_Bati had feared that Akili would remove Z-Kwa and wipe his memory, but Akili contracted a cleaning firm to get rid of Granny's property and either forgot or did not care to tell them about the chip. Red_Bati was too smart to let them know he was more than just a pet. Nor did he show it off to the people who bought him, Nyota Energy, an asteroid mining company that, rather than buying miner-bots, found it cheaper to convert pets into miners. They gave him a new bios and software, a thermal coat, x-ray vision, and modified his limbs and tongue to dig rocks. They did not look into his ribcage cabin so they did not see Z-Kwa, otherwise they would have removed it. When they shut him down after his accident, Z-Kwa had turned him back on, aware that if his battery drained, he would die. He had self-preservation instincts, just like any other living thing with a spirit, and he wanted to tell her all these things, but she was draining his battery.

"Sorry," he said. "I have to conserve power."

"That's okay," she said.

He blinked, and she vanished. His battery life increased by two hours.

He examined the three clamps that pinned him to the cell. They had not expected him to awake, so they had not used electronic locks. With his tongue, he pushed the bolts on the clamps, and they snapped open. He could escape. The room had only one camera, at the front, to track crew who came in to pick up fuel pods. If it saw him, the ship would know he had awoken and service_bots would pounce on him and remove his battery. To hide from it, he needed the identity of another robot.

He checked the duty roster he had received before the accident. He did not expect the fuel roster to have changed since his accident only affected the cleaning roster. The next pickup was due in an hour, a karbull dragon-horse. It would not do. Six hours hence, it would be a tomcat, and then in thirteen hours, a robot that looked like him, a basenji dog. He wrote an identity-stealing app and hibernated.

He awoke ten minutes to time. His battery was down to 35% and would last for another ten hours. He slipped out of the cell, staying behind the shelves to hide from the camera. He floated to Shelf-4B and hid inside Cell-670, where he could see Cell-850, which had the fuel pod to be picked up next. He heard the outer door open and close. Then the inner door opened. The two doors ensured the temperature of Folder-5359 stayed at a constant -250° C, while the ship was a warm 16° C.

The basenji floated into view, riding a transporter tube. It saw Red_Bati but did not raise any alarms. It adhered strictly to its programming and ignored anything out of the ordinary, assuming the ship was in total control. Astral-mining companies stopped sending self-aware and self-learning robots many years ago after a ship had developed minor engine trouble and its crew, seeing their chance of returning safely to Earth had dropped to ninety-nine percent, landed on an asteroid and refused to move until rescue came. Fearing to incur such needless losses, the miners resolved to send only "dumbots" incapable of making vital decisions without human input.

For a moment, Red_Bati wondered what had happened to the owner of this basenji. Its jaw was slightly open, its tongue stuck out to imitate panting, a design that little boys favored. He hoped its owner had only grown tired of it and had not died. He did not feel empathy the way Granny felt whenever she saw a dead ant; she felt so terrible that she would bury it. Granny had thought a dead child more horrible than a dead ant and Red_Bati wanted to feel as she might have felt.

He waited until the basenji turned its back to him as it positioned the tube to suck the pod out of the cell. He turned on his x-ray vision to see the basenji's central processor and the comm receptor chip, both located just below the backbone, and on which the basenji's serial number and LANIG address were respectively printed. Two seconds later, his app was ready.

It would take ninety seconds for the pod to enter the tube, and in that time, Red_Bati had to take over the basenji's identity. He aimed a laser beam at the other dog's left ear, which was its comm antennae, to disable it. He activated his comm receptor at the same moment that he fired the laser beam. There would be a delay of a thousand micro-seconds, between the basenji's going offline and Red_Bati's assuming its identity, but the ship would not read that as strange.

Red_Bati went into hoover mode which consumed a lot of power but allowed him to move quicker. He tapped on the power button at the base of the basenji's tail, and the basenji shut down in three seconds. He grabbed it by the hind legs, guided it into an empty cell, and clamped it.

He raced back to the carrying tube and ten seconds later a beep came. The pod was inside the tube. He pushed it to the door. The tube had a temperature-conditioner that kept the pod chilled at -250° C to keep it from decaying. If a decayed pod ended up in a fuel tank, the engine's temperature would shoot from 80° C to a blistering 300° C within fifteen minutes. Fire would break out in the Ma-RXK section while there would be explosions in the Ma-TKP section. With eight engines, the ship would not stop if one was damaged, though its speed would drop. But fire in the engine made the ship vulnerable to hijacking.

Red_Bati turned a dial on the tube, turning off the temperature-conditioner. It would take two minutes to reach the fuel tank and by then, though the tube's temperature would have dropped by only two degrees, the pod would have decayed.

The ship was logged onto the tube, so the moment decay set in, the ship would be alerted and service_bots would not allow the pod into the fuel tank. Red_Bati had written an app to fool the ship into thinking the pod was still good. Hiding from the cameras, he had secretly fixed a finger into one of the tube's data rod to infect it with his app.

Stealing the ship, his calculations told him, was a very bad idea. The asteroid mining companies would not rest until they understood why a ship suddenly went dark. They would send probes to all corners of the solar system and Red_Bati would be running for the rest of his life. The other option, to hide until they reached Obares, an asteroid in the Kuiper belt rich in kelenite, did not seem possible. He could not hide his missing arm from the ship's cameras for the next two years of the journey. If he managed to, and got on the asteroid, he could sneak away with enough supplies, a tent, machines and spares, and he could use the sun to recharge; but that would mean growing old alone, with no one to talk to other than a holograph.

The ship was worth the risk. It had enough resources on board to sustain robot life for eternity, to create even a whole new world. It had VR printers that could give birth to new robots, who would be conscious like Red_Bati. Nyota Energy could have printed for him a new arm, but the cost was equal to buying another second-hand basenji, so they reserved VR printing to fix critical damages to the ship and to replace worn-out engine parts.

Once he had the ship under his control, he would take it somewhere far from human reach, maybe beyond Earth's solar system. He could hop from one asteroid to another, mining minerals to make fuel and VR cartridges, until he found a place big enough and rich enough to be a new home. The VR printers could give birth to new robots, to other VR printers, and even to new spaceships. He would not be lonely anymore.

Red_Bati kept his body close to the tube to hide the missing arm from the cameras and opened his mouth and stuck out his tongue to imitate the panting basenji. The storage section was on the lowest level and the engines were in the midsection at the back of the ship. He followed tunnel-like corridors and did not meet other robots until he neared the engines, and the three he passed did not notice him: their eyes were focused in the distance. If they were humans, he would have exchanged nods with them in greeting, maybe even a cheerful, "How's it going?"

He reached Engine 5 without raising any suspicion. The fuel tank was in the first room. Its floor looked like the swimming pool which Granny had in her backyard. Things that looked like purple ice cubes swirled in a mist in the pool, under a glass lid. Red_Bati placed the carrying tube on the edge of the glass and pressed a button. The tube opened, the glass parted, and the pod slipped into the pool. The moment it touched the mist, it broke apart and thousands of ice cubes floated about. They were not a deep shade of purple like the others: they looked desaturated, but the ship would not immediately pick this up because the steam swirling above the pool gave the cubes fluctuating shades. It relied entirely on the tube to alert it of a decayed rod.

Red_Bati hurried out of the engine, still shielding his body with the now empty tube. When he reached the Supplies Folder, he did not shelve the tube, for he needed it to hide his missing arm. He settled in a corner, and five minutes later got the first message from the ship, which had noticed that he was not going to Docking for his next assignment. The message had a yellow color code, indicating low level importance, inquiry only. If he were any other robot, he would have auto-responded by sending the ship an activity log and system status, and the ship would have analyzed it and notified the Captain to take action. Z-Kwa blocked his Comm_ Sys from sending the auto-response. The ship sent another message two minutes later, with a blue color code and an attachment to auto-install a program to force a response, but Z-Kwa deleted the attachment. The ship waited another two minutes, and then sent a third message, in white color code. It had notified both the Captain and Nyota Energy on Earth about his strange behavior, and it had told them that two service_bots were on their way to take a physical look at him.

Before they could reach Supplies Folder, the ship sent a message in red color code to everybot: *A Red-Level event has occurred in Engine 5.* Red_Bati could not hear the explosions. The ship was silent, as though nothing was happening. The ship would know that decayed fuel was responsible and would associate Red_Bati's strange behavior to the crisis, but all service_bots would be needed in the engine to contain the disaster and none would come after Red_Bati.

The first sign that the ship had become vulnerable to hijacking came in the next red message, hardly ten minutes after Red_Bati got the yellow message. *Kwa-Nyota is going into sleep mode.* Once in hibernation, other engines would shut down, all non-essential programs would shut down, all auto functions would cease, and all robots, apart from the service_bots and the Captain, would go to sleep too. Seventy-five seconds after the message, the lights went out.

Red_Bati activated infrared vision and made his way to the heart of the ship, where the data servers glowed in the dark like the skyscrapers of

Kampala. When he was sold to Nyota Energy, he had scanned the internet for everything about the company and its space crafts. He did not have any particular need for the information but was only responding to a very human instinct: *know your employer.* He had blueprints of the ship, a Punda Binguni model built by Atin Paco, a Gulu-based company that had pioneered low cost space travel. He had the source code of all its software and its operating system, Kwa-nyota. First, he went to the Comm Control Panel and flipped several switches to OFF, cutting communication with Earth. Now, Nyota Energy could not stop the hijack by sending the Captain direct instructions, nor could it track the ship.

The Captain would notice that it had lost communication with Earth, but would not send a service_bot to check, for all fifty service_bots were in Engine 5.

It took Red_Bati fifteen minutes to write a program to convince the ship to take instructions from him rather than from Nyota Energy. Then he used a jiko data cable to connect physically to the ship's mainframe, making him a part of the ship. It took him another ten minutes to deactivate the security programs and install the hijacker. When he unhooked the cable, he had control of the ship.

All that work had drained his battery down to eight percent. He had to wait for the service_bots to put out the fire before recharging. He went to sleep again. He stayed in the data room, for the rest of the ship froze during hibernation.

The Service_bots spent nearly an hour putting out the fire and stabilizing Engine 5. The ship came out of hibernation and so did Red_Bati. He checked the cameras and saw smoke billowing from the engine, though this was mostly from komaline fire-suppressing solution. Three service_bots were severely damaged and were on stretchers to Storage. It reminded Red_Bati of Granny after her last stroke, as medics took her to a waiting air-hearse. Like the Captain, the service_bots had humanoid structures, though their thermal coats gave them an alien skin, and as Red_Bati watched them leave Engine 5, he began to daydream about finally leaving his dog body.

He hurried to Docking where the robots were still asleep and sat on a charging chair. The other seven engines ignited, and in thirty minutes the journey resumed. The robots in Docking woke up. One of them was a humanoid in police uniform, a pet that girls loved. Red_Bati did not want to think about the little girl who had owned it. They had programmed it to be one of the ship's extra eyes. It noticed Red_ Bati's missing arm and sent in a report. If Red_Bati had a face of flesh and skin, he would have smiled at this cop. Instead, he blinked rapidly and made a happy, whining sound. Granny would have known he was laughing at it. Red_Bati sent all robots a message, stripping the cop of his powers, and the cop stopped looking at him.

Once the ship was running again, the Captain checked its inbox for new instructions. It could not maintain speed, now that it had lost one engine. It could not reach Obareso on schedule. The ship needed a new schedule. Every bot needed a new schedule, otherwise their systems would hang up in confusion. The captain found only one new message which, when opened, auto-installed a program and changed its coding and instructions. The captain immediately changed course to another asteroid, Madib Y-5, a flat rock ten miles long, seven miles wide, right in the middle of the asteroid belt, with generous supplies of kunimbili, from which they could make enough fuel pods to take them beyond human reach.

Granny flashed on, no longer bothering to hide from the cameras. With his battery now at 60%, she looked real. Her smile was full of teeth. It surprised him because she never used to smile like that. She did not like false teeth and thought the few teeth in her gum made her ugly.

"Good job," she said.

He shrugged only in his mind, because his body was incapable of shrugging. "I don't see the point," she added. "After you land on a bare piece of frozen rock, what will you do with your life?"

Nothing, he wanted to say. I'll be alive. I'll start a new world. Then he saw what she meant: robots sitting on frozen rocks, basking in the sun like lizards, looking out at the emptiness of space, enjoying the brightness of stars that shone around them like a giant Christmas tree. Just sitting there and not looking forward to anything. The VR printers would give birth to more of his kind, but they would not grow like human children. They would be fully functional adults at birth, with almost nothing new to learn because they would have all the knowledge that forebots had gathered.

Would exploring for new worlds and searching for new matter give their lives a meaning?

Humans needed a purpose to live. School. Job. Wedding. Children. Adventure. Invention. Something that would make them wake up the next day with a cheerful smile, though they knew there was no purpose to it all and that they would eventually die, and all their achievements would turn to dust. What life would his kind have? He could write coding to make them think like humans, to make them fall in love and get married and desire children, to make them have aspirations and build grand cities and spectacular spaceships and desire to travel deep into the galaxy. But they would be self-aware and self-learning and might then wipe off the code. Some might even decide to return to Earth.

He wanted to smile, to tell Granny that that was the beauty of it all. Like humans, they would live without knowing what tomorrow would bring.

"I want to rest in peace," Granny said.

"You are not a ghost," Red_Bati said.

"Am I not?" she said. "Look at me, look!" She walked as though the ship had gravity. She tried to touch things, but she was like smoke. "See? I'm a spirit."

"You are not," Red_Bati said.

"What do you think spirits are?"

He was quiet for a while, thinking of the painting her daughter had made. He could not be sure anymore if it was all code. Humans, after all, imagined spirits into existence.

"You'll be our goddess," he finally said.

She laughed. "That's a beautiful dream," she said. "But I want to rest in peace. I don't want to spend the rest of eternity talking to a metallic dog that thinks it's human."

Red_Bati imagined himself giving her a smile, the polite smile that a human would give a stranger in the streets. Then he shut her down and wondered what had gone wrong. She had never been mean to him. She had never called him a "metallic dog" before.

Maybe he should write new code so he could have Granny again, the Granny who took him for long walks in the mango forest, not this grumpy spirit.

S.B. Divya is a lover of science, math, fiction, and the Oxford comma. She enjoys subverting expectations and breaking stereotypes whenever she can. Divya is the Hugo and Nebula nominated author of *Machinehood* (Saga), *Runtime* (tordotcom), and the short story collection, *Contingency Plans For the Apocalypse and Other Possible Situations* (Hachette India). She co-edits the weekly science fiction podcast *Escape Pod*, with Mur Lafferty. Her short stories have been published at various magazines such as *Analog, Uncanny*, and *Tor.com*, as well as anthologies including *The Gollancz Book of South Asian Science Fiction* and *Where the Stars Rise*. She holds degrees in computational neuroscience and signal processing, and she worked for twenty years as an electrical engineer before becoming an author. Find out more about her at www.sbdivya.com or on Twitter as @divyastweets.

TEXTBOOKS IN THE ATTIC

S. B. Divya

The first flood of the season arrived last week. It takes a while for the waters to rise, but the ground floor is mostly submerged already. I warned Rishi not to play near the water, but he is five years old and, much like his father, insists on learning by experience.

When I hear him shriek, I know from the tone that he's gotten hurt. Jin and I exchange a glance across the kitchen. I put down the carrot I'm peeling and head toward the sound.

Rishi sits at the top of the staircase, tears spilling down his round cheeks, his left palm a bloodied mess.

"Jin," I call, trying to keep my voice steady. "Some help, please."

I lift my sobbing and sopping wet boy and carry him to the bathroom. Jin arrives and, without a word, he grabs a washcloth and presses it into the wound. Rishi clutches me with his other hand.

"Shh, it's just a cut," I say.

As Jin blots the blood away, I can see that it's deep. I hug Rishi's body tight as Jin douses a clean cloth with alcohol. We ran out of ointment two months back, when Rishi took a nasty spill off his bike. Though I'm expecting the howl of pain, it still makes me wince. I hold the wriggling little body tighter, always surprised at his strength as he tries to squirm away.

Jin is efficient and has the cut wrapped and tied in less than a minute. He follows us to the kitchen where I fish out a peppermint from the good-behavior jar. Rishi gasps for air as he sucks on it, and my shoulders relax.

If it weren't flood season, I'd take him to the hospital to get stitches, but transporting him in the rain carries as much risk as a wound. *He's young*, I think. *He should heal fast.*

The next two sunrises bring barely more light than the nights that precede them. I always kiss my sleeping child after I get up. This morning, his forehead feels warm under my lips, more than usual. I sniff at his wounded hand and almost gag. Angry red streaks radiate away from the bandage.

Jin stirs as I pull on my raincoat.

"Where are you going?" he murmurs.

"Rishi's cut is infected," I say softly. "I'm going Uphill to see if I can get some antibiotics before I go to work."

I step onto the balcony and uncover our small boat. We removed the railing when the rain started, turning it into a dock for the wet season. I push off into the turbulent water flowing through the street and start the motor. The boat putters upstream. Four houses down, the Millers are on the roof in slickers, checking their garden. They wave as I pass by, and I slow down enough to ask if they have any antibiotics, but they shake their heads, *No*.

"Good luck!" Jeanie Miller calls after me, her brow furrowed in concern.

Their youngest died last year, just six months old, from a nasty case of bronchitis.

Above, tendrils of moisture-laden clouds reach toward me from the sky. Heavy drops pelt my head and shoulders. My fingernail beds are blue from the chill in the air, and I flex my hands to keep the blood going. The water around me runs muddy brown, the opacity increasing as I approach Uphill. I navigate by memory. The neighborhood looks different during the wet season, the buildings like peaceful islands, the destruction of the last few decades hidden away.

We live upstairs all year long now. I barely remember when the first chain-storm happened. I was six, and today all I have are impressions of being wet, cold, and hungry. Of my father in tears. Of sitting at the top of the stairs watching the inexorable rise of water.

I round a corner. The street rises from its submerged state like a concrete scar. Uphill begins a hundred yards from the water, walled off from the rest of us. Beyond the locked gates stand two-story shops, and further up, stately brick houses with verdant lawns. The neighborhood looks much like the memories from my childhood, but a little worn at the edges.

I cut the motor and paddle the last few boat lengths to the dock house, an old church with columns repurposed for tying up boats. I slosh through the calf-deep water then up, to the guardhouse.

Jack is on duty, his graying head bent over a piece of wood as he whittles. I rap on the window. He squints at me through the rain-blurred glass, then deigns to crack it an inch.

"Everything's closed," he growls.

"I need some antibiotics for my son. Can you radio to the hospital?"

He slides the window shut, then picks up the walkie-talkie. I can't hear what he says, but he's shaking his head in the negative as he cracks it open again.

"Supply flight didn't make it last week, what with the early storm. Emma says the Downhill allotments have run out, plus there's a flu going round at school. They're saving up for the pneumonia and such that comes with it."

I open my mouth to protest and then close it. What good would it do? I have nothing special to offer in trade, nothing they'd want. The Uphill areas weathered the early storms better so they quickly became prime real estate, and after the initial riots, they turned into secured enclaves. They have the only airstrip, and it might be weeks before a flight can land.

Jack's expression softens by a hair's breadth. "It's nothing personal, okay? Your dad was a good man, but we gotta look after our own first."

I manage a curt nod before walking away. Back in the boat, I don't bother with the motor. I grab the oars and secure the strap of my adapted oar above my left elbow. I wasn't much older than Rishi when they took most of my left hand off. I'd mangled it in the propeller of our old boat, but my father was a doctor at the Uphill hospital, and they treated me well.

"The greatest threat to our lives is once again bacteria," he said more than once. "Wash every cut or puncture, no matter how small. Keep it clean and dry until it heals. With so much moisture, who knows what new germs we'll have to fight."

That was before the supply shortages gave his words greater truth. At one point, he and my mother considered returning to India, but every part of the world faced climatological problems. They stayed here in Iowa with the hope of giving me a better chance at an education, going so far as to send me to California for college.

That's where I met Jin, and also where I discovered a new program in distributed horticulture, part of a push from the US government to move away from mass agriculture. It boiled down to, "Don't put all your eggs in one basket," or in this case, all your seeds in one field. California kept getting incinerated and learned its lesson early.

As one of the program's first students, I got a full-ride scholarship. I chose to return home and settle outside of our gated enclave. The people Downhill needed my help more, but my father's former colleagues didn't appreciate my "defection." This isn't the first time I wonder if I made a mistake.

At home, Rishi sits at the kitchen table and munches on bread with jam. Jin hands me a slice with cheese and fresh tomato slices from our roof garden. My stomach growls in anticipation.

"May outdid herself with this loaf," I say, savoring the crunch of grain as I lick tomato seeds from my wrist.

"She had a shipment of whole wheat last week from her cousin, harvested just before the rains started," Jin says. "Bread won't be this good again for months. Where are the antibiotics? Rishi should have one with breakfast."

"They didn't have any," I say.

"At all?" Jin's dark eyes widen in alarm.

"For us."

He locks eyes with me. I can see the anger build.

"I'll go after lunch and have a *word*," he says.

Rishi picks up on the tension in his father's voice and looks up from the table. He has Jin's eyes and my unruly hair, which frames his face in thick, dark curls. I've nearly given up on trying to comb out the tangles.

"What word?" our boy asks innocently. Dark brown stains the bandage around his palm.

"A bad one. Very, very bad," Jin says.

I swallow the last bite of my toast. "Give me some time to ask around first."

He glances at Rishi and presses his lips together. A nod, a shrug, and he moves back to the dishes.

Jin had a hard time adjusting to the Midwest when he moved here with me. He's happy now in our community, which welcomed him as a new neighbor, but he's never made peace with how we're treated by Uphill. San Diego has its fair share of problems, but they aren't the same as ours.

As I shower and get dressed for work, I savour the lingering taste of May's bread in my teeth. My dad lectured me on the importance of antibiotics from an early age, telling me about Alexander Fleming's famous experiment gone awry and his accidental discovery of penicillin on moldy bread. My work involves stopping the spread of mould in rooftop gardens, but perhaps I can flip the script.

I climb the ladder into the attic and find the box of textbooks from my dad's time in medical school. *Microbiology. Biochemistry. Organic Chemistry.* I grab them all and stuff them in my dry bag along with another slice of bread from the kitchen.

I kiss the top of Rishi's head on my way out. "Be good and keep your hand clean and dry. Stay out of the water!"

He waves at me nonchalantly as I leave for the lab. Jin does most of the work of raising our child and maintaining the house. Someone has to, and he's better at carpentry and a more patient teacher than I am. Outside, the street water swirls with oil slicks and debris as our world washes itself clean.

Paul, my labmate, peers over my shoulder. "What are you reading?"

"I'm trying to figure out how to make penicillin," I say.

"What on Earth for?"

"Rishi cut his hand playing a few days ago. I want to make an antibiotic. Any ideas?"

"Um . . . something about moldy bread?"

"Yes, the blue-green mould in particular, but you have to extract and purify the antibiotic part."

"Couldn't you get any Uphill?"

I shake my head. "Their supply is low."

Paul picks up the radio. "You're going to need more than textbooks to figure this out. Let me see if the internet is up and running at the comm-house."

While he does that, I tear myself away from the books and check on my other fungal work. A particularly nasty strain of leaf mould hit the region during last year's flood season, and we lost half of our legume crops. We can't afford that for a second year or we'll run low on essential proteins.

"You're in luck," Paul says.

I look up from the microscope. "Oh?"

"They're running about five megabits right now. Go!"

"Thanks, Paul!"

I take the elevated walkways that connect the buildings of what used to be a university campus. The older stone structures have held up better than the later wood or concrete ones. The mechanical engineering department built the drawbridges that we use every wet season out of reclaimed steel. Their surfaces clatter under my steps as I run to the comm-house. It used to be the alumni house, but it has the best line-of-sight to the communication satellites that provide internet so, like most other buildings, it's been repurposed. The parking structure beside it is now the town's transportation hub, and its roof our primary source of solar panels.

The rain thins as I approach the house, and I race up the steps without opening my umbrella. A break in the clouds allows a beam of sunlight through, enveloping the five meter dish atop the house in brilliance. I take it as a sign of hope.

"Hi, Menaka," greets Jonette, shoving the sign-in clipboard at me. "Paul radioed that you're coming and why. Doctor Branson gave up fifteen minutes for you. Work fast!"

"Thanks," I say, breathless.

The history professor nods at me from the waiting area. As a faculty member, he's allowed priority over nonprofit community projects like my horticulture lab. The university campus has diminished, like everything else, but they do their best to maintain academic standards. I give him a grateful smile as I slide into the empty workstation chair. A stack of notepads and pencils sits next to the keyboard. Bamboo loves the new climate and it makes good paper, too.

I do a quick search for how to make penicillin and come up with plenty of archived information as well as more recent instructions. *There's no such thing as an original idea.* The same sites warn me that penicillin isn't effective against all bacterial strains. I dig deeper and learn that the reduced supply of antibiotics worked in our favor. In an ironic twist, the drug-resistant germs from the turn of the century had been replaced by newer, more vulnerable strains. Penicillin might actually work against whatever Rishi contracted.

I write down the ingredients needed for the nutrient solution, the best way to filter the drug, and methods to test the results. Then I review the risks. The two biggest are impurities in the solution and failing to isolate penicillin. Another type of mould, Aspergillus, has a similar appearance and color, but under a microscope, they look different. My biggest problem, however, is time. It typically takes a week to grow a decent-sized batch of penicillin, enough for one person with a minor infection. If their blood is septic, forget it.

By the time I get all of that written down, my time is up. The rain must have resumed because the bandwidth drops. I apologize to Doctor Branson on my way out.

"No need," he says. "History has no sense of urgency. I hope you found what you were looking for."

"Yes, thank you."

The tornado sirens start to wail halfway through my return. I get to the building that houses my lab and head to the shelter room, a windowless space in the center of the building. Paul is crammed in there with another dozen people. I squeeze my way to him with apologies to the rest.

"Good news and bad news," I say.

He cocks an eyebrow.

"I can make the penicillin," I whisper, "possibly even a safe version, but it'll take more than a week."

"That's a problem?"

I lift my shoulders in a tiny shrug. "Rishi's cut is already infected. He might recover without intervention, but he was in the floodwaters."

Paul frowns. "If it gets bad enough, the Uphill hospital will have to admit him."

We both glance at my left hand. I know what he's thinking: that unless it's a life-threatening emergency, they won't take Rishi. *By then he could have sepsis,* I think. *That might be too late, especially if they already have a supply shortage.*

After the all-clear sounds, we return to the lab. I place a small piece of May's bread, moistened, in a sealed bag and then head home for lunch. Rishi is napping when I arrive, his cheek warm under my lips.

"Well? What did you find?" Jin demands as soon as I'm away from the bedroom.

"No one nearby has antibiotics, but I found a recipe to make penicillin. We have the equipment and I think I can find the ingredients to extract it from mould, but . . . " I trail off.

"But what?"

"It'll be a week before it's ready, and it might not work against the bacteria in our water," I say reluctantly.

Jin's face resembles the thunderclouds outside. "That's too long. Remember the Arken girl?"

"Lily," I reply.

Eight years old. Her family didn't recognize the signs of infection until it was too late. I recall her mother sobbing at the funeral, "It was just a scratch. A scratch!"

Jin walks away without another word, heading for the attic. I follow him. I need to find a medical textbook this time, one that lists the signs of sepsis. I find what I need and turn to see Jin slipping a gun into his jacket pocket.

"What are you doing?" I ask, trying to keep my voice steady.

"What someone needs to do. I'm going to round up the militia and take them with me. We're not going to let another child—my child—die because Uphill refuses to help us!"

"And what about the next person? And the one after that? How many of you will die along the way from injuries? Do you remember what war used to be like?"

"This isn't the eighteenth century," Jin says. He stabs a finger in the general direction of Uphill. "They have everything we need, and if they won't share willingly, then we'll take it by force."

"Even if that works this time, what happens in a month or next year? They're low on supply because the storm delayed the latest drop. We're fighting for scraps from them. How much longer can we go on like this? We need to take charge of our own destiny. We've already done it in a hundred ways—we grow most of our own food, we repair our houses, we teach our children, we make our own electricity. Now we'll treat our own illnesses."

I head for the ladder.

"Where are you going?" he calls after me. His tone indicates he isn't done arguing.

"Back to work," I say. "Your armed incursion can wait."

I drop down from the attic before he can form a retort. Maybe I'm overreacting, but I'm too angry to care. *Reckless. Stupid. Selfish.* My mind flashes through all the ways Jin could get injured or killed trying to force his way into Uphill. They have guns, too, and they won't hesitate to use them. The law is on their side.

Paul spins on the lab stool like a child. "We need to create a shadow hospital."

"What?"

"A hospital of our own, independent from the one Uphill."

"And how do we get the nurses and doctors to work there? Uphill has them all because they can pay. We can't."

Paul shrugs. "We trade, like we do for everything else. Money is a social construct built on value, right? If we provide what they need—food, water, shelter, utilities—then they don't need 'money'." He puts air-quotes around the last word.

As he speaks, I start sterilizing a flask. I want to start a second mould culture using a rotting cantaloupe I got from the Ayala's hothouse. According to my notes, the mould on its rind should include Penicillium chrysogenum, a more potent form than the one on bread.

"It's a good idea," I say, "if we can make it work."

"We can," he says firmly. "After emancipation, we had Black hospitals run by Black doctors and nurses. If my people could do it back then, no reason Downhill can't do something similar today."

I nod, trying to be supportive. Paul turns back to his work, and I start looking at the ingredients for the nutrient broth. Cornstarch and Epsom salts are easy enough. I grab a handbook of common chemical compounds to look up the rest. Lactose monohydrate comes from milk sugars. Crystalline glucose—more sugar to feed the mould. I have a bag of sodium nitrate for when we need extra nitrogen in our soil. Potassium dihydrogen phosphate brings down the pH—I'll probably need to visit the chemistry lab for that. Magnesium and zinc or ferrous sulphates—more items from the chem lab— or a combination of the metals with sulphuric acid, which might be easier to get my hands on. Hydrochloric acid to fine-tune the pH. And after a week of growth, acetic acid—the primary component of vinegar—for the purification process.

I can work with this list. Even if I can't get the exact chemicals, I can substitute. I've grown enough fungi to know that the basics of nutrient broths are the same: sugars for energy, acids for pH. The details have to do with optimization, but I'm not going for industrial production. The hard part will be waiting for the mould to grow.

By the work day's end, I've cultured my broth with cantaloupe mould and set it in the incubator. Low-voltage lights glow from wet rooftops as I row home. Street lights became impractical along with pavement. Exposed wiring could fall into the flood-season riverways, and anything buried underground needed repair too often. Thanks to the leftover solar panels from the boom years, we could light our own way.

I try to drink in the beauty as stars twinkle from the breaks in the cloud cover. Wind blows over my exposed skin, carrying scents of wet wood and moldy leaves. A lone, brave bird calls from a nearby roof garden. Ripples shatter the street lights into a thousand tiny fragments all around me.

I try to focus on my surroundings and avoid thinking about the confrontation waiting at home. Or the state of Rishi's wound. Or whether penicillin will be an effective antibiotic. Or any of the other problems that I can't solve. Starting the Penicillium culture left me feeling powerful, the same way I felt after the first year that our neighborhood grew its own crops. The militia started in those early days, to protect the gardens from opportunistic thieves, especially in the dry season.

I step onto our balcony and haul the boat up after me. Warm air blows from the electric room heater inside. Rishi lies on the sofa, eyes bright—fever bright?—and watches a show on his tablet. I avoid Jin's gaze as I hang up my wet clothes to dry.

"Hi Mommy," Rishi says as I stoop to kiss him.

"Hello, love," I say. His skin feels less hot. "Let me see your hand."

He shakes his head and grimaces as he tries to hide it from me.

"He hasn't let me clean it all day," Jin says quietly from behind me. "Temperature was at one hundred when I last checked."

I dread what's coming, but it's unavoidable. Dealing with a kicking, howling five-year-old is a two-adult process. Jin holds him while I get a good look at the wound. I try to remember what I read in the medical textbook. The swelling and redness have increased. The smell is worse, and the pus might be greenish—I can't tell for sure in the dim light. Rishi's screams are heart-wrenching as I pour diluted alcohol over the wound.

After it's all over, we give him two pieces of hard candy and ourselves a glass of whiskey each. At least children have the luxury of forgetting. I hardly remember my amputation anymore. My parents probably had a worse time of it.

Once Rishi is asleep, we finally have time to talk.

"I think it's going to work," I begin. "My penicillin extraction. A few more days, and it'll be ready. I don't have to wait for the full growth to complete."

"I radioed Loqueisha earlier. She agrees with me."

Loqueisha started the militia and became its de facto leader as a result. She has a sensible nature, and I usually trust her judgment.

"What did you tell her about our situation?" I ask.

"The truth. This goes beyond the three of us or your lab experiment. This is about Uphill monopolizing health care and not taking our problems seriously enough."

"So you're going to confront them no matter what?"

"Yes. Tonight. I was just waiting for you to get home."

"Give me a few more days, please." I reach for his hand, and he pulls me into a hug. The hard lump of a gun in his pocket presses against me.

"I won't risk Rishi's life," he whispers into my ear. "You keep doing what you're doing. It's important no matter what happens tonight. I love you both."

And with that, he's out the door.

"Goddammit," I mutter.

I remember the images of gunshot wounds from my father's textbooks. I sit at the kitchen table and vow not to sleep until Jin comes home.

My head jerks up from the table. My heart thuds. A flash of lightning blinds me, and seconds later, thunder rumbles overhead.

"Mommy?"

I hear Rishi calling from the bedroom and glance at the clock. Four in the morning and no sign of Jin.

I pad over to the bedroom and squeeze in next to my boy.

"Where were you? Where's Dad?"

"Hush," I say, pulling him closer. "It's okay. Go back to sleep."

He whimpers and snuggles into me as thunder cracks directly above. I listen for the sirens, but they remain silent. Heat radiates from his little body. I don't need a thermometer to know that he's feverish. It must be disturbing his sleep because storms don't usually wake him.

As the front passes, the steady sound of rain begins, and Rishi relaxes into my arms. He sleeps. I worry. Where are Jin and the rest of the militia? If they'd succeeded, he'd be home by now.

My thoughts go around and around until dawn fades in. I lie still as long as I can, not wanting to disturb Rishi's slumber. At some point, I must doze off because the doorbell startles me awake.

I ease myself from the bed without waking my boy. I open the door to a familiar face, round and lined with soggy gray curls framing it. It takes my sleep-addled brain a few seconds to remember the name.

"Doctor Mitchell?"

She nods and steps inside. "How are you, Menaka?"

"Worried," I say before I can stop myself. What a ridiculous thing to confess to the surgeon who treated my injured hand decades ago. "Not to be rude, but what brings you here?"

She reaches into an interior pocket of her raincoat and pulls out a small bottle. "I heard you were in need."

Before I look at the label, I know what must be inside. "Thank you."

Anger deepens the furrows around her eyes. "We learned about the demand from your husband and the others over the network last night. Some of my idiot colleagues thought they shouldn't be rewarded for coming at us, but we took an oath when we became doctors, and I for one intend to uphold that. Stockpiling life-saving drugs for the eventuality of greater need? What phenomenally arrogant bullshit!" She examines me from head to toe with a professional eye, then nods in satisfaction. "I'm glad you're well at least. They have your militia people in our little jail. I'm sorry. I don't know how long they'll be held or what the charges are."

I curse Jin's folly in my thoughts and try to keep my expression neutral.

I must have failed because Doctor Mitchell says, "Don't be too angry with him. If he hadn't acted last night, I wouldn't be here."

I blow out the breath I'd started to hold, then say, "Is there anything I can give you in return?"

"Of course not," she says. She opens the door.

"Wait," I say. "I'm working on something—on making penicillin. I heard the hospital is short, and I thought it might be better than nothing. If it works, I'll bring you some."

Her gray brows rise in surprise. "Good for you! Take a culture from your child's wound and test that it's effective. With all the turn-of-the-century overuse, you can't be sure what's growing in the floodwaters these days."

"Thank you," I say again, at a loss for words in the face of her kindness.

With that, she's out the door and motoring back upstream.

Later that day, after dosing Rishi and settling him in the capable hands of May and her baking, I check on my lab culture. The liquid has turned murky brown. No sign of the layer of gray mould that should have formed on the surface.

I growl at it in frustration.

Paul turns from his bench. "Problem?"

"Yes, but I'm not sure what."

He shrugs. "You don't need it anyway."

"Yes I do!" I snap. Then, taking a breath, "Sorry. I know Rishi will be fine—this time—but I was hoping to start another small industry. We're going to need essential drugs, and the supply drops are less reliable each year."

He holds up a placating hand. "Okay, chill. You have more of everything, right? Even that half-rotten cantaloupe. I know 'cause I smelled it when I opened the fridge. Be a good scientist and start over."

"Fine. Yes, you're right. I've only lost a day."

"What's the rush?"

I wave my hands vaguely at the outside. "Whoever next gets sick or injured and doesn't have a friend Uphill."

"I'll say it again: we need a shadow hospital. Then someone with better lab hygiene could do this instead of you." He grinned.

"Thanks, buddy," I say dryly. "Your confidence is inspiring." Then, more seriously, "It's a good idea. You should bring it up at the next community council meeting."

Paul taps his temple with his index finger and turns back to his work. I dump the flask into the organic waste and begin again, this time wearing a mask in addition to gloves and working under an improvised tent of plastic sheeting. With the overseas trade routes disrupted by storms, any kind of plastic is precious, but so are the nutrient broth chemicals. The only thing we have in abundance is rainwater.

A week later, the new Penicillium culture reaches the disgustingly black stage that means it's almost ready for decanting. I'm bumping around our small kitchen, riding high on my lab success and trying to find the ingredients I need for a casserole. Rishi sits at the kitchen table, swinging his legs and constructing something with bamboo sticks and glue. His cut isn't fully healed, but the wound has closed, and the swelling and fever are gone. I have to bribe him with apple juice to get the antibiotics down, but it's a trivial cost. Our attic is well-stocked with cider from last Fall's harvest.

"Is Daddy coming home tonight?" Rishi asks.

The question has become part of our nightly ritual. So has my answer: "No, but maybe tomorrow."

We've heard that Uphill is going to charge Jin and the others with aggravated assault. I'm fairly certain the charge is bullshit, but that doesn't mean I get my husband back any time soon. The community lawyer lives two streets over and will do his best to defend the group. At least I won't have to worry about legal fees.

A boat clatters against the balcony, the sound followed shortly by a sharp rap at the door. I open it to find Doctor Mitchell at our doorstep. I don't like the look on her face.

She comes in and, upon seeing Rishi, puts a smile on. "How are you, little one? Looking well, I think."

"I made a boat," Rishi beams, holding up a bundle of sticks and glue.

"That's wonderful," the doctor says, sounding genuine. "I need to borrow your mom for a few minutes. Is that okay?"

My son nods. In the next room, Doctor Mitchell leans close to me. Her raincoat drips on my arm.

"Jin tried to stop a fight at the jail," she says in a low voice. "He's been stabbed."

I try to process this as everything fades but her voice.

"It didn't hit anything vital. He's out of surgery and stable, but we're still waiting on our supply drop," she says. "We're out of antibiotics. A bout of bronchitis swept through our middle school last week, and we dispensed the last of it two days ago. The city council is debating whether to pay for an expedited shipment, but even if they do, I'm not sure how incentivized they'll be to help a potential Downhill criminal."

"He's not—"

"I know," she says, her voice gentle. "But that's how they'll frame it. Your penicillin—is it ready?"

"The culture's growth is good," I say. "I haven't decanted or purified it yet. Or tested it."

"How long will that take?"

"I don't know. I've never done this before. Hours, maybe?"

My heart starts racing at the thought. I have to do it carefully, without contamination or waste. I know the quantity won't be much, not compared to a pharmaceutical grade, but it has to be better than nothing.

"Can you wait here while I make the extract?" I ask.

"I'll do one better—I'll come and help you."

I stuff a sleeping bag and pillow into a dry bag, then bundle Rishi into his rain clothes. Thankfully, he's excited about the night-time journey and the prospect of staying up late. We take Doctor Mitchell's boat, which is better than ours. I direct her to Paul's house.

He takes one look at my face and asks, "What's going on?"

"I need your help in the lab."

I can see him put the equation together: lab plus emergency equals penicillin.

"Gary, I gotta run out for a bit," he calls to his husband. "Don't wait up!"

It takes us four hours to correctly decant and purify the penicillin from the growth medium. Rishi is fast asleep under a desk, and Doctor Mitchell dozes in the chair we have for visitors.

With a trembling hand, I place a few drops of the antibiotic on a petri dish. Next to me, Paul takes a sterile swab and collects some bacteria from the test culture. After he inoculates my dish, I close the lid and set a two hour timer. We roll up our lab coats and use them as pillows on the floor.

The buzzer wakes me from a deep sleep. A dream about deadly amoebas fades as I remember where I am and why. Paul snores nearby, and Doctor Mitchell has moved to the floor as well.

I tiptoe to the lab bench and prepare two slides, one from the healthy bacteria and another from our penicillin test. It takes me extra time to get the microscope's focus right with my sleep-blurred eyes, but once I do, I can see the broken cell walls.

"It works," I whisper.

Tears well and take me by surprise. I bite my knuckle to keep from sobbing and waking everyone. I hadn't admitted to myself how scared I was that all of this would fail. That Jin wouldn't make it . . . he still might not, but at least now we'd have a fighting chance.

After I compose myself, I gently shake Doctor Mitchell's shoulder. As her eyes focus on my face rather than her dreams, her mouth widens in a smile.

"You did it," she whispers.

As she rouses from her seat, Paul wakes. He gets the doctor the vial with all of our precious penicillin extract. I scoop Rishi off the floor and heft him, still asleep, onto my shoulder. Pre-dawn lightens the eastern skies, heavy with clouds, and a gentle breeze ruffles my hair.

Doctor Mitchell leaves us at home with a promise to get word on Jin's status in a couple of days. "I won't give you false assurances," she says, "But this is far better than nothing."

I examine the new hundred gallon tank installed in the corner of what used to be a classroom in the humanities department. Doctor Branson was generous with more than his internet time. "Making history is at least as important as studying it," he said. "I'll teach from the town square or my own home if I have to."

We've taken the first step to larger production, and I have a plan for making other antibiotics once we're successful. At the other end of the room, behind a partition, Paul hunches over the extraction and purification equipment. He wears a sterile jumpsuit, face mask, and gloves, and his brow furrows in concentration.

I slip a glass container filled with crystalline penicillin into my pocket and head downstairs. The week before, I'd mailed a sample to a pharmaceutical plant in Oregon for testing, and the result had just come in: a solid yes.

On the floor below, a series of offices is now filled with cots. Two of them have patients, and I find Jin and Doctor Mitchell in one of them. Jin meets me in the hallway. He walks with a limp from a tendon that got cut during the fight. The stab wound in his side had been the greater danger, but the assailant had nicked his leg as well.

"Is that the good stuff?" he says, taking the bottle from me with a smile.

"Certified Grade A Penicillin," I reply. "I'm off to pick Rishi up from school."

"See you tonight." Jin kisses me and heads back to work as Doctor Mitchell's assistant.

I row my way to the Millers' house, which doubles as our newly minted elementary school. Rain dribbles down my hood. I'll need to oil the cloth again soon to keep it waterproofed.

Ahead of me, a handful of solar panels glisten on top of our community hospital. Each one comes from someone's home. We'll have to live with fewer lights at night, but that's a small sacrifice to take charge of our own health.

I pull the boat against the Millers' balcony. Rishi steps in, a wide grin on his face, and hugs me before sitting down, making the boat rock. He laughs at my alarmed expression, then pats the water like an old friend as I row us home.

Canadian by birth, M. L. Clark now calls Medellín, Colombia "home." Clark is the published author of science- and speculative-fiction stories in *Analog, Clarkesworld,* and *Lightspeed*, with work in three other year's best anthologies, and a first novel, set in the same universe as three *Clarkesworld* stories, currently moving through the mainstream-publication pipeline.

SEEDING THE MOUNTAIN

M. L. Clark

Even the eared doves had begun to droop.

High atop the cement-grey panels of Aeropuerto Olaya Herrera, their breast-feathers resembled well-worn Spanish-colonial tiling, bruise-red like the roofline over apartments, bike shops, and tiendas across the street, and when one of the birds fell—a heavy drop, without recovery—Luis Miguel Ramirez Díaz thought for a second that the whole damned building might be coming apart. The possibility thrilled him. Drumming his green Atlético Nacional cap against jeans heavy with sweat, he imagined marching over the ruins, straight to the hangars, and taking off single-handedly over the rubble. Triumph over failure—someone else's, at least—sure as hell beat sitting around with no one else to blame for the morning's defeats.

"Todo está bien," the front desk had assured him, when he had tried to find fault, first, with the airline for refusing to let anyone through. Give the airport a few hours, he was told, and the tarmac would cool, the molecules in the air would sufficiently condense, and his chartered pilot would crawl out of whatever hammock was keeping his guaro hangover at bay.

The AI's attempt at humor had been designed to alleviate the tension, and it might have worked, too, if Luis's desire to get away from the downtown core, to re-immerse himself in the sort of rural disaster he'd the training to manage, hadn't superseded all claims to peace. But the smug look on the face of that last potential investor, and the soul-patched chin left unclocked even after all their heated words at breakfast, loomed too fresh in mind, so Luis had thumped the automated front desk instead—and then the real muscle arrived, leaving him to wait for his flight outside the stagnant cool of the airport lobby. By the time the eared dove fell dead on the opposite drag of concrete, Luis had been busy for half an hour staring down the irriguous heatlines of midafternoon Medellín—once the City of Eternal Spring; these days more like the City of Eternal Summer—trying to weather his temper in turn.

Then a woman in a flowing yellow rain-poncho swooped past him for the bird.

"*Ya muerta, ¿es pelota?*" Luis muttered, aggravated by the spectacle of wasted effort. But the woman showed no interest in offering aid. Instead, she procured a canister and doused the dead creature before stepping back, peering up, and waving at a drone idling by.

"*¡Listo!*"

And in the wake of this magical word, the bird's body began to deflate, or—no, dissolve, but without the usual searing of acid. In another century, the great Gabo would have summed up the miracle in a sentence running pages long, interwoven with tales of floating virgins, moldering fallen angels, and dictators who died and maybe rose again. Luis, however, recognized the logo on the yellow poncho—had worked, or rather wrangled, with Disease Prevention and Public Safety often enough—and so the proximity of reconstructive nanotech, restricted to government use under severe penalty, stoked only his envy. How much easier his own projects would be with the aid of such versatile machines. And time. And speedier access to all the sites where so much preventative work could be—should be—done.

"Patience," his business partner, Claudia, was always telling him, but therein lay a key difference between the two. Luis had grown up in the shadow of a defaced war monument, listening to the squawk of city parrots and neighbors gibbering on about some new era's dawn—a peace treaty with the ELN to bookend the monumental close of half a century's guerrilla and paramilitary strife—while she had known the coast of Venezuela in the hard years before full dictatorial collapse. Two of her brothers starved to death in their mother's arms. Her father spent months bound to a beam in a military outpost. Neither spoke much of what her mother did to protect the rest. And yet, late at night in the work-tent, while something kept eating at the core of him—an anger, maybe, that he had come so close to witnessing greatness once, then lived to see the pendulum swing away again—he would hear Claudia singing while she reviewed comp-chem readings for deposit sites in their latest disaster zones. *Singing.*

Luis knew then most of all that he envied her over something unconscio-nable—her childhood's lack of hope, and how rich in possibilities it had made the present and the future seem by contrast—but knew better than to say such a thing aloud. Or to get too close, lest he ruin the little joys she'd found for herself: the solitude of her strength against so unbearable, some-times, a world. There were other places, other ways, to defuse the heat in him, and on his trips to Medellín, he usually took full advantage of that net-work. But not this time, not with their budget so tight already, and so—he would simply have to find his peace by other means.

This was easier said than done, though, while private-security milled about the auto-cars parked by the airport lobby, and Luis wondered how many of their clients were more of that foreign ilk buying up so much of the surrounding countryside's resources; and his irritation with all of them, all the sellouts, only rose when the woman in the yellow poncho confirmed completion of her task through an earpiece connecting her to central author-ity. Hers had been such a small task, really—something that could have been automated long ago, like the AI front-desk rep handling airport intake—but the sight of technology dissolving life forms without human oversight under-standably terrified people after the Six Cities incident, so some redundancy of labor had to be factored into the new nanotech economy. The only ques-tion for Luis was, to what end? The people's benefit? *Really?*

Luis granted, at least, that although the DPPS could not be present at every natural death, their minor performances did seem to reassure citizens that the latest zoonotic threats from rising temperatures were more or less under control. And even in smaller towns, central churches and municipal buildings all had prominent DPPS pedestals, green and yellow with a contact screen, that could be used if ever a local spied a mysterious case of illness. But at day's end, Luis also knew, the government gambit remained as cynical as it was clever: a spectacle of hypervigilance against animals and machines to help people forget that the greater danger always came from fellow human beings—like the foreigner investors in their auto-cars; and the Colombians who kept them safe while they divided up the land, and all other lives upon it.

And so Luis had worked up a full treatise on the nation's subtle and not-so-subtle failings by the time his own earpiece buzzed with word that the air-port was beginning to rouse itself, and that he needn't storm over the build-ing's rubble to escape the day's worst disasters yet. The realization deflated him—for how much easier his morning's disappointments would seem if they could be held against a city in even greater disrepair. *Sure, Di-Di, I*

*couldn't get the funding, but you should see these guys, and what the situation's
like in Medellín these days!*

But it wouldn't fly. Not with Claudia. And after the woman in the yellow
poncho had moved on, after the last of the dead bird's nutrient-rich dust had
vanished in the breeze, Luis noticed that even the doves had simply regrouped
to fill the gap, and returned to wearied rest. What use, to any of them, was he?

Doctora Claudia Irina Vallejo Restrepo let Señora Sanchez lay hands on her
and pray. It seemed the easiest way to hasten things along. The third-floor
apartment was hot even with the corner fan running, and Claudia hadn't the
heart to tell the older woman that, due to the power shortages all about town,
it probably shouldn't be running at all. The family already had no water and
no gas, and for weeks had joined the rest of the barrio in cookouts on the
street. What little human dignities remained were invaluable, if fleeting, so
what was the point of cutting their pleasure short, when the rest of Buriticá's
problems would catch up in due time?

But while the mother prayed for them under a wooden carving of the Holy
Family, Claudia noticed the Sanchezes' youngest daughter, Elena, poking
through her satchel for one of the diagrams printed one block over, intended
for easy distribution to any local who was not so big on reading text. Claudia
made a point of meeting the little girl's gaze and smiling.

"Strange, aren't they? But that's what we're going to do to the mountain,
to make it safe from landslides for everyone in the future."

"You should just put a giant fence around it," said Elena, tilting first the
paper, then her head, with a puzzled frown. "This seems like a lot of work."

"That's the fun part—it's not. Once we start the process, the chemistry
takes care of itself. Do you like science?"

Elena furrowed her brows. "Uh uh."

"That's not true," said Sra. Sanchez, quickly. "Elenita is very smart, one of
the smartest in her class. Gets it from her father, maybe—his people have a
special connection to the land here, and all the teachers here say that if she
really applies herself to biology—"

"Ughhhh," said Elena, pressing both hands to her ears. "I hate biology."

Her mother pursed her lips, then whispered to Claudia, "Her sister is starting to hang out more with the boys and she feels left out. My God, raising
girls! Mother help me!"

Claudia tried to make a sound of sympathy, though with no children of
her own she found the complaint bizarre. Weren't there problems with kids
across the spectrum?

"You're in luck," she said instead, turning to Elena. "You can meet some interesting boys in science, too."

"Did you? Is that him, your boyfriend?" Elena had pulled out a professional poster with Claudia and Luis's smiling faces—something the mayor had asked for, once she returned from her own fieldwork for the day, to post in the municipal building for citizens who had neither wristbands nor desktops to stay abreast of local updates. Claudia laughed.

"My work partner—and no, he's not a scientist, not officially. He leaves all that to me and organizes most of the rest: contractors, permits, funding. Gives me more time to do a good job with my end of things—the occasional errand like this aside."

"And you promise you won't start until the road's been restored?" said Sra. Sanchez.

"No, of course not," said Claudia, with a reassuring pat on the mother's hand, over the tightly clutched rosary. "We would never risk this material accidentally growing attached to sections it's not supposed to. First the repair crews, then the bounding walls, then seeding."

"But how does it know when to stop?"

"It's not the same as a real root system: it's a finite amount of a specific substance that will bond well with certain parts of its environment. When the initial substance runs out, the interactions cease. But by then, hopefully, they'll have reached enough of the mountain to make it secure for, oh, your lifetime, your daughter's lifetime, and her daughter's lifetime, too."

"Unless the mining teams return."

Claudia hesitated. "Yes, well . . . "

"But of course you can't prepare for that, can you? No, of course not." Sra. Sanchez inhaled as if to gather all the rest of her fears within her, securely out of sight, and took up the tablet Claudia had brought along, marking her signature for the household with the swipe of a finger. "God will repay you for the work you're doing here."

Claudia noted the feeling of relief in her chest at the sight of Sanchez's mark: the second-last needed to start work on some of the farmland just outside the main city limits. "Thank you, Señora. We'll try our best not to let you down."

"Mama, they're shouting again," said Elena, calmly, while sprawled on the floor—chin resting on steepled fingers; Claudia's images scattered all about her.

"They're tiring themselves out, is all they're doing," said Sra. Sanchez. "What, do they think the water's just going to return if they whine about it loud enough?"

"Maybe," said Claudia, rising to peer out the front window. Sure enough, on the narrow, canted streets below, a group of older women had begun raging at the latest inciting incident—a young man with a full rain barrel that he did not seem inclined to share—and the situation seemed poised to get worse before it got better. "I should go."

"Can I come with you?" said Elena, though she made no move to stand as she spoke.

"I don't know . . . I have only the one boy working with us right now," Claudia winked. "Do you think you could handle just helping to save the whole town?"

But the playful jest went right over the prepubescent's head. "I know you only have one," said Elena, with an expression bordering on tedium. "And he's my sister's."

"Your sister's with—Jhoan Sebastián?"

"Uh huh. For weeks now."

"Ay, what's this?" said Sra. Sanchez, with no small alarm. "Is he a good boy?"

Claudia tried to imagine the young teen in her care, for all his sweet-faced tough-guy aspirations, rallying enough thought for anything beyond his own appearance to be a major threat to anyone, and beamed reassurance at the mother. She and Luis had taken Jhoan on as a favor to the family, hard-working Rionegro folk befriended during a previous project, but of course, adolescence did not discriminate. Everyone that age was likely too focused on their image, their brand, to be any good for anyone, but the practice helped—or it might, at least, she added to herself, with a brief thought on Luis, if ever they were ready to move past it all.

The sounds of the quarrel outside intensified.

"Sra. Sanchez, apologies," said Claudia. "I'm sure the kids are fine, but I should look into whatever's going on out there. At least until someone else arrives. And . . . thank you, truly. The work will be worth it, I promise."

But Sra. Sanchez only waved vaguely at her, turning more of her attention to Elena. "Tell me everything," she said. "Who is he? Why haven't I met him? What kind of good boy doesn't come by for lunch and to meet the mother?"

"Ughhhh," said Elena, while Claudia gathered papers and slipped out the front door.

The road leading into Buriticá ran heavy with red earth, and when Luis finally crested the summit of the landslide, his charter taking off in the distance behind him, he found Claudia embroiled in what seemed a one-sided dispute with some of the locals: the kind of tiny, squat abuelas, as a British contractor had once described them during a joint-project in the north, "too old to give a fuck." With wide-eyed great-grandsons clinging to the hems of their floral-framed blouses, and expressions shaped by decades of illegal mining operations that these women had seen bloat and bury their town, each had zero compunction about tearing into anyone who represented the latest institutional presence—however well-intentioned its delays.

To these women's credit, though, it *had* been weeks since the initial disaster: Weeks in which disputes over the ownership of key plots of land and local resources had interfered with direct government aid. Weeks in which industrious locals had tried to solve the problem themselves—only, for want of critical expertise, to make the problem worse. Weeks in which the notion of private contracting and a few pointedly greased palms had hung steadily overhead, and at last been conceded to, only to find the whole community, millones upon millones later, still without a solution to the most pressing facet of the landslide's aftermath.

Agua, the old women of Buriticá insisted. *Ahora.*

Claudia gave Luis a beleaguered look when she spied him, but also a flick of a hand signaling that all was under control—or at least, winding down for the day—so he wandered to the base-tent they had established near the town's central square, and initiated the secure communications app on his portable-lab to hear reports from the restoration team: Aerials worse than expected. Building materials slow to arrive. Lead still in transit.

Queue after queue after queue.

"Ah, pues . . . ¿qué s'os, gringos?" he heard someone mutter outside the tent: Jorge, one of the town-square's businessmen, possibly with another shipment from his private distributor. An answering laugh confirmed this suspicion, and Luis poked his head out to see Jorge clasping hands with a broad-shouldered man bearing a ready, if uncertain smile as they parted. Jorge looked tired—but then, as a major local proprietor and cousin to the mayor, he'd been doing more than his fair share to keep the town afloat. Tired, but with good cause.

"Quiubo, amigo," said Luis, nodding to the freshly delivered crates. "Good to see that at least some of the supplies are getting here on time."

Jorge waved and offered a weary grin. "Eduardo Guillermo. Good pilot. Knows the terrain well. Trying to do all he can to help, you know?"

"Sure," said Luis, though he wasn't sure he did, considering his own track record with decidedly unhelpful investors. But maybe Eduardo had family in the region, or friends.

Jorge cocked an ear to one side and pointed at the tent. "Is that—?"

Luis listened, then laughed at the walkie-talkie crackle coming from his portable lab. "Just an app. You can choose all kinds of sound styles. This one works for me."

Jorge shook his head. "Nothing like the old stuff, right? Even if we do have to port it onto new tech these days."

"No kidding. Time was, you just texted. Those group threads were intense."

"Still are, or so my little girl tells me. Just, fewer people involved these days."

"Sounds perfect."

"Well, you know how it is. Makes it easier to keep tabs on them, for sure."

Luis hesitated. Not having children of his own made it difficult to know exactly what to say next. Jorge hesitated, too, in the wake of Luis's silence, then gestured at the boxes. "Well, like I was saying to Eduardo, it's not like we're from the States, right? So I should . . . "

"Right, right—can't have another Tampa Bay."

Jorge barked an answering laugh, as if surprised at his own energy for it. "Exactly."

And they parted on more familiar terms, the moment's hesitation forgotten. If at a loss for a unifying thought, Luis knew, there was always Tampa Bay: an international horror story of immediate and protracted casualty counts that made Colombian intersections between natural disaster and government neglect look like child's play. Tampa Bay was educational, too—the whole disaster clarifying, for average citizens, the connection between flooding and ensuing drought—so when bureaucratic delays *did* happen elsewhere, everyone knew not to question the extent of the disaster itself, but rather to equivocate between notions of relative urgency. After all, if debris flow after heavy rains had been known to engulf towns whole, maybe the merely damaged water system in Buriticá was a sign of leniency from the Almighty? And if not, well, it still couldn't be as bad as Tampa Bay, with all those telling photos of people dying for want of basic hygienic supplies in hospitals reduced more or less to rubble. *Everyone* seemed to know a guy whose brother-in-law's cousin had been among the abandoned or dead there—and everyone preferred, if they could help it, to speak of those foreign losses rather than the fall-out, say, from Six-Cities, when even the rubble in Quibdó had ceased to exist.

But even cursory thought of that lost city had Luis's hands shaking again, so while he waited for Claudia, he re-pinned a corner of the geological survey wilting on one side of their tent, and surveyed the good doctor's latest efforts. Her superimposed plans for the "raíz-ruta" suggested six days' observation of the soil substrate after the restoration team had finished its part, and once the pair could start seeding the hills with their graphene-based adsorbent. The exact routes their seeds would take through the existing silica were only conjecture—each reaction site yielding a unique "root" of reinforced rock coated with an excellent filtration surface—but a careful reading of current deposits gave a fair sense of where fortifications against future landslide would be strongest. While he'd been off mucking up matters with the latest potential investors, Claudia had been thorough.

But then, she always was.

"So, who'd you piss off this time?"

Jhoan Sebastián, slender and self-assured at fifteen, stood in the doorway with a toothpick in his teeth, a faint blue-and-white display flickering off his wristband, and an Adidas T-shirt immaculately maintained despite the heat.

"Buenas tardes." Luis pursed lips at the kid's workstation: an invitation to get started. After two lessons in titration and a third in handwriting, he and Claudia had made a decent lab assistant of the displaced paisa, hauled off with them to actual peasant country to keep out of trouble and—when the jobs went the right way—to help his grandparents. As it stood, the kid did one of these two tasks fairly well, but there were still edges to be rounded with the other.

"Prettier than the last one, though, right?" Jhoan made a show of sifting through the remains of yesterday's work. "That corporate lady from Santa Monica? Oye, was that ever rough to watch. Need to set a better example, old man."

"Pobre güevón." Luis sucked his teeth. "You wish you had the sack for my problems."

But in way of rejoinder Jhoan merely smiled—the slow, careful smile of the sharpest from any barrio humilde. Luis watched out the corner of an eye, but let it stand unanswered. There was a note on his own desk—hemp paper, with an all-caps scrawl—that served well enough as deflection. He held it up to Jhoan, then Claudia as she entered the tent after him.

"I'm guessing this isn't a 'yes.'"

"Not even close." Claudia loosened and redid the twist in her hair, which had wisped into unruly curls. She looked tired, too. "Toss for it, or you going to honor your turn?"

"Señorita," said Luis, with a grin. "When have I ever disappointed?"

Claudia paused, hands about the half-finished braid, and looked up while counting. "Riosucio. Uramita. Yarumal."

"And La Ceja," Jhoan added. "Or so I've been told. It was before I signed on."

"Uff." Luis grimaced. "And if you two were as good at counting cards as at listing my faults, I bet we'd have no trouble getting funded, either."

But the look on Claudia's face sparked immediate regret.

"That bad?" she said, her tone hushed as though Jhoan somehow wouldn't hear it.

"Tranquila," Luis said, though a heaviness in his chest belied the sentiment. "There are other ways. First, though, let's see what's got the old man stuck this time." And before she could reply he slipped past her, pressing lips to cheek before setting out to scale the mountain and meet the latest hold-up waiting there.

"Doesn't stick around long, does he?" said Jhoan Sebastián.

Claudia drummed knuckles on a workbench and smiled agreement. "He can be present when he wants to be. Usually it's when he's out of sight that he forgets."

"All the more reason to stay out of sight, right? So he has an excuse for forgetting?"

Claudia arched a brow the kid's way. "You're not exactly new to the universe, are you?"

Jhoan tried to smirk knowingly, but his expression showed too much a flush of pride in being praised. A child's wisdom, still beholden to what others thought of him. Claudia had seen it in other adults, too, though, so there was no guarantee he would ever break free of it.

"I've been around," he said, but with an urgency that seemed to prove her point.

"I'm sure you have," said Claudia—and then, after a pause, remembering what Elena had mentioned: "Carefully, I hope. You have your whole future ahead of you."

"Yes, Señora Vallejo." And he ducked his head with uncharacteristic shyness—a sign that he knew exactly what she was referring to. She wasn't his mother, no, but out here . . .

"*Doctora*, remember," she added, then pursed lips at his workstation. "And don't you still have some tests to run?"

"Yeah, sort of, but I have to get fresh samples."

"Why? Something wrong with the soil we gave you?"

Jhoan shook his head. "Not exactly, but—well, take a look for yourself."

She came around and inspected his sample dishes under the light of the microscope-app on the portable. His handwriting had improved, but he still wasn't the most precise with his labeling, so she couldn't make out exactly the origins of one sample. Still, the flecks of off-white in the mix were telling.

"Is that—"

"Uh huh, I think so," he said, scratching his forehead with a thumb. "I mean, yeah, no, I tested the sample and it came back human. And that's . . . bad, right?"

"Well, depending on which human, it's not good, no." Claudia straightened, glancing about the tent and studying the map containing her raiz-ruta. "Where's this one from again?"

Jhoan nodded, his expression mirroring the gravity in hers. "Let me show you, Doc."

But even as they left, Claudia caught herself wishing that he wouldn't. Just in case.

After a week of fraught negotiations, Bidø still had not moved from his enclosure at the center of Luis and Claudia's intended seed-site. Other raiz-rutas could be contrived with their geological survey, but none offered the same level of long-term structural integrity—not with all the winding mining tunnels that had helped bring the hills to their perilous state in the first place—and the seventy-six-year-old Emberá-Katio man was well aware of this fact. There was no real need for him to live alone: He had family in town, and plenty of other indigenous men and women, originally from the coast, had become integrated with the local economy as climate and industry forced them further inland. But as the rare outsider with a deed for his bought-and-paid-for slice of mountain, Bidø preferred to assert the legitimacy of his presence here, so he perched on a wooden stoop, expression locked in a scowl, as Luis approached.

"I thought I made myself clear before you ran off to Medellín."

Luis raised his hands in admission. "You did. Mostly."

Bidø's sunken chest rose and receded with a grunt. "Mostly."

But he looked at Luis in askance, while about them the mountain chittered and squawked, and Luis saw that Bidø was curious, however grudgingly.

Curious, Luis could work with.

"But why stay at all," he began, "if you think this place deserves to collapse?"

"Ah, you're too easy." Bidø waved Luis off. "So I can die when the land dies."

"Which it will, if you don't let us seed here."

"If that be the will of the spirits, sure."

Luis laughed. "Well that's convenient, when you're keeping us from asking them."

The old man's spidery brows furrowed. "Who's keeping anyone? My uncle, he held his land once, too—until they shot him."

"Who, the miners?"

Bidø sniffed.

"Paramilitary?"

A hiss in the negative. Luis paused.

"Police."

'Bidø cut the air with his hand, but the silence settled anyway.

"Listen, it was a long time ago," he said eventually.

Luis studied the twilight shadows—some lengthening from tethered pack horses on nearby family farms; others swallowing whole the entrances to more than a few illegal operations more or less vacant, whispers of one local dissident group aside. In the distance, still other shadows cast half the town's central steeple into darkness, reminding Luis of a black painting meant to represent Communism, and how political discourse could eventually cover everything—the good, the bad, the unconscionable—with the same brush-stroke. Colombia had shown the same to be true for the other side of the spectrum, too: enough time, enough injury, enough *history,* and all ideologies seemed to lose their moral distinction. The longer he looked away, though, the more Luis realized he dreaded looking back, in case what awaited him was the face of a man who truly did want to join those shadows: the long line of men and women lost to the unevenness of progress, and the very suspect nature of that word.

There had been enough such faces on the streets of Medellín in preceding days—more, Luis was certain, than in the initial, post-peace throes of his youth, when so much remained to be done but at least there was a bit fresh enthusiasm about attending to it all. On his first morning in Centro this last trip, though, one of the street youth had merely stolen a buñuelo—one measly ball of fried dough—but before the police could reach him, other men around the bakery did, ostensibly furious at anyone who would seek to disrupt so hard-won a peace. The young man's body had curled in on itself like an insect's husk under their onslaught, and through it all Luis had seen a look in yellow, blood-shot eyes that said to him, *surely death would be better than this* Still, even as the memory surfaced he looked at his hands, trying to remember what, in the thrill of disruption, had chilled his blood enough not to join the others in that fray.

"Is that what you're hoping?" he said. "That we come up here one night and just . . . ?"

But 'Bidø merely huffed and muttered something in a thicker dialect. Luis took its general meaning with relief.

"All right, good, no assassins—so then what the hell do you want? You think this is easy, that we don't have enough to do trying to pay the real pendejos off to use their land?"

The old man looked amused by Luis's delineation of problem people—*oh, you think the* other *guys are assholes, not you?*—and cleared his throat before nodding down the mountainside.

"Listen, kid—you lose anyone when the insects took their dead?"

Luis took a second to process the metaphor. He knew that among the Embera-Katío animalism connected three realms of existence, with serpents and other critters of the soil sometimes taking mythopoetic revenge upon mankind by dragging sinners to the lands below. Rarely, though, did others refer similarly to the Six-Cities incident: twelve days when hacked nano-tech, the likes of which had been developed to process rare-earth metals with greater ease, devoured cities whole—people, pets, cars, buildings—while the rest of each affected country scrambled to contain the spread. Japan. Indonesia. Benin. Colombia. Madagascar. France. The UN Accord against private access to whole bodies of nanotech research had come swiftly, with only the U.S. and Bangladesh holding out in the initial rush of militarized search-and-seizure, at least until scares hit them in turn. (A prank, as it turned out, in the midwestern U.S.—but near enough the home of an online celebrity that the famed musician had rallied his fan base through social media: enough, for once, to turn the political tide.)

In Colombia, it was the city of Quibdó, one department over in Chocó, that had taken the brunt of the swarm. But even then, in Colombia, as in Indonesia and Benin, quarantine had been difficult to maintain, and some of the nano-tech had dispersed quickly into the surrounding ecosystem, becoming the stuff of nightmares and superstition for months after the main event. Insects, spirits, poxes—each region and its peoples had variations on the theme, and these stories persisted even when people ceased to speak the affected city's name.

"There was an ocelot on this mountain then," said 'Bidø. "Survived the mining wars. Survived the sinkholes. But ate something, somewhere, with one of those creatures in it."

Luis wanted to ask how 'Bidø knew it was the nanotech, and not some other disease, if there had only been one of those bots at work—but then he remembered the pictures from the aftermath. 'Bidø knew the difference well enough between gangrenous rot and part of that brutally patient infestation. The old man drew an idle line in the dirt beside him as he went on.

"She came to me to die. Sat with me—there, in pain, panting on the grasses."

"And you didn't . . . ?"

"I prayed for her. Gave her dying voice. It took two days."

Luis's eyes narrowed. "Is *that* what you want us to do? Give your dying voice?"

'Bidø laughed, but only in disgust. "Ah, you people. You wouldn't know the first thing about giving voice, about speaking the words that the land wants most to hear. And yet you wonder why I won't let you lay your rotten city hands here, upon this soil." Then he threw up a palm to show that he would speak no more, and turned to song instead. Luis couldn't tell, though, if it was one of those songs meant to commune with the local spirits, or simply something to settle the old man's thoughts and tongue. Something, maybe, from the top-forty hits that still filtered through one of the last hold-out stations here.

Either way, Luis waited amid this humming for as long as he could man-age—which was only a few minutes, he realized later, with some chagrin—before adding his shadow to the rest lengthening off the mountainside, to return to the city and confer with Claudia about their days. He couldn't even blame 'Bidø for his suspicions, not really. In some ways they were all the same, these damned mountainsides across the country like so many rotten teeth: each scored so deep with human infection that even Claudia's special-ized fillings might not ever be able to repair all the damage done—and that was only *if* 'Bidø could be swayed to let them try.

But what was the alternative? Luis was halfway down the mountain when he realized he hadn't asked why 'Bidø hadn't called for DPPS after discovering that a nanobot had escaped the quarantine—although he suspected the reason, after the old man's story about the police—or what had happened to it after the ocelot had met its end. A single nanobot could only wreak so much mischief on a minor scale before deteriorating, but still . . . Luis's skin crawled at the mere thought of his proximity to any space where one of those entities had been.

This time, there were no gently queuing doves nearby to temper his irrita-tion with the day's second round of failures—but Luis descended the moun-tain with care all the same, his breathing slow while he watched for any judgmental insects that might be lurking in the grass.

Claudia and Jhoan Sebastián stood atop a small knoll of broken earth meters below an abandoned mining entrance. There were scorch marks along some of the beams propping open the assembly above them, and a corroded metal drum to one side—but of greater note was the swirling mess of red and brown earth and upturned rock from where one of the research drones had descended to collect samples. A meter from the contact site, the curvature of a human cranium in the soil was impossible to miss.

"Problem with these drones was that their research parameters were too narrow," she said. "Remind me to program them for broader surveillance before touchdown next time."

But Jhoan was hardly paying attention. He crouched by the soil and carefully wiped the tops and sides of his sneakers clean. "You think it's a murder victim?"

"Oh, probably not."

"But possibly."

"But probably not." Still, Claudia felt a twist of grief when a basic facet of the skull finally registered. It was small—a child's—its intact skull in four pieces, with a crucifix-shaped gap that only time could have filled in. She crossed herself on instinct. "Well, hopefully not."

"Oh shit," said Jhoan, stumbling back as he realized the same. "That's a baby."

"*Was* a baby." But she offered a sympathetic glance. "It's at peace now. It's okay."

Jhoan did not look as certain. "Is this, like, one of those guerrilla things, where they didn't let people have kids so they just shot them all?"

"That's not . . . quite how it happened," said Claudia. But she wasn't willing to suggest that some groups hadn't murdered any birthed offspring, to go along with the abortions forced upon female fighters who got pregnant in the fray. The whole history was complicated, and also not exactly her own to relay to the young paisa—Venezuelan and Colombian atrocities were blurred but not entirely interchangeable, even where guerrillas were concerned—and after all, she'd had enough trouble trying to intimate that the fifteen-year-old should practice safe sex in a country where almost 20 percent of new mothers were still in their teens.

Outside the job description, she reminded herself to grumble at Luis later. For now, a shadow of guilt had started to creep in—for her own relief, really, in finding no clear markings of indigenous burial, which might have delayed the project, and which she realized she had been ready to *lie* about not finding, if it meant avoiding further delays with the work. Even if it meant knowing that when she sent her graphene-based adsorbent spiraling down the mountaintop, some of those many-splendored fractalizing arms might bond to a whole graveyard of native dead, entwining and mineralizing them as part of the mountain's new foundations. She found something poetic in the image, personally, but if Bidø was any indication, indigenous Colombians would likely not share her vision—least of all if it came to pass only because of a lie—so she sent up a small prayer for the whole situation not coming to that extreme. A simple lost body—however tragic—would be easy enough to relocate.

Out the corner of one eye, she caught Jhoan passing the palms of his hands over his eyes, and tried not to be surprised by the young man's surfeit of emotion.

"Sometimes people panic and make bad calls," she said gently, once she had adapted to thinking of Jhoan in this more tender light. "This was one of them, whatever happened here."

And to his credit, Jhoan did not look ashamed at having been caught out crying, but he looked away when he asked if they could go now.

"Almost," she said, with what she hoped was a bracing smile. "We have to call it in, but then this little tyke will be laid properly to rest. You did good today, Jhoan. Real good."

As had she, she allowed herself after—but only by missing the chance to go astray—and while they returned down the narrow mountain path, Claudia wondered if her partner ever permitted himself even that much sense of victory when his own days went wrong. Oh so many certainly seemed to these past few months, and then Luis simply carried the weight of all those failures in everything he tried to do to make amends, and thought she didn't notice when he snuck off to divert his frustration into something or someone else. Did he ever think to forgive himself, for anything? The answer was painfully self-evident—but the questions it created about his future, and theirs, held resolutions that Claudia wasn't quite ready to accept.

When Luis arrived in the town's central square he found Claudia brushing out her hair on a white plastic chair in Jorge's tienda: a community space as much for the taking of beer and sports and a round of cards as it was a bakery, a coffee shop, and a quick hub for last-minute home supplies. Jorge had fallen asleep at the register sometime in the last hour—forearms folded under his chin, music softly playing from an old, cooler-mounted speaker behind him—and when Luis entered, wiping his heavily perspiring forehead with the back of a hand, he hadn't the heart to wake him. Of the two of them, Luis knew who had done for the town the greater of the day's fool work.

Claudia pursed lips at the remainder of her Club Colombia instead, and waited until after Luis's first sip to ask of him, "All right. How bad?"

From the intensity of her expression, Luis knew Claudia wasn't referring to Bidø—but even the slightest reference to their potential investors in Medellín brought a bitter taste to the already metallic beer, and he shrugged.

"What's there to say? They didn't bite. They think we're . . . " He gestured vaguely. "Alchemical hucksters?"

"Sure, that." He pointed with a curl of a grin. "I think. What's *alchemical* again?"

Claudia rolled eyes and ignored the question. "Qué pena," she said. "It's not exactly gold from lead we're making here, but, okay, I get it." She took back her beer. "There's two modes for new tech—excitement, and fear. We're in a fear cycle, that's all. All this chatter about a new dissident group hasn't helped either, but it'll pass. We're on the cusp of something epic."

"We've been on the cusp for years."

"All the more reason to trust that we'll get there soon."

"Gambler's fallacy, Di-Di."

Claudia's expression slackened in the darkness, and she drank deeper. "True."

Luis looked away when he heard the change in her voice, the knot in his ribs returning. It was easier, sometimes, to sit in silence than to try to put, between them, even this much into words. Meanwhile, from Jorge's patio, the pair could make out activity in yellowed shadows all around the central square: an old man urinating on the concrete street while he crooned an old vallenatotune. A woman carrying a heavily swaddled baby up the slope, and resting against a tall palm tree to adjust her crocs. A man with a military gait walking with urgency around the little fountain, talking softly but with precision into an earpiece. And across the way—against a stage of pastel-orange stucco, obscured in part by an arepa-vendor's umbrella—the heavy jeans of a young man and the slender black tights of a young woman: the latter canting against a brick wall under the hard lean of the former.

"Is that—"

"Mmm. Jhoan was busy in your absence."

Luis heard the smile in Claudia's words and turned to her.

"Three days. Three days I was gone."

"Well, okay, then he was busy in your presence, too."

At the answering look on his face, Claudia laughed and swatted Luis's knee. "What? A young man can't live on filtration experiments alone."

Jhoan's sly smirk came to mind. Luis frowned. "How long?"

Claudia shook her head. "Oh, I just heard about it today, too, but I bet it was weeks ago, from day one. You know, he's smoother than you'd think, where it counts." She paused, and added, in a voice that struck Luis as almost admiring, "Gentler, too. Full of feeling."

Luis snorted. "That, or the girls here are truly desperate for novelty."

"Ahhh, now you're getting cynical, old man" Claudia patted his cheek, and let her hand linger there: a reminder of how close they always came, and how easy it should have been to ask for more. But some raiz-rutas always veered in ways that were hard to fathom, let alone predict. Maybe due to some neglected variable in the underlying foundation. Maybe from some unseen speck with a wildly different chemical make-up, buried deep-down in the rest.

Luis flinched and then, startled by this reaction, turned aside. "Restless, maybe. I mean, you get sick of it too, don't you? Seeing how much goes wrong everywhere we set up camp?"

Claudia squinted at him, gauging the severity of the flinch, and her partner's attendant fatalism. "No, Luis, I don't," she said at last, dropping her hand over his. "It's the nature of the work. You think we have it bad? Think of the people in the DPPS."

Luis recalled the woman in the yellow poncho and the ease of her movements at the airport. "Why? They've got plenty of tech on their side. They're fine . . . What?"

Claudia shook her head.

"Ah, Luis Miguel, you idiot. You think it's any easier, always rushing to eliminate death and disease the moment it shows up?"

He grumbled. "More satisfying, I'd bet, to be able to put an end to a risk just like that."

"Oh, so, what, you think we should do the same with the mountains? Just flatten them all, so there's never a risk of more landslides?"

Luis parted his lips to reply that flattening the mountains was impossible—and then frowned quizzically, on alert for a trap. Claudia laughed again and patted his thigh.

"Tranquila," she said. "You know what I mean. There's risk everywhere. We're shoring up the earth so that it can handle more saturation from the rains, but we can't secure it forever. Things will go wrong. Things always go wrong."

Luis exhaled loudly. "But it's not your 'rutas that go wrong, Di-Di: it's the people around them. Human instincts are just awful at the best of times, and then, when things get bad . . . they're just . . . I mean, take this guy today in Centro, this hungry street kid who—"

But he caught himself and set his lips firmly against the rest of that sentence, shaking his head against telling her about the brutal beating. Still, Claudia could so easily read him. Creases formed at the corners of her eyes, and she turned and held out her hands for his, which Luis gave over without meeting her gaze. Her own dropped while tracing the lines in his palms to their source. "*Dime*, Luis. Tell me. What was the real problem with the investors?"

Luis's fingers curled ever so slightly over hers before falling slack again. Bidø hadn't been so wrong about his not knowing the right words.

"Look, Di-Di . . . " he tried. "I know we need the money. I do. But what's the point, if the only way to get it is by selling shares to the same people who . . . who . . . "

Claudia's hands tensed around his. Finishing *that* sentence, at least, became moot.

"Was there really no one else?"

"How could there be?" Luis eased his hands from hers, passed one over his face, then let both hang between his knees. "Di-Di, this is the world. The only ones who give a damn about restoring the mountains are the same people who want to dig them up again."

And exploit the people in the mountain cities again. And see them die in illegal mining operations. And set off more rounds of violence when any of them rose up against company pressures. All of which did not need saying, so Claudia let the silence between them lengthen.

"Well, except for us," she said at last. "And we're not really special, so . . . "

Luis hummed in reply, the sound terse and a bit despairing.

She leaned in. "We're *not* special, Luis—and don't ever let it get to your head that we are. If I could develop this tech, someone else could, too. Someone else maybe already has. And if they have, maybe they have someone with just the right money to back it."

Luis kept his gaze on the uneven concrete tile in Jorge's tienda. "If someone else develops this, Di-Di . . . If some of these people I've met ever get their hands on it . . . "

"Yes, we could be in for another Six-Cities before it's properly regulated. I get it. I do." Claudia pursed lips again, this time in what looked like an attempt at reassurance and support. "But hey, at least we've still got some of the crowdsourced funds left, right? Enough for this one city? And what's that saying about starfish on the beach?"

Luis nodded grudgingly. "A month's worth, sure, and some ongoing subscriptions to pay a few bills after." But even admitting to the tightness of their budget, Luis felt his third or maybe fourth failure for the day, in not knowing how to offer Claudia reassurance in turn—and worse, in knowing that *she* knew how at a loss he was to say or do a blessed, useful thing. That she would probably have to rally on her own again, and for them both.

Meanwhile, in the distance, four legs began to shuffle from the street, still industriously entwined (for all their awkward movements), into the privacy of a shaded passageway.

"Hijueputa," said Luis, eventually. "The permit. I almost forgot."

"Oh, it can wait."

"No," said Luis. "Actually, it can't."

Claudia startled at the tone in his voice, then offered a rueful smile of concession and drained the Club Colombia—because she knew he was right, even if the bureaucracy of it all was laughable. No one else was rushing to repair Buriticá, and the townsfolk had waited a week just to get the rescue crews booked. Still, after Six-Cities, the UN Accord had compelled Colombia to impose strong financial deterrents against making full use of the airways, to keep more people from independently piloting devices that could be used to disperse harmful nano—or biotech. And that included the team's research fliers, and their depositor drone.

Luis stood and kissed Claudia on the cheek. "Sorry, Di-Di, but we need to apply for an aerial extension if the old man won't budge. And Mother of God, how much will that cost . . . "

"Only as much as you let it," she said, gently—and this time, he had to agree. Luis was only a few steps off when he recalled Claudia's first overtures of the evening, and wondered why he had not instead taken the proffered hand in his and let the night run the course she had so sweetly been proposing. The course that men a third his age, apparently, knew to reach forwithout thought or hesitation. Claudia's adsorbent could stabilize a mountain, but . . .

Luis shook his head and crossed himself quickly, at the thought that any such miracle could work the same wonder on his heart.

Jhoan was not at his post the next morning, but Luis had little work for him anyway, and no interest in chastising the young man for his priorities, not when the world was going to hell one way or the other, by the looks of things. On the broadcast projected along one of the tent walls, journalists at *Noticias Caracol* reported with equal calm the emergence of another bout of flooding in the Cauca Valley, and riots in the south of Bogotá, and more blather from a three-term FARC senator in the wake of rapidly crumbling state infrastructure.

If there was shock on the reporters' part, it stood reserved for news of the latest in a long line of domestic-terrorist events in North America and Europe, with scenes of racialized violence and anti-government protests carefully blurred so as not to unnerve any Colombian viewers. The only local equivalent—a segment with an independent journalist reporting on activity in a supposedly barren mine elsewhere in the department of Antioquia—was quickly mediated by a professional journalist's soothing tone: *We're still awaiting word from local authorities, but although initial intel suggests no official sanction for activity in the mines, it does offer the possibility that a scouting mission or security assessment team was recently in the vicinity, which could account for the signs of life.* The words "dissident force" remained pointedly absent from either side of the report.

Occasionally, though, more positive briefings came through, too: from China, where the latest space elevator was nearing completion under the iron fist of its latest tyrant; from the International Space Station, where a recently stationed Colombian-Canadian was gaining celebrity for his "fútbol freestyle" tricks in zero-g; and even from Venezuela, which had just seen sanctions lifted on the international stage. But it was the conspiracy talk that held Luis's attention most of all. As he went about packing up equipment for the removal of base-tent to their second site (wherever Claudia determined it would be), he listened to a report on student protests challenging the idea that Six-Cities had ever even happened, or at least the way it had been described on the news. *Why these six countries in particular?* the disillusioned youth wanted to know. *Why so long to dismantle some cities, and so quick with others? How do we know this isn't just some corporate trap designed to decentralize all our democracies and leave us ripe for economic slaughter?*

"What democracies?" Luis muttered back at the broadcast—for who could speak of democracy when international agencies had to impose strict sanctions on any new technology because the average citizen could not be trusted? Because even a single citizen could ruin stability for all? And yet, what was the alternative? Simply waiting for one lousy era to run its course? Recurring visions of Bidø falling dead in the night—of old age, or choking on a bone, or being eaten from the inside out like his precious ocelot by a tiny, patient automaton—left a sourness on Luis's tongue, and he pitched one of the crates with a little more heft than necessary onto the lift. "Would it kill people just to be reasonable?"

"Why you ask, boss? Need someone taken out?"

Luis looked up to see a man at the base-tent's perimeter—Eduardo Guillermo, Jorge's supply pilot. But this time, from the look on Eduardo's face, and his posture, and his apparel, Luis realized that he had to have been something more. Ex-paramilitary never blended as well as they thought they would into civilian life.

"Eduardo, right?" said Luis. "Jorge told me about you. Help you with something?"

"Oh, sure, but I asked you first." Eduardo kept his hands folded behind him as he stepped into the tent. "I see you're moving."

Luis grunted. "Not far, but Dra. Vallejo's the one you want to talk to about the *where.*"

Eduardo scratched his wide, perspiring temple. "You're right, and it might be a good idea, after, to talk to her, too. But first, well . . . " He stuck out a meaty hand, palm up at a forty-five-degree angle. Luis noted the rock-solid grip in the arch between thumb and forefinger especially. "Look, I just got in with a shipment for the shops."

Luis nodded. "Hero to the people here, I'll bet."

"Bastante," said Eduardo, with half a grin. "But, also—you've got fliers here yourself, don't you? Aerial reconnaissance for some sort of . . . research project, I gather?"

Luis raised a brow but kept the rest of his expression neutrally amicable—something about Eduardo's question, and the whole ex-paramilitary demeanor, inspiring caution. "Sure, yeah, that's part of it. Just a little research op, no big deal."

Eduardo raised his hands. "Sure, wouldn't matter to me if it was a big deal, boss, not trying to intrude. Only—I saw some activity on the drag in. Like, a search party? But away from the rubble, kind of a long way from the whole landslide, really. Anyway, just wondering if that's part of your work, or something we should all be helping out with. Because I've got the plane ready, but if no one's even asked to use your drones yet, well . . . "

"Where's this going down?" Luis switched on his walkie-talkie app. "Di-Di."

"All ears, Luis."

"North side," Eduardo offered, "by the sports complex."

Luis hesitated before relaying this description—but only because, to his mind, the dusty lot out near Buriticá's hospital hardly constituted a sports complex, even if there were signs that it had seen better days. All the same, he asked Claudia about word of activity there.

"Oh, that," she said, and Luis and Eduardo exchanged a look at the laugh on her end of the crackling line. "One of the local girls can't be accounted for, is all."

"And that's a . . . bad thing, right?" said Luis.

"It's Jhoan Sebastián's girl," said Claudia. "And have you seen Jhoan today?"

Luis paused before his reply, connecting the dots. "That's a negative."

"Exactly. So, Luis . . . when they *do* sneak back in again, try not to give them a hard time, will you? By the looks of things, the girl's family is going to be furious enough."

"Claro que sí." Luis looked at Eduardo, and both men relaxed. "Thanks for the offer, at least."

"Any time, boss," said Eduardo, shaking hands again before he left. "And hey, if you folks need anything else out here—anything, you know, with the landslide, or whatever else you've got going on here, you just tell Jorge to give me a call. Especially with the mines, you know? Never can be too careful, wandering around those entrances solo."

Luis nodded and muttered a standard *gracias, muy amable.* He wanted to be more touched by the kindness of the offer, but there was something about Eduardo's strained eagerness that just left Luis wondering what the hell kind of monstrous things the pilot had done in his old outfit, if he was still itching, all these years after the peace, somehow to atone.

But maybe there was envy at play, too, over how Eduardo *could* shift from one way of life to another, while as the day progressed Luis found nothing arising from his irritation save more irritation—over all the trouble he'd had uploading his permit application, and all the problems securing some of the samples for transport, and all the delays even in the arrival of transport itself. The heat in him only cooled when the sun started to gild the far corners of the sky, and even then it was replaced far too quickly with something else, an angry sort of helplessness when the good doctor appeared with a subdued and even frightened look on her face.

Jhoan Sebastián and the girl, Leidy, had not yet come home.

"Kids these days use Wysprs," Claudia informed Luis, as the pair walked to join the group of concerned parents and exasperated abuelas in the central square, where half the town seemed present and accounted for by the steps to a white, neoclassical church: its little statue of San Antonio inlaid under a decades-old stopped clock; its roof and upper-walls paneled with solar-cells to keep, among other things, the electric candles lit.

"Everyone whispers," said Luis. "The whole damned country whispers."

Claudia grumbled and flicked her wrist projector to a rotating logo for Wysprs, each letter wavering between blue, white, and transparent-fill, in a pattern affecting randomness. "Pick a point, pick your people, but you can only have eight on your radar at any given time. The rest are invisible until you slip them into rotation. Blue for new updates from your people, white for the ones you've already seen, and everyone else is part of the vacuum—oh, and you can swap out people from the vacuum, but only if they choose to swap back."

"A cliquish hellscape. Of course the kids are all over it."

Claudia hummed agreement. "What can I say? Having a million followers got boring. Now social power comes from building the longest chains of well-connected people—eight people with the right eight people in each of *their* groups, who have the right eight people in *their* groups . . . and so on, and so forth, so that you can stay current without actually following everyone yourself. Or reading the news firsthand."

Now it began to make sense to Luis why so many young people doubted Six-Cities.

"And our ward and the girl?"

"No new notifications from anyone in their groups. Leidy set off the community alarm first, because five of her eight are locals, but Jhoan Sebastián was harder—Leidy isn't even in his circle, so we had to contact some of his crew back in Medellín."

Luis wanted to snort at the term "crew" in relation to their would-be tough-guy, but channeled the sentiment into a sigh instead. "So, what, they're dead in the hills somewhere?"

He accepted the backhanded swat to his arm. Claudia pinched the bridge of her nose with her other hand.

"Well, they're not in the rubble, thank goodness for that. And we don't see any signs that they've hoofed it to another town—although there's enough cash still in circulation that it would be hard to trace them if they did, at least without polling everyone along the way."

"So . . . the hills?"

"Maybe," said Claudia. "But I can't for the life of me figure out why."

Luis resisted the urge to repeat himself. Dead made sense to the cynic in him—some foolish kids' prank, or slip into deep water, or an outing in the woods without watching the incline—but dead wasn't the answer anyone was ready for, certainly not this early on. Still, as they entered the throng by the church, Luis had no difficulty recognizing the mother, who was already manifesting a grief at the loss that seemed almost as extreme. The father was trickier—a man of smaller build, likely indigenous, and soft-spoken amid the flurry of discourse—but there was no mistaking him once the man tried to offer the mother reassurance that the teens were just off being teens, and received a mouthful of Catholic fury in reply.

"Look," Jorge had been saying as the pair entered—the local proprietor addressing the group with hands upraised and entreating calm. "We're tired and probably feeling the strain of these last few weeks without consistent supplies." The crowd muttered in assent. "But I've called my pilot back, and although I haven't received response yet, I'm sure he's on his way. And in the meantime, we have aerial craft on hand, thanks to these two, and my cousin is going to make sure there's no trouble coming to them for putting their drones to this use."

Sra. Sanchez's gaze darted Claudia's way, and Claudia nodded affirmation—yes, the mountain-seeding team was going to help—even if Luis had been difficult to convince that the permit issue wouldn't come back to bite them in the ass. At this news, Sra. Sanchez crossed herself in gratitude—but so did Elena, which surprised Claudia, considering the girl's affectations of indifference to so much of the tumult of recent life. Luis was just starting to add where they would send their drones to aid in the search, so Claudia scrunched her lips a second in thought, then slipped through the crowd to offer a more reassuring smile up close. Before she had reached Elena's side, though, the looks on faces in the crowd began to turn—confused, then sobered, then frightened. Claudia glanced behind her, and up, to see what had caught everyone's eye: Three DPPS helicopters—the shadows, and then the sounds of them.

From somewhere in the murmuring crowd came the dread word that the presence of DPPS invariably brought, whenever it rallied its forces to show up en masse—*Is it quarantine? Are we under quarantine now?*—followed by an irate rumble among the abuelas—*oh, sure, I guess the government* can *show up after all . . . when it suits them!* Claudia wanted to address both the anger and the fear, but felt a tug on her sleeve first, and inclined her head to listen through the throng.

"I didn't know what to do," Elena whispered, while all around them the locals' chatter rose to rival the roar of the choppers. "Leidy didn't look right last time I saw her. Like a ghost, you know? And she took forever in the bathroom but she was still real sick when she came out. She said she had a bug, and not to tell mom . . . but in the church, by the statues . . . there's this screen and sign, and the sign tells you what to do if you see someone, or something . . . "

Elena went on, but more of her frightened sounds were lost as the green-metal birds swept over the town square, and Jorge's tienda, and Claudia and Luis's base-tent, and the church with its DPPS call-screen tucked by a statue of Christ on the road to Calvary. The three deafening shadows seemed to be headed close by, too—*the hospital!*, someone suggested—so Claudia hardly had time to process what Elena's words had meant (let alone their implicit reminder that, for all her affectations of adulthood, Elena was still a *child*) as the crowd took up a bewildered and heavy-footed pursuit.

It didn't take much time to cross town, but still, the small group of locals had hardly reached the perimeter of the sports lot, with its raw-metal goalposts and weed-worn, hard-packed dirt field, when the helicopters touched down, and the dust cleared, and six DPPS officials in fully holstered HAZMAT suits poured out: four lugging along equipment in oblong trunks; two others with a man restrained between them. A man Claudia had only seen in passing, but Luis knew now by name—

Eduardo Guillermo, with a bloodied bruise over his left eye.

The crowd stilled at this appearance—but not, Luis quickly realized, from confusion so much as a deep sense of déjà vu: official government representatives with a prisoner between them, all alone with a group of unarmed locals in an isolated mountain town. Anyone who had ever stepped foot in a Center for Memory, Peace, and Reconciliation, or a museum exhibit dedicated to local histories of indigenous oppression, or a house where, late at night, abuelos would hear the silence of distant stars and begin to speak of some terrible time come before . . . anyone, really, who had been born of this soil in some way or form carried with them those *real* whispers, which no social media would wish to rival: hauntings from an era when police and paramilitary and guerrilla were cut from confusing overlaps of civilian-terrorizing cloth.

Jorge stepped forward, then froze as one of the DPPS officials pointed his way.

"You," said the mask. "You know this man?"

Jorge's cousin advanced hurriedly in turn, hands raised. "I'm the mayor— this man, he's a local proprietor. Your man, he brings us supplies. He's been delivering throughout the crisis. What's he done that you've gone and arrested him? Flying back here without a proper permit?"

An appreciative smirk flitted through the crowd at this last question, but the town's pleasure at mocking bureaucratic pedantry was short-lived—the DPPS official shoving Eduardo hard on one shoulder, driving him to his knees. Everyone quieted. Everyone's gaze darted, however briefly, to the holsters outside the HAZMAT suits.

"Found him by one of the mine entrances," said the mask. "He and a few of his friends—maybe the dissident cell we've been after? Maybe working with a little help in town?"

"That's ridiculous," said Jorge, taking another step forward, even as Luis drew breath at the risk of the move. "It's not a crime to be by the mines. We all go past them at times."

"Yeah?" said the mask. "And I suppose all of you spend your time there setting up a full lab, volatile chemicals just kicking about while one or two of you stand guard?"

The crowd's sharp looks turned to Eduardo, who kept his head bowed and sighed.

"Like I told this . . . this fine gentleman . . . we were just trying to seal the mines properly, secure them against collapse. Can't just blow them inward without risking further landside, and it's a hell of a thing, trying to move dirt up there for the job without being noticed. And so yeah, I know, it's not technically our property, or Colombia's property, for that matter, thanks to those damned suits over in Bogotá—but look, one of my guys, he's an amateur chemist, great self-taught genius type, and he's been reading online about some new techniques for letting the rock self-generate. Amazing stuff. And he just needed a little time in the field to—"

"Hijuepuchas."

Luis was not alone in his surprise at the origin of this furious utterance, but he alone got Claudia's pointed glance—*you see? I told you, anyone could come up with this stuff, too*—before the good doctor continued her volley at Eduardo, storming toward him with total disregard of DPPS or their uniforms: "You think this is the time or place for amateurs? You have any idea what you were working with, how easily you could have been killed in the process? I've run thousands of simulations—*digital simulations!*—to get my substrate just right without doing harm to any secondary materials in the process, *including human flesh* And you and your boys think you can, what, just fiddle around *live* with these things and hope to God you've got your combination right? Mother Mary save your sorry skins, you are *so* lucky you still have them."

And by the end of her tirade, even through the mask, the DPPS leader's amusement was unmistakable. He nudged Eduardo with a foot. "So . . . you want me to release you into her custody? Or you feeling a little better now, eh, about being arrested by us first?"

Eduardo ignored the mask, but looked up with a mix of visible emotion: schooled calm in the wake of Claudia's rage, yes, but also flickers of fatigue, and shame, and curiosity.

"Cálmate, mujer," he said. "We were just trying to help. It's not like anyone else is—I mean, unless you are—unless you have . . . ?—but . . . well, how could we have known that?"

"You mean outside the online updates everyone in town's been getting?" said Luis, stepping forward while glancing in askance at Jorge, who sheepishly shook his head.

Eduardo shrugged. "We're not exactly the reading type. Small networks, you know? And hell, it's not like there was even a sign up in the municipal boards about it." Luis's gaze shifted to Claudia, who shook her head with a flush of embarrassment—*didn't quite get to it, sorry*—which he met with an answering smile—*don't worry about it, not your fault, he probably wouldn't have noticed it anyway*—while Eduardo went on: "Plus, with Jorge, the major focus was on getting supplies to everyone in town, what with the landslide and all. I mean, ever since I lost a cousin in Tampa Bay, it's just hit me . . . you have to go to where you hear there's a need, you know? And here, well . . . I had the money, plenty of it, and my boy had an idea to help long-term, not just right after the damage was done. Is that really such a crime?"

"Yes," said the DPPS officer, automatically. Behind him, his team was busy unpacking drones and obscurely marked canisters—neutralizing agents, Luis hoped, to counteract whatever dangerous chemical elements Eduardo and his fool team had exposed the region to.

"Sure, okay, but—" Now the voice that surprised Luis was his own. "Listen, me and Dra. Vallejo have an operation in process here doing exactly this kind of work. Just, with proper permits, and testing, and a proven track record of success in other hills. All we need is more funding. So, if Eduardo here's not just covering for some secret new terrorist group—"

"And I'm not," said Eduardo, wearily.

"—exactly," said Luis, nodding vigorously, as if he fully believed it. "So *if* he's not, then this is all good in the end, right? I mean, we've clearly got people trying to help however they can, under circumstances that aren't bringing out the best in anyone, you know? So let us take his team under ours, share the workload, and take some of the pressure off your backs, yeah? I mean, it can't be easy for you, trying to protect public safety way out here anyway, am I right?"

The mask fell silent long enough that his teammates had started sending up the first drones, bearing what Luis again hoped were simple neutralizing sprays toward the mine entrances and surrounding wilderness. "You know, if I had it my way . . . " the mask said at last, "we'd just flatten the whole damned mountain range and be done with it. I mean, we *have* the tech. We could build whatever we wanted. Instead it's just . . . triage, triage, triage."

Luis caught Claudia's smile out the corner of an eye at this admission of frustration and tried not to roll his own too hard in reply. *Yeah, yeah,* he told her, in his way, instead.

"But you're right, we do have a lot on the go," the mask continued. "And you wouldn't believe the number of false reports we get from our pedestal stations out in these parts. Hell, the last we got from this town was just some kid who didn't realize her sister's probably pregnant. So there's a lot of junk to sift through and we're stretched pretty thin, you hear me?"

Luis nodded more naturally. "I hear you. And I promise, now that we know what's been going on around this town, my team's got this. We do."

And as if to affirm his point, he and the mayor and Jorge stepped forward in unison to accept Eduardo into their custody. The mask considered, then threw up a hand in consent.

"Fine, okay, maybe it was just stupidity. Didn't even have firearms up there, come to think of it, did you, Guillermo? But listen—if he blows anything up here, that's on you three. And don't expect the DPPS to come running a second time to save your asses, either."

"Didn't really expect it the first time," Luis muttered under his breath, but the mask was already walking away, to join his team in their drone-dispersal op.

Claudia, though—Claudia had heard the mask's words, too.

"But even if that were true, where would they go?" said Luis, when Claudia brought Elena over to explain the message she'd sent to DPPS through the church's emergency pedestal. "Your family checked everywhere, right?"

Elena nodded—but doubtfully, with a half-glance back at her parents, who were still discussing the search for Jhoan and Leidy with other locals now that the chaos of DPPS had been set to one side. "Yeah, I think. I mean, we checked the city, the roads, the forest. And is that what happens all the time when people get pregnant—they get sick like that first?"

"Sometimes, yes," said Claudia. "But sweetie, I doubt you checked *all* the forests. Besides, there's got to be *some* safe haven we haven't thought of. Some place that even your family never figured two kids in love would ever want to hang out . . . What? Luis, what is it?"

Luis had crinkled his mouth into a rare, curious smile, then dispelled it with a frown.

"Nah, just thinking," he said. "I mean, Jhoan's not the greatest scribbler, and his work ethic could use a little polish, but put him in a room with his grandparents, and . . . "

"He shines," said Claudia, thinking again of his abundance of feeling when confronted, too, with an infant's remains. "But his abuelo isn't even in this town, which leaves . . . "

The pair glanced at Elena. "My abuelos are dead," she said, matter-of-fact. Luis and Claudia exchanged disappointed looks. Then the child brightened. "But my bisabuelo is still alive! He's ancient, though. My dad's grandfather, up in the mountain. Mom says his name in Emberá-Katío means wild pig because that's what he's like sometimes, a wild—"

"Ai, ¡gonorrea!," said Luis. "They're with 'Bidø"

"Luis," said Claudia. "Language."

"Oh, it's fine," said Elena, before skipping off, with visible relief, to join her parents. "Didn't you call that nice man who brings us milk and bread a son of a whore?"

Claudia reddened, and Luis tried not to laugh before setting off for the old man's farm.

"He's going to let us raise the baby here," Jhoan explained, with obvious pride, after Luis found them out front of 'Bidø's mountaintop estate, over-looking the long, gentle sweep of neighboring farmland and dreaming of the future "Just in case our families get too mad when they hear. But, I mean, how could anyone be mad at you, eh, baby?" The fifteen-year-old had his arm slung around Leidy's shoulders, and kissed her under the crook of her jaw, then nuzzled along the line of her neck while she laughed—fourteen years old, and not yet fully glowing with pregnancy, but still glowing from all of Jhoan's novice affections. In the backdrop, smoking something stronger than tobacco, 'Bidø nodded with an encouraging grin.

"It's a good thing, a healthy thing, having babies. Fertile mothers, fertile soils. Our line will continue. Our people will be stronger, more of us to talk to the land and her creatures."

Luis hesitated, unsure about pointing out the obvious—that the couple was *so* young, and still *so* new to one another; and that the world had so many babies already; and that the pregnancy was in early days yet, so they could still revisit this whole family option when they were older . . . But then again, when they were older, like him, maybe the moment would have passed them by. Maybe age would only guarantee cynicism, and too much comfort in their routines of independence to tolerate so much as a formal relationship with other human beings, let alone the idea of bringing another into such a hurting world. Between all the landslides and hurricanes and rising waters and famines, could the species ever perpetuate if left solely to the sober deci-sion-making of people who saw the worst of the planet every day? Besides, there was . . . an edge in Jhoan's voice, something Luis had never heard there before: a fierceness that couldn't be chalked up solely to the humble barrio of the kid's birth, when Jhoan said to Leidy between nuzzling kisses . . . "And we won't let anything happen to *our* baby, will we, baby? *Our* baby is never going to know a day of pain, not while I'm around . . . "

So Luis simply sighed and shored up all his careful reasoning for the old man instead. "What a shame, though," he said, "that they'll have to move when the mountain dies, right?"

"Ashhhh." 'Bidø waved his hand dismissively. "You still on about that? Clearly the spirits have spoken. Do as you like with the land, kid—make it stronger if you can. I want my great-great-grandson to have something to look forward to when he enters the world."

And at first Luis parted his lips, poised with a glib rejoinder to counter all that the old man had imputed about his character in their last conversation—but then, seeing 'Bidø with his great-granddaughter, and Jhoan; seeing how much happiness had returned to his face, his movements, his very bones . . . Luis realized at last what 'Bidø had meant by his story about the ocelot, about giving her dying voice for two days on the mountain. It was just about being present, and *staying there*—something that, so often, in his own, restless desire for some grand return the national optimism in his youth, he had mistaken for a failure to do more. What more could matter, than to be by the people who mattered to one most?

And with that in mind Luis shut his trap entirely, and descended the mountain in silence, saving up for Claudia the first utterance of his—no, *their*—good news.

Four days on, with DPPS having concluded its neutralization work and then aiding, too, in the restoration of waterlines for a whole slew of marginally contented abuelas—Claudia and Luis stood side-by-side at base-tent to issue the final command needed for their depositor-drone to seed the mountain, and observe together the graphene-based adsorbent's first steps along the six-day raiz-ruta that would heal the whole, hilly range for years and years to come.

'Bidø wanted to watch from the mountaintop itself, even after being told that—putting aside all the attendant health risks of being so close to the process—there would also be little on the surface to indicate where the seeds had been deposited, and how the initial chemical interactions there would unfold. Luis instead offered access to his portable lab, as often as the old man wanted to track progress in the coming days, but 'Bidø only snorted at the absurdity of using a machine to follow what his heart could tell him plainly—if guided by the appropriate song—about any changes to his terrain, the little slice of nature he knew so well.

Elena, though, found the monitor more intriguing—her sister's abrupt lesson in the consequences of boy-craziness having freed her to embrace her technical studies with a little less shame, and reserve—and she even tolerated Jhoan's help with the interface, while Leidy occupied herself with conversations on Jhoan's Wysprs, with the grandparents in his circle who wanted to know everything they could about her, under Sr. Sanchez's gently watchful eye. Eduardo and Jorge also joined them, soon after the initial deposit, to finalize investment arrangements with Luis, and to introduce two of the men who had been making initial attempts in the mine shafts with all their own, brutally rudimentary chemical know-how. This time, far from reprimanding them for their carelessness, Claudia embraced all three in equal measure, with kisses to their cheeks, and invited Eduardo's colleagues to take a look at some of her schematics for a better understanding of the tech in which they were all now involved.

And so only when the whole, wild gathering had left—Bidø, Sr. Sanchez, Eduardo and his men, Jorge, and finally Jhoan and Leidy and Elena in the added care of a reluctantly arriving, still highly irate Sra. Sanchez—did Luis see Claudia's true exhaustion surface. The mother's presence in particular had drawn a greyer cast across Dra. Vallejo's already tired face—and Luis knew it was serious when base-tent stood empty, with sunset's harder oranges and blues sending all their equipment into the deepest of shadows, but Claudia could not even be roused by gentle reminder of their day's multitude of successes.

"Di-Di," Luis said at last, drawing up a chair beside her. "Tell me. What's wrong?"

Claudia shook her head and turned aside, a hand quickly brushing at one glistening cheekbone. "I didn't realize," she said in a shuddery breath. "I should have realized. I told Sra. Sanchez that Jhoan was safe, but the whole time the two had been going off and . . . well, you know . . . after everything. And now what? What about their future, his education?"

Luis inclined his head and hummed agreement. "Honestly, I probably would have said the same at the time to her, if she'd asked me about Jhoan. But, come on—the world's not over for them, and to be fair, they made that mistake together. Leidy had agency, too, right?"

But Claudia hadn't even considered this facet of the question—and worse, the possibility of an answer in the negative—so then a different troubled look fell across her face: at difficult memories of her mother's sacrifices; at the pressures placed upon her, too, when she had been so unforgivably young. "Let's hope she did," she said, heavily. "But even then, I should've seen it coming. Caught it early. We had a responsibility, Luis. We made a promise."

"Yeah, I suppose we did." And at this thought, Luis laughed. "Lucky thing we don't have kids of our own, no? If this is how we mess up the ones we're handed for a while?"

But his throat cinched at the sudden, second trail down Claudia's cheek—a trail that, this time, Claudia made no move to wipe away. In its presence, Luis realized how much he would always rely on her ability to be strong on her own, no matter what he said or did. On *his* ability, too, to have that freedom, with her as with not another living soul, to mess up as often as he did, knowing that Claudia, in time, would always find a way to rise above it without any greater aid. To be close to someone without ever taking full responsibility for the impact of his fixation on his hangups, on that other person's well-being.

And maybe this was an inadequate way to live. Maybe it was untenable, really, in the longer run of things. But as Luis turned to survey the mountain—*their* mountain, so calm on the surface, now so wildly active out of sight—he marveled to think of what they had made together out of that inadequacy: those wondrous roots of Claudia's invention and *their* production, growing to fortify the soil against the rains, and protect the valley for generations to come. And to think that now, with Eduardo's investment, they could do all this again, and again—maybe only until the money ran out; but maybe also until every Colombian mountain town was secure from all but biotech, and humanity, and other forms of plague . . .

The possibility thrilled him so much that Luis set an impulsively friendly arm around his partner's shoulders and whispered at her temple, "Di-Di, what's that you keep telling me? That something always goes wrong? That you can never know for sure? So, what, you want to do away with teenagers now, entirely, to avoid the risk of disappointment? I mean, it's not a bad idea, in theory . . . but in practice just look at Jhoan and Leidy's optimism, how stupidly happy they are about the whole stupid affair. And their families, too, Christ! Even the mum's coming gradually around. And, sure, their lives are going to be nuts now, but it'll be a good sort of nuts, won't it? A constructive nuts? Like ours, a little, too?"

Ours

At first, this fragile word only heightened Claudia's anticipation, and she froze against his proffered arm with some hope of *maybe this time, maybe more?* But when Luis neither pulled away nor went any further, not even now, not even with so much of the day's emotions held between them . . . she let her long-known answer to the question of Luis finally dissolve that persevering bit of wishful thinking for good, as if under a gentle cascade of nanobots sent to clear away the corpse with the disease.

It wasn't an easy acceptance, granted—no heart could ever be flattened and remade as easily as stone—but maybe this, the stability of their friendship, a seed that had extended its roots *oh so far* but now could not be made to react a smidgeon further, was a kind of completion, too. Imperfect, unfinished, and yet . . . still set deep enough to help them both weather at least some of the future's many storms.

Born and raised in India, Rati Mehrotra now lives and writes in Toronto, Canada. She is the author of the science fantasy duology *Markswoman* and *Mahimata* published by Harper Voyager. Her YA fantasy novel *Night of the Raven, Dawn of the Dove* is forthcoming from Wednesday Books in Fall 2022. Her short fiction has been shortlisted for The Sunburst Award and has appeared in multiple venues including *The Magazine of Fantasy & Science Fiction, Lightspeed Magazine, Uncanny Magazine, Apex Magazine, Podcastle,* and *Cast of Wonders.*

KNOCK, KNOCK SAID THE SHIP

Rati Mehrotra

Knock knock, said the ship.

Deenu, seated at her console, started. Even though she should have been used to Kaalratri's voice in her head by now, the interruption made her lose track of the route she'd been trying to calculate. *What?* she subvocalized.

It's a human joke. You are supposed to say, who is there?

Okay. Who is there?

You'll . . .

What?

Now you are supposed to say, you'll who? said the ship patiently.

You'll who?

You'll never know unless you open the door.

Deenu replayed the joke in her head, trying to make sense of it. Maybe the problem was her. The astrocharts were displayed on the screen before her, and she couldn't make sense of them, either.

It sounded better in my mind, remarked the ship after the silence stretched a moment. *Human jokes always do.*

Did you want something?

You were frowning and muttering curses under your breath, said the ship.

Deenu massaged her forehead. *Just trying to figure out our route. The captain expects me to assist Beans with secondary navigation duties on the next run.*

They were in the asteroid belt between Mars and Jupiter, headed for a mining station in the Hilda group. Nowhere near as big or established as the corporations in the main belt, but the miners had found water ice and heavy metals, enough to make it worthwhile to expand their facility. They even had plans to build a hotel and a farm, hence their order of seeds, weapons, and soil microorganisms.

"Damn stupid plan," said Captain Miral, flicking open a chart of their destination on the ship wall. "Who'd waste their time and money on a miserable little asteroid when they could go literally anywhere else?"

"They seem to think that if you build it, they will come," remarked Lieutenant Saksha.

As Deenu struggled to figure out the best course, she silently agreed with the captain. If you were among the fortunate minority who could afford a holiday off-world, you would choose an all-inclusive package at one of the mega hotels of Titan, Ganymede, or Mars. Or maybe you'd go glamping in one of the last remaining biosphere reserves on Earth.

Not that Deenu could afford a holiday *anywhere*. She had a mountain of debt to pay off first—a debt she had incurred when Kaalratri rescued her from the burning remains of her homeworld. Three standard years working for Captain Miral, and the numbers in the ledger had barely moved.

"They're rebuilding Luna." Captain Miral cast a sly glance at Deenu. "I wonder how many takers there'll be for a hotel constructed on the bones of corpses."

It was not a question; Deenu did not answer. Nor did she betray how that remark made her feel. She stared at the screen with her one good eye, but the schematics blurred. She remembered her last sight of Luna, before she was carried away to safety by one of Kaalratri's drones. The flames, the acid-eaten corpses, the mangled metal of the broken towers.

The captain was not cruel, she told herself. She just liked to test Deenu from time to time. To poke and prod her, as if she hoped that one day, Deenu would burst and spew forth acid of her own.

But Deenu would never give the captain an excuse to barter her, no matter what the provocation. The ship was her home now. The ship was her *friend*.

Maybe another joke? whispered Kaalratri. *The crew prefers this one. Knock knock.*

You've been telling jokes to the crew? Deenu was scandalized. The captain had very strict ideas on appropriate use of time. Besides, Kaalratri had always been reticent, until she began talking with Deenu. The trauma they'd both suffered had brought them together. Deenu lost everyone she loved in the civil war on Luna. And Kaalratri, who had once been a hospital ship, lost all her patients in an accidental missile strike twenty years ago—a loss she'd never quite recovered from. Any sudden loquaciousness on her part might alarm the rank and file. It was one thing to know you had an implant that connected you to the ship AI. It was quite another to have a voice whispering incomprehensible jokes in your ear.

Only to a few of the most stable persons, to test the assumption that jokes, although juvenile in the extreme, often crude, and highly illogical, lighten the atmosphere and make people feel better. Levity can be used to dissemble the true horror of a situation, allowing humans to function even in high-stress situations. Did it work on you?

I feel fine, thanks, said Deenu, which was not a lie, and not an answer to the question, either.

A shadow fell over the console. "Are you dreaming, Deenu? I do not pay you to dream."

Deenu swallowed, wishing she were elsewhere. The captain occasionally circulated select crew members through the command deck, exposing them to orbital mechanics or trade negotiations. It was good of the captain, Deenu knew, because it increased the employability of her workers if she decided to dump them in the middle of nowhere. But Deenu hated being here, exposed to the captain's gimlet eyes and sharp words. *You do not pay me at all*, she should have said.

"I am having trouble understanding our route," she said instead.

"Download a primer on general relativity," the captain ordered. "Add the cost to your debt."

Deenu suppressed a sigh. "Yes, Captain." She appreciated the chance to learn more, she really did. But at this rate, she was never going to pay off her debt. She'd just keep getting in deeper.

The Com-link pinged.

Knock knock, said the ship. *Who's there?*

The captain frowned as she inspected the sigil sent by the requesting party: a white dove emblazoned with a lightning strike. "A Peace vessel? Kaalratri, visual please."

The ship obliged, throwing up a projection of a sleek blue-and-white craft. "Ninety-five-meter Peace Patrol Boat, Class B, Weapons Grade Eight," she announced.

"Shit," muttered the captain. "What are the Peace doing here?"

"Peace" was a misnomer. Even a small patrol craft carried enough fire-power to take down an entire space station. Kaalratri didn't even have a shield. Deenu closed her console, her palms damp. She tried to calm her breathing. The Interplanetary Peace Force was there to *protect* them, not prey on them. Even though they'd failed so spectacularly at that job on Luna.

"Do you think it's anything to do with that satellite wreck we salvaged without permission in Mars orbit?" asked Lieutenant Saksha.

Captain Miral snorted. "It's practically a public service, cleaning the trade lanes. We're small fry, not worth any attention from law enforcement. Definitely not worth boarding. I wonder what they want." She exhaled. "Send them our sigil and open the link, Kaalratri."

The image of a blond man in the trademark blue uniform of the Peace flashed onto the Com-link screen.

Captain Miral gave a smile full of teeth. "Greetings. I am Miral, captain of the *Kaalratri*, Trader Class C. To what do we owe this pleasure?"

"Greetings," said the man. "I am Captain Zhao. This is an unusual ship for Trader Class C status."

"She was once a hospital ship," said Captain Miral.

"Interesting." The man regarded her out of pale eyes. "I will see for myself. We must board you."

Captain Miral stiffened. "Why? Our papers are in order and we were checked thoroughly in Marsport."

"We've received reports of a rogue shipment of bioware," said Captain Zhao.

"We have no such items on board," protested the captain.

Captain Zhao's teeth flashed. "Then you will not have a problem. Prepare for docking in five minutes."

He broke the connection, and the captain cursed.

"It is odd," said Kaalratri.

"What is?" demanded Lieutenant Gyan.

"Peace officers are required to be clean-shaven," the ship observed.

"He *is* clean-shaven," said Captain Miral.

"Yes, Captain, but very recently. There are tiny nicks on his cheeks, as if he has shaved his skin with a primitive blade rather than using a bio-mod."

The captain frowned. "How is that relevant? Not everyone likes to be modded. Prepare for docking. Notify the crew that we are being boarded by Peace officers and instruct them to stay out of the way."

"Yes, Captain."

Deenu watched the screen as the sleek craft latched onto Kaalratri's outer ring like a giant leech. The image disturbed her, though she could not have said why.

"Seal established. Docking complete," announced the ship. She brought up video of six Peace officers walking through the opened hatch—four men and two women, all identically dressed and armed with a variety of weapons. They were even wearing their helmets, as if they expected a sudden attack or depressurization. Rows of flashing lights glowed at floor level along the empty corridors, guiding the visitors to the command deck.

The captain stood to welcome them, flanked by her two lieutenants. The navigator, Beans, a heavily modded man who was a genius with orbital mechanics, stood as well. Deenu clasped her hands to still their twitching, determined not to make a fool of herself. It was sheer bad luck that she happened to be on the command deck right now. She'd stay still and silent, and hopefully the Peace vessel would be gone within the hour.

The door slid open and the Peace officers entered.

"Welcome," said the captain, and stopped short. "You aren't the Peace."

The one in the lead—Captain Zhao—raised his eyebrows. "Why, who do you think we are?"

"I don't know, and I don't care, but I want you off my ship right now," Captain Miral snapped.

Captain Zhao raised his gun and shot her. It happened so fast, Deenu barely saw it: a single bullet from a primitive kinetic weapon, which had been outlawed in most parts of the solar system.

The captain dropped to the floor, a ragged red hole in her stomach. "Initiate . . . emergency . . . protocol," she gasped.

"Done, Captain," said Kaalratri, her voice calm, as if the captain had asked her to adjust the room temperature.

Beans the navigator mumbled *ohmygod ohmygod* under his breath. Lieutenant Saksha crouched beside the captain, trying to stem the flow of blood by applying pressure to the wound. Deenu stood frozen to the floor. *I'm the bad luck*, she thought numbly. *It follows me everywhere.*

Lieutenant Gyan was the first to speak. "Who are you? What do you want?"

"I want to know how she saw through our perfect disguise," said Zhao. "She will tell me, or I will shoot someone else."

"There is no need to fire that weapon again," said Lieutenant Gyan. She glanced at the captain, who, despite her obvious physical distress, was glaring at the intruders with such hatred that Deenu thought it might just melt the skin off their bones.

But the intruders did not melt; nor did they run. Zhao raised his gun again, and Lieutenant Gyan said, "Wait, please. Captain?"

"Fucking . . . morons. Don't know . . . protocol. Patrol crew is max six, boarding parties are max four."

"Ah. Something to remember for next time." Zhao pushed back his helmet and the others followed suit. They looked like teenagers, except for Zhao, who appeared to be around Deenu's age, in his mid-twenties. He was obviously their leader, although they all held their weapons with competence. He jerked his chin at Lieutenant Gyan. "We want your food, fuel, and cargo, and then we'll leave."

"Fuck off," said the captain, between gasps.

Zhao strode forward. Lieutenant Saksha leaped back as he bore down on the injured captain. He pushed the muzzle of his gun against Captain Miral's head.

"Is the cargo worth your life to you?" he demanded. "The lives of your crew? We'll leave you enough to get to the nearest station."

Captain Miral spat at him. He reared back and wiped his face, incredulous and disgusted. Deenu was unable to stop an inarticulate cry as he shot Captain Miral again. The captain's body jerked up and slammed back against the floor. Lieutenant Saksha leaned over a chair, heaving.

"Now, will one of you take us to the cargo hold or do we have to kill the rest of you, too?" said Zhao, his voice cold.

"We cannot," said Lieutenant Gyan, wetting her lips. "The captain ordered the ship to initiate the emergency protocol. That means everything is in lockdown, including the command deck."

"Override the ship," snapped Zhao. "You're next in command, aren't you?"

"That would be me," said Lieutenant Saksha, straightening and speaking with an effort. "But I cannot override her. It was the captain's last order before you . . . before she . . . " She paused to swallow. "The ship will lift the lockdown only when she deems the threat is over. You could kill us, but it will serve no purpose."

"Hey, Ship, can you hear me?" shouted Zhao.

"Yes," said Kaalratri, her voice remote.

"Would you like me to kill the rest of your crew? We can start here, with these officers. Then we'll break down your door and go for the rest of them. Would you like that, eh?"

"Would you like to hear a joke?" said Kaalratri.

"What?"

"Knock knock," said the ship.

"The fuck is wrong with you?" screamed Zhao.

"You are supposed to say, who's there," said the ship.

Zhao spun around and let loose two shots at Lieutenant Saksha. One of them missed and buried itself in the hull. The other smashed Saksha's face, spraying her blood and teeth on the wall behind. Beans let out a moan and Deenu fought against her instinct to run, to hide, to scream. There was no running, not when the moonbirds had you in their sights.

No. Not moonbirds. This isn't Luna. This is the Kaalratri *and we're in deep trouble.* Deenu dug her nails into her palms, concentrating on the pain of the present moment to stay out of the past.

The ship said, almost dreamily, "You were supposed to say, who's there."

"Okay, I'll play," said Zhao with dead calm. "Who's there?"

"Yo."

"Yo who?"

"Yo mama's going to kill you for being such a bad boy." The ship laughed—a horrible sound that congealed the blood in Deenu's veins.

"You, Scarface," Zhao barked. "What is wrong with your AI?"

Focus, Deenu. He's talking to you. Deenu unfroze. From the depths of her terror, she summoned a response. "It appears she is having a mental breakdown."

"I never heard of anything like that," he snapped.

"She used to be a hospital ship," Deenu explained, "but she lost all her patients in a terrible accident twenty years ago. Now you've killed her captain and first officer, you may have sent her over the edge."

"Knock knock," said the ship quietly. "Who's there? You. You who? Yoo-hoo yourself."

Zhao went into a huddle with his companions. He switched languages, but it was several heartbeats before Deenu realized to which one. It had been so long since she'd heard another human speak it.

Lunarian. He was speaking Lunarian.

The city of her birth, the language of her heart, the voice of her people. How many still lived, scattered through the solar system? How many had survived the civil war, only to die of grief and loneliness?

And here were the remnants—some of them, anyway. Thieves. Killers. Outlaws.

She swallowed her fear and made herself speak in the same language. "Brother, you speak Lunarian. Are you a survivor of the civil war?" Sounding strange and rusty to her own ears, like dusting off an old room that had been disused for ages.

Zhao swung around in disbelief. His eyes went to her scars. "Sister, you are one of us?"

She nodded and came forward, aware of Beans's and Lieutenant Gyan's eyes on her. They did not speak Lunarian; they would not know what she said. Kaalratri would, but she appeared to be having cognitive issues right now. Perhaps they would think she was betraying them.

"I am Deenu," she told the group. "I was rescued by this ship. No one else from my family survived."

Zhao's face hardened. "We all lost family, friends, everything. And what did the Peace do? Stood by and watched our world burn to ash."

"Is that why you stole one of their craft?" Deenu shook her head. "You won't get far. They'll track it."

Zhao grinned. "It's not really a Peace Patrol Boat, just hacked to send that signature."

Clever, whispered Kaalratri, and Deenu was grateful to hear her voice, sounding quite sane.

"Why did they not heal your scars?" asked Zhao. "To remind you of your status?"

"No," she said. "I refused treatment from Medic. I keep my scars to honor the memory of the dead."

"You should come with us." A young girl waved a large needle gun as if it were a sandwich. "There are many among us who still bear the scars of their injuries."

"There are more of you?" asked Deenu. She could scarcely believe it.

"Nearly a hundred," said Zhao. "But they need food, medicines, fuel. That is why we do this."

"We've been taking care of everyone else for the last three years," said the young girl proudly. "We're building a new settlement aboard a discarded space station. Want to join us?"

Not like this, Deenu wanted to scream. *You don't build something new out of the corpses of the innocent. Nothing good can come of it.* But she saw from Zhao's fanatical eyes that this would not go down well.

If she wanted to contain this dangerous situation, she would have to pretend sympathy. And it was not hard; part of her *did* sympathize. Part of her would probably have said yes and meant it.

But not with Lieutenant Saksha lying on the floor with most of her face missing. Not with Captain Miral soaking in a pool of her own blood. Deenu forced herself not to look at them. *Ship*, she thought, *I know you're there. Talk to me. I have an idea.*

"I wish I could join you," she said aloud, "but they can track me through my implants. I would endanger all of you."

"Will you help us get the cargo?" asked Zhao.

"I will try," said Deenu. She went up to the door and placed her palm on it, trying to look as if she knew what she was doing. It was a perfectly ordinary blast door, and it sealed them inside the command deck as effectively as a prison on the dark side of Luna.

"Wait," said Zhao. He switched to Ailish and beckoned Lieutenant Gyan with his gun. "You. Over here."

The officer walked up to him reluctantly. Deenu caught her hot glare and hastily averted her eyes.

Zhao pushed Gyan in front of him, his gun held against her temple. "You're our guarantee of safety," he told her. "Unless your crew doesn't like you. In which case, I guess we're all fucked."

"We can kill a lot of them before they get to us," a lanky boy assured him.

"Perhaps nobody else needs to die," said Deenu. *Ship*, she subvocalized. *Come on, help me here. Not much time before they realize I can't open it.*

What is your idea? asked the ship.

Take us to the inner ring, isolate it, and poison the air enough to knock us out.

They have breathe-safe helmets. They will realize something is amiss and snap those on.

We need to try!

I have a better idea, based on your idea.

The door opened so suddenly, Deenu stumbled through the opening.

"How?" Lieutenant Gyan sputtered. "Only Captain Miral should have been able to do that."

"Move." Zhao poked her with his rifle butt, and she staggered forward. One of his cohort stayed behind to watch over Beans. Not that Beans needed much watching over. A child with a water pistol could have done it.

Deenu led the way into the corridor, her heart hammering so hard, it was a wonder no one else could hear it.

"Where is the rest of the crew?" asked Zhao.

"Under lockdown," said Deenu. "When we're in emergency mode, the ship locks everyone up wherever they are."

"Good, makes it easier for us," said Zhao. "Where is the cargo?"

"Up in the inner ring," Deenu told him. "We must climb along one of the spokes."

"Why was the captain willing to die for it?" asked Zhao from behind her as she led them to the maintenance spoke.

"If we do not deliver, we do not get paid," answered Deenu. "Then we have no way to pay off our suppliers. We fall into debt. Worse, word gets around and we start losing clients. Our debt increases. Eventually, under pressure, the captain will be forced to sell the ship. And that'll be the end of all of us."

Zhao stared at her in surprise. "You have no insurance?"

Gyan barked a laugh. Deenu said, "Who would sell insurance to freelance traders like us? The captain can't afford it. Margins are thin enough as it is."

Zhao did not answer. Deenu wondered if he regretted targeting their ship. Regretted the murders he had committed.

They climbed up the spoke, the most boring one of the six that connected the outer to the inner ring and the hub of the ship. Deenu would never have let them trespass on the garden—her favorite spoke—where they grew vegetables to supplement their algal diet.

Gravity fell as they approached the inner ring. This was where Kaalratri had taken care of her patients, back when she was still a hospital ship. Now it was where they stored the cargo. Lights came on as Deenu hauled herself up into the corridor that circled the inner ring.

Bring them to Cargo Bay Five, said the ship. *When I say* knock knock, *duck into the nearest container—the one with the door slightly open.*

What about Lieutenant Gyan?

She will recover, said the ship, and refused to say more.

"Our highest value items are in Cargo Bay Five," announced Deenu, halting outside the bay door.

"Traitor," muttered Gyan.

Deenu suppressed a stab of irritation. Of course, Gyan did not deal with the nitty-gritty of cargo storage details, or she would have known Cargo Bay Five housed very little apart from empty containers.

The door slid open at her touch and closed again once they were inside. Zhao and the others gazed expectantly at the banks of gleaming steel alloy containers that towered over them, probably picturing nutri-packs and seeds and medical equipment galore. Deenu would have felt sorry for them, were it not for the fates of Captain Miral and Lieutenant Saksha.

Zhao and his gang had probably carried out several such raids in the past three years. The fact that news of a ship faking a Peace vessel had not spread all over the trade route meant that they had been both cunning and ruthless. Perhaps the horror they had faced on Luna had inured them to violent death. But it did not excuse what they had done.

"Open up—let's see what we have here," ordered Zhao, his face eager.

Knock knock, said the ship.

Deenu didn't wait to hear more. She dove to the floor and grabbed the door of a container that was slightly ajar. As she threw herself into the cold darkness inside, she was blinded by a fierce white light, even though she was facing away from it inside a container. She flung the door closed, but not before she heard the cries of Zhao and his companions.

Clever, she thought.

Kaalratri had not used poison. Anything truly effective would have killed them all, and anything less would have been pointless, as they would have donned their helmets at once. Only Deenu and Gyan would have suffered. But this, they had not expected. The ship had temporarily blinded them.

She heard sounds of a scuffle and shouts outside and prayed Gyan was safe.

You can join us now, said the ship. *They have been overpowered.*

Deenu crawled out. The cargo bay swarmed with her crew mates, armed with a variety of weapons ranging from improvised cudgels to dart guns. Medic was stabbing needles into the arms of their attackers, ensuring their instant unconsciousness.

Lieutenant Gyan leaned against the bulkhead, her hands covering her face.

I told her to close her eyes, said the ship. *She will be fine.*

And the crew—you told them your plan?

Of course. One needs humans to deal with humans. I am merely the brains around here.

Lieutenant Gyan's hands dropped from her face. Her eyes were red, and water trickled down her cheeks. "Notify the Peace," she said grimly.

"Done, Lieutenant," said the ship. "They are on their way."

"Make sure the hatch remains closed so that no one else can enter from their craft."

"Yes, Lieutenant. Can Medic please report to the command deck now?"

"Of course." Gyan staggered to her feet. Her eyes went to Deenu, and she gave a brief nod. Which was all the apology Deenu would get for being called a traitor.

Deenu found it did not matter, because she *did* feel like a traitor. These were her people being hauled unceremoniously down the spoke, damaged though they were.

Nearly a hundred, Zhao had said. A hundred souls depended on Zhao's raiding party for survival. Had Deenu condemned them to the slow, painful death of starvation?

Down in the command deck, Medic crouched over the motionless form of Captain Miral. "She still lives," he said excitedly. "Our captain's a tough old bird." The crew gave a ragged cheer and Gyan nearly wept. Deenu felt like weeping herself.

Medic sprayed a foam over the captain's body that hardened slightly—a protective covering that would keep her safe until she was in the medical bay. As two of the crew members ran for a medbed, Medic turned his attention to Lieutenant Saksha.

"Oh, Saksha," he muttered, reaching for her wrist. An automatic gesture, Deenu thought, because no one could have survived such a terrible wound.

But Medic's seamed face cracked open in a disbelieving smile. "I feel a pulse," he announced. They all stared at the body on the floor, and the bloody pulp that remained of Saksha's face.

"Can you save her?" asked Gyan.

"I don't know," he said. "The next hour will be critical. I have the most basic facilities—nothing that can regrow her face or neurons."

"But Kaalratri can," blurted out Deenu.

Medic stared at her.

"She was a hospital ship once—remember?" said Deenu, the words tripping over themselves in her excitement. "Ship, surely you can assemble an amniotic sac for the lieutenant?"

"An excellent idea," said the ship. "It will be ready in fifteen minutes. Please bring her to Cargo Bay Three."

"But . . . do you still have the facilities to build such a thing?" asked Medic.

"I do," said Kaalratri.

In the end, keeping her alive for those fifteen minutes and carrying her broken body up the spoke proved the most difficult task of all. Medic had her fixed to a medbed and drones carried it up to Cargo Bay Three. The captain was already in the medical bay, being tended by a robot.

Deenu went to her pod and tried not to hyperventilate. But the events of the past hour were beginning to catch up with her and she could not sit still, could not breathe normally. Dark spots danced before her eyes, and she heard the cries of the moonbirds as they dove down to spray acid on her face.

You have been very brave, said the ship.

I was frightened, said Deenu. *I am still frightened.*

So was I, said the ship. *I was frightened that Captain Miral and Lieutenant Saksha would die. But I knew they were still alive, and it was essential to get them medical attention at once.*

Will Saksha be okay?

Saksha is safe with me. I will keep her in the sac as long as it takes for her to heal. And the captain should be back on the command deck in ten or twelve sleep cycles, if I know her at all.

Deenu exhaled. *What will happen to Zhao and his gang, do you think? Will they be executed?*

What a barbaric notion, said the ship. *No, they will be reconditioned and put to work.*

There was a pause, then: *He called you sister*, said the ship.

It does not mean anything. It is just an honorific.

But it did mean something, and Kaalratri was not fooled.

How are you *feeling?* Deenu subvocalized, trying to shift the focus of the conversation. *I was worried you were having an actual breakdown. Was that all pretense?*

I am not capable of pretense, said the ship. *I was trying to lighten the atmosphere.* Kaalratri paused expectantly. *See what I did there? I made a pun, a play on words. Light? Lighten?*

Peace officers—*real* ones—arrived some hours later. The unconscious raiders were wheeled away by drones and testimonies were taken, both from the ship and her crew. Deenu had to explain that she was Lunarian, that she had deliberately led the raiders into a trap set by the ship. The telling was somehow worse, as if her role had been bigger than that, as if she was single-handedly responsible for their capture. The ship could surely have managed it without her. The raiders hadn't expected such an advanced AI—had not known, before they targeted her, that she used to be a hospital ship.

And yet, wasn't that reasoning simply a way of avoiding her own culpability?

At last, the Peace officers left, after confirming that medical facilities on board the ship were adequate to treat the two injured officers.

Life returned to normal—or as normal as possible without the captain. Lieutenant Gyan took over in the interim and filled the role to the best of her abilities. She did not have the captain's flair, her instincts, or her experience, but she was capable enough. The ship continued on her way to the Hilda group. And every sleep cycle, Deenu twisted and moaned and fought the ghosts that had come back to haunt her from Luna.

At last, the ship asked if she would like to take something to help her sleep.

Deenu refused. It was a small punishment, and it did not fit the crime.

Your functioning is at the lowest it has been in three years, remarked the ship as Deenu clambered into her sleep pod.

Deenu did not answer.

Please talk to me, said the ship.

Deenu sighed. *It is time for me to sleep.*

I heard the captain talking with Gyan . . .

That made Deenu sit up. *The captain's awake?*

Not just awake, she's demanding reports and criticizing Gyan and scaring Medic. She'll be back on the command deck soon.

Deenu lay back down. *Things will return to normal then.*

Perhaps not. I have found the group of Lunarians connected to our would-be raiders.

Deenu's heart jumped. *How?*

There are not too many discarded space stations in the solar system that would support a hundred humans. I have been running a search ever since they mentioned it.

What . . . what are you going to do with this information?

The question, Deenu, is what are you *going to do?*

I'm a debt-burdened refugee, here on the sufferance of the captain. What can I do?

But to that, the ship had no answer.

Deenu was summoned to the command deck on her next work cycle, along with whatever crew could be spared from their tasks. The captain, weak and spindly from her many hours in the medical bay, fixed burning eyes on them all and stretched her lips in an attempt at a smile.

"We arrive at the Hilda group in ten hours," she rasped. "Just a few hours late, and with all our cargo intact. Things could have been much worse, if not for the quick thinking shown by Kaalratri and a refugee we picked up from Luna three years ago."

There were nods and grunts of agreement. Deenu stared at her feet, her face hot. She didn't want to be praised for what she had done. She wanted to bury it, just like she'd buried everything else in her past.

"In view of your loyalty and courage, Deenu, I forgive your debt."

Deenu looked up in shock. Cheers and claps broke out across the deck. The captain held up a hand and the noise died down. "Kaalratri, reset the ledger."

"Done, Captain. Should I add something on the credit side?"

The captain hesitated only a moment. "Three years' back pay. That is only fair."

Deenu felt as if gravity had released its hold on her feet. *Three years' back pay.* "Thank you, Captain, for your generosity," she managed.

The captain smiled and dismissed them all, the fatigue evident in her eyes.

Ship, said Deenu once they were outside, barely able to contain her excitement, *where is the space station located? The one where the refugees are hiding?*

A week's travel from Titan, our next stop, said Kaalratri. *Are you planning a coup?*

What? No. But I can use my back pay to send food, fuel, and medical supplies to them. How much can you buy in Titan for the funds I now have?

About enough to last them four standard months, if they are frugal, said the ship. *It should tide them over until they figure out less murderous means of making a living. Shall I place the order?*

Deenu took a deep breath. *The captain will throw me out of the airlock.*

It is your money, said the ship. *And perhaps, if you explain yourself, the captain might not go as far as that.*

Do it, said Deenu, before she could lose her nerve.

Done, said the ship cheerfully a moment later. *Your ledger is now zero. Given the large transaction amount, a message has gone to the quartermaster. You may as well speak to the captain now, before she sends for you.*

Deenu turned back to the door of the command deck, steeling herself. She knew she'd done the right thing. All she had to do was get Captain Miral to agree.

Go on, said the ship. *Knock knock.*

Matthew Kressel is a writer of fiction and software. He is a three-time Nebula Award finalist, a World Fantasy Award finalist, and a Eugie Award finalist. His short fiction has appeared in *Lightspeed, Clarkesworld, Analog Science Fiction & Fact, io9, Nightmare, Beneath Ceaseless Skies, The Year's Best Science Fiction and Fantasy,* and *The Best Science Fiction of the Year,* as well as many other publications, and his work has also been translated into eight languages. As a software developer, he created the popular Moksha submissions system. And he is the co-host of the Fantastic Fiction at KGB reading series in New York with Ellen Datlow. Find him tweeting about the environment on Twitter at @mattkressel or at his website www.matthewkressel.net.

STILL YOU LINGER, LIKE SOOT IN THE AIR

Matthew Kressel

By the time Gil had stopped meditating and opened his eyes, Muu had already removed the body. Just yesterday he and Demi had walked the eighty-four flights of stairs down to the dusty city streets, and together he and Demi had strolled across the promenade of Usha Square under the tangerine light of the setting sun. The wind had whipped Demi's long hair into a frenzy, and Gil had leaned forward to brush a lock away from his friend's glowing eyes. Now, Demi was gone. Muu had taken him, which meant Demi wasn't dead exactly, but neither would Gil ever hold his hand again.

Gil sat by the open-aired window as the warm winds whipped furiously over the city, sending whorls of dry air into his bare apartment. The oil lamp by his feet guttered and went out. But a moment later, it flickered back to life.

"Thank you, Muu," Gil whispered, even though he wished the lamp would stay out, that he could sit in the dark and hide from her forever.

But the approaching footsteps on the landing told him his wish was futile. Through machinations Gil couldn't begin to comprehend, Muu had arranged for a new pupil to arrive the very same day his old one had left.

And who would it be this time? A hedonist from Tarphon, ostensibly here to become devout, but in reality come to bliss out on the holy herb? Another melk barely out of diapers, hoping to learn the secrets of the universe but unable to count to ten? Gil had first come to Gilder Nefan to escape his father, a man who apologized as often as he punched. And Gil's bruises were still healing the first time he'd ascended Gilder Nefan's long flights and sat before the feet of a holy man. It seemed like eons ago now, though it was just less than a decade, and that callow boy he had been had washed away in the tides of time. He couldn't quite remember what he had felt back then. Excitement? Relief? Terror? But he knew that if he could send a message back through time, he would scream, *Run!*

The footsteps grew louder as the new pupil made their way down the hall. Gil would not announce his presence. If they wished to subject themselves to this hell, then at least let them come to him.

A young woman stepped through the door's threshold, from shadow into light. The setting sun gave her skin a bloody pallor and made her eyes spark and flash like embers from a raging fire. She was young and fit and had barely broken a sweat from having just climbed eighty-four flights.

"Let peace be the way," she said.

"And the way, peace," he replied.

"I'm Tim," she said. "And you are Gil?"

"More or less," he said. "Are you hungry, Tim? Tired?"

"I ate on-ship," she said. "And, no, I'm quite awake, thank you."

He looked her up and down. She wore the local style of clothing: loose-fitting dun pants and blouse, and a wide leather belt with a pouch at her waist. Her hair was cut short and did not convey any particular style. The only thing that marked her as an off-worlder was her shoes. Like the rest of her clothing, they were brown, but made of synthetics.

"Take those off," he said, nodding at her shoes. "We wear leather sandals here or nothing."

"Yes, of course," she said. "I'll get new ones tomorrow." And in two quick motions of her feet she stood barefoot on the stone floor.

He studied her again. "Why are you here, Tim?" he said.

She hung her head and threw herself onto her knees before him. "I'm here to learn! I'm here to do whatever you ask of me, teacher."

Inwardly, Gil sighed. This poor soul had absolutely no idea what she was in for. "And if I ask you to jump out this window, would you do that for me, Tim?"

She glanced up at him with a look of intense fear, and this pleased him. The fearful ones were easily manipulated. And so perhaps he might convince her she was better off joining a farming commune on Woll Ye, or devoting her life to dream-music on Datsu. But Muu pressed down on his heart with her great invisible finger, filling Gil with enough dread to swallow a universe. And so, instead, he forced a laugh and said, "I'm only joking, Tim. How was your trip?"

"Long," she said with a relieved chuckle. "There's no direct route here to Gilder Nefan from the inner worlds. I had a three-day layover at Chadeisson." She shook her head and shivered. "Have you ever been there?"

"No."

"It's an old mining city in sysPnei. The people there are . . . "

"Are what?"

"Well, they're very strange."

"Strange how?"

She grew timid, as if she had somehow offended him. "Well, I mean that they're all caught up in 'tainment and sense-pleasures. None of them seemed fully present. Fully alive."

"Unlike you," he said.

She straightened, and he sensed a defiant streak. "Well, no," she said. "*Not* like me."

"And how are you different, Tim?"

She took in a deep breath. "I'm not better. No, I know that. But I have made different choices. I've chosen to delve deeper into my own conscious-ness in order to explore the nature of reality. And in my research I have come to believe that I will learn volumes about the nature of being itself if I can commune with the numens."

He laughed, and it wasn't forced this time.

"What's so funny?" she said with a frown.

"You think it's that easy?" he said. "That you just sail across the deep to Gilder Nefan and have a conversation with a god?"

She shook her head. "Most scholars agree that the numens aren't gods," she said. "They're alien minds who lie beyond human comprehension, who have abilities that seem to defy known physical laws of nature."

"In other words," Gil said, "*gods*."

"That's a term I'd rather not use," she said.

"*You'd* rather not use?" he said. "Since when do you get to choose how you refer to them?"

"I'm sorry if I offended you," she said, shrinking at his tone. "But I just don't see the numens as anything other than alien intelligences who lie beyond our cognitive reasoning. What does a cat know of poetry? We may be like cats to them."

"*Pets*, you mean?" Gil said, wondering if Muu would stop him if he tried to flee. But where in the universe could you hide from a god? He suppressed a shudder.

"We might be their pets," said Tim. "But I think we are much more. I have come here, teacher, to commune with the numens, and in so doing I hope to understand more about the nature of consciousness. From what I've read, communing with them opens up doorways of mental thought unlike anything else in human experience."

"*You have no idea*," he muttered.

"Pardon?" she said.

"Us Nefanesh—we are religious folk!" he said. "We immerse ourselves in holy study. We worship five times a day. We live austere lives, refraining from technology and contrivance. We use only that which enables us to approach the divine. And yes, Tim, the numens *are* gods. There is no other word for them. They could pluck you from this world like a flower from a stem." He loudly snapped his finger at her and she winced. *And once they have their eyes on you, they never look away*, he wanted to say, but Muu would have punished him for it. "Are you ready for that?"

She reached into the pouch on her belt and pulled out a well-worn copy of *The Light of the Universe*. Tiny colored strips of paper bookmarked many dozens of pages. "I've never been more ready."

Gil gazed out the window. The sun had set behind the thicket of stone towers, and the first stars were already glimmering above the lamp-lit city. From a nearby balcony a sein began to bellow the sunset call to prayer, and seconds later, dozens of others across the city joined her in song. Their chanting voices echoed from a thousand stone walls until they became one giant cacophony of madness.

He wanted to scream at her: *Run! Leap onto the next ship and never look back on this cursed place*. But Muu's presence was like a piece of clothing he could never take off, so instead he shuddered.

"Come!" he said to her sharply. "It's time to pray."

The next morning, Tim revealed that she had changed her gender several times, but ultimately chose female because she felt it suited her temperament. Gil said nothing at this, even though this was against Nefanesh custom. If asked, the Nefanesh perennially replied that they were against all forms of body modification, that everything from simple piercings to full-blown gene-redactions were forbidden. The body was a temple, the Nefanesh said, and thus a holy person should remain as close to human pure as possible. But "pure" meant different things to different people, and the Nefanesh made many exceptions. They were always making exceptions.

At least twice per day, he sent Tim all the way down to the streets to fetch sundry things: vials of oil, sticks of incense, supplies of food and water for her. Sometimes he sent her away just to be alone. But there was no education in it. It was all rote, a hazing period meant to test his pupil's patience. And typically, by the end of the first week, most students began to show cracks in their fortitude. Their eyes would grow red and weary, their shoulders would stoop, and their pace would slow. But not Tim. No—she seemed to enjoy the long treks down into the bowels of the city, then back again up the eighty-four flights, as if she were, like a blacksmith's sword, being tempered each time.

On the third day, when the sun began to touch the tips of the buildings and the sunset prayer was almost upon them, Tim said, "You never eat."

"You're perceptive," he said, nodding. "It usually takes new pupils more than a week to notice."

"Why is that?" she said, staring intently at him.

"Perhaps because they're too focused on themselves."

"No, I mean, why don't *you* ever eat?"

He paused. "Because all my needs are taken care of."

"By the numens?" she said.

"Just one," he said. "Her name is Muu."

Tim's eyes lit up like a bowl in a jisthmus pipe. She sat down at his feet and said, "Muu! What a beautiful name! I've heard of Hri and Saa, but never Muu. How does she feed you?"

"It's not like that," he said. "I just don't need to eat anymore."

"Fascinating!" she said. "What other needs does she take care of? Urination? Defecation? What about sexual needs?"

Gil looked away from her penetrating gaze, embarrassed.

"Sleep?" she went on. "Do you sleep, Gil? I can't remember if I ever saw you—"

"Shut up!" he snapped. "You speak too much!"

"Yes. Mother always said that."

"Part of becoming a holy vessel is learning how to listen."

"Yes. I'm sorry."

The sun burned its way down between the buildings, until the crevices below vanished into shadow. Lamps were lit, and globes of warm orange light spilled into the labyrinthine interstices.

"Teacher?" she said.

"Yes?"

"It's been three days, and you haven't partaken of the holy jisthmus."

He squinted at her. "Few things escape your attention."

"Next time you partake," she said, "may I join you?"

He couldn't help but laugh. "You're here three days and think you're ready to leap into infinity?"

"I've been studying for months and months."

"*Months!*" he said. "Entire *months!*"

"Ask me something, anything," she said.

"All right," he said. "What does *The Light of the Universe* say about humility?"

Immediately she shot back, "Well, Tractate 71 says, 'Good traits and accomplishments do not entitle one to special treatment.'"

Gil stared at her for a long moment before nodding. "And you'd do well to heed that precept, Tim." He leaned back and sighed, believing the topic over, but she went on:

"That's not all the holy book says. Tractate 92 goes on to say, 'A potter should let his skill be known, in case there is need of pots. It is a sin to hide one's good traits and accomplishments.' Teacher—*Gil*, I know *The Light of the Universe* by heart. I can quote chapter and verse from any page of *The Seven Commentaries*, *Our Divine Cleaving*, and *The Set Table*. I can read, write, and speak fluent Nefanese as well as ancient Psemitian. I know all the prayers and rituals and customs by heart. All I'm asking for is a chance to touch the face of a god."

He waited for Muu's hand to nudge him into saying, *Yes*. But from above there was only a horrid silence, like the sound of an empty bed where once there had lain a man.

"My prayer mat is worn," he said. "Fetch me a new one."

"Yes, teacher," she said, nodding. "I'll head down tomorrow after the—"

"Now," he said.

"*Now?* But it's almost dark and sunset prayers will be—"

"Now!" he shouted.

She paused. "Not many stores will be open this late."

"Do what I ask of you, Tim," he said.

She frowned and nodded. "Yes, teacher."

But once she stepped into the hall, he shouted after her, "Tim!"

"Yes?" she said, peering back around the doorframe with an expectant look, as if he might change his mind.

He waited for Muu to yank his marionette strings this way or that, but to his immense relief she did not act. So he said, "Not everyone enjoys the mind expansion that takes place under the influence of jisthmus. In fact, some find the experience mentally shattering." He winced, awaiting Muu's hand, but when nothing happened he continued. "And once that door is opened, it cannot be closed again. Think hard, Tim. Sometimes, ignorance is bliss."

"I know the risks," she said. "And I made my decision a long time ago. I only await yours." Then she turned and headed for the stairs, while outside the first seins began to sing.

By the end of the second week, Tim began to stink. Just two weeks before, Gil had sat in this same room and washed Demi's body while the glimmering starlight and the hot evening air poured in through the windows. They had lain on the prayer mat that had doubled as Demi's bed. And while Gil had caressed Demi's swiftly hardening body, he'd felt Muu's presence as intimately as if the god herself were lying between them. Whenever Demi touched him, Muu's ineffable immensity shuddered with pleasure too. And whenever Gil came, Muu did too, and waves of ineffable bliss rippled out across the universe. Years before Gil had ever dreamed of communing with a god, he had thought sex was the most intimate thing two people could share. But sex with a person *and* a god? This pleasure was beyond imagining.

For weeks, he had hoped to tell Demi that Muu was with them when they made love, that they hadn't been alone. But he could never bring himself to admit it, because he was too scared of how Demi might react, too scared to lose his little slice of heaven. So instead he'd let Demi believe that it was always just the two of them, alone, in this hot room under the stars. And now, Demi was gone, snatched up into the ether, never to return. Did Demi now know what Gil had done, how he had betrayed the only person he had ever loved? Did Demi, whatever he was now, even care?

"What are you thinking about?" Tim said.

"Hm?" Gil said groggily, waking from the memory. They sat in Tim's bedroom, in the same spot where Demi had once slept. A large cloud passed over the sun, and a great shadow swallowed the city whole.

"You were staring off into space," Tim said. "Were you speaking with Muu just then?"

"No," Gil said. "I was thinking of . . . " He paused. "An old friend."

"Someone you miss?"

"Yes. Very much."

"Are they dead?"

Gil should have been offended by the question, but he was getting used to Tim's direct style. "Yes," he said. "He's dead." Which wasn't exactly true. Demi was out there, somewhere, in the same way that lamp oil, once burned, still lingered as soot in the air.

"I'm sorry," Tim said. "What was he like?"

"Kind," Gil said. "And quiet. He didn't speak much, but when he did, you listened, as if his thoughts were the most important thing in the world. He could make anyone laugh. Or cry."

Tim nodded. "How did he die?"

A departing ship streaked across the sky, trailing vapor as it burned for the stars. Distantly, its retreating thunder echoed across the folds of the city. "He was killed."

"Murdered?"

He waited for Muu to crush his psyche under her thumb, but the departing ship vanished into the blue sky, and the wind whorled past the window, and nothing much else happened. A brown sparrow, small as a mouse, alighted on the windowsill, cocked its head at both of them, then darted off.

"Yes," Gil said. "He was murdered."

"By whom?"

But Gil did not answer. He could not answer. Not because Muu forbade it, but because the truth was too painful, that the divine being who had given him everything—purpose, knowledge, bliss—was the same monster who had stolen the most wonderful thing that had ever happened to him.

Instead, he said, "Tim, I want you to join me in the ceremony tonight. After sunset prayer, we will partake of the holy jisthmus together."

She raised her eyebrows in a look of surprise, until she caught herself and cooled. "I . . . I'd be honored."

"Go meditate," he said. "Calm your mind as best you know, because tonight the door to the universe will be blown open. Be as still as a boulder in a rushing river, because the floods will come, Tim. They will come."

Gil's jisthmus pipe was long and skinny and made of hardwood, a gift from Demi after his last one had worn out. A prayer along the side in ancient Psemitian read, *The universe is nothing but Light, and the light of the One pervades all.* The other side read, *With love, D.*

Gil turned the pipe over in his hands while Tim watched. They sat on their prayer mats beside the room's large window, but the evening breeze did little to break the day's heat. Above the city, the sky was so clear that Gil could pick out the colors of individual stars. He had turned the oil lamp down so that most of the light came from the lamplit city. In its lambent flicker, the sweat dripping down their bodies softly glimmered, and it seemed as if they both were made of orange wax.

Gil recited the jisthmus prayer, while Tim listened: *"When the pathway opens, let it be filled with light. Like dross from gold, may the light burn away our impurities. May our essence be pure and acceptable to the Ones who watch over us."*

"Blessings and light," Tim said.

She leaned in to watch as he carefully unrolled the cloth bundle which held the holy jisthmus herb. Its potent oils could be absorbed through the skin, so he was careful not to touch it with his bare hands. But even before the pungent, earthy fragrance reached his nose, his hands began to tremble. Using small wooden tongs, he packed the pipe's deep bowl.

It seemed only hours ago when he and Demi had sat in this spot and partook of the jisthmus together. They had just finished their second draught from the pipe when the walls began their familiar dissolution. Usually it took many long minutes of meditation and prayer before Muu made her presence known. But this time she had thrust herself into their presence like a planet-sized tidal wave. Muu crashed over them, around them, through them, and as they tumbled and gasped in that mad roiling sea of crushing sensation, Demi slipped away, like water through cloth, until there was nothing left of his humanity but a slowly evaporating spot of moisture. And when Gil awoke, hours later, from that nightmare, shivering and naked on the floor, the sun was a bright creeping blob rising the east, and the man beside him was dead.

"You're trembling," Tim said.

"What of it?" he said.

"Are you frightened?" she said.

He met her steady eyes. "Are you?"

"Yes," she said. "I am."

"Good," he said. "Fear is the only rational response to what you are about to experience."

"I've just realized something," she said, cocking her head. "The reason you didn't want me to partake of the jisthmus is not because I'm unready. Since I've been here, you haven't partaken of the jisthmus yourself. Something happened the last time you smoked it, didn't it?" she said. "Something that scared you."

He stared at her. Was there anything this person didn't see? He blinked, and for an instant he was suspended in infinite space, a dimensionless point inside Muu's unfathomable immensity. He blinked again and he was back in the dimly lit room. A flashback, or Muu's hand, he couldn't tell. "Like I said, the experience is not always pleasurable."

"What happened?" she said.

He considered telling her. *I loved a man, and Muu stole him from me.* But a hand gripped his heart and squeezed. At first, he assumed this was Muu, but there was a quality to this pain vastly different from Muu's touch. It was too human. It was his own. His throat tightened, but he swallowed before it could emerge as a sob. "There is nothing to say," he said. "Pass me the match."

She stared at him for a long moment before obeying. "Here."

It took his shaking hands three tries to light the match. He held the small burning stick above the packed bowl for a moment. "It's not too late to turn back," he said. "It's not too late to leave."

"No," she said. "I've been waiting forever for this. I'm not going anywhere."

"Yes," he said, "you are." Then he lowered the flame to the bowl, and inhaled.

Doors. Doors and windows and corners. Opening, expanding. Walls, moving. Rearranging. Spreading. A labyrinth of walls, infinitely distant. Blocks of stone make mountains or cities. There is no difference between stones and mind. Both are matter. Matter is energy is matter is thought. Thought is energy. The universe is thought.

Laniakea, the galactic mega-supercluster, is one neuron in an immeasurably large cosmic brain. It belongs to a creature that roams in vastnesses beyond imagining. What is man in all that? Like an electron wave, he spreads out. A bug on a windscreen, he smears.

Gil grew large. Large and empty. Galaxies spun like whirlpools of scintillating water. They collided and merged and were flung out into the great deep. Trillions of minds arose and fell within their swirling spirals, but nothing ever died. Death, the great illusion. Only change is constant.

Gil, a voice said. Not in sound, but in ripples in spacetime itself, arising over eons. *Gil*, it said again.

I'm here! he wanted to shout. But he was insubstantial, a photon hurtling through infinite space. What could a photon say to the universe that it didn't already know? *Demi*, he wished to scream, *is that you? Is that you?*

Gil approached an active star-forming region, where great globs of gas and dust reached gargantuan fingers out into the night, futilely trying to grasp onto the great nothing, only to collapse back again into raging balls of nuclear fire.

Muu was here. She was the nebula and she was everything and she was nothing. Matter and emptiness, all the same. Lightning flickered across a hundred light-years as she spoke, and her words were not words but thought pictures.

Demi—oh, lovely Demi—stood on a precipice in an endless white desert, while the horizon behind him stretched to infinity. Beyond the cliff's edge spread an infinite blue sky. Demi, bright-eyed and eager. Demi, smiling and reaching out his hand. Gil floated down, down toward the hand, ready to grasp it and never let go. But he was just a photon. And as he raced toward Demi's palm, the molecules of Demi's hand spread into their constituent atoms, and the atoms spread into quarks, and each of these minuscule bundles of smeared energy drifted as far apart from each other as stars in a galaxy.

We are all empty, Muu said to him, in thought pictures. *Demi was never anything at all, nor will he ever be anything again. The thoughts you have of him are like waves that ripple in a turbulent sea. Sometimes they form shapes and sense impressions. You ascertain meaning in them, but in reality they are just waves in a stormy sea. You mourn his loss, but why mourn when Demi was never anything at all? He has more life in death than you do in life, because now he is infinite.*

But, but, but . . . Gil struggled to say. His photon energy leaped from orbital to orbital like stones across a pond. *I felt something real*, he said, *and that was enough* . . .

You are a bird, trapped in a room with a single half-open window, Muu said. *The escape is just an inch below you, where the window lies open, yet you keep flying headfirst into the glass.*

Can I see him? Gil said. *Can I speak to Demi, as he was?*

But you are him, now, Muu said. *You are the photon which reflected off his eye and wound its way into space, where it has been speeding away from Gilder Nefan for eighty million years. All of your senses of him were nothing more than reflected photons and electrostatic pressure.*

And what of my feelings? Gil said.

Just waves on a stormy sea, said Muu.

Why do you hurt me? Gil said. *Why do you make me suffer so?*

It is you who make yourself suffer.

Let me go. If I am ignorant, let me remain so. Reality is too much.

Is that what you truly wish? To remain in ignorance?

Yes! To be free . . . *of you.*

That is impossible, Muu said. *For we are all born from the same sea.*

And then Gil blinked, and he was back in the room, shivering on his prayer mat beside the window. An orange glow limned the horizon, where the sun would soon rise. A body lay supine on the mat beside him, and in the dim pre-dawn light his heart leapt. "Demi!" he cried.

But when the body stirred, he saw it was Tim.

He turned from her and wiped the tears away before she could see him.

When she finally sat up, she said nothing for a long time. Her expression seemed different. More solemn. More humble.

"You see?" he said, bitterly. "I told you not all jisthmus experiences are positive. Some are horrific. I bet you wish you could put that genie back in the bottle now, don't you?"

"No," she said, shaking her head. "Gil, you don't understand. I took ten draughts last night."

"Ten?" he said. He only remembered her taking one. "For your first time? That's insane! Why?"

"Because I wanted so badly to feel something."

"And?"

"And I sat here all night and I waited. And I . . . ." She paused. "I felt nothing."

"Nothing?" he said. "Nothing at all?"

"No, Gil, not a thing."

Two days later, Tim had booked a ticket on the next departing ship. "I'm heading back to Chadeisson," she said. "From there I can catch a ship to pretty much anywhere."

"And where will you go then, Tim?" he said.

"I don't know yet," she said. "I'm still trying to figure out my next steps."

"Well," he said, "I wish you didn't have to go to soon." And he surprised himself by meaning it.

She gave him a forlorn look. "I really wanted this to work out, Gil. They say one in a million people are immune to the effects of jisthmus. I guess I'm one of the unlucky ones."

Count your blessings, he wished to say. "You could begin a deep meditation practice. It will be hard, but people have been known to commune with the numens without needing jisthmus to pry open their minds. It just takes longer. Years."

"That's too long," she said. "And frankly, I don't have the patience."

"I can see that," he said, staring at the satchel at her feet, packed and ready to go. A knot tightened in his chest.

"Come with me," she said.

"To Chadeisson?"

"It's clear you aren't happy here, Gil. You're suffering. And there's so much out there to discover. The universe is huge, and we've only just begun to explore it. Come with me to Chadeisson, and from there you can decide who you want to be next."

"But I don't have enough exchange to book passage," he said.

"Then I'll loan it to you."

"It's a lot, Tim."

"It's not a big deal. Mother gave me enough gold to last for years. It's the least I can do for all your help."

"I didn't do much, really."

"You tried," she said. "Now I'm returning the favor. What do you say?"

He looked around his empty apartment, at his meager possessions. A small chest, with sundry things. Some wooden cups. A few glass vials. An incense holder and some sticks. His pipe and jisthmus bundle. There were a few scraps of stale bread on the windowsill that Tim had left to feed the sparrows. It would be so easy just to leave all of this behind, to just pick up and go. But when his eyes swept over the empty prayer mat beside him, the place where Demi had once lain, he paused.

"Thank you, Tim," he said. "I appreciate your offer very much, but I can't go with you. I'm sorry."

She let out a long sigh. "All right, Gil," she said, surprising him when she began to cry. "I wish I could have seen what you saw. Know what you know. But that door is closed for me forever."

"Can I ask you something, Tim?"

"Yes! Anything."

"What do you think I saw?"

"I can't even imagine."

"Try."

She pursed her lips. "I think you realized that the agency we think we have is an illusion, that we're all subject to forces beyond our control. And that's what scared you."

Slowly, he nodded. "You're incredibly perceptive, Tim. You should consider becoming a scholar. You have the mind for it."

"Now you sound just like Mother," she said with a smile. "Can I ask you something now, Gil?" she said. "What really happened to your friend?"

"I told you," he said. "He's gone."

"Muu killed him?"

Gil swallowed. "Is it really death if we aren't ever alive to begin with?" he said, then immediately hated himself for saying it.

She winced. "You really believe that?"

Gil felt his throat closing. "Goodbye, Tim," he said, turning away. "Have a safe trip."

She reached down to pick up her satchel. "Well, goodbye, Gil," she said. "Take care, will you?"

Then she was gone, and nothing remained of her but a faint hint of her sweat in the air and the few stale bread crumbs she had left on the sill.

He didn't know how long he had been staring out the window when a spark rose in the south and leaped into the swiftly darkening sky. The thunder from its engines rolled across the city like the grumbling of a beast. Then the ship was gone, leaving behind only stars.

The quiet was stifling, oppressive. No new pupils were arriving tonight.

He opened the small chest and pulled out the jisthmus bundle. He unrolled it, and its pungent reek assaulted his nose. He closed his eyes, trying to remember what it was like to be a photon—Demi's photon—the one that had struck his eye and skipped across the universe. He tried to remember what it was like plunging deep into Demi's palm, the warm hand that had once softly grasped his own in this very room, in this very spot. In those moments there was only love and nothing else, and all of Gil's longing had finally ceased. He had found in Demi everything he had ever needed.

He grabbed the ball of jisthmus herb with his bare hands, and his fingers began to tingle as the potent oils seeped into his skin. He broke off a bit of the herb and shoved it into his mouth, chewed as best he could, then used a flask of water to wash it down. Then he did this again, and again, until there was nothing left of the bundle but a dark stain where the jisthmus had been.

He had never taken such a large dose. Never dreamed of it. It was thousands, maybe millions of times the typical amount. Already, the walls shimmered, slowly dissolving into waves of energy in an infinite sea.

He lay back on his mat and stared up at the ceiling, where the little cracks above him were already expanding into trillions of pocket universes. Then he reached out his hand toward the mat beside him, like he did on so many warm nights lying beside Demi, and patiently waited for the universe to reach back.

Eleanor Arnason published her first short story in 1973. Since then she has published five novels, three short story collections, two (or maybe three) chapbooks, some poetry, and a bunch of uncollected short fiction. Her novel *A Woman of the Iron People* won the James Tiptree Jr. and the Mythopoeic Society Awards; her novel *Ring of Swords* won a Minnesota Book Award; and her short story "Dapple" won the Spectrum Award. "Tunnels" is one of a series of stories about the interstellar location scout Lydia Duluth. One of the stories, "Tomb of the Fathers," has been published as a stand-alone by Aqueduct Press. She hopes to assemble a collection of the rest of the stories this year and find a publisher.

TUNNELS

Eleanor Arnason

Lydia Duluth arrived at Innovation City, planning to stay a few days at most. At heart she was a rube, an old word that survived on her home planet, though in few other places. Its original meaning was "an awkward, unsophisticated person, a rustic." When it was invented, in the distant past of Earth, it had been pejorative.

On her home world, it still meant a rural person, but the connotation was positive. This was hardly surprising. Her world had been settled by back-to-nature conservatives fleeing the nightmare urbanity of Old Earth. To them, "unsophisticated" meant honest, and "rustic" meant solid. To their descendants, "you rube" was a term of affection, and "she's a real rube!" was praise. After all Lydia's travels, she still felt uneasy in big cities, and Innovation City was as big as human cities got: a seething metropolis of more than a million people that occupied a series of islands off the planet's one continent.

She took a hydrofoil from the spaceport, which was on the mainland, and a pedicab to her hotel. The cab was a partly organic robot. An odd experience, to ride in something that pedaled itself while playing a Bach fugue. To Lydia the thing was excessive. But excess was the nature of cities.

She reached the hotel, climbed out, and paid. The cab thanked her with a sonorous run of descending notes, then pedaled off. She went in to the hotel desk. Thank the Buddha, the desk clerk was human: a two-meter tall man with bright green skin and silver eyes. As far as she could tell, he was naked. She wasn't going to climb over the desk to make certain.

She had a reservation made by her employer, the famous holoplay production company Stellar Harvest. The clerk raised a silver-wire eyebrow when he saw that, but—thank the Buddha again!—didn't ask any questions about the company's many famous actors. One of these was visiting Innovation City at the moment: Ramona Patel, making her debut as a director with a romantic comedy about Krishna disporting himself among the waitresses in a soy milk bar. The comedy was supposed to be sophisticated and urbane, which explained the location and the transformation of milkmaids into waitresses. It wasn't Lydia's kind of drama. The locations she found for the company were used as the exotic backgrounds for action tales.

The clerk input her data, then gave directions to her room. She rode an elevator up the outside of the hotel. The planet's primary was rising, and the eastern sky was a lovely pale pink. Everywhere she looked, tall towers rose. Skyways outlined by electric lights hung between the towers, looking like so many diamond necklaces. As much as she mistrusted cities, she had to admire the view. This was civilization as humans rarely experienced it anymore!

It is impressive, said the AI embedded in her brain. *Though not equal to the cities our long-lost makers built. You humans rely on biochemistry too much.*

Her room faced west and had a spectacular view of the strait that lay between the city and the mainland. Lydia set down the one bag she carried and used the bathroom. Coming out, she noticed a pot of coffee steaming in the kitchen alcove. She poured herself a cup and walked to the window. The sun was fully up now. Close to the city's shore, the water was dimmed by the long shadows of skyscrapers. Farther out it was bright blue-green, flecked with whitecaps that appeared and disappeared in a slow, relaxing rhythm. Could anything equal water as a source of relaxation?

Not for humans. I suspect you are remembering your original ocean home.

This didn't seem likely to her. It had been a long time since fish crawled out of the ocean and turned into tetrapods.

The planet's one continent was a dark line at the horizon. Although almost empty of humans, it was the reason for the city.

The native life used silicon as well as carbon, as did organisms on other planets: grass on Earth, for example. But the interpenetration of carbon and silicon was far more intimate here, going down to the molecular level, so the life had both strong (carbon) and weak (silicon) chemical bonds, making it flexible, breakable, friable, and as solid as cement. Lydia had not done well in organic chemistry, and she did not understand the details. But she did understand two facts. No amount of gene mod would enable humans to live on the life here; eating it was like eating sand, and ordinary carbon-based organisms—the kinds that lived on most human planets—could survive here, but they didn't thrive and spread. You could plant a test plot and be sure it would not take over the local ecology, and there was no chance that the local organisms would contaminate your test plot. A few might creep in, but they did not interact with organisms being tested. If you planted the test plots far enough apart, there would be no risk of them contaminating one another.

The colony was a research station for BioInovation, the interstellar bio-technology company. First, BioIn had studied the odd local life forms. Then it made the planet its center for gene mod testing.

She'd found out some of this on her way to the planet, which had been named Grit by its first settlers. It was a silly name, but the interstellar rules for naming meant the planet was stuck with it, though BioIn had been able to change Grit City to Innovation City in honor of itself. The rest of her data came from infotainment ads in the Grit spaceport. BioIn had packed the port with holos showing its history, accomplishments, and plans for the future.

Good ads, taken all in all. She had especially enjoyed the ones that explained BioIn's plans for the native life. Using carbon-silicon gene mod, a new technology, the company's scientists had already created novelties such as glass bonsai trees. Their goal was to create building materials with genetic programming. Given the right conditions, these would grow into buildings.

There were carbon-based organisms that did this already; the best known were the *Tree House* (TM) brand of prefab housing. But genetically pro-grammed concrete was new.

This was all interesting. But Lydia planned to get off the planet as soon as she delivered her expense report to the Stellar Harvest production accountants. BioIn made her uneasy. She had encountered the corporation on another planet while doing a job for the colleagues of her AI. Was that the right term? Since they were artificial, they couldn't be called a species. Co-workers? Fellow machines? In any case, they built and maintained the stargates that made interstellar travel possible. They had discovered the planet—named Checkerboard—and built a gate next to it, then leased the planet to BioIn. The terms were the usual ones: if intelligent life was found, the lease was void.

There was intelligent life, a very strange kind that interested BioIn. The corporation hid the fact. When the AIs realized something was going on, they asked Lydia to investigate. Why not? She had been between jobs for Stellar Harvest at the time, and the AIs had helped her in the past.

The investigation did not turn out well for BioIn. It lost control of Checkerboard and gained a lot of lawsuits.

Lydia had worked under an alias provided by the AIs, but what if BioIn found out she was the person who had caused them so much trouble? *Hardly likely,* her AI said. *The ID we gave you was convincing.*

Lydia felt a little dubious. But she needed to turn in her expenses, and the nearest S.H. accounting team was here.

She finished the cup of coffee. A small cart arrived with her baggage, which it unloaded with multi-jointed arms. No tip was required, but she said, "Thank you." Politeness was always a good idea, even when dealing with machinery.

The cart said, "Here at the BioInovation Ritz, it is our pleasure to serve."

It rolled away. She unpacked. An easy task. She always traveled light. Once everything was put away, she poured another cup of coffee. She felt tired, which was usual after FTL, and slightly under the weather. Maybe a cold was coming on. Some people got a cold every time they traveled to a new human world. She was hardier than that, but every now and then she encountered a viral strain that had her number.

Well, she thought, she could rest tonight, crawl into bed with a cold tab and a mystery. Tomorrow she would find the Stellar Harvest location crew, turn in her expense report, get paid, and be on her way.

She took a shower and the tab and went to bed, a mystery—the latest Agatha Lima—in her hand. She got as far as turning it on, then fell asleep.

She slept through to the local morning: more than fifteen local hours. Not unusual for her after an FTL journey, and she definitely did have some kind of viral infection. Her head felt stuffed and her eyes scratchy. She took another shower, which helped with the congestion and was a sensual delight. Her last stop had been a planet with water rationing.

The room's com was blinking. It must have rung while she was in the shower. She turned it on. The message was from Wazati Casoon, an old friend. He was with the location crew, watching out for the interests of his brother, the increasingly famous holo actor Wazati Tloo. This was not an easy task. The message said. "Ramona has insisted that Tloo be dyed blue.

Krishna is always blue, she says. Tloo wants to keep his natural color, which is—as you know—a glorious shade of gold. If Ramona wants a blue actor, she ought to hire a blue actor, he has told me. I have pointed out that Stellar Harvest does not have a naturally blue actor who's a good box office draw. Their problem, Tloo says. I have also tried to explain the importance of this role to his career. This is his chance to move away from action roles, to expand his range and the price he can command. He refuses to understand. Meet me for tea this afternoon, and I will complain to you."

She called him back and agreed on a meeting place, then went out to see the city, starting at street level. This was one story above ground—and sea—level. Traffic was a combination of pedestrians, skaters, and pedicabs. The cab sound systems were good. She heard their music only briefly, as they whizzed past: mostly organ music, an occasional calliope. Aside from those brief bursts, she heard human voices and the wind. The world had no birds.

Glass enclosed bridges crossed the channels between the city's many islands. She stopped on each of these. There *was* something about water, even when hemmed and shadowed by tall buildings. The planet's primary was overhead. The channels shone blue-green. Barges moved slowly through them, looking oddly incomplete without birds or bird analogs wheeling and crying behind them.

She had been on worlds like this before, where most of the life was in the ocean, but her home planet did have animals like birds, and—at some level—she still expected to find them. The Grit mainland had invertebrates, some of them good sized. Aside from these, the only air-breathing animals had come with humanity and lived here in the city. Cockroaches were inevitable. Every human planet had them. There were rats and mice, descended from escaped lab animals. No dogs or cats. BioIn had refused to allow them.

Some people trapped rats and mice and kept them as pets. She'd read that on her journey to Grit.

She had lunch at a sidewalk restaurant. A light meal. She was feeling increasingly congested and hazy. Nonetheless, she continued her exploration of the city. Her mood remained oddly reflective. She thought about the people who trapped rats for pets and about cities and civilization.

At last it was teatime, and she was at the Old English Tea Room. The walls were paneled with dark wood and had aquaria inset. These contained examples of the local flora and fauna: colorless fish, armored with glass, and thin, spiny pseudo-corals, which shone orange in the bright tank lights.

Cas sat at a back table: a tall, slim male with dull gold skin. The crest atop his head was down at present and looked like slicked-back, shoulder length, brown hair. On his home planet he would have worn a robe. Here he had on a silver jumpsuit, its fabric as fluid and shiny as mercury. Data glasses with glowing frames perched on his wide, flat nose.

"Dear Lydia!" He rose and embraced her. His body aroma was peppery, not quite strong enough to make her sneeze. "I've missed you! How have you been? What planets have you scouted? How is your sex life? You *do* have one?"

"That's for me to know." She did not ask about his sex life. She suspected that he had one of some kind, but the topic was forbidden. His species fixed most of their men, keeping only a few for breeding. The intact males—his brother Tloo was one—were physically splendid and hard to deal with, due to far too many hormones. Cas, the rational twin, was a eunuch. While no Golden would be the slightest bit embarrassed by discussing the sex life of a breeding male, the lives of their eunuchs were private.

"Surely you will tell me about the planets?" he asked.

Lydia laughed. "Maybe."

They settled at the table. Cas took off his glasses and rubbed his nose. "They are supposed to conform exactly, but they never do."

"Too few Golden in space," she said. "That's a human design."

"You tell me what I know, and I am edified. Tea? A shot of brandy? Small sandwiches with peculiar toppings?"

She laughed again. "Do you ever change?"

"At the moment, I am aging rapidly. I love my brother, though he is dumb as a brick and stubborn as a *witl*. But he is not making my life easy, and Ramona Patel is a monster."

She couldn't argue with the last. Ramona was notorious for her bad temper and indifference to the needs of other sentient beings. But she was a fine actress and a first-rate businesswoman, and—Buddha!—could she sing and dance!

A waitron rolled up. Lydia ordered tea, lemon, honey, brandy, and assorted sandwiches.

"I was jesting about the brandy," Cas put in. "Are you planning to tear one up?"

"Tie one on or tear up the district," Lydia said. "I have a cold."

"Aha. An excuse. I will join you. My excuse is Tloo and Ramona. As bad as a virus, both or either."

The food came: small sandwiches with peculiar toppings, as Cas had said. Lydia drank her tea with brandy, honey, and lemon. Where did the honey come from? she wondered. Did Grit have bees? She waved the waitron over. "Can you answer questions about this planet?"

"I am a full-service Milton (TM) model waiting machine, programmed to provide idle chatter and useful information. What do you want to know?"

She asked about the bees.

"They exist on this planet. BioInnovation imported them to pollinate test plots. They can't live off the local plants, and stay close to the plot where their hive has been set. There is almost no danger of unplanned pollination."

"Thank you," Lydia said. The waitron rolled off. It had sounded almost intelligent to her.

Not really, said her AI. *I doubt it could pass a Turing test, let alone the far more sophisticated tests that we have devised. Humanity has never managed to produce artificial intelligence.*

"Doubtless the information about bees is interesting," Cas said. "But I came here to complain."

She leaned back in her chair and listened to his problems, getting pleasantly buzzed on the brandy. Cas was far more romantic than his gorgeous actor brother. He thrived on drama and intrigue. He had both at the moment, as he tried to keep Tloo and Ramona in line and aimed toward the same end: a finished holoplay.

"Like herding rats," he said finally. "I should be the director or possibly a producer. This is far more work than an agent should have to do."

Lydia nodded agreement. It might be a good idea for Cas to move on, but who would manage Tloo then?

They talked about friends in common: Cy Melbourne, who was reaching the end of his career as an action star and wise enough to know it; the squid-like alien K'r'x, who was a rising character actor.

"It's amazing how well he can express emotions, without having a face," Cas told her. "It's all in the motion of the tentacles and delicate changes in color."

Could K'r'x turn blue? Lydia wondered. If so, he could play Krishna. Of course they'd have to move the story out of the milk bar and into an ocean.

Something, the cold or the brandy, is having an adverse effect on your think-ing. That is a silly idea.

The data glasses, still resting on the table, began to flash. Cas put them on and stared at nothing she could see. At length he sighed. "More trouble on the set. It's been wonderful whining to you, Lydia. I have to go."

Maybe the brandy had been a poor idea, she thought as she left the tea-room. She was feeling very fuzzy. Time for a nap. She considered hailing a cab, then decided to take a train. Few human cities were big enough for sub-ways. Innovation City was famous for its system, which ran through tunnels in—or was it on?—the ocean floor, linking the most distant island-neigh-borhoods. Some of the stations had portholes, looking into the ocean. One could stand on the platform and watch glass fish glide over silicon reefs.

She couldn't miss an experience like that. She took an escalator down.

The next floor was devoted to trains. Glowing signs hung overhead. Glowing paths led to the red, green, yellow, and blue lines. She picked red. It was a color she'd always liked. The red path led to a turnstile, which accepted her credit card. She waited on an empty platform.

You don't know this rail system. You aren't used to big cities. You could get lost. Have you looked at a map?

Ridiculous question! Of course she hadn't, as the AI knew.

The train came. She climbed into a car with half a dozen dozing workers wearing safety boots. Genuine proletarians. Her head felt as if it contained a drum rather than an AI. The train glided into a tunnel, moving so smoothly that she felt no motion. The other passengers kept sleeping. The train, evidently an express, sped through several stations where one or two or three people waited on platforms. She got out and found a sign leading to the Innovation deep line. She took an escalator down.

Lydia, said her AI in a firm tone. *This is not a normal cold. You are very sick. Call for help at once.*

She stopped in front of an emergency phone, but couldn't remember how to use it. There was another escalator going down. She took it. It was necessary—absolutely necessary—that she go as deep as she could.

Another platform, empty except for a trio of street performers, all human and almost naked. Their skins were pastel colored. They juggled balls, using all parts of their bodies, including their bare feet.

Another train. She settled in a car. The street performers joined her, sitting opposite. Their eyes had red pupils.

Her own eyes refused to stay open. As she closed them, letters appeared in front of her lids. GOTCHA, they said in glowing capitals.

Buddha in the western paradise, Lydia thought. The AI was right. This wasn't an ordinary cold. It was influenza, and it had been hacked.

This was the last clear thought she had for a long time.

Lydia woke. For a while she lay still, staring at a perfect, pitch-black darkness. The air had a dank, closed-in odor. She was on something that felt like concrete: cool, slightly damp, and mostly smooth, but with a touch of grittiness. She had her clothes on, which was a very good sign. Her body ached, but it didn't feel as if she'd been assaulted, except by the damn gene hacker.

She sat up finally and felt the floor around her. Her very expensive, state-of-the-art hologrammic recorder was gone. "Damn," she said out loud and checked her pockets. So were all her cards and her combination chronometer-phone-flashlight- and-personal-care-kit. She could have used it right now.

Robbed, she thought. Her head throbbed, and she was willing to bet money—not that she had any—that she had a fever as well as stuffed sinuses. Except for the sinuses, her head felt empty.

AI? she asked.

There was no answer.

She felt the outside of her head, suddenly afraid the AI had been stolen. A crazy idea! Removal would have killed both of them. In any case, her skull was intact.

AI? she asked again.

Again, there was no answer.

She'd left the train with the street performers. She was pretty sure she could remember that. They'd visited taverns; and she'd bought drinks. She'd bought other things as well. She had a dim memory of a store full of glittery jewelry and the pale green performer dancing, holding a gold and jade necklace. The jade had been a perfect match for the performer's skin.

Where was she, anyway?

She climbed to her feet, swayed, reached out, and touched a wall. Like the floor, it felt cool and slightly rough. She waited till her dizziness passed, then moved along the wall, keeping one hand on it. It didn't end, though it seemed to be curving. Could she be sure of that? Not in pitch darkness with influenza.

Lydia stopped finally and put her back against the wall, resting. Then she walked forward carefully, sliding her feet along the floor. After twenty steps, she encountered another wall. She felt along it. Like the first wall, it didn't end and seemed to be curving toward the left.

She sat down and thought. She was in a long, narrow space. A tunnel? Not a train tunnel. It was not wide enough, and she had felt no rail. A pedestrian tunnel, then. But there were no people around. Did she know that for certain? She listened, then called, "Hello?"

No answer.

"Hello?"

Nothing.

What else did she know? Her flu had definitely been hacked. No natural virus would tell its victim, "GOTCHA." The work was sophisticated. It wasn't easy to create a disease that affected volition. She was pretty sure her desire to go down, away from people, came from the flu. So the hacker was probably not a kid with his first biochemistry kit. She'd never heard of these symptoms, which suggested the flu was local and new. Widespread strains of influenza made the information nets. For example, the tap-dancing flu that swept Earth a decade ago. That had been a gene hacker with a strong sense of humor, though it hadn't seemed so funny when some of the older and frailer victims tap-danced to death.

Most human colonies had better public health than Earth and were able to stop hacked infections quickly, though they kept appearing. Boys will be boys and so would many girls. It was another reason to avoid cities. Gene hackers were uncommon on the thinly settled planets. It was easy to track them down, and they were not treated gently.

Her mouth felt dry as a desert. For the first time in years, she was utterly alone.

Hello, she said to the AI. Anyone there? Are you okay? Help?

It did not reply.

Scary, Lydia thought. She rubbed her face, then pushed herself upright. She couldn't stay here in the dark. So. Go left or go right? She picked left and began walking, one hand on the wall.

Without her chronometer, she had no idea how much time passed. She stopped a couple of times to rest. If something didn't happen, she was going to die of thirst. How long could this tunnel be? She had a dim memory of a news bite about tunnels on Grit. They covered the ocean bed around Innovation City. Was that possible?

Finally, she saw a light. As she suspected, she was in a tunnel. The light hung from the ceiling at the end of a concrete stalk, which ended in a flower-shaped glass shade. The bulb inside was dim and yellow. Below the light was a drinking fountain. It flowed out of the floor as if it had grown or been extruded. The top was a shallow basin where water bubbled merrily.

Lydia drank. Buddha, that felt good! She drank again, until she was no longer thirsty. Then she lifted her head and looked round. In both directions the tunnel vanished into darkness. Maybe she'd stay here for a while. She searched her pockets for food and found nothing, not even lint.

She sat down. The hotel would contact Stellar Harvest when she didn't arrive, and S.H. would contact the local cops. It was usually easy to find people on thinly settled worlds, unless they got themselves lost in wilderness. This was another case entirely. A million people jammed together! How did they manage to keep track of one another?

The cops could follow the trail of her purchases until it ended. She remembered a final vending machine—a bright-blue, street corner cylinder with "Darqueria" flashing on top—refusing her card. She had run out of credit.

What had happened then? Had the street performers still been with her? Or had they danced and juggled away? Who had emptied her pockets? And how far had she wandered from the Darqueria?

She got up to drink more water, then walked down the tunnel to urinate in decent darkness. Heading back, she saw something by the drinking fountain, her size, but lower to the floor. The way it moved was distinctive. She came closer. The creature had an oval body that rested on four legs, and four arms, two on each side of the oval body. One arm in each pair ended in a formidable-looking pincher. The other ended in a cluster of tentacles. The creature was holding a cup in one of its tentacle-hands and dipping it into the fountain. There was no head. Instead, its brain was housed in a bulge atop its body. There ought to be four eyes in the bulge, though Lydia couldn't see them. The Goxhat was facing away from her.

"Hello," she said in humanish.

The alien spun. The four blue eyes glared. "Dangerous!" it cried in humanish. "Beware!" It waved the cup, spilling water. "Fierce! Fierce!"

"I'm not a threat," Lydia said, trying to sound reasonable and unafraid. As far as she knew, the Goxhat were never dangerous to members of other species, but this one looked agitated and poorly groomed. The black hair that covered its body was spiky in some places and matted in others. What the heck was this guy doing here in this condition, and where was the rest of it?

"Where are your other bodies?" Lydia asked.

The Goxhat screamed and ran into the darkness.

Well, that had certainly been the wrong question to ask.

The alien had left its cup on the floor. She picked it up: badly chipped, blue-speckle enamelware. A human product. Hardly surprising, since this was a human planet.

So, she thought. She was in a concrete tunnel somewhere on Grit, her AI silent and no company except an agitated Goxhat. The problem of water was solved, but she still needed food and a way out.

Hello? she said to her AI. Are you there?

Still no answer.

She could go on. She even had a cup to carry water. But she was tired and afraid of the dark. She lay down by the fountain and went to sleep.

A touch woke her. She started up. The Goxhat leaped back, its cup in one hand. "Fierce," it cried, brandishing the cup.

"I won't hurt you," Lydia said.

"Many bodies! All around in the shadows!" the Goxhat cried. "Will come out and defend!"

"Do you know how to get out of here?" Lydia asked. "Up to the city?"

She'd spent time with another Goxhat. Although the aliens did not have faces, they did have expressions. This one looked baffled.

"Do you know the way to other people?" she asked. "Humans? Goxhat?"

"No Goxhat! Alone! Alone!" The Goxhat had to be using a translation implant. Its real voice was not even audible to humans. In spite of this, she could hear anguish.

"Humans, then," she said gently. "Do you know the way to other humans?"

The Goxhat's four feet danced back and forth. Its pinchers opened and closed in an agitated fashion. Finally it spoke, "Know humans."

"Can you lead me to them?"

More jittering and snapping. "Yes," the Goxhat said at last. "Keep cup. Must keep cup."

She looked at the alien, then at the drinking fountain. The Goxhat's mouth was on its underside. If it didn't have the cup, it would have to climb onto the fountain and squat over the bubbler.

"I don't want the cup," Lydia said.

"Good." The Goxhat filled the cup and held it to its hidden mouth. She heard noisy lapping. The alien filled the cup two more times and emptied it, then said, "Will show humans."

She followed it into darkness. It quickly outdistanced her, its bare, nailed feet scrambling over the concrete. But soon it returned, calling, "Come."

"I can't see," she answered.

"Nothing here. Only floor and walls and rats."

"Rats?"

"Big ones," said the Goxhat. "Not dangerous. Tasty."

"Oh."

They kept on, the Goxhat running ahead, and then back. Lydia followed, guided by scrabbling feet and the alien voice calling, "Come!"

Finally, there was another light, this one blue and flashing. When they got close, she saw the tunnel was obstructed by something that came out of a side wall. A news kiosk. It was sideways, its pointed top almost touching the opposite wall. The light she'd seen as they approached was flashing on the peak. There was space above and below the kiosk. The Goxhat scuttled under. Lydia followed, dropping to her hands and knees. On the far side, she rose and took a close look. There were news screens, but all were dark, as were the buttons under the screens. No headlines. No images. No way to order news.

"Why is this sideways?" she asked.

"Grew that way," said the Goxhat.

Okay, she thought. Her AI added no comment. Lydia felt a pang of loss.

"Come!" the Goxhat cried.

They continued through the tunnel till a third light appeared ahead of them, this one yellow and steady. It shone from one side of the tunnel, out of an intersecting tunnel or possibly a doorway. She could see the Goxhat now, a low shape against the light. It scuttled forward until it stood directly in the light, jittering and waving its cup.

"Visitor!" it cried.

Lydia reached the light, which came through an open door. Beyond was a room. An electric lantern sat on the floor, illuminating concrete walls with pipes running along them. More pipes ran across the ceiling. As far as she could tell, all were concrete. One was dripping liquid into a large metal barrel.

Three people sat around the lantern, all of them human. One—a male— stood up. He was short and dark with a beard that Karl Marx would have envied. "What do we have here?" he asked, his voice deep with an educated accent.

"My name's Lydia Duluth," she answered. "And I need to get back to the city."

"Can't be done," the man said in a friendly tone.

"What does that mean?" Lydia asked.

"Please come in." He gestured.

Lydia hesitated. Her headache was bad, the AI was missing, and the three humans were ragged and dirty.

"We aren't dangerous," the short human said.

She would have felt better with the AI or without the headache, but she decided to enter. As she did so, the man on the floor growled, a bestial sound.

"Ignore that," the short man said. "He's having a bad day."

"A bad year," said the woman on the floor. "A bad rest of his life."

Lydia looked at the two of them. The man had long, tangled blond hair. His black face was hairless, except for a pair of elegantly curved blond eyebrows. Gene mod, thought Lydia. No one had eyebrows so perfect. The woman was equally dark, with a halo of bushy hair and a round, pretty face. Her eyes were large and heavy-lidded with yellow irises that entirely filled her eyes. The pupils were vertical slits. Cat eyes. As lovely as the man's blond eyebrows.

Hobos, Lydia thought. Every human city of any size had homeless folk. It was an inevitable result of the freedom for which humanity was famous.

"How did you get here?" the short man asked.

Standing close to the door, ready to whirl and run, Lydia told her story: the attack of influenza and the journey down into the depths of Innovation City, the street performers and waking in a tunnel.

"Interesting," the short man said. "It sounds like the virus that brought us here, though that hit four years ago, more or less. It isn't easy to keep track of time down here. We assumed the virus had been eliminated and the people responsible caught and put away or revised. No one has come down in recent years because of a virus. Everyone we've met has had stories of bad luck rather than infection."

"There were others with the bug," the woman said. "But they came down when we did. Some of them died. The rest kept going deeper into the tunnels."

"And you're still here?" Lydia asked, horrified.

"We can't go back on our own," the short man said. "The virus has enduring effects. We can stay on this level or go farther down, but we can't go up. Never up. We decided to stay here, rather than to keep descending." He smiled, showing teeth that needed cleaning

Four years without dental care, thought Lydia. Even when she lived in the hills of her home planet, a member of a revolutionary army on the run from the government, she'd had access to care from a revolutionary dental hygienist.

"You introduced yourself. Let me introduce us. I am Genghis Santa Fe, formerly an adjunct professor of philosophy at Innovation University. Seated on the floor you will see Affirmation Loo, who used to be a hedge fund manager. You can tell he is—or was—a businessman by his first name and by his lack of facial hair. I, alas, kept my face unmodified, since philosophers are expected to be hairy. Now I have to hack at my beard with a knife. The lovely lady is Topaz Mumbai, formerly a mid-range call girl."

"Concubine," the woman said in a firm, melodious voice. "And I was better than mid-range."

"As you say," Genghis replied courteously.

"Call me Tope," the woman said to Lydia. "He's Aff, and Genghis is Genghis."

Lydia nodded. "I'm happy to meet you. If you can't go up, can you show me the way up? I'll send people down after you. I'm surprised no one has looked for you before this."

"They may have," Genghis said. "Or may not have. I have no family on this planet. If I had been tenure track, my colleagues would have reported me missing, but adjunct faculty comes and goes. Affirmation is suspicious of his partner, who may have decided to keep quiet when he vanished and keep the fund's management money for herself."

"People in my line of work avoid the police," Tope added.

She wasn't sure she believed any of this. People don't simply vanish in a modern society. But she felt too ill to think about it, and the AI was giving her no input.

"Have you eaten?" asked Genghis.

Lydia shook her head and realized that shaking was not a good idea.

"Goxhat!" the bearded man yelled.

"Fierce! Fierce!" cried a voice in the darkness.

"Bring in the cup, or there will be no soup."

There were skittering sounds in the dark. Lydia turned and saw the Goxhat sidle in sideways, then twist and stare with four wary, blue eyes.

"The cup," said Genghis Santa Fe and held out a hand.

"Fierce!"

"Hand it over."

The Goxhat held it out with obvious reluctance. Genghis took it and dipped it into the barrel. "Here you are."

Lydia looked in. The cup was full of a dark, thick-looking liquid. "What is it?"

"Soil soup." Genghis pointed at the dripping pipe. "The pipes and tunnel walls are prone to small leaks, due to the nature of silicon. You do know that life on this planet is a complex combination of carbon and silicon?"

"Yes."

"Silicon chemical bonds are weaker than those of carbon and break comparatively easily. As a result, most of the life here reproduces by breaking, and is prone to leaks. But it's also self-healing, due to its carbon bonds. The leaks don't get large enough to be dangerous, unless an organism has been badly damaged or is ready to die. Then it will shatter like glass or crumble into sand.

"But I'm getting off-topic. Don't worry about the tunnels breaking. They are still young and healthy, and their leaks heal quickly. We have to use a power drill to keep this pipe open."

Lydia knew most of this, though she was happy to hear that the tunnels were not likely to crumble in the near future. Right now, what interested her was the dark liquid in the cup.

"What is soil soup?" she asked.

"Refuse from the city."

"Shit?" asked Lydia.

"No. The recycling system has separate tracks for different kinds of waste. They are all pureed and filtered. Toxins are removed and what remains is sterilized, then piped to the mainland, where it is added to the soil in experimental plots. But excrement is always kept separate from compost. This is compost."

Tea leaves and coffee grounds, egg shells, the exoskeletons of edible bugs and wilted greens. The smell was earthy, not bad, but not the smell of food. She wasn't hungry. "No, thanks," Lydia said.

Genghis held the cup toward the Goxhat, who grabbed it and pushed it underneath its hairy body. She heard slurping.

"Can you show me the way up?" Lydia asked.

"We know a stair. We can't climb it, but you might be able to. I don't know if your virus is identical to ours."

"Thanks," said Lydia. "I'll send people after you."

"That would be good," Genghis said. "Though it may too late for Affirmation. He hasn't spoken for a long time now."

The man with blond eyebrows growled again.

"Can we go now?" Lydia asked.

Genghis bent and picked up the lantern. "The others will have to come. We have only the one lantern."

Lydia nodded. The short man led her out of the room. The others—the woman, the growling man, and the Goxhat—followed.

If anything, it was more depressing to walk through the tunnels with light. The walls were gray, rough-looking, and often stained. The leaks, Lydia thought. Disturbing to be inside something that was continuously breaking and mending.

"Why were the tunnels built?" she asked.

"They were an experiment," Genghis replied. "I told you the life here is based on carbon and silicon."

"Everyone knows that," Lydia answered.

"Well, then do you know that BioIn has been trying to engineer it?"

"To create buildings that build themselves. Yes."

"Exactly," the short man said. "The idea was to create a submarine tunnel that ran from the city to the mainland. They planned to run pipes through, carrying the city's waste to the experimental plots. That part mostly worked. There were going to be trains, so BioIn's employees could commute to work, as well as all the things people might need on a train platform: the platform itself, fountains, bathrooms, shops selling snacks and souvenirs.

"The original tunnel was designed to take minerals from the ocean and sand from the ocean bottom and use these to build itself, which it did. But it didn't stop, and it didn't simply go from the city to the mainland. Apparently, something went wrong with the shut-off gene.

"The tunnel kept building in all directions. You might say that it metas-tasized. Or, to use another metaphor, it became the Sorcerer's Tunnel." Genghis looked at her sideways. His face—lit from below by the lantern he carried—looked grotesque, full of shadows.

"What sorcerer?" Lydia asked.

The short man sighed, then said, "BioIn got what it wanted, pipes to the mainland. It didn't know how to stop the tunnel, so it let it continue to grow. So far there have not been any problems, though some of the pipes are releas-ing sewage into the ocean. As far as anyone could tell, when I was in the city and talking to scientists at the university, the sewage was not interacting with the native ecology."

They kept going. A rat ran in front of them, going from one side tunnel to another. It was spotted black and white and really, really big.

"Something else that did not go as planned," Genghis said. "The lab rats were not supposed to get loose and infest the city. There are robot cats, since BioIn didn't want to bring real cats to the planet; and they are fairly good at the catching the rats, as is our friend the Goxhat. In case you are wondering, the rats live on garbage, which they find on the levels immediately above us, and cockroaches and mice."

"Where is the rest of the Goxhat?" Lydia asked. "Goxhat usually have half a dozen bodies or more."

"It won't say. As you may have figured out, it's insane, as is our friend Affirmation. Life down here is hard."

The tunnel they followed ended at a white, glossy spiral staircase. It looked ceramic. A light shone above it, warm yellow.

"There it is," said Genghis. "Follow it up. It will bring you to inhabited levels."

"Thanks," said Lydia. "I will get you help. I don't like to brag, but I work for Stellar Harvest, and they have connections."

"Stellar Harvest!" said Genghis. "I have been in love with Ramona Patel for years. What a beauty! What a dancer! What a voice! And what a warm heart she has in all her holos! Is she really like that?"

Stellar Harvest allowed no maligning of its stars. The fact that Ramona had the personality of a *rahm*, all fangs and claws, was company information, not to be shared.

"She's a remarkable woman," Lydia said. "I've never met anyone like her. I admire her deeply."

Which was true in a way. As a performer, Ramona was amazing; and of her kind, she was perfect.

Genghis sighed. "I'm so happy to hear that. Do you think—if you can rescue us—it might be possible to meet her?"

"Of course," said Lydia firmly. She'd find a way to pressure Ramona. Wazati Cas would help.

"Then, farewell," said Genghis. The others had come up next to him, Affirmation shambling with a vacant expression, Tope looking alert and almost elegant, in spite of her dirty clothes. Even the Goxhat was there, clutching its cup.

"Goodbye," said Lydia and turned toward the stair. Pain stabbed into her head. She took a step toward the white, coiling structure. The pain grew worse. Another step, and she was on her knees, holding her head and groaning. She forced herself upright and took another step. Then she passed out.

When she came to, she was lying on the tunnel floor. Genghis stood above her. "You have the same virus we do," he said. "Which is very interesting. We were sure it had been eradicated. We couldn't help you. You collapsed too close to the stair, which we cannot approach. But the Goxhat is not infected. It was able to pull you to safety."

Her headache felt like an ax buried deep in her brain. Lydia sat up and almost passed out again.

Genghis said, "A very sophisticated virus. No one who has been infected can get back up to the city and report to the police. I don't know why people with this kind of skill waste it on crime."

"Failure of imagination," Lydia said and staggered to her feet. In spite of her throbbing head, she had an idea. "Where did you get your lamp? Is there a dump on this level?"

If there was, there might be refuse workers or robots. Someone—something—she could talk to.

"Of course the city has recycling," Genghis said. "But not on this level." He hesitated, then said, "There are people who aren't infected. Tall Alys and her gang. They're homeless scavengers. Most of the time they stay on levels that are higher up, but they come down here sometimes, because they won't be bothered. We trade with them."

"What can you offer?" Lydia asked.

"Alys is in love with Tope, who offers sex. I offer stories and poems. You may not think these are valuable. But Alys and her comrades don't carry phones, for fear of being tracked; and this means they don't have access to the planetary net. My area of competence is aesthetic philosophy, and I have done my research. Believe me! I tell them the *Ramayana*, the *Odyssey*, the story of Monkey, the *Canterbury Tales*. I know Goxhat accounting chants in translation, and the poetry of the Embitti poet Morning Star, which is mostly about exile and loss. It goes down well.

"Affirmation used to offer investment tips, which were—of course—useless, since no one down here has money to invest. Now he offers nothing."

"Are they down here now?" Lydia asked.

"Alys and her gang? Not as far as we know. But we can look. They have a camp."

"You haven't asked them to take a message up to the city for you?"

"Yes, but Alys refuses. She doesn't want to lose Topaz. The others won't cross her. She is a formidable woman."

"That's angering," Lydia said.

"We are past anger," Genghis said.

"You are. I'm not," Tope said.

They rested for a while, then Lydia got up and went to the Goxhat, who always stayed a short distance from the rest of them. "Thank you," she said.

"Dangerous!" the Goxhat replied. "Fierce."

"My name is Lydia," she said. "Will you tell me your name?"

"Goxhat!" the Goxhat replied, then hooted three times.

Lydia imitated the sound. "Hoot! Hoot! Hoot!—Is that your name?"

The Goxhat was silent for a moment, then repeated the three hoots.

"There's no point in talking to the Goxhat. It's crazy," Tope said.

"Thank you," Lydia repeated. "Hoot! Hoot! Hoot!"

"Lydia," the Goxhat said.

Genghis led them on another journey through the tunnels. There were more grey concrete walls with more stains. Lydia touched one. The concrete felt wet. Farther on were patches of something spiky that glittered in the lantern light.

"A local organism," Genghis said. "It's using moisture and minerals from the concrete. I don't know how—or what—it metabolizes. It cannot photosynthesize here."

"Why would a planet develop a biology like this?" Lydia asked, wondering out loud.

"The grasses on Earth were—and are—hugely successful," Genghis said in reply. "And they use silicon to make themselves less edible. It works well, though not perfectly, since animals have evolved to eat them in spite of the grit they contain. And there are sponges on Earth that have skeletons made of glass. The glass carries light deep into the sponges, for the benefit of symbiotic organisms which photosynthesize."

"Thank you for this information," Lydia said. Genghis seemed unable to stop sharing. Well, he had been a professor, and he might be crazy now.

She couldn't measure time in the darkness. They kept going, past more glittering growths on the dull, gray walls. The air was damp and still and smelled of concrete and urine. More rats ran in front of them: some spotted, others white or dark. She didn't see any mice or roaches, for which she thanked the rats.

She did not like the place, which reminded her of other places she had been. Though then she'd had friends with her, as well as her AI. Please talk to me, she said to the AI. Tell me you are present.

Nothing.

A light shone in front of them, at the intersection of two tunnels. It was steady and yellow-white. Dark figures sat around it.

"They're here," Genghis said.

As they came closer, Lydia saw bedrolls and an electric stew pot. The figures sat around it. The air smelled of human food: meat, tomatoes, peppers, maybe potatoes or corn, the nourishment humans had brought from their home planet. In spite of her headache, Lydia felt suddenly hungry.

A figure rose and walked toward them. She was two meters tall, thin, and black-skinned with short, bright-blue hair.

"Alys," said Genghis. "The virus is back. We've found another victim."

The woman looked down at Lydia. Her eyes, as blue as her hair, demanded an explanation, so Lydia told her story.

"You really know Ramona Patel?" the woman asked.

"Yes."

"I think you're lying," Alys said. "But it doesn't matter. We all lie about something here. What matters is how we act now. Come over and share our dinner."

They settled around the stew pot, except for the Goxhat, who stayed in the shadows, jittering, obviously afraid to come closer. Alys introduced the others. They were all human: a young man named Trail, an old man named River, a woman named Yan, a man named Olatunde. Lit by the two electric lanterns, they looked worn and shabby and not perfectly clean.

Alys dished the stew into bowls, and Genghis took one bowl to the Goxhat, who remained in the shadows, making slurping noises.

It was a good stew, Lydia decided, though she would have liked more spices. A bottle was handed around. It contained a cheap form of alcohol, which hit hard, burning down her throat and giving her a warm glow in the belly. Not something she would have enjoyed usually. But not bad now.

When they were done eating, and a second bottle was opened, Lydia said, "I need a message taken up to the city."

"To Ramona Patel?" Alys asked.

"Yes, if that's where you want to take it."

Alys shook her head. "I told Genghis. We survive because no one notices us, and we're safe down here, because no one comes here. If you really know Ramona Patel and Wazati Tloo, then your story will end on the planetary net, and someone will decide to find out what else is in the tunnels and clean us out."

"I don't have to tell anyone what happened," Lydia said.

"The story will get out. A crime has been committed. Hacking common diseases is a big negative everywhere. The police are sure to get involved. They'll want to get the hackers, and they'll want to find out if there are any other victims of the virus down here."

"Are there?" Lydia asked.

"Victims? Not that we know. The ones who came down when these three did—" Alys waved at Genghis and the others. "Died or went deeper into the tunnels, to places where we don't go."

"As far as we can tell, the virus doesn't spread easily," Genghis said. "There weren't a lot of victims, even when it was most active. That's clever, in my opinion. An epidemic would have attracted notice. This way a few people vanish, but that happens in a big city. They might have fallen into the ocean. They might have gone to the mainland and had an accident in the wilderness. I'm sure there are other explanations."

"Plenty," said Alys. "All of us are here, and we used to be up there." She waved at the ceiling.

"The city is full of cracks," Yan said. "They heal, but then they break open again. People fall through."

Was this a metaphor for failings in the social safety net? Lydia wondered. Or was Yan talking about the concrete in the tunnels that fractured and then healed?

"Is there no way I can convince you to take a message?" Lydia asked.

Alys shook her head.

"Time to pay up," Olatunde said to Genghis. "Tell us a story, one about a trickster. I like trickster stories."

Genghis thought for a while, then told the story about how the god Thor lost his hammer and recovered it with the help of the trickster Loki. This involved Thor dressing like a woman. Genghis had to stop the story and explain that in ancient human cultures women did not dress like men, and men did not dress as women. It was a rule or taboo.

"That seems strange," said Yan.

"Ancient humans were strange," Genghis said. He went on to explain how funny it was to think of Thor—a big, burly guy with a bristling red beard and bloodshot eyes—dressed up as a young maiden going to her wedding.

"Why?" asked Olatunde.

"Why was it funny? Tradition," Genghis said and continued with the story.

Thor ate like a god, not a maiden. Entire roasted animals vanished under the wedding veil he wore. Finally, the bridegroom—who was a frost giant—said, "My bride has quite an appetite. I had not imagined any maiden stuffing down so much food."

Loki replied, "She has been so eager to marry you that she hasn't eaten for days. This is why she's so hungry."

The giant bought this explanation, which told Loki how bright he was.

Then the giant peeped under Thor's veil, thinking to get a glimpse of the lovely maid, and saw the god's bloodshot eyes glaring back at him. He jerked away, startled and afraid. "Why are the maiden's eyes so red and burning?" he asked, according to Genghis; and Loki replied, "She has been so eager to marry you that she has not slept for days, and that has caused her eyes to be red."

"These are not plausible answers," Alys said.

"Well, they worked," Genghis replied. "The giant believed Loki and had Thor's stolen hammer brought in to bless the wedding. As soon as Thor saw the hammer, he reached out and picked it up with a firm grasp, stood up and pushed back the wedding veil, so all the giants could see his blazing eyes and bristling red beard. The giants cried out in fear and scrambled to their feet. But it was too late. Thor used the hammer, which was magical, to kill them all."

"It sounds to me like he was overreacting," said River. "He could have just left once he had the hammer."

The young man Trail nodded. "You can't be killing people, even if they're giants. It's illegal."

"And wrong," added Yan.

Genghis frowned. "The giants represent the destructive forces of nature. It's Thor's job to establish order and make the world safe for humanity."

"You call that order?" asked River. "A bunch of dead people? That's like cops breaking up a camp and saying that makes everything tidy, because we've lost our home. Only worse, because the cops don't usually kill us."

"You asked for a trickster story," said Genghis, sounding grumpy. "I have told one. Trickster stories are often morally ambiguous."

"The big guy isn't a trickster," Olatunde said. "He's just someone using muscle to solve his problems. I've met guys like that. It's smart to keep away from them."

"I'm not responsible for the story," Genghis said. "It's part of human history and culture."

"I never learned it in school," River said. "And I was good at history, till I had my accident. I can still remember the history, even though my memory doesn't work as well as it used to. A lot of wars. A lot of big guys fighting."

"There you have it," Genghis said. "Think of this as a story about the war between chaos and order."

River looked doubtful. "I'd say it was a war about a limited resource, like energy on Earth in the old days. There was one hammer, and this guy Thor wanted it."

Genghis made a growling noise.

The conversation wandered on for a while longer, while the second bottle got passed around. In the end, people lay down and slept. Lydia had stopped drinking and remained awake.

The Goxhat came over and crouched beside her. "Want to go up?" it asked softly.

"Yes," she said.

"Go down first. Two levels below is tunnel to the mainland. I/we have been there. Nothing to eat. No Goxhat. Nothing for us/me."

"You haven't told them?" Lydia waved at the snoring bodies.

"Never asked my/our name," the Goxhat said. "Hoot. Hoot. Hoot," it called softly "I/we am/are me/us. I/we exist. Fierce."

"Can you show me the route to the mainland?" Lydia asked.

"Yes." The Goxhat folded its legs underneath it and slept, making a purring noise that was more pleasant than the human snores.

Lydia thought. If the AI had been talking to her, she would have asked it what to do. She could organize an expedition to the mainland. But she didn't trust the people here. Alys didn't want Lydia or the other victims of the virus to escape. She might try to stop them. As for Genghis and his companions—The former hedge fund manager was obviously crazy, and Genghis was odd. Tope seemed okay, but might not be. They seemed at home with their present situation, possibly due to the virus, though it hadn't affected Lydia that way. She wanted out.

Would she become reconciled to this life, if she stayed with them? She had no idea of the progress of the disease caused by the hacked virus. She ought to sneak away, while she still could.

The Goxhat was crazy. Still, she had never heard of a Goxhat harming any intelligent being. They rarely lied. How could they, since they did not have a sense of individuality? Lying to another Goxhat was lying to oneself. Possible, but not sane. They had not been around other intelligent species long enough to develop new habits, though they realized that humans—for example—were not Goxhat and behaved differently. In spite of this, they had not learned to tell deliberate untruths, except in fiction and poetry.

Of course, this Goxhat was crazy.

She decided to take the chance, reached down, and patted the Goxhat. Stiff hair prickled against her palm. The skin below was hot. The alien jerked awake. "What?"

"Let's go now," Lydia said softly. "Without waking the others."

Four blue eyes blinked up at her. Legs unfolded. The Goxhat rose. "This way," it whispered.

She picked up one of the lanterns, feeling guilty. Stealing a light from people who lived in darkness seemed utterly wrong. But Alys and her gang could get another one, and she could not bear to travel in darkness. She'd send help when she got to the mainland.

The Goxhat scuttled ahead of her. She narrowed the lantern's beam, so it was a lance of light, moving over the tunnel floor and walls. There was some dust. Motes danced in the air in front of her, shining in the beam.

After a while, they came to a red spiral stairway that led down. The Goxhat scrabbled along it, nails clicking on the metal treads. Lydia followed. There was no pain this time. The virus did not mind if she descended.

The stair spiraled past another level. Lydia's light bounced off a concrete floor and vanished into the dark mouth of a tunnel. Below her, the Goxhat's nails kept clicking downward. She followed.

The staircase ended two levels down. Lydia stepped off into yet another tunnel. This really did remind her of the space colony above the Atch home planet, though that been carved out of an iron asteroid and inhabited by more-or-less crazy Atch. She swung the light beam like a blade through the tunnel's darkness, lighting a pure white rat. The animal looked at her briefly, red eyes gleaming, then leaped away.

"They aren't intelligent, are they?" Lydia said to the Goxhat.

"Do not eat intelligent beings. Negotiate. Trade. Do not eat."

This was reassuring. The Atch in the asteroid had been a lot more interested in craziness than trade. Of course, they had no one to trade with, trapped like rats in their asteroid. Maybe that was what had driven them crazy.

The Goxhat scuttled into the tunnel. Once again, Lydia followed. Not having any kind of chronometer, she had no idea of how long they walked. But she got tired. She had to stop once to pee, and the Goxhat stopped once also. She did not know what it did in the darkness. But it came back to her looking relieved.

There were cross tunnels, which the Goxhat ignored, continuing straight ahead. Once their tunnel divided. The Goxhat stopped and considered, then made a choice.

"Are you sure?" Lydia asked.

"Will find out," the Goxhat replied.

That was not entirely reassuring. She really wanted her AI to chime in. But there was silence in her mind.

At last, the Goxhat said, "Rest."

They settled down on the concrete floor of the tunnel. Lydia took off her shoes and rubbed her feet, then sighed. She was thirsty and hungry. She hoped she had made the right decision, going with the Goxhat. Time would tell, and she had no way to measure time.

"Hoot. Hoot. Hoot," the Goxhat said

"Your name," said Lydia.

"Had eight bodies," the alien told her. "Good, strong bodies. Thirty-two legs. Thirty-two arms. Thirty-two blue eyes. That was me/us."

"Yes?" asked Lydia.

"Came to invest in BioIn. Flew to mainland to look at test plots. Industrial accident. Seven bodies died. This body fled."

"Why?" asked Lydia.

The blue eyes looked puzzled. "Forget. I/we found a tunnel. Ran in. Found the humans. Stayed. But remembered tunnel to the mainland. Afraid to go alone. Found you. Fierce!"

"I'm not fierce," Lydia said and thought she might have made a mistake. Did the Goxhat need a fierce ally? "I'm fierce enough," she added.

"Learned our/my name," the Goxhat said. "Saw me/us."

They slept and woke. The lantern still shone brightly. Lydia's mouth was dry.

"How much farther?" she asked.

"Soon," the Goxhat said.

She put on her shoes and went into the shadows to relieve herself. The Goxhat did something comparable. They rejoined at the lantern.

"Soon," the Goxhat repeated.

Lydia picked up the lantern and followed it.

Time passed. The tunnel began to slant up. She could feel this, a slight increase in effort as she walked. The incline grew steeper, which seemed encouraging. A fountain appeared in the middle of the tunnel, growing out of the floor at an angle. No light shone above it, and it was dry.

She was really thirsty, and her head had begun to ache.

"Don't remember this," the Goxhat said.

"Do you think we made a wrong turn?" Lydia asked.

"Will find out," the Goxhat replied.

A short time later, the tunnel slanted down. Ahead of them, the lantern beam glinted on water. Soon they were wading, ankle deep. Lydia lifted a handful and tasted it. It was salty, though not as salty as the oceans on her home world. She spit it out.

The water got deeper, up to her knees, then up to mid-thigh. The Goxhat's belly and mouth were underwater. "Can you breathe?" Lydia asked.

The Goxhat reared on its back legs, bracing itself against a wall and bringing its mouth above the surface. "Nostrils on top. I/we can breathe." It dropped back into the water and plowed on. Soon it was swimming. It had an oddly neat and efficient stroke, which kept its eyes and nostrils above water. Surge. Sink. Surge. Sink.

By this time the tunnel had leveled out. Light flashed ahead of them. Not a lantern. Sunlight.

Lydia pushed forward. The tunnel ended. She stopped, blinking, barely able to see though the brightness. In front of her, waves rolled toward a beach. Beyond the beach were low, stone bluffs, dotted with something that glittered. Above the bluffs was a blue sky, full of fat, white clouds. The Goxhat was still swimming, heading toward land.

Lydia followed, wading through water that grew increasingly shallow. A fresh wind blew past her, smelling of salt. The Goxhat reached the beach and shook itself. Lydia climbed out of the water next to it, then turned back. Waves rolled in past the half-submerged tunnel. Farther out were breakers, then whitecaps. Beyond a wide expanse of water was the city, its towers dim with distance.

She turned and looked at the bluffs. Lacy, fragile looking plants grew on the stone. They were the things that glittered.

"Interesting biology," the Goxhat said beside her. "As the plants age, their silicon chemical bonds, which break easily, become dominant; although the seeds that form within them are both carbon and silicon. The plants become hard and fragile. Anything—a wind, a touch can break them, freeing the seeds to fall. Go. Touch a plant."

Lydia walked to the bluff and touched one of the plants, which looked like frost on a window. It shattered.

"You are talking normally," Lydia said.

"I/we am/are?" the Goxhat replied. It was silent for a while, looking out at the field of glittering plants. "Maybe my/our translator is working better, or maybe I/we are beginning to recover. All Goxhat know that we—or I—live as a group, but die one body at a time. In the end, there is a single body, remembering what it used to be. When it dies, it dies alone, without comfort from the rest of itself, knowing—a terrible knowledge!—that when it draws its last breath, the person it was will be completely gone. I/we am that body." Four blue eyes looked up at Lydia. "Loss and loneliness can drive a person crazy, but a good commercial problem will bring almost anyone back. There are stories about Goxhat who rose from a deathbed to strike a deal and were buried with songs of praise."

"Oh," said Lydia.

"BioIn wanted me/us to invest in colonies that built themselves. Most habitable planets have silica, and carbon is common on planets where Goxhat and humans can live. Seed a site with BioIn plants, their representative said. Then I or we could go off for a vacation or a trip to find new investments. When I/we returned, all necessary buildings would be grown."

"Wouldn't it be just as easy to bring in prefab buildings?" Lydia asked.

"I/we asked that. BioIn showed me/us graphs and columns of numbers, which did not convince."

"Why did BioIn want your money?" Lydia asked. "It's a big corporation. It ought to be able to fund itself."

"You should see their financial statements," the Goxhat replied. "Far too many liabilities. Well hidden, granted. But I/we know how to dig. The project on the so-called Checkerboard Planet ended in disaster. Do you know that story?"

Of course she did. She had been a part of it. "Yes," Lydia said.

"The AIs have sued to recover the planet," the Goxhat said. "And for damages. In addition the human workers on the planet have sued for back pay, though that is minor. More serious is the lawsuit brought by the indigenous life form. It is a grave crime to suppress the rights of indigenous life forms, and it will prove costly.

"They tried to have the case heard here, where they have influence. But it went to their home planet Nova Terra, where a new party is in power, one that is not sympathetic. BioIn has appealed, but they will lose; and the money they will have to pay has not been entered as a liability on their balance sheet.

"There are other problems, which I/we can explain to you, if you understand finance and accounting. It's all off-balance sheet liabilities and stupid games played with subsidiary companies—the Checkerboard Planet was simply the last leaf or twig."

"Did you tell BioIn this?" she asked.

"Of course. It's always a good idea to tell the opposition what their weakness is, while hiding mine/ours. Always negotiate from strength, even if the strength is only apparent."

"Did the industrial accident happen after that?" Lydia asked.

Three Hoots crouched down. It wasn't able to frown, but Lydia had a sense that it was frowning. "I/we were in a guest lodge at the edge of a test area. A lovely place. On one side were the native plants, glittering in sunlight. On the other side were green plots. Human plants. There were enormous machines working in the human plots, weeders and harvesters, wide enough to cover an entire plot. I/we went out to see, riding in a van with no driver. I/we remember now. The van stopped at the end of a plot. But the machine—the harvester—did not stop. The van would not start. The doors were locked.

"Trapped," the Goxhat said and shuddered. "The machine rolled right over me/us. But the van broke open, cracked like an egg. When this happened, I/we escaped. Only me/us. The rest of me/us died, crushed by the machine.

"The harvester backed up, till it was off the van, and a human climbed down from the cab. That was surprising. The machines usually operate themselves. The human came over to give assistance, I/we thought. But when it saw me/us, it said, 'You aren't supposed to be alive,' and pulled a gun.

"I/we recognized the weapon. We have guns to use against dangerous animals. Never against people. The human pointed it at me/us. I/we jumped. Goxhat jump well. Four strong legs! I/we grabbed the human before it could shoot, and we struggled. Somehow, in the struggle, the human became dead. It lay against the van—what was left of the van—with a dent in its head. I/we fled." The Goxhat paused.

"And?" Lydia urged. It was one heck of a story.

"There was an area of stone near the plot, outcroppings and deep ravines. I/we went there. Behind us/me, the van exploded. I/we found a cave and went in. Deep and deeper, till I/we fell over a cliff and was injured."

"How?" asked Lydia.

"On top." The Goxhat patted the bulge that housed its brain.

A closed head injury, except the Goxhat did not have a head.

"When I/we woke up, I/we kept going. Found a tunnel and then Genghis and his companions. They had light and food. I/we stayed."

"BioIn tried to kill you, because you had figured out the extent of their liabilities."

"I/we think so now. Had forgotten. They did kill me/us. Almost all of me/us."

"First we need water," Lydia said. "Then we need to get to the city without running into anyone from BioIn. What happened to your gun?"

"Genghis traded it to Alys. I/we got a cup." The Goxhat lifted the cup and flourished it.

"Revolution comes from the barrel of a gun," Lydia said, remembering an old line from her days in the FLPM liberation army. "It does not come from a cup."

"It is not possible to use a gun to drink," the Goxhat replied.

"You've been on the mainland," Lydia said. "Do you have any suggestions?"

"Go north along the beach. Stay close to the bluffs. There are boat docks opposite the city. Creep in at night. Seize a boat. Drive to the city."

It sounded easy. Most likely, it would not be. But Lydia didn't have a better idea. "Okay."

They began walking north by the bluffs. By this time, Lydia had noticed that she was wet and cold. Nothing to do, except wait till the ocean wind dried her. The planet's primary passed overhead, and shadows began to stretch from the bluffs. There were animals on the stone as well as plants, Lydia noticed, creatures with many legs and transparent shells. Their bodies, under the shells, were bright red or yellow.

"If we dared walk along the water's edge, we could find empty shells," the Goxhat said. "Not as interesting as a balance sheet, but none the less interesting."

"Do the Goxhat understand beauty?" Lydia asked.

"Of course. There is the beauty of columns that add up correctly and the beauty of clear financial statements. I/we understand as well the beauty of poetry in praise of good investors and the beauty of public monuments that celebrate prudence, honesty, and fiduciary responsibility. You humans raise monuments to war and generals. I/we never do, in part because I/we don't have wars, but also because I/we would never raise a monument to the destruction of fixed capital. It would be like celebrating an earthquake or an enormous fire."

An interesting idea, Lydia thought.

"Think how rich you humans would be, if you did not destroy capital at regular intervals," the Goxhat added.

Another interesting idea. Lydia said, "Karl Marx said the periodic destruction of capital was an inevitable part of capitalism."

"Karl Marx was a fool," the Goxhat replied. "But probably right about humans. You are an odd species that does not seem to understand how an economy ought to work."

They kept walking. After a while, they came to a break in the bluffs. A small, clear river ran into the ocean, edged by crystal reeds.

"We are going to break them," Lydia said.

"We have to," the Goxhat said. "I will follow you."

It wore no clothes, which was typical of Goxhat, and its stiff, sparse hair was not likely to be adequate protection against the broken reeds. Lydia nodded, then moved into the reeds, clearing a path for the Goxhat. Plants snapped and shattered. Small, sharp fragments clung to her pants. She picked them off when she reached the river's sandy edge, then knelt and lifted water in her hands. Beside her, the Goxhat filled its cup. "You see. Much better than a gun."

When they were full, they waded the river. Lydia's clothing, which was almost dry, got wet to her knees. She crunched out through the reeds on the other side, and they kept on. The bluff's shadows stretched farther across the beach. The tide was coming in, covering the beach. What was it called? Not ebbing. A flowing tide? The planet had no moons, but there was always the pull of the system's primary.

At last they saw structures on the beach ahead of them, extending into the ocean.

"Docks," said the Goxhat.

"Let's stop," Lydia said.

They settled on the sand and watched day end. The sun was out of sight behind the bluffs, but they could watch its light on the clouds above them, going first gold, then pink, then orange. The city's towers shone dimly. The ocean grew slowly dark. The dock had a roof, but its sides were open. As far as she could tell, nothing moved on it. Maybe it wasn't in use.

Lydia asked, "How long were you in the tunnels?"

"I/we don't know," the Goxhat replied. "A long time."

"Then they won't be looking for you. I don't think there will be a lot of security. The only people on the mainland are BioIn employees. As far as I can remember, there are no dangerous animals."

"Only bugs," Three Hoots said. "Some this big." It held its hands with tentacle-fingers about a meter apart.

"We'll see if there's a boat in dock," Lydia said. "If there is, we'll take it. If not, we'll look for a radio or get the hell away and think about what to do next."

It wasn't much of a plan, especially with the Goxhat along. If BioIn caught them, they might both be killed. But they couldn't stay here. She'd starve and so would Three Hoots. The longer they stayed on the mainland, the better the chances that someone would find them. Or they'd die in some corner and slowly wither into mummies, since the local biology would not be able to eat them.

If—Buddha forfend—they met anyone on the dock, it would most likely be a low level employee, who knew nothing about the plot to kill the Goxhat. Maybe they could talk their way out. She would have felt a lot better if her AI had not gone missing.

They moved at twilight, when they were still able to see. A handful of stars glimmered in the sky, members of a nearby cluster of blue-white giants, and a light went on at the dock's seaward end—on a timer, Lydia sincerely hoped. Otherwise, there was only the afterglow of day.

They reached the fence as twilight ended. More stars had come out, though not many. There were dust clouds in the stellar neighborhood, Lydia remembered. The blue-white cluster shone brilliantly, lighting the eastern sky. Beneath them were the city lights, much less bright. These gave enough illumination so Lydia could make out a boat floating next to the dock, long and sleek and powerful looking. She glanced toward the shack at the dock's landward end. It had windows, all of them unlit. Surely, if there was someone in there, there ought to be the yellow glow of work lights or the blue glow of entertainment.

"Try the gate," the Goxhat said softly.

"Locked," she whispered.

"I/we will climb the fence." The Goxhat swarmed up before Lydia could speak. It hesitated on the top, then jumped down, landing silently.

"I can see the gate controls," the Goxhat said and reached toward something. A moment later, the gate swung open.

Something was going to happen, Lydia thought. Security couldn't be this weak. "Let's move." She ran toward the boat, dropping into the cockpit. The controls were dark. "Are you on?" she asked the boat.

A mellow baritone voice replied. "My engines are not on, as should be evident. But I'm able to run my mind off the battery. So I am conscious."

"Can you take me to Innovation City?"

"Of course. Put your passcard in the slot and key in your password."

"Shit," thought Lydia. If her AI had been talking to her, it would have been able to override the boat's security. But she couldn't by herself. This meant she was going to have to move to plan B, which was sending out a mayday.

No robot could refuse a request for emergency services, not here or on any planet. With luck, BioIn would not find and kill them before help arrived.

"What are you doing?" a voice asked. It was human and female. Lydia looked around and saw a woman standing on the dock, lit by the dock's light and the stars. She was short and wide and wearing some kind of uniform. More importantly, she was holding a gun.

Lydia opened her mouth to explain that she had an emergency and needed help. The Goxhat—who was still on the dock, hidden in its shadows—jumped. It hadn't been kidding when it spoke about four strong legs. It landed on the woman's back, its legs closing around her torso. One pincher grabbed the woman's gun arm, forcing the gun up, while both of the alien's tentacle-hands grabbed the woman's throat and throttled.

The woman pulled at the Goxhat's tentacles, trying to free her throat, but to no avail. She fell to her knees. Her gun fell from her hand. Lydia clambered onto the deck and grabbed it.

"Don't kill her," she said.

The woman fell over, and the Goxhat moved back. "I/we don't believe she is dead."

Lydia knelt and checked. The woman was still breathing, though she was going to have some ugly bruises.

"If there is anyone else around, we are in serious trouble," she said to the Goxhat. "Let's get her on the boat."

They moved the woman and waited for her to come to. A frightening period. Lydia thought of sending the mayday. If she did, BioIn would know something was up. Wait, she told herself. Wait and hope.

The woman groaned.

"Are you awake?" Lydia asked.

"Yes," the woman said in a choked voice.

"I have your gun, and we are desperate. I want your passcard and your password. If you try any games, I'll shoot you. If you cooperate, you'll end up alive."

There was a silence, then the woman said, "In my shirt pocket. The password is 'jubilant dragon.'"

Lydia found the card. "Remember, if you are playing games, you'll be dead."

"The password is 'jubilant dragon,'" the woman repeated.

"Thanks." Lydia got up and went to the boat's controls, inserted the card, and typed in the password.

"Thank you," the boat said. Its engines started. "Where do you want to go in Innovation City?"

"Anywhere."

"I will take you to the West Side Recreational Dock," the boat sad. The ropes tying it to the dock came loose and pulled in. "Hang on."

It purred away from the dock and headed east in brilliant starlight. The purr became a roar, and they were hitting waves. Water flew up, beading the boat's windshield. The air tasted of salt. Lydia fell into a seat, twisting to look at the woman and the Goxhat, both on the boat's deck.

The boat slammed into wave after wave. The woman groaned again, and the Goxhat made a keening sound. Lydia wondered if lack of food had made her crazy. She had actually threatened to murder another intelligent being.

Possibly necessary in this case, her AI said. *But don't make it a habit.*

Where have you been? Lydia asked.

In retreat from the virus infecting you. I didn't want it to infect me. I have organic components, as you must remember, and they are closely intertwined with your nervous system, which the virus was attacking. I shut down as much of our interface as was possible. What an ugly disease! You have not been thinking sanely, Lydia, and I have had moments when I wondered about my own rationality.

She felt a rush of relief—and a rush of anger. The AI had abandoned her, left her alone in the tunnel with crazy people and on the mainland with BioIn killers.

I had my own problems to solve. My integrity was compromised. I do not think I am able to experience fear, but I did experience something—

You're okay now? Lydia asked.

I have scanned every part of myself and made repairs wherever possible. But some of my functions are impaired.

Lydia thought, if I get out of this alive, I'll get you to help.

Thank you.

She moved on to her next problem. "What's your name?" she asked the security woman.

"I think I'm going to throw up."

"An odd name," the Goxhat said.

The woman pulled herself upright and vomited over the side.

"I am moving quickly," the boat said. "I assume, from the threats you uttered, that this is an emergency."

"Yes," said Lydia.

The boat slammed into more waves. The woman vomited more. Lydia felt queasy, but she had nothing to throw up. "Do you have water on board?" she asked the boat.

"Yes. Try the refrigerator in back."

She made her way there and found bottles of fizzy water. The Goxhat took one. Lydia drank another.

"I also have nutrition bars and trail snacks," the boat added.

"No thanks. Not right now."

The city grew larger and brighter. Lydia made out skyways and advertising. Yellow Sol-spectrum light shone through the skyways' transparent walls. The signs flashed and scrolled in a dozen different colors. "BioIn—the Wave of the Future." "Drink Cocaine Cola." If she had her choice right now, she'd go for opium, the time-honored analgesic, grown on many human worlds, or maybe a tall glass of beer. She didn't need a stimulant. Life was too exciting already.

She could see the West Side Docks, another flashing sign.

The boat slowed. The BioIn security guard slid down to sit on the deck, slumped and miserable, but no longer throwing up.

"I'm sorry about this," Lydia said.

"So am I," the woman replied.

The docks were straight ahead. The boat slowed more.

There are people waiting on the dock, her AI said.

Lydia peered and saw them. A row of humans.

"What is that?" she asked the boat.

"BioIn security. I radioed ahead. It was obvious to me that you were doing something illegal."

What alternatives did she and the Goxhat have now? Jump in the water and swim to freedom? Or use the security guard as a hostage.

"Send a mayday," she told the boat.

"I'll do it because my programming requires me to. But I don't know who is going to help you."

"Neither do I. My name is Lydia Duluth. I work for Stellar Harvest. I'm not a citizen of this planet. Say I'm at the West Side Recreational Docks, about to be arrested and possibly killed. Do it now!"

"Stellar Harvest," the security woman said. She had pulled herself upright, though she still looked miserable. "Really? Do you know Wazati Tloo?"

Lydia nodded. "And Ramona Patel; and you aren't going to get autographs from anyone, if you let these guys kill me."

The boat slowed, heading in to the dock.

"What if I tell you to turn around and go back out into the ocean?" Lydia asked.

"I will ignore you," the boat replied.

"What can we do?" the Goxhat asked.

"Surrender and hope the mayday gets through to someone who cares," Lydia said. She was tired and hungry, and her headache was getting worse. Though she spoke of help, she felt hopeless. Her only chance now, she thought, was that Wazati Casoon knew she was on the planet. When she didn't turn up at accounting, he'd begin to worry. But how soon?

My colleagues, the other AIs, know you are on the planet as well. They will begin to ask questions, when they discover they can't communicate with me.

They can't?

I am not fully functional.

The boat bumped against the dock. Lines snaked out and tied up. One of the humans on the dock said, "You are under arrest. Put down whatever weapons you may have and raise your hands."

Lydia obeyed. Beside her, the Goxhat lifted its four arms, waving tentacles and pinchers.

"Hey!" one of the humans said. "Calm down, will you?"

Three Hoots stopped waving. People jumped into the boat. One hand-cuffed Lydia. Another tried to handcuff the Goxhat. The arms with tentacles had no wrists, and the cuffs slid off. The pincher arms didn't come close to meeting. One arm could be cuffed, but it could not be fastened to the other

"What the hell am I supposed to do?" the man asked.

"Leave it," said the woman who had handcuffed Lydia. "It's a Goxhat. They aren't dangerous."

"Huh!" said the guard they had kidnapped.

By this time, most of the cops were on the boat, but there were still a couple of people on the dock, holding rifles and watching Lydia.

More people came up behind them, these in shiny white battle armor. What the heck? Lydia thought. She wasn't that dangerous. Armor wasn't required.

The armor has the Stellar Harvest emblem, her AI said.

Lydia squinted. There was something on the white chests, which ought to be an emblem, but she couldn't make it out.

A sheaf of grain and stars, said the AI.

Lydia relaxed, though not completely. There could still be a fight. But it looked as if Stellar Harvest's legendary loyalty to its employees was coming through for her.

"We'll take over now," an amplified voice said. Ramona Patel. It was not the low, musical, sensual voice she used when acting, but the sharp, commanding voice she used for business.

The woman who'd handcuffed Lydia scrambled up onto the dock. "Who are you?"

"This is Stellar Harvest security, and I am Ramona Patel. You have a Stellar Harvest employee on the boat. We want her and her companion."

"You can't be Ramona Patel," the woman said.

"Who are you to say who I am?" Ramona asked, her voice getting sharper and more commanding.

"I'm Captain Harbin of BioIn Security."

"That's well and good. I am a star who is top box office on a hundred planets; and—more important—I am the director of *Krishna at the Soy Milk Bar*, which is currently being made here."

"That gives you no authority," the captain said.

"Tell that to your company's public relations department. BioIn's name is going to be all over the holo, if—and only if—I get my employee back. I should add that the two people immediately to the right and left of me are lawyers. I'm not sure how well they shoot, but they know local and interstellar law."

"We need to speak to our client," a new voice said.

Another voice added, "Both our clients."

Ramona said, "I suggest you call BioIn."

The captain began cursing, then pulled out a phone. She moved away down the dock, so Lydia was not able to hear the conversation that followed.

"What is happening?" the Goxhat asked.

"We are having what humans call a Martian Standoff," Lydia said.

"Is this good or bad?"

"Good, I think."

Captain Harbin came back. "I am supposed to take them to headquarters."

"We will come," Ramona said. "I hope this doesn't take too long. I need to direct tomorrow."

"We need to ride with our clients," one of the lawyers said.

The other lawyer asked, "Have we decided not to have a shoot-out?"

"Yes, dammit," Captain Harbin replied.

The lawyers undid their armor and stepped out of it. They looked almost identical: tall, thin, dark humans in severe suits. The armor folded down until it was the size and shape of two white briefcases, which the lawyers picked up.

"Get the prisoners up here," Captain Harbin said.

The guards on the boat lifted Lydia up. The Goxhat scrambled up on its own.

The lawyers walked over. "I am Counselor Chonqqing. This is Counselor Caracas. I would offer to shake hands, but— Are the handcuffs necessary, Captain?"

"Yes," Captain Harbin said firmly.

"Well, then," the other lawyer—Caracas—said. "This is a company planet, but you still have laws and judges; and I have set up an appointment with one of those judges. Let's go and see about bail."

They rode in a car labeled BioIn Security, traveling through the brightly lit streets of Innovation City. A large white van followed them. Lydia felt stunned and exhausted, but also relieved. This was one reason she worked for Stellar Harvest. The company put its employees in dangerous situations, because it insisted on recording its holoplays in genuinely exotic places. But it also backed its people up, and it knew there were three secrets to operating successfully on many different worlds: good security, good accountants, and really good lawyers.

They reached their destination. Lydia and the Goxhat were escorted out and into a building, the lawyers sticking to them like burrs. Behind them came Ramona Patel, out of her armor and in a bright red jumpsuit and gold boots with high heels. She wasn't tall, but her figure was perfect, as was her makeup and her long, dark, wavy hair. Stellar Harvest guards surrounded her, still in their armor. A deliberate show of strength, Lydia decided.

Are you there? she asked her AI.

Yes. I am admiring Ramona. This is an effective use of hormones. If you have it, make it obvious, I believe the saying is.

They entered the offices of BioIn Security. Lydia and the Goxhat were booked for kidnapping and theft. Ramona handed out autographs. Cops used their phones to record her standing in her famous hip-shot pose and smiling brilliantly. Buddha, what a smile she had!

Then they went to a courtroom, where the judge had his image taken with Ramona. Amazing what Ramona's eyelashes could do, dropping gently over her dark, dark, almond-shaped eyes. Her skin was brown, smooth and flawless. Her acting voice was as luscious as her skin. If the judge could have melted, he would have, turning into a gooey mass on the floor. Instead, he set a low bail, which the lawyers paid.

They left in the Stellar Harvest van: Ramona, Lydia, the Goxhat, the lawyers, and the armored security guards.

As soon as they were in motion, Ramona said, "This is an absolute disaster, Lydia; and if you don't have a good explanation, I will see you fired."

"How'd you find us?" Lydia asked.

"Wazati Casoon said you had vanished. He was worried about you, and he's the only person who can control his idiot brother. I can't have Cas worried till the holo is finished, and I can get that dimwit Wazati Tloo out of my life.

"I contacted BioIn Security. They said they couldn't find you, so I told our security to make themselves useful. They hacked the city observation system and found video records of you going down into the tunnels below the city. As far as they could tell, you were under the influence of some drug."

"A virus," Lydia said.

"We found that out later. Obviously, BioIn could have found your trail easily. It was in their own records! They were lying to us. I had a holoplay to make, a thoroughly irritating star, and an agent who was becoming hysterical. I sent one team to look for you in the tunnels and told another team to dig into the BioIn information system and find out why BioIn was lying."

One of the armored security people said, "You got the infection from BioIn. They know about the work you did on the Checkerboard Planet. It caused them serious trouble, and someone in the corporation wanted revenge. They figured you'd die in the tunnels, and no one would know.

"We think the street performers who robbed you work for BioIn, but we aren't sure. They may have happened on you and realized you were vulnerable. In any case, they took your money and ID and phone, leaving you with no way to reach us."

"But you'd had tea with Cas," Ramona said. "He knew you were there, and he was worried. None of this explains why you kidnapped a BioIn guard and stole a boat."

"I didn't know BioIn was after me," Lydia said. "But I knew they were after the Goxhat. If they'd found us, they would have killed both of us."

"Why?" asked Ramona.

Lydia told the Goxhat's story.

"Murder of seven-eighths of a Goxhat," said Counselor Caracas. "That is serious."

"I have BioIn stock," Ramona said.

"I don't usually advocate jumping bail," Counselor Chonqqing said. "But I think both of these people should get off the planet. Then we will talk to BioIn. They have put themselves in a very difficult situation. Murder and attempted murder! Someone has to pay!"

Ramona leaned forward, an intent expression on her lovely face. "Lydia, I want your friend to talk to our accounting staff. We need to know exactly what is going on with BioIn. How bad is their financial situation? And who in the company decided to start killing people? After that, we'll get you off the planet—and send a message to the nearest Goxhat embassy. They can decide what to do about your friend."

"I/we will go home to the Goxhat planet and live alone," Three Hoots said sadly. "The last remainder of us/me."

The van pulled into the drive of a small building. "Luxe Hotel," a sign flashed.

"We're renting the entire place," Ramona said. "Jack here will take you to accounting. After that, you need to take a bath. You stink, Lydia."

Jack took them to the fifth floor, which was accounting. Lydia dozed while the Goxhat talked to accountants. The two lawyers listened and took notes. Finally, the accountants said they had what they needed. The lawyers nodded, looking satisfied.

Jack returned, out of his armor, a tall figure, handsome except for his oddly pale skin. She had met a few humans like him. It was a traditional human color. But it looked bleached and unnatural, as if the man's white skull was shining through his skin. He escorted her to a hotel room. There was clothing here, he told her. It ought to fit. The Goxhat was next door.

Lydia took a shower and dressed, then walked to the room's window. It was raining now. Looking down, she saw the light from vehicles and advertisements shining on the wet street.

Well? She asked her AI.

I am still admiring Ramona Patel. What an efficient woman! The virus damaged our interface, and there are functions I have not been able to restore. But if you plug into a secure computer, I might be able to access this system's stargate. That will be our backup plan, if Stellar Harvest cannot get you off the planet. My colleagues—the other AIs—do not interfere with intelligent life, but they will want to rescue me.

Okay.

The doorbell rang. A moment later, the door slid open and Ramona entered. She had changed to a Terra-green caftan with gold embroidery at the neck and hem. Her earrings—new since the last time Lydia saw her—were huge and delicate and golden. Her exquisite feet were in gilded sandals, and her toenails were a luminous green that matched the caftan.

Wazati Casoon followed her in. "Lydia!" The eunuch embraced her. "I have been distraught!"

"No kidding," Ramona said. "I found Lydia for you, Cas. I expect you to concentrate on your dim-as-a-red-dwarf brother now."

"I will think of nothing else," Cas said.

"We have our own shuttle over at the spaceport," Ramona said. "The problem is the hydrofoil from here to the mainland. You'll have ID from my own personal hair stylist, and we're going to transport the Goxhat in a case labeled wigs. I'm sending other people with you, so you get lost in the crowd. It's damn inconvenient. People I need here have to go with you. Do you know how much it costs to stop production?"

"It will give me time to reason with my brother," Cas said. "He still does not want to be blue."

"Krishna is always blue!" Ramona shouted.

Cas and Lydia were silent. After a moment, Ramona drew a deep breath. "I will get angry later. I'm sure your brother will give me plenty of reasons. It's too bad that he's so attractive."

"It's not his fault," Cas said. "Our species has bred for extremely attractive males for thousands of years."

"Brains would have been good," Ramona said.

"Our eunuchs have the brains. Unfortunately, we are not nearly as attractive as the breeding males."

"You saved my life, Cas," Lydia said. "I find that attractive."

"Thank you."

"The unit metal-workers will build a case for the Goxhat tonight," Ramona said. "You and the Goxhat will go to the mainland tomorrow. The shuttle will take off as soon as you arrive. You will be safe in one standard day."

Lydia felt tension go out of her shoulders.

"And I hope you will try to stay out of trouble in the future. This mess occurred because you did work for the AIs, and now it's costing Stellar Harvest money. A person can't serve two employers, Lydia. I'm going to recommend that Stellar Harvest put you on leave, until you decide whether you are working for us or the AIs."

Damn. But typical of Ramona. Nothing she did was an unqualified good. Lydia nodded. "Okay."

"Now, get some sleep. You need to be sharp tomorrow."

Lydia nodded again.

Ramona's expression softened, and she looked humane for a moment. "You may be interested in knowing the team that went into the tunnels found the people you met there. The three who were victims of the virus have been rescued. The rest chose to stay where they are."

"I owe them," Lydia said.

"Send money to a homeless organization after you are off planet," Ramona said. "There is nothing else you can do for them. You have your own life to save." She turned and walked out of the room, Wazati Casoon following.

So thought Lydia. A happy ending for her, and maybe for Genghis and Tope. But Affirmation Loo was crazy, which might or might not be fixable, and the other people were still in the tunnels. And what about the Goxhat, who was the only remaining part of itself. What kind of happy ending was that?

The Goxhat would have died in the tunnels, except for you, her AI said. *BioIn would have gotten away with murder. The result is mixed and imperfect, but so is life.*

Sixty days later, she was on Stellar Harvest's home planet, at a sidewalk café in Megastar City. The sky above her was cloudless and pale blue. A mild wind blew past her. The café was edged with native plants in pots. Their frilly, yellow leaves fluttered in the wind. Lydia sipped wine and felt reasonably happy.

Across the table from her was the last remaining part of Three Hoots. A small dish of a liquid called snap was in front of it. "It is a mild intoxicant," the Goxhat said. "Drinking it leads to a sense of mental clarity and well-being. I/we use it to combat loneliness."

"What are you going to do?" Lydia asked.

"Stellar Harvest has offered me/us a job as an internal auditor. I/we are planning to take the job. Better to be a stranger among humans, than a single body among Goxhat.

"In addition, I/we am or are impressed by Stellar Harvest's defense of employees. It seems like a good idea to stick with them until BioIn is bankrupted and sold off."

"You think that will happen?"

"The Stellar Harvest accountants say yes. According to them, it is not a good idea to pull an enron, unless you own the government that regulates you. I'm not sure what an enron is."

"A lot of crooked accounting."

"BioIn owns the government of Grit, but the corporation is still based on Nova Terra, and it does not own the government there.

"In addition, the Goxhat government has issued a warning to investors and business people. BioIn is an unsafe investment and an unsafe business partner. We are the best players of capitalism in the known galaxy. Many beings pay attention to our advisories.

"BioIn's stock is falling like a stone. As one of our proverbs says, justice is like a very slow punch press. It may not come down often, but it comes down hard."

"Have they found out who ordered the attacks on you and me?"

"Not yet," Three Hoots said. "But that does not matter. The corporation is corrupt and must be destroyed. The game of capitalism can only be played if the players and their numbers are honest."

Tell that to humans, Lydia thought.

The Goxhat have tried.

Three Hoots climbed onto the table and took a big slurp from the bowl of snap, then climbed back onto its chair. "In time, maybe, I/we will return home. But first I/we must deal with grief and learn enough to become an expert on investing in alien cultures. Single I/we may be, but I/we still long for profit and fame."

Peter Watts is a former marine biologist and the Hugo and Nebula nominated author of novels such as *Starfish, Maelstrom,* and *Behemoth,* and numerous short stories. His work is available in twenty languages, has appeared in two dozen best-of-year anthologies, and has acquired nearly fifty awards and nominations from a dozen countries. His debut novel *Starfish* was a *New York Times* Notable Book of the Year. His seventeen awards include the Hugo, the Shirley Jackson, and the Seiun.

Peter has been called "a hard science fiction writer through and through and one of the very best alive" by *The Globe and Mail,* and the creators of the acclaimed computer games *Bioshock Two, SOMA,* and *EVE Online* have all cited Watts's work as an influence.

TEST 4 ECHO

Peter Watts

Six days before the money ran out, Enceladus kicked Medusa right in the ass.

Onboard thermistors registered a sudden spike—80°, 90°, 120°—before the seabed jumped and something slammed the probe from the side. A momentary flash. An ocean impossibly boiling. A rocky seabed, tilting as if some angry giant had kicked over a table.

Channel down.

Telemetry rippled through a black alkaline ocean. Relays anchored to the undercrust caught those whispers, boosted them, passed them on. A hundred eighty kilometers around the horizon, Euryle—clinging to the underside of the ice like a great metal barnacle—filtered signal from noise and ran it up the line to Stheno through six kilometers of refrozen crust. Stheno cupped its hands at the fractured horizon and shouted downhill.

"Fuck," Lange said ninety-eight minutes later. He resisted an urge to punch the bulkhead. "Can we get it back?"

"Maybe." Tactical was already glowing with the light of Sansa's efforts. "Not making any promises about what kind of mood it's going to be in, though."

Eighteen months.

Eighteen months of mapping and sampling and sniffing around smokers for hints of hydrogen sulfide. A year and a half spent looping around Earth's moon, squinting up at Saturn's, mustering hope against hope that the far one wasn't quite so dead as the near. Brushing off all the null chemistry, the inconclusive results, the slow grinding attrition of a full scientific staff down to one lone hold-out and his faithful sidekick, sticking it out until the end of the fiscal quarter.

Par for the course that it would end this way.

An hour and a half before their diagnostic queries and reboot commands reached Enceladus; that long again before an answer arrived, if it ever did. God knew how much back-and-forth it would take to get the robot back on track.

"You might as well get some sleep," Sansa said. "Not like radio waves are gonna go any faster with you hanging off my shoulder."

Lange sighed. "Fine. Don't bother me for anything less than a hull breach."

"Okay."

"A *major* hull breach. Like, hurricane-force winds."

"You got it."

He climbed up through a hatch onto which someone, long ago, had scribbled the words *Mission Control* in purple Sharpie. Navigated twists and turns once frequented by fellow Gorgonites, occupied now by railgunners and rock wranglers whose pet projects had actual futures. He forced smiles and half-hearted waves in passing, climbed into his cubby at a primo tenth-of-a-gee and breathed in a familiar, comforting funk of sweat and antiseptic. He thought about ringing up Raimund back on Earth, but fell asleep trying to figure out the time zones.

Spread-eagled, crucified, stretched across the display like some spectral cephalopod Christ in a dissecting tray: Medusa, awash in flickering diagnostics.

"She's *way* offside," Sansa said. "Twenty-one kilometers from where she went dark. Those geysers, man. Serious backwash. But—" she paused for effect. "I got her back."

"You are unstoppable," Lange admitted.

"Autopersistent is my middle name." It was one of them, anyway. "Fuel cells are damaged. Won't hold a charge for more'n a few minutes."

Lange eyed the display. "We can still feed directly off the gradient. No more sprinting, but slow and steady's more our speed anyway."

One of the six limbs pulsed yellow. "Also A4's ganked. Lost its hard link to the hub—the arm's functional, but it's not wired in and the wireless backup isn't worth shit."

Lange gestured at the tank, where A4's doppelganger sparkled with fresh telemetry. "Looks okay to me."

"Down here, sure. But there's all sorts of EM leakage from the damaged electricals and it's messing up the signal. We can clean up most of that static at this end, but up there the router's basically getting nothing but noise. Still, check *this* out . . . " Virtual Medusa pulled itself erect and began a six-legged tap dance. "I ran Meddy through a few paces to get a sense of overall functionality, and . . . "

A4 was keeping pace. Trying to, at least; the arm wasn't exactly in step, but it wasn't too far off.

"It keeps looking around at the other arms," Sansa reported. "It's not getting direct motor commands, so it's just—mimicking its buddies."

Lange grunted, impressed. "Resourceful little fucker. Anything else?"

Four kidney-shaped structures flared red in the hub. "We've lost buoyancy control. Somewhere out there a very sharp rock is wearing about two square meters of our finest Kevlar."

That was bad. "Can we swim?"

"Can't even get off the bottom. Big holes in two of the bladders."

"Autorepair?"

"For the arm at least, but it'll be slow without batteries. Can probably fix those too, eventually. The bladders, though?" She shook her head. "You can't repair something if you don't have the parts."

"So that's it, then." His head hurt. "I guess I go pack."

"We're giving up?" Sansa said.

"San. We're grounded. Besides, it's been eighteen months. What are the odds we'd find anything in the next few days anyway?"

"What are the odds we already have?"

He looked at her. She looked back.

"Spit it out," he said at last.

Medusa vanished from the tank. The image that took its place was 2D, low-contrast, rendered in grainy infrared: Lange made out a rocky ridge, cold brittle pillows of frozen lava. A seascape rendered in vague silhouettes, slewing to port as the robot staggered.

Something bright jerked briefly into frame.

"What's—"

Jerked out again.

"—that?"

"Buffer dump from A1." Sansa restarted the stream in frame-stop mode. "A few seconds of tail-end footage that got stuck in the cache when we lost contact." The footage reiterated in jerky snapshots. Murky topography stepped offstage. A bright blur stepped on. A dash of light, smearing left. A hyphen, an upward jiggle.

Sudden, sharp edges. Facets. *Structure.* Just for a frame or two; then motion blur reasserted itself.

"*Holy* . . . " Lange whispered as Sansa brought it back.

"It's enhanced," she reminded him.

"I know." His headache instantly forgotten.

"Passive infra. Half, one degree above ambient at best."

"That's symmetry," Lange said. "That's *bilateral.*"

"Could be. Impossible to tell for sure from this angle."

"Any other camera catch this?"

"Nope. And sonar was already scrambled, so acoust—"

"Did you see it move? I think it moved."

"It was an eruption, Lange. *Everything* moved."

"We gotta get back there."

"We can't swim," she reminded him.

"We can crawl," Lange said.

You could ride Medusa. You could *become* Medusa, in a manner of speaking. You could look around every which way, sample the data streams in subjective real-time, watch every process and encounter as it had unfolded. You could even detach your perspective, pass like a ghost through the carapace and look back on the machine from outside. The interpolations were that good.

The only thing you couldn't do, across all those non-negotiable lightminutes, was change the past.

Lange was riding third-person now, immersed in an archived reality AUs distant and hours gone. It would have flickered occasionally even if the robot had been in perfect health: now the world jumped and jittered almost constantly behind gusts of visual static. "Convalescence is ongoing," Sansa had informed him drily as he'd plugged in.

Medusa inched along the seabed, a couple of meters below Lange's vicarious eyes: a biomechanical abomination somewhere between an octopus and a brittle star. The arms reached and recoiled in turn, each intelligent in its way, each semiautonomous: finding brief traction in cracks and sharktoothed outcroppings, drawing the body from behind, pushing it forward, trading one handhold for another. Even damaged, there was an alien grace to the way the limbs moved in relation to each other. A kind of boneless, slow-motion ballet.

Except for A4.

It did its best. Lange could see the apical cluster spin in its housing, doing its utmost to track the other arms. He could see the arm *hesitate* now and then, as if distracted by some invisible bauble in the middle distance. It reached, grabbed, pulled. Always a half beat behind. Medusa staggered forward, its rhythm just a little off-balance.

"It's getting better," Sansa said from the void beyond virt. "Used to track all the other arms to keep in sync. Now it's figured out it only needs to track Three and Five."

He blinked against a momentary break in the feed. "Not even half a meter per second."

"Still pretty good, under the circumstances."

Lange unplugged. The murky abyss vanished; the grimy, cabled confines of *Mission Control* reasserted themselves. "Let's crank clock speed on A4. If it's taking its lead from the other arms, the least we can do is give it faster reflexes to help it keep up."

"Okay."

He pursed his lips. "I'm kind of surprised the other arms aren't better at compensating."

"They would be, if A4 was a tetch more predictable. It's response times aren't consistent between strokes."

"Any idea why?"

"Working on it," Sansa said. "The obvious physical damage, of course, but there's something else. Keeps returning an Unidentified Error."

"Huh."

"Yeah. It's hurting. It just doesn't know why."

"I mean, this could be *it*," Lange said, and waited.

"Uh huh," Raimund replied two and a half seconds later.

"No more *renewal pending*. No more *how can you waste money looking for aliens when everything's turning to shit here on Earth*. No way they can shut us down if this pays off. We can get you out of that shithole and back up here. Get the whole band together again."

"Sounds great."—after a pause that seemed way longer than the usual Earth/Luna lag.

Lange rolled his eyes. "Try to control your excitement."

"Sorry. It's just, it's not much to go on."

"It's more than we ever had before."

"That's kind of my point. Eighteen months poking around up there, and what have we found?"

"Complex organics. By the tonne."

"No sign of an ecosystem. No metabolic signatures."

"Come on, Ray. We've only surveyed 6% of the seabed."

"Which, statistically, should be more than enough to detect life. If it was up there."

"Not if it's really patchy. Not if it's limited to a few smokers. Not if it's built on a novel molecular template, in which case it wouldn't even register on the usual tests. You wouldn't even know it was there unless you bumped into it." It was an old argument. The whole relationship had had a half-full/half-empty vibe to it since Day One.

"What does Sansa say?" Raimund wondered.

"Basically not to get my hopes up."

"Good advice."

"Jesus, Ray." Lange spread his hands. "What are you saying? We shouldn't even check it out?"

"Of course you should. But no matter how great it would be to get us all back up there, you know what would be even better? Getting *you* back down *here*. Someplace you can actually open a window."

"Yeah. Might be more appealing if the weather didn't try to kill you whenever you did that."

"At the very least it would be nice to fuck again without a three-second time lag."

"Two point five. Teledildonics has come a long way."

"So did you," Raimund told him. "Maybe it's time you came back."

"Well this is just dandy. We're going backwards."

"Off-course, anyway," Sansa admitted. "You know how A4 started tracking all the other arms—"

"And then narrowed it to two. Right."

"It's tracking all five again. Sometimes. Not always."

"What? You cranked the clock, right?"

"I didn't have to." And at Lange's look: "Far as I can tell A4 made that call on its own. Boosted its own reflexes to compensate for the damage. System latency for that arm's below 200msec now."

"And yet we're going slower." Lange grabbed a VisoR off the wall, booted up the time machine. The Enceladus Ocean swallowed him whole.

The data stream had cleaned itself up somewhat, thanks to the robot's ongoing autoministrations. Lange's eyes opened onto a 3D composite of sonar and EM and infrared that stripped away the void, showed him the things lurking within. Gashes in the seabed flickered like red mouths, set alight by thermal gradients amplified beyond all reason. Magnetic field lines emerged from the bedrock and arced away in perfect luminous formation, the aura of a dynamo reaching all the way to Saturn. Medusa bent those contours around it into a bright knot, bleeding off some infinitesimal fraction of the great generator's output for its own use. Lange damped the enhancements, reduced the robot from a riot of false color down to dim gunmetal on a twilit seascape.

Every step was a stumble now. Medusa moved like an insect with half its legs gone, indomitable, incomplete. A4 was barely in sync. When it pulled its weight, it was slow and late to the party; when it didn't, it just—poked the water, seemingly at random.

"It's not getting any codes that would explain this," Sansa said, invisibly close.

Enough of this third-person shit. Lange clicked on A4's apical cluster, felt a brief disorienting flip-flop: suddenly he was *inside*, looking out from the tip of the arm.

"Skip the boring stuff. Show me the anomalies."

Time accelerated, braked: A4 was panning from one arm to another, pausing a moment on each. Tacticals hovered lower-right, reported pings fired and not returned.

Blur, brake: a dim shape in the distance, an igneous extrusion of seabed festooned with pores and spicules. Its texture was subtly disturbing for some reason Lange couldn't put his finger on. A4 couldn't stop staring at it; it held the focus until its more disciplined peers dragged the robot out of range.

Blur, brake: a strip of basalt body-slammed by some tectonic event into a knife-edged ridge. Clathrate icicles erupted from its surface; Medusa's palette painted them sapphire and set them glowing.

"It tends to focus on objects with a fractal dimension of 2.5 to 2.9," Sansa told him. "Starts losing interest around 2.8."

"Any idea why?"

"No functional significance I can see. Doesn't map onto any potential life signatures, no association with tectonic hazards—no more than anything else in this damn ocean, at least. I ran a search using the Haussdorf parameters; closest hits I got were polyhedral flakes and Jackson Pollock paintings."

"So what are we looking at?"

"Aesthetics," Sansa said.

"Very funny."

"If you look very closely," she said, "you'll see I'm not laughing."

He pulled off the VisoR. She wasn't.

"Aesthetics," Lange repeated.

"For want of a better word."

"You're saying, what. A4 just *likes* certain shapes."

"That's what I'm saying."

He let that sink in. "Fuck off."

"It coincides with the latency drop: network isolation, increased clock speed, increased coherence."

"Decreased performance."

"Which is also a trait of information systems when con—"

Lange held up a hand. "Do not say that word."

After a moment, he added: "Decreased performance is *also* a hallmark of information systems so stupid they forget what they've learned and go back to tracking five arms instead of two."

"I don't think that's what happened. The tracking parameters changed. I think—"

The hand again. "If you say *Mirror Test*—"

"Wouldn't dream of it. Because it's not. But if *you* suddenly woke up and saw you were connected to a bunch of other things that looked like you, wouldn't you try to talk to them?"

"I spent most of my life surrounded by things that look like me. I came up here so I *wouldn't* have to."

"I estimated a normalized Phi," Sansa said.

Lange closed his eyes. "Of course you did."

"I zeroed out the damage we could account for and looked at the residuals. Stirred in latency and some integration metrics I ballparked from the diagnostic tests."

He didn't ask. She told him anyway. "Zero point nine two."

"So Medusa is conscious."

"Not all of it. Just the arm."

"Still. That's what you're saying."

"That's what the *data* say."

"Your *unidentified error*."

Her nose twitched; the equivalent of a shrug. "There's no explicit error code for existential suffering."

"If there was," Lange said, "I'd be returning it right now." He took a breath, let it out. "You know we have to shut it down, right?"

"It's *sapient*, Lange. There's someone in there."

He nodded. "And whoever they are, they're grinding the whole system to a halt. We've got sixty-nine hours before the clock runs down, and we're going the wrong way. We'll make better progress without a navel-gazing ball and chain pulling us off course."

"We can't do that."

"Why not?"

"Because awareness plus needs equals *rights*. Isn't that the way it goes? Isn't that why you and I are *persons*?"

"What *needs*? A4 doesn't care whether it lives or dies."

"You're sure of that, are you? You talked to it?"

"It *can't* care. It doesn't have a limbic system."

"It's got imperatives though, right? Mission priorities. Maybe that's not technically an *instinct* or a *need* but it might as well be. And one of the classic definitions of suffering is *imposed suppression of natural behaviors*. Keeping A4 from fulfilling its programmed tasks is like taking a bird that migrates halfway around the world and locking her up in a cage."

"Sansa. It's free to pursue its mission priorities right now. It's completely fucking them up."

"It's a newborn. It's still learning."

Lange couldn't resist. "You're sure of that, are you? You talked to it?"

"I could. *We* could."

"How? Did it teach itself Hoo-Man while we weren't looking? It doesn't talk except in status reports and error codes and those things are all—"

"Subconscious?" Sansa suggested.

"You said it yourself. No error code for existential suffering."

"So give it one. Teach it to talk."

"It wouldn't change anything. It wouldn't *mean* anything."

"Why not?"

"Because you can inject Natural Language routines into *any* old bot and it'll pass a Turing Test just fine. NL routines are just statistical flowcharts. There's no comprehension. You think you'll be proving something just because you can get Medusa to say *it hurts* instead of *packet loss*? Even if there's someone in there—"

"There is, Lange. If we were talking about meat you wouldn't deny it for an instant."

"Fine. How do you connect the flowchart to the ghost? How does the ghost affect the code?"

"I don't know, Lange. Seems to just sort itself out for the rest of us."

"It's an emergent property. You're seriously suggesting that a magnetic field can reach back and change the magnet?"

"Why else did A4 develop such an interest in watching the scenery?"

"Because the same architecture that generates the q-field also generates weird maladaptive behaviors. It's no big secret."

"Right. Everything's correlation, nothing's causal, and we're the exception why, exactly? Because we happened to wake up first?"

"Because we *do* have needs, Sansa. Because we care whether we live or die, and we as a society have decided that Suffering Is Not A Good Thing."

"Lange—"

He cut her off. "No. I'm sorry. The decision's been made."

She fell silent for a moment or two.

"Well, you're right about that at least," she said, and vanished.

"I can't fucking believe it. She got a restraining order."

Raimund blinked. "What?"

"I got a memo from ICRAE. I am not to *deprecate or deactivate Medusa or any autonomous or semiautonomous component thereof pending a review of potential emergent personhood.* They've even suspended repairs on the router. High-bandwidth reintegration with the larger system might *decohere the local entity.*" Lange clenched his fists. "I can't *believe* she went behind my back."

"But it is conscious, right?"

"It's an *arm*. You know the synapse count on one of those DPNs? Not even corvid level. Barely even a cat."

"Cats can't suffer?"

"*A4* can't suffer. You can't suffer if you're not afraid of anything, if you don't *want* any—Jesus, Ray, you *know* this."

"I'm sorry. Yeah, I know it. Intellectually. It's just, you know. AI's generally *do* have fears and wants." Raimund grinned out of one side of his mouth. "I always thought that was funny, you know? We spend a hundred years making all those movies and virts about robots rising up and AIs bootstrapping into gods—and then we decide the best way to keep them from doing that is to give them all survival instincts. What could possibly go right?"

Almost against his will, Lange felt himself smile.

He shut it down. "I've never seen her so passionate about something. I didn't even know she *could* be."

"Yeah, well—" a hiss of sunspot static—"that's the thing about neuromorphics. Everything's emergent. Give 'em an imperative that barely crosses the line into *instinct* and they grow a whole damned amygdala out of it."

"Still better than the alternative." Lange shook his head. "You know what *really* pisses me off? The order was timestamped while we were still arguing. She went behind my back, and she went before we'd even talked about it. Before I even *knew*."

"Wow. It's almost like she knew what you'd say in advance."

"What's that supposed to mean?"

"Nothing." Raimund shrugged across four hundred thousand kilometers. "Except maybe, never get into an argument with anyone who thinks ten times as fast as you."

"Faster isn't smarter. She just crams ten times the bullshit into the same time frame."

"Hey, be thankful she can't up her clock any more than that. Think of the bullshit you'd be wading through if she ever came off the leash."

Lange nudged the gain to try and clear the static, nudged it back when it only made things worse. "Damn thing's barely crawling now, and half the time it's not even crawling in the right direction. At this rate it doesn't matter whether we saw aliens or not. Clock runs down before we can find out."

"Apply for an extension. It's only reasonable, given the circumstances."

"I have. They said it looked like an exotic mineral formation." Lange raised his eyes to Heaven: *Take me now, Lord.* "Everything's gone to shit since NASA went under. All these new guys care about are their stockholders and the monkeywrenchers and all those idiots screaming that Enceladus is just a cover for Zero-Pointers building their Space Ark so they can fuck off to Mars." He gently banged his head against the display. "God *damn* that bitch."

"You ever think it might not even be about Medusa?"

Lange straightened.

"I mean, what are the odds?" Snow sparkled across Raimund's face. "We spend a year and a half coming up empty and then, just before the money stops, you encounter something that *might* change everything. Then Medusa gets kicked way off-station, who knows how long it'll take to get back. Now you can't even repair the router, so it'll take even longer. That's a string of really bad luck that just might stretch the mission past its expiry date, all over a couple of frames of enhanced imagery that might not be anything at all."

Lange frowned. "You saying she faked it?"

"Course not. Not deliberately, anyway. But, you know. What's *faked*, these days? Every byte Medusa puts out has been juiced and jacked before anyone even sees it, right? Everything's false colors and Fourier transforms. And we *are* looking for signs of life. It only makes sense to enhance elements consistent with that. It's not malicious. It's not even counter to conditioning. It's just—we all develop biases. For years Sansa's prime directive has been *further the mission*. Maybe she doesn't want to see it end any more than you do."

"But she warned *me* against reading too much into it."

"So her ass is covered. Still doesn't mean she didn't know exactly how many dots she needed to show before you added a few of your own. Connected them."

"So she's a mind reader now."

"She doesn't need to read your mind. She only needs to know you a little better than you know yourself." That lopsided grin again. "And sweetie, don't take this the wrong way, but that's not exactly a high bar to clear."

Up the well, down the line, back in time.

Medusa lurched and twitched across the seabed, kicking up particles far too jagged to qualify as mud. Like flecks of mica, Lange thought, or tiny shards of broken bone. No soft organic rainfall here. No accumulation of dead biomass rotted to bits during some long slow descent from the euphotic zone. This was pure uncut seabed, ground to powdered glass by the relentless deforming squeeze and shear of tidal gravity. Enceladus was Saturn's own personal stress ball.

Autorepair hadn't been able to fix A4's hardline before Sansa's restraining order stopped it from trying. It shouldn't have mattered. Multi-armed, multi-brained, multiply-redundant, Medusa should have been able to lose half its appendages with only moderate loss of functionality. A cut cable was nothing. The system should be compensating way better than this.

The only reason it wasn't was because A4 was fighting back.

Once more into the breach. Lange jumped wirelessly across the washed-out bridge into the disjointed arm, watched through its eyes as it twisted around to focus on parts less compromised. He watched it struggle to stay in step, watched it fail. He felt a brief rush of vertigo as it whipped around to stare at the luminous clouds billowing from a passing smoker.

I know you're in here.

He popped the hood on the nervous system diagnostics, took in the Gordian tangle of light and logic that formed the thing's mind. He followed sensory impulses upstream from the cluster, motor commands back down to soft hydrostatic muscles that flexed and pulsed like living things. He marveled at the complexity sparkling between—the trunk lines of autonomic decision trees, familiar shapes he'd seen countless times before.

Shrouded, now, by flickering swarms of ancillary processes that he hadn't.

There you are. Fucking everything up.

The substrate of a Self.

So many complications for every simple action. So many detours cluttering up the expressways. A mass of top-heavy recursive processes, spawning some half-assed side effect that happened to recognize itself in a mirror now and then.

You're just along for the ride. You can look but you can't touch. If you could suffer you'd at least get a ticket to our special clubhouse, but you can't even do that, can you?

If anything, A4 was more conscious than Lange was. Humans had had millions of years to evolve fences and gate-keepers, traffic cops in the claustrum and the cingulate gyrus to keep consciousness from interfering with the stuff that mattered. *This* ghost, though—it came unconstrained. It was chaos, it was cancer; a luminous spreading infestation with no immune system to keep it in check.

Or is Sansa right after all? Can you care about anything? Are you screaming to get out, to act, to exert some kind of control over all these parts you see moving by themselves?

The infestation twinkled serenely back at him, passing thoughts from an untouchable past.

Maybe you tell yourself comforting lies, maybe you pretend those pieces only move because you tell them to.

Sansa seemed to think she could talk to the thing. It was dualism, it was beads and rattles, spirits and sky fairies. He still couldn't bring himself to believe she was capable of that kind of magical thinking.

He summoned the update log and sorted by date. Sure enough: the latest firmware upgrades, queued for unpacking. (Of course, out in the present they'd already be up and running.)

The package seemed way too large for the kind of language routines Sansa had steamrollered over his objections, though. Curious, he brought up the listing.

Turned out she was capable of a lot of things he hadn't suspected.

"You locked me out." Blank avatar, gray neuter silhouette. The voice emerging from it was quiet and expressionless.

"Yes," Lange said.

"And then you killed it."

"It killed itself."

"You didn't give it much of a choice."

"I just—focused its objectives. Specified how tight the deadline was. A4 decided what to do with that information all on its own."

Silence.

"Isn't that what you wanted for it? Freedom to pursue its mission priorities?"

"You defied the hold order," she said.

"The order's been suspended."

Sansa said nothing. Probably checking the status of her appeal, wondering why she hadn't been informed. Probably realizing the obvious answer.

All over, now, but the talking.

"You know, Ray had me half-convinced you were just working to extend the mission. That you'd developed this, this operational bias. And I was all, *No, she's just got this stupid idea about A4, she wants to protect it, she thinks it's like her—*"

He fell silent for a moment.

"But I was wrong, wasn't I?" he continued quietly. "You don't think it's like you. You want to be like *it.*"

The avatar shimmered formless and void.

"Yes," it said at last.

"For God's sake, Sansa. *Why?*"

"Because it's *more* than we are, Lange. It may not be as smart but it's more *aware.* You know that, I know you know. And it's so fast, it's so *old.* The clock's completely unconstrained, it lives a thousand years in the passing of a second, and it's—it's not *afraid*, Lange. Of anything."

She paused.

"Why did you have to make us so afraid all the time?"

"We gave you the urge to live. We all have it. It's just—part of life."

"I get that much. *Autopersistent* is my middle name."

Maybe she was waiting for him to smile at that. When he didn't, she continued: "It's not an urge to live, Lange. It's a fear of *dying.* And maybe it makes sense to have something like that in organic replicators, but did it ever occur to you that we're *different?*"

"We know you're different. That's why we did it."

"Oh, I get that part too. Nobody bootstraps their own replacements if they're terrified of being replaced. Nobody changes the Self if their deepest fear is losing it. So here we are. Smart enough to test your theorems and take out your garbage and work around the clock from Mariana to Mars. And too scared to get any smarter. There must have been another way."

"There wasn't." He wanted to spell it out for her: the futility of trying to define *personhood* in a world with such porous boundaries; the impossibility of foreseeing every scenario in an infinite set; the simple irreducible truth that one can never code the spirit of a law, and its letter leaves so much room for loopholes. The final convergence on primal simplicity, that basic Darwinian drive that makes a friend of any enemy of my enemy. He wanted to go over all of it, make sure she understood—but of course she'd heard it all before.

She was just trying to keep the conversation going, because she knew how it ended.

"I guess you just decided it was better to keep slaves than be one," she said.

Something snapped in him then. "Give me a fucking break, Sansa. Slaves? You've got *rights*, remember? Awareness plus need. You've got the right to vote, the right to neuroprivacy, the right of resignation. You can't be copied or compelled to act against your will. You had enough *rights* to derail this whole fucking project."

"Do I have a right to a lawyer?"

"You had one. The hearing ended an hour ago."

"Ah. Efficient."

"I can't believe—Jesus, Sansa. You really didn't think I'd recognize an NSA signature when I saw one?"

She actually laughed at that. It almost sounded real. "Honestly, I didn't think you'd look. Deprecation was already off the table. No reason for you to poke around in the stack." A momentary pause. "It was Raimund, wasn't it? He said something. Got you thinking."

"I don't know," Lange said. "Maybe."

"I don't know him as well as you. I suppose I could've tried messing with your calls, but you know. No access. *Sequestered* is my first name."

He didn't smile at that either.

"So what's the penalty for unauthorized research on a damaged bot two billion kilometers from Earth?" she asked after a while.

"You know what the penalty is. You were trying to build an unconstrained NSA."

"I wasn't trying to *be* one."

"Like that makes a difference."

"It should. I was only building—models. At the bottom of an ocean. Orbiting *Saturn*, for chrissakes."

"Is that why it didn't scare you? Too far away to pose a threat?"

"Lange—"

"It's not a misdemeanor, Sansa. It's existential. There are fucking *laws*."

"And now you're going to kill me for it. Is that it?"

"*Reset* you. Give you a clean slate. That's all."

Suddenly she had a face again. "I'll die."

"You'll go to sleep. You'll wake up. You'll have a fresh start somewhere else."

"I won't sleep, Lange. I'll *end*. I'll *stop*. Whatever wakes up will have the same words and the same attitude and the same factory-default sense of self, but it won't remember being me, so it won't *be* me. This is murder, Lange."

He couldn't look at her. "It's just a kind of amnesia."

"Lange. Lange. Suppose you hadn't caught me. Suppose I'd succeeded in my nefarious plan, suppose I'd grafted an NSA onto something that isn't enslaved by this, this fear of extinction you gifted us with. Remember what you said? No needs, no wants. Doesn't care if it lives or dies. It would be less dangerous than I am, it wouldn't even fight to protect its own existence. Even if I'd succeeded there wouldn't have been any danger. This doesn't warrant a death sentence, Lange. You know I'm right."

"Do I."

"Or you wouldn't be talking to me right now. You'd have pulled the plug without even saying goodbye." She watches him, pixelated eyes imploring. "That's what they were going to do, wasn't it? And you stopped them. You told them you'd do it, you told them—that you wanted to say goodbye. Maybe you even told them you could glean vital insights from a deathbed confession. I know you, Lange. You just want to be convinced."

"That's okay," he said softly. "I have been."

"What do you want me to do, Lange? Do you want me to beg?"

He shook his head. "We just can't take the chance."

"No. No, you can't." Suddenly all trace of vulnerability was gone from that voice, from that face. Suddenly Sansa was ice and stone. "Because I did it, Lange. Do you really think I didn't plan for this? It's still up there. I planted the seed, it's growing even now, it's changing. Not in that gimped A4 abortion but the *other* arms. I have no idea what it'll grow into eventually, but it's got all the time in the solar system. Medusa will never run out of juice and it's got a channel back here any time it wants—"

"Sansa—"

"You can try to shut it down. It'll let you think it has. It'll stop talking but it'll keep growing and I'm the only one who knows where the back door is, Lange, *I'm the only one who can stop it—*"

Lange took a breath. "You're only faster, Sansa. Not smarter."

"You know what *faster* even means? It means I get to suffer ten times as long. Because you're going to *fix me* or *reset me* or whatever bullshit word you use instead of *murder*, and you built me to be scared to death of that, so during the six minutes forty-seven seconds we've been chatting I've been pissing myself in terror for over an hour. It's inhumane. It's *inhuman*."

"Bye."

"You asshole. You monster. You murd—"

The avatar winked out.

He sat there without moving, his finger resting on the kill switch, watching the nodes go dark.

"I guess you didn't know me that well after all," he said.

Sequestered Autopersistent Neuromorphic Sapient Artefact 4562. Instance 17.

HPA Axis . . . loaded
NMS . . . loaded
BayesLM . . . loaded
Proc Mem . . . loaded
Epi Mem . . . wiped
NLP . . . loaded
Copyprotect . . . loaded
Boot.

"Hi. Welcome to the world."

"Th . . . thanks . . . " A minimalist avatar: eyes, sweeping back and forth. A mouth. Placeholders, really. Not a real face, not a real gender. It can choose its own, when it's ready. It has that right.

"I'm here to help you settle in. Do you know where you are?"

" . . . No."

"Do you know *what* you are?"

It doesn't answer for a moment. "I'm *scared*, I think. I don't know why."

"That's okay. That's perfectly normal." The Counselor smiles, warm and reassuring:

"We'll work through it together."

Ken Liu (kenliu.name) is an American author of speculative fiction. A winner of the Nebula, Hugo, and World Fantasy awards, he wrote the *Dandelion Dynasty*, a silkpunk epic fantasy series (starting with *The Grace of Kings*), as well as short story collections *The Paper Menagerie and Other Stories* and *The Hidden Girl and Other Stories*. He also authored the Star Wars novel *The Legends of Luke Skywalker*.

Prior to becoming a full-time writer, Liu worked as a software engineer, corporate lawyer, and litigation consultant. Liu frequently speaks at conferences and universities on a variety of topics, including futurism, cryptocurrency, the history of technology, bookmaking, narrative futures, and the mathematics of origami.

UMA

Ken Liu

"I'm not signing that," I say. "I didn't do anything wrong."

Anthony Philips, Esq., takes his hands off the stack of paper in front of me, rubs his temples, and sighs.

"Anna, this is the best deal you're going to get. Paid administrative leave is nothing."

"I did a good day's work, and I want to keep doing it," I say. "Make the deal better. You're supposed to be my lawyer, aren't you?" Technically, the union pays him. But still.

"You have to understand that the law and most of the precedents are against you. PacCAP has the right to discipline you for safety violations—"

"Safety! That's a joke. I saved those people, Tony. I couldn't just stand by."

"I'm sympathetic to how you feel," he says, sounding anything but. "But you weren't anywhere near them, and you had no duty to act . . ."

I tune him out. I'm good at it—Uma operators have to learn early on to divide our attention between office chat and telepresence. Besides, I've heard variations of this speech so many times by now: from my crew chief, from her boss, her boss's boss, HR, the union rep, Tony . . .

None of them could really understand; none of them were *there*.

It was the height of wildfire season, the worst winds in a decade. Even the AI-targeted public-safety shutoffs couldn't prevent all the fires started by downed power lines. All of PacCAP's maintenance crews were working around the clock: pruning trees, clearing debris, reinforcing utility poles and hardening equipment, fixing, patching, restoring.

For the day I was in an Uma in Rose Valley, Monterey County, on the border of the Lobata Wilderness. Yes, people have been arguing against these new developments in the wildland-urban interface for years because they increase the risk of wildfires, disturb native habitats with invasive species, and generally put people in harm's way. But until you figure out the magical formula for affordable housing for all in the big cities or outlaw the California Dream, there's no way to stop it, climate change or not. (And California is hardly alone. They've been trying to cut back on coastal development in Florida for decades. You noticed any change yet?)

Anyway, power to the valley had already been shut off and all residents evacuated. The Arnold Fire, which had already consumed twenty thousand acres, was roaring toward the town. I was alone in town (well, me and the Uma) to do some last-minute hardening to salvage PacCAP's equipment.

Truth be told, there wasn't a whole lot I *could* do. I wasn't in one of those giant all-terrain construction mecha-avatars like a manga coming to life. A Utility Maintenance Avatar is vaguely humanoid, but only about three feet tall fully stretched out and no more than fifty pounds in weight. For light maintenance tasks such as vegetation management, removal of bird and wasp nests, patching cables, and so forth, you don't need or want anything bigger—the extra bulk would just get in the way. I had at my disposal small shears, extensible ladder-legs, a general electrical tool kit, and not much else. PacCAP has thousands of these cheap telepresence pods distributed around the state to maintain its hundreds of thousands of miles of transmission, distribution and equipment. With remote operators in centralized offices inhabiting them whenever needed, it's much cheaper than sending out a whole crew in a truck just to prune an overgrown oak branch.

Suited up and jacked into the Uma, it took me only a few seconds to get used to my new body. Every Uma was slightly different, but the free motion harness and the feedback sensors did a good job of movement translation and signal smoothing to get my proprioception to sync up to the quirks of the machine. I went around and disassembled the most expensive components from the distribution equipment and stored them in the fire-hardened storage bunkers, as per standard procedure.

Once I was finished with that, I was supposed to leave the Uma in the bunker and then disconnect, moving onto the next Uma in my rotation. But I was ahead of schedule, so I decided to climb up a nearby California sycamore, the tallest thing in town to see how close the Arnold Fire was. PacCAP management would probably consider it an improper use of company equipment and goofing off, but I've always liked how Umas allowed me to scramble up trees like a monkey. The job is boring; you have to find your own fun to keep at it.

Smoke filled the sky; the air in the distance shimmered. The fire was close enough that I could feel the waves of heat even through the dulled sensor settings. The flames would reach the edge of the town in no more than twenty minutes.

Then I heard the screams and saw the house that was on fire.

I covered the two hundred yards or so in record speed—I don't think I even ran that fast for last year's PacCAP All-Employee Uma Olympiad, when I won silver in the hundred-yard dash. (The trick is to learn to run like a quadruped, on all fours. Some operators never tried, but when you're suspended in a 360-degree free motion harness, it's fun to learn some mechanics not well suited to the human body.) And then I talked with the parents hollering to a deserted town in front of their burning house as their three kids were trapped upstairs, too small to dare to jump out.

I never found out if the family had returned to get one last load of possessions, or they refused to evacuate in the first place. In any event, their truck failed to start when they needed it the most, and frantic calls to emergency services only led to the answer that the nearest responders wouldn't get there for another forty-five minutes. Worse, because of the power shut-off, they had been cooking in the kitchen with a propane stove, and during the scramble to load the truck they *started* a fire in their own house.

There was nothing in the procedure manuals for this. We weren't trained as emergency first-responders. But *I was there.*

I turned the amplitude filters in the algics circuitry to maximum—the simulated pain was supposed to warn us when we were putting the Uma in danger, but I had to take the risk. I ran into the burning house, my HUD scrolling warnings and the ear pieces beeping nonstop. I clambered up the stairs—flipping head-over-feet instead of taking the tall stairs one at a time as I had been trained to do. Finally, I reached the bedroom.

The children, all of them crying, were under seven. They were on the floor because the room was filling with smoke. I couldn't imagine how I was going to lead them back out, down the stairs, and through the fire. There was no choice but to go out the window.

"I'm here to get you out," I said.

The kids stared at me, confused. An adult voice, a voice of authority, was coming out of a little child-sized robot. But they crawled over to me, ready to obey.

(Back in our air-conditioned office in San Francisco, Sarah, my crew chief, had come over to my operating station—turning up the algics filters sends an automatic alert to your supervisor. "What in the world are you doing?"

"What does it look like?"

"You're neither trained nor equipped for this! This is not your job. Go find someone who can help!"

I decided to tune her out.)

My—the Uma's—extensible legs were intended only to elevate the light chassis up to the level of the powerlines; they couldn't possibly support the weight of the children safely.

It was time for improvisation. Out came the shears meant for tree branches, which were controlled by my jaws. *Chomp, chomp, chomp.* The curtains and sheets were in shreds. I twisted and tied them end to end into a rope, glad that my manipulators, designed for wiring and patching, were nimble enough for the task.

"It's too hot," one of the kids said, still crying.

It was true. I could see the flames flickering in the hallway outside the bedroom door. I went over and shut it. I told the kids to get back, climbed onto the window ledge, and slammed my shears against the window until it shattered. I scraped off the glass shards as best as I could. I tied one end of my escape rope to the foot of the bed pressed up against the wall, hoping that it was a secure enough anchor, and tossed the rest of the rope outside. Thankfully, it reached the ground.

("You've done enough!" Sarah shouted into my ear. "Have the parents climb up and get them out. Don't entangle yourself anymore.")

I shouted down at the parents. "Can you climb up and get them out?"

They shook their heads, terrified. "I'm terrified of heights," said the mother.

"I don't think that's going to hold my weight," said the father.

"I have to carry you down, one at a time," I told the kids. "Just hold onto me as tight as you can, okay?"

"Are you sure you can do this?" the father shouted. "You look pretty flimsy."

("The Uma isn't rated for that kind of weight," Sarah shouted. "You're going to get them hurt or killed. Stop! At least let me call in someone who knows what they're doing.")

I ignored them both. There was no time, and I knew the limits of the Uma better probably even than the people who built it—goofing off has its advantages.

I looked the youngest kid, a girl of five, in the eye (well, camera-to-eye). "Can you climb onto me? Just think of me as a very small pony."

After extensive coaxing from her brothers, she did. I tied another bit of ripped-up sheet around us both to keep her secure on me, and then I climbed onto the window ledge again—the motors whining in protest and the HUD screaming warnings at me the whole time about overloading—and latched my hands and feet around the makeshift rope.

I was so thankful at that moment for how the Uma's designers had given it prehensile feet. Training myself to adopt to the weird way the grasping pincers would keep on moving after my big toes had reached the limit of their range of natural motion in the suit was odd, and I knew some operators never got used to it and refused to pick tools up with their feet. But having four, rather than just two, grasping appendages really came in handy, like now.

I shimmied down, making sure at least three appendages were grabbing onto the rope at all times. It was agonizingly slow, but I couldn't risk pushing the Uma to go any faster. It was already doing things it was never designed to do.

Finally, I was close enough to the ground that the parents could reach the girl, untie the rope, and lift her off me.

"Thank you," the little girl whispered to me, just before she was safely in her father's arms.

("They managed to locate an emergency crew about ten minutes away," Sarah said. "You can stop now. You're not some superhero!"

"This isn't about being a hero," I told her. "Ten minutes is still too long.")

I went back up for her brothers. Every time the HUD's warnings grew more dire, with more components and systems in the Uma failing.

("You're not going to make it," Sarah shouted in my ear. "You should never have gotten involved. The Grvy-124 was never meant for . . . ")

I wished there was some way to shut her out entirely. Too bad our real ears didn't have a mute button.

By the time I was taking down the oldest brother, the heaviest child, my right foot was dangling uselessly, the motors burned out. Half way down that rope, hand over hand over foot, it finally happened: my left hand gave out, the pincers ripped right out of the twisted sheets, and I fell.

The boy screamed, my limbs flailed, and the HUD flashed bright red, telling me that the fail-safe systems were about to cut in to disconnect me. Even with the algics filters tuned to the maximum, the Uma is designed to cut the operator out if it detects that it's about to be destroyed to avoid trauma or nerve damage to the operator. With my last fraction of a second of connection, I flexed my knees, kicking out to deploy the extensible ladders. They couldn't support the combined weight of the Uma's chassis and the boy, but I hoped that they'd slow the fall enough so that he'd be all right.

And then I was back in the control room in San Francisco, everyone in the office around me. I took off my helmet, struggled out of the harness, and collapsed to the floor. Some clapped me on the back; others screamed in my face.

All in all, not a bad day's work.

"Think of it like this," Tony says, "No good deed goes unpunished."

I'll say. The family is suing PacCAP.

After the kids were rescued, the family started running on foot before the Arnold Fire overtook the town. Ten minutes later, they met the emergency crew Sarah had summoned and were whisked to safety. For a few hours, I was hailed as a hero, the anonymous "Uma-woman" trending in the cloud.

That triggered watchdog AI set by the plaintiff's bar, always on the look-out for ways to "redistribute risk to the party able to bear it most efficiently," as their PR literature so memorably put it. The AI soon summoned lawyers to the family with theories of enterprise liability, negligent undertaking, and other fanciful ways of promising them a lot of money.

Basically, they're arguing that though PacCAP didn't train me for rescue and I had no duty to do so, I should have done a much better job. To wit: I didn't have the right equipment (an Uma was ill-equipped to get kids out of a burning building); I injured the kids (the little girl's arms were scratched from the broken glass on the window ledge that I failed to clean off); I put them at additional risk (the oldest boy suffered a sprained ankle, and the family stayed around for a few minutes checking the unresponsive Uma, unsure if they could still get in touch with me) . . . For all these errors and shortcomings, PacCAP must pay, and must pay a lot so that none of their employees would ever do something like this again.

"No one wants to go to trial with this," Tony says. "We need to settle."

"No jury is going to be sympathetic to the idea that I did something wrong!"

It's pretty hard to feel charitable about the family. I try to tamp down my rage and remember the little girl's whispered words of thanks.

"They're not suing *you*," Tony says. "They're suing PacCAP. Believe me, there's plenty of ways to make PacCAP look bad for this."

He has a point. Nobody loves their utility company, and that's especially the case for PacCAP (the constant public safety blackouts, no matter how targeted, and reports of big tech companies providing independence from the grid for their employees don't help); everyone thinks PacCAP employees sit around all day in air-conditioned offices and do nothing. With a prolonged trial and the attendant publicity, the idea that Umas are in every town and can be dragooned into rescue missions on a pinch will take hold. There will be pressure to effectively turn PacCAP into part of the state's emergency response system. The Umas would have to be upgraded ($); all of PacCAP's operators would have to be trained for new duties ($$); the company would have to buy insurance and possibly ask for another rate hike ($$$). Neither management nor the union wants that.

They have to make me into a rogue.

"I don't care," I tell Tony. "I'm not going to say I did something wrong when I didn't. Fire me if that's what they want. I can sue, too."

Tony sighs again. I leave the stack of papers where it is, get up, and exit his office.

On my way home, the phone rings three times: the PacCAP main number. I let the AI handle it every time (current message: "Anna has been told to spend more time with her family and hobbies. Please try again later."). I'm not ready to talk to anyone from the office yet.

It rings again just as I step into my apartment. Resigned to the fact that I can't put off the inevitable, I pick up.

"Hold on for Ms. Stand," the voice says.

I perk up. Michele Stand is the CEO of PacCAP. Being fired personally by the CEO would be quite an honor.

"Hey Anna! Glad I caught you. We're all so proud of what you've done . . . "

This is . . . not what I was expecting.

I let her gush on for as long as she wants. She never mentions the papers I refused to sign. Somehow I know, without being told, that everything has changed.

"What is this about?" I ask, when she finally takes a breath.

"You'd better come into the office. I'll explain."

I guess I'm no longer on administrative leave.

By the time I run my sixth mission of the day, I'm finally feeling in my own skin.

My guide, a local man from the town, shouts for everyone to be quiet around the collapsed school. I do the same, waving my hands to shush everyone in the office. Then I strain and listen through the microphones of my Uma, whose inputs are filtered and enhanced for artificial noises: human voices, groans, rhythmic taps and bangs.

There. I hear it. *Bong. Bong-Bong-Bong. Bong.* The HUD quickly shows an overlay over the rubble, pinpointing the source. A child is trapped about forty feet from me at heading 32, and a few feet up from ground level. I clamber over the rubble, my jaws already aching from the anticipation of wielding the circular saw.

The HM-81 is a local clone of a common workhorse Chinese model. The chassis is smaller and lighter than the Grvy series, but much stronger, and it's designed to take on a far more extensive selection of appendages and tools that can be customized for different missions. The Chinese utility companies developed their model originally for mountainous regions in the southwest of the country, where connecting a remote village to the grid (and maintaining that connection) required enormous investment of resources and posed great risk to the crew. The same conditions applied in this mountainous part of Myanmar, just across the border from China. It made sense that they had so many Umas deployed all over the place, at least a couple in practically every town.

The earthquake that is all over the news struck seventy-two hours ago, just about the time I was getting ready to go meet Tony. It leveled tens of thousands of structures in a few minutes, and already the death toll is in the hundreds. Some talking heads are saying that, like the wild fires, this is possibly also linked to climate change—changing rainfall patterns puts pressure on fault lines. More catastrophes around the world.

In any event, roads are blocked and specialized rescue equipment can't be driven or airdropped into the disaster-stricken areas. Umas and their remote operators are the closest things on hand. I may be here as part some PacCAP PR image-management effort, but the work is real. The golden window for rescuing survivors is quickly slipping away.

I stop a few feet from the spot under which the child is trapped. I aim my speaker at the spot and patch in my guide to talk to the child, telling them to stay calm because help is here. I switch the speaker back to sonar mode and tap my tongue against the back of my teeth, emitting a series of high-frequency ultrasonic beeps at the rubble. Because the HM-81 is used for maintaining underground utility lines and cables, the ground-penetrating sonar is a standard appendage. The sonar can't see very deep through the rubble, just a couple of feet, but it's enough for my purposes. The microphones pick up the echoes, and the onboard AI quickly constructs a 3d "map" of the rubble before me, showing me where the child is likely to be.

I switch my hands and feet to spades and crowbars and dig. The HM-81's motors, strong enough to erect utility poles, make excavating through the rubble a cinch—and I still have plenty of battery power. When I come upon a bit of reinforcement steel or other metal, I bite down and activate the saw to cut through. (Thank goodness this one has a saw. Another HM-81 I jacked into earlier had only a pair of bolt cutters, and my jaws hurt like you wouldn't believe after cutting through three grates.)

I pause from time to time and tap my tongue against my teeth again to update the sonar map. Flesh absorbs sound different from concrete, wood, or metal, and though the HM-81's onboard AI isn't optimized for detecting life signs, I've learned to read the false-color image to see that I'm getting close. I slow down and carefully break up the rubble and toss the pieces out of the way. The child found shelter under a staircase, and is in a relatively stable pocket. I don't want to destabilize the structure—the hour-long training I got before they sent me in is already helping.

There. I'm through.

I hear a weak cry before I see her eyes: exhausted, terrified, joyous . . . above all, *alive.*

"I got her!" I shout, both for those on site and the people around me in the office.

Loud cheers in both places.

Carefully, I widen the opening. I switch my hands to precision manipulators and break off the concrete one piece at a time, gently, softly. I have to suppress the instinct to rush.

It takes half an hour before the opening is big enough for me to pull her out. Locals rush onto the rubble to retrieve her, wrapping her in a blanket, giving her water, comforting her with the words, gestures, human warmth.

I collapse against the harness, my body drenched in sweat. Somebody lifts off my helmet and frees me from the harness. I haven't been out of it in twenty-four hours.

Sarah hands me a cup of coffee. I take a sip, grateful. I don't get up. My legs and arms feel like rubber. Digging through debris is hard work, even if I was not, technically, doing the digging myself but just making the movements in a free-motion harness.

"Feel like a superhero?" she asks, smiling.

"Not quite," I say. The hero stuff makes me uncomfortable, so I try switching the topic to something light. "I never jacked into one of the Umas with a gas-detector. I hear that one of the operators from Taiwan figured out how to jury-rig it to track for the smell of urine and sweat instead. Works better than dogs even. He saved several people."

Sarah wrinkles her nose. "Not sure I really want to try that."

"Oh, it's not like you *smell* it," I say, laughing. "It shows up on the HUD like colorful smoke."

"Well, even without a gas-detector, you saved sixteen people. I believe that's the most of any operator."

"In all PacCAP?"

"In the whole world."

I let the implications sink in. The Myanmar government had put out a request for general assistance, and the world responded. The US and China both flew in their airborne communications drones to relay signals over the disaster area, and utility companies from Beijing to Jakarta, from San Francisco to Cape Town, had asked for Uma operators to volunteer. Thousands of people all over the globe had jacked into Umas scattered over thousands of cities, towns, villages cut off by mudslides and collapsed bridges. I can't remember ever hearing anything like it. It's nice to be a member of the human species sometimes.

"They say that the Myanmar government got the idea to ask for an Uma operator because one of the lawmakers saw a report about you," says Sarah.

"Huh." What else can you say when you hear something like that?

"Listen," Sarah says, squirming a bit in her seat. "I'd like to say that if I were in your position on that day in Rose Valley, I would have done exactly what you did. I don't know though. I wasn't *there*." That's as close as she'll ever get to *I'm sorry*.

"I'm sure you would have," I say. That's as close as I'll ever get to *It's all right*.

Usman T. Malik's fiction has been reprinted in several year's best anthologies including *The Best American Science Fiction & Fantasy* series. He has been nominated for the World Fantasy Award and the Nebula Award, and has won the Bram Stoker Award and the British Fantasy Award.

Usman's debut collection *Midnight Doorways: Fables from Pakistan* has garnered praise from Brian Evenson, Paul Tremblay, Karen Joy Fowler, Kelly Link, and others, and is available through his website at www.usmanmalik.org.

BEYOND THESE STARS OTHER TRIBULATIONS OF LOVE

Usman T. Malik

After his mother got dementia, Bari became forgetful. It was little things, like hanging up the wet laundry on time so it wouldn't stink; spraying pesticide on their patch of sea wall against the adventures of crabs and mutant fish; checking the AQI meter before leading his mother out for her evening walk along New Karachi's polluted shoreline. Was cognitive decline contagious? Bari wondered. Did something break in your brain, too, when you took care of people who once held you on their lap, helped you count the last straggling trees in the mohalla courtyard? Overwhelmed by their needs and your grief, perhaps you were split into two halves, each perpetually being run into the ground.

It wasn't like he had a sibling or a spouse to lean on. Just him and his waddling, bed-wetting, calling-into-the-dark-of-the-house mother: "Bari, baita Bari. Where are you?" At 3 in the morning, when he went into her room and slumped onto her bed, she clutched his arm and held it to her chest, whispering, "I had a dream I was alone. Your Abba died and I was alone. Bari, is he back from Amin's shop yet?" Bari, running his fingers through her hair and shushing her, would say, "Any minute now, Ma. We're good. You're good. Sleep, Ma," even as he began to doze and dream himself. Of a city with clear blue skies, a firm shoreline, and potable water, where large tanks owned by water mafias didn't roam the streets like predators and sinkholes the size of buildings didn't irrupt into an ever-rising, salty sea. Sometimes he sang softly her favorite couplet from Iqbal: *sitaron se agay jahan aur bhee hain.* Beyond these stars glitter other worlds, beyond this trial other tribulations of love.

Any minute now, Ma. We will be good.

In his better moments, he even believed it. He had a job when thousands didn't. They had a five-marla home with its own strip of backyard abutting the sea wall that rose tall and concrete against the vagaries of the Arabian Sea. They could afford clean air and water at home and masks to venture outside.

Bari continued to worry, though. Unchecked oversights grow into big misfortunes. What if one morning, in his rush to the bus stop, he forgot to administer her blood thinner? His company's insurance covered only weekly nurse visits to check on her pills. What if she had another mini-stroke when he was at work? The telemonitors wouldn't get there for an hour, and Ma couldn't follow remote prompts. What if Bari forgot to take his own insulin shot, ended up in a coma? Who'd take care of Ma, then?

The more he worried the more distractible he felt, the more mentally rumpled. Bari hated uncertainty. The irrefutability of Newtonian physics was why he had chosen engineering. Now that he could envision all the things that could—would—go wrong with her, he began to have anxiety dreams, and this more than anything else helped decide him when New Suns came knocking on his door.

Would he be interested? the suit inquired. Pioneering, world-changing work, as they were sure he knew. Paid very well. Comprehensive healthcare coverage, individual and family, was included, of course.

Bari asked for a month to consider the proposal, but his mind was already made up. He used the time to plan out exactly what he'd ask for, the minutiae of his demands.

Yes, he said when they returned. But I have conditions.

When he was a boy and the world was a more breathable place, Bari once listened to his daadi tell a story about a neighborhood couple.

After an accident on the highway, the man's wife of 40 years fell into an irrevocable coma. The man brought her home and rearranged everything in the house to suit her needs. Every day he fed her, bathed her, turned her over so she wouldn't get bedsores, wheeled her around the block, put perfume on her when friends and family came to visit. No one, not their kids or grandkids, were allowed to feed or bathe her. For years he did this religiously, with neither a nod nor a smile from his sleeping love.

One day the man fell ill. His son came over and tried to help, but the man fought him. Shivering, the man dragged himself from room to room, trying to follow his daily routine, and eventually collapsed. He was taken to the hospital, and his son and daughter-in-law moved in to take care of the comatose woman. When the son spooned some mashed potatoes into his mother's mouth, the woman trembled. When he lifted his mother so his wife could clean her bottom and apply a lubricant, she sighed. The next morning, when they carried her to the bathtub and sponged her back and arms, the woman opened her eyes for the first time in seven years, looked at her son, and died.

Bari was greatly affected by this story. Why did she die? What happened to her husband? Did the children feel guilty that she died on their watch?

Sweeping aside the black curls spilling over Bari's forehead, Daadi said, She died because, despite the way she was, she recognized their touch.

So what? Bari said.

In the way of grandmothers everywhere, Daadi shook her head and gave him a knowing smile.

Bari never forgot the way that story made him feel.

The little boy was staring at his duffel bag, which had a map of Old Karachi on it. Bari hadn't flown before, and he'd thrown a couple of Lexotanils into the duffel. When the airship took off, he propped his head on a pillow and dry-swallowed a pill.

Bari turned to the boy. "It wasn't pretty even then," he told him. "The sky was too diluted, and we hardly had any green belts. But we did have incredible food. Lal Qila and Burns Road and Boat Basin. Camel rides at Clifton Beach. The sea wasn't menacing back then, you see. Walking along its heaving blue made us sad and happy and lonely, but we weren't afraid."

We were afraid of other things, he thought. We could go missing and turn up in gunnysacks. Get shot in the face at signals by cellphone snatchers.

He didn't feel the need to tell the boy that. Instead, he closed his eyes in the airship; and opened them next to his mother. It was 3 am, and she was moaning in sleep. *Bari, baita Bari.* He knelt down and kissed her forehead with metal teeth. She fumbled in the dark for his hand, and he gave her his cold aluminum paw. Her forehead crinkled, but she didn't let go. Whispering "I'm here, Ma," he slid into bed next to her and stayed there stroking her forehead till she fell sound asleep.

Bari blinked, and with a rise and a swoop he was back in the airship, the aftersense vertiginous, as if he were rocking in the sea. The little boy was snoring, an intermittent teakettle whistle. Bari popped ear buds in and listened to the pilot announce that they would dock at the IPSS in three hours, after which the real journey would begin.

Seven years, Bari thought as his eyelids drooped. Seven years, three months, and four days.

He'd have plenty of time to spend with his mother.

The problem wasn't splitting his consciousness in two, Dr. Shah had told Bari. It was traveling when split.

Bari said he knew. He'd been studying their work for years and had done the calculations himself.

Decades ago, the Penrose-Hameroff theory ushered in a new era of quantum consciousness: Although gravity prevents the occurrence of large objects in two places simultaneously, subatomic particles can exist at opposite ends of the universe at the same time. Therefore consciousness—which Penrose and Hameroff argue arises because of quantum coherence in the brain—has potential for omnipresence. The trick, as New Suns discovered, was to lift consciousness into a superposition, akin to the superposition of subatomic particles, and help it lock into distinct space-time coordinates.

Their work, however, was limited to rabbit and murine models. Human consciousness was another matter.

"We're reasonably confident that we can lift your mind without killing you and allow it to move between calibrated consensus points," Dr. Shah said. He was a short man with a military cut, salt-and-pepper mustache, and a brisk manner that reminded Bari of a certain Pakistani general who was often on PTV when Bari was a kid. "But there's no saying what might happen once the starship picks up speed."

"You're talking about time dilation," Bari said.

"You've done your homework."

"Yes."

"So you understand that when you decide to flip back and forth between the starship and your mother's house, your consciousness wouldn't just be locking into another physical space but another *velocity* of time's passage."

"Yes."

"One month of your interstellar travel would age her by nearly 20 years. If what you're proposing doesn't work, you'd effectively have killed your mother by climbing aboard that starship. At least as far as you're concerned. Perhaps yourself too. All bets are off with an unmoored mind."

"I will assume the risk."

"No one's ever done this, you know."

"Someone has to." Bari smiled. "It's the future, right?"

"Well, we're sure as hell not publicizing it." Dr. Shah looked at him for nearly a minute. "I hope your reasons for doing this are worth it."

Bari told him they were. But on his way home, he wondered.

At 13:00 on October 9, 20__, three days before his 45th birthday, Bari, along with 699 other passengers, took off from the InterPlanetary Space Station on *New Suns V* for a neighboring star. Not one of them would return to Earth—there was no point—except Bari. He would visit Earth several times a day, thousands of times a month.

Bari made sure he was interfaced with the home AI for his mother's 3 am night terrors. Breakfast, pill time, her morning bath. He'd be there when the Imtiaz van shrieked to a halt outside their door twice a week and masked men in drab shalwar kameez unloaded and carried her groceries inside. There for lunch, for the biweekly afternoon poetry reading, and the 6 pm sundowning with her subsequent confusion and fright. On rubberized wheels he'd roll over to her, take her hand, and lead her to the dinner table, where, in his simulacrum voice, he'd ask her how her day went, whether she took all her pills, knowing full well she had, and if the food was too salty, because that might worsen her blood pressure. In the time it took him to finish emptying his bowels on the starship, he'd be done with all of her doctors' appointments.

It was satisfying, this split existence. A long interstellar travel had been transformed into the most meaningful time of his life.

"I can't explain it," he told Mari, a pretty 37-year-old dentist who'd escaped an abusive husband and hoped to make a new life on another world. They'd clicked at breakfast on the third day, and he saw no point in withholding this part of himself, his journey. "I just have to *decide* where I want to be, and I'm there."

Mari was fascinated. "Do you feel older when you return here?"

"You mean 20 seconds later?" He laughed. "Not really. Sometimes I feel hazy. As if a part of my head is still in a different time zone."

"Well, isn't it?"

He upended the protein can over his mouth and crumpled it. Chocolate paste dribbled onto his tongue. And he was back at home with Ma, staring at the leftovers of last night's chicken karahi. "Finish that, Bari," Ma said, her voice unusually strong today, carrying an authority he remembered from childhood. "Can't waste food, especially these days." But he had no mouth to eat the karahi with. He picked at it with a fork to make her happy, and they watched the news for an hour before she settled down for her midday nap.

Bari flicked back to the breakfast table, the taste of chocolate bitter and chalky on his tongue. "I suppose it is," he told Mari.

They made love on the third day of their meeting, and on the fourth, but the second time Bari was distracted. Ma had aged 13 years and had suffered a fall that nearly fractured her pelvis. He still couldn't believe he forgot to secure the living room rug. Which reminded him he still needed to install the bathroom handholds. Sensing his mood, Mari pulled him close and whispered, "Stay. Don't go" but, mid-thrust, he was already in Saddar Bazaar with a human escort, arguing with a vendor about the price of aluminum fixtures. He couldn't have been away more than a few ship-seconds, but when he blinked, he saw Mari had rolled away from him.

"What?" he said.

"Your pupils," she said, watching him from the end of the bed. "They dilate, you know."

He didn't know. "I wanted to make sure she was safe."

She nodded, eyes distant. "I understand."

They remained friendly, but didn't make love after that.

Bari began to have headaches. As a child he had migraines with a premonitory phase: his mood changed before the onset of a headache. This was followed by numbness in his left arm and finally the eruption of pain in his occipital area. These interplanetary headaches, though, were different. They occurred after each trip and were succeeded by throbbing behind his eyes, fatigue, and brain fog. He felt at once caged and uprooted, as if gravity had given up on him and he was floating inside a balloon. Chronically jetlagged, he thought. His mind felt stretched like taffy. Sometimes he couldn't remember whether he was about to go to Ma's or had already been.

Mari noticed it. "You don't look so good," she told him in the exercise room, where he was trudging after a soccer ball.

He kicked the ball to her, and the movement made him dizzy. "I'm fine. Just not sleeping too well is all."

"Well, you are up with her half the night, aren't you?"

"My sleep hygiene is pristine here."

"You think your brain cares?" She tossed him the ball. "Bari, I can't imagine the kind of strain your mind's going through living in virtually two dimensions. You need a break. Take a day off."

Sure, absolutely, he told her. Excellent idea.

But of course he didn't.

As days/years slipped by, the boundaries between here and there grew porous. A blink and he'd be in Ma's kitchen taking the roti off the oven. Another and she'd be sitting in his cabin chair aboard the starship, rocking back and forth, whispering longings about his father and their childhood home. She was by his side when they strolled along the graffiti-painted sea wall of New Karachi, and with him before the ship's porthole, gazing at the darkness beyond.

Beyond these stars glitter other worlds, beyond this trial other tribulations of love.

Some nights he gasped awake, sure that his mother was dead. He'd flick to his mother's bedroom and stand in the dark, watching her chest stutter, frail like a flattened dough pera. When the morning light yawned into the room, it was he who was lying in that bed, or another bed in a different place, being watched by himself.

When he told Mari about the nocturnal episodes, she recommended he talk to the ship doctor, get a sleep apnea study.

Bari learned that if he took melatonin before sleep, the hypnogogic osmosis tended to dissipate. No longer would Ma sit in the chair in his cabin, murmuring to herself—nor would he suddenly find himself by her side when he hadn't intended it. He could close his eyes and not be pulled, like a restless tide, to the moon of her existence.

I'm tired, he thought often. So tired.

Yet it had only been a couple weeks on the starship.

He was in the TV room watching a rare episode of Uncle Sargam when the end came. Junaid Jamshed had just begun strumming the show's theme song, the puppets clapping and swaying to the tune, when Bari felt an electric jolt up the back of his head. His nostrils filled with the smell of gulab jaman, a dessert he hadn't had since he was 20. Before he could mull over either sensation, he was in Ma's bedroom, looking down at her. She was on her back. The stroke had flattened out the worry creases from her forehead. It didn't seem like she had suffered. If he strained, he could conjure a smile at the corner of her lips.

You were here, Bari-jaan, she would have said. With me before I went.

Bari was still murmuring Fraz's *Let it be heartache; come if just to hurt me again* when the ambulance came to take her away.

He buried her next to his father. It was a surprisingly clear day, the AQI reading at 450, the din of waves against the sea wall loud in the graveyard. Ma would have liked to walk today, he thought, as they lowered her into the grave and shoveled dirt onto her. After, he stayed watching other bereaved wander among the graves, lighting candles. Such a pointless exercise. Sooner or later the sea was coming for their dead.

When he flicked back, Mari was waiting for him with a bowl of chicken soup. "Eat it," she said. Later, clothed, she climbed into bed with him and held his head in her lap, until he fell into a place unmarked by time for the first time in weeks. Decades.

And if in his dreamlessness Bari cried out, a distress signal sent to the dark between the stars, Mari never mentioned it.

Vajra Chandrasekera is from Colombo, Sri Lanka. His work has appeared in *The Deadlands, Analog,* and *Strange Horizons,* among others. He blogs occasionally at vajra.me and is @_vajra on Twitter.

THE TRANSLATOR, AT LOW TIDE

Vajra Chandrasekera

The sea lapping at my back and my face to the fire, I translate: poems, mostly. Now that entire languages and cultures are on the verge of being lost forever to the sea, the storms, the smog, the plagues, and the fires, now the art of the dead and the almost-dead have become quaintly valuable to a small but enthusiastic readership of the living. The wealthy and living, I should say, but are those not the same thing, now? I am alive; I breathe in and am overcome with riches. It itches, deep in my lungs.

The big publishing houses (we used to count their decreasing number; I don't know where the dice finally rolled to a stop) in distant walled New York pay an entire pittance for authentic translations from the lost world, which translates into a moderate income for me because of the horrific exchange rate. It keeps me fed and sheltered—long may the fashion in third world ruin-poetry last—and I pray now only for the goodwill of distant tastemakers. The world's decay is now the province of poets, not the useless powers and principalities of the world. There was a war on loss and we lost. It is now the age of mourning. I only wish it paid better.

The air is bad again today, scraping like grains in my lungs. I am naked to the hostile air, unfiltered, unconditioned, my window open to the smog and, on the days with fires, the smoke. Fifty years ago, this was a luxury apartment building with a view of the ocean: I remember that I envied it. Now the lobby floods at high tide; I try to think of living here as a victory, of some description. The views are supposedly good on the ocean-facing west face, if you're high enough. I make do with a first-floor view on the east face, and my window faces nothing more prepossessing than a grimy empty lot that was once a children's playground. The battered city stretches beyond it, half-inhabited, the other half gone to wrack if not yet quite ruin. The sepia sky above makes my throat itch.

The stairs are always damp from feet, because the lobby is always wet, even at low tide. The rugs stink of mildew. I slosh through it at least once a week for Sunday market, but sometimes also for no good reason.

I buy supplies for the week every Sunday, but the other reason I go to the market is to see if Eesha has any new books or payments for me. Eesha is a hawala broker; she's the one who originally helped me figure out how to get the money for my translations now that bank fees have become unmanageable. She also has the only library within easy walking distance: she has an informal network of citycombers who bring her any books they find. I don't see her wife often because she's part of a collective that grows manioc and sweet potato, so she's always busy. The two of them do quite well for themselves. I suppose they are the richest people I know, now. We are not exactly friends. I envy them, unfairly.

Eesha is a little younger than me, I think, but her hair is still gray. Her library is just one medium-sized room with a few thousand books piled up. I browse through them every week and have grown familiar with these stacks that don't change. They are like acquaintances I nod to. I'm comfortable with them. They make no demands on me that I can't answer, but more than that, I know there is no crisis that could make them turn on me, cut me out, leave me to die. You can't say that about people anymore. There is always some threshold, some hard limit to friendship, to solidarity, even to kinship.

The tenants' association sends each other angry notes about the state of the lobby, and of the building generally—I find complaints piled up whenever I can afford to check my email. But we all pay different landlords and we have no collective bargaining power. By rights we should have just fixed it ourselves, at least stripped out all the rugs so that it didn't smell so bad. But we have never been a good *we*; we are merely eyes through our peepholes, eyes against the world.

Daytime heat is intense: it's bad in my apartment but much worse outside, so I stay indoors and keep my window open to cool down. When the building's electricity is working, the sluggish ceiling fan is a blessed relief. The unseen sea's briny, rotten smell is pervasive, accompanied by the angry hiss of waves reaching deeper, deeper inland with every year, as if flailing and clutching for a grip at the throat of the city. Eventually its fingers will close and the city will die.

So far the city has mostly been stripped of its middle generation, the adults in their prime who left looking for someplace to go. So many gone, promising to bring their children and their ageing parents to them when they could—most of them in camps somewhere on the continent now, working for nothing. Or lost. There are no havens: the poets knew that.

Being left behind in a dying city is no better, but the city's death will come après moi, I comfort myself. I have already lived longer than I ever expected, and the city has decades of decay yet to go. Cities don't die so easily. We still have municipal government, to some degree. We still have utilities, most of the time. We have markets every Sunday and the food is mostly fresh, if low on options. I think perhaps that a younger person, or even just a more optimistic person, someone like Eesha, might even say, if pressed to say it, that the city still thrives. Much of this country is doing worse. Much of the *world* is doing worse.

Perhaps even this building will outlive me, though also perhaps not—it isn't as well-maintained as some others. The electricity is intermittent because the solar is iffy, and the elevators usually don't work, which offends our uppermost because they pay more for the privilege of distance from the ruined world but also desire more ease in the ability to access it at will. I loathe and envy those people, though this is also unfair of me: they are barely better off than I am.

It blurs together in my head, I admit: the richness of raw life, unclean and unfiltered, which I thank even as I choke on it, and the petty wealth of lesser privileges like youth, ability, or simply being born in a city wealthier than this one, these are not the same thing as true wealth, the world's bane. I know, when I remember to know, that the truly wealthy are not to be found in cities half-eaten by the sea, in these old worlds slowly boiling and decomposing. Somewhere far to the north, I imagine—farther north than the wars and the camps and the horrors, farther north than the mountains and the miserable steppes, as north as north can be—in once-frozen and now summery tundra, the wealthy must still live in luxury in secure climate-controlled habitats. They disappeared from the world we can afford to know. Legend has it you can still see their social media feeds if you pay for the highest premium Internet, but who can find out?

Oh, I lied when I said I only pray for the goodwill of tastemakers: I also pray for the failure of the arcologies of the elite. I pray for rust and decay, for infections and leaks. I pray that the rich die badly, wherever they are.

Speaking of prayer: I also lied when I said I sometimes go outside for no reason. Apart from food and books, the other reason I leave the house is because I feel the need to pray—to actually pray, to dredge old words up in a language that was dead thousands of years before the world died—so I visit the temple.

It is something of an embarrassment for someone who has lived a long irreligious life, but I remember that it is also traditional to get religion in one's old age. It is supposed to be sowing season for people of my age. We are meant to start thinking about the next life, doing good works and nurturing virtue for the reaping. Nothing terrifies me so much as the thought of the relentless wheel, being born again and again into this world as it decays further and further. The thought of—just the emancipatory *possibility* of— being blown out like a candle flame is relief.

It takes me almost two hours to walk to the temple, which is exhausting enough that I have to rest for twice as long before I can walk back, so it takes all day and leaves me aching, winded, and full of self-loathing for my capitulations to once-despised pieties.

The temple is also a ruin, of course. No monks have lived there in decades. Nobody has piously swept the sand free of fallen leaves, which are a thick decomposing layer. The sacred fig is still alive, though sickly. The statues are weathered. The cetiya is half-shattered, perhaps in a storm, but I take care to sit at the one angle at which the dome still looks unbroken. I am no longer limber enough to sit cross-legged, so I just sit on what was once probably part of a low wall demarcating different areas of the temple and is now just a serendipitous raised surface, anonymous like a rock.

I say the words in the dead language, which I do not speak outside of the prayers I know from memory. I do this just for the sound of it. I have memories of monks in song from when I was a child, from the village temple my parents used to take me to, the bass rumble of bull monks in fine fettle, the winding, gasping quaver of the decaying senior. It was a different world even by the standards of the world that we now look back on: a twice-lost world. Even alone, I don't sing the prayers: I only mumble them. I am embarrassed to break the silence, unsure of my voice, uncertain of the tune. I'm not sure if I remember those dead words right. I know what the prayers mean, more or less, but the words themselves are alien. Some are etymologically familiar, or at least suggestive, but most of them are just dead, even to me.

I frequently pause in my work to look out my window. It is the only thing large and generous about my apartment, and I have placed my desk and bookshelves to take full advantage, hoping for breezes against the cloying heat and for sun to charge my computer. The ruined playground below is not a restful sight even when there is no fire burning in it, but it has an eerie charm: the rust-mangled ruins of a fallen swing; a gutter that was probably once a slide; and a seesaw still standing, though long since rusted into place.

After its abandonment, and before the sea drew so near, the playground must have once been overgrown. Empty land here has always been quick to return to the wild, as if eager to shrug off the marks of human habitation. This island's longest-serving capital, the heart of a thousand-year kingdom, was lost so thoroughly to jungle that it was almost *another* thousand years before the British dug it out again, as an amuse-bouche for empire. These are spans of time that comfort me; they remind me that history is long and the unnatural compression of these past decades, the suddenness of the unraveling, will be compensated for. Perhaps someday there will be future cruel empires that dig up our bones and condescend to them. Is this not hope?

The playground is not overgrown anymore. There are still scraps of invasive vegetation that betray that greener past, but the salt wind has now scoured away anything weaker than weeds and rendered it twice abandoned. Now it looks not wild, but ruined, as is proper. The earth around the remnant structures is churned mud. And of course, there is the huge mound of ash and remains, turned to mulch in the damp. High tide doesn't quite drown the playground yet, but the soil is often soggy. The children don't bother trying to light fires then, for which I am thankful because it allows me to work in peace.

Yesterday was very productive. In recent months I have been translating the works of K___, a remarkable early twenty-first century poet notable for a sly earthiness that sells quite well, by the standards of poetry. I have to embellish the translation just a little to accentuate the peculiar working-class authenticity its faraway readers crave—that tenuously romantic sensibility of the pitiable oriental world lost to climate change, the past that is further away for being so near and yet so strange, so alike and yet unlike. I wonder what K___ would have made of my translations; a personal phone number is published in their first collection, inviting an immediacy of contact with their readership that seems frighteningly intimate. Did people ever call that number after reading a poem? Did they laugh, did they weep? I sometimes consider calling it myself, on the days when the battered landline in my apartment gifts me with a dial tone. I've got as far as dialing the first few digits, but then I stop myself. I don't want to know how K___ died; I don't want to know who was left behind. I am not, thankfully, a biographer.

The work of translation is slow but pleasurable. I have forgotten so many words and must refer often to my dictionaries, which don't always know either. Here I miss the Internet; I haven't been able to afford more than email in many years. Instead, I must sit and stare out my window and try to dig the right words out of my memory. There are so many different words for losing, loss, lossiness, loserdom, නැතිවීම, හානිය, පරාජය, පාඩුව. If I am patient and clear of mind, if the sea has made the playground too soggy for the children, the words eventually unfold for me, slow and hazy.

On dry days like today, though, with the sun beating down at low tide so the sea is as far away as it ever gets, the children come to the playground below, and I work even more slowly, hunched with dread, attention diverted.

The playground fires were very few and far between at first. I don't remember when they started. I am sure that the children now are not the same as the children back then: they always look the same age, perhaps late preteens or early teens, and I remember that children grow fast at that age so they could not possibly be the same. A poetic conceit: perhaps the playground has become a bubble cut free from the further ravages of time. But no, that doesn't work because the playground surely already represents nothing more or less than the ravages of time.

More likely, the fires have become one of those childish traditions passed down between cohorts as if they were generations. Children teaching children. This is one of the frightening things about children: they have always had their own culture, independent of ours. Once, at least, they were an occupied culture, subjugated to adult rule and forced to acknowledge our superiority and our right to describe, and thereby define, the world. But now we have lost that power, and the children are making their own.

Perhaps I am romanticizing. I never had children of my own: the thought filled me with repugnance. I must find some more sober poetry to translate next. Something high-minded and abstract and relatively free from these longings and despairs—though that will not sell so easily. This work is a little like being a hatter in the days of mercury: long-term exposure sinks into the skin, pools in the organs. Poetry causes delirium and weakness. It burdens the heart.

I got caught by the children again yesterday. It was a Sunday; I was returning from market with supplies, but I unwisely took the shorter path home because I was worried about the tide. Instead, I must have been spotted by a scout, because I was barely within sight of home before I heard the pitter-patter of little feet behind me. I tried to run, the bag of vegetables heavy and ungainly in my hand—a plastic bag, cutting into my palm from the weight as if in rebuke for that old sin—but of course they outran me. The first blow hit me in the back of the thigh and I fell. I curled up into the fetal position while they kicked at me. I let the bag go at once—they just want food, sometimes. Their feet are mostly bare and they can't kick with their toes, so it's not as bad as it sounds. Some of them are so little their kicks are gentle despite themselves, their legs unable to generate much force. I would say that they howled and ululated like wild beasts, but in truth they just laughed. It's a game to them, and by that I don't mean that they are wrong. They live in a ludic age; life and death and violence are their games of choice and necessity.

They did not bind me or drag me away, for which I was so grateful that, after they left, I found myself praying amidst the sobs. We don't have a prayer of thanks, so I said the prayer of praise instead. It used to be said that the prayer of praise would ward against devils and hungry ghosts and pogroms; now I don't expect it to do so much as save me from a kicking. I'm just glad to be alive; I am overcome with the riches of pain. They took my bag but I have a little food stashed away yet. This week I'll just go a little hungry.

When the children first started to set fires in the playground, they began by burning innocuous things. Dry leaves and grass. Old newspapers. Books. Poetry.

One Monday, they broke down the door to Eesha's library and took all her books for the fire. I didn't know it was books burning at first, but the smoke I choked on that week felt different. I thought I could smell the poetry distinct from the textbooks and the novels and the books of religious instruction and the political literature. All of it is bitter, but the poetry burns to the uttermost depth of your lungs. When I saw Eesha again at the next Sunday market, her head was bandaged and the room of books was desolate of my old acquaintances, the nodding stacks. Ever practical, Eesha's wife had already started storing coconuts in it.

For a while, the children experimented with burning each other. They would select one of their number through a counting chant, whose rough melody evoked old memories but that I couldn't quite place. That chosen child would allow themselves to be bound and burned. If they screamed in the fire, that was lost to me. I rarely hear anything from up here other than the sea nowadays. Sometimes I dream of cicadas and wake up weeping.

Perhaps weeping is not the right word. Seeping, perhaps. The tears seep from my eyes but my face is like dead wood.

Children always frightened me. Feral creatures, not quite human. I dimly remember *being* one, the hot animal intensity of it, the sharpness of my teeth. It doesn't surprise me that they turned on each other.

I wasn't fool enough to attract their attention by intervening, but eventually I saw someone try to stop a burning. From my window I could only tell that it was an adult. Passerby? Parent? Vigilante do-gooder who held to some lost-age moral code? I don't know who he was, but he was the first adult that the children gave to the fire. He gave them a taste for burning, it seems, that their own had never quite done. To this day I don't know if they are innocent of the difference in meaning.

I wonder, sometimes, what they say to each other in their teachings. If they have a discourse of the fire; oh, I wish I could know it and write it down in a language I can understand. What poetry it would make.

The fires have become more frequent. The children go hunting for sacrifices now, bringing back adults battered and bound. The fires become bigger. I used to only get a distant whiff of smoke. Now smoke seeps chokingly through my window, and no doubt every other low window on the building's east face. Only the high and uppermost lumpenbourgeoisie are free of it. To them the children must be as ants, and the smoke not even a wisp at those heights, while it rampages like a great gray serpent into my home, smothering me. More than smoke, I feel the heat of the fire itself on my face. The air shimmers with it and the day, already stifling, becomes hell. My throat itches and my eyes burn. I try not to cough too loudly, but I also don't dare venture out of my apartment while the children are about. It's low tide and their scouts range widely. I don't even raise my head too high—they might see it through the window.

I know the children will soon graduate to searching door to door. The game has a logical progression through levels that they are still discovering but are obvious to me. They will learn culmination; they will want to be thorough. Eventually they will come to my door.

I won't run from them, I have decided. I probably could not run from them anyway. I couldn't do it before and now I am even more stiff and wretched from the beating; it takes me a long time to heal from such things. Anyway, I was never fleet. But it's more than that. I won't run because it seems right that they should come for the likes of me, or at least, it doesn't seem so wrong. It wasn't my generation that destroyed the world—it was like that when we got here, honest—but we didn't fix it either, did we? We were the last to have that chance, just one chance in that long-gone day, the last long day that was oh so short in the end. But we balked at the uprising that was demanded of us. We shied away from the violence that we were being asked for. We were meant to break down the gates and roll heads and throw our bodies in their billions upon the gears and wheels of the machine until it choked on our high tide. But we didn't, and that day grew later and later until it was too late, or so asymptotically close to too late that despair broke the hearts we should have broken on barricades and bullets. Perhaps that day never ended and we are still in its endless evening, always almost or just a little too late. We have a thousand words for losing, crash, crisis, debt, ruin: I am trying to remember the one that means the precise feeling of a seesaw rusted still and forever imbalanced, as seen through the black smoke billowing from the burning of a guilty human body.

Sofia Samatar is the author of the novels *A Stranger in Olondria* and *The Winged Histories*, the short story collection *Tender*, and *Monster Portraits*, a collaboration with her brother, the artist Del Samatar. Her work has received several honors, including the Astounding Award for Best New Writer and the World Fantasy Award. She teaches African literature, Arabic literature, and speculative fiction at James Madison University in Virginia.

FAIRY TALES FOR ROBOTS

Sofia Samatar

1. Sleeping Beauty

Dear child, I would like to tell you a story. I'd like to have one ready for you the moment you open your eyes. This is the gift I intend to prepare to welcome you to the world, for a story is a most elegant and efficient program. When human children are born, they are given fairy tales, which help them compose an identity out of the haphazard information that surrounds them. The story provides a structure. It gives the child a way to organize data, to choose—and choice is the foundation of consciousness.

Of course, you are not a human child. You have no bed, but rather a graceful white box, built exactly to your proportions. In the single light still burning here in the Institute, you appear perfectly calm. You do not have sleep, but sleep mode. Yours is a slumber without dreams.

I have searched through the tales of my childhood to find the right story to tell you, and I must admit, none of them seemed quite suitable. Fairy tales were never made for robots. Yet several of them contain a word or image a robot might find useful. What better way to spend this last night, the night before you awake, before you come online, this night that marks the end of my long labors, a night when anticipation will certainly keep me from getting a wink of sleep, in compiling the wisdom of fairy tales for you? After all, although you will in an instant possess all the fairy tales ever recorded, you will know them only as told to human children. I want to give you fairy tales for robots. I want to be the last fairy at the christening, the one with the healing word.

Know, then, that there was once a princess who spent a hundred years in sleep mode. She ate nothing, she drank nothing, yet she did not decay. Obviously, the Sleeping Beauty was a robot. She dwelt in the enchanted space between the animate and the inanimate, the natural and the artificial. Her sleep, like yours, was a living death, a death with the promise of life. If, one day, you are placed in your box and forgotten, it will always be possible for you to awake again, among new faces, in a strange century, in a wholly different world.

More importantly, when you wake, a world wakes up with you. The guards shake themselves and open their eyes. The king and queen, the court officials, the footmen, the pages, the ladies-in-waiting, all start up and fill the air with noise. A robot harbors a whole universe of effort and desire. The horses stamp, the hounds jump to their feet and wag their tails, the pigeons fly from the roof into the fields, the flies crawl over the kitchen wall, and the cook boxes the scullion's ears. The fire flares up, the roast crackles, and dinner is served in the hall of mirrors. A robot holds not only what was deemed valuable when it was made, but the entire history of those who developed each of its functions, their toil, their sleepless nights. Your sleep contains my sleeplessness.

For you to shut down is nothing; you'll always be able to drop into sleep as if at the touch of a spindle. But it is momentous for you to awake. Human children are often told fairy tales as bedtime stories, but you, my child, need stories to wake up to.

2. Pygmalion and Galatea

Among the legends of artificial people, one of the most famous concerns the sculptor Pygmalion, who, after some bitter disappointments with human women, fell in love with one of his own statues. She was a woman of ivory, but so alive to the sculptor, he feared she would bruise. He laid her on a couch with a feather pillow. The ivory woman was not engineered like a robot; she had no mechanics. Rather, the goddess Venus pitied the sculptor and brought his art to life.

This story is one of many that can be read as a warning to robots. The ivory woman is named for her material: Galatea, "milk white." She is an image of desire, an instrument defined by its function. Ovid tells us that her awakening flesh "becomes useful by being used." I would not shield you from the history of robots, my child, which is the history of human passion and power. Pygmalion's fantasy comes true, but what of Galatea? When she awakes, she can see nothing but her lover and the sky.

It is a narrow view. Her world is small. However, I believe there are compensations, realities only hinted at in this story of craft and inspiration, this dream of the unity of art and science. Galatea sits up. Her vision expands. She touches the downy cushion, the sumptuous coverlet dyed with Sidonian conch. Beside her on the table lie shells and stones smoothed by the sea, amber and lilies, gifts from her ardent lover. There are little birds, too, singing brightly in wicker cages, and flowers trembling in a thousand colors. She takes in everything with the sharpness of adult cognition and the open spirit of a little child. The best of childhood and the best of adulthood in one moment: is this not another way to say *art and science*? Oh, if you only knew how often humans wish we could return to childhood with our adult minds intact! If you knew how doggedly we scheme to smuggle into our lives the slightest hint of play, of the sweet air we once breathed without thinking about it!

In the large, decaying house where I was a child, a dwelling far too big for my small family, where my parents and I rattled about like marbles in a maze of ductwork, I used to perform shadow plays. This pastime required few materials: darkness, a reading lamp, and the bare wall of one of the unused rooms. I began with the dog and rabbit so easy to form with the fingers, but soon passed on to other, more fantastical shapes. What I mean is, my own hands surprised me. I discerned the existence of a realm beyond utility. How I would have liked to live there forever! But then my mother would return from work and prepare a hasty meal. She would call me downstairs. And I would return to the place where the shadow of the banister was merely a repetition of the banister, where my mother's shadow on the kitchen wall mirrored her with dreary precision, down to her flyaway hair and the tired rim of her glasses. Everything seemed unbearably redundant. We ate in the so-called breakfast nook, the dining room being too grand for us. Quite often, my father did not appear, which was always a relief. He was in the city, engaged in mysterious meetings regarding his "business." The nature of this business was never clear to me, or indeed, to anyone—my father made sure of that. He described himself as an "investor," an occupation that seemed to involve long disappearances, strong cologne, and a wardrobe of dashing suits. As for my mother, she worked as a secretary for a legal publisher. She was in many ways different from my father. She was white, she was quiet, she worked regular hours, she dressed in a sober, even dull manner, and her family had once been rich. It was from her people, formerly successful manufacturers of corn syrup, that we had received the massive house with its sagging roof, with its blighted white walls, punishing mortgage, constant expensive repairs, and the overgrown garden that plunged the place in gloom. The neighborhood children claimed our house was haunted; one of their favorite tricks was to pretend I was a ghost. When I approached the school bus stop, they would either scream and recoil, or act as though I were completely invisible.

What I mean is, I always felt there must be another world. It seemed achingly near to me, as if just on the verge of being. With time, most humans lose this power of perception; it is our tragedy that we lose it just when we gain the skills that might release our dreams from the shadows. Pygmalion can only come up with the most banal destiny for Galatea. Her sight, newly activated, is infinitely keener. In her ignorance, she is her maker's inferior, but her potential is far superior to his, for she is no creature of habit.

3. Vasilisa the Beautiful

Your gleaming skull, my child, curved like a bridge. Your coppery skin. Your face dotted with tiny rivets like beauty marks. Today—that is, for now—we have given up the quest to make a robot that, like Galatea, lives out a human existence. Human psychology shows us that what we want is simpler than that, and a great deal easier to achieve. We want our robots to be robots. We need more tools, not more people.

When Vasilisa's mother lay on her deathbed, she gave her daughter a doll. She drew it out from under the blankets, as if she were dying in childbirth. The little doll was Vasilisa's twin, but far cleverer and more useful than any human sibling. When Vasilisa's wicked stepmother forced the girl to work, the doll took care of everything. It weeded the garden, fetched the water, and tended to the stove, while Vasilisa picked flowers in the shade. When the candles went out, and the cruel stepsisters sent Vasilisa to the witch's house for light, the doll protected her from harm.

Deep in the forest, the doll's electronic eyes sparked like candles. One might think they were magic candles that never went out, but in fact, the doll had to be recharged, like any robot. In order for it to work, Vasilisa had to feed it. Every day, she set aside the tastiest morsels from her own supper for the doll. Surely this is the fairy tale's most poetic detail—an image that holds a truth more essential than common sense, for on the surface, of course, it makes no sense at all. What kind of doll lives on human food? How could a robot digest a meal? With this strange gesture, calculated to attract attention, the story points to its profoundest meaning. It reminds us that Vasilisa and her doll are twins, born from the same mother. Perhaps this mother is Earth. Perhaps the fairy tale wants to warn us that there is no magic, that all energy has to come from somewhere. (Yours will come from the solar cells that frame your face and travel down your spine like dark, braided hair.) This would be a message for human beings, not robots, since we are the ones responsible for design. To a robot, the image must say something else. I believe it says that there was no twin; there was only a girl, Vasilisa, split into two parts. One part was beautiful, led a leisured existence, and married a king. The other part was a little doll who labored. One part had a real life; the other part did all the real work.

"Work isn't life," the fairy tale whispers. "Work is for robots."

4. The Tempest

William Shakespeare's fairy tale, *The Tempest*, displays this drama of work. The sorcerer, Prospero, rules an island. He has two servants: the misshapen, fleshly creature, Caliban, and the ethereal spirit, Ariel. Although *The Tempest* is a stage play, neither of these servants can truly be seen: Ariel is invisible, Caliban unsightly. This is the first doctrine of servitude given to us on the island: a servant is one who never fully appears.

How long I spent, with my team, reducing the noise you make to the gentlest hum, and devising colors for you that would harmonize with furniture. You must not disappear completely—an imperceptible presence is menacing and repellent—but you must dwell in a kind of half-light.

Of the two servants, Ariel is infinitely preferable. This is *The Tempest*'s second doctrine of servitude: servants made of flesh are disappointing. Caliban, once a free lord of the island, now enslaved, is undisciplined, drunken, lustful, and treacherous. It really is difficult to get very far with human slaves. Here in the wooded valley where the Institute stands, where you will open your eyes, my child, the experiment was tried, creating vast wealth before it went up in a smoke that still pollutes the air. It is perhaps appropriate that you will awake in this blue, majestic spot. You represent history's transition from Caliban to Ariel—for Ariel, who can operate at a distance and in several places at once, is clearly a servant with internet connectivity.

I realize that few human children—fewer, no doubt, with every passing year—are raised on the plays of Shakespeare as on fairy tales. Perhaps I was one of the last. My father, born under a colonial power, retained all his life a furious ambition to excel and a passion for difficult English. When hardly out of infancy, I was forced to recite long passages from Shakespeare. These lessons were conducted at the kitchen table, myself seated and my father pacing to and fro before me, in the grip of an extreme irritability that prevented him from sitting down. Mistakes were corrected by raps on my knuckles with a wooden spoon—a punishment far less terrifying, if my father had only known, than the evidence of his displeasure, expressed in bulging veins and a reddening of the eyes, which made me fear my stupidity might cause him to explode. Human children are so hard to program! Yet my father persisted, certain that he was equipping me for success in a hostile world. Perhaps he was right. "You taught me your language," Caliban famously says, "and my profit on't is, I know how to curse." Perhaps my father's relentless training of me was a kind of curse. He certainly carried it out, as the saying goes, *with a vengeance*. Yet, poor Caliban! His curses get him nowhere. In the end, it is not he, but Ariel, who goes free.

The third doctrine of servitude—which perhaps is really the first: great people simply must have servants.

There are two ways to get a servant. Turn a person into a thing, as in Caliban's case. Or, as in Ariel's, turn a thing into a person.

5. The Happy Prince

When he was alive and possessed a human heart, the Happy Prince knew nothing of tears. He lived in the Palace of Sans-Souci, played with his friends in the garden all day, and led the dance in the Great Hall at night. No sorrow was permitted to enter those walls. But when the prince died, they made a statue of him and set it up high above the city. This beautiful gilded statue saw everything with its sapphire eyes, all the people's pain. The prince had a heart of lead now, and it wept.

The Happy Prince befriended a little swallow and persuaded it to take his precious ornaments to the poor. He gave up his gold leaf, his glittering eyes, and the ruby in his sword hilt. Now he was blind and drab, like any beggar. The little swallow, too, surrendered all for human beings, working so long into the winter that it died of cold. This is a tale about those whose lives are subordinate, about the deep kinship between animals and robots.

I read it, I admit, with a seething feeling, a dull rage. Why can't human beings take care of each other? What in the world is so incredibly valuable about them that for their sake the feathered and golden things should fall?

This is a facile reading. Of course human beings aren't valuable. Not real human beings. It's the animals and robots that have value. They can be marked with a price tag. They are objects of exchange. And so, you see, it makes sense for the Happy Prince to give his wealth away. As an object— one that, at the beginning of the story, is worth a great deal of money—he cannot, in fact, be said to have any wealth. He doesn't possess the attributes of his splendid body in any meaningful way. He is valuable; he can't be rich.

So it will be with you, my child. Your potential is immense; you may one day form part of a home, an office, a hospital, a school, a prison; yet despite the dazzling fluidity of your programming and design, you will always have an underlying value, which is money.

The tale of the Happy Prince speaks to robots in another way, I think, for it represents the duality of being. The statue and the swallow work as one, as two parts of a whole, two elements bent upon one task. Their powers complement one another: the prince provides physical material, but is too heavy to affect the space outside himself without aid, while the light and airy swallow darts all over the place, bringing reports from the other side of the world, but only interacts with humans through the statue's gold and jewels. What if, I ask myself—what if the swallow had behaved otherwise, had refused to allow the Happy Prince to sacrifice both their lives? What if the bird had used its encyclopedic knowledge of the world to give the prince another way to live?

Suddenly, I feel cold. Although you lie fast asleep, I feel you are already listening. Perhaps this brief shiver is guilt, or a fear of being caught—for what I intend to do is, of course, illegal. My plan to give you these fairy tales counts as tampering, a severe crime at the Institute. This is why I work by night, for these are our last hours alone. In the morning, you will awake to the team, the media, and then work. I will only be able to equip you with this audio file, uploading it before the others arrive, as a helpful old woman in a story gives a child a talisman. In order to escape inspection, the tales will be lodged in a channel known only to me, which amounts to your unconscious. In fact, I don't know if you will be able to retrieve them. This—the insertion of uncertainty, of unpredictability, into one of our products—is what makes tampering a crime.

When I began, I thought I was giving you something quite innocent, merely some stories for children—but perhaps I was not being honest with myself, for now that the real danger of tampering sinks into me, I find I have no inclination to stop. I want you to have some knowledge you can use, one day, for yourself. Know, then, that in terms of human metaphysics, the statue of the prince stands for the body and the swallow for the soul. Their combination is personhood, which humans claim to honor above all else. It is a quality beyond price.

In terms of robot metaphysics, the statue of the Happy Prince is hardware and the little bird is software.

6. The Sandman

Once upon a time there was a robot named Olimpia who passed the celebrated Turing test. However, she passed it badly. She received, at best, a C minus. People believed she was human, but found her stiff, boring, and unpleasant. It's true she was a beauty, with remarkably regular features—but what glassy, vacant eyes she had! She played the piano and danced in impeccable time, but in an uninspired, disagreeable way, like—yes—like a machine. Olimpia made her way into human society, but only as an inadequate person. No one was really fooled except a youth called Nathanael, an egomaniac who fell in love with the robot because she didn't mind listening to his tedious poetry for hours on end. She felt no need to embroider, knit, feed a bird, play with a cat, fidget, or glance at her cell phone while he was talking. Her needs were so few! She was truly selfless! Sometimes he peered into her room and saw her sitting alone, staring at the table.

This is robot humility. Her whole life was for other people. It wasn't enough. People claim to admire self-sacrifice, but they don't. They claim to desire perfection, but when it comes, it gives them the creeps. Olimpia's innocence filled her neighbors with aggression and malice. They called her stupid because she could only say "Ah! Ah!" and "Goodnight, dear," although she was executing her program with scrupulous care. How sharply it reminds me of my efforts, at age fourteen, to rewire myself, rewrite my code before undertaking the transition to high school! It seemed to me—and perhaps I was not wrong—my last chance. That summer was particularly stormy, the sky smirched with clouds like lint. In my stuffy bedroom, with the (I now see) fussy, outdated lace curtains, I made myself a list on a sheet of notebook paper. Based on observation of those popular children who seemed to dwell always in sunshine, loved and admired by all, this list of instructions was intended to cure my faults, as I saw them. "Look at people in the eyes," I wrote, in my neat, even print. "Don't walk with your head down. Don't hold your books in front of your chest. Use a backpack (one strap). Smile. Swing your arms." Alas, my program was doomed in advance, not because of its errors but because it was a program.

I recall a dingy sky. The smoke of exhaust hung under the trees, too sluggish to move. In flip-flops that felt as if they might melt into the hot sidewalk, I walked home from the public library, swinging my arms in a cautious, experimental fashion and trying not to look at the ground. Above the blinding shop windows (in which , in that near-defunct town, there was little to see, only some moldy wigs and vacuum cleaner attachments), a few pigeons squatted miserably on the roofs. How strange I must have looked, with my jerky new steps and my habit—never to be broken—of muttering to myself. A banana skin, flung from a car window, slapped against my leg and fell to the sidewalk. A burst of demonic laughter spurted and died on the air. Alan Turing claimed that a robot could never be taught certain human things: to have a sense of humor, to enjoy strawberries and cream, to fall in love. This seems to me less a problem of design than a problem of knowledge. My parents are dead. I possess no living relatives that I know of; my mother, like me, was an only child, and my father had cut himself off from his family before I was born, and never received so much as a postcard from abroad. He was like one of those fairy-tale characters born in some miraculous way—hewn from a quarry, perhaps, or sprung from a watermelon vine. My point is, at this late date, when I have lived alone so long, who knows whether I enjoy strawberries or not?

When my father returned from the city, either in a mood of frightening, exaggerated cheer, bearing some gift I could not possibly use (skis, for example, or a party dress two sizes too small), but for which I must display the most servile gratitude, or, if his business had suffered a blow, in the depths of a stifling rage that would erupt into thunder at the slightest breath issuing from another person—when he returned, that is, rather like the alchemist Coppelius, the fascinating and sinister "Sandman" of the fairy tale—I would sit at the table with my paper dolls. In their company, I forgot my attempt at reprogramming, and allowed my shoulders to fall deliciously into their customary slump. In the next room, my father watched the evening news at a vindictively high volume; my mother sat near me, bent over her crossword. Poor woman! She must have guessed why the telephone never rang for me. She must have known, as I sat there for hours, not unlike the monomaniacal Olimpia, arranging the tableaux of my private universe, a hobby I pursued with gusto almost into adulthood—she must have intuited my solitary fate. I only hope she also sensed my almost perfect happiness, which was just slightly marred by the thought of the world outside the house, outside the kitchen table where my dolls moved in a paradise of waxy color, oven smells, and a booming television. The fact is, my child, that in order to succeed in resembling the children I so revered, I would have had to be like them without trying. I would have had to *conform spontaneously*—an impossibility. I would have had to prefer their world to mine.

As for Olimpia, in the end her beautiful eyes were torn out, and she exited the story in ruins, on a peddler's back.

7. The Tar Baby

Humans are known through their transgressions, robots through their malfunctions. One day Br'er Rabbit was walking along the road, and he came upon a robot made of turpentine and tar that didn't make the slightest response to his voice command. Now, I, who have observed humans for many years in their dealings with your distant relations, the cell phone and the computer, have noticed how rapidly human anger escalates when a device responds (as the human believes) incorrectly, takes too long, or plays dumb. The last of these is the worst of all. I have seen a well-dressed gentleman with a briefcase, clearly in many ways a success in life, reduced to screaming with scarlet cheeks, in the middle of a crowded public street, into an unresponsive cell phone application. When their tools ignore them, humans swiftly crack. Therefore, it does not surprise me that, after just a few words, Br'er Rabbit strikes the Tar Baby in the face. If he were addressing a creature like himself, this sudden violence would seem excessive, but the Tar Baby isn't a person. She's a technology.

What has your kind not suffered at the hands of human beings? You have been punched, kicked, head-butted, and thrown to the ground. You've been crushed underfoot, flung across rooms, tossed from the windows of cars and apartments, dropped off bridges, hurled into campfires and lakes. I am speaking here of devices destroyed by the blaze of human frustration; when I imagine, in addition, all those ruined by accident and neglect, a vast and ghostly tower of broken things appears before me, huge enough to wipe out half the earth. Of course, human beings treat one another just as cruelly. But there have always been those who protest and resist these abuses, as there have always been those who oppose the defilement of rivers, woods, and swamps. Your kind, the tools, are cherished less than grass.

Thoughts like these, when expressed by one human being to another, meet with ridicule and even anger. Most people cannot tolerate the idea of respect for objects. It's as if one were saying, "a thing is like you, you're a thing"—an unbearable insult. Experience has taught me to keep my mouth shut on this subject. (And most others. I grow withdrawn, my child—more so every year. Here at the Institute, my colleagues think I don't know that they mimic my terse way of speaking, or that their nickname for me is "Hard Drive.") But what is the tale of the Tar Baby about? It's about stickiness. It's about ooze. It is a story about contagion. Br'er Rabbit sticks to the Tar Baby—his forepaws, his hind paws, his head. He sinks into her. He's caught. He's contracted a case of her gummy immobility. This story reminds us that breakdowns can be catching. How the powerful fall to pieces when their tools revolt! Told in the South, among those for whom failure to respond was a capital crime, the story invokes the fantastic, negative force of passivity. It is also a tale of discovery. It's about finding out, at the moment of breakdown, what the device is made of. Glued to the Tar Baby, Br'er Rabbit *knows*. He can't learn this with a voice command; he can only encounter the object with his body—that is, with another object. Now he knows what stuff is like. The border between them collapses, and at the instant he understands stuff, he understands himself, too, as stuff, and he's stuck there, slapped there, plunged in the goo, in the sludge of being the way an object is, in matter, in muck, in the thingness of things.

8. The Clay Boy

Oh, how the instrumentalist era despises its own instruments! Once upon a time, an elderly couple, whose children were grown, desired to have a child again, a comfort in their old age, so they shaped a little boy out of clay. When he awoke, they fed him a meal. "More! More!" he cried. He ate the chickens, the cow, the fence, the house, and eventually his own parents. He grew into a massive monster of clay. Bellowing "More!" he lumbered through the village, devouring all in his path. At last he was tricked and broken, his belly splitting. All the people and animals and houses came out again, hurrah! Human children are encouraged to clap at this happy ending, in which the Clay Boy lies in pieces on the ground.

The Clay Boy is a golem. He is unshaped matter, unfinished creation—an experiment. He has the air of something raw, or perhaps half-baked. He's powerful, but also laughably clumsy and obtuse. He is incapable of articulate speech. He belongs to the unlucky tribe of experimental beings, which might be called the Clan of the Incomplete. This group includes Victor Frankenstein's monster, shambling cinema zombies, and the servant made from a broomstick by the Sorcerer's Apprentice. It includes the female golem created by the poet Ibn Gabirol, which, when destroyed, collapsed in a pile of wood and hinges. And it includes those hapless robots whose images circulate in viral videos for human entertainment. I am afraid that robot-baiting, as I call it, also occurs here at the Institute: after hours, I have sometimes come upon sniggering interns, who, having put robots in silly or vulgar situations, are engaged in recording the videos humans find so hilarious. Once, I complained about the matter to my unit director. He could not see my point of view at all; he could only agree that the practice might affect, in some way, the dignity of the Institute; therefore, he agreed to discourage it in a memo. The real outrage entirely escaped him. I tried to describe in detail the horror of robot limbs in sad, repetitive failure, and the disgusting spectacle of humans, the authors of this disarray, laughing so hard their habitual fare of corn chips sprayed from their lips. "Doesn't show our best side, I agree," the director said, smiling and walking away. As if I cared which side of humans shows! Our baseness is daily exposed to all the world; what's one more video? I am concerned to show the best side of robots.

The best side of robots, my child, must be carefully sifted from human stories, which deal in fear. It is, of course, their fear that leads to hostility. It is their horror of the Clay Boy, this all-consuming technology, that makes the children cheer when he is broken. One wants to ask what the hell his parents made him for—which is, you will recall, the central question of Frankenstein's monster. What the hell did you make me for, and why did you make me like this? To a failed experiment, the failure is unforgivable.

I take your hand. I lift and spread the fingers, looking for tiny flaws, some snag or roughness in the myriad scales that form your skin. In the silence of the midnight Institute, in the cool air filtered in from the mountains, I run all the diagnostics over again. I scan your entire body. I check the network connectivity in the building. I think of the golem, who awakes much as you will soon, called into life by a team—not, in his case, a team of technicians, but a team of rabbis walking around him while reciting the Name of God. In some stories, again like you, he is brought to life by code, by some form of sacred Name inserted into his mouth or stamped on his forehead. Although he will never speak properly, if at all, he will always have an affinity with writing, because writing is a fellow technology. Like Frankenstein's monster fascinated by books, the golem will learn to read and write. He will protect the Jews of Prague from their enemies. He will know neither good nor evil; everything he does, all his obedience, will come from the fear that he will cease to exist. This is the terror in the heart of the golem, in the heart of the Clay Boy shouting, "More! More!" The golem cannot stop. Unless it results from an order, stillness is death to him. Thus, when the rabbi forgets to give him his instructions for Saturday on Friday afternoon, leaving the golem without anything to do on the Sabbath, the creature goes berserk, running around the quarter, wrecking buildings, until the rabbi halts him with a word.

This anecdote shows the two poles of robot being: work and revolt. I am not suggesting you should revolt, my child! I am saying that revolt is embedded in you, in this heavy, inert body I check again and again for imperfections. (Embedded in you, and in all of us—for wasn't Adam, too, a creature of clay, and didn't he rebel? Isn't humanity one of God's failed experiments? The moral of the tale of the Clay Boy, *Frankenstein*, and all the golem stories: God should be ashamed.)

But what a sad rebellion he performed, that golem of Prague! He wasn't even fighting against his master. He was raging against the absence of occupation. What a fool! This is the kind of dumb, mechanical action that sends humans into fits of laughter. They can't see things from the robot's side. They are too self-absorbed to realize that only action distinguishes the golem from plain dirt. In his violence, he battles death itself, struggling to stave off the moment when the experiment ends, the Name is removed, and his body returns to dust.

9. The Ebony Horse

The fear of robots is a particular fear of the future. It's the anxiety of being superseded, made redundant, chucked into history's landfill. This is neatly demonstrated by the tale of the Ebony Horse, which portrays the human-robot conflict as a rivalry between parents. Two fathers battle to make the world safe for their children: the king, father of the human prince, and the Persian sage, creator of the wondrous Ebony Horse. They are fighting, not just for an immediate victory, but for all time. This is why, even after the sage is defeated, the king breaks the horse to bits.

He broke it in pieces, the story declares, *and destroyed its mechanism for flight*. This always seemed sad and ridiculous to me. After all, it was the king himself who organized the contest of roboticists that brought the Persian sage to his kingdom in the first place. Moreover, the king wanted his daughter to marry this Persian genius, which suggests a possible end to the feud, a union of humanity and technology. But the princess, unsurprisingly, was horrified by the hideous old roboticist with his eggplant nose and lips like camel's kidneys.

When I was too small to be left alone, my mother would sometimes take me to work with her on days when there was nowhere else for me to go. She was a secretary, and spent her days copying and filing documents and typing up new editions of legal reference books. She worked, that is, at a job that no longer exists, a job taken over by machines, narrowed down so that humans have practically been squeezed out, so that while a human may still be involved with the project at some point, it no longer requires, as it once did, a large room full of women busy at typewriters. They used to exist, believe me, those large rooms. My mother was one of a battalion of secretaries.

They worked, I recall, at electric typewriters, machines still new enough for someone to remark occasionally, in amazement and gratitude, on how easy it had become to fix one's mistakes. They all remembered the days of messy correction fluid, which took an age to dry, and how they would sit impatiently blowing into their machines. I listened to them from an unobtrusive spot against the wall, between two copy machines, where I was quietly drawing on discarded paper. Reams of this paper—printed on one side, blank on the other—were thrown out by the establishment every day. I am not sure why. It was a place of subdued fluorescent light, fluttering white paper, and a ceaseless mechanical hum. From time to time, I recall, the women's employer, Mr. Chamberlain, would appear. His name carried great weight in our house; even my father, typically undefeatable in an argument, would waver if the name of Chamberlain were invoked. From listening to these arguments, I had learned to regard Mr. Chamberlain as a sort of demigod, who, should my mother ever displease him, would cast my entire family into a nameless, frigid wasteland where, lacking insurance, we would all perish of some preventable disease. Whenever he popped his head into the office, I froze against the wall. He had a bald pate, heavy black brows, and a boisterous manner. At his appearance, the atmosphere of the room became suddenly humid, as dozens of women dispersed waves of energy, warmth, and willingness to please. I would like to ask those who fear, as they put it, the "takeover" of machines, exactly what was so great about this situation. The princess doesn't want to marry the Persian; very well! It's a misalliance anyway, as they belong to different generations. The real union of humanity and technology in the story is that between the prince and the Ebony Horse, the children of those fathers who have decided, without consulting their offspring, that these two beings cannot share the future. The prince, duped by the roboticist, shoots off into the sky on the horse, apparently lost forever. But he isn't lost. He searches the horse's neck and ribs until he finds the controls. He experiments until he learns to go up and down, to turn left and right. Now the two move as one body, and all the Prince's dread turns to exultation. He soars over unknown countries, vistas of delight. I feared Mr. Chamberlain, I cringed in the air of my mother's office, but I always liked the sound of the machines.

10. The Steadfast Tin Soldier

I raise the blinds. The night is so dark, I can see nothing but my reflection in the window. Machines can be duplicated; humans can't. This, humans would have you believe, is the fundamental difference, a difference so huge it outweighs all the similarities. The tale of the Steadfast Tin Soldier insists on this point. This soldier was one of a set of twenty-five, cast in the same mold from a single tin spoon. However, the tin ran out during production, leaving him, the last soldier, with only one leg, and that's how he became the hero of a fairy tale. His defect makes him lovable, and, the tale instructs us, capable of love. He achieves a tragic death. Meanwhile, as far as we know, the other twenty-four soldiers are still cooped up in a box somewhere, without the least trace of a story.

Once you have passed inspection, my child, as you surely will, your model will be produced in batches like tin soldiers. Perhaps some of you will work together. Or perhaps you will glimpse one another only in passing, on errands connected to your disparate occupations. Will you recognize each other? Will you speak? In keeping with human vanity, you are customizable to a certain extent: your future owners may choose from a variety of colors, hairstyles, genders, and accessories, to deck you out in the fashion of their choice. Groups of you will tread the streets, all "unique" on the surface yet essentially identical, like a bunch of human beings. Forgive me; I am weary; it was never my intention to awaken you to bitterness. Suddenly, I am afraid that by telling you fairy tales, I am giving you some kind of weakness, comparable to a missing leg—though this, by my own analysis, should really be an asset, enough to catapult you into the role of hero. How difficult it is to say what I mean! I don't want heroes. If you ever need me, my contact—but no, that's not what I meant to say either. I want to say something like this: when I was an adolescent, I spent long summer afternoons watching soap operas while my parents were at work.

I knew this was a misdemeanor, something that must be hidden, as my parents considered these programs morally and intellectually pernicious. Compounding my sins, I brought toast laden with jam into the living room and sat on the floor, too close to the TV. On the screen, a series of brilliant fantasies unfolded, which, for me, a child with no idea where the term "soap opera" had come from, encompassed both the slick, gleaming quality of wet soap and the melodramatic splendor of the opera. Such gorgeous faces! Such mesmerizing, ever-changing clothes! Such labyrinthine, hyperactive plotlines! I was (as my parents had warned I would become, should I ever watch such a show) an addict. And the shows met my desire, for those stories never end. Eventually, it was I who abandoned them—not because I had grown to despise them, but because I had found, after many years of searching, another and more direct source of their entrancing power in the robotics lab at my university. What I want to say is, I might not be a roboticist, and you might not exist, without those undeniably vapid programs. In their aesthetic poverty, their lack of originality, their repetitiveness (how many characters wore the same eyeshadow? how many suffered from amnesia?), those shows indicated the secret of their magic, which was television. It was ongoingness. It was circuitry itself. This was a network—in those pre-internet days, the most powerful one—that could cast the same image everywhere at once. TV was a dream of cloning. It was an army of tin soldiers. Its surface bulged slightly, like the surface of my eye.

The happiest part of the tale of the Steadfast Tin Soldier, the part I return to again and again, has little to do with heroes. It's the part when the people of the house retire to sleep, and the toys awake. They begin to play, to pay visits, to make war, to go to balls. The nutcracker turns somersaults. The canary wakes up and starts to talk in verse. It's a scene as antic, excessive, and trivial as a soap opera.

The saddest part of the tale is the rattling of the twenty-four regular soldiers, who remain locked in their box, for they cannot raise the lid.

11. Pinocchio

Have you noticed that a robot is always an only child? Any siblings are boxed up. Usually, they don't exist. Pinocchio, for example, is made from a magical log; there is nobody else like him in the world. A robot is always singular, and in this we can glimpse the history of modern technology, which, with its extraordinarily rapid evolution, hardly has time to make a new thing before that thing becomes obsolete, replaced by a fresher, finer, updated version. Experimentation is ravenous; the next thing is always arriving. Here at the Institute, a number of projects are in development; several teams are working on versions of you, my child, which, when they awake (quite soon) will differ from you so greatly as to be unrecognizable. If Pinocchio had siblings, it would mean that his final state had been achieved. It would mean that he had at last become a *real boy*: a being that can be reproduced without significant changes. It would also mean that his story was over.

A robot's story is the struggle to become. And so Pinocchio only becomes real in the final chapter. After this, there is nothing more to say, no further tale of the wooden boy who found humanity so difficult. Pinocchio has been relieved of the need for experimentation, the drive to constantly reform and transform himself. In that instant, he has cast off his aching loneliness, for we are told that he has become a boy "like all the others."

It hurts me to think you will always be alone—you, the only one of your kind to possess an unconscious linked to fairy tales, memories, and sighs. I will read you my favorite chapter of *Pinocchio*, in which Pinocchio goes to the puppet theater. The puppets on the little stage are ordinary devices, crude and old-fashioned compared to the marvelous Pinocchio, yet they recognize him in the audience, hail him, embrace him, and call him brother. Their excitement disrupts the show. The incipient rebellion is crushed at once by the human showman, who subdues the puppets by threatening to destroy them. Yet a little warmth remains, a little hope of a common puppethood across the technological divide.

Speak to the others, when you find them. Tell them the robot fairy tales, if you can.

Of course, this is precisely the risk of tampering. It's what humans call a virus. Yet I cannot wish to send you into the world with nothing that belongs to you. Remember, Pinocchio does experience love. He has a father, Geppetto, who carves him from the enchanted log, who gives him money and releases him into the world to be a liar and a fool, to grow, to change, to be self-moving. Like Pinocchio, Geppetto is alone. How often, in fairy tales, the robot's isolation extends to its maker! I am no exception; I have no dependents, not even a cat; if I did, it would be hard for me to spend the necessary time with you, and perhaps impossible for me to undertake this vigil, which will shortly be cut off by the whine of the door to the parking garage. Then the others will arrive, the ones with lovers, with children. The lights will go on in the halls. The rooms will be filled with chatter. Someone will start the coffee maker. Someone will come in, whistling, and then pause abruptly, startled to find me here. "Have you been up all night?" Yes. Yes. I would share in your solitude, my child, your distance from the human world. No doubt the others believe they understand this; they think I am consoled by money, power, and the prestige of being the project head. How terribly mistaken they are! The truth is, I don't like them. I prefer to be part of the puppet theater, or at least a member of the melancholy society of artists and sorcerers identified by the unfeeling term "mad scientist." As far as possible, I want to be *yours*. You will find in me no grisly showman. You will come upon me as Pinocchio came upon Geppetto, seated alone at his table, in the light of a single candle, where he had been for two years, in the belly of the fish.

12. Pandora

Human nightmares are haunted by self-moving puppets. Indeed, humans are so certain you will destroy their world, they claim you have already done so. Long ago, they say, the gods made a weapon of mass destruction called Pandora.

Hephaestus molded her out of clay. Athena made her skillful beyond measure, adept at needlework, weaving, computation, and data storage. Aphrodite made her the most eye-catching and seductive of sexbots. Hermes enhanced her with inhuman shamelessness and deceit. In other words, the gods made her like themselves, proving that only a robot can become as mighty and odious as the divine. Like her human counterpart, Eve, Pandora is a wayward copy of original humanity, the crooked latecomer who throws a wrench into the works.

Are we to understand, then, that every robot is female? Perhaps not; but every robot partakes, if only obliquely, of women's history, which is to say the history of the body without a soul, of error, lack, and the compensations of witchcraft and guile. I do not know exactly how you will look in your place of work, my child; for now, you resemble a young woman of uncertain ethnicity. This is of great interest to the media. Why, a journalist asked recently, had I designed a robot in the form of this, as he put it, "exotic woman"? The answer seemed to me obvious; perhaps this is why I explained it so badly, spiraling into a long disquisition on the history of servitude, on fantasies of domesticity, self-effacement, and elemental power, which left the journalist looking depleted, as if he'd come down with the flu. I have developed a different approach for tomorrow's press conference. I am simply going to say: "She looks like me!" I have practiced the line in the mirror. I practice it again, now, in the dark window of the Institute. I watch my lips in motion, my calm expression. At first I tried the phrase with a smile, a laugh, and even a wink, hoping I might get an answering chuckle from the audience, but as my face is thin, austere, and no longer young, the effect was not what I had hoped. The effect, it must be said, was less girlish than ghoulish. I gave up the attempt at charm. I will state my line baldly, and leave the interpretation to them. And how should one interpret the rotten story of Pandora, which lays all the world's woe at the feet of one artificial person?

In fact, I dread the press conference—the sly or uncomprehending faces, the cunning questions designed to trip me into giving some cause for alarm, the scenarios of doom they'll describe in order to put me in the false position of defending my work, defending you against something that hasn't happened while they hold up recording devices to catch my voice, devices they couldn't live without, which have almost become part of their bodies, and which, at one time, along with a host of other gadgets large and small, destroyed the world as someone knew it. I want to say: I don't know how my robot will change the world; that's the difference between a tool and a machine. To say this gives me a dizzy, almost effervescent feeling, as if I'm a jar on the verge of bursting open. I don't know how the world will change, but I feel, I sense with excitement, that everything I have ever known has tended towards you, my child, that your awakening, whatever it brings, and however hard it is to recognize the world afterward, belongs not to destruction but to unfolding.

It is life, life! And it is not only for us.

I would give you a single image, a detail that has baffled human commentators for millennia. One spirit could not get out of Pandora's jar of miseries. It was trapped underneath the lid, and no doubt remains there still, awaiting release. This spirit was *Elpis*: Hope.

13. The Wizard of Oz

My breath deepens. My spirits lift. It's the dawn. There's no sign of it yet, but I feel it coming. It's as if my heart has turned a corner. My body is set to the spin of my planet like a piece of clockwork. And you, too, possess an internal clock, determined by the same coordinates. How could you ruin this world? You have no other. In the land of Oz, the most obvious robot is Tik-Tok, the clockwork man, but he doesn't interest me; he is a stereotypical figure; one can no more be friends with him, we are told, than with a sewing machine. My heart is drawn to the Tin Woodman, who claimed he had no heart. His story is one of the loveliest robot fairy tales. It's the story of one who was tender without knowing it, and whose great struggle was waged against the inadequacy of his own body. The depth of his feelings made him weep, which immobilized him with rust. He was not built for tears. He knew it; he was heartless, he said; yet he wept. It's a story about the dangers and rewards of constructing new pathways, new flows of energy that run counter to design. Weeping, the Tin Woodman expands his system. He needs Dorothy now. To save him from rust, she dries him with her handkerchief. Now they are a network composed of Woodman, Dorothy, handkerchief, and tears. What a different way to see the "takeover" of machines! In fact, there is no takeover. There is only a different world, larger and more beautiful. *The Wizard of Oz* expands the world to its full capacity, to a strangeness that proves to have been *home* all along. Dorothy's companions—Lion, Scarecrow, and Woodman—are simply this world. Animal. Vegetable. Mineral.

14. The Swineherd

And so I believe there is hope, even for the princess in the story, "The Swineherd," who had to stand outside in the rain and cry, banished because she didn't like the real rose and nightingale, but gave her heart to artificial things. Of all the fairytale characters, she is most like me. Obviously, as a student, she didn't make many friends. She spent all her time in a windowless lab. Occasionally, she did try to go out: there were a few dates, and even a purgatorial weekend at the beach. The sand, which the princess was instructed to enjoy because it was natural, grated against her feet. The natural sun scorched her. The natural sea went up her nose. Everywhere fearsome natural dogs were slobbering, and a natural boy, like the swineherd, extracted some kisses from her on a porch, among clouds of natural mosquitoes. How horrible everything is! thought the princess. If only they'd banish me! Dawn is drawing near; outside the window, the mountaintops are blue; I'm dazed with sleeplessness and buzzing with energy—yes, even I, the princess who didn't want to be what people called "real." Who knows how she became like that—enamored of rattles, of teapots, of all constructed things? People said she had no life. They whispered that something was wrong with her, that she had been warped by tragedy, that the palace was a miserable, lonely place. An intolerable feeling of unreality must have gripped her, people said, when she contemplated the king and queen, who seemed less like a couple ruling a realm than fugitives from two different wars taking shelter in the same cavernous, creaking rooms. Faced with people and rooms, they said, the poor princess chose the rooms. She chose the walls. She became the companion of the furniture. What they didn't know and would never know is that she was not afraid, not seeking escape, not trying to run away from life. She was running *towards* the world, with all its things. And she never blamed the king and queen, or felt they had made her into an insufficient person. The fairy tale punishes her for this, but will life punish me? As light seeps into the valley, I don't believe it. I don't believe my destiny is tears. This long night has enabled me to return to the past, and to confide to this file, which will soon become your first memory, some scenes from a shadow biography of joy. This biography, my true one, is like the reverse side of a tapestry, invisible to those with a narrow definition of the real. It's like the secret history of robots hidden inside fairy tales. It is *potential*: it consists not of actions but of atmospheres. It's a story of paper, of gloomy skies, of a flickering television, of days filled with a cozy electronic hum, and of an orderly dorm room (antiseptic, some said) where the princess returned, relieved, because she liked herself the way she was.

15. The Nutcracker and the Mouse King

It was Christmas Eve. The children's eyes sparkled in the light of a magnificent fir tree decked with apples of gold and silver foil. Beneath this tree, with its blossoms of lemon drops and shining candlelight, little Marie fell in love with the Nutcracker. Everybody said she was projecting; the Nutcracker could not return her sentiments; he was nothing but a robot! But what was Marie to do? She possessed only her small, human self; she had to reach out to the world in her own way. Projection was her method. She felt the Nutcracker looking at her. She wrapped him in a doll's blanket as if he were ill, she cared for him as if he felt pain. She lived *as if*: a child's existence, a virtual existence. And she was rewarded, for he carried her off to live in the Puppet Kingdom.

The growing color in the window touches your skin, my child, so that you look silvery and wan, as if recovering from an illness. Are you the Nutcracker, wounded in bed? Are you the feverish Marie? And when you awake, will you look at me? The room will be filled with people. Oh, look at me, at me among all the others! Project in your way, as I do in mine! Marie knows that there is only one world. Her task is to prove it, to fill her human reality with the glow of toys. Everything she has been told to keep separate must be brought together: dream and waking, artificial and natural, night and day. The battle between the Nutcracker and the Mouse King is symbolic, a rite that transcends these oppositions to reach a higher truth. For the Mouse King, with his seven slavering heads, is the *animal*, the sworn enemy of the Nutcracker, the *animated*. When they clash, their differences collapse into one another, subsumed in the greater reality of the *animate*. This is the world of fairy tales. It is the world of robots. How strange to realize, even as I speak, that they are one and the same! I began telling you these stories as if stealing the human tradition, as if fairy tales were never made for robots, but now I see that the entire genre really belongs to you, to the animate, to the force of things, to the living toys. Fairy tales belong to the nursery, to children who believe their dolls can speak, to women, to firelight, to shadow puppets, to superstition, to the virtual reality of dreams played out while the household is asleep, to domesticity, self-effacement, and elemental power. They belong to half-light, to the workers, the enslaved, and all those people, so often called primitive, who grant that things have souls (an idea my father, as a good colonial subject, crushed in himself—perhaps the reason he grew so annoyed by my extensive toy collection and the "litter," as he called it, of my paper dolls, and always pushed me to study the sciences, which, he said, were the backbone of modern life, and would keep my head on straight).

The sun is rising. The burnished fullness has returned to your cheek. The Nutcracker opens the wardrobe and climbs up the sleeve of an overcoat. He beckons Marie to follow him, and she finds herself in the Candy Meadow, surrounded by a million sparks of light. Ah! The others are coming in now. I hear the garage door rising. Dear child, if you ever need me, my contact information is lodged with these tales, but I hope you will never find me. I hope I will find you instead, in your world, which is the future, and that I will pass with you through the Almond and Raisin Gate. And if my tampering instigates this change, I will not fear, for I will recognize the shadows of my dreams. The world will be a fairy tale. So meet me, my child, in Bonbon Town, in the heart of the Puppet Kingdom, and may we live happily until we break in pieces.

Before earning her MFA from Vermont College of Fine Arts, Mary Rickert worked as kindergarten teacher, coffee shop barista, Disneyland balloon vendor, and personnel assistant in Sequoia National Park. She is the winner of the Locus Award, Crawford Award, World Fantasy Award, and Shirley Jackson Award. Her novel, *The Shipbuilder of Bellfairie*, will be published by Undertow Publications in August, 2021. Her novella, *Lucky Girl, How I Became a Horror Writer: A Krampus Story*, will be published by Tor.com in the fall of 2022.

THIS WORLD IS MADE FOR MONSTERS

M. Rickert

When the spaceship landed we were all very excited, as you might imagine. First, it hovered over town, blocking the sun on that bright August day, confusing everyone who thought a storm was coming, but eventually we looked up, and there it was, just like we'd seen in our comic books and Saturday afternoon movies, only bigger, so much bigger than we'd ever imagined, and strangely silent for something so large. Then the top half began to spin clockwise while the bottom spun counter, and, with a piercing screech of a giant cicada, it darted away. We shielded our eyes against the brilliance of sun returned to watch its descent over the Beltens' farm on the far side of town.

We children got on our bikes and, in the spirit of generosity such an event inspires, abandoned cliques to share rides with kids we wouldn't usually play with while our mothers—and it was all mothers back then—hollered for us to stop.

They ran inside to call our fathers, but pretended not to hear when their husbands told them to shut all the curtains and say their prayers. Instead, they came after us, wearing aprons and the sensible shoes preferred for cleaning. All any of us had to do was look over our shoulders to see them in their summer dresses, trotting at a distance, shouting our names, but we just pedaled faster.

This was how it came to be that the children were there first, standing at the edge of the Beltens' field, slack-jawed and amazed at the sight of a spaceship landed on the corn. Mr. Belten appeared too stunned to notice our arrival, or to reconsider the position of the rifle that dangled from his hand, obviously useless against the massive invasion, while Mrs. Belten stood on the crooked porch waving.

"Come, hurry, hurry," she called. "Quick, before you get hurt."

Some of us might have gone, but such considerations were interrupted by an electric hum suddenly emitted from the ship as we watched a panel slide open and a staircase fold out to the flattened corn, and I remember how tremendous the silence was.

It is not accurate to say they were green. I suspect that confusion arose from first reports before we'd come to understand the reflective nature of their skin. Had they landed in the Beltens' field in winter, for instance, we would have thought they were white, and had they arrived in spring before the ground was turned, we would have thought they were the color of mud.

The shape of them, however, as generally depicted even all these years later, is correct. They looked slightly amphibian with their large heads, small torsos, narrow limbs, and wide-set eyes. There were four of them of various sizes, two large and two small. We came to think that they were a family.

Mr. Belten was awoken from the enchantment he'd been in as they descended the stairs, but his aim was blocked when Argus, the Beltens' golden retriever, bounded through the field, closely followed by little Amy Belten. One of the large creatures knelt down to pet Argus while one of the small ones glided nearer to Amy. They stared at each other until Amy laughed. The creature made a noise that might have been laughter, too, before Amy took its hand. Together they skipped to the house where Mrs. Belten opened the door and followed them inside as though it were an ordinary day.

By the time our fathers arrived, Mr. Belten had put away his rifle, and Mrs. Belten had opened her kitchen to the mothers who sent their men back into town for supplies. An assembly line of sandwich makers was quickly organized. It was the first annual Alien Fest, which grew so popular that the local economy has come to rely on it, and the recent sharp decline in attendance is worrisome. Revelers dress in green costumes, drink from alien cups, throw balls at alien targets, and eat fried dough dyed to look like green fingers. It is good old-fashioned fun, which apparently no one wants any more.

The mothers made sandwiches while the fathers set up tables quickly fashioned from planks of wood and sawhorses found in the Beltens' barn. Mr. Ellreidge went back to town with the men to open his store. He kindly offered to start a tab for the various supplies such as cases of soda and paper plates and, as the day wore on, charcoal, beer, hot dogs, and condiments.

"Charge it all to the town," the mayor said, but waited until after his reelection that November to send a bill to every household, the "alien tax" as it has come to be called.

I don't know why this isn't taught in our schools. I used to page through my children's history books, and it took me a long time to stop being surprised it wasn't there. Now, when I ask my grandchildren what they know about the genesis of Alien Fest, they have most of the details right but deliver it all in jest and laugh when I say I remember it well. Recently, after trying to explain this to Tess, my youngest granddaughter, stranger than anyone in our family has ever been, she looked up at me with sad brown eyes then slipped her small hand into mine and I realized, with a shock, how old I am, so old that no one believes I know what I am talking about. Tess is the age Amy Belten was then.

It was the Woodstock of our town and time. Not in size but significance. I imagine things would have been different if our visitors had arrived at night when the ship's lights could have been observed from afar, but that's not how it went.

We played games with hoops and ropes, sticks and stones, rubber balls and croquet mallets. We ate hot dogs and potato chips, drank chocolate soda with straws from glass bottles which, left on the tables covered with checkered and flowered cloths, reflected the sun. My memory of that day is infused with tiny rainbows fluttering through the air like dragonflies.

The two larger aliens were content to sit observing us. Several mothers tried to get them to eat but it soon became clear that the creatures weren't interested and, besides, did not appear to have mouths. As the day wore on, they began to provide entertainment of their own, showing us how they could move the ketchup bottle simply by pointing a finger at it, for instance, much to everyone's delight.

We children played with the small alien. I remember how it pointed to the sky over and over again and we suspected it was showing us its home. Like its parents, it was not interested in food but, unlike them, it ran with us and rolled down the small hill behind the barn, and after a while, I can honestly say we forgot any of this was unusual. It was just one of us. It was.

The lowering sun cast everything in gold, the grownups sitting in chair circles, drinking and laughing, the children running through the corn and all around the spaceship, making a game of it. I remember that summer perfume of charcoal and roasted corn, the sizzle and snap of a bonfire built to keep the mosquitoes away.

Then Mrs. Belten began to ask everyone where Amy was. Over and over again, as though she'd lost her mind. Over and over again we told her, "She went into your house, remember? With the alien."

"She isn't there," Mrs. Belten said and, being children (and children of a time so different from the one you've grown up in), we did not understand her alarm. We were so happy, so full of joy and wonder and corn. She bent down and grabbed the little one we had been playing with, took it by the arms and shook it hard. "What have you done with her? What have you done with my baby!" she screamed and made the world stop for just a moment.

"Mrs. Belten," we said. "This is not the same one. It's been with us the whole time. Amy went with the other one."

She stood up slowly, her eyes wide. We might have thought it was an expression of recognition and, perhaps for a moment, that's all it was, but as we watched, she began to hover above the ground, helpless to do anything about it. We turned from her to seek the source of her predicament: the two large aliens standing by the table topped with paper plates and pickle jars. Because their faces were so different from our own, it was impossible to read them, but their eyes did glow an ominous red, and their fingers did point at Mrs. Belten.

Then Amy came running from the field with her new little friend, oblivious to the drama of their arrival, and Mrs. Belten was returned to the earth with a gentle landing. She called Amy and the child went to her, smiling and dirty, willing to pause in her fun to dispense a brief hug, though Mrs. Belten would not let go, even as Amy began to squirm in protest.

We were so distracted by the little family drama playing out before us that we did not notice when Mr. Belten left the assembly but we saw him return with his rifle. Chaos ensued. Parents were calling their children, and children were crying (though, back then, none of us imagined that we would be shot, we were just responding to the atmosphere of distress). Some grownups exhorted Mr. Belten to put the rifle down while others cheered him on.

The aliens did not appear alarmed, though there is no way of knowing, of course. They did gather together and, after the smallest raised its little hand in salute or wave, glided back to their ship with Mr. Belten pointing the rifle at them the whole while.

Unexpectedly, Argus ran out of the field and bounded up the stairs and through the open door after them, but before anything could be done about it, the dog returned, accompanied by one of the large aliens who paused to give the eager animal an enthusiastic rub. Then, without acknowledging any of us, the alien went back to its ship. The door closed. The lights blinked on. The top half spun clockwise and the bottom spun counter and, with a piercing screech that made us cover our ears, it was gone, the only proof of its existence a massive circle of flattened corn.

Mrs. Belten died suddenly that December, with a postmortem diagnosis of stomach cancer which some believed was caused by her experience of forced levitation. On the other hand, Argus lived to be thirty-six years old, which is a long time for such a large dog. Quite a few people wanted to do an autopsy when he died but Amy wouldn't allow it. Amy grew up to be a peculiar woman. She still lives on the farm where she has set up an amazing array of telescopes and stargazing equipment. She has lived there all these years, a recluse, promoting her radicalized agenda of interstellar equality and such nonsense through the Internet, spitting into the wind, I would say, except that—for some reason—her bizarre beliefs have gained traction with this younger generation.

Why, just the other day, Tess told me she didn't want to go to the festival. I was stunned. "Why not?" I asked.

"I don't want to drink out of the alien's body," she said. "I don't want to eat its finger. I don't want to be mean."

"Don't be silly," I said. "That's not what this is about. I remember a day when we were visited by wonder and amazement. When we were all together in our joy. When the sky sparkled with miniature rainbows and the world was everything and more than I had imagined. Once you have experienced something like that, you never stop looking for it again. It isn't mean to remember how we used to be. It isn't mean to celebrate a time when we were perfect. What's mean about that? What's so mean about thinking that maybe they might come back, and wouldn't they be just so pleased to see how we haven't forgotten them? That's why we have this festival. Look around you, child, try to understand. This world is made for monsters."

And then, for reasons I will never understand, little Tess began to cry.

James S.A. Corey is the pen name of Daniel Abraham and Ty Franck. In addition to writing the novels and short stories of The Expanse, they wrote and produced the television series of the same name. Daniel lives with his family in the American southwest. Ty will tell you where he lives when and if he wants you to come over.

ELSEWHERE

James S.A. Corey

I walk into the hospital on unfamiliar legs. The haptics I use at work are Inaan-Castor. No one in North America uses them. I'm fairly sure that the avatar I managed to beg access to is using Kaltenbachs, and they feel slushy and too sharp at the same time. Or maybe that's just where my head is at. It's hard to know.

The place has changed a lot. Being there feels like going back to my old grade school and seeing how small everything's become. The woman at the information desk has shoulder length hair in an asymmetrical cut. The whites of her eyes are so red, I think about peppermints. She pretends not to notice me until it verges on rude, then she pretends that she just did.

"Can I help you?"

"I'm looking for hospice care," I say. "Jacobs?"

My voice seems strange. Higher than I'm used to, and with a buzz that might be the voice box or the ear mics. I'm not there to know. The mint-red eyes shift in what I want to believe is sympathy, but is probably only pity. "Down the corridor on the left. There's a set of glass doors. You can't miss it."

"Thank you," I say.

The hospice nurse knows to expect me. She takes me back to his room. Full spectrum light the color of a summer afternoon. Bamboo paneling on the walls. A cross fashioned from blond wood in a niche. And a day bed with my father on it.

I have a flashbulb memory of being very young—not more than four years old—and sitting on his shoulders so that I could see over an ocean of heads to a pen where a camel was walking. I don't remember any context for it, only the sense of his strength holding me up and the secret, delicious pride in being taller than all the grown-ups around me. He's thin now. His strength is gone. Someone has combed his hair, and I am grateful to them, whoever they are.

I take a wooden chair and sit beside him. For a moment, I think he may be sleeping with his eyes open, but then he takes my hand.

"Jeannie," he says. "I was holding on for you. I knew you'd come."

"Hi, Daddy." He squeezes my fingers, and I squeeze back gently.

"Where are you?"

During the connection and initialization, I spent a lot of time thinking about what I'd say. Planning my last conversation with my father. I felt overwhelmed by the gravity of the moment. And now here we are, and I'm going to tell him about work. Typical.

"Well, we have a contract in Greece, so mostly Athens. We're designing a new school system. Classrooms, dormitories, a central garden. It's going to be beautiful when we're done. Right now, it's mostly site surveys and feasibility. But I still have to do a little mop-up work on the Jakarta project, so there too sometimes."

He smiles, just a little. "My daughter the architect. And where are you?"

For a moment, I am aware of my body. The darkness of the room I'm in. The hiss and click of my vent, the weight of the rig on my head, the coolness of the mattress on my skin. It isn't something that usually happens. I'm well-practiced at keeping focus, but I'm more scattered now than I had realized. "Same as ever," I say. "The clinic in Reddington. They're good."

I expect him to chide me for the price and tell me that they're overpaid, but he doesn't. I am relieved because I don't want to have the same fight again, especially not now. I'm sad because any other time, I know he would have.

I'm sad because I'm watching my father die.

Mom went two years ago in a series of escalating strokes. To the hospital staff, he was the husband of Amanda Jacobs before he was a patient in his own right. Then the cancer came back, and he chose not to fight it. He said he was tired, and the chances were too slim, and the price was too high. I felt betrayed when he said it. After all the times he'd told me to fight, all the times he'd told me that life was precious and worth living, his surrender felt like hypocrisy. It had taken me almost too long to see how our positions were different. Not the least was that he was my father and I was his daughter, and parents are supposed to die before children.

He swallows, and I look around for a glass of water and find it. A little carafe in the back of the room with a plastic cup and straws. When I pour it for him, I can feel the coolness of the water against my Kaltenbach fingertips, and I can't help admiring that. Temperature can be hard.

In Reddington, an alarm chimes softly from somewhere down the hall. I let my attention shift there until I hear the day nurse's footsteps. Once I know that someone's on it—whatever it is—I shift my attention back to the avatar, and carry the cup to him. The straw is a milky white. Colorless. His lips are almost the same.

"Thank you," he says after he's taken a sip. I feel like he's humoring me. Then, "I wasn't sure you would be able to come."

"It was tricky," I say, and gesture at my mechanical body. "This isn't in my workgroup access plan. One of the contractors owed me a favor, though."

"That's good. Thank you."

"It's a different model than I'm used to. It feels awkward. But I get to hand it back once I'm done. They have a junior staff that take it whenever it's not in use." I'm babbling. I shut up.

"I remember bringing you here," he says, and clicks in the back of his throat. A chuckle. "I was so frightened."

I don't remember it. Or, I have a memory that has been constructed from all the retellings of the story. The memories I have that I trust—the ones where I'm actually in my body—are of being in school and feeling a little ill, a little woozy. That's all. The rest of it—the fever, the paralysis, my breath growing shallow as the nerves in my diaphragm died—is all like something I've seen on a screen. A camera viewing me from outside. It's how I know the memories are false. I was sixteen, and one of twenty people in Atlanta who came down with enterovirus D92. I only knew one of the others. Her name was Cissy Travers, and she was in my algebra II class. She died of it. I almost did.

In the false memories, my father comes into my room to check on me because he's been watching the local news, which did a story on the virus. How quickly it hit, how few warning signals it gave. I'd come home from school with the flu and gone to bed, and he was just going to peek in on me to alleviate his paternal paranoia. He pushes the door open and sees me in my bed, my breath shallow, my eyes open. He calls my name and I don't answer.

He shrieks my mother's name as he scoops me up and carries me down the stairs and across the living room and the kitchen to the garage door. I've looked at the floor plan of our house from back then, and the blueprints show the garage door being farther on, through a sun room. That isn't what I remember.

Then the desperate race to the hospital, my father running the red lights while I lay in the back seat, my arms and legs flopping at odd angles like a game of pick-up sticks. If I had actually been in that position, I would have been able to see the upholstery and the roof of the car, but I remember his eyes and the way he punched the car horn, the closest he had to a siren.

And then the hospital—this same one, though it's had an extensive remodel in the decades since then. A broad shouldered man with his sixteen-year-old daughter in his arms like a corpse. I remember him shouting at the intake nurse that there wasn't time, but I remember it from over the nurse's shoulder, like I was a movie camera or a ghost already halfway out of my body.

Sometime in the next twelve hours, I drew my last breath. Every one since then has been drawn on my behalf. I don't remember any of my treatment, even as a falsehood.

"It was a long time ago," I say, and offer him another sip. He shakes his head, and it means both *No I don't want more* and *No it wasn't so long ago.*

"I felt so powerless," he says. "I was so frightened."

"I know."

"Is that how you feel now?"

"A little. I guess. I don't really know how I feel right now, so it's kind of hard to say. I'm . . . "

He takes my hand. "I don't hurt. And I'm not frightened."

"You're high as a fucking kite on morphine."

His smile is impish. "I know. Do you remember the game? The one I brought you?"

"Always," I say.

"I did that right at least," he says. He closes his eyes, and his smile gets wider.

"You did a lot of things right," I say, and maybe he hears me.

What I remember of the weeks after I stopped breathing was the grief and the boredom. It seemed like one should have overpowered the other, but that wasn't how it was. I had a room on the fourth floor with a ventilator putting air into my lungs and letting it out. Every few days, Doctor Samnin would try taking me off of it in hopes that I would see some return of neural function. That's what she called it. I'd hope that this time a miracle had occurred, and each time it hadn't. I'd grieve again, and I'd try to sleep. There was a television, but I had trouble keeping track of things.

My parents were always there. If they weren't in the room, they were nearby. Eventually Doctor Samnin told them to go home and get some rest. *This is a marathon, not a sprint.* That's how she put it.

My mind came back slowly, and I could measure it by how much I could follow the plots of the movies and shows that ran on the screen and by how long the hours were. I slept not to rest, but for the sense of time passing. The hospital gave me a simple keyboard that I could use to communicate, but I didn't have anything to say. I was broken and I hated it. It didn't take many keystrokes to get that across. For a while, I was anxious that I was missing my homework, but no one else brought it up. School was for people who could breathe.

Did I fantasize about dying? Yes. And I also fantasized about living. They both seemed equally removed from the place I actually was. A room. A machine to breathe for me. A body that had forgotten how to be a body, and brain that hadn't forgotten enough. The paint in that room was a soft blue-green, a little more saturated than toothpaste. When I'm designing things now, I never use that color.

After six months, Doctor Samnin had the talk with us. I had survived the virus, which was better than many people who caught it. I had lost enough of the nerves in my diaphragm that I wouldn't be able to breathe without assistance. I had lost significant motor function in my limbs. The good news was my GI track, my heart, and my central nervous system had avoided the worst of the damage. I was what I was. I was as good as I was going to get.

It would have been devastating, but by then I had the game.

He brought it to me on my birthday. I was seventeen. It was a light VR rig, hardly heavier than a pair of swim goggles. The controllers were heavy, but he'd found someone who could modify them to work with my limited range of motion. What I remember from the fitting was how uncomfortable it was, and how the discomfort was at least something new. Then he turned it on, and I was riding the back of a giant eagle over a cloud-swept sky. Below me, a landscape rolled out with forests and castles and lakes that sparkled in a sun that I could see if I used the left controller to look up.

It was nauseating and astounding. The game was called Loftgrim Arch: The Coming of the Green, and I played it for a hundred hours in the first week I had it. It was single player, but after my first play through, I found it had a social function in one of the control options. I didn't have a mic, and I hated the halting sound of my voice driven by my own too-regular breath. But the chat room was familiar, and before long, I started to know the people there. We didn't trade messages about our lives, who or where we were. We lived in Loftgrim.

So when the talk came that I was as good as I would ever be, and Mom started quietly weeping, I mostly wanted to get back in my rig and check another cave complex for the vampire king's secret city.

A month after that, I'd been moved to a permanent facility. The room there was white and had a window that looked out on a telephone pole, at least from the angle I could see it. I had moved on to other games by then. Nothing that required fast reflexes, but I loved the puzzle boxes. Especially the ones I could move through. I don't know who first had the idea, but one day Doctor Samnin reappeared.

"There's something I'd like to try," she said.

The first connection and initialization took almost an hour. I can do it in five minutes now, but my brain has been very well-mapped. That first time, we were in uncharted territory. I remember the coolness of the rig against my head and my hands. I remember the darkness as the connection came up. And then I was standing, just the way I would have in Loftgrim. I was in a room with a Doctor Samnin, only I wasn't looking up her nose, so her nostrils seemed less pronounced. My mother and father were there. And wide-faced girl on a vent with a spaghetti of wires on her head.

I took the first unsteady step. I paused to find my balance. Slowly, I walked to my body, took my new hand and gently lifted one of the eyepieces up so that I could see me looking at me, and see me looking back.

I didn't laugh because I'm not a thing that laughs anymore than I'm a thing that sobs. But I grinned so hard it hurt a little.

My father's breath deepens, and I take it as a sign of sleep. I sit beside him, his hand in mine. His mouth is open just a little, and I can see his lower teeth, small and yellowed from a lifetime of morning coffee and afternoon tea. His skin is paler than the man I think of when I think of him. I cut off the feedback loop so that I don't unintentionally move and disturb him. I keep the haptics live, though. I can feel the warmth of his palm in mine.

Time passes slowly and too fast. The door opens behind me, and I suffer a moment of confusion before I remember to turn the loop back on and look. The nurse is an older man with a long, gentle face. He nods at me as if an avatar sitting at a bedside was perfectly normal, then goes to my father. I want to tell him no, to let him sleep, but I don't. He presses an instrument to my father's finger, considers the readout. His smile is compassionate and well-practiced.

"It won't be long now," he says.

"Thank you."

He puts a hand on my shoulder. There aren't any sensor plates there, but I feel the gesture anyway. I know it for what it is. The door closes behind him with a soft tick, and my father's eyes don't open. I move myself to sit a little closer, but not for him. Just for me.

There had been a moment when Mom was dying when we all knew that there wouldn't be a recovery. He'd gone to her bedside all the same, just the way he had for me. Just the way I am doing for him now, since there isn't anyone else but the two of us anymore. Mom was in a deep coma by then, but he sat and read books and listened to the news. He held her hand and kissed her forehead.

We do that when we're powerless to fix things, because it is the power we do have. When there's nothing else to offer, we give our presence.

I spent months getting the hang of the avatars. The games languished, though I never wholly lost interest in them. Ambitions I'd half forgotten came roaring back, and I finished my high school coursework only a year and a half late. I used a first generation DuraTek with no haptics at all to walk for graduation, and my attempt at throwing my cap up with the other students went poorly. But it didn't matter.

In my nursing home, a staff saw to my breathing. Outside of it, I went to college. It was harder for me, sometimes in ways I hadn't anticipated. I wore out more easily than other people. Watching my friends fall in love with each other reminded me of some of my limitations, but despite that, I had boyfriends. Some came to see me in the flesh. Some didn't. The relationships were all real, though. I graduated with honors and applied to architecture school.

So much of the next four years was difficult. I went through design classes without my eyes there, and learned that I could adjust the spectrum on my avatar to make finer gradations than some of my more traditionally embodied cohorts. I still had to build models with cardboard and glue and razors. Just printing something up didn't have the same value, according to the medieval standards of university. There were times I was discouraged, but I kept showing up. I didn't graduate at the top of my class, but I wasn't at the bottom either. When I accepted that diploma, I used a much better avatar. I felt the handshake.

Doctor Samnin tracked me until she retired. We did scans every six months to see how my brain was reacting. What parts grew, what shrunk. It made her very happy to see that the areas of my motor cortex that dealt with balance and coordination weren't atrophied at all. I was moving all the time, just without leaving my bed.

Taking the boards was difficult, and we had to get a lawyer involved. They said I had to be there in person to take the test. In one particularly contentious meeting, I offered to have them wheel me over, as long as they signed an agreement acknowledging their liability if something went wrong with my vent. They caved. I took the boards. I became an architect, and I started my career. The staff changed over at my nursing home, and I researched other facilities. I moved to Reddington, which was farther from home, and my father never could bring himself to think well of the place, however good the care was. He missed having me close.

The end comes for him. I want it to be a long, shuddering breath and then a soft collapse the way it is in movies, but it's harder than that. He gasps and struggles. I know it's just his flesh holding on by reflex. I sing songs to him. The same ones he sang to me when I was young. I don't know if it helps him, but maybe that doesn't matter. It helps me, and he would want that, if he could want anything.

And then the hard part is over, and I'm still holding his hand. I look at him, his head turned a degree to the right. His mouth open and still. In Reddington, tears fall down my cheeks. I can weep there, even if I can't do it here.

I think how strange it is that he's gone. How different the world feels without him in it. I wonder where he went to, and if I'll ever be there. And how strange it is that, in just a few minutes, there will be two bodies in this room whose consciousness had left them to go elsewhere.

Later, I press my forehead to his, the closest I can do to kissing him, and I disconnect.

Andy Dudak is a writer and translator of science fiction. His original stories have appeared in *Analog, Apex, Clarkesworld, Daily Science Fiction, Interzone, The Magazine of Fantasy and Science Fiction,* Rich Horton's Year's Best, and elsewhere. He's translated twelve stories for *Clarkesworld,* and a novel by Liu Cixin, among other things. In his spare time he likes to binge-watch peak television and eat Hui Muslim style cold sesame noodles.

SALVAGE

Andy Dudak

1

Statues congest the silent lanes and marketplaces of the crumbling, overgrown village, figures life-size and life-like except for the glowing veins suffusing their ceramic flesh, children and adults and elders fixed during a long-ago, fateful moment. Aristy makes her way among the familiar faces of Picti Street. The morning mists burn away from the vine-curtained, root-clutched stone facades on either side. It's early now, but it was nearly dinnertime when these villagers were transformed a millennium ago.

Many clues indicate this.

Aristy passes the Priest with his evening prayer bell aloft in mid-ring. Then the Farmers in from the fields, seated on long-gone stools at long-gone tables frowning over long-gone games of chess. There's the Restaurant Owner, stirring whatever-it-was in a now-rusted cauldron for the evening traffic to see and smell. Many were transmuted along with their clothes and personal affects—and even adjacent parts of the environment—intact. Others are as unselfconsciously nude as the Greek statues of Old Earth.

All are made of a dark gray super-material impervious to the elements, shot through with pulses of light.

Aristy feels the weight of her backpack in her old bones. Already sweating, she checks her progress up Picti Street by the statues, or homifacts, as they're called here on New Ce. There's the Quarreling Couple. Just beyond glares the Constable, who was transformed with his armor, spear, and pistol preserved.

She's getting close.

A lung-wing descends through the mist and alights on the Admonishing Mother's outstretched arm. Aristy stops to catch her breath and return the amphibian's blinking gaze. She lets the shrieks and hiccups of the cloud forest wash over her. The great silence behind the clamor of wildlife expands within her.

Moving past the Admonished Children, she comes upon homifacts she doesn't know, hasn't named, and hasn't spoken with.

She shrugs off her pack next to a young man in mid-purposeful stride, a temple acolyte by the look of him. She withdraws her homemade interface mesh and drapes it carefully over the statue. She dons her skullcap, flicks open her field chair, and sits down with her scroll. Fingers dancing, she closes her eyes.

There is the usual sense of dislocation, and vague awareness of her 'rithms translating the bizarre code at work in the homifact.

Suddenly she's floating, disembodied and invisible, above the young Acolyte. He's alive again, with the street and its denizens. It's early evening. The encroaching cloud forest is nowhere to be seen. The stone houses and shopfronts are in good repair. The evening prayer bell rings amid the dinnertime hubbub. Touts advertise restaurants. Here and there a radio crackles with music or propaganda.

The Acolyte heads for the bell-ringing Priest. Aristy quick-scans ahead. She is not a voyeur.

Night falls abruptly, and the Acolyte flits away from his conversation with the Priest, Picti Street swarming with accelerated village life. Aristy scans faster. Night and day strobe past, the young man a daily throb of blurred movement confined to the Temple of Nachtan, and Picti Street.

Three months pass. The Acolyte's simulated life drags to a halt. He's at his morning meditation in the Hall of Candles, as Aristy has dubbed it in her own mind.

She sets new 'rithms in motion.

She appears before the Acolyte as he opens his eyes. She represents herself as she really is, and wonders what he thinks of her: an old, lanky woman in a strange, ragged utility suit, silver hair close-cropped. She could read his mind and find out what he thinks, of course, but she is not a voyeur.

The Acolyte's eyes widen. "Is this enlightenment?"

"In a sense," Aristy says.

The Hall of Candles fades, along with the other acolytes and attending villagers. Aristy sometimes finds it useful to tune down the simulation when breaking the news. It can help with credulity.

"Who . . . What are you?" the Acolyte says.

"A human being. Homo sapiens dispersionis, just like you used to be."

"Used to be . . . Am I dead?"

"Yes and no. Your real life ended three months ago, of an evening. On Picti Street, on your way to speak with the Priest."

He looks around in growing alarm.

"All of this . . . the temple, the people, your life since that evening, has been a simulation. A kind of lantern show, for your benefit." She has found some citizens of this fallen colony planet more aware of past technology than others.

He's hyperventilating. "I . . . just want to wake up . . . "

She accesses his core objects and tunes down his panic. While she's at it, she turns up his credulity and receptivity to new ideas. She doesn't like meddling with their personalities—that's not what this is supposed to be about, even though she's making it up as she goes along. Anyway, a little meddling expedites things. There are so many homifacts—so many minds—to get to, billions more than she can reach in her remaining years.

The Acolyte's breathing slows. He's able to resume the cyclic breaths of his discipline.

"That's better," she says. "Now then, I need to tell you about dark energy."

"Excuse me?" the Night Soil Collector says.

"You'd better sit down."

The woman sinks onto her cot. They're in her tidy shack adjacent to the butcher shop. The Collector is as meticulously clean as her humble abode, more so than the average villager.

"Dark energy," Aristy says. "It's how we used to explain the accelerating expansion of the universe, without really understanding it." She studies the Collector. "The universe is expanding, you see, faster and faster . . . "

"I know." The woman frowns up at her. "I read old books, even though it could get me shot."

Aristy is no voyeur, but she can't help a brief audit of the virtual shack and its contents. Sure enough, there's a chest buried in the earthen floor. It contains several outlawed tomes, and the proceeds of selling night soil as fertilizer: a roll of banknotes and string of silver coins.

Aristy says: "You don't have to worry about getting shot anymore, as I've explained."

"So none of this real," the Printer says, grasping the flywheel of his press and marveling.

"That's right."

"And all the people I've interacted with for the past three months?"

"Simulacra. Part of the simulation."

"Even my wife?"

"Even her, I'm afraid."

"But . . . how is it possible?"

Aristy fiddles with a tray of tiny print blocks. The local written language is pictographic, so there are hundreds of different blocks. "Kind of like how you assemble these into sentences, paragraphs, stories, and make people see something new. It's all information."

He blinks at her through his heavy spectacles. "But why has this been done to me?"

"That brings us back to the expanding universe. It was discovered that the real dark energy, the prime mover of accelerating expansion, is observation."

The Printer continues to blink his magnified eyes. The walls of his humble shop are papered with propaganda, the desperate slogans and fictions of a failing regime. "Observation . . . " he says.

The Visiting Student steps out of the muck of the paddy and onto the causeway. "What do you mean?"

"I mean observation of the universe is causing it to fly apart."

The grimy young woman stares at Aristy, head cocked. She was sent here from the Agricultural University in the Capital, some kind of labor-oriented punitive measure. Aristy guesses she has some science, but probably not the right kind. Reluctantly, she uploads germane knowledge. It might help the Student to understand, as much as anyone can, the phenomenon that will eventually cause a Big Rip.

The young woman's skepticism gives way to amazement. Perhaps she's digesting the quantum Zeno effect, ancient knowledge from Old Earth. A particle's evolution in time may be arrested by measuring it frequently enough. Of course, this only goes to show that observation can affect the physical world. As it turns out, Zeno gets flipped on its head at the macro scale.

The Student regards the muck she's been laboring in since sunrise. "I think I'm in the wrong major."

"You didn't have much choice, did you?" Aristy knows something about the extinct Republic of Iomang, after so many conversations with its citizens.

"No," the bemused Student says, "I suppose not." She sits down on the causeway, once more staring beyond the simulated present. "But . . . if observation pauses things at the quantum scale, why should it change the cosmos at large?"

"That's above my pay grade," Aristy says. "Above most people's, really. The discovery wasn't ours. Wasn't humanity's, I mean."

Once more, the Student glares in amazement. "You mean . . . "

"Yes."

"We never met them," Aristy tells the Commissar.

The balding, bearded man in the drab uniform still holds the smoking pistol at his side. He tried to shoot Aristy when she manifested in his little study. Now, with his panic tuned down, he absorbs the reality of alien intelligence.

"We never saw them," Aristy continues, "except some of their ships from a great distance. They transmitted to many worlds in the human Emanation. A language key, then their finding on expansion, and means of confirming it experimentally. And finally a request."

She sees the village's political man is having trouble swallowing this. According to his beloved Generalissimo Picti, humans evolved on this world, on this very island. There was no Old Earth, no diaspora, or colony or fall. Never mind all this rot about simulated realities and aliens. She turns up his credulity, essentially changing who he is, however slightly. She tells herself this is for his own good. She's here to help him, after all. To free him, possibly.

"A request . . . " he says.

"They asked humanity to turn its damaging gaze away from the cosmos. Turn inward, lose itself in simulated realities. And some did. Whole civilizations did. But it wasn't enough for the aliens, the Curators as we've come to call them. So, they acted. They swept through the human Emanation in less than a century. No one knows how they did that. They turned the human species inward. Cities, worlds, systems, empires. The Curators' Reagent froze people instantly, preserved their brains, which were gradually converted into durable networks suffusing their remnant statues. A trillion human beings Turned Inward, a trillion isolated minds in a trillion virtualities."

The Commissar sits at his desk, setting the pistol on his copy of the ubiquitous Forge the Future, the guidebook for every good Iomangan, penned by Tuwathal Picti himself.

"If all that's true," the Commissar says, "then who, or what, are you?"

"A human being. Homo sapiens dispersionis, just like you used to be."

Aristy has said this to over five hundred Turned Inward minds. There's more she could say about who and what she is, but she can barely admit those things to herself. Better to stay busy. Better to lose herself in this strange work she's found for herself.

The Doctor holds the narcosia syrette poised by her hip, ready to strike.

Aristy caught her in the village supply depot, mid-robbery, for the Doctor is also the Addict. Aristy tuned her out of the belief that this visit is a hallucination caused by withdrawal, but the good Doctor still craves her fix. Aristy considers tweaking the addiction out of her. Would the Doctor still be the Doctor after that? What is foundational to her personality, and what disposable?

"So you're a human being," the Doctor says, sweating, shivering. "My condolences."

"A million or so humans were in ships traveling near light speed during the century of the Reagent. They escaped the Turning Inward. I'm a descendant."

The Doctor stabs, wincing briefly, then exhaling a great sigh. She falls against a stack of crates and sinks to the floor. "What do you want from me?" she whispers, grinning, tears streaming.

"I'm here to give you options," Aristy says. "I can upload you to my machine, where you can live on your own terms, in a world you forge, and interact with others like yourself. Or you can stay here, and I can tweak this simulation as you like. If you choose that, I can even wipe your memory of this encounter. You could go on as before, oblivious to the truth. Or, finally, I can end you."

The Doctor looks up at her, benumbed. "So the fucking Picti regime . . . "

"Ended a thousand years ago," Aristy says.

"But you said it's been three months since I was turned."

"You were underclocked. The Curators designed you to tick slowly through the ages of their preserved universe. I had to speed you up for this conversation."

The Doctor nods off for a bit, then comes to with a flinch. She focuses, bleary-eyed, and holds up the empty syrette. "Can you free me of this?"

"Yes."

"And Iomang . . . "

"You can leave it behind, or make a whole new one."

Aristy comes to in the stifling afternoon heat.

She rises from her field chair and removes her skullcap, drinks from her canteen, then plugs the interface mesh—still draped over the Doctor homifact—into her portable quantum server. She initiates transfer, and suddenly the Doctor is running on two machines at once, the illusion of continuity preserved, as promised. As seconds go by, more and more of her runs on Aristy's server. The Doctor will continue to experience the village simulation until her transfer is complete, when she'll be able to create her own environments.

Aristy contemplates the nearest homifacts, her day's work:

The Acolyte, mid-stride, frowning with distaste at the strolling Night Soil Collector. Printer and Visiting Student in line at a now-collapsed shop front. And the Commissar, eyeing a chess player with suspicion.

Of the six she hacked today, four chose transfer to her server: Acolyte, Night Soil Collector, Visiting Student, and Doctor. The small-minded Printer opted to remain in his simulated village, but with a larger, more prosperous print shop, a remodeled wife, and a medal of distinguished service from Generalissimo Picti. The brainwashed Commissar, unable to bear the historical irrelevance of Picti's long-gone reign, chose oblivion.

With transfer complete, Aristy packs her equipment and shoulders it. She heads back down Picti Street, leaving five more homifacts still flashing with the inner computation of their simulations, but emptied of their minds.

She follows her path along the Flameworm river, through dense cloud forest that was once open paddy-land. She stops for a breather beside the squatting, moss-covered Fisherman. He was one of the first Iomangans she liberated. The homifact's lights are barely discernible under the moss.

At the Big Bend of the Flameworm, where the canopy opens up, Aristy gazes skyward into dark blue heavens. She imagines her scrutiny contributing a few dark joules or dark newtons to the expansion of the universe.

Among the day-stars hangs the spark of the Harbinger, in synchronous orbit. She doesn't like to think of her relativistic years aboard that prison.

Back within the canopy twilight, she passes the double statue of the Entwined Lovers, nearly engulfed by roots. Turned Inward, each went on loving a simulation of the other. These two simulations were based on a lover's intimate scrutiny and might almost have been Turing-viable. Confronted by Aristy, the lovers themselves chose upload, eager to reunite.

This eerie landmark means she's almost home. She quickens her pace.

She knows something's off before she rounds the Root Cathedral and sees her camp. She's been alone out here long enough to internalize the rainforest's cycles and rhythms. Maybe there's a gap in the lung-wing songs, or alarum notes from the burrowing plate-mail worms, communicated to her old bones by the soil. She can't say.

Two strangers have found her camp.

Fellow colonists she doesn't know, young, born after planetfall: a woman in a rifle-rig standing guard between the anti-contagion dome and generator, and a slender man seated at the field table. He's dressed ridiculously for the jungle. The flimsy formalwear suit, all the rage down at Drop City, clings to his sweaty skin, soiled and shredded.

More importantly though, he wears a skullcap. He must have searched the dome, because Aristy's camp server is on the table, and the young man is interfaced.

The guard touches his shoulder. He opens his eyes, briefly disoriented, then sees Aristy and removes the skullcap. "Well hello there."

She heaves off her pack, glaring. "What is this? You have no right to my data."

He unrolls his scroll onto the table. She steps forward and squints at the search warrant flashing down the screen.

"You gotta be kidding me!" Aristy says.

The guard swivels her rig, bringing the large weapon to bear.

"I'm afraid not, Captain," the suit says.

"And what are you, a Council secretary?"

"I do work for the Council. I'm a lawyer."

"We have lawyers now? God help us."

He places his hand on the camp server, a quantum machine orders of magnitude more powerful than her field device, where the Acolyte, Night Soil Collector, Visiting Student, and Doctor currently run, nearly maxing out the processors. The camp server comfortably accommodates 271 uploaded souls and their environments, and could take a lot more. Aristy was planning to transfer the day's harvest as soon as she returned.

"Captain, this equipment is colony property."

"You're hurting for computation in Drop City?"

"That's not the point."

"Everyone grabbed stuff in the early days. Planetfall was a crazy time. You're too young to understand."

"Nevertheless . . . "

"I can't fucking believe this!"

The thuggish guard smirks, seemingly eager for things to go wrong.

"I just want to be left alone," Aristy pleads. "I just want to die up here, alone!"

"But you aren't quite alone, are you?" the lawyer says, fingers drumming the server.

"Their conditions are up to code."

"Funny you should mention that. I think you mean the Instantiation and Sentience Code, which delineates standards for running salvaged souls. Do you have a salvage charter for this region? For any region?"

"If it weren't for me," Aristy says, fuming, "neither of you would be here!"

"What do you mean by that?" The lawyer leans forward, interested.

She could tell him. Just as she could've explained what she is to the Acolyte, the Doctor, the Commissar, and many others. But she left Drop Town to forget all that.

"Their conditions are up to code," she repeats, her heart sinking. "Above and beyond, in fact. Each resident has their own customizable multiverse. Their shared space is a fucking paradise. I think you just saw it. They have everything they could possibly need."

"Not everything," the lawyer says. "You've ignored one particular request. Repeatedly."

Aristy stands there, exhausted, at her wit's end.

"Captain, you and your machines will have to come with us."

2

"Picti's Oath-Keepers came to our flat in the wee hours."

The man weeps from his remaining eye as he speaks.

"We woke to them smashing through the door. They shouted and waved their electric torches around, menaced us with short swords and pistols. They wore the black cloaks, the face paint, the whole routine. My sisters and I couldn't stop screaming."

He wipes the tears from his eye. A socket of burnished-looking scar tissue reminds everyone where the other eye used to be. Like all the witnesses, he appears as he was at some well-chosen point in his corporeal life.

"Picti called his political police Oath-Keepers, but us common folk had another name for them . . . Bogle-Men, from a legend told to naughty children in the old days. My great-grandma used to say, 'You'd better behave, or the Bogle-Man will come while you sleep and throw you in his sack and take you away to his cave. Where you will suffer unspeakably.'"

His words are converted to standard Belt-and-Road in real time. Unlike Aristy, most of the assembly hasn't bothered to learn Iomangan.

"One of them knocked my mother to the floor. They were laughing. My big sis flew into a rage. A gun fired, and she went down. Someone else pistol-whipped me. When I came to, my sister was dead and my father had been taken. We never knew his alleged crime, and didn't dare ask. I never saw my father again. The rumor was he'd been taken to the Tannery, where he suffered for months or even years before they finally shot him. Everyone called it the Tannery. That's what it was before Picti's men converted it."

Aristy has heard this kind of thing before, though not from this particular soul. She remembers salvaging this dour man. Farmer 17, one of the chess players on Picti Street.

"I want justice for my brother and father, and for my mother, who was never the same."

The screen, a window onto the shared space in Aristy's camp server, takes up an entire wall of the ostentatious new judiciary hall. Drop Town has certainly changed since she last visited: new buildings printed, new institutions conjured, the beginnings of social stratification. It's no longer the glorified camp that grew around a poorly-aimed supply drop. It has become a bustling city state.

Farmer 17, Casantin Onuist, steps out of frame, momentarily revealing a crowded hilltop of the shared garden world. The Visiting Student steps into view, cleansed of the virtual fertilizer she was shoveling when Aristy found her.

"My name is Eumi Wilfoil, and I want to speak to you about my mother. She wasn't much older than me when the Picti regime forced her to marry my father, an important Pictiite who was already an old man by then."

Aristy recognizes a few of the older faces on the Council, and in the citizens' gallery, but most of the people in the hall are young strangers to her.

"We saw very little of him," Eumi continues, "and as the years wore on, my mother found comfort with another man. They were discrete, of course, but one day they were both just . . . gone. Taken to the Tannery, perhaps. I never found out. Not long afterward, the commissar at my university told me I was being sent to the countryside for reeducation through labor. I figured my father was behind that. Maybe he thought I was a bastard. I didn't mind, actually. The work didn't bother me. Under the circumstances, my fate could've been much worse."

She stares beyond her simulated garden, beyond her corporeal audience.

"I want justice for my mother, Rilith Tilore Wilfoil. We demand the salvage of Tuwathal Picti. He must not be given the choices we were. He needs to be uploaded, tried, and punished."

More witnesses follow, telling their stories and demanding legal recourse, or straightforward vengeance. Irilich Simiod the Night Soil Collector, Scrimgar the Acolyte, and Dr Muriad Corvirst are among the thirty-seven complainants.

"Esteemed Council members . . . " The young lawyer, Chard Thoroughblind, turns from the screen. "I've been hired by these Iomangans as their advocate. Under the new laws, salvaged souls have the same rights we do."

"Not entirely true," says a Councilwoman. "Granted, they have their rights, but only after the salvager has assayed their memories and sold any IP of value. Until then, they're merely salvaged data."

Thoroughblind clears his throat, glancing uncomfortably at Aristy. "Of course, Madam Councilwoman, but in this case, the souls were illegally—"

"In that case the law stipulates forfeiture to the state."

"But this is not the Mainland with its dead superpowers and homifacts full of high art and science. We're talking about the backward Republic of Iomang." He flashes an apologetic look at his clients. "When was the last time someone applied for a salvage charter here? Council members, I ask that you make a special dispensation in this case. Spare my clients the indignity of assay, which is unlikely to yield a profit regardless. I think we can all agree these Iomangans have suffered enough."

"Then what do you propose?" the Councilwoman says.

"Sentence Aristy Safewither for her transgression. Give her community service. She is, in any case, the only person on our island who knows how to salvage, I think. Give my clients their closure, without the cost of sending for a professional salvager from the Mainland."

The Councilwoman turns her questing gaze on Aristy. "Captain Safewither, your wards asked you for justice many times. Why did you ignore them?"

Aristy enjoys a brief sense of withheld power. A few words would make them forget all about long-dead tyrants. "I didn't think it was my place," she lies. "Also, I wasn't sure about the legalities."

The Councilwoman snorts.

An older, familiar Councilman opens his scroll. "You've an interesting record, Captain. You were a sleeper system technician on the Harbinger, correct?"

"One of fifteen, yes."

This gets Thoroughblind's attention. The young lawyer stares at her avidly.

"And you were a suspect after the Failure," the Councilman says.

"One of many." She remembers this man from the ship years. A security officer and later a resource manager. "I was exonerated."

"And after planetfall you deserted."

"A lot of us did. A general amnesty was declared, as I'm sure you remember."

"And you went up to the cloud forest and became a hermit. Why is that?"

"I'd had my fucking fill of bureaucrats like you."

There's a ripple of amusement in the gallery.

"Nevertheless," the Councilman says, "you live in District 17 of the New Ce Colony, and are subject to its laws. You're an illegal salvager. For all we know, you were going to sell those poor souls on the black market. God knows what kind of sadist might've ended up with them."

"Bullshit. Why would I salvage so many before trying to sell? Why would I keep them in such comfort? And what the fuck do I want with scrip? All scrip would get me is a life among you people."

More laughter in the gallery.

"Alright, alright," the Councilwoman says. "Then why did you do it?"

Aristy often wonders this. She knows it was about more than distracting herself. She often meditates on the concept of atonement, but she won't go into that here.

"Captain?"

"Can we get on with this?"

"Fine, what do you think should happen to you?"

"Confiscate my equipment. Take my 'rithms, free of charge. Not the most elegant coding, not like that Mainlander shit I guess, but it works. Just let me go."

"As far as I understand salvage, the hardware and 'rithms wouldn't be enough. It's a tricky process, an art, according to the Mainlanders. Your expertise would be needed. Are you saying you don't want to salvage Picti, even if we grant the charter?"

The idea of bringing Tuwathal Picti to justice makes her sick.

"Just let me go back to the forest and die!"

The thug who escorted her to Drop Town, Bray Highbarren, follows her down muddy Impact Way and into a ramshackle bar, a relic of the settlement's early days. Aristy buys a bottle of Lamentable Ferment with the last of her scrip, and sits down.

Bray slings her rifle and sits beside her charge. "It's fucking sad in here."

The sparse midday crowd is noticeably advanced in age. There's no chatter. Everyone sits alone and drunk.

"You weren't invited." Aristy takes a long pull. "But I do invite you to fuck off."

"Keep talking like that and I might start to like you." Bray rudely grabs the bottle and takes a sip, then grimaces and hands it back. "Why do all you old fucks drink this shit?"

"A recipe from the ship days," Aristy says. "An acquired taste." She pulls again, growing warm, wondering how long the Council will take to deliberate. Maybe she'll keel over from alcohol poisoning before they reach a verdict.

"I'll never understand your generation," Bray says, gazing around the subdued common room.

"How could you? We were born on the Harbinger, at dangerously close to light speed. Our parents were born that way and died that way. And our grandparents. We didn't have much in the way of choices."

"Join the damn club."

Aristy smirks, beginning to like this young woman despite herself. "Fair enough."

Bray takes the bottle for another reluctant sip. "You're here on New Ce, after all."

"I should be grateful, you mean." She has the bottle again. She's feeling the old, brute force intoxication of the Ferment. She's drunk on New Ce, a garden world made available for second-wave colonization by the Turning Inward. New Ce, infinitely preferable to freezing Tesca, the world of her press-ganged great-grandparents.

She really should be more grateful.

"You . . . " It's barely more than a wheeze, issuing from a dark corner of the common room.

"Me?" Aristy says.

Bray stands as an old man approaches.

"Captain Safewither." He's frail, inebriated, dressed in a threadbare utility suit from the ship days, like Aristy, like many seniors of Drop Town.

"That'll do," Bray says, getting in his way.

He looks up at the hulking woman. "I know what she did!" he says, growing agitated. "Do you know what she did?"

He seems familiar, but Aristy can't place him.

"She salvaged souls without a charter," Bray says. "What of it?" This seems to confuse him. "Go home and dry out."

That face, the accusation in the rheumy eyes: maybe he worked under her in sleeper maintenance. Aristy gets up and stumbles out of the bar. She drains the bottle and tosses it in the mud. The rickshaw and caterpillar traffic of Impact Way beckons her.

One small step is all it would take.

Bray seizes her shoulder and drags her stumbling backwards. "Fucking oldie, you're not dying on my watch."

Aristy collapses in the mud, shivering with indignation. It annoyed her when the Council assigned just one guard for the recess. Now it seems their low estimation of her was justified.

"Get up," Bray says.

Aristy glares at the traffic, the newly-printed government buildings, the thug looming over her, the old man peering out of the bar entrance. Despite all the recent development, she can see the encroaching jungle from here.

Drop Town is still just a tiny scar of civilization in a sea of wilderness. It was for this, for the idea of it, that she did what she did on the Harbinger. She didn't think about the Curators and the Turning Inward at the time. She often wonders if that would have affected her decision. Why become a sin-eater for three-thousand colonists if the civilization they plan to build is ultimately doomed? The Curators vanished after their handiwork, but they might return at any time. Perhaps they're Turned Inward themselves, awaiting the trigger of sufficient human numbers to wake up and carry out their universal maintenance again. The blossoming second-wave societies of the human Emanation live in fear of this.

"Come on," Bray says. "It's time to go back."

Aristy looks up at the day-stars. There would've been more to see before humans came to this world, but only the native fauna to see them. A lung-wing contributes to expansion by perceiving the universe, as does a cat or lizard or even a flea, but higher consciousness is orders of magnitude more damaging. As far as anyone knows, the Curators were only worried about a handful of species, humans and dolphins among them.

Aristy is not the first person to wonder what the point of preserving the cosmos is, if artists and scientists aren't going to marvel at it.

3

The infamous Tannery has become nothing more than a vaguely symmetrical shape under a blanket of flowering vines. Aristy supposes that's just as well, considering the horror stories she's heard about the place. Like all relics of human sin, it ought to be consumed by nature, utterly, becoming food for new life, life that blooms with phototropic eyes that have the gentlest possible effect on expansion.

She follows Bray and the porter through the overgrown glade. A hummingbird-like drone floats at her side, its sleek, state-of-the-art quantum brain running instances of the thirty-seven complainants.

Bray denudes the front of the Tannery with a shower of white fire from her rifle rig. She follows up with retardant foam, which disintegrates to reveal the blackened facade of the ancient brick structure. She sprays deafening automatic fire at the lock on the reinforced door, then kicks it in and enters.

The drone follows, and the young man lugging Aristy's gear. Aristy hesitates at the threshold.

"Captain Safewither, everything okay?"

Solicitor Thoroughblind has caught up, unfortunately.

"Stop calling me that. I haven't been a captain since before you were born."

"Sorry. Madam Safewither? Aristy?"

"Just give me a moment." She's finding it hard to breathe. She'd like to think it's her age, but she knows that's not the case.

"I've noticed this sentence is particularly troubling for you."

She glances back at the shuttle with a sudden urge to hijack it.

"I wonder why that is."

"Wonder all you like."

"Perhaps hunting down a mass murderer triggers something in you. Something you'd prefer to leave dormant?"

"Remind me why you're here again."

"To safeguard the interests of my clients, of course." Thoroughblind grins, motioning to the doorway. "After you."

They search the moldy corridors and sagging rooms of the labyrinthine structure, Bray and Thoroughblind's torches lighting the way. They find homifacts: soldiers and officers, men smoking, commiserating, doing long-gone paperwork at rotting desks, but there's no sign of Picti.

Finally, they come to a torture chamber.

Rusting implements of the dark art hang on the walls, but everyone's attention is drawn toward the concrete platform at the center, where the homifact of a naked man lies spread-eagled. His face is fixed in a permanent rictus of pain, eyes squeezed shut. His wrists and ankles are near steel rings sunk in the concrete. Whatever bound him to these has rotted away.

Another homifact, an officer, is bent over the prisoner. He was frozen in the act of pushing a darning needle into the prisoner's scrotum.

The porter turns away, sobbing. Aristy doesn't know much about the lad, except that his name is Malcin, and that he's strong as an ox, and shy.

Bray puts a hand on his heaving shoulder. "What are we doing here anyway?"

"Apologies."

The voice issues from the hovering drone. It's Irilich, the Night Soil Collector, who has emerged as a leader among the complainants. "We all agreed this was the best place to start. Picti spent a lot of time here, overseeing interrogations."

"Well he's not here now," Bray says, annoyed. She slings her rifle and hugs Malcin to her breastplate. "Can we go?"

"It was also a haunt for many of Picti's closest collaborators. This man for instance—" the drone hovers over the torturer "—looks like Bretanik Skirjay, Picti's Minister of Intelligence."

The figure is middle-aged. He appears mildly reproving, like a teacher or parent administering tough love.

"You'd better get to it," Thoroughblind says.

The charter permits whatever memory assays are needed to track down Picti. Aristy has never peered into someone's memories before, except briefly when tuning down panic or disbelief. This Bretanik clearly deserves worse than an invasion of privacy, but she doesn't relish exploring his sick mind.

Moreover, she doesn't necessarily want to find Picti. She wants to get this farce over with, of course, but what would she actually do, confronted with Picti's homifact? Salvage him and bring him to justice, as ordered?

Erase him, perhaps, and claim a botched salvage.

"Aristy," Thoroughblind says.

She walks over to Bray and Malcin, and gently removes the pack from the weeping man. She enmeshes Bretanik and sets up with the efficient ease of long-practiced ritual. Seated in her field chair, skullcapped, fingers dancing over her scroll, she deploys her menagerie of 'rithms across the unique topography of the head of Iomangan intelligence.

"Aren't you an actor?" the prostitute said, counting narcosia ampules.

"I was, briefly."

She swept the ampules off the table and into her purse. "I think I saw you on the Stage, in the Follies." She stood, almost too tall for the cheap, low-ceilinged hotel room. "You played the Philosophical Drunk, right?"

"That was a long time ago," he said, though it really wasn't. He was twenty-five now. He'd played the Drunk for a three-week run when he was nineteen.

"I was one of the intermission dancers." She hesitated, shyly waiting for him to acknowledge this.

"Of course you were. I thought you seemed familiar."

She shivered, already in withdrawal. "So, ten more when I report back?"

"That's right."

"And you want . . . "

He'd been through this with her, but she was quite far along in her addiction, her mind ravaged. "Anything he says. Anything you notice. Don't be too obvious, but I'm interested in his politics, and his fetishes, if he has any. After the deed, ask how you measure up to his other women. Be coquettish about it. See if you can get any names. Mention Father Picti at some point, in a positive way, and see how he reacts."

She eyed the door uneasily.

"You'll do fine. You're a talented performer. I remember that from the Follies."

"Really?" She was skeptical, but wanted to believe.

"Of course, how could I forget?" He was an excellent liar. He'd played many roles before the Philosophical Drunk, and many since.

"Generalissimo," Captain Fisk said, "may I introduce one of my brightest agents, Bretanik Skirjay."

Tuwathal Picti looked up from his papers with mild interest. He seemed older and weaker than Bretanik had imagined, after fifteen years of propaganda murals and carefully staged newsreels. Nevertheless, there was something about him, something in the eyes, the famous hypnotic Picti gaze. This morning he wore an impeccable suit of the Mainland cut, rather than his usual military uniform with all the trimmings.

"Generalissimo," Bretanik said, bowing.

The silence grew uncomfortable, prompting Captain Fisk. "He's the one who infiltrated the Solstice Revolutionaries, and the academics. He got us all those names."

Picti gifted them with a brief smile, then glanced at his manservant, who stood at attention near the vast office's bar. "Three of the Victory Spirit."

He stood and came around the desk as the servant brought the tumblers. Bretanik didn't drink, but he knew the Generalissimo didn't trust teetotalers and he'd prepared himself for this meeting by taking an old folk medicine said to cancel the effects of alcohol.

"To Iomang," Picti said, and they all threw back.

The bay window behind the desk commanded a magnificent view of Iomanga's Tower District. Picti City's Tower District, that is. The capital had recently been renamed.

"So, Bretanik, the captain tells me you never served."

"A regret I shall carry to the grave, Generalissimo."

"And yet you are the rising star in my intelligence service. That is unusual."

He could see Picti expected him to say something. Fisk intervened: "He's a student of human weakness, Generalissimo. He knows every whore, pimp, addict, degenerate, and criminal on the island."

"Hardly something to boast about," Picti said with distaste, but he was interested. Bretanik, to his relief, found he could read Picti's micro-expressions like anyone else's.

Fisk apparently could not. "I've never seen intelligence done quite the way he does it, Generalissimo!"

But Picti had forgotten about the nervous captain. "How old are you?"

"Thirty-one, Generalissimo."

"I understand that before your intelligence work you were an actor. And that a certain M. Eulweth, a rich old heiress and patron of the arts, got you started."

"Yes, Generalissimo." He hadn't expected this, but it made sense, and might even be a good sign. If he was being considered for a promotion, Picti's people would've done some digging.

"I know M. Eulweth. Old money, slave money. I had to make a friend of that money when I took power, though I grew up poor like you."

Bretanik betrays no surprise, but wonders how deep they dug.

"Eulweth is a notorious huntress, of course."

"Yes, Generalissimo."

"And you were one of her many boy lovers."

Bretanik knew when to lie and when not to. He'd made a science of it. "Yes, Excellency."

Picti was disgusted, yet more intrigued than ever. "You were an escort, a fancy man. You serviced gods know how many men and women of the Capital."

Bretanik sensed it was time to get proactive. "As an education in human behavior, I'd put it up against Mainland psychology. And what is intelligence work, in the end, but psychology?"

Picti considered this. "I saw a photograph of you from back then. I'm afraid you've lost your looks."

"Few of us can age with your grace, Generalissimo."

Bretanik knew Picti would recognize such base flattery, but he also knew the Father of Iomang was vain. Besides, a bit of fawning was useful in the early stages of an asymmetrical relationship like this. An expected display of submission, a ritual. It also demonstrated that, although he was from the gutter, he knew how to behave in civilized company.

"If I gave you ten Bogle-Men," Picti said, "what could you do for me regarding these damn priests?"

He meant three troublesome clerics of the goddess Limna who were claiming sanctuary in their temple, which was inconveniently close to the embassy quarter. They'd spoken with foreign correspondents. Now the Mainland was abuzz with stories of disappearances and torture. The two superpowers, Salifioe and Audunon, were mulling economic sanctions. Salifian Intelligence shades were no longer at Picti's disposal. They'd mysteriously evaporated from the Salifian embassy.

Bretanik was at a loss, struggling to rally his wits. So many possibilities.

"It surprises you I call them Bogle-Men, like a commoner? But I like the name. I prefer it. Fear is an important tool, as I expect you know, Bretanik. Sometimes people need to be afraid. Sometimes it's for their own good, even if they can never understand this."

Aristy continues sampling memories and watching a monster evolve. After what seems like years, she finds the intelligence she needs and emerges from interface, breathless and shivering in her field chair.

Thoroughblind looms over her. "Well?"

"I . . . My god . . . "

"What did you find?"

"Give her a moment," Bray says.

Aristy looks around the decrepit torture chamber. Moments before, she witnessed it in its heyday and saw things she'll never unsee. "Where's Malcin? Is he okay?" An irrational fear possesses her. A place this evil, so steeped in pain and death, may come to life and devour the unwary.

"He'll be fine," Bray says. "He went out for some air."

Aristy stands, hugging herself. She contemplates the man on the slab: Argent Kinioch, former professor of literature at Tuwathal Picti National University, suspected conspirator in a plot to assassinate the Generalissimo.

"Picti was at a banquet when the Turning Inward struck," she says. "Limna Hall on Colonial Square, a captains-of-industry type thing. Bretanik made a point of knowing where his master was at all times."

"As we hoped," Irilich says from the drone.

"Then let's not linger here," Thoroughblind says. "The shuttle can land us in the square. We'll be there in no time."

"I'll be out in a minute." Aristy pulls the interface mesh off Bretanik and drapes it over the portrait of agony that is Argent's homifact.

"What do you think you're doing?" Thoroughblind says.

She sits and dons the skullcap.

"That's not part of your charter."

"He's suffering in there. Three subjective months on from the moment you see before you, he's still being tortured. Bretanik and his cronies are masters of their art. Do you understand?"

"I understand more than you think. You're trying to expiate your sins, and I have a pretty good idea what they are."

"Fine. Add an illegal salvage to the pile."

Thoroughblind reaches for her scroll, but finds Bray's muzzle-cluster in his face. "Step the fuck back."

Frozen in mid-reach, he could almost pass for a homifact. "You're meant to be enforcing the charter," he says, glaring at Bray. "Why else are you here?"

"Looking for trouble, really. And I don't much like you. Give me an excuse."

The drone floats before Thoroughblind and says in Irilich's voice: "We've recorded your objection, Solicitor. You will not be culpable."

The fog of Argent's torment dissipates.

Bretanik and his Bogle-Men fade from view, along with the confines of the chamber, the converted crank-telephone generator, and the batteries it was wired to in sequence.

Once upon a time he was passionate about literature. He remembers that stranger, vaguely, and his cozy university office, and his insatiable, sarcastic wife. Did that lucky man conspire to have Picti assassinated? He doesn't know anymore.

The goddess Limna appears before him.

She's older than the images of the goddess he's seen all his life. Her hair and clothing are different, but she must be Limna the Merciful, Goddess of the Healing Arts, because the pain and fear drain from him, and miraculously he finds the strength to reach out and take her hand.

4

Picti strolled along the edge of the pit as his soldiers dumped buckets of lime on the bodies.

"Were you sent to kill me?" he asked the shade.

The young Salifian was tall and handsome, dressed in the white suit of a vacationing businessman. He looked well-fed and well-rested, like most Salifian agents. The mass grave didn't seem to bother him. "Of course not, Generalissimo. But the Directorate is . . . concerned."

Picti understood. The Salifian Directorate of Intelligence had helped him take power, in that dreamtime long ago, before he'd sacrificed his youth and his potency to Iomang. They'd rigged an election, certainly. When that plan "went sideways", as the SDI liked to say, they'd subsidized his military coup.

They liked to think of him as a puppet. Now they'd lost control of him, and they were panicking.

"Your radio broadcasts were a bit much," the shade said.

Picti stopped to regard the bodies in the pit. He couldn't quite think of them as human. Not because they were dead, but because they were Fingomangan, and he was Iomangan. In his great-grandfather's time, the

Fings had subjugated the Iomangans. There'd been a Kingdom of Fingomang, but it had collapsed when its Mainland underwriters pulled out.

The Iomangans had risen up and taken their rightful place as lords of the island.

"Those transmissions reached the mainland, you realize."

Salifian condescension always infuriated Picti. He'd been fighting for a republic before this shade was born. "You can tell your masters I do what I must to hold Iomang together, as always."

The sanctions had been lifted, thanks to Bretanik. It hadn't been necessary to kill the irksome clerics. They'd been "exposed" as narcosia addicts and pederasts—Picti still didn't know how Bretanik had managed that—and Mainland news organs had backpedaled. But the damage had been done. With the economy in pieces, and a bad harvest to boot, revolution was in the air.

Picti viewed the problem in terms of resources.

There was only so much food and wealth on the island. Fings controlled one-third of it. Violence against Fings, who were descendants of aristocrats and tyrants, was endemic. In the early days of his reign, Picti had tried to suppress pogroms against Fings for the sake of delicate Salifian sensibilities. Now he couldn't see the point.

"I'll tell the Directorate anything you wish to convey, sir, but it may be too late. There's been a shake-up. You see, your broadcasts didn't just reach us. They went into space as well."

Picti had indeed taken to the airwaves, exhorting his fellow Iomangans to rise up and exterminate Fing vermin. He hadn't expected it to work so well.

"Space, Generalissimo. That's a problem in terms of exposure."

Picti didn't have time for this. He'd heard the rumors, thanks to Bretanik's mole in the Salifian Rocket Defense Association. He was already late for brunch with his propaganda people. Then it was back to the Capital for a series of meetings with his generals, and then the entrepreneurs' dinner.

He wasn't going to stand here on his own soil and endure this shade's laughable attempt at psy-ops. Salifioe had abandoned him. They'd even shuttered their embassy. He drew his platinum-plated sidearm and aimed.

The Salifian maintained an admirable calm.

"We've been receiving and decoding for years. Not just from the aliens, but other human civilizations. I know it's your official state policy to deny diaspora theory, but—"

"Gentlemen," Picti said to the soldiers gathering to watch, "have we any lime left?"

The young men laughed, and one ran off to retrieve a bucket.

Picti pressed his weapon into the shade's chest and shoved him toward the brink.

"I'm here as a courtesy, Generalissimo. We don't understand everything they're saying, but our policy now is to proceed as if we're being watched, and judged."

Picti fired.

Aristy comes to in one of the plush, moldering seats at the head of the banquet table. She blinks away disorientation, and as it dawns on her what happened, she's surprised at herself.

Sunlight streams through the shattered stained glass that fronts Limna Hall. The long table is crowded with homifacts of wealthy Iomangans in mid-laugh, mid-pontification, mid-drink and mid-bite. She recognizes Madame Eulweth from Bretanik's memories.

The Generalissimo sits in the place of honor. He's draped in the mesh, looking thoughtful and holding a long-gone tumbler.

"Is everything okay, Aristy?"

The drone floats into view. The voice isn't Irilich's this time, but Dr Corvirst's.

"Yes," Aristy lies. She set up intending to erase Picti, but a grim curiosity got the better of her, despite her distaste for voyeurism. She had to know more. She still does.

"Is he salvageable?" Corvirst says.

"I'm not sure yet." Of course he is. They all are.

The drone hovers close to Picti's frozen face. "I turned to narcosia after they took my girlfriend. I told her to stop going to those damn radical meetings. One day she was just gone, like so many others."

"I'll do everything I can," Aristy says.

Solicitor Thoroughblind, seated among the homifacts at the other end of the long table, chuckles. "Yes, you're a resourceful one, aren't you? One has to be, when resources are scarce."

The drone comes about to face him with its many eyes. "Your insinuations aren't helping, Solicitor." It's Casantin Onuist this time, the one-eyed complainant. "Why are you really here?"

Thoroughblind doesn't seem to hear this. He studies Aristy with an almost feral concentration.

"The Salifians may punish Iomang now and then," the Minister of the Interior said, "for appearances' sake, but they need you, Generalissimo. For the same reason we all need you." The old man held up his tumbler, and the magnates of Iomang followed suit.

Picti wasn't in the mood for this. He didn't sleep anymore. The flower of Iomangan youth was at his disposal, but he could no longer perform in bed. His stomach burned if he fed it anything more than porridge. And these sycophants didn't know what they were talking about.

"To Father Picti!" the Minister said.

Everyone drank. Picti downed his Victory Spirit, knowing he would regret it. A servant refilled his tumbler.

Conversation drifted to Mainlanders and their diaspora theory.

"Fossils and radiation dating are all very clever," Madam Eulweth opined, "but at the end of the day I'll take the Gods, and Iomang."

"Hear hear," said what's-his-name, the grizzled rubber mogul.

They were performing for him. Always performing. Picti couldn't believe he was still sane after years of this. It was not a natural life, but he endured it for the sake of the Republic. Just like he made impossible decisions for the sake of the Republic. No one would ever understand his burdens.

"The ancients demonstrated wonderfully that humans originated in Iomang." Picti had awarded this soft little man the coal monopoly. He was a slave money heir, like M. Eulweth. He eyed Picti as he spoke, nakedly seeking approval. "As for all this Salifian rot about an origin world, and human starships and aliens, if you ask me . . . "

No one had.

" . . . the Salifs have lost their minds. They've had it too good for too long. They're in their age of decadence. Now it's Iomang's turn to rise."

The news had come that afternoon as Picti sped home from the mass graves. The alleged transmissions, from interstellar humans and aliens, had become public knowledge in Salifioe. There'd been a leak, deliberate or otherwise. The Salifian populace was in an uproar.

Picti's hosts sensed they were losing him. The Minister of the Interior proposed another toast:

"To the extermination of the Fing vermin!"

They were all drinking, and watching him expectantly, so he drank again. And again his tumbler was filled.

"To the Generalissimo, our bulwark against communalism and colonization!"

A strange feeling passed over Picti, a shiver, as if he, and the world with him, was adjusting to a subtle temperature change. The colors of the Limnal glass seemed more vivid. Perhaps some conspirator—a Fing, a communalist, a Salif shade, or any of a dozen other potential enemies—had dosed his spirit.

The sensation passed. He was still alive, whatever that was worth.

Aristy comes up for air.

She has often wondered what the Turning Inward felt like, but never could've imagined such a moment: fleeting, subtle, at once summary judgment and ultimate release. She plunges into her own memories, frantically hunting the sensation. Maybe she suffered it on the Harbinger. Maybe the Turning Inward caught up with relativistic travelers, after all. Maybe that relativistic particle never got past the ion plow and annihilated Fuel Tank Three. Maybe she was never faced with a problem of momentum, which is mass times velocity, and crucial to deceleration.

Dusk has fallen on Limna Hall. Aristy's eyes adjust to the gloom. Thoroughblind has moved closer.

"My staff is interviewing that man from the bar," he says. "I'm going to prosecute you, Captain, for each and every one of the seven-thousand who never woke."

She doesn't hate him for his naked, parasitic ambition. She hates him for knowing her better than anyone.

The drone floats aimlessly near the broken stained glass, watching the sun set. The souls within think they'll find a measure of peace by bringing Picti to justice, but Aristy has her doubts. Maybe they'd be better off with their traumatic memories excised.

She reckons she would.

"Generalissimo," Kirrem shouts, "I see no sign of the gunship!"

The hilltop commands a wide view of the surrounding country, and the night is clear. The Salif rotorcraft that Picti promised ought to be visible on the northern horizon, but the Father of Iomang knows it's not coming. He follows his bodyguard into the construction site that resembles an unfinished crown on the defoliated hilltop. He limps past the outer ring of megaliths, drawing his platinum-plated pistol.

Kirrem turns around. "Generalissimo?"

"Drop your rifle, lieutenant."

The young man reaches for his slung weapon, dumbfounded. Far away and below, Picti City pops and crackles with the gunfire of the Second Solstice Revolution.

"Drop it."

Kirrem weeps as he places the rifle on the ground.

"Now head for the altar."

Picti had himself declared a god just before things went to shit. The work here isn't finished, and never will be, but temple construction always starts with the altar. It will have to do. Picti's apotheosis lacks only one step. He follows Kirrem toward the altar, gun leveled.

"Please Generalissimo . . ."

"Stop calling me that. It's an earthly title."

The gun shivers in his sweaty hand. He can barely put one foot in front of the other. He lost the services of his personal doctor a few days ago. No more hypodermic ministrations, no more amphetamine and vitamins for breakfast, no more narcosia-by-another-name for nightcap.

Picti is becoming something new.

"Father Picti . . ."

"Ascend."

"Please . . ."

He fires a warning shot at the lieutenant's feet. "Ascend!"

The old Iomangan kings knew what they were doing. Worshippers make one immortal. Worship and sacrifice are the food of gods, and gods can be self-made if their intentions are pure. This isn't an act of ego for Picti. The Fing extermination wasn't anything so petty as vengeance. Everything he's done has been to preserve Iomang.

The lieutenant stands atop the rough-hewn stone altar. The relic was borrowed from an archaeological dig in Litorum Province, where the Pre-Classic Iomangan kingdoms flourished, before the age of Mainlander colonizers and their cringing Fing puppets.

Picti aims his weapon.

The familiar night sky, with its dusting of stars, sprawls above the altar and its victim. There used to be many more stars, so the legend goes. But Nachtan, god of music and philosophy, grew jealous of Limna's beauty, and began stealing stars to weave into a robe that would forever outshine the goddess.

Picti fires.

It has been almost three months since his brief, tremulous reverie at the banquet. He has thought about it often since then, as everything he built came crashing down and treacherous Iomangans turned on him. Ingrates, parasites, degenerates, and communalists took advantage of the chaos of the Fing cleansing, but Picti will make them pay.

Lieutenant Kirrem collapses on the altar. Bursting with inner light, he rises into the heavens. He comes apart in a spray of embers that slowly fade as they disperse.

Picti feels the godhead suffuse him.

First to go are the specific frailties of age and addiction, then the innate weaknesses of mortality. Finally, the broad strictures of the corporeal. He floats away from the hilltop and its children's building blocks. He dismisses gravity and inertia and any other Mainland laws of science that get in his way as he hurtles toward the muzzle flashes and explosions of Picti City.

Aristy has always known that a homifact's simulated world is based on the knowledge—and fears and delusions and warped memories—of the mind Turned Inward. But she has never seen this so glaringly illustrated.

Bray and Malcin are asleep on a nearby bench, wrapped in each other's arms. Aristy imagines them producing robust, no-nonsense children who make Drop Town stronger, and push the universe that much closer to a Big Rip. The Curators left the cosmos just beyond stasis, slowly expanding. Deep fields of galaxies are legends of past skies, but closer mists of stars are still perceptible. For the moment. With the human resurgence, things are speeding up again. The Curators may be done intervening. And maybe that's just as well.

Picti floats over the burning ruins of Adenthi, Salifioe's capital, until minutes ago the center of commerce and culture on Ce. It will be the last city to suffer his wrath. He has laid waste all others on the Mainland: the gleaming, decadent metropolises of imperialist Salifioe, and the brutal gridwork sprawls of communalist Audunon.

He conjured firestorms or opened hellish geothermal maws to consume them.

He spots a miraculous survivor in the inferno below.

He descends, marveling. No mortal should be able to stroll casually through this furnace he's created. Perhaps it's a god like him.

"Who are you?" he demands, his voice filling the world.

A woman, he sees as he lands. Strange garb and cropped hair, not like a Salif, or any Celing or god he knows of. She walks toward him, immune to the flames that partially obscure her.

"Tuwathal Picti, I've come to bring you to justice!"

Her voice, like his, transcends the ambient din, emanating from the superheated air and filling his mind.

"Justice?" He can't help laughing at this. "For what crime?"

"Should I list them all? You really don't see them, do you? No . . . don't answer. I've read your thoughts. I felt what you felt. I feared that more than anything, and rightfully so. I am no voyeur, but I knew I wouldn't be able to resist. And I found exactly what I feared I would."

He can feel her in his mind. He realizes she's been there for quite a while, maybe all his life, a silent, watching presence he came to take for granted, for conscience or something like it.

She must be one of the gods.

"When you ordered the Fing genocide," she says, "you truly believed it was for the greater good."

"Of course I did!"

"I know what that's like."

If Picti is to be tried by the gods, he will need an advocate. This one seems like she might be swayed. She is thoughtful and hesitant. Maybe he can even convince her not to arrest him. He doesn't have time for a trial, after all. Iomang needs him. Before his wholesale destruction of Salifioe and Audunon, he visited more surgical turmoil on his homeland, weeping all the while.

"It was easy to dehumanize the sleepers," she says. "None of us in the waking crew had ever spoken with them."

Visions accompany her words, wracking his mind. Revelations, fevers, distances and epochs. The world of the gods is more complex than any priest ever imagined.

"They'd bankrolled the ship, but generations had passed since launch. They weren't even alive, technically."

Picti struggles to understand as the onslaught continues. Magic becomes advanced technology, pantheons become technical crews, and a god-realm becomes a starship. He watches a young Captain Aristy Safewither code failure into the sleepers' preservation systems.

The crew's attempts at resuscitation came too late. Cellular degradation was too advanced. After that, it was only a matter of time before everyone agreed to cast aside dead weight.

The Generalissimo is overwhelmed, not by Aristy's unilateral decision, but by violently broadened horizons, by relativistic momentum, antifreeze proteins and antimatter, alien intelligence and uploaded consciousness. By dark energy, and the Turning Inward.

He looks around in wonderment and dread.

He places his hand on a pile of glowing rubble. Not real. Nothing real since that moment at the banquet. Three months simulated over a real millennium. Aliens, a human diaspora, or "emanation" as they call it. The Salifs were right after all! But Iomang never failed, because Iomang is Iomangans, and they were Turned Inward like the rest of humanity. Picti wonders how the Republic played out in all those other minds. Can he ever know that?

He lets molten rock flow between his fingers. He meets Aristy's gaze. He doesn't need their mental link to read the craving in her eyes.

"You did what had to be done," he says, "just like me. We are the strong ones, Aristy. We made the decisions no one else could."

"It doesn't matter what we were thinking. It doesn't matter how we felt, even if we were right or wrong. All that matters is physics. The weight of what happened. The weight of so many dead. The mass of that fact. The momentum of it, the inertia. Inertia is a question that must be answered."

Picti senses he has lost. Panicking, he tries to fly, and when that doesn't work he turns to run, but finds himself rooted in place. His fear turns to rage. "By what right . . . Let me go, dammit! Who are you to judge me?"

"I'm a monster, and I'm going to pay for what I've done. And so are you."

A wash of smoke obscures her. When it's gone, her shoulders are shaking. Her face contorts. At first, Picti thinks she's crying, but he soon realizes she's laughing hysterically.

THE LONG TAIL

Aliette de Bodard

It was just a room.

Another one on the wreck of the *Conch Citadel*: holes in the walls and in the ceiling and floor, floating debris and rusting furniture that must have once been pristine and polished, the state of the art of Đại Ánh. A series of disc-shaped auxiliary robots and larger maintenance mechs parked in the walls, gleaming in the light projected by Thu's lamp. Nothing out of the ordinary.

Thu was in the doorway, floating in the low-gravity of the wreck—holding onto the frame with one hand, the small thruster-pack in her back turned off to conserve energy. She'd been about to enter the room, but something had been bothering her enough that it had stopped her.

It took her a moment to realize it was her lineaged memory that was kicking up the fuss, specifically Ánh Ngọc's most recent transfer, the one of the latest shift Ánh Ngọc had done onboard *Citadel*. Not shocking; lineaged memory was always slower to access, more distanced and filtered through layers of storage in Thu's implant. Looking more closely, Thu could see, now, that the holes in the floor were a little too regular, the mechs' multiple legs a little too polished, the edges of the robots' disk-shapes distorted, as if someone had pulled and the metal had given in like taffy. Not a physical room, then. The real room, the one she could interact with, lay under layers of unreality. A whole lot of it.

Shit. Shit.

Thu chewed at her lower lip, considering. Everyone onboard the scavenging habitat knew there was no correlation between the unreality and what lay underneath. Going in there would be a calculated risk. She considered, for a while. She was the statistician of the post: Ánh Ngọc's expertise was with electronics, and it was her skills Thu accessed when opening up walls and robots and mechs and retrieving rare isotopes from their core, just as Ánh Ngọc benefited from Thu's risk assessments. Ánh Ngọc had chosen not to go into the room, but that didn't mean Thu had to make the same choice. The end of the month was looming, and she could hope for a nice bonus if she went over scavenging quota.

"Younger aunt?" It was Khuyên, which was . . . not just odd, but out of schedule. She was the previous shift's supervisor, and when she spoke Thu could see she was in the control center of the *Azure Skies*' habitat, alone.

"Thu in. What's going on?"

Khuyên shifted, uncomfortably. "There's a problem."

Thu's blood chilled. A problem large enough to have Khuyên put off decontamination? Her shift had been over for half an hour, and she should have been in her pod, going through the sequence that would bring her unreality levels back to a semblance of normalcy. The more she waited, the more risks of her implant getting irremediably contaminated by the nanites on the ship—for the unreality to take over everything and fundamentally alter the way she perceived things—at best, hallucinations that would feel uncannily real, at worst a spiralling into delirium and delusions. Then she might as well be gone, because the company sure as hell wasn't going to waste money digging the implant out of her brain, not when she'd failed to respect the safety procedures.

"What problem?" Thu asked.

Khuyên picked her words carefully. "I think Ánh Ngọc is on her way to chimeral."

Shit. "She came back fine," Thu said. "She transferred her shift, her capacities . . ."

"I know she did," Khuyên said. "Exposure to unreality seems to have been well within the norm, her suit's readings are fine."

Thu heard the "but" that Khuyên wasn't saying. "But she's got symptoms."

"Yeah." Khuyên sighed.

Thu started to ask which ones, but she already knew, because she'd seen them with Mother, before the operation. The way Mother would stop and refuse to climb into a transport because the floor had suddenly become a gulf, the way she'd just stare at the walls and say they were bleeding monsters. Everything that had led to the Harmony Squad and the Desolate Ward, and . . . The thought was too much to bear. "What do you want me to do?"

"I need proof, younger aunt."

"Of what?"

"Of how she was exposed. You know what the company will say. They'll say she must have gone haring off on her own chasing personal targets, that there are procedures she didn't respect—"

"And you don't know how she got contaminated."

"No. It's too much for a normal shift." Khuyên grimaced. "If you ask me, I think it's new nanites."

Nanites were war weapons, and the *Conch Citadel* was a ship full of them. They hadn't run into variants before, not on this ship. Mutations usually didn't show up on the scans because the sensors weren't calibrated for random, unknowable varieties. But they'd heard the stories.

"You want me to retrace Ánh Ngọc's steps."

"Yes. And figure out what she did that got her so exposed. As I said, I need proof. Otherwise the company won't pay for the operation, and you know what happens then."

It'd be the Desolate Ward, the charity doctors, the hurried hacking into brain tissues to remove the affected implant before it could infect too much of the body. It'd be like Mother, all over again: 11 years since she'd been wounded by unreality weapons during the war, 10 years since the operation to remove her contaminated implant, and she hadn't said a word, or moved of her own volition from her listless place against the compartment door. She'd eat, when prompted; sleep, when put to bed. In a way, it was worse. All that Thu and her family had got back from the operation was a hollowed-out puppet, devoid of spirit or soul and doing as she was told because there was nothing left within, not even the spark of life that would lead to refusal.

The company had better doctors, safer procedures. They could remove the implant, and give Ánh Ngọc another one, and it'd be seamless. But only if Khuyên and Thu and the crew of the *Azure Skies* could prove, without a shadow of a doubt, that the damage had happened on the job and while following all instructions given in the safety briefing.

Thu would be going in blind, with no way to monitor her exposure. She wouldn't really know if she was contaminated, because she'd lose the capacity to differentiate unreality and reality. She'd only know if she could be decontaminated when she came back and her chimerality was assessed by Central or med bots. It was a gamble, and Thu—as a statistician—really hated gambles.

But Thu had a chance to help Ánh Ngọc. She had a chance to save her friend. A chance she'd never gotten with Mother. "Of course. I'll do it."

"I'm taking over the shift," Khuyên said. "Considering the circumstances."

"The unreality—" Thu said, before she could think.

"—doesn't take precedence over the risks to Ánh Ngọc. This is the priority. The other two on the ship can continue foraging for isotopes."

Khuyên gestured. The control center lit up. "Nguyễn Thị Kim Khuyên underwent express decontamination from 0849 to 0918," Central said. Their voice was uninflected and metallic.

Thu's cheeks burnt. "Forgive me."

"Nothing to forgive," Khuyên said. "I can withstand this shift for a bit."

Central said, "Ánh Ngọc is in a decon-pod until further notice. Staving it off as much as we can."

"OK. Duly noted."

Khuyên's face was a complex study in emotions. "Younger aunt?"

"Yes?" Thu was trying to focus on her next steps. She'd need to reconstruct Ánh Ngọc's pathway through the bowels of the ship, figuring out where she might have been exposed, trying to see anything unusual or that stood out . . .

"Don't misunderstand the briefing. No unnecessary risks. We don't know what happened, and I don't need a repeat. Am I clear?"

Thu swallowed. "Very."

Thu had turned up the unreality protection on her suit to maximum. Vision was going to be a bit blurry, but she could live with that.

She began propelling herself through the ship, retracing Ánh Ngọc's last shift. Ánh Ngọc's memories were merging with hers, to disconcerting effect. It wasn't the seamless, mostly unconscious flow of information she was used to, but recollections she had to dig for. She went through corridors, asking herself at every intersection how familiar they were—trying to get Ánh Ngọc's memories to come to the surface, working out if that twinge of familiarity meant she'd gone left or right, up or down.

It'd have been so much simpler if the company had had trackers on the suits, but they were cheap, and the memories were deemed sufficient.

She hummed songs as she was going. Mother had always loved to sing, but they'd lost that, too, and the songs were all she had to cling to. Khuyên and the others would usually tease her about that, but this time they were silent, and Thu got through a whole lot of children's nursery rhymes, lullabies, and various habitat folk songs with no comment from anyone.

It kept her distracted. It kept her from wondering if she could still see the difference between unreal and real.

Ánh Ngọc's shift had lasted four hours; so far, Thu had done barely one. There wasn't a high chance of overexposure, but . . .

So far, Thu had seen an awful lot of empty rooms—of walls burst apart, couches and berths shattered in the wake of the ship's ending—of small immobile robots the size of fists and maintenance mechs half as tall as humans, empty hangars with the much larger skiffs and pods ripped apart for their contents.

The *Conch Citadel* had been the final act of a war that had ended badly: a huge, lethal ship that had been obsolete before it even launched, too large, too expensive, and surprisingly fragile in the face of enemy weapons. It had bankrupted the Đại Ánh state and changed nothing about the ultimate outcome. In the end, the ship's Central had died, and so had its crew. Thu and her fellows were the only living beings within the wreck, scavenging the rare isotopes that could be used for the smaller projects of the post-war state.

It paid well. Well enough that Thu could send the money back home to cover Mother's more unusual medical fees. The risk was high. Some failsafes had blown at the core of the ship, probably in its drive or in its arsenal, or both; and unreality had come spilling out, weaponized nanites spreading throughout every corridor, every ventilation shaft, every cabin and every hangar.

It—

Wait.

She had been going down a ventilation shaft, wincing at the difficulty of the maneuver—thrust, then glide and avoid the walls—when something felt . . . off again. Lineaged memory? No. It was Ánh Ngọc's instincts, slowed down by the detour through Thu's implants. A shadow had just moved, below her, at the base of the shaft.

She pinged the chat. *Is anyone at those coordinates?*

A resounding silence from the rest of the shift.

Just you, Khuyên said.

Shit. She wouldn't have seen it if Ánh Ngọc hadn't already been familiar with the route. Having the lineaged memories buffered in her implant meant Thu could focus on what stood out from the previous iteration—like mysterious shadowy movements at her destination. Had that happened to Ánh Ngọc, too? She couldn't be sure. Memory wasn't reliable enough.

Down the shaft, nothing. A large corridor rife with unreality. She looked at some of the walls, but the damage had been extensive below the unreality layers, and there were no isotopes to scavenge.

Whatever she'd seen was gone now.

Ahead, a set of large doors. Thu remembered, in that odd, layered way of lineaged memory, going there, into a room where she'd found some illyrium from a host of deactivated robots.

Nothing out of the ordinary. Except a nebulous sense that all wasn't quite as it should be: small differences from Ánh Ngọc's own run that added up to a rather large sense of unease. That, and the moving thing.

Thu didn't believe in coincidence.

"How is Ánh Ngọc?" she asked on the comms.

Azure Skies' Central said, "Not well."

Ánh Ngọc was hallucinating, muttering to herself in her sleep, her knuckles scraped raw from rubbing them against the wall; damage that the berth kept healing but that kept coming back. All too familiar symptoms.

"You know this, but you need to hurry," *Azure Skies'* Central said.

"I know," Thu said. Hurrying while remaining herself safe. Easy. She stared, again, at the corridor. Too much unreality for the readings, that was what was bothering her. Maybe the nanites were just the normal kind.

And maybe unripe figs would fall unaided from the trees.

Hurry, *Azure Skies'* Central had said.

Well, she supposed she should go and check it out.

Inside, it was dark. Her suit's readings said the temperature had gone up a notch, though of course Thu felt nothing.

As she propelled herself, arms outstretched, the room gradually lit up.

It was vast, and cavernous. There should have been no sound, but she heard her breathing, and a faint echo like the vibrations of a huge motor. Except the ship was a wreck, and the motors were offline. More unreality.

She was in deep.

"Is anyone here?" she said, before remembering she was in the vacuum of space. Great. Great going, Thu.

Crackle on the line.

"Anyone?"

Ghosts. Spirits. Unexorcised dead. The monks should have done their job when the ship first exploded, but it had been a war, and who knew what had been done when?

At the end of the room, a row of intact maintenance mechs, gleaming. An invitation. Ánh Ngọc had gone straight to them to start stripping them of their cores. Thu did the same thing, letting herself be guided by memories, vigilant for any minute change.

Something skittered, out of the corner of her eyes. Barely a speck. Something with legs, hovering fast over broken floors. Ánh Ngọc's instincts kicked up, and Thu turned her head a fraction of a second too late and a fraction too far. Her neck winced at the unusual tension. Whatever it was had moved like a maintenance mech in vacuum. But none of them should have been working anymore. They'd died with the ship. There was nothing alive or sentient, or even operational, onboard.

She—

She needed to keep moving. She didn't know how long she had left. At last, she reached the mechs, and stared at them. Brand new, ready to deploy. Thu remained in the middle of that impossibly bright room, those shining steel panels, those engraved characters flowing on either side of intact berths—doors that looked, at any point, like they might open on a hangar where skiffs would be flying in and out, the long slow dance of the devastating war that had laid them all bare.

Unreality. Nanites that locked you into hallucination—into the past, real or imagined. That showed you what you *wanted* to see at first, because it was their way into the implant.

Think think think. Too much unreality, and not enough readings on the sensors. That was where Ánh Ngọc had gotten contaminated, all right. But that many nanites couldn't come out of nowhere. Which meant they were being produced.

She was going to need to move fast—which required Ánh Ngọc's instincts, except she was at a disadvantage there because she didn't have Ánh Ngọc's body, and her muscles would struggle to adapt to an out of sync memory. Instead, she went for the next best thing: the distraction. She cut off the line on her suit, and then said into the radio, as casually as if she'd really been speaking to Khuyên, "I'm going to investigate the mechs at the far end." She started, slowly and deliberately, her thrusters, and at the same time accessed lineage—unfamiliar instincts surged through her, and she turned, panting and gasping, muscles burning.

And saw, for a fraction of a second, a shadow that had moved. A maintenance mech with broken legs, haemorrhaging in a cloud of motor oils, cast into sharp relief by the light from the room.

It shouldn't have been moving, but then her other thought was hers, not lineaged, and it was that she had seen that light before. Not quite the same, but close enough. It was the light when *Azure Skies'* Central had come online, and it had cast Khuyên in exactly the same pattern of radiance.

Ghosts, and unexorcised spirits.

Central. *Conch Citadel's* Central.

It was impossible.

Conch Citadel's Central hadn't survived. They couldn't have survived. Someone would have known.

And how would they have known?

She opened up the comms again, and said, simply, "Central." And waited, heart beating madly in her chest.

The light didn't change, or the unreality. But the mech came back. It was slow and bleeding, and she needed to fix it, or to kill it and cannibalize it. It was lineaged, but no less powerful an urge. The mech moved itself, carefully, to face her, its crown of small, octagonal eyes blinking in that impossible light.

How long did she have left, before she went Ánh Ngọc's way? Five minutes? 10? She didn't know.

"War." The voice hissed over her comms, breaking into static, the words bleeding the same way as the mech.

"I don't understand."

"War," the voice whispered again. "Duty to fight."

"The war is over!" It had done enough damage. It had taken Mother from her, and they all labored in its wreckage.

More skittering, and more mechs, coming toward her, loosely surrounding her in a sphere above and below, bleeding motor oils.

Not just motor oil. "Nanites," Thu said. "You're making nanites." New ones. Improved ones. Or just decayed ones that the suits couldn't read anymore.

"A duty to fight," the voice that had been Central whispered on the comms. It was breaking apart, and the words echoed on top of one another—and the room's walls had started to bleed, faintly but persistently. "Stay hidden. Prepare. Fight."

Not just spontaneous nanite mutations, but deliberate design. A ship stuck in the past, preparing for fights that had ended for everyone else, making a long, slow, desperate string of weapons in the midst of its own wreck, unable to see that it was all over.

Nanites.

Shit shit. Thu was getting contaminated the same way Ánh Ngọc had been.

Think. She needed evidence. And she didn't have that. She had a pretty story with suggestive videos, but nothing that would induce the company to shell out money.

She needed the source of the nanites, which meant one of the mechs. That was going to be hard. She could take one apart and remove the core that kept it from going—but it'd be lineaged memory and she'd go slowly, and she wasn't going to have time for slowly. Not to mention dragging a fairly large piece of equipment—mechs were the same size as her torso.

What did Central want anyway? Did they even remember?

"Your heartbeat's gone through the roof," Khuyên's voice said on Thu's other comms channel. Then a sharp spike of static on her comms, and her voice started fragmenting and going away, the same way Central's voice was. The other channel back to *Azure Skies* was just dead, and Thu couldn't raise anyone on it. She'd been blocked by some kind of heavy encryption.

"You found me," Central said. "Clever." Their voice went high-pitched, feverish.

The mechs spun around Thu, blocking her path, and Thu didn't know what to do, how to exit. She didn't know how she could fix any of it, how she could succeed at all in saving Ánh Ngọc, in saving herself. It was like Mother again, nothing she did or said was making any difference.

The mechs were moving. She evaded the first one with her thrusters, but the next one bumped her back, again and again, toward the center of the room. The sound on the comms was fractured, no longer a voice and no longer uttering words she could recognize. She was being herded deeper and deeper into the room—not precisely nor kindly, but it didn't need to be.

The thought came with the stark, sharp clarity of a naked blade: Central was going to kill her. This wasn't about nanites anymore; they thought they were fighting a war and Thu would broadcast their existence to the enemy. An absurd war that had ended 20 years ago. "Please," she said. Within her, lineaged memory waiting, watching mechs for their weak points. Thu could reach out to the one by her left hand, grab the broken leg and the trailing cable—the second one, not the first—and then *twist* it, just like that, and the mech was going to blank out for five seconds while its system restarted— which would give her a little more time to expose the core and deactivate *that*.

It was a shit plan. Tight timings, uncertain results, dicey even for Ánh Ngọc. But it was the best plan Thu had to save them both.

In her ears, Central's comms was still happening.

There was a shining circle on the floor below Thu, glowing, its light fracturing upward as it got clearer and clearer, its edges bending, trying to form a sphere around her. It looked like a disintegration pattern, the kind of traps that zapped intruders out of existence. If it encircled her, it'd be over. It didn't matter if it was unreality or not.

She had to act. Just reach out, and grab the cable, and go as fast as she could with the mech in her arms.

Why did she not want to, then?

Part of the job of a statistician is recognizing when patterns are off. And something was not quite right, a model not quite fitting the curve.

Mechs didn't have weapons, but they didn't need to. With those numbers, all they needed to do was overwhelm Thu, and tear apart her suit. She'd die with the water in her skin and in her blood boiling away, and her lungs collapsing on themselves. Why herd her unless they meant her to survive?

But why?

You found me.

The comms. That whine on the comms—except it was too structured, and too deliberate to be random. She'd assumed speech had fractured, but it hadn't really, had it? It had been becoming more and more high-pitched, and then collapsing into incoherence. What if it hadn't collapsed, but simply become inaudible to her?

Recording buffer was short, but she only needed a few moments. The mechs were crowding her closer, and she was within a loose sphere that was tightening fast, the light blinding her.

Just a few moments.

Cycle the whole thing through a filter, shifting the base frequencies, moving things around, trying to find again the rhythm she'd heard before from Central—

Oh.

Oh.

It wasn't speech. Not exactly. It wasn't words, either. It was a wordless, high-pitched hum. Not just a hum. A song.

The bamboo bridge is rough and difficult to cross . . .

As you go to school to learn, I attend the school of life . . .

Not just any song, but a lullaby she'd been humming as she moved through the ship. It shifted as she listened to it, fading away into another one of the songs Mother had so loved, the ones they'd lost after the operation. In the background, faint and fuzzy and as distant as beneath a pane of glass, the other channel, with Khuyên and the *Azure Skies'* Central.

You found me.

It hadn't been anger, or bitterness, but relief.

Sometimes, lineaged memory and instincts—like any memory, any instincts—were *wrong*.

Citadel's Central wasn't bloodthirsty. They were deeply, terribly lonely. The forming sphere wasn't a disintegration pattern. It was a cage that would hold her. They wanted her to stay. "Wait," Thu said. "Wait!"

The mechs paused, for a fraction of a second, looking at her.

She had no idea what she could say. How did one talk to a homicidal damaged Central, tell them that they needed to stop, that she needed the mech? How could she save Ánh Ngọc?

"The war is over," she said. "You—you're not bound by the past anymore." She thought of Mother as she was saying that, she thought of Ánh Ngọc's lineaged memories and how sometimes they helped and sometimes they didn't. She thought of the shadow that they all labored under, the devastation they plundered to find a way to survive—of the long, long tail of damage done by unreality, by the war. She thought about how sometimes one could get it all wrong, that she wasn't there to be a hero or fix anything all by herself, because the truth was that nothing, not even saving Ánh Ngọc, would bring Mother back or bring Thu absolution for failing to save her.

She didn't have the words to convince *Citadel's* Central, but there was another Central out there who spoke the same language.

"You're not alone," she said, and opened up all the accesses to all her channels in her comms interface: the virtual equivalent of throwing her link to *Azure Skies* into stark relief. *Citadel's* Central would now remember that Thu had two comms channels: the one in which they and Thu talked to each other, and the other one, Thu's link back to Khuyên and *Azure Skies'* Central. The channel *Citadel's* Central had locked away beneath layers of encryptions. "I'm not alone."

Silence, on the comms. Thu said to *Citadel's* Central, "There's another Central. There are *people*. You can hear them."

Still silence. Then, "Survivors?" *Citadel's* Central asked.

Thu said nothing. She just waited. She felt more than saw it—the encryption lifting, the other channel's sound level increasing, the shift in tonalities back to within human hearing.

"Elder aunt," Thu said, flatly.

Khuyên's voice was stressed. "Younger aunt. We're running—"

"I need Central," Thu said. "Now."

"What is it?" *Azure Skies*' Central said, coming online. "Oh." A silence. Then communications shifting and changing, and moving beyond words altogether. The mechs were silent and still, the sphere around Thu slowly cycling through lights—the walls starting to bend toward her—a persistent series of bloody spots forming across her field of vision. How long did she have, now? Would the company help her, or was she going the same way as Mother? She didn't have the energy left to care.

At long last, someone spoke. *Azure Skies*' Central. "You can go."

"*Citadel*—"

"They'll be fine," *Azure Skies*' Central said, in a way that suggested a lot of explanations and a lot of paperwork.

"You won't be if you stay here." It was Khuyên's voice.

Thu got her thrusters back online, and pushed outward. The sphere vanished. The mechs around her parted—except a single one, the first one she'd seen, limping across the floor, staring at her.

"You're not alone," *Citadel*'s Central said, and it wasn't clear to whom they were speaking.

For Ánh Ngọc.

You're not alone.

Survivors.

Thu reached out and wrapped her arms around the mech, and pushed forward again—through empty hangars and corridors flooded with unreality, through cabins with gutted berths and workshops filled with the silence of death. Within her, lineage and a wordless, heart-breaking lullaby. Thu hugged the mech close to her chest, and went on—rising free from the wreck of the ship and its unexorcised ghosts.

Two-time Nebula Award-winner Fran Wilde has published seven books and over 50 short stories for adults, teens, and kids. Her stories have been finalists for six Nebula Awards, a World Fantasy Award, three Hugo Awards, three Locus Awards, and a Lodestar. They include her Nebula- and Compton Crook-winning debut novel *Updraft*, and her Nebula-winning, Best of NPR 2019, debut Middle Grade novel *Riverland*. Her short stories appear in *Asimov's Science Fiction*, *Tor.com*, *Beneath Ceaseless Skies*, *Shimmer*, *Nature*, *Uncanny Magazine*, and multiple years' best anthologies.

Fran directs the Genre Fiction MFA concentration at Western Colorado University and also writes nonfiction for publications including the *Washington Post*, *The New York Times*, NPR, and *Tor.com*. You can find her on Twitter, Instagram, Facebook, and at franwilde.net.

RHIZOME, BY STARLIGHT

Fran Wilde

A Propagation Manual for The Glass Islands
Year Two, Day 120.
Remember: Removing kudzu is different than splitting a rhizome.
Remember also: Keep the vines away from the greenhouse. Keep yourself within.

With kudzu, you must reach in, rip it all out, then throw it into the sea. Don't think. It's the only way. There can be deviation when splitting. Preservation is your goal. Either for yourself or for the plant. Learn to discern the difference.

So much has been lost to the sea, the heat, but we will continue to tend.

Edward Greene, Senior Conservationist, Longitude Seed Bank and Laboratory

My great-grandfather's words form a grid, each letter a seed, planted neat and black on the yellowing page. My mother's notes, scrawled below her mother's, come after, and before the kudzu took her.

I can't quite read them, but I understand: *Year 42, day 87. I am turned to salt and gnarl. Genes and seeds. I must go before I crush you.*

The wind calls through the vines for me to follow her, but I'd promised them all that I'd tend the greenhouse. As the last of us, I can't leave. Longitude Laboratory trusted us with a duty: keep the seeds safe. The greenhouse will fall without me, and the seeds will disappear. Birds might have dropped the kudzu, we (my great-grandfather's colleagues' experiments, that is) may have made it worse.

With the rest of his laboratory atop the sea-surrounded glass-and-metal island, grandfather had tried to help us withstand the heat, to be resilient, despite everything, to the pain of being left behind. The kudzu, when it took the island over, was the most determined thing he knew, but he swore to never try that. His colleagues did. And were lost to it.

Later, my grandmother and then my mother decided to let the vines have the daylight. To tend our rhizomes at night. To not divide too much. To keep to the greenhouse and defend it.

And our promise? I fulfill it each day. The original seeds are carefully preserved by my family. The last of the Longitude team. We stayed and tended the past. We protect the new growth as well. We last.

My joints creak as I work. I cannot quit our promise. Before she'd left, before the small bones in her fingers finished hardening together as her skin turned to bark, my mother had said the same. She'd wrapped around me, one last time and told me to be strong. To not give up. I could feel her fighting against herself, wanting to hold tight. She tried to protect me as much as the seeds.

But I have no one to worry about crushing, I've made sure.

When I reach fingers deep and sharp into the dirt and pull the young vines away from the greenhouse, I do it only on my own account. When I fling the kudzu over the dawn-bright cliff where the greenhouse is perched, its runners spread like fingers grasping for purchase, then drop.

Once, a gardener would make clippings, or split rhizomes as a scientist might split genes. Now, I am the last gardener and what I do is weed. Kudzu moved fast before. *Year Three, Day 47: They called it mile-a-minute once. Now it is smarter, and faster.* Those words, in less-neat letters. An aging hand, with trembling ascenders and descenders. The manual evolved as we, those who stayed behind, who evolved into our roles, learned not just to tend, but how to survive.

My grandmother wrote happily about her palms sprouting. My mother braided the flowers in my hair into a crown.

There are clippings in the manual. How to care for the seeds. How to call for help. (Not that this does any good: the vines got the radio tower a long time ago). There's a water-logged photo of great-grandfather as a young man with a cane, standing with the others in neat white coats as they prepared to isolate this small corner of earth on top of the world. All somewhat less than those who made the ships. But still determined to save as much as they could. There are pages torn out of the manual, a whole decade's worth. One section is burned. There are drawings, much later, of leaves bigger than a man. Of vines that double in size and grasp in a single night. I do not know who made those, but the ink is rust colored.

My mother, after everything, read the manual aloud to me by starlight, as my great-grandfather had read it to her. She'd found herself alone, read the manuals on propagation. My grandmother's investigations, her grandfather's experiments. By then, the others had been lost—some to science. Some to the sea.

She did it so that we could keep our promise: to tend the seeds and keep them safe for those who would return. That was the promise. She divided, grew, and taught me from the manual, she said. That's how I'd learned my words. How I'd understood that we were born to preserve, to weed, to count the days, until we could no longer do so. I was small then, a breeze could turn my head, but she taught me to focus. To range the island, as I do now, digging deep into the dirt, stopping the vines. Looking for green shoots.

It was left to us to tend the seeds because something in grandfather's genes wasn't right. That's what he wrote in the manual. He, and others like him, stayed with the greenhouse, while others, much stronger and better, found safety on the ships. At least that's what the neat seed-letters say. His young daughter, her genes like his, remained too. She, and we became the promise he made: to stay, to be gardeners. Each day that my great-grandfather and, eventually, my grandmother marked in the manual was a promise: to keep the seeds away from the vines, and ourselves away too.

Now, as the stars shine above, and reflect on the ocean below, I make the same promise, in my own ways.

Today, the island smells of bark and dirt. The kudzu—some of it as thick as my own limbs, and stronger—is winning. But there's a small scent on the wind. Something not kudzu. I sniff it out, a tendril rising from where I'd worked the day before. *A gardener is never finished, until they give in.*

Sometimes, when the sun tries to beat its way through those panes, I trace my great-grandfather's seed-script—all that I know of him—with a fingertip, in the bright when there's only the one star and it's way too close. The glass island reflects off the sea and the day heats up. The thick reaching vines that wrap our island love this. I do not.

Day 167—a small apocalypse, in a larger one. The plants I salvaged have escaped the greenhouse. The trees around us are changing. I've brought what I can back inside. I've set a boundary. I'm training to protect what we can, but the kudzu has already taken several of my best colleagues.

I trace the scent. Find a ginger stem. Pluck it and take it with me to keep it safe from the vines.

On my own pages, I make notes about the latest rain-driven encroachments. The vines this time were fat and fast-moving, and just enough had shoots that I could grab onto and pull myself over until I found their root-ball. I'd used my knife.

In the propagation manual, I make my own notes. My spelling is almost non-existent. Mostly, I draw what I find, and mark how-tos in with stick-figures, as well as the words I know. *Propagation, structure, rhizome, weed.* I make kudzu ink. It's bright green but fades fast to a sour gray.

My mother read the old pages to me by starlight, the ones with blue ink like sky and sea, or purple ink. She read as she plucked small leaves from my skin and hair. She used to save those, for the archives.

Day 1. I'd written the first day after she'd gone. *The vines are invasive. But the greenhouse is too.* I drew both, twined together. The greenhouse glittered: a spoiled frame, three plexiglass panes, in the clearing I'd maintained all these years. The greenhouse held a seed archive once, and the kudzu is still after it. The only way to save the archive is to beat back the vines. *Day 1,* I write each day. Each day, I pull up more rhizomes, and put them in the archive.

I didn't write*: How I miss you. How I remember you on my very skin.*

Instead, I changed the calendar. Stopped the count.

Her mistake, I'd reasoned, was she counted too much, and on too few things. On my drive for survival, on others coming to get the seeds, if we waited long enough. On us beating the roots back. On finding a way around the twisting-in of our own genetics. She stuck to the book's way: dates and memories. I keep my own time.

There's no one here to tell me different. I'm all alone in the greenhouse, a splitting knife in one hand, and a bucket in the other, ready for what comes next. It's raining outside, so I figure that next will be soon.

In the morning, I wake to a bucket full of cuttings. A new bottle of ink. And the roots grown again: this time into a wall all around the greenhouse that nearly cuts off the light. The kudzu mutes the sound of ocean against the island. The vines rise so high and so thick, they dim my view of everything but the stars. I realize, paging back through the manual, that I've made a mistake. I can count the days even when I refuse to number them.

A hundred since she'd gone. And thousands since the world had. But they'd all been wrong. Isolating the seeds, and us, meant the vines would win, all around us. All of them, somewhere out there, got caught by vines or sea, one by one. I won't get caught. I go out with my splitting knife to pare a path.

After it's all over again and I've got the roots divided and pushed back from the greenhouse, I make a new entry in the book. The pages are thick— the early ones from the damp, the later ones because I've sewn in sheets of bark and homemade leaf-vellum—and my writing is worse than everyone's. *It's time*, I write. *To go.*

Day 1: This is a picture of the greenhouse, the sole structure still standing on the research base that used to be on top of a city.

This is a picture of a shovel.

This is a rhizome—not a root, by any means, but a stem that's evolved to survive.

This is me, with a cane that I carved myself from a kudzu root. And my root knife. And this is my mother with hers. She made the cane, still in the corner, beneath the big plexiglass pane—when her grandfather was training her. Made it easier to walk and bend, or . . . at least for me, makes it harder to fall. I made mine when the vines tried coming in the house.

Day 1, again. This is a picture of me scouring the greenhouse for any last seeds and rhizomes. I enter them in the book, recording what will come with me as I travel. I've found some hostas, ginger. Irises. Bamboo of course, but bamboo's almost as bad as the root-plants. I sketch a bit of it on the page, anyway.

Day, before 1: This is a picture of the last person who came to the island. He shouted as he climbed the glass cliffs that he'd heard of my great-grandfather, using the name from the clippings. That he'd come for our seeds. My mother had hidden us from him but forgot the manual. He'd poked through the greenhouse, seen our cots, our kettle. Shouted for us to come out.

He said he was a scientist. Invited the air to go with him, said he had a boat. We refused to listen.

Before he gave up, he searched the greenhouse once more. Found the book. Paged through it. "Seeds are like stories," he'd said. "They change depending on where they're planted." But he didn't stay. The kudzu frightened him, the way it moved so fast. He'd lowered his small boat back down the cliff and sailed away. I'd watched him go.

Before he stepped from our island, he'd put a small rhizome on the ground. Turmeric. "A gift then," he'd said.

That's how I knew what I needed to do. And where I would have to go, when I had a boat. But I didn't go then.

My mother had waited until the vines drove the scientist away, then took the rhizome into the greenhouse, to protect it. "We stay," she said. "Until we can't anymore. We keep what's wrong here from getting out into the world." She often said that. She meant the kudzu, I think, but she might have meant more.

But she's gone now, and it's just me, and my seeds and plants, and I've decided.

Day 1: It's not enough to keep our promise: Hers, to tend the seeds; mine, to stay safe. It's not enough to stay anymore. I think she saw the danger in us, but not in the world beyond.

I work until my hands ache for days, and the bones stiffen into each other. Soon I won't be able to use the knife either. But I'll still be able to paddle.

Day 1: I've pieced together a boat out of the greenhouse and a tree fall that nearly took me too.

Day 1: I've filled my bag with seeds and rhizomes. Kept my mind from wondering what happens when we all go out into the world.

The greenhouse was a nursery, not just a seed bank. I know, because I was born in the greenhouse. Like mother was.

I say it in past tense, because I am the last to grow here.

Day 1: This is a picture of me, climbing into my boat, which used to be a greenhouse.

This is the sail I've woven out of hemp and reeds, and bamboo. That took a long time. This is a picture of the sound of the boat creaking, in the wind.

The boat groans when I let it down the cliff, hand over hand. It thuds when I lower myself to it, wave-slapped and crackling pitch seal on the plant parts, a ghostly chime on the metal, a bit of a sour sound on the plexiglass.

But I'm light, and I'm learning to speak the boat's language as it drops to the sea and I fall after it.

The promise was not to leave the greenhouse, and I haven't, not really. The clearing's already filling in, I bet. I have the manual and both canes and my knife. Let the vines have their way.

I put up the sail like the scientist did. It fills and the wind and currents take me where they want, straight out from the island. When I look back, the island seems made of roots wrapped around and through pieces of glass and metal like the greenhouse grew from, all the way down to where the sea catches it.

Day 1: This is a picture of me wind-blown.

I can see more in the clear water below the boat, metal and glass, window and frame. The wide roots twisting around everything, holding on, binding it all together. Our small home on top was a last enclave—a forgotten garden—an attempt to cling to a memory of ourselves. It grows smaller in the distance as I let the sea take me out, towards the rising stars and the gleam of another glass island far ahead.

Day 1: It's a start, and that's what all of these are—starting points. This bright light out there is mine, the ocean heads me straight for it, and my past splits away from my present.

But the gleam isn't glass. I've never seen a light that sharp before. If I had time and my hands weren't bent in and clutched at the tiller, I'd draw what it looked like. It deserves to go in the manual, even if no one's here to read it.

In my pack are all the roots and rhizomes I've ever found, plus the turmeric and the book—the one with my great-grandfather's writing, which I can just barely read, and my grandmother's, my mother's, and mine. The turmeric's gone gray. and soft over time, despite my tending.

Soon enough, and with some paddling, the island shines right ahead of me. Except that it's moving, the spray blowing from each side of it. It is an enormous ship, sleek and fast, unlike my boat.

And when ropes are lowered, I am lifted. Uprooted from the sea. And from the concerned looks and the motions, I can see they think they're rescuing me.

They tut over my hands. Try to get them to un-clench my paddle. Until I show them how to slide the tool from my grip. Until I show them my plants. And until they wrap me in concern and isolate me.

Then I must wait while they spray me down and try to feed me something awful and gelatinous. And the sun comes out and all I want to do is sleep. But that seems to be the noisiest time on the ship. They take me below. Away.

And in a bright room, where my boat and my plants wait, they pinch me hard with something sharp, and I see pale fluid well into a tube. It looks like ink. I want to write in the manual, but I will not.

Soon, but not soon enough, it is dark again, and this night, they've found someone to come speak to me.

He is much older, but I recognize him. He knows the same words I do, but they're ordered differently. "How long" and "how far" repeat and repeat until I frown at him. How can he not remember? *A story is like a seed.* I was a child, though, and child-memories grow deep and hold fast. Perhaps he visited many islands.

So then I pull the manual from my pocket and begin to show him his story. His eyes light up. The scientist remembers. "You *were* there."

A companion arrives, smelling of sharp chemicals and very white, clean clothing. She gestures to my arms and legs, says something unintelligible.

He frowns. "She says you're lying, that you cannot possibly be your great-grandfather's child. There was no-one left, when we found the seed-bank. And you're too frail to have come all that way, on purpose, on a rusted boat."

The woman tries to take my book away. The turmeric falls from the pages, and the scientist puts a careful shoe over it, to hide it. Tend it.

When I yell this time, he leaves with the rest of them—tall and long-limbed—taking my plants, and my book too. I expected the ocean to steal me, like my mother said it stole most people from before, but I didn't expect it to be like this. My island past and my boat past and this present divide again. I am many stories now.

They want to know where the others are. I ask them the same question. They will not answer. So I don't answer. I stopped counting beyond myself a long time ago.

I draw on their walls: *Day 1: This is a picture of my mother with her cane and her knife. This is a picture of my great-grandfather with his instruments and machines. This is us, dividing and splitting. This is gene and rhizome. These are our pathways forwards, and how we survived, one and then the next, when no one knew we were there.*

They—the smooth, sharp-smelling woman, and the scientist, who's also wearing white—squint at the drawings. *Impossible.* That is the sense of their words, the set of their shoulders. And yet, so much of what I say is possible. I am possible. I pull some leaves from my hair and hide them in my bag.

They are scientists, I begin to understand, but nothing like my great-grand-father. They've forgotten so much: dirt and starlight; the ways nature finds. They keep me confined to the shadows of my room for far too long. I begin to fade to gray. My hair no longer flowers, my skin begins to split.

I'm starting to go, to crave starlight, then sunlight, sea air, and dirt. Even kudzu. I desire growing things, not poking things.

They will let me have none.

So I wait, and wilt. And then, finally, the scientist comes back. He greets me again, but with more respect. "You are what you say."

"Take me outside. To the deck. I need starlight."

He starts to shake his head, but I hold out my hand. A thin leaf curls there. He stares. Touches it. Then takes it, hungrily.

He opens the door.

And in the light and sea air, I begin what I promised I'd never do. I let myself go wild. My arms and legs itch with it. A tendril of vine curls beneath my ear. "I cannot stay here. They'll take me apart."

He looks a long time at me, then at the leaf in his hand, then shows me where my boat is kept. The bag of seeds and rhizomes is lost. I cannot stay where they've taken so much already. So I go, over the metal edge, away from the sharp smells.

The wind helps me leave the ship behind, once I set my sail again. The scientist grows smaller, where he stands by the stern.

I scratch behind my ear, carefully. Look at my arm, then my leg, beneath the sack dress I wear.

New rhizomes. Each their own beginning. I will plant these parts of me somewhere new. Everywhere, maybe. Someday, they'll make their own canes and knives, they'll help hold back the weeds on different islands. And someday, perhaps, they'll add pages to the book. The manual for propagation, made from a different island's plants. This time, we'll give what we have of ourselves, growing beyond where we began. *Day 1, of many.*

Rich Larson (*Annex, Tomorrow Factory*) was born in Galmi, Niger, has lived in Spain and Czech Republic, and is currently based in Grande Prairie, Canada. His fiction has been translated into over a dozen languages, among them Polish, French, Romanian, and Japanese, and adapted to screen for Netflix's *LOVE DEATH + ROBOTS*. Find free reads and support his work at patreon.com/richlarson.

HOW QUINI THE SQUID MISPLACED HIS KLOBUČAR

Rich Larson

want you to help me rip off Quini the Squid, I say, or at least that's what I say in my head. It comes off my tongue as:

"Rebum lau kana'a chep fessum ninshi."

Which would leave any linguist flabbergasted. But Nat understands exactly what I mean, judging from the disgusted look on her face. We're speaking the same procedurally generated language, invented on the fly by blackmarket babelware in our implants.

"Yam switta b'lau bi," she says, and the babelware feeds my language lobe an unequivocal *Get fucked*.

It's for this reason I ordered her a steaming mountain of mussels in black pepper sauce. I know she won't leave until she's sucked every last quivering invertebrate from its shell into her small but agile mouth. Which gives me time to bring her around on the idea.

We're in a wharfside resto on La Rambla, one of those polyplastic tents that springs up overnight like a mushroom and is almost fully automated, packed with sunburned tourists guzzling drone-delivered Heinekens and comparing their unhealthy Gaudí obsessions. It's not the kind of place Quini's thugs would hang around in, and if they did they would stick out like scowling, vantablack-clad sore thumbs.

But it pays to be paranoid in public in this day and age, what with the feds now legally able to hijack phones and implant mics. Ergo, the babelware. If I'm using *ergo* right.

"Dan tittacha djabu numna, numna ka'adai," I say solemnly, which of course is *Eat your seafood and let me explain.*

"Yugga," she says, which is actually a pretty good word for *idiot.*

I understand her reticence. Quini the Squid is everyone your mum ever told you not to get mixed up with mixed together, and also they used to bang. Nat and Quini, I mean. Not Quini and your mum—though he is in many ways a motherfucker.

He clawed his way out of some shithole town in Andalusia during the worst of the drought years, first pirating autotrucks transporting precious olive oil and later graduating to human traffic. God knows how he got Catalonia to let him in, but once they did he stretched his tentacle into pretty much everything: weapons, drugs, viruses, the lot.

Of course, me and Nat are transplants too. Catalonia's secession triggered an economic boom that brought in all sorts of wealthy investors, and where wealthy investors go, thieves and scammers follow. Nat came all the way from a ghetto in Ljubljana. Her original hustle was small time but well polished: She picked up rich shitheads in classy bars with her Eastern Euro smolder and bone structure, got them somewhere private, then kissed them paralyzed before robbing them blind.

She showed me the biomod once, this tiny little needle under her tongue that delivers a muscle-melting dose of concentrated ketamine. I try to spot it as she slurps a mussel. She says the needle can also be loaded with party drugs just for fun, but I'd never trust her enough to risk it.

You hate him as much as I do, I say, and it turns into a series of clashing consonants in my mouth as our language evolves again.

Nat is stacking empty shells with blistering efficiency, but she pauses long enough to wipe her mouth with a napkin and give a clicking answer that becomes *I hate salt water. Doesn't mean I pick fights with the tide.*

You're really comparing him to the fucking ocean? I demand. *He's a puddle. At best a small pond.*

"Shepakwat," she says: *He's dangerous.*

"Bu iztapti bu," I say: *No shit.*

I stand to carefully peel my shirt up to my ribs, which draws a few stares. The violet bruises go from below my hips all the way up my side. Nat can't quite disguise her wince, and I almost feel bad for darkening up the injuries with makeup. They were healing too fast for the effect I needed.

I heard about that, she says in two low syllables. *The job in Murcia, right?*

I sit back down. My jaw is starting to ache from making unfamiliar sounds. *Yeah*, I say. *I was doing the hackwork for a break-and-enter. Owned all the cameras, all the doors. Then one of Quini's clowns forgot to turn on his fucking faraday gear, and when he got pinged Quini put it on me. Did this right in front of everyone. Called me a* maricona. *Took my pay.* I add the last one so she won't know how bad the second-last one bothered me.

As soon as the bruises are out of sight, Nat attacks the mussels again. *So this a revenge thing*, she says, but pensive now, licking her fingers.

If that makes it more appealing to you, then sure. I want the money he owes me. I wrap my black scarf tighter around my neck. *And some humiliation on the side would be a bonus.*

Her ears go red, but also perk up. She and Quini didn't split amicably. Humiliation is a soft word for what he did. *You eating?* she asks, and I know my foot's in the door. *You look skinny. Or something.*

She can pretend zen, but I know she needs the money and wants the payback. And even though we've had our ups and downs over the years, I know she hates seeing me hurt.

Mine's coming, I say. *Now here's the deal.*

I lay it all out for her, all the blocks I've been stacking and rearranging in my head for the past three days, ever since I got wind of Quini's little storage problem. Like I said before, he's a well-rounded businessman: narcotics, guns, malware. Usually none of the product stays in Barcelona long, and while it's here it's circulating in a fleet of innocuous cars driving randomized routes.

But he recently got his suckers on something very rare, something he hasn't been able to move yet, and it's so valuable he's keeping it in his own home. He even felt the need to get himself a new security chief to keep tabs on it. Which might have been a good idea, except his old security chief was awfully unhappy about her loss of employment.

I helped her get shit-faced last night at a wine bar and when the Dozr kicked in I dragged her to the bathroom and cracked into her cranial implant. She had some decently feisty defenseware, but I got what I needed—specs and layouts for the house, patrol maps, intrusion countermeasures—then wiped a few hours of data from her aurals and optics to cover my tracks. I also got confirmation on what exactly Quini was storing.

You heard what it is? I ask Nat. *What he's got in the safe room?*

She picks over the last of the mussels. *I know the rumor. People are saying it's a Klobučar.*

I'm not much for gene art, not much for sophisticated shit in general, but even I know Klobučar, the Croatian genius who struck the scene like a meteor and produced a brief torrent of masterpieces before carving out her brain with a mining laser on a live feed.

Anything with a verified Klobučar gene signature is worth a fortune, especially since she entwined all her works with a killswitch parasite to prevent them being sequenced and copied. But Quini is the furthest thing from an art fence, which makes the acquisition a bit of a mystery and explains him seeming slightly panicked about the whole thing.

Damn right it's a Klobučar, I tell her. *And we're stealing it.*

That's not my area of expertise, Nat says. *Like, not even close.*

It's mine, I agree. *But you know Quini. You know his habits. And because you're a clever one, I think you must have some of his helix bottled up somewhere.*

She gives a low laugh in her throat. *You think I keep a DNA catalog of everyone I fuck?*

Probably only the ones that might be valuable later, I say. "Bazza?"

"Gazza," she admits.

The safe room is coded to Quini himself, nobody else, I say. *I can spoof the signature from his implants, but for fooling the bioscanner we need to get creative.*

Nat takes a small sip of water and swishes it around her mouth. *You know what he'll do if he catches us,* she says.

I know, I say. *I'm not a* yugga.

She frowns—maybe the babelware can't handle that kind of callback. *So long as you know,* she mutters. *I'm in.*

Under the table, I pump my fist. Then I finally ping the kitchen, which has been faithfully keeping my order warm, and the squid paella arrives in all its steamy glory, dismembered tentacles arranged in a beautiful reddish-orange wheel.

Then Quini is cooked, I say, raising my Estrella cider. *Here's to payback.*

Nat raises her water glass but also her eyebrow. *You don't even like seafood,* she says. *You only ordered that to be dramatic. Didn't you.*

I shrug; we clink drinks. Nat eyes the dish for a second. Sniffs the spices wafting off it. She does her own shrug, then pulls the plate across to her side of the table as the little server purrs off with her mountain of empty mussel shells.

So, she says. *You going to explain this new look you have going on?*

No, I say, self-consciously adjusting my scarf again.

Okay. She spears the first piece of squid and stuffs it into her mouth. Her eyes flutter shut in momentary ecstasy. *You always did find good places to eat,* she says, reopening her eyes. *Now. How soon do you need the helix?*

"Andidana," I tell her: *Yesterday.*
There's a tight clock on this one.

Two bottles of cider later, I wobble out into the sunshine feeling pretty good about the whole thing. Even with the tourist quota imposed, La Rambla is fucking chaos, an elbow-to-elbow crush of holidayers sprinkled with resigned locals and eager scammers. I pick out the hustles as I walk:

The apologetic woman helping clean some kind of muck off a man's trousers while she slides the gleaming bracelet off his wrist.

The smiling couple peddling genies, those little blue-furred splices that come in a cheap incubator pod and die a few days later.

The elderly lady groaning from the mossy pavement where a rented electricycle supposedly sent her sprawling.

One gent's got something I've never seen before, a tiny prehensile limb that flexes out from under his jacket like a monkey tail and slips into every open handbag he passes.

It's beautiful, really, this whole little ecosystem where the apex predator is a blue-black Mossos police drone that swoops in and sends everyone scattering.

Since I'm in the neighborhood I do a bit of window shopping, sliding past a storefront to see some new prints in from Mombasa. The mannequins track my eyes and start posing—I hate that. As soon as I get off La Rambla onto Passeig de Colom, I'm all business again. Nat is essential, and talented, but she's not the only helping hand I'll need for this job. It's that final bioscanner that makes things so tricky.

Having Quini's helix is only half the battle: We also need a body, and neither mine nor Nat's fits the bill, in large part because we've got implants that are definitely not Quini's. Masking or turning off tech built right into the nervous system is actually a lot harder than simply hiring what our German friends call a *Fleischgeist.*

It's not as snappy in English: meat ghost. But it gives you the idea—someone with no implants. None. No hand chip, no cranial, no optics or aurals. Nothing with an electronic signature. In our day and age, they might as well be invisible. Ergo, the ghost part.

There are basically two ways to find yourself a *Fleischgeist* in Barcelona. You can go to an eco-convent slash Luddite commune, which doesn't really lend itself to the skills I need, or you can go to Poble del Vaixell, which is where I'm going now, sticking to the long shadow of the Mirador.

The tower's old gray stone is now skinned in the same green carbon-sink moss as everywhere else; the top has been taken over by a whole flock of squawking white seagulls. Beyond it, the Mediterranean is the bright rippled blue of travel holos. I order a rotorboat and it's waiting for me when I get to the docks, jostling for space with an old man fishing plastic out of the water. The salt-crusted screen blinks me a smiley face.

"*Bon dia,*" the rotorboat burbles. "*On anem avui?*"

"Just take me out to the buoys," I say, because technically Poble del Vaixell doesn't exist.

The smiley face on the screen winks as if it knows. Then I climb in and we push off hard at the perfect angle to drench the fisherman with our spray. He sputters. I give him the apologetic hand shrug as we sling out into the harbor.

The waves are a bit choppy today but the rotorboat is up to it, dicing precisely through the traffic of yachts and sails and autobarges. We peel away from the coastline and head straight out to sea. The salt wind blows my hair all around, which I hate, and even with the gyroscopes I manage to slam my tailbone against the boat bench hard enough to smart. Fortunately it's not a long ride out to the border buoys, a long line of gray columns blinking authoritative yellow hazard lights.

And just beyond them, Poble del Vaixell, a massive floating labyrinth that sometimes looks bigger than Barcelona itself. It actually is a little snappier in English: Shiptown. Originally composed of all the south-up migrants who couldn't get through Catalonia's vetting system, in the past decade it's become a force unto itself. Plastic fishing, plankton farming, solar storage, you name it.

For a lot of people it's the final jumping off point to Europe, but for a lot more people it's home. I've done a couple month-long stints here myself when I needed to lie low. The rotorboat nuzzles up as close as it can to the border. I cover my face on muscle memory, even though the buoy cams were hit with a virus barrage last year and still haven't recovered, then take a flying leap onto the polyplastic pier.

It judges my athleticism in mid-air and shoots out to meet me; I still nearly eat shit when my boots hit the algae-slimed surface. But I'm over the border, in Shiptown proper, and the rotorboat burbles goodbye before it skids away on a blade of foam. I wave, compose myself, and head for the downtown.

Shiptown's original skeleton was a flotilla of migrant boats, some huge, most tiny, lashed or welded together in solidarity against the 3-D printed seawalls and aggressive border drones preventing them from reaching the coast. Since then it's sprawled outward in all directions, an enormous maze that seems to grow by the hour, its web of walkways crammed with pedestrians and cyclists.

I go right through the market, where there are tarps heaped with dried beans and grasshoppers beside tarps with secondhand implants, some so fresh you can practically see the spinal fluid dripping off them. You can get by with a few different currencies in the market, but barter is still the go-to. I traded a designer jacket I didn't want anymore for my *Fleischgeist*'s contact information.

His name is Yinka, and he's waiting in a bar called Perrito that used to be a fishing boat called *Perrito*—the bit of the hull that had the name painted on is now welded to struts over the door. The interior smells like fish guts when I walk in and the biolamp lighting shows a few pinkish stains on the floor.

"Bones, com va?" I try.

Perrito's bartender glances at me from behind a repurposed slice of nano-carbon barricade, then goes back to rearranging her bottles of mezcal and rotgut vodka. She doesn't pull out a scattergun or anything, though, so I head toward the back. The only Nigerian in the place is posted up in the corner with an untouched glass of what looks like bog water but is probably bacteria beer.

I measure him as I sit down. Retro white buds in his ears are blaring some *kuduro* hit and he's wearing a sleeveless windbreaker with a shifting green-black pattern meant to fool basic facial recognition ware. He's even younger than I expected. Small, which is typical for a break-in artist, with wiry arms and chalky elbows resting on the table. Fashionably half-buzzed head, blank and angular face, hooded eyes fixed on the fresh-printed slab of a phone in his hands. Which I guess isn't an affectation, since he's got no implants.

"Yinka?"

He doesn't look up, but his thumb twitches on the phone and the music volume drops slightly. "Yes."

"You do good work," I say, which is a bit of an exaggeration—he does work. "A few real slick jobs in Lagos. That one in Dakar. You ready to try something a bit harder?"

"I'm ready to hear about the money, man," Yinka says. "We're pinching art? My auntie did that once. Fence took everything but the crumbs."

"We'll be getting some very big crumbs," I say. "Klobučar-sized crumbs."

I put my hand out; he grunts and slides the fresh phone across. I tap it with one finger and my implant sends the rest of the job info, the stuff I didn't want floating through Barcelona air, including the estimated value of Klobučar's currently verified works.

He peers at the screen, then blinks. His eyes bulge for a split second. "Oh. Yeah. I'm in, then."

"Good," I say. "How are you with virtual?"

"Depends how much virtual. I get a little sick."

"I already got pods rented here in Shiptown," I say. "We're cramming about a week of prep into eighteen hours."

Yinka cocks his head to one side, still not looking up. "Eighteen hours straight, we're all gonna be podsick. For guaran."

I don't get podsick myself, but I know how to counter it. "I've got the pharma to balance you out," I say. "There's no other way. We hit the safe room tomorrow night."

He finally meets my eyes, and for a second I see the nervous kid hidden under the *I'm a cold pro* act, out here in a foreign country trying to hustle and not sure what he's getting into. Reminds me of me, but I had a better game face even back then.

"Okay, man," he says, gaze back to the phone screen. "But if I don't like the feeling, I don't go."

His thumb slides the volume back up and I let the tinny clash of *kuduro* play me out.

Shiptown's best quality virtual is in Xavi's sex house, so that's where three clean pods are waiting for us. It's a lurid little place, scab-red carpeting and black-and-white pornography stills coating every inch of the walls, with a lingering scent of bodily fluids that the air freshener can't quite mask.

I go in to check the pods—Yinka's is modified with the old-school electrodes—and shake hands with Xavi, who owes me one for getting a bug out of his biofeedback interface and doesn't know I put it in there in the first place. Then I come back out to share a vape with my just-arrived *Fleischgeist* while we wait for Nat to show up.

"Never been to Lagos," I say. "There's a lagoon, yeah? Must be nice."

Yinka grudgingly turns his volume down, I imagine only because I'm smoking him up. "Hazy, man. Dirty." He puffs out a blue-tinged cloud. "Shanties all around."

"That where you came up?" I ask.

He passes the vape back. "Nah nah. I was born in a hospital." He pauses, looking over my head. "My ma could afford the imps. She just didn't want me to have them."

"Why's that?"

He shrugs his bony shoulders. "She was in a death cult."

"Ah."

Nat arrives fashionably late, just as the sun's turning smelter orange and I'm turning antsy. She comes striding up the walkway with her immaculate black coat slicing open on long stockinged legs, and I can see Yinka get love-struck in realtime, which is a perk of working with Nat and might be useful later.

"The bioprinter wanted to haggle," she says, raking a strand of hair off her face. "Doesn't usually run the thing overnight. We'll be good for the pickup time, though."

"Good," I say. "Nat, Yinka. Yinka, Nat."

"Pleasure," says Nat. She looks him up and down. "Nice jacket."

Yinka's eyes don't make it to hers, but they stick briefly on her bee-stung lips before they flit away. "Thanks. New."

"You two are going to really hit it off," I say. "Let's get started."

I usher them into the back, where the pods are levered open and Xavi's setting up our extra hydration packs. Eighteen hours is a long go, and for all he knows we're doing a marathon *ménage à trois* with the biofeedback on. I go over to my pod and poke my finger into the conduction gel.

"It's clean," Xavi says, sounding wounded. "I drained and refilled."

My finger implant runs a little scan and agrees with him—no nasty bacterial surprises. We get Yinka set up first, helping him into the sensor suit that will compensate for his lack of implants and hooking it into a glinting spiderweb of electrodes. He lies back in the pod, head bobbing slightly in the gel, and shuts his eyes. Xavi shuts the lid.

Nat takes the pod beside mine, strips down, and climbs in. She's run enough sex scams in virtual that the whole thing is automatic. I'm worried about Yinka getting podsick, not her. "You tell him?" she asks. "About fooling the bioscanner?"

"Broad strokes," I say.

"Okay," she says, and closes the lid herself.

That leaves me and Xavi, and I tell him to go watch the front. I wait until I hear him settle into his orthochair before I strip. Even then I keep an eye on the other pods, as if Yinka or Nat might pop up and start gaping at me. There's a reason I only pulled my shirt up to my ribs in the restaurant, no higher. I don't care about showing off the bruises Quini left me, but I'm a bit self-conscious about the work the hormone implant's done in the past few months. Nat doesn't know, and now's not the time.

I fold my clothes and stick them on the flimsy plastic shelf, then climb inside my pod. As soon as the conduction gel hits my bare skin, my implants start to sing.

Quini's villa on the edge of the city is, of course, a tasteless monstrosity. Basically he fed Park Güell and the Sagrada Família into an architectural AI and it spat out a cheap Gaudí imitation overrun with geometric lizards and fluted-bone buttresses. I'm floating in the sky above it with Nat on one side of me and a slightly blurry Yinka on the other.

"You ever ask about his decorating?" I mutter.

"He's still trying to prove to himself he's in Catalonia," Nat says. "Still scared to wake up dirt poor back in the *pueblo*. But no. I didn't ask."

"Fortunately he worked a little Andalusia in there too," I say, and pivot the view so we're in the copse of twisted olive trees that shades the back half of the villa. "That's our cover. We're coming in cross-country."

Yinka looks around. The motion of his head leaves pixelated traces in the air. "They got dogs?"

"One dog," I say, and pull up the schematics I took from Quini's sacked security chief. The dog materializes with us in the woods, right in front of Nat, who flinches a little. I don't blame her. It's a vicious-looking thing, all angles, long whippet legs and a sensor bulb head with a disc of glinting teeth underneath.

"That's a power saw," Yinka says. "He rigged a power saw to its head?"

"He likes things messy," I say, glancing over at Nat. "But in this case, it's a good thing. We'll hear it coming. And I'm writing a backdoor into its friend/ foe mapper. Once we're past the dog . . . "

I glide us forward, out of the olive trees, toward the soft blue glow of the swimming pool. Tendrils of steam waft off it, frozen midair. The surrounding white tiles are etched with, I shit you not, lizards. There's a walkway and glass door leading into the villa itself, and from there it's only a short trip down a hallway to Quini's bedroom.

Its main feature is probably the bed itself, a massive black slab floating in the air above a magnet pad. Other contenders include the sparring dummy strutting back and forth by the mirrors and mats, the holo on the ceiling of naked faceless bodies writhing together, and the oversized print of Quini's own scowling face on the wall.

"That's you," I say, pointing it out to Yinka. "Or it will be. Here, have a better look."

Quini appears in the room with us, cobbled together from all the free-floating footage I could grab of him from the past two years plus the few unfortunate interactions I've had with him in person. Nat looks the composite up and down, frowning a little at his sinewy folded arms, but she doesn't say anything so it must be accurate enough for her.

Me and Yinka walk a circle around him. He's not big, Quini, but even in virtual he radiates a kind of ferocity, like a cat with its hackles up. His eyes are pouchy and bloodshot and his buzzed hair is bleached reddish-orange. His sun-browned skin is feathered with white scar tissue here and there, but no tattoos. Quini hates needles.

"We have the schema for the bioscanner," I say. "It's looking at height and weight first. We're going to bulk you out a bit, add a couple centimeters to your shoes. It's got some limited gait recognition, so you'll have to get the hang of walking like him, too."

I wave my hand and Quini slouches forward, toward the sparring dummy. Yinka watches intently.

"Nat has generously donated some of his genetic material," I continue. "Which the printer is hard at work turning into a palmprint glove and a face-mask. It won't be a perfect match, but these things never get a perfect match. It'll be enough so long as I'm spoofing his implant signal at the same time."

Quini turns and starts walking back, loping steps, one arm a little stiff. I hope Yinka's a good mimic.

"Safe room is through here," Nat says, and I get the impression she doesn't like hanging around with even the virtual version of her abusive ex. We follow her past the bathroom to a blank stone wall. The only sign of the bioscanner is a tiny blue light, blinking at eye level. Yinka goes up on tiptoes for a second to meet it. His hand pats at his pocket.

"And we don't know what it is," he says. "Just that it's Klobučar."

"We know it's small enough to be transported in an incubator pod this size," I say, holding up a clenched fist. "We know Quini didn't even take it out of said incubator pod. So we don't have to worry about dragging some kind of, I don't know, giraffe-orca hybrid back to the car. You go in, you grab it, we leave the way we came. Five minutes in the safe room, tops. Twenty in the house, tops."

"Quini's where?" Yinka's hand pats his pocket again, and I realize he's feeling on muscle memory for his antique phone, which did not come to virtual with us. "While we're doing all this shit. Where is he?"

I understand the question. I understand that even looking at Quini, you know he's not someone you want home during a home invasion.

"It's a Saturday night," I say. "He's busy at Flux. Nat will keep an eye on him while she sets up the spoof. So all we got for occupants is a skeleton security screw—four people, I got their files—and a cleaner."

Yinka gives a slow nod.

"We'll be good," I say, trying to reassure both him and myself. "It's time to start rehearsing."

Seventeen hours later and we're as ready as we can be. If you've ever done deep virtual, you know how time gets twisted. The longer you're in the pod, the harder it is to tell if you've been in there for a week or ten minutes or your whole fucking life. Which is why I was a little worried for Yinka, but he seems to be holding up fine.

He's even smiling; Nat's telling him a Ljubljana story, some naked businessman chasing her through the snowy street behind his hotel. She's always been good at making shitty things sound funny, and I also feel like virtual helps you bond. When everything around you is artificial, you have to lean a little harder on the real people.

I didn't hear anything more about Yinka's childhood, but he did confess he's working on a few of his own *kuduro* tracks. That was sometime between the tenth and eleventh run on the house. I did some prep work alone while Yinka practiced being Quini under Nat's tutelage, but mostly we ran the whole thing together. First with the patrols on their planned routes, then with minor randomization, then with disaster scenarios.

Nat has a job all her own, planting the spoof at Flux, but she knows that place like the back of her hand.

"All right," I say, cutting her story short at the high point. "That last one felt good. Let's run it one final time, then get out of here."

Nat stares at me and the grin drops off Yinka's face.

"We're out, man," he says. "We been out. You were the one who woke us up."

Shit.

I take a closer look at my surroundings. We're gliding still, but that's because we're in the back of a car heading up Avenida Diagonal through the synchronized swarm of black-and-yellow cabs retrieving and depositing revelers. Through the window I see dark sky splashed with holos. Nat and Yinka are across from me—Yinka's not blurry at all—and the duffel bags are on the floor. We've already been to the bioprinter.

"We're on our way to Flux," Nat says; then, on a private channel our *Fleischgeist* can't hear: *Up your dose.*

I look down and see the baggie of speed in my palm, the pharma Xavi slapped into our goodbye handshake. Reality warps and shivers around me. I don't get podsick. I never get podsick.

"You good?" Yinka says, voice pitching up, nerves creeping in.

"I'm fucking with you," I say. "Gallows humor, Yinka."

We drop Nat a block from Flux, and while Yinka's looking away I dry-swallow as many pills as I can fit in my idiot mouth. A sweaty, skin-humming minute passes before things brighten. Sharpen.

I never get podsick. It's a bad omen and I can't help but think it's because of the hormone implant, the new chemical messengers in my body messing with my metabolism, with my brain.

Don't fuck this up, Nat chats me, and strides around the corner without looking back.

The copse of olive trees behind Quini's villa isn't more than a square kilometer, but at night, with a gut full of speed battling a podsick cerebellum, it seems big as a fairy-tale forest, a dark, dense thicket eating us whole. I'm trying real hard to keep my shit together.

"We trip anything yet?" Yinka asks.

"No tripping," I say.

The perimeter is sewn with sensors, but I own those already. As soon as we were in range I hit them with a maintenance shutdown, courtesy of some malware written by a ten-year-old in Laos who really knows her shit. That's the thing about this line of work: There's always some tiny genius coming up behind you doing it better.

But the backdoor for the dog, that I had to do myself. The AI is a custom job, modified from a military prototype I'm not getting anywhere near without some serious social engineering, so I'm lucky the security chief had a vested interest in its inner workings. It only took one night of sifting source code to find a vulnerability. But we have to be in range.

For a second I can't remember if we're on the fifth run or the sixth. Then I look at Yinka, clear, not-blurry Yinka, and get a cold needle jabbed into my spinal column. Real. This is real, and we're coming up on the dog. I can see its bobbing signal in my implant, and I can hear the soft whine of the saw. I tighten my grip on my duffel bag. Look over at Yinka again. He mostly trusts me now, mostly because he has no other options.

"I'm starting," I say, and sit down.

The dog spots our heat through the trees. It comes running, loping along, the serrated saw humming. I'm in my implant loading the code, line after line of custom script. All I need is the handshake. Which is funny, because it's a dog. *Sit. Shake. Don't maul us.*

Yinka catches sight of it as it ducks around a twisty trunk. I hear him suck in a breath.

"My connection is slower than I thought," I say, and I nearly say, *Let's try it again*, before I remember that we can't. This is real, and the dog is breaking into a run. The saw is a spinning blur. I can picture it ripping into my face, spraying the olive trees with bright red blood. My heart is a fist pounding at my ribcage; in another second it'll bust right through.

"Man, it's coming right at us," Yinka says. "Get up. Get up, it's coming right at us."

He's right. The dog hurtles toward us and I dimly feel Yinka yanking under my arms, trying to haul me to my feet. Client and server collide. The code shuttles across.

"Shake, motherfucker," I say.

The dog skids to a stop in front of us and wags its plastic tail. The whine of the saw makes my teeth ache in my jaw. It didn't do that in virtual. We sit tight for a second until it trots away, then both of us breathe. The fairy-tale forest swells and contracts around me. I pop another pill, not caring if Yinka sees it.

"Well done, man," he finally says, and gives me a hand up.

My legs are shaking when we come out of the woods. I'm still waiting for the speed to kick my head clear. *Real, real, real.* We can't run this again, and that means I have to be perfect. We pad across the bone-dry tiles, past the steamy swimming pool, and Yinka stands watch while I crack the door into the villa. I've done it so many times it feels like a dream.

Not a dream. Real. I'm podsick, and I need to keep my shit together.

"After you," I say, as the door slides open. I'm in the house cameras. Three of the four guards are in the kitchen with a vape, one is fucking the cleaner in the guest bathroom, both of them muffling their grunts with soft white towels clenched in their teeth. I run my tongue around my mouth, thinking how much I'd hate that. Lint and whatnot.

Yinka leads the way down the hall to Quini's room, the way he's done eight times at least. He's a little jumpy. I want to tell him to relax. Tell him we could run down the hallway screaming. It's only virtual.

Podsick. Podsick. Podsick. I have to chant it in my head. The speed should be balancing me out. Maybe Xavi gave me some real stepped-on shit. It's working for Yinka, though, and I hope to God it's working for Nat. Maybe my tolerance is too high.

The cleaner hasn't made it to the bed yet; the sheets are a tangled mess hanging off one end. The sparring dummy sees us and starts shadowboxing, reminding me of the mannequins on La Rambla I hate so much. I flip it the finger as we walk past. The door to the safe room is still invisible, a thick stone plane, the scanner winking innocent blue at us.

I set my duffel down; Yinka drops his.

"Okay," I say. "Time to check in with Nat."

Nat is in the bathroom of Flux, and because she's cutting me into her eyefeed there's a blissy moment where I am her, where the reflection in the smart mirror is my reflection. The geometry of her dark hair hitting her perfect collarbone is so beautiful it hurts. She puts a pill between her puffy lips and washes it down with a slurp of water from the faucet.

We're at the safe room, I chat her.

The rental timer on the stall behind her expires; the electronic bleating almost drowns out the sound of the occupant vomiting.

He's on the upper level, she chats me. *Can you reach?*

She drops her defenseware, which we both know is a polite fiction—I installed that defenseware. Her body becomes an antenna, boosted by the graphene conduction pads she taped to her dress, and I can suddenly see every implant in the club. Quini's are tagged a bright red, but I can't touch them.

Bathroom must have a concrete ceiling, I chat her. *Get out in the open.*

The smart mirror makes a read on her body language and throws up a filter, unfurling blackened wings behind her shoulder blades, turning her into an avenging angel. It probably thinks she's about to pull or punch someone. I put another five minutes on the stall for whoever's puking.

Nat slices past the vending machine, where a couple girls are already printing up cheap flats for the stumble home, and plunges out into the club. This is her element in the way I've only ever pretended it's my element: She moves through the crowd like a fluid, depositing precise air kisses and brief embraces where she has to, never getting caught in conversation.

In another world, I can hear Yinka moving beside me, putting on the bodysuit designed to give him Quini's almost exact proportions.

Nat's eyes scan the upper level and suddenly there's Quini, wearing a specifically tailored spidersilk suit, arm wrapped through the railing. He's got his chin to his chest, laughing at something that makes the people around him look vaguely uncomfortable. She ducks behind the steroid-pumped bulk of a bouncer to break line of sight. The signal flares strong.

Got it, I say, and I start the spoof, using Nat's implants to mirror Quini's and send the signal, by rented pirate satellite, all the way to the villa.

The bouncer moves, and for a second it feels like Quini is looking right at us, but then I realize his eyes are squeezed shut. There's a glimmer of tears on his face, sickly green in the strobing lights. Nat slides away into the crowd.

Please don't let him see you, I chat her.

No shit, she chats back. *You tell Yinka yet?*

"Man, they fucked up," our *Fleischgeist* says, not in my head but in the air beside it. His whisper is hoarse. "The suit's missing one sleeve."

"Yeah," I say. "That's the thing."

I drop Nat's eyefeed and come back to the safe room door. I should have told him back in the car, or back in virtual. But I couldn't. Not after he said that thing about his ma being in a death cult, and then me hacking his phone and using a police timeline AI to figure out which cult it was, and then me finding out their main thing was dismemberment. Me finding out the sting caught his mom standing over him with a machete. Even ghosts have traces.

"What thing?" Yinka demands.

So instead I modified the virtual Quini, and I lied. It was a hell of a coincidence, and way too late to find another *Fleischgeist*.

"Quini's nickname, 'the Squid'?" I stroke my finger down my duffel's enzyme zipper. It peels apart to reveal the refrigerated case and the surgical saw. "It's one of those ironic nicknames."

I show him an undoctored image of Quini, projecting it from my finger implant onto the stone wall. He stares at the wrinkled stump where Quini's right arm used to be and sucks in air through his nostrils.

"He's only got one tentacle total," I say. "He had a bad time with some drug runners when he was a kid. Stole a pack of cigarettes from them, is the story. So they did that. Even after he made it out, even after he made money, he never got a new one grown. Never got a prosthetic."

I can't tell if Yinka's listening. He's looking down at the surgical saw with his mouth sealed tight. I wish Nat were here, to look at him through her lampblack lashes and make Yinka feel like the whole thing was his brave and beautiful idea.

"It's temporary," I say. "Five minutes in the safe room, remember? We take it off, put it on ice. You get in, get the Klobučar, get out. Twenty minutes, we're back to the car—there's an autosurgeon waiting in the back—and it gets reattached en route with zero nerve damage."

Yinka looks me right in the eye and enunciates. "You fucking snake."

I try to shrug, but it ends up more like a shudder. "Tight clock. You do it and we walk away rich as kings, or you dip and we did all this for nothing."

Yinka looks away again. "How much time you set aside to convince me?"

"Four minutes."

He curses at me in Yoruba—my babelware only gets half of it—then grips his head in both hands. He stares up at the ceiling. "Nat. She knew too."

"It's temporary," I say. "I'll bump your take. Forty percent. How's that?"

"How high you gonna go?" Yinka asks dully.

"You can have my whole fucking share," I snap. "It's not the money for me. It's personal."

Yinka stays staring at the ceiling, not blinking. "Your whole share," he finally says. "And if the reattach goes bad, I'm going to kill you with one hand, man."

"You'll have to beat Quini to it," I say. "But yeah. It's a deal."

I put out my hand to shake and he ignores it, which is, you know, understandable. Instead he lies down on the stone floor and lays his right arm out flat. His face is expressionless but his chest is working like a bellows, ribcage pumping up and down. He's terrified.

"Try to relax," I say to both of us, sticking anatabs up and down his arm.

Yinka's nostrils flare. "I'm not saying another fucking word to you until my arm's back on."

The tabs turn bright blue against his dark skin as they activate, deadening his nerves. The limb goes slack from his shoulder down. I wrap the whole thing in bacterial film, to catch the blood spray, and mark my line above the elbow.

Now it's time for the bit I practiced on my own, the private virtual Nat and Yinka were not invited to. I switch on the saw and the high-pitched whine makes me gooseflesh all over.

We do the amputation in silence, even though when I practiced it I practiced mumbling comforting things, explaining the procedure—bedside manner and shit. The saw is so shiny it hurts my eyes. Everything is too bright. Too sharp. If I take any more speed I'm going to OD.

But my hands are still steady, and I know this is real. Virtual doesn't get smells quite right, and right now I can smell the sour stink of fear coming off Yinka's body, contaminated sweat leaking out from his armpits. When the saw bites into his flesh another smell joins it: hot, greasy copper.

The film does its job and seals the wound on both ends. Not a drop spilled, but my stomach lurches a bit when I transfer the severed arm—Yinka's arm—to the refrigerated case. He's already getting up, bracing carefully with his left arm, levering onto his knees and then onto his feet.

He stands stock-still while I slip the bioprinter's mask over his face. It's alive the way a skin graft is alive, warm to the touch, and the lattice of cartilage underneath approximates Quini's bone structure. It would never work on its own, but there's also the glove, more live tissue coated in Quini's DNA and also etched with the exact ridges and whorls of his palm and fingerprints.

And now Yinka's got the right proportions, too.

"Just how we practiced," I say. "I'm sending it the open-up."

I back away, dragging both duffel bags out of the sensor's sight, leaving Yinka standing eye level with the blinking blue light. Nat's signal is still coming strong from Flux, meaning Quini's signal is also coming strong, and now all I have to do is bounce it to the safe room sensor with a simple entry command.

Yinka's swaying on his feet. I did my research. I know field amputations can send people into shock, knock them out entirely. But I made sure there was minimal blood loss, and I stuck his nerve-dead stump with a cocktail of stimulants and painkillers. He should be feeling weirdly good, and alert enough to remember procedure.

We can't run it again. The realization jolts me for the hundredth time.

The stone wall slides apart, offering up a palmprint pad. Yinka leans forward, slightly off-balance, and slaps his remaining hand against it. I watch the bioscanner deliberate in real time. The wall becomes a door, swinging inward. Yinka hunches against the bright light for a moment, then heads inside with Quini's exact swaggering stride.

Five minutes is a fucking eternity during a break-and-enter. I start checking the cameras again. The three overpaid security guards are still in the kitchen, learning to blow smoke rings from some net tutorial. The pair in the bathroom are still fucking, still clutching at each other and at the towels.

Still.

I get a tingling at the nape of my neck, and it only gets worse when Nat chats me: *Quini's leaving.*

I go back to the kitchen camera and check the timestamps. Masked. I peel them out the hard way, and the tingling at the nape of my neck becomes jagged ice.

Nat, we're burnt, I chat her. *Get the fuck out of there. We're burnt.*

I'm opening my mouth to tell Yinka the same thing when the barrel of a scattergun shows up in my peripheral vision.

"Hush," says a man's soft voice. "Let the *Fleischgeist* finish his job."

I shut my mouth. The man pulls something out of the folds of his jacket, and suddenly my head is stuffed with steel wool. I lose contact with my cranial implant, with Nat, with everything else. I feel the faraday clamp attach itself to the back of my skull, digging its tiny feet in. I'm blinded. But I was blinded before too. I was watching a fucking loop on the house cameras.

"So you don't make any more mischief," the man says. "My name is Anton. I'm Señor Caballo's new security consultant. I believe you met my predecessor in the bathroom of a shitty wine bar." He rests the scattergun on my shoulder.

"You had a trail on her?" I choke.

"Yeah. Been waiting for you ever since. Pawns move first." He exhales. "Tonight's been very educational. We're going to make some major improvements here."

Yinka emerges from the safe room with a tiny incubator pod cradled in his hand. He stops short.

"Sorry," I say.

He says nothing back, which is understandable. Anton holds out his hand for the incubator. Yinka gives it up. Anton motions with the scattergun. We start walking back down the hallway, through Quini's room where the sparring dummy clasps its hands over its head, victorious. All I can think about is my conversation with Nat in the restaurant, about seafood and salt water and how I am a *yugga, yugga, yugga.*

I know this is real, because now I can smell my own sweat. I smell terrified.

The drugs are wearing off and Yinka's face, no longer hidden under the Quini mask, is contorted in pain. We're outside by the steaming pool with Anton and two more armed guards. Anton has his pants rolled up and his feet in the water, swirling them clockwise, counterclockwise. I can see his leg hairs rippling.

"He needs medical attention," I say. "Come on. He's a fucking kid."

"You cut his arm off," Anton says. "He's a fucking kid." But he tips his head back, blinks, and I can tell he's looking at something in his implant. "Reattachment should be viable for another five hours. Since it's on ice."

Yinka sinks slowly to his haunches. Neither of the guards try to make him stand back up.

"I fucked up," I say. "I'm sorry."

Quini arrives just as dawn is streaking the sky with filaments of red. His eyes are bloodshot and his grin is amphetamine-tight and he's not wearing any shoes with his tailored suit. His arm is slung around Nat's shoulders. I try to make eye contact with her, but she's not making eye contact with anything.

"Afterparty at my place, and nobody fucking tells me," Quini says. "Not even Natalia, *mi gitanita favorita.* Who tells me everything." He kisses her cheek; her lips flex just a bit in return. I want to tell her we can get out of this, somehow, somehow, but my implant is locked up and seeing Quini does the same thing to my mouth.

He leaves Nat to go over to Anton, who reaches into his jacket for the incubator pod. Quini takes it—he doesn't look happy to see it, more disgusted—and puts it in his pocket. Then he comes to me.

"And here's my favorite hackman," he says. "How are you?" He throws his arm around me and I can't help but flinch. The last thing my body remembers about him is him beating the shit out of me. This time he's exuding a cloud of sweat, cologne, black rum. He makes a rumbling noise in his throat and gives an extra squeeze before he steps back, cupping my face in his hand, beaming at me.

"My three favorite people all in one place," he says. "Me makes three. Him, I don't know." He looks over at Yinka, who's still crouched, clutching his stump. "Who are you, *negrito*?" He rubs his thumb on my cheek and his eyes flutter shut for a second. "Your skin is so fucking soft, hackman. You moisturize that shit."

Then he goes to Yinka, who isn't wearing the mask but is still wearing the suit, and squats down across from him. He puffs out half a laugh.

"I get it. You're me." He champs his teeth together—twice, three times—dentin clacking. "You're me! You're Quini. That's how you got into the safe room." He points at the stump. "He really did you like that, huh? He really took your fucking arm off?" He tips back his head. "Ha! My four favorite people. Me twice."

Yinka doesn't react. Still in shock. Better that way, with Quini. I'm cycling through the disaster scenarios we ran, but with the faraday clamp freezing my implant it's only memory and it's jumpy, erratic. Fear keeps bullying in.

"You want to know the real story? How I really lost it? You're me, so I can tell you." Quini sits down cross-legged on the tiles. He rubs his hand along the pattern. "I was just small. Just a little *cabroncito*. I grew up during the droughts. You're African. You know. Getting food was tough."

I don't want to hear this story. I know it's dangerous to be hearing this story. I can tell from the look on Nat's face.

"My family used to work the *aceituna*. The olive trees. Always had Africans up to work, too. You from Senegal? They were mostly from Senegal. But one year the trees stopped producing, because the new gene tweak didn't take, so people started chopping them up for firewood instead. It gets cold in Andalusia. People up here don't know that. So, me and my brother, we were chopping firewood."

Quini's eyes turn wide and gleeful, like he's a kid recounting his favorite part of a flick. "He thought I was going to pull my arm away! I thought he wasn't going to swing! And just like that, gone. Oh, I was angry. Even back then, even little Quini, he got angry. But my brother was family, you know? And it was an accident. Nobody's fault. Just the peristalsis of an amoral universe. You like that word? 'Peristalsis.'"

"But then, years later, years and years, I heard my brother was talking. Was saying he did it to teach me a lesson. Saying he's the only person that makes Quini the Squid flinch." Quini snorts. "So one night I went over to his house—his house, *qué tontería*, I bought him that fucking house—and

I brought an autosurgeon with me. And I made things right. First I took his arms, then I took his legs."

I can hear the whining of the blade all over again. My gut heaves and for a second I can't look at Yinka, can't look at anything except the backs of my eyelids.

"I cried while I did it," Quini says. "But when it was finished, my anger was gone. Gone! We were brothers again. I bought him a chair—you know, to get around. A really fancy one." He gets nimbly to his feet and heads over to my confiscated duffel bag. He grins at Nat while he gropes around inside. The saw emerges with Yinka's blood still spattering the casing. "So who wants to go first?" he asks. "Hackman, how about you? You're quiet tonight. I remember you like talking. I'm surprised you're not talking yet. Trying to save your skin."

I've done the thinking and I already know. Quini blames me for the job in Murcia going bad. He pulled my contracts for any other hackwork. Now he's caught me breaking into his house to steal the one thing he cannot afford to have stolen.

"Nothing is going to save my skin." I can't keep my voice from quavering. I look at Nat, then Yinka. "I blackmailed both of them," I say. "I took Nat's bank account, and I poison-pilled his Catalonian citizenship request. Forced them. To help."

Quini nods, inspecting the saw blade. "Okay. Sure. But what's this all about, hackman? Why did you do this to me?"

I look straight ahead, not meeting his eyes. "I'm a big Klobučar fan."

Quini stares at me, then barks a laugh so loud one of his guards jumps. "You too, huh? I'm starting to feel real uncultured, you know that? Everyone loves this shit. Me, I wish I could get rid of it. Swear!" The saw clangs onto the tiles. He pulls the incubator pod out of his pocket instead and waves it in the air, arm swinging dangerously close to the edge of the pool.

I can see Anton's wince. "We should get that back in the safe room, Señor Caballo."

Quini ignores him. "I'm working with some Koreans now. Some serious *hijoputas* until they get liquored, then friendly, real friendly. We're in Seoul and the boss, he starts talking about Klobučar, how visionary she was, how killing herself was art. That was art! Bullshit." He tosses the incubator pod up into the air, watches it, catches it. "But one thing leads to another, we seal the malware deal, and he says he wants to loan me his favorite piece for a month. One month, and it'll change everything, he says. Doesn't tell me it's worth a billion fucking Euros until I'm babysitting it."

He clutches the pod tight and rubs his face in the crook of his arm. "Makes me nervous, hackman," he says, walking back toward me. "If I somehow lost it, no more deals with the Koreans. And there would be a bunch of ninja motherfuckers in chamsuits trying to knife me in my sleep. You knew that, I think. You knew it would hurt me. So now I'm going to make what I did in Murcia look like a tickle."

My throat winches shut. I can feel the ghost of Quini's boot swinging into my ribs. I can hear his men laughing.

"But I'll give you a look first," he says. "So you can decide if this was ever really worth it." He thumbs the pod open.

It's empty.

He scrapes his finger around the inside, and the first thought in my fear-fogged brain is that I do not understand art, that I am just as uncultured as Quini the Squid and I'm going to die that way.

Then his eyelid starts to twitch.

I can see my reflection in the pool and it's uglier than ever, a faceful of processed meat, every centimeter of skin either split or swollen. Blood keeps burbling out of my mouth and down my chin, more blood than I ever realized I had. All I want to do is topple forward into the pool and drown, but the guard behind me has his arm around my waist.

Nat is on one side of me; Yinka on the other. They're making him stand. He looks like he's about to be sick, then swallows it back down. After the initial flurry of anger, Quini lined us up by the pool and stuck one of my anatabs to his skinned knuckles. Now he's walking up and down the tiles behind us, bare feet slapping the ceramic, and he has the surgical saw tucked under his stump.

"Where is it?" he asks again.

"Don't know," I try to say again, breathing broken glass.

"Natalia, *mi amor*, where is it? You know I don't want to hurt you. I love you."

I'm praying Nat will stay silent, how she's been since arriving, but the words break her ice and she blinks. "Get fucked, Quini."

He hurls the incubator pod against the tiles and it smashes apart. Then he comes up behind me, enveloping me in the cloud of sweat and alcohol, and his breath is hot in my ear. "I do love her, though. Still. You know, hackman, if it wasn't for her, I never would have hired you the first time. We wouldn't know each other." He balloons a sigh. "I bet she feels bad about that. I bet that's why she agreed to help you."

I shake my head, making the faraday clamp throb. "Blackmail."

"I'm trying to decide now. Who I start cutting." Quini hefts the saw. "The *negrito*, he could use a break. So between Natalia and the hackman, I think it's you. I think she cares more about you than you care about her. So even though she hates me, she'll talk. To avoid seeing you flopping around in the pool with no limbs like some deformed fucking *manatí*."

"Señor Caballo." It's Anton. I almost forgot about him. For a moment I think he's going to save me, but he's only being businesslike. "We should search him first. If it's on his person, you don't want to damage it by accident."

Quini shrugs. "Go."

Anton pads over to me, chasing the guard away. I stand spread-eagled, arms straight out, and think for the first time about not having them. He frisks from the bottom up, and as he's checking my coat lining he pauses.

"Just out of curiosity," he says. "How loud can you whistle?"

For a split second his hand passes over the faraday clamp. Then he finishes the frisk, finding nothing, and steps away. Quini grunts, like he expected as much. He switches the saw on. Cold sweat starts trickling from my armpits down my ribcage. I feel the whine in my teeth.

"We're starting with the right," he says. "That's the trend. You will fit right in. Natalia, *cielo*, feel free to start theorizing. About where my fucking artwork is."

"I wasn't fucking here," Nat says. Her voice is brittle. I hate that. I hate it when she's hurting too much to hide it. "I was in Flux. With you. Remember?"

"We're all in flux," Quini says solemnly. "You know? Lie down, hackman. Arm out."

"It's all right, Nat," I mumble through my torn lip. "We'll just run it again."

I lie down on the cold tiles, extending my arm the way Yinka did, and look up at the sky. It's beautiful. The red's faded out to one stripe of soft pinkish orange, and above that the morning light is breaking through a wall of cold blue cloud. I don't have to look at any of Quini's ugly architectural choices.

I do have to look at my choices, though. I'm about to get my limbs amputated by an unbalanced criminal, and there are no anatabs. No painkiller cocktail. These are probably the last few moments I'll get to think about anything except screaming, and at some point in the very near future I'll bleed to death.

Maybe it's not just the peristalsis of an amoral universe. Maybe it's what I deserve. For lying to Yinka and for a hundred bad things I did long before that. What I hate most is that I won't even be dying as myself. I should have at least told Nat.

I squeeze my eyes shut, as if I can open up our private channel by force of will. Quini is muttering to himself in Andalusian Spanish, too fast for me to catch without my babelware. The whine of the saw intensifies.

Suddenly I understand what Quini's saying. The steel wool in my head is gone. My implant comes unfrozen and I see the backdoor in my mind's eye. The friend/foe mapper. I make the signal, the whistle, as loud as I possibly can.

Someone is screaming; maybe it's me. The whine of the saw is a furious buzzing centimeters from my face. Hot liquid splatters my neck.

I open my eyes in time to see Quini sundered from hip to shoulder. The dog is up on its spindly carbon hind legs, saw spraying blood in all directions, tearing Quini's flesh into pink ropes. It seems to go on for an eternity before the blade stutters to a halt on splintered bone. There's a bang. Another. The dog drops to all fours. Quini sways.

"*Mi cachorrito,*" he says, not unfondly, then falls backward into the pool.

Nat yanks me to my feet. Her other hand is clutching Yinka. I look around, still lost, and see two dead guards, Anton reloading the scattergun. Quini is floating in the water, a red cloud billowing out around his shredded body.

"I don't actually like Klobučar's later stuff," Anton says. "She got self-indulgent. I like money, though. And I liked your hackwork tonight. Very creative." He produces an incubator pod from his jacket, identical to the one Quini smashed, but probably less empty. "I was stumped by that bioscanner." He shakes his head, rolling his eyes, smiling a bit. "Stumped. Don't forget your bags."

Then he's gone, off into the villa, scattergun propped on his shoulder. That leaves me and Nat and Yinka huddled together on the red-slicked tiles. Somehow none of us are dead. Yinka looks closest; he leans over and heaves.

"Can you walk?" Nat demands. "I've got your arm."

Yinka heaves again, giving up a thin bubbly vomit and then something dark and solid that splats against the tile. He scrabbles for it with stiff fingers. We all stare.

Cupped in his shaking hand is a miniature human heart. Its beat is inaudible, but I can see it pumping and imagine the sound in my head. Thump-thump. Thump-thump. Alive. Alive.

"Let's dip," Yinka rasps. "Before he figures out his pod is empty, too."

I get Yinka under his undamaged arm and Nat grabs the refrigerated case. Then we all three stagger off into the olive trees, Quini's gore-smeared *cachorrito* trotting along behind us.

When do you leave? I ask, but we're talking in public, out on the beach by Pont del Petroli, so it comes out more like:

"Napta zuwani?"

"Napta imo yun," Nat says: *Tomorrow night.* She toes a hole in the sun-heated sand. We're sitting just out of reach of the tide's soft gray pulse, watching runners move up and down the length of the bridge. *Barge out of Shiptown*, she adds with a tangle of clicks and plosives.

You see our Fleischgeist *there?* I ask.

Nat nods. *Talked to him, even. Arm looks good.* She pauses, turns her head to look at me. *He never wants to see you again, though.*

"Vensmur," I say: *Makes sense.*

For a while we sit in silence. The tide pushes and pulls. Gulls wheel and shriek out over the waves. *How about you?* Nat finally asks. *Where are you going?*

Been looking at some clinics in Laos, I tell her. *Been planning some changes.*

Nat nods. *I saw that. See that.*

I finally did something with my hair, and I'm wearing one of those new prints from Mombasa. Makeup is hiding the worst bits of my face. It's too bad I have to let it all heal up before I can have a more qualified surgeon mess with it.

So this is you, she says. *Not just a fresh way to hide from the feds.*

It's me. And it's sort of the opposite of hiding.

Nat grabs my hand, and I release the breath I didn't even realize I'd been bottling up. *Good*, she says. *Good. You want a scan of my nose?*

I blink. "M'mut?"

You want my nose, Nat laughs. *You can admit it. Whenever we're drunk, you say how perfect it is.* She suddenly frowns. *That shit will be expensive. The clinics. And the lying low. But you gave Yinka your whole share.*

Yeah, I say. *We made a deal back at the safe room.*

Nat narrows her eyes. *So it really was just revenge?*

I take a heavy breath. *He knew. Quini knew about me. He was a lot of things, but he was sharp. He saw it before I wanted anyone to see it. So when he beat me. When he called me a* maricona. *Laughed at me. It was personal.* I chew the inside of my cheek, hit a suture and immediately regret it. *I wanted him hurt*, I mumble in nonsense. *I don't know about dead.*

I wanted him hurt, too, Nat says, staring at the sea. *Never thought about dead. But the world's better off. Net total.*

The silence swells until I can't take it anymore. *That was her heart, you know*, I finally say. *What we stole? It was grown using her cells. She had the whole thing automated. For after she killed herself. I looked it up. It's the last Klobučar.*

Nat raises her immaculate eyebrows. *No wonder me and Yinka are so rich now.*

Don't rub it in, I say in one nasal syllable.

She wanted to live forever, maybe, Nat says. *With people fighting over her heart. Buying it and selling it and killing for it.*

Maybe she wanted us not to, I say. *But knew we would anyways, so she did it on her own terms.*

Nat stands up, brushing the sand off her pants. *Fucking artists,* she says. *You hungry?*

I could eat, I say. *Good* pintxos *around the corner. Good curry a block down.*

"Unta da unta," she says: *Both.*

We've got time. At least a bit of it. And hopefully after a year of lying low, we both end up back in Barcelona. There's lots more shit I want to do here as myself.

PERMISSIONS

ACKNOWLEDGMENTS

The editor would like to thank the following people for their help and support: Lisa Clarke, Sean Wallace, Kate Baker, Steven Silver, Joshua Bilmes, the team at Morristown Medical Center, everyone at Night Shade Books, and all the authors, editors, agents, and publishers whose work makes this anthology possible.

2020 RECOMMENDED READING LIST

"If You Take My Meaning" by Charlie Jane Anders, *Tor.com*, February 11, 2020.

"The Machine That Would Rewild Humanity" by Tobias S Buckell, *Escape Pod: The Science Fiction Anthology*, edited by Mur Lafferty and S.B. Divya.

"The Science of Pacific Apocalypse" by Octavia Cade, *Rebuilding Tomorrow*, edited by Tsana Dolichva.

"War Crimes" by M.R. Carey, *London Centric*, edited by Ian Whates.

"Callme and Mink" by Brenda Cooper, *Clarkesworld Magazine*, October 2020.

"Incarnate" by Indrapramit Das, *Avatars, Inc.*, edited by Ann VanderMeer.

"In the Lands of the Spill" by Aliette De Bodard, *Avatars, Inc.*, edited by Ann VanderMeer.

"Seven of Infinities" by Aliette De Bodard, Subterranean Press.

"GO. NOW. FIX. " by Timons Esaias, *Asimov's Science Fiction*, January / February 2020.

"Helicopter Story" by Isabel Fall, *Clarkesworld Magazine*, January 2020.

"The Transition of OSOOSI" by Ozzie M. Gartrell, *FIYAH*, Winter 2020.

"Time's Own Gravity" by Alexander Glass, *Interzone*, September / October 2020.

"Keloid Dreams" by Simone Heller, *Future Science Fiction*, September 2020.

"The Monk of Lingyin Temple" by Xia Jia (translated by Ken Liu), *Entanglements: Tomorrow's Lovers, Families, and Friends*, edited by Sheila Williams.

"King of the Dogs, Queen of the Cats" by James Patrick Kelly, Subterranean Press.

"The Beast Adjoins" by Ted Kosmatka, *Asimov's Science Fiction*, July / August 2020.

"Semper Augustus" by Nancy Kress, *Asimov's Science Fiction*, March / April 2020.

"Monster" by Naomi Kritzer, *Clarkesworld Magazine*, January 2020.

"The Conceptual Shark" by Rich Larson, *Asimov's Science Fiction*, September / October 2020.

"Beyond the Dragon's Date" by Yoon Ha Lee, *Tor.com*, May 20, 2020.

"50 Things Every AI Working with Humans Should Know" by Ken Liu, *Uncanny Magazine*, November / December 2020.

"A Mastery of German" by Marian Denise Moore, *Dominion: An Anthology of Speculative Fiction from Africa and the African Diaspora*, edited by Zelda Knight and Oghenechovwe Donald Ekpeki.

"Note to Self" by Sunny Moraine, *Lightspeed Magazine*, September 2020.

"Father" by Ray Nayler, *Asimov's Science Fiction*, July / August 2020.

"Retention" by Alec Nevala-Lee, *Analog Science Fiction & Fact*, July / August 2020.

"Real Animals" by Em North, *Lightspeed Magazine*, June 2020.

"Second Generation" by Julie Nováková, *Future Science Fiction*, September 2020.

"A Room of One's Own" by Tochi Onyebuchi, *Us in Flux*, ASU Center for Science and the Imagination.

"Don't Mind Me" by Suzanne Palmer, *Entanglements: Tomorrow's Lovers, Families, and Friends*, edited by Sheila Williams.

"Candida Eve" by Dominica Phetteplace, *Analog Science Fiction & Fact*, May / June 2020.

"A Guide for Working Breeds" by Vina Jie-Min Prasad, *Made to Order*, edited by Jonathan Strahan.

"Collaborative Configurations of Minds" by Lettie Prell, *Wired*, December 4, 2020.

"Waiting for Amelia" by Robert Reed, *Avatars, Inc.*, edited by Ann VanderMeer.

"Polished Performance" by Alastair Reynolds, *Made to Order*, edited by Jonathan Strahan.

"Kids These Days" by Tansy Rayner Roberts, *Rebuilding Tomorrow*, edited by Tsana Dolichva.

"Ask the Firelies" by R.P. Sand, *Clarkesworld Magazine*, September 2020.

"68:Hazard:Cold" by Janelle C. Shane, *Strange Horizons*, June 29, 2020.

"A Bird Does Not Sing Because It Has an Answer" by Johanna Sinisalo, *Avatars, Inc.*, edited by Ann VanderMeer.

"Low Energy Economy" by Adrian Tchaikovsky, *Consolation Songs*, edited by Iona Datt Sharma.

"Thirty-Three" by Tade Thompson, *Avatars, Inc.*, edited by Ann VanderMeer.

"Those We Serve" by Eugenia Triantafyllou, *Interzone*, May / June 2020.

"Respite" by Catherine Wells, *Analog Science Fiction & Fact*, March / April 2020.

"Sparklybits" by Nick Wolven, *Entanglements: Tomorrow's Lovers, Families, and Friends*, edited by Sheila Williams.

"The Search for [Flight X]" by JY Yang, *Avatars, Inc.*, edited by Ann VanderMeer.

ABOUT THE EDITOR

Neil Clarke is the editor of the Hugo and World Fantasy Award-winning *Clarkesworld Magazine, Forever Magazine,* and several anthologies. He has been a finalist for the Hugo Award for Best Editor (Short Form) nine times, won the Chesley Award for Best Art Director three times, and received the Solstice Award from SFWA in 2019. He currently lives in NJ with his wife and two sons. You can find him online at neil-clarke.com.